SHATTERED SOULS

THE GUARDIANS OF THE MAIDEN

SHATTERED SOULS

BECK MICHAELS

PLUMA
PRESS

Trigger Warning: This book contains strong violence and gore, violence against women, death and murder, addiction, heavy grief and loss, inappropriate language, attempted rape (not shown and stopped), child abuse (whipping), captivity, suicide attempt, and sexual situations. Please don't continue if you find these themes uncomfortable.

PLUMA PRESS
P.O. Box 341
Camby, IN 46113
Visit Us at PlumaPress.com

Published October 2022

Author: Michaels, Beck

Title: Shattered Souls / Beck Michaels

Series: The Guardians of the Maiden; 3

Genre: YA Fantasy Fiction

Summary: Dyna and her Guardians race against time to leave Azure as they grow and learn about the bounds of love, duty, and power.

Identifiers:
ISBN 978-1-956899-03-0 (hardcover)

| ISBN 978-1-956899-04-7 (softcover) | ISBN 978-1-956899-02-3 (ebook)

www.BeckMichaels.com

Printed in the United States of America

For all those who are broken.
Don't surrender.

GLACIAL OCEAN

JERASH

SKATH

UNITED CROWN

THE THREE
RIVERS

EDYM

XIAN
JING

HARROMAG
MODOS

DRAGON CANYON

NAL
ME

LEDOGA

RED
HIGHLANDS

LANGSHAN

THE VALE OF

SUN
GUILD

LEVIATHAN OCEAN

MAGOS

MOUNT IDA

LUNAR
GUILD

LAND OF URN

MONTEZUMA

ARGYLE

HERMON
RIDGE

**DWARF
SHOE**

AZURE

FLOATING ISLANDS
OF NAZAR

HILOS

GREENWOOD

THE ELVES

SAXE SEA

MISTY
ISLES

EMPIRE

EARTH
GUILD

KINGDOM OF AZURE

GLACIAL
OCEAN

EVERFROST

TROLL BRIDGE

BERYL
COAST

HERMON RIDGE

TANNER'S
COVE

BLACK
WOODS

HALLOW'S NEST

INDIGO
BAY

RULEM

CROWN'S
HARBOR

SEANA

TANZANITE
KEEP

ZICRO

MARINER'S
HAVEN

EMBERDIN

ADHARS
COVE

KYANITE

WILLOWS
GROVE

THE BLUE CAPITAL

THE PORT
OF AZURE

LAZAR

SAPPHIRE
MINES

OREM

ARGOS VALLEY

THE MOORS

ZAIFRO MOUNTAINS

KAZER
BLUFFS

CORRON

GAMOR

ELMS
NOOK

LANDCASTER

NORTH STAR

HILOS

LYKOS
PEAK

GREENWOOD

SAXE SEA

MISTY
ISLES

THE SEVEN GATES

Each soul passes through the gates at their beginning and their end.

HEAVEN'S GATE

LIFE'S GATE

SPATIAL GATE

TIME GATE

MORTAL GATE

NETHERWORLD GATE

DEATH'S GATE

Seek the Maiden with emeralds for sight and tresses of fire,
for she holds the key to the Unending thou desires.
Beware the Guardians who come to shield her from thee.
She will be protected by one of divine blood
and a dweller of the moon howling to break free.
Thus follows a warrior bestowing his vow,
and a sorceress grants her sorcery.
A familiar face vies for vengeance,
and a creature with the strength of ten eradicates the forgery.
Great peril in the venture thou art pursuing.
Be not swayed by love, lest it be thy undoing

PART I: CAPTIVE

PROLOGUE

Dynalya

The Shadow was coming.

Dyna felt its presence behind her as she ran into the night. The relentless blizzard whipped around her, blinding her vision as her numb feet sank into the thick snow. *Keep going.* She had to keep going. A faint white glow rose beyond the dark forest.

She only needed to get to the *Hyalus* tree. It would protect her.

Her mother once told her its light held great magic. The thought elicited flashes of her mother's torn body, Thane falling into smoke, and her father...

Tears froze on Dyna's lashes. He died protecting her with a smile on his face. His voice still echoed in her mind, telling her to keep running.

Her heart lurched with fear at the roar sounding in the distance. Dyna pumped her legs faster. Her body spasmed from the cold, her lungs burning. She was almost there. The tree seemed to call her as if it were exactly where she needed to be. Oh please, let her reach it.

The frozen forest seemed to stretch endlessly, but the white light grew brighter and it pushed her numb feet onward until she stumbled out of the trees and came before the *Hyalus*. It glowed vividly, its translucent leaves shimmering like glass stars in the night.

Dyna whimpered in relief. She made it—

The ground vanished in her next step. She screamed as the earth sucked her down into the darkness and her body hit the bottom of a steep ravine. Sharp pain shot through her ankle and knee. Any attempt to stand made her shriek. She couldn't walk, but she wouldn't die like this. Not when she was so close. Biting back her cries, Dyna clawed back up the ravine. Icy mud burned through her bleeding fingers, desiccated roots cutting her legs.

When she reached the top, something moved behind her.

The sound of claws on stone seemed to scrape her skin. Dyna's heart sped, her breath heaving in the air. A low, crackling growl rumbled within the trees, stealing the air from her lungs. Terror clamped on her limbs, freezing her in place, but she couldn't stop herself from looking over her shoulder at the molten red eyes watching her from the darkness.

The Shadow found her.

Dyna couldn't scream or call for help. No one would come now.

She curled into a ball and squeezed her eyes tight. Claws skittered across the ground, inching closer. And closer. Her heart nearly gave out at the growl rumbling above her head. Cold smoke brushed against her cheek, wafting through her hair. She covered her mouth to smother her screams.

A sudden beam flashed through her eyelids, and the Shadow roared in pain. Its cold smoke whipped away in a freezing gust. Dyna held up a hand to screen her vision from the blinding light streaming through her fingers. The *Hyalus* tree. It blazed with light, keeping the demon at bay.

She stumbled to the tree, and one of its low-hanging branches seemed to reach out to her. As soon as she took it, the branch gently wrapped around her hand and pulled her close. The tree's light flared, washing away the darkness in a swathe of white.

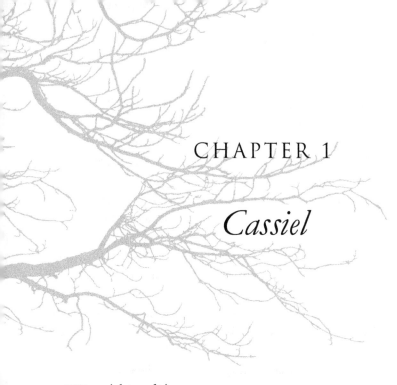

CHAPTER 1

Cassiel

Cassiel was dying.

His throat burned with his screams as his soul shredded apart. He couldn't move. Couldn't breathe. Someone called his name, but he barely heard it. The unbearable pain of the severed bond reduced him to a wretched thing on the ground, begging for the nothingness of death to take him quickly, merely to ease the agony.

"Cassiel!" Rawn dropped next to him. He removed the branch pierced through his left wing, though the pain didn't register under everything else. "Prince Cassiel, what has happened?"

He couldn't form the words to answer. The trees above spun in and out of focus. Everything hurt. He'd broken several bones when he fell out of the sky, but nothing compared to the pain in his chest where his other half used to be.

A massive black wolf anxiously zigzagged with his nose in the leaves. It spun in erratic circles, sniffing and whining.

"Zev has lost their trail," Rawn said.

The wolf howled at the sky, and the maddening sound rattled within the emptiness inside of him—because it wasn't there. The warmth of her life. His connection to her every heartbeat.

It was gone.

"Prince Cassiel." Rawn shook his shoulders when he gasped for air. "What is wrong with you?"

"Dyna," he rasped. "I can't feel her."

"What?"

"Our bond, it's gone. I can't feel her anymore. She...she's dead."

Zev went still beneath the patter of rain.

Cassiel's chest felt as if it was caving in, but it was the fragments of his soul that had collapsed. Tears he had no control over endlessly spilled. He finally had his mate, only to lose her on the same day.

Lord Norrlen stared at him. His long blond hair stuck to his face in wet strands, making his pointed ears more prominent. "No. It cannot be."

"The bond is broken. That only means one thing."

Zev's fur gave away to skin as he shifted, his wide yellow eyes on him. Cassiel wouldn't have minded if the Lycan had killed him then. Anything would have been better than this unbridled torment.

Zev turned away and slashed into a tree as he roared a cry. Cassiel covered his face. The world was crumbling around him, piece by piece until he was falling into an abyss with no end.

"Lady Dyna is not gone," Rawn said firmly. "I do *not* believe it."

Rawn moved ahead, his agile steps careful as he studied the ground. He held out his hands as if to search for something in the air. Cassiel stilled, holding his breath. Zev watched him, too, both of them grasping at the subtle rise of hope. When the elf went further into the trees with Fair they scrambled after them.

Stopping in a small glade, Rawn pressed his palms flat in the mud, and they glimmered a teal blue with magic. "I feel the workings of a spell here. The mage must have cloaked their tracks with a veil. It's a powerful concealment spell. No trace of Lady Dyna can be found outside of it."

A spell.

Cassiel clung to Rawn's words like a thorn. He inhaled the relief it gave him, even as doubt threatened to drag him under.

"Lucenna cast something similar when protecting our camp," Zev said, quickly yanking on a pair of pants. "It must be how Tarn hid from the Azure King all this time."

Cassiel had to do something. He needed to move. Now that there was a chance his bonded was alive, wild desperation took root. His wings twitched as his blood worked on healing them. "I will fly overhead."

"They will have cloaked their camp as well," Rawn said. "You cannot find it by sight alone."

Damn it all.

Rawn sighed. "If only I had learned more magic, I could track her now."

Cassiel and Zev locked eyes. "Lucenna," they exclaimed together.

"We can ask her for help," Cassiel explained to Rawn. "She told us once only she had a lock on Dyna's Essence."

Optimism entered Rawn's face, but then he frowned. "Lady Lucenna wants no part in our opposition with Tarn."

"Then what else do you propose?" Zev said. "Dyna is her kin. Do you think she wouldn't help?"

After the way they parted, Cassiel wasn't so sure. But Lucenna cared about her. "Whatever her feelings, she could aid us with a spell, at the very least."

They watched Rawn wrestle with a decision. It went against his ethics to pursue her after she asked them not to. Cassiel respected the elf's morals, but he didn't have time for them now.

"I'm going after her. She couldn't have gone far." As Cassiel said it, he knew the chances of finding her quickly were slim. They had parted three days ago. She could be anywhere.

"Tomorrow," Zev said, his voice full of heavy lament. He sank to his knees before a large oak tree and dropped his head against the trunk. "We will search for her tomorrow."

Cassiel looked up at the dark sky as the moon rose above the parting clouds. They could go no further today. His skin crawled at the reminder of the Other.

"Did you bring his things?" he asked.

Rawn removed Zev's flat pack from Fair's harness, setting it down. It appeared to have nothing, but Cassiel stuck his hand in the vast space and thought of the silver shackles. The cold, rough chains landed in his palm, and he heaved to pull them out until there was a large mound at his feet.

Rawn regarded them warily. "What will you do with those?"

Cassiel glanced at Zev for his reply, but he didn't answer. "It's for him."

Thinking about something else besides his missing bond gave him a moment's reprieve as he took the time to wrap the chains around the tree, the links clinking in the silence. When he finished, Zev limply held out his scarred wrists. His head remained lowered, dark hair falling over his face. He looked as defeated as Cassiel felt.

Do you despise me? He wanted to ask. *Do you hate me for losing her? For being the one to do this?*

He wasn't brave enough to give the words shape.

Cassiel latched the shackles closed around each wrist and flinched at the loud clang. Zev cried out and fell forward on his hands and knees, gritting his

5

teeth. Smoke rose from the manacles, his skin audibly sizzling. He tried not to breathe in the burning scent.

"I'm sorry," Cassiel whispered. How awful Dyna must have felt doing this to him every month for years. "Is this safe? You nearly died from silver poisoning not an hour ago."

"I have no other choice," Zev growled. "Now go before I end up killing you."

Cassiel didn't know if he meant as the Other or as himself. Zev couldn't have forgiven him yet for bonding with Dyna. He had yet to forgive himself.

Cassiel stumbled away. He sensed Rawn had questions, but was wise enough not to voice them yet. They stopped a quarter of a mile away when he found a small cave on a cliff side surrounded by dense trees.

Rawn tied Fair's reins to a nearby bush and stroked his muzzle. "You did well, old friend."

The white stallion neighed tiredly in reply.

The cave was shallow, with barely enough room to fit them. It protected them from the windchill, but they were soaked through. They both quickly changed into dry clothing. Darkness was coming fast, but there was no firewood available after the rain drenched the forest. Rawn pulled out a few candlesticks and lit them with a snap of his fingers.

Cassiel sat against the cave wall as he fought the panic that urged him to keep going. He focused on breathing in the cold fresh air to calm himself. Every second he was away from Dyna seemed to fracture another piece inside of him. His heart hardly beat. His lungs barely breathed. There was no strength in his body. He sat with his arms laying limply over his knees, his head hanging, telling himself it wasn't real.

Dyna was out there. She had to be.

If she wasn't, then he truly had nothing left.

His wings twitched, and a faint ache passed through them. His broken bones had mended, but the rest of him wouldn't. Not until he found her.

A howl rang in the distance, and he dimly looked up at the full moon glowing in the night sky. Its light slipped through the cave entrance, making the rock walls glimmer.

"How are you feeling?" Rawn asked.

It was a senseless question. He was furious. Scared. In so much pain, he should be unconscious.

"I feel as if I'm split in half," Cassiel muttered. "I tell myself she is not dead, but my soul mourns the loss of her."

"She lives," Lord Norrlen reassured him again. "Your bond is not broken."

Not broken. Not broken.

He closed his swollen eyes and repeated it over and over. His hand shook as he pressed a fist to his chest. Their bond had to be there somewhere inside of him, hidden under the curtain of magic.

"You will not be well until you truly believe her to be," Rawn said. "You must be stronger than your consciousness, Prince Cassiel. Say it."

The words shook on his lips. "She is alive."

"Yes. Again."

"She is alive." He dropped his face into his hands, wetness slipping through his fingers. "She is alive."

Please be alive.

Another mournful howl filled the forest. Zev remembered nothing as the Other, but Cassiel wondered if it could see his memories. Fair nickered nervously at the cave entrance.

"The chains. Every full moon, he..."

"Yes." Cassiel wiped his face and met Rawn's grim expression.

"You have done this before." Rawn frowned thoughtfully at the moon. "He cannot control the change. I should have realized it when I saw the scars. I assumed they were old."

"Some are. Zev has not mentioned it?"

"He did not."

No, he wouldn't. To do so would bring up his past. The death of one's father wasn't an easy burden to carry. Cassiel couldn't imagine bearing that weight.

"I did not know either until I witnessed Zev's change during the last full moon. He has a hard time speaking of it."

"I understand." Rawn didn't comment more. He laid down and rested his head on his pack, closing his eyes.

There would be no sleep for Cassiel tonight. His body trembled with the urge to find Dyna. His sanity depended on it. But he couldn't leave while Zev was bound by his chains. Still, Cassiel fought to stay put. He couldn't get Dyna's frightened expression out of his mind. She hadn't been afraid for her life. She feared for theirs and gave hers up willingly so they could live.

Stupid human.

But how could he be angry with her? Dyna did exactly as he had done for her in the Port of Azure. It was his turn now to be forcefully separated from her. He hated it. How could he keep his promise to never leave her alone in the dark if he wasn't with her? He hoped there was light wherever she was.

Rawn peeked open one eye at the restless bouncing of his knee. "Rest. You will need your strength come dawn."

"I cannot sleep."

"Tarn will not harm Lady Dyna. He needs her."

"And what will happen when he finds out she lied about the map?" Cassiel asked. When they met Tarn for the first time, there had been a chill in the air. That man with those pale, unfeeling eyes had no remorse or conscience. "There are ways of hurting her without killing her."

Rawn looked up at the cave ceiling without replying. He sat up again, and they both held vigil beneath the moonlight, listening to the howls in the night.

Cassiel curled over his knees. He had to find Dyna alive and whole. For if anything happened to her, he may set the world on fire—and burn with it.

CHAPTER 2

Dynalya

Since that night on the frozen hill, both darkness and light had walled Dyna's life. Right now, it was dark—and so dreadfully cold. The wind wailed outside, blowing against the tent like a spirit demanding to enter. She couldn't see anything, but she felt Tarn's vice-like hold on her body, his frosted breath on her cheek as he waited for her response to his revelation.

Immortality.

The word repeated in her head in an echo that wouldn't fade.

He wanted to become immortal.

But her mind latched on to two things. Her chest was cracked open and hollow from the bond taken from her—and they were sitting in pitch-black darkness.

Panic bubbled in her chest. She shoved Tarn away, but he was unyielding, and the force pushed her off the bed instead. Her back hit the hard ground. She clawed at the heavy metal brace on her throat as the darkness swallowed her.

Hard fingers grabbed her arm, quickly letting go at her scream. "What is this? What's wrong with you?"

"I can't breathe...I can't...I can't..." She gasped for air as the walls of her reality closed in. The sound of her heartbeat thudded in her ears. She yanked on the brass collar, but it only seemed to squeeze tighter. "I..." She wheezed on the ground and curled into herself. "Please, I...can't..."

A dance of purple lights broke through the dark, illuminating Tarn crouched in front of her, frowning.

"Maiden." He reached out, making her recoil.

Von entered the tent, and his wide eyes bounced between them. "Master?"

There was a snap of a match, then fire flared in the brazier, and the tent's interior filled with warm light. Dyna weakly clawed at the metal strangling her. Her vision dimmed.

"She's suffocating," Von said in alarm as he rushed over. "The witch collar. You must remove it."

Tarn's pale eyes narrowed at him.

"She will die, Master."

He watched her struggle to breathe, perhaps enjoying the sight of life leaving her body. Idly rising to his feet, Tarn went to his desk and took out a brass ring with several brass keys, each with sharp teeth and small red gems embedded in the bow at the top.

His icy fingers slipped around her neck, then there was a click, and the collar fell with a heavy thud by her head.

Dyna sucked in gulps of air, panting with each one.

"There, lass." Von helped her sit up. "Are you all right?"

Dyna didn't answer. Her tender throat was bruised and raw from her nails and from all the screaming she had done in the grove. She closed her wet eyes, relishing in the heat of Essence refilling her veins. It immediately banished the cold that had settled over her, and it hummed on her skin—ready. Dyna braced her legs, calculating how fast she could escape. But she kept seeing Zev's face, the black blood spilling from his eyes. Her shaking fists clenched with the anguish building inside of her.

He couldn't have survived the silver poisoning without her.

They killed him.

The exit was at her back, and all she had to do was run, but two of her enemies stood before her, and she wanted them to suffer as much as Zev did.

She wanted them to *bleed*.

Static crackled above her head, and the charms on the ceiling flickered. The wards. A blood-red crystal clutched in a clasp of dark talons glowed bright red, making the hairs rise on her arms.

"I thought so," Tarn said derisively, in his northern brogue accent. "You're a wonderful performer, Dynalya. However, I don't recommend what I suspect you are about to do."

She bared her teeth and shot a blast of Essence at Von. The flare of green threw him back into the table, and she stood.

Tarn's ice-blue eyes gleamed as if he enjoyed this challenge she was presenting.

Von groaned as he pushed up on his arms. "Lass." He shook his head. "Don't."

"I will never allow you to be immortal," she hissed.

Tarn's mouth faintly curled at one end. "I'm amused that you think you can stop me."

The mocking on his face, the snide arrogance—it filled her with a blinding rage.

Magic flamed in Dyna's hands. It fired up her arms, and the inside of the tent seemed to hum. The blood-red crystal smoldered, and it picked at her being like a thousand needles. But she didn't care how much it hurt as long as she hurt them, too.

Dyna released a blast of green Essence at Tarn—only for it to disintegrate into nothing but a waft of smoke.

Then the needles impaled through her body, and every nerve was on fire. Screams tore from her throat. She was on the ground, completely immobile beneath the power of the glowing wards as they peeled her open and dismembered every fiber of her being.

Pain throbbed all over Dyna's body. Groaning, she sat up in a cot with a scratchy gray blanket, once again in another stranger's tent. This one was a fourth of the size and humbler than Tarn's. A second cot across from her held neatly folded quilts. A chest sat between them with an oil lamp flickering on top. She turned to sit on the edge of the cot, and her feet landed on a bamboo mat covering the ground.

Where was she now?

Dyna swallowed thickly and pressed on her aching head. Water, she needed water.

On the left of the entrance was a chair and a table with a small mirror and a pitcher. Dyna staggered to her feet, and the sound of jingling made her glance down. A chill licked down her spine. Tarn had traded her collar for two brass bangles on her ankles, and they were engraved with odd symbols. By her lack of Essence, it could only mean they were enchanted, too.

The pitcher shook in Dyna's hand as she poured herself a cup of water and swallowed it in one gulp, the cool contents like a balm in her parched throat. Her reflection stared back at her from the small wood-framed mirror. A mess of mottled bruises had flowered on her neck. Angry, raw lines marked her chest where her nails had dug last night when her bond with Cassiel broke.

She lifted a trembling hand to her torn skin, and fresh tears sprang to her eyes. The emptiness in her chest turned her body into a shell. A thing that was decaying without that presence that had somehow become the life she breathed.

They had cleaved him from her soul. The only way Dyna could swim out of the sorrow she drowned in was to remind herself of the cloaking spell placed to separate them.

Her mate was out there. *Alive.*

But everything that mattered was gone.

Her bond.

Her magic.

Her freedom.

Her cousin.

Grief ripped into her, gnawing its way through her heart. Images of their childhood as they grew up together filled her mind. She heard Zev's laughter, felt the warmth of his embrace, and saw the sadness in his green eyes at the end.

She would never see him again.

Dyna's legs gave out, and she sank to the ground. A broken cry lodged in her throat, and she wrapped her arms around herself. One minute. She gave herself one minute to cry. The dam holding back her pain lifted, and her whole body heaved with wracking sobs.

Everything will be fine, Zev told her that at the fjord, when she had been in another helpless situation. He had believed in her, and so had Cassiel. It wasn't until she also believed in herself did she find the strength to get up.

That's what she had to do now.

Dyna exhaled a heavy breath and wiped her tears. Her one minute was over. She buried everything in a deep pit somewhere inside of her being and stood. Cassiel and Rawn must be searching for her, but she couldn't wait to be rescued. She was Dynalya of North Star, a descendent of Azeran Astron, and she had people counting on her.

She left her home to fight for them.

This time, she would fight for herself.

A quick search of the tent proved there were no weapons here. She found her satchel resting against the cot she'd laid on, but it was empty. They'd taken her notebook with her inscriptions on plants, her balms, and other nonessential things. They weren't leaving her with anything that could be used against them. But if they were being so careful, why leave her untied and unguarded?

Dyna went to the tent entrance and peered through the flaps, listening to the activity outside. They had camped in a clearing in the middle of the woods. Judging by the sun's position in the sky, it was early morning. The distant hum of several voices and the nicker of horses reached her. Rows upon rows of black tents circled a massive one at the center. It stood tall, with a sharp peak, towering above them all. That had to be Tarn's. *This* tent was set away from the others.

Rather...convenient.

Waiting until the area was clear, Dyna slipped outside into the brisk morning. She pulled up her hood and moved quickly, avoiding tents and dodging Raiders. Her torn dress dragged through the mud. She kept going, staying quiet and alert. Her heart jumped with each neigh or barking curse, every nerve anticipating someone would grab her at any second.

But as she passed the latrines, she realized no one was truly vigilant.

Men dressed in all black passed by, going about their duties, brushing down horses or polishing weapons. Others huddled around campfires, laughing and eating. One of the men broke out in a merry song about big-bosomed women and their flapping skirts.

Dyna kept going until she looked up. Her steps slowed as she gaped at the massive translucent dome spanning the sky. It contained the entire camp like a soap bubble, shimmering and whirling with iridescent colors in the sunlight. It must be some sort of shield, much stronger than the one she'd seen Lucenna make.

And it had to be the way out.

Only two guards patrolled the perimeter at an idle pace as they talked. As soon as Dyna was beyond their line of sight, she ran for it. The touch of magic crackled in the air as she neared the edge of the dome. It rippled and hummed with a power that made the hair rise on her arms. The land beyond it was visible but hazy and discolored, leached of pigment.

As if it wasn't part of this realm anymore.

She tentatively reached out, hovering her hand a foot away from it. An electric charge prickled against her palm.

"I wouldn't."

Dyna jumped and spun around at the sound of the voice. A familiar young man sat in the shadows of a tent by a dying campfire. His brown hair fell over his face as his amused, dark eyes met hers. A staff rested on his lap with a jagged orange crystal at the top.

"If you attempt to cross the veil, it won't go well for you."

Dalton, she recalled, recognizing that cocky face and the brown robes on his reedy frame. A mage.

Veil? Her mind worked to recall where she had heard of that spell, but her thoughts were too jumbled.

"Do you mean to stop me?" she asked. Perhaps he was extra security.

His smirk grew. "Oh, no. We're all *very* curious to see what you will do, Maiden."

She turned to find a growing group of Raiders watching her silently. They made no attempt to stop her. The veil's power continued crackling at her back. It felt the same way Tarn's wards had, and Dyna sensed if she touched it, the veil would attack her as well.

She stepped away.

Dalton chuckled and poked at the fire with a stick. "Wise choice. The veil is in place to keep us in as much as it's to keep unwanted people out."

It reminded her of a containment dome, but this felt different.

Raiders frowned and left, seeming disappointed that she didn't attempt it. If the veil was anything like the wards, she imagined the pain would feel a hundred times worse.

Dalton shifted in his seat, causing the bangles around his ankles to clink.

"What are these?" she asked, looking down at her own.

"Witch bangles. Pretty, aren't they?" His smile turned sharp. "The badge of a slave. They're enchanted with different uses, depending on the wearer, but all keep us confined in some form. In your case, it prevents you from using magic."

"But not yours," she guessed. "You cast spells in Landcaster when you had those on. How did you leave the veil?"

"Some of us are occasionally afforded privileges, but everyone always returns. Even those of us without bindings." Dalton looked past her, and she followed his gaze to where Von stood a few feet away.

Dyna's heart jumped at the sight of him, and a churning twisted in her stomach. He looked the same as usual, dressed in all black with several knives strapped to the bandoliers on his chest with a hard expression that looked both tired and almost...

He approached. "Did you explain to her what would happen if she touched the veil?"

The young mage stood and propped his staff across his shoulders. "We all learn by experience, Commander. It would have been rather amusing to see her discover how well the spell works." With that, Dalton strode away, winking at her as he passed.

"Dyna," Von called.

She stared at a spot past him, seeing the image of the knife in Zev's stomach. The way he fell to the ground kept flashing in her mind, the black veins webbing beneath his ashen skin, his black tears. Dyna ground her teeth as her eyes burned.

"How are you feeling?"

She almost laughed at the question. The only thing she felt was bitter anger and the constant stark pain in her soul. Dyna looked at the weapons strapped to Von's chest and a dark thought rose in her like bile. She had never wanted to kill someone before, and the vileness of her thoughts frightened her.

Von glanced down at her clenched fists. "Are you hungry? The Master is preoccupied at the moment, so I will take you to Sorren. He's a good cook. I'm sure he will have something for you."

His sea-green eyes were bloodshot, but open and concerned. Pretending to care wouldn't work on her. Yesterday, he stabbed her cousin and now he was offering her a meal?

"Come along, lass."

The last thing she wanted was to be anywhere near him, but she might find another way out without having to sneak around the camp. And it wasn't as if she had a choice.

Dyna trailed behind Von as he led her through the maze of tents. There were hundreds, it seemed. Tarn truly had a small army at his command.

Her boots squelched in puddles left from last night's rain, giving her a glimpse of her pale face. Her hands hadn't stopped shaking. She was surviving on pure adrenaline.

A frigid breeze blew through her clothes and splinters of the broken bond seemed to tremble with her. Dyna's fingers brushed her lips, feeling the phantom caress of Cassiel's last touch.

Wait for me.

Always.

CHAPTER 3

Dynalya

When Dyna had first left North Star, she knew she would see many new wondrous things. Some would be dangerous, some awe-inspiring, and others...frightening. So at Von's warning not to scream when she met Sorren, Dyna halted. They had left the campsite and were in a short clearing leading to a lonesome tent. It was bigger than the others in both width and height. The scent of baking bread drifted with the smoke billowing from the opening at the peak.

"Why would I scream?" she asked. If he expected her to be afraid, then why would she go in there?

Von saw her expression and his mouth twitched. "Sorren can be gruff, but there's nothing to fear—unless you insult his cooking."

Dyna didn't know how to react to that. Was this his attempt at a jest?

They reached the tent, and he parted the flaps for her to enter. She couldn't make herself move. Von placed a hand between her shoulder blades and led her inside. A displeased growl rumbled in the stuffy tent. Dyna stiffened, and her gaze climbed up...and up. She gaped at the large Minotaur glaring down at them.

Sorren stood a little over eight feet tall with the face of a bull. One thick horn curled above his head, and where the other should have been was a sawed stump. A golden ring hung from his snout, and earrings decorated his long, floppy ears. Sandy fur covered his hulking body.

"I think she might spew," Sorren said. Dyna stiffened at the coarse sound of his deep voice. He set down a stack of dirty dishes and scrutinized her with dark eyes.

"Then try to appear less menacing," said the pretty woman beside him.

She looked small compared to the massive creature. Long auburn hair framed her face in soft waves, and she offered Dyna a kind smile. The skirts of her olive dress swished around her feet as she approached, every step jingling. She wore witch bangles, too.

"Oh, you poor thing." The woman wrapped her in a hug. "You must be so frightened."

Dyna's first instinct was to shove her away, but the compassion in her gentle voice had her eyes watering again.

"Bring her closer to the fire. She looks cold." Dyna glanced at the young man standing at another table in the middle of chopping vegetables. He wore a long apron with a white kerchief tied over his head. Geon, she remembered. He gave her a small wave.

The woman led her to sit in a chair near the fire that burned in a deep hole dug into the ground. Above the dancing flames hung a gigantic cauldron, its contents loudly bubbling. Long tables lined the left and right boundary of the tent with several chairs. The air held a potent scent of garlic. It drew her attention to the roof, where dried herbs, smoked meat, and pots and pans hung.

There was no other way out other than the way they came in.

"What did you do?" the woman asked Von in a clipped tone. Dyna tensed, bracing for the backlash, but the woman held his gaze with no fear.

"I didn't hurt her," Von replied, a weight in his words.

"But you hurt someone, didn't you?"

He didn't answer.

Dyna closed her eyes and willed herself not to cry. Not in front of them.

The Minotaur growled again, and this time it sounded menacing. "When will this end, Von? How many more people must you kill for that filthy cur?"

"I will do my duty, and you will do yours," Von replied curtly. He glanced at Dyna, and his features creased before they fell back to his usual stoic demeanor. He introduced the woman. "This is my life-servant, Yavi."

He had a slave while also being one? Yavi smiled, though it was tight and didn't reach her hazel eyes. A small sign she hated being called that.

"She will help you familiarize yourself with the camp and how we run things," Von continued. "See her for whatever you need. I will come find you later." To the others, he said, "Have her eat something."

Then he swiftly left, and they watched him go until he fell out of view.

"Here. Have something to drink, Dyna." Yavi poured water into a wooden cup and passed it to her.

"You know my name," she muttered.

"We have heard a lot about you and your Guardians. Geon told us how he helped him in Corron."

Geon flushed when they locked eyes, and he fidgeted with his chopping knife. "Thank you for what you did. Master would have thrown me back on the streets if I couldn't walk."

Would they merely toss him aside with a broken leg? Tarn's cruelty shouldn't surprise her after everything he'd done.

"And I-I'm sorry about what happened in Corron." Geon winced. "And for Landcaster..."

That felt like so long ago. Before all of this, life had seemed easier even with the burden of her past, for the journey hadn't been tainted yet. Back then, she'd been naïve and optimistic...and she still had Zev.

Dyna wiped her cheeks. Everyone was looking at her.

The Minotaur snorted a heavy breath, and his thick brass bangles clanked against his hooves when he made a threatening step forward. Geon flinched away.

Yavi rubbed her back. "Stop spooking him, Sorren. You've turned him into a skittish cat."

"I'm not skittish," Geon huffed as he continued to chop greens.

Sorren went to stir the contents inside the cauldron, a long tail lashing beneath his apron. He poured something into a bowl before placing it in front of her. "Eat, girl."

It looked like mushrooms and other vegetables in a brown broth. It smelled good, but Dyna's stomach churned in protest. She couldn't consume anything right now.

Sorren crossed his hairy arms. "I prepared it without meat, as instructed."

How would he know her eating habits? Then she recalled Von mentioning they had spied on them before.

Yavi saw her face and pushed the plate to him. "She doesn't want it, Sorren."

"Then I will make something else for you." Geon hurried off to dig through the baskets of fruits and vegetables on the counter behind him.

"No, thank you...I'm not hungry." Dyna's voice came out like a rattle of dry leaves.

Yavi looked at her with sympathy. "This must all be a lot for you. Come. Let's take you somewhere quiet."

For whatever reason, Dyna followed her outside and walked through the camp again. Most of the Raiders stole glances at them, others gave them a wide berth. Yavi walked on with her head held high, glaring at anyone who lingered too long. But an older Raider sitting by the fire openly stared at them with a lascivious leer, leaving a sickly oily feeling on Dyna's skin.

Yavi's eyes narrowed. "I'm sure you remember what happened the last time someone crossed the commander, Haran," she told him icily, her voice projecting loud enough for everyone nearby to hear.

Haran snorted. His dark, contemptuous eyes stayed on her as they walked away. To Dyna's surprise, the other Raiders no longer looked at them, as if they were afraid of Yavi...or the warning. For a slave, she was unusually outspoken.

"You're safe with me." Yavi winked. "Von won't let anything bad happen to us."

Why did she think that? She must have his favor, since her warning had been enough to keep the men at bay.

With every step Yavi made, her bangles danced. They seemed to be engraved with different symbols. "A gift from Master Tarn," Yavi said when she noticed her studying them.

Dyna heard the bitterness in that statement. They arrived at another tent a bit away from the others. When Yavi opened the tent flap for Dyna to go in, she recognized it as the same one she had woken in that morning. "This is our tent. I know it's not much. I used to...share it with someone else, but it's your home now, too."

Everything in Dyna went cold. "This isn't my home."

Yavi winced and smiled ruefully. "You're right, it's not." She brought her to sit on a cot, then sat in the opposite one. "I know how you feel. It took me a long time to accept that I was a slave."

"I'm not a slave," Dyna said stiffly, scowling at the bangles she wore. "And these don't make me one. I'm going to get out of here. My friends are looking for me and I know they will find me."

Yavi sighed, and there was only sad pity on her face. "Benton has veiled this camp. If your Guardians were to arrive, it would be futile. They cannot smell you, hear you, let alone touch you. Not even if you stood right in front of them. Why do you think they haven't caught Tarn? No one can find us."

Something inside of her quivered as the floor threatened to tilt. Dyna shook her head. There had to be a way out, because she refused to accept this new reality.

Yavi looked at the flame flickering in the lantern. "I was stolen away from my family in the middle of the night. My parents don't know what happened to me or where I am. They probably think I'm dead."

Dyna felt guilty for snapping at her. "I'm sorry."

"It's all right. I have Von." Seeming to catch herself, Yavi quickly added, "I mean, the commander is a kind master. He treats me well."

It was an odd thing to hear. Slaves tended to be abused, but by Yavi's clothing and lack of bruises, she wasn't. She spoke freely with him as well, without fear of retribution.

"He murdered my cousin," Dyna said. "Kind isn't how I would describe him."

Yavi's eyebrows curled, and she laid a gentle hand over hers. "I'm sorry that happened."

Dyna tried to focus on the woven patterns in the bamboo mat so she wouldn't break down again. The last thing she said to Zev was that she wouldn't forgive him if he died. She was so furious at him for wanting to take his life. She wanted to force him to live, and some raw, desperate part of her thought guilt might work. But he had passed away with her last angry words. She wished with all her might that she could take them back.

"He didn't want to do it." Yavi came to sit by her and wiped the tears from her cheeks. "Don't let his demeanor fool you. Von doesn't like to kill, but he does as his master orders."

"And you think that would make me forgive him?" Dyna stood. "You think that is a valid excuse?"

Yavi lowered her gaze. "In this place, disobedience means death. Von, along with a fourth of the men, are owned by Tarn. He makes a sport of collecting people." She shook her ankle, causing the bangles to clink. "And he likes to remind us of that. These are enchanted to keep me no more than a mile from the Crystal Core in his tent. The mages wear them too, so they can't attack him with their magic. Sorren's bangles confine him to his kitchen."

The Minotaur was a prisoner more than a slave. She made a note of that detail. It might be useful.

"Why?" Dyna asked.

"Because if he was ever freed, Sorren would tear through everyone in this camp to kill Tarn."

Definitely useful information, then. "Why did Tarn want a Minotaur?"

"That had nothing to do with it. Tarn simply needed someone to feed his men. He offered to employ him into his service, but Sorren had his own establishment and a family, so he refused. Tarn never accepts refusals."

Dyna shook her head at the incredulity of such a wicked man. "Why did he collect you?"

Yavi motioned to the wooden box sitting on the floor by her cot. "I'm a linguist. I speak, read and write several languages, including ancient Urnian."

Dyna gasped softly. "You know the old tongue?"

"I'm a descendant of the acolytes that once served in the temples of the God of Urn." Her brow furrowed as emotion filled her eyes. "My father taught me how to read the Sacred Scrolls."

Which was astonishing. The scrolls and the old tongue were a lost part of Urn's history, for so many were destroyed a thousand years ago.

"But why would Tarn care about the scrolls?" Dyna asked. "He doesn't strike me as a virtuous man."

Yavi smirked. "Believe me, he is far from it. The only time Tarn calls on the God of Urn is to claim a life-debt. Not even I know exactly what he wants with the Sacred Scrolls. Only that he's searching for a specific one with information on the…"

She trailed off, but Dyna knew what she meant to say. "The Unending."

"He told you?"

"Not everything."

He was too smart for that, so why reveal his goal for immortality? He said the Tree of the Unending was on Mount Ida, and her map had the location. Then what was the purpose of searching for the Scroll of the Unending? Becoming immortal couldn't be as easy as finding the hidden treasure island.

Nothing ever was.

"What are you thinking?" Yavi asked, watching her pace in the tent with wide eyes.

Dyna hesitated to answer. This woman might have been sent to watch her, but the harsh way she spoke of Tarn dwindled that suspicion. Or maybe Dyna wanted to believe that because she needed an ally in this place.

"I have a sense that immortality isn't the only thing he wants, or as simple as we think it is," she said. "It must be on Mount Ida, but…it's not enough." She halted when she came to a realization. Tarn told her one truth to distract her from the ones he omitted. "He needs something else. Something hidden in the scrolls."

The color drained from Yavi's complexion and she pressed on her stomach, looking like she might spew. "Of course he does. The Sacred Scrolls hold secrets of the very fabric from which our world was created, the essence of life itself. Whatever he wants, you can't let him have it," she said, pleading earnestly. "Can you imagine what he would do with immortality in his hands?"

Some tension eased out of Dyna's shoulders. "You don't want that?"

"No one wants that. Not even Von. We're all bound to that man's whim, but not you." Yavi took her hands, her mouth trembling with a watery smile. "I have waited a long time for you, Dyna. Since the moment we learned you were coming, we have been waiting."

She stared at the woman, taken aback by the look on her face. It was so full of hope and wonder as if she were some sort of miracle. "What do you mean?"

"Because you, dear Maiden, will be Tarn's undoing."

CHAPTER 4

Zev

No matter how many times Zev was burned alive, he could never get used to it. He woke feeling feverish, his face and body heated as white-hot pain stole the last of his strength. Every inhale smelled of mud and scorching flesh. He could hear nothing outside of his heavy breaths that clouded in the air. Smoke rose and hissed where the silver touched him.

Why did he wake? He didn't want to wake up yet.

Zev's heavy eyelids slid closed, wishing to return to the black void of his dreams. It was a boundless plain, the ground perfectly reflective, like a mirror made of black water, rippling with each step he walked into nothingness. Until he had looked down. A white wolf gazed back at him with the most vivid blue eyes, as if looking in from the edge of another realm. But when he took a step forward, he sank through the water.

"Zev!"

He jerked awake again. Had he even woken in the first place? He grunted a curse and fought against his restraints. But it only made his skin melt into the chains snaked around him. Rawn held down his shoulders as Cassiel quickly shoved the key into the shackles and unlocked them. His wrists were covered with pus-filled boils.

"God of Urn," Rawn murmured.

"Ready?" Cassiel asked him.

Zev clenched his teeth and nodded. Cassiel tried to be gentle, but it didn't stop the chains from peeling away his flesh like sodden paper. His vision swam, and his screams echoed through the forest.

Once he was free, Zev buckled to the ground. The pain throbbed through every nerve, and his mind tried to bury him away, but his hazy thoughts jerked his body with earnestness to get up. He needed to find his cousin. And Lucenna. Both. Both of them.

But he couldn't do more than shiver violently. Rawn threw a cloak over him, and Cassiel supported his arm over his shoulder. Together, they helped him to his feet. His body leaned heavily against them, with no ability to stand on his own. His wolf had been chased off by the silver, comatose somewhere inside of him.

He tried to say Dyna's name, but all that came out was a garbled moan.

"You must heal first," Rawn said, somehow understanding.

Zev wanted to protest, but Cassiel's grim expression agreed. He was no good in this state when he could hardly stand.

They grunted under his weight as they carried him away, his feet stumbling under him. Zev fought to stay conscious. His ears filled with the chatter of the forest and the rattle of the chains straggling behind them. They brought him inside a small cave that smelled of wet stone and earth and carefully lay him down on layers of blankets. He drifted in and out, catching snippets of their muffled voices. His head was burning, and sweat beaded on his body.

Everything seemed to shake.

"His fever is climbing."

"I'm afraid I carry no medicine. Not even for the pain."

"He barely survived the silver poisoning yesterday. This is too much. We need a healer. We need Dyna."

Dyna...

Where was Dyna?

Zev might have called out for her, but his mouth didn't work. He couldn't stop shaking. The pounding in his heart raced faster. He tried to hold on, but he was floating away like a leaf in the wind.

"Is it not against Celestial law?"

"At this point, I am beyond any reprieve."

His mind fogged as he thought of the vivid blue eyes again.

Then he was gone.

The reflective black floor rippled beneath Zev's paws. Every step echoed, the soft sound of clinking following him. The silver chains hung around his neck like a collar he couldn't escape.

Hours seemed to pass before he caught the flash of a white tail and gave chase. Zev ran and ran through the void, even as he lost sight of what he was chasing. He ran faster and his surroundings shifted into a dark forest. His paws tore through the frozen dirt, icy wind slipping through his fur as he raced past the trees.

The moon streamed in through the branches and formed a path as though to light the way. A howl broke through the forest. Then another and another, melding into a chorus of voices, announcing a hunt. But for once, not for him.

Zev threw back his head and howled back.

A white flash darted past him. He gave chase again. Snow fell and soon it coated the ground. Zev bounded into the winter storm, making his way up a hill. Whatever waited at the top, wherever the moon was taking him, it didn't matter. There was no push against his mind, no hissing presence. No guilt. No pain.

Nothing but the hunt.

Something moved among the shadows of the trees. A man was walking ahead with a pack on his back. Zev halted. He didn't need to see his face to know who it was.

Zev whined. *Do you forgive me?*

His father turned and smiled at him. It held no blame. Only a fond greeting that spoke of warmth and affection.

"What are you doing here?" he asked, frowning playfully. "Are you lost?"

Lost? Zev looked around the rise. The black sky glittered with snowfall, and the horizon stretched on endlessly. His steps somehow left no prints. The snow was a perfect layer.

Untouched. Unmarked. Clean.

Zev wasn't sure how he got here, but he liked it. He didn't want to leave.

Kneeling in front of him, his father reached for the chains. *No.* Zev moved back. If he lost them, he would be insubstantial. They were the only thing solid of his being. Losing that was frightening.

"These chains were never meant to be a permanent part of you." His father stroked his head. "If you keep holding on to the past, you won't catch up to the present, son." He nodded for him to look at the white wolf waiting for him at the top of the hill. "And I never taught you to give up."

25

Zev groaned out a long yawn and rubbed his face. It felt dry and tight, like he had been stretched thin. He blinked blearily at the cave ceiling, listening to the chirping of birds drifting from the trees outside. Fire crackled in the campfire beside him. What a strange, lucid dream.

A pang went through his chest as Zev thought of his father. He was trying to tell him something or show him something. What did the white wolf mean?

He'd never seen one before since they were an arctic breed. Was it symbolic? Or was he simply hallucinating from the fever?

Zev scratched absentmindedly at his smooth chest. *Smooth?* At the unexpected feeling, he glanced down at himself and froze. His skin—the scars from the silver chains were gone. Every single one. His wrists held no proof he ever wore manacles.

"Good. You are awake. I was beginning to worry." Cassiel and Rawn watched him from where they sat on the other end of the campfire.

"What have you done?" Zev grated. "Why did you heal me? I didn't ask you to heal me!"

Cassiel frowned. "No thank you this time? Your whole body was burned."

"It's meant to be that way. Those were my scars to bear!" He forced himself to stand, swaying on his legs.

Once his vision stopped spinning, Zev stormed away from the cave, naked as the day he was born. He shoved his way through the thick foliage. The Madness was always there below the surface. He waited for its cackle. For its hiss. But it merely prowled, quiet and listening.

He lifted his trembling, clawed hands. They looked clean and unblemished, like the snow in his dream. It was all wrong. Zev sank to the ground, hunching over his knees. The hands of a killer shouldn't look this way.

A faint rustle in the bushes was the only announcement Rawn gave to his presence. With the breeze coming downwind, Zev wouldn't have noticed him.

"May I approach?" Rawn asked.

Zev didn't answer. His wild, dark hair blew over his eyes as he stared blankly at the dead leaves stuck to his muddy feet. His legs were also unblemished. Every full moon he endured; the proof of his torment meant to pay for his sin—it was all…wiped away.

Rawn draped a blanket over his shoulders before sitting beside him. He didn't ask more of him. He simply kept him company as the morning arrived.

"He shouldn't have erased my shame," Zev eventually whispered, not able to hide the misery hovering beneath his anger.

"Do you say this because you cannot control the change?"

"No." If only that was the only reason. He dug his sharp nails into his palms until he bled. Maybe he had become used to the pain. Needed it to feel something other than remorse. "I...killed my father one night that I turned. The silver chains, I deserve the torture they mark on my body. It's my penance for what I have done."

The quiet expanded with the rise of his lungs and he waited for the weight of that fault. And it did come, but it somehow felt...

"I am sorry, my friend," Rawn said softly. He didn't look very shocked or appalled. Cassiel must have told him.

Zev pressed on his swollen eyelids. "You have no need to be. I don't mean to make you uncomfortable."

A brisk wind blew through the trees, causing the few remaining dry leaves on the branches to rustle. He almost didn't hear Rawn's quiet confession.

"I, too, have killed my kin. My mother."

Zev's next breath halted in his throat. They didn't know much about Lord Norrlen, but the little he did reveal always seemed to be heavy and private. Like parts that were a deep, integral part of what made him. And this was another heartrending piece.

"She passed whilst giving birth to me...leaving behind five other children." Rawn gazed at the trees as though he were seeing something else. "My brothers were never close to me. I think...they despised me for taking her away from them. My sister... she was kinder due to being too young to remember her. I knew my father held me at fault as well, although he, by no account, admitted it. I did all I could to gain his favor." He twisted the gold military ring around his finger with a sigil Zev didn't recognize. "I became a soldier as he wished and progressed rapidly through the ranks of the army. Despite all my efforts, my father remained discordant. I did not complain. I felt his resentment was warranted."

Zev shook his head. "But...but it wasn't your fault."

Rawn smiled at him sadly. "Likewise, you did not intend to harm your father. Werewolves are not sane of mind when they turn. You had no control over what occurred that night. And you should not give up your life because of it."

Zev looked away. "You heard our conversation yesterday."

Sometimes he forgot how well the elf could hear. He was in a dark cloud when he confessed to Dyna about wanting to die.

"I did." Rawn looked up at the clear blue sky through the tree branches. Scattered clouds rolled past, leaving behind shapes on the ground. "No matter how hard we try in life, there is no guarantee of a perfect ending. Living is the greatest adventure there is, and it would be a great shame for you to miss it."

It was difficult to go on with his life when it hurt to breathe in a world that didn't allow it. The moment of nearly dying filled him with the need to survive, but to continue, Zev had to accept what he had done to his father.

"I'm weighed down by my grief," he admitted. "It's burrowed within me so deep it has become my marrow. The truth is, I'm not ready to let that go yet..." He picked a desiccated leaf off his leg, and it crumbled in his hand. "Because if I were to yank it out, my bones would have nothing to hold on to, and I would simply...break apart."

To say it out loud brought a sudden clarity of something he hadn't known about himself.

Rawn nodded, as though he understood, because he had felt the same at one point. "Pain is not meant to break you. Enduring it is in itself a cruel trial of strength. It will take some time to heal, if that is what you wish. It's not an easy road, nor a short one, but do not dwell on how long the journey is. The top of one mountain is the bottom of the next. Therefore, keep climbing. Eventually, you will arrive where you are meant to be."

It was times like these when Zev realized why Lord Norrlen was their Guidelander. It wasn't merely about knowing the land. He let them make their own decisions, even if he didn't agree. But in these dark moments when they felt so lost, he simply guided them back. And not once did he ever make Zev feel judged for it.

"Thank you, Lord Norrlen. For your ever-present wisdom."

A soft smile rose to his face. "I merely share what I have learned."

"And thank you for not questioning my ability to shift during the day. You have been among the first not to find it strange, other than—" His eyes widened. "Dyna." The reminder of her had Zev leaping to his feet. "Gods, we need to go."

"Yes." Rawn quickly got up and followed him back to the cave. "Why should I find it strange?" he asked curiously as they hurried through the trees. "I have met many Lycans during my travels."

"Lycans?"

"Half-human werewolves. They call themselves Lycans and can shift freely as they wish. I heard the largest Pack of them dwell in Xián Jīng."

Zev halted, shock falling over him like icy water. There was more like him?

Rawn's eyebrows rose high. "My friend, did you believe you were the only one?"

Yes, he had...

"God of Urn, forgive me. If I had known, I would have mentioned it sooner."

But Zev wasn't upset. He was swimming in relief. He wasn't alone in the world, and the fact was so overwhelming he had the urge to both laugh and cry. All this time, he thought he was an abnormality, but now he found there were *Packs* of his kind.

He continued through the bushes. "Have you…met the Pack in Xián Jīng?"

"I have not, unfortunately," Rawn said. "The Garou Pack keeps their territory hidden in the Lángshān Mountains. But there are a few others in Urn. I once met the Lupin Pack while passing through Emberdin. They've laid claim to the plains there."

Emberdin was the grasslands of Azure, only three days to the east. Zev turned his head in that direction as if he might catch a glimpse of them. It was enough to know that they existed. Maybe when this was all over, he could go in search of them.

"I had yet to meet a fully grown Lycan who could not control their Other," Rawn continued with a heavy sigh. "Hence, I assumed you had a hold of yours. However, you never knew there were more like you out there. Your Pack has greatly neglected you."

Zev slowed when they came out of the tree line, stepping into the sun. It reflected off the gilded embellishments in Rawn's scabbard. "What…" He breathed. "What did you say?"

"Pardon if I offend. I merely meant the Other is very dangerous if left unattended. The Pack Alphas must teach the young pups from a very young age how to master it. Some have never had to use chains."

"No—" Zev shook his head sharply. He had to swallow before he could speak. "You said *control*. It's possible to control the Other?"

Rawn frowned, as if it were an odd question. "Of course it is."

He couldn't do more than stand there in stunned silence. His father had been right, after all. *These chains were never meant to be a permanent part of you.*

"Zev." Cassiel stood outside of the cave holding Fair's reins. Their bags were all packed and tied to the harness.

He clenched his teeth, a growl rumbling in his chest. "Don't speak to me."

"Zev—"

"God of Urn help me, Cassiel. If you don't leave me be, I swear I will beat you within an inch of your life. Then let you heal, and do it again."

"Do it if that would make you feel better," he said. "I'm sorry about the scars, but you are angry about more than that."

"Oh, I'm furious. So beyond it, I'm trying to restrain myself from—" Zev broke off in a frustrated snarl. "Healing me when I didn't ask for it is one thing, but I cannot forgive you for bonding with Dyna and keeping it from me as well."

29

"Seven Hells, Zev. I never planned for it to happen!" Cassiel snapped. "I saved her life, damn it. You need to get over yourself and point your anger somewhere else." He beat a fist over his heart. "Tarn took her. And every minute I don't see her, I have to fight against the instinct telling me she is dead."

Zev narrowed his eyes. "She's not dead."

"It feels that way."

"Because you cannot feel her." His fangs extended, fur growing along his arms. "That must mean she cannot feel you either."

"Probably not." Cassiel squared his shoulders, acceptance in his cool gaze. "Now is your chance, Zev. Do your worst—"

Zev slammed his fist into Cassiel's jaw. He staggered, but braced his legs to remain standing.

"Cease this," Rawn said, moving to intervene.

"Leave him." Cassiel wiped the blood from his nose. "Feel better?"

A deep growl rumbled in Zev's chest. "Hardly."

"Come on, then." The next punch landed in Cassiel's gut, and he doubled over, but he motioned for him to keep going. When Zev didn't, he scowled. "That is all? We're not finished. Hit me!"

Desperation swarmed in his bloodshot eyes. He wanted this. He was punishing himself, as Zev had done many times before. For not saving Dyna and perhaps for other things. The need to feel some sort of pain other than the one torturing him now. But he had long learned no one else could carry that weight.

"We each must bear our own burdens, Cassiel. This is yours."

Cassiel slumped back and looked up at the cloudy sky, his wings hanging limply. He looked so lost. Zev wondered if that was how he'd looked to others all these years.

"It hurts," Cassiel rasped, curling a fist over his heart. It shook, and Zev caught a brief flicker of blue there, a dance of light passing through his taught fingers, gone in a blink. So fast, Zev wasn't sure if he had truly seen it. "I...I need her, Zev. I need her back."

The brokenness on the prince's face made his own eyes water. Zev had always been there for Dyna, but for all of his strength and ability, he felt so powerless.

"Aye, I know you do." Zev crouched in front of him. "But you have to get up, all right? We have to keep going because she needs us. And I need—" His voice cracked. "I need you to keep hoping for the both of us. Understand?"

His sanity was hanging by a thread. It lured the Madness, and Zev felt it lurking in the edges of his being. If he lost another member of his family, he was done for.

Cassiel's weary eyes looked up at him. Whatever he saw made him take a deep breath and nod. Zev helped him up.

"Do not despair," Rawn told them. "We *will* find Lady Dyna."

Cassiel dragged a hand down his face. "Not without Lucenna."

"We don't have a choice right now, Lord Norrlen," Zev groused at the disapproval on his face. Every inch of his skin tugged with the urge to shift and search for the one thing they couldn't find. "You cannot magically track Dyna. I cannot catch her scent, and Cassiel cannot sense her. I think Lucenna will understand us coming to her for help."

"I don't care if she understands or not." Cassiel expanded his large wings, the wind ruffling the black feathers.

"Then we should return to where we saw Lady Lucenna last," Rawn said, finally agreeing. "There might still be a trace of her there."

Zev met his eyes and knew they were thinking the same thing. It had been days since Lucenna went her own way. The rain might have washed away any traces of her, and if it did, then hopes of crossing paths with her dropped to near impossible. The further they went, the further they were from Dyna, but right now, their best chance of finding her was to go east first.

He called on his wolf, and his body ached as the shift rippled through him. Fur sprouted from his body and his paws hit the ground.

Tarn may have won for now, but Zev would never stop hunting.

CHAPTER 5

Von

The Maiden's presence had changed the atmosphere of the camp. Von felt the tension from the quiet men as they went about their duties, as if they were holding their breath for whatever would come next. He was on his way to find her and dreaded every step, but when Von arrived at his old tent, he halted at the sound of Yavi's voice reciting the divination.

"'Seek the Maiden with emeralds for sight and tresses of fire, for she holds the key to the Unending thou desires. Beware the Guardians who come to shield her from thee. She will be protected by one of divine blood and a dweller of the moon howling to break free. Thus follows a warrior bestowing his vow, and a sorceress grants her sorcery. A familiar face vies for vengeance, and a creature with the strength of ten eradicates the forgery. Great peril in the venture thou art pursuing. Be not swayed by love, lest it be thy undoing.'"

His eyes widened. Yavi could be flogged, or worse, for telling her that.

"That was the Seer's prediction when Tarn asked her how to obtain immortality," she said. "Don't you see? It's fate, Dyna. You're going to stop him."

"Pardon, what?"

"Be not swayed," Yavi said excitedly. "It means—"

Von entered before she said more. They jumped apart and stared at him with wide eyes, like they had been caught conspiring or discussing things they shouldn't. "The Master will see you now."

Dyna nodded stiffly and slipped past him outside.

"Don't let him hurt her," Yavi said earnestly.

"I'll be there." Von couldn't promise more than that.

Knowing the way, Dyna walked some paces ahead of him to Tarn's tent. Her back was stiff, every line of her body tense.

Von kept thinking about the last line of the divination, but he knew Tarn would never be swayed. The only thing he cared about was his ambition, and damn anyone who got in his way. The Maiden was only a means to get what he wanted. Then Tarn would crush her as well. The thought of such a thing befalling her made Von's stomach pitch.

Dyna's gaze fixed on the Hermon Mountains in the distance. Sensing she may attempt to run, he grabbed her arm. His long strides forced her into a quick gait. Tarn didn't like to be kept waiting.

"Yavi said you're a good man," Dyna said tightly, pulling against his grip. "If that's true, then you need to let me go."

"She shouldn't have said that." He wasn't a good man. Not anymore.

The wind blew fiery red locks across her face as she studied him. "Do you want him to become immortal?"

He looked away. "I serve my master as the God of Urn commands. I don't have the right to want anything." Noticing her arm, Von turned it over to inspect the tree tattoo spanning her forearm to her wrist. The roots wove around her fingers, as if tethered to her. "What's that? You didn't have that in the port."

"It's a geas."

Which only came about one way.

He hauled her to a stop. "Why did you make a deal with the fae? They are not to be trusted."

"It was done unwillingly," Dyna said, her tone cutting. She tried to jerk her arm from his grasp again. "I prefer you not to touch me."

"I will let you go if you promise not to run."

"If I attempt it, will you stab me as well?" Her words were a blade in his ribs. Then it twisted and ripped free with her next reply. "Killing seems all you're good for."

Von released her. Dyna's skin looked pale beneath the cloudy day, but Zev had turned gray as soon as he had plunged the silver knife through his gut, as though it had drained the color out of him. He pushed back the memory of Zev's veins turning black beneath his skin and the black blood spilling from his mouth.

"I told you not to move," Von had said.

Why did he move?

Did it matter? Tarn wanted the Lycan dead. The pure distraught on Dyna's face at that moment and her broken scream had torn through Von. The weight of regret was a boulder on his back. He'd taken many lives at Tarn's orders, but this one left a stain bigger than all the rest. His actions broke another family. He had slayed Zev right in front of her.

Von wished he could take it back. "Dyna, I—"

"There is nowhere for me to run, Commander." The edge of hatred sharpened her emerald eyes. "Go on. Take me to your master."

He couldn't expect anything else from her, and it was no more than he deserved.

Von continued, and she followed until they reached Tarn's tent. He inhaled a low breath before opening the flaps for her to go in.

Dyna peered up at the hundreds of protection spells and crystals hanging from the roof, then at the charred outlines of runes that marked the canvas walls of the tent. The spells were old and faded, but their power pulsed in the air, ready to strike should she attempt anything again.

The glowing amethyst crystal hanging above stopped spinning, and the scatter of purple lights it made on the walls faded as they fully stepped inside.

"A Forewarning Crystal..." Dyna muttered to herself.

Von let her peruse as her eyes continued to roam over Tarn's bed and desk, covered in artifacts and scrolls. By it rested chests of clothing and gold. A large dining table was on their left with a platter of roasted chicken, vegetables, fruit, and baked bread. At the farthest end of the table sat the Master.

The white-blond locks of Tarn's hair were slicked back, leaving every sharp angle of his face exposed. Including the distinct scar that coursed diagonally across his face, between his right brow to the left of his jaw.

His cool eyes were fixed on the journal set in front of him, seeming to be offended by it. Von pulled out a chair at the opposite end of the dining table for Dyna.

Tarn's gaze lifted to her. "We have much to discuss."

She raised her chin. "Remove the bangles. Then we'll talk."

Von was impressed by the flash of defiance on her face, even if her fists trembled at her sides.

"Such hubris and coming from someone so fragile. *Sit.*" Sharp authority lined Tarn's tone, and Dyna immediately sat. He glanced at him next.

At the silent command, Von lifted the carving knife off the table and shaved off slices of chicken, then plated it with some greens. After taste-testing each item, he set the plate in front of his master.

"It seems you are correct. My mages cannot open the journal without you," Tarn said. "I find it incredulous that they cannot bypass your spell."

Dyna did her best to keep her expression aloof. Though, from Von's vantage point, he noticed her fingers fidgeting on her lap. Her complexion was more pallid than usual.

"I didn't place the spell." She glanced at the truth rune shaped in a horizontal hourglass. She must recognize the wards.

Tarn paused, considering her answer, as he glanced at the rune as well. It glowed bright blue in confirmation. "Who placed it?"

"Azeran Astron."

He slightly raised an eyebrow at the name. "He was quite the famous mage in his time. How did you acquire his journal?"

"It's mine." She shifted in her chair uneasily as Von served a plate and a cup of water for her next. She stared at the rolls of bread, cheese, butter, and berry compote, then at him. He nodded at her to eat, then moved to his post by the entrance.

"I won't play word games with you," Tarn said. "Speak plainly. Where did you get the journal?"

Dyna seemed to freeze under his icy stare. He had that effect on people. Von caught her eye, giving her an encouraging look that hopefully said it would be all right. She only needed to answer the question.

"It was passed down through my family," she finally replied. "I'm one of his descendants."

Tarn linked his fingers together and leaned back in his chair. "How well are you versed in the magical arts?"

"I don't know any magic," she said carefully.

The rune for lies glowed red. Von tensed at the cold smirk rising to Tarn's mouth.

"Well, I know a few spells, but I can hardly use my Essence," Dyna blurted. "And not enough to be useful."

The truth rune lit up, supporting the claim.

Tarn observed her intently. "To channel Essence means you have magic, and we all saw evidence of it yesterday."

She had struck them with a powerful green blast in the grove when Zev fell. It had thrown Von clear across the hill.

From the look on his master's face, he was greatly interested in that. Von suspected this would happen as soon as Tarn discovered her abilities. He would never let her go now.

Von couldn't remember when his obsession with magic first originated. Many enchanted relics were strewn about the tent, the more valuable ones kept on the desk. They had spilled blood for most of them. Some were stolen, and a rare few were bought. His gaze landed on a small, antique wooden chest. It was intricately carved with a palace garden scene and a winding dragon. It had gold-plated corners and was sealed shut with a locked clasp shaped with the sigil of Xián Jīng. To this day, he still didn't know what was inside.

"I'm willing to bet you hold quite a bit of power in you," Tarn said. "All you need is instruction, Dynalya."

She grimaced. "Don't call me that. Only my friends may call me by name, and you're no friend of mine."

"Then what shall I call you?"

"Maiden. That's all I am to you."

Von glanced back and forth between them. The crackle of burning wood was the only sound in the dragging silence. Their staring match was interrupted by the sound of Dyna's growling stomach. Her face flushed bright red.

"Before we discuss other matters, have a meal first." Tarn motioned at her plate, and she glowered. "Not to your preference? As I understand it, you prefer not to eat meat."

Dyna glanced at the food warily.

"It's not wrong to eat at your enemy's table. You betray no one but yourself to go with an empty stomach." Tarn raised his goblet, nodding to him. "If you think the food is poisoned, then Von will be more than happy to taste it for you."

Von felt her eyes on him as he lifted the flagon from the sideboard table and poured wine into Tarn's cup, the spiced, fruity aroma drifting to his nose.

"Is he truly happy?" Dyna asked after a pause, and Von met her gaze. "To risk his life in favor of yours?"

"He lives merely to serve me. Is that not right, Von?"

Von lowered his head, emptying his mind of all else but the reason he was here. "Yes, Master."

The image of long, golden brown curls lying in a pool of blood flashed in his memories. He briefly closed his eyes and took a breath. When he opened them again, Tarn's soulless eyes were on him.

They had learned a long time ago where they stood with each other.

From his coat pocket, Tarn drew out a glass vial. The black contents swirled inside as he poured six drops into his goblet. They hit the surface and gleamed silver before disappearing.

Dyna watched the action as well, following the cup to his lips when he drank it. "You say he serves you willingly, yet you don't trust him or the others enough to sleep around them."

Tarn paused.

She leaned forward, mouth hitching at the ends. "Why else would you drink Witch's Brew?"

CHAPTER 6

Dynalya

Dyna forced herself not to look away from Tarn's piercing stare. His eyes may as well be orbs of ice, lacking any warmth. Despite the scar across his face, he possessed a merciless kind of beauty. Hard and sharp. Not able to look at him any longer, she let her eyes drift over the elegance of his fine black jacket, the lapels, and cuffs embroidered with gilded detailing. The ensemble was completed with a formfitting vest over his tunic, with thin chains and gold buttons.

Everything he wore spoke of wealth and nobility. As they analyzed each other in the silence, curiosity peaked through her unease, and she found herself wondering about this man. Was he truly a descendant of the Ice Phoenix? Why was he pursuing immortality? How did he become the most wanted man in Azure?

She tried not to squirm as his pale blue eyes flickered over her messy hair, to her torn clothing, briefly pausing over the scratches on her neck and chest before falling to the geas. Dyna tugged her cloak around her to hide it.

He turned the glass vial in his fingers. "You know what this is?"

Not able to ignore her hunger, Dyna slathered a dollop of fruit compote on some bread with a dinner knife. "I'm a Herb Master. I studied the medicinal use of every plant in the region, including their witchcraft use. There aren't many potions I wouldn't recognize."

"Good. Then you will tend to the captain of my spies."

She frowned. "What?"

Tarn took a drink. "Your elf injured mine. Therefore, the task of tending to him is yours."

It was a test.

Thanks to his spies, this man knew everything there was to know about her, so he was already aware of her trade. He merely flaunted the potion to see how knowledgeable she was. Dyna bit into her bread and chewed slowly. This could work in her favor.

"And if I refuse?"

Tarn answered with a heartless, cruel chuckle. The sound raised the hair on the back of her neck. "Well, should treating the ill no longer be in your interest, we can move on to an interest of mine."

She glanced at the journal. "Why not force me to open it?"

Standing, Tarn came around to sit on the edge of the table beside her and held out his palm expectantly. "All in due time."

Dyna's pulse sped as they stared at each other for a moment. Then she reached into her cloak and dropped the dinner knife in his hand.

"Have you ever killed before, Maiden?" Tarn asked, tapping a fingertip against the dull, rounded point.

"No."

"You would have failed tremendously with a dinner knife."

She leaned back in her seat and let her gaze drop to his throat. "I think with the proper motivation, it wouldn't take much to puncture a vital artery."

The statement came out casually, but Dyna's heart beat wildly. She couldn't let on how much he frightened her.

Tarn's stare leveled on her face, and his mouth quirked as if she didn't fool him at all. "In that, we agree. Do you plan to be difficult? You promised to come willingly."

"And I came. Staying is another issue entirely."

He hummed. "I don't think you would like to know what I do to those who defy me. By all means, the choice is yours. But I'm curious. Von mentioned you're from a hidden village somewhere among the Zafiro Mountains."

She stiffened at the mention of her home.

"It must have farmland, I take it. Land to cultivate, cattle for food and labor."

Dyna nodded slowly, not sure why he cared to know.

"Tell me, how do you tame a wild horse?" Tarn asked, his voice suddenly so deathly quiet. "They are willful. Stubborn to the ways they lived before. Eventually, they are broken in and fitted with the bit and bridle." Bracing his hand on the table, he leaned forward until their faces were inches apart. Her next breath lodged in her throat, and frosted air filled her lungs. "You have a willfulness that you believe cannot be broken. It will be interesting to see how long it takes to tame you, little colt."

She inhaled sharply through her nose, anger sparking in her chest.

He headed back to his seat. "Dismissed."

She had expected him to make demands, to order her beaten or...defiled. Yet Tarn's tall frame settled into his chair, and his attention fell on a stack of parchments. At her hesitation, his glacial stare swept back to her.

"That's all?" she asked.

"Did you expect more?"

Her brow furrowed. "I don't know, but I expected a great deal from the fearsome Tarn."

"I don't need to make threats, Maiden," he said. "By your education, you're clearly intelligent. You understand the bangles will inhibit the use of magic. Any attempt to remove them and the outcome will result in unpleasant pain. Attempting to cross the veil will be far more excruciating than anything you ever experienced." He rested his elbows on the table, steepling his fingers. "In the unlikely event you manage to escape, I will hunt you down."

How did he express himself so eloquently, yet intimidating, at the same time? That statement sounded precisely like a threat. He wouldn't send Von or his Raiders. Tarn would come himself. The edge in his voice assured he truly would be *hunting*. Slipping through his talons was going to prove challenging.

She rose from the table. Tarn handed Von the journal, and he took her arm to lead her to the exit.

"Von." Tarn's eyes locked on him. "No one is to touch her."

He quickly let go.

"Be sure the men are aware."

Von bowed. "Yes, Master."

Dyna followed him outside, feeling as shocked as the commander looked at the protection Tarn extended over her.

He cleared his throat. "This way."

She trailed after him quietly, her steps lightly squelching in the mud. Raiders passing by saluted him in greeting. A few glanced at her, but one warning look from Von sent them on their way.

"All right, lass?" he asked.

"I...I had expected him to torture me," she mumbled, still confused.

"Perhaps tomorrow if he's in a foul mood."

"That's him in a good mood?"

"Should the day come that you're the target of his displeasure, you will know."

There was something in his tone that made her wonder if Von spoke from experience. She had a feeling he did.

They came to the northern edge of the camp, where another tent stood with the forest at its back. It was about the same size as Sorren's. An electrical pull of power prickled on her skin, making Dyna gasp. The magic in the air was more potent here.

"This tent belongs to the mages," Von told her.

The feeling became stronger as they neared, and dread swarmed through her.

She shook her head. "I cannot be around mages."

"I know about the customs of the Magos Empire, lass. They won't harm you. On this, I can swear." They looked at each other for a long minute. Did he say this because of Tarn's order?

The entrance flap parted, revealing the old mage who had attacked her friends outside the grove. Long brown robes flowed to his bare feet. When he saw her, and the glower replaced itself with an intrigued smile. It sent a spike of nerves through her pulse. He stepped aside to let them enter.

Once she crossed the threshold, a prickle of static coursed from her scalp to her toes. The heady scent of damp soil and a sweet floral aroma infiltrated her senses. The soft ground was a plush carpeting of grass spotted with tiny white flowers and red toadstools. Vines had overtaken the walls and the roof. A line of several crystals of different colors and shapes hung like a banner overhead. Three cots lined neatly to the right of the entrance. Opposite of it was a large desk constructed of massive tree roots that had sprouted from the earth. Scrolls and stacked books of magic littered the surface.

"This is Benton," Von introduced, motioning to the older mage. "And those are his sons, Clayton and Dalton."

Two young men sat at a table in the far corner. Clayton had to be the eldest. He looked older than Dalton by a few years, perhaps in his twenties. Both shared the same dark brown hair and narrow features as their father.

Benton eyed Dyna down his thin nose. "Am I to believe you come from Azeran's line? Pitiful thing, aren't you?"

"My name is Dyna," she replied shortly. Were all mages this rude?

He reached for her face, and Von had a knife at the mage's bobbing throat faster than she blinked.

"Don't *touch* her." Von's harsh voice carried the clear promise of spilled blood. His sharp eyes flickered to the startled brothers, who were frozen mid-rise from their seats. "The day any of you lay a hand on the Maiden will be the last day you draw breath."

Dyna might have hated him a tiny bit less for that.

"I merely wanted to examine her features, Commander," Benton said tersely. He stepped back, making his bangles clink. "But yes, I see it. Unfortunately, you look like her. Helia of House Fuego. Disgusting. To mix the bloodlines like that is an atrocity."

She glared at him.

"Pardon if you find that a slight. It's merely a fact."

"To be slighted, I would first need to value your judgment, old mage. And if you must know, I don't."

A snicker burst on the other side of the tent. Dalton quickly smothered it under a cough when Clayton elbowed him.

"I'm a Grand Magus, born of House Slater, sovereign of the Earth Guild," Benton said to Dyna, curling his lip. "I won't tolerate such impudence from a girl, regardless of your ancestor."

Dyna rolled her eyes. Still, the title of Grand Magus was of note. It marked him as having a chief position in the mage government, a step below the Head of the Guild.

"Here." Von handed him the journal. "Keep trying to open it."

"Hmm." Benton carefully accepted it, caressing the embossed crescent sigil of House Astron on the worn black leather. "To hold his memoirs in my hands is a real honor, despite him being a traitor. Azeran was a powerful mage and discovered several innovative ways to use magic." He glanced at her from the corner of his eye. "Is your family powerful?"

"I'm afraid not, Grand Magus," Dyna said, humoring him. "My family passed away a few years ago."

"I see. What of your ancestors?"

She knew where he was going with this. "Azeran's descendants took humans for life-mates."

Benton tossed the journal on the table and wiped his hands on his robe as if they were now filthy. "A sad waste to sully such a prominent bloodline. But how is it you can open his journals when I don't have the power to do so?"

"Oh, she has magic, Father," Dalton said, winking at her. "Geon said she healed his broken leg after the clash with the Guardians in Corron. I've seen the scar."

From the corner of her sight, Dyna noticed Von stiffen.

Benton crossed his arms as he continued to scrutinize her. "Azeran was a renowned healer. By restoring the kitchen boy, does that mean you can perform Essence Healing as well?"

Dyna hesitated to answer, but it was the look of mocking on his face that made her nod.

The mages glanced at the crystals dangling above them, but none reacted.

Benton's mouth curved with a devious smile. "You're a sorceress."

"No," she immediately denied out of both habit and apprehension. A white crystal glowed red, and it cast a faint sheen over their faces. Dyna had always identified as human, but Lucenna told her she was a sorceress, and this confirmed it.

The mages laughed as if the truth was a grand joke.

"I felt your power in Landcaster," Dalton reminded her. "You are indeed a sorceress."

"If you can perform such a complex spell, then you must be powerful," Benton said. "I may give you to one of my sons to see what offspring you would produce."

Dyna gaped at him. "I beg your pardon?"

Von growled a curse at him.

With a snap of Clayton's glowing, yellow fingers, grass sprouted across the tabletop until it became a meadow of wildflowers. "For you."

Was this his attempt at courtship?

"Yes, my eldest is the best match," Benton nodded proudly. "He's talented in the arts of magic. My younger one is obviously inept."

Dalton slammed his hand on the table, and all that was green shriveled up and died.

Clayton retorted. "Don't be a child, Dal."

"Piss off, Clay."

"Need I remind all of you of your places?" Von snarled at them. "The Maiden isn't here for you. Make such suggestions again, and I will have your tongues removed."

Benton's eyes sparked red. Dyna bet if it wasn't for the bangles, the mages wouldn't be so obedient. "Then why is she here?"

"She's a Herb Master. I brought her to treat the captain."

"Her?" The question dripped with skepticism. "What would she know?"

Dyna squared her shoulders. "Since I'm here, apparently more than you."

Von's mouth twitched. "Where's Elon?"

The old mage waved his hand and the far tent wall parted, revealing a separate section with more cots. The elf lay in one. Dark brown hair stuck to the sweat on Elon's pale forehead. She glanced at his hand pressed over the bandage on his shoulder. The back of it had a perfect circular scar.

Two others kept him company. She recognized the man in a cavalier hat. Beside him was a girl with dusky skin, her long black hair pulled back in braids. Beneath their cloaks, both wore black leathers and were strapped with weapons.

Dyna took a tentative step forward. "May I see?"

Elon's amber eyes studied her for a moment, then he nodded. The others dutifully stepped back for her to approach.

"Not sure what you could do," Benton said. "I tried healing him. The spell won't take. If anything, it causes him more pain."

Dyna kneeled by Elon's side and carefully pulled back the bandages. He gritted his teeth, but otherwise didn't make a sound. The cut was inflamed and beginning to puss, red veins sprouting from the wound site. It was a sign of magic clashing with the body's ability to heal. "You cannot treat elf magic with mage magic."

"We know that," Clayton said. "He was hit with an arrow, not a spell. I think it's poison, but none we have seen before."

"May I see the arrow?" she asked.

Dalton brought it to her. She scraped off the dried blood from the arrowhead to reveal an upside-down protection rune.

"I hadn't thought to check that," Benton said.

"I should have known." The man in the cavalier hat scowled. "Their elf nearly killed Len with a similar arrow. It had pierced through her enchanted armor."

It must've had the rune for dissipation, the one that broke spells. Similar to Rawn's enchanted sword. Dyna did her best not to react to that tidbit of information.

"Do you have it?" she asked casually. "It may provide more insight on the damage inflicted."

Von held her gaze. "It's in the Master's possession."

Of course it was.

"This one is a hindrance rune." Dyna traced her thumb over the ridges. "The type that thwarts spells."

Which might have been Rawn's attempt to stop Elon from casting any more magic during the battle. She secretly sent her thanks. His arrows might be what she needed.

"Any attempt to use magic on the wound will make it worse," Dyna said as she stood. "This will require a potion to counteract the rune's spell. For that, I will need royalrod flowers. Also, yarrow to treat the pain and echinacea for the infection."

"We have none of that here," Benton said.

She turned to Von. "Then I must gather them in the woods, if I can find them in bloom."

His brow furrowed. "They are most likely out of season now, lass. Winter is nearly upon us."

He held out his hand for the arrow. Dyna reluctantly surrendered it, and he tossed it back on the desk. Von and Tarn would be watching her carefully after getting caught with the dinner knife.

"Well, as long as I can find one flower, it will be no problem for the mages to magically grow more, correct?" She smiled at them brightly. "If they are as powerful as they say."

Clayton smirked. "With a mere seed, I could grow you a bushel."

Dalton rolled his eyes.

"Go and make sure she doesn't inadvertently poison the elf with her concoctions." Benton waved them away.

Dyna left the tent with the young mages eagerly accompanying her. Von followed behind.

"How did you know about the rune?" Dalton asked.

Dyna shrugged as if she hadn't seen Rawn spend his mornings carving them. She was highly aware of the arrowhead left behind and the other one that must be stored somewhere in Tarn's tent. Like a secret fortune meant only for her.

"A simple guess."

CHAPTER 7

Dynalya

The air was chilled with the briskness of the coming winter, but it smelled like spring. Dyna lifted a royalrod stem with her gloved fingers, admiring the rich color of the tiny midnight blue petals. Thousands of them fluttered in the field she kneeled in.

"These are beautiful," Yavi said, carefully clipping another. She'd been called to help with the harvesting. "They look similar to goldenrod flowers."

"Royalrods are their cousins," Dyna told her. "Without magic, we're unlikely to find them like this."

"The boys certainly outdid themselves. I think they were trying to impress you."

Good. Dyna was willing to take advantage of that if it helped her escape. She was working on a plan, but some details were complicated. Like the pesky veil.

There had to be a way to bring it down.

The dissipation arrowhead might do it. The other option was black clovers, and Tarn wore three of them strapped to his wrist. But Dyna didn't want to meddle with black magic, so they were a last resort. Besides, the clovers wouldn't work on physically removing her bangles, so the arrowhead was her best chance. Possibly the hindrance one might be of use.

"What are you making with these?" Geon asked on her left. He had volunteered to help, too, since it released him from kitchen duty.

"A potion to treat Elon's wound and ease the pain," Dyna said. "The magical properties in the royalrods will help remove any remaining traces of the spell ailing him. But they have other uses." She lifted a stem, letting the sunlight catch on the deep blue petals. "It can treat sores, infections, and some rather fatal venoms. But likewise, it's also poisonous."

"Don't touch the leaves," Yavi warned him. "It will give you a horrid rash and blisters." She tucked her dress around her legs, covering her ankles.

"And if you burn the petals, it creates a toxic smoke that causes temporary blindness," Dyna added.

"Good thing we're not burning them." Geon chuckled as he lifted a full basket.

He carried it to the barrels they were slowly filling on the edge of the field, and he stopped to talk to Novo. The spy had been sent to keep an eye on them, but all he did was lay in the grass and observe the sky.

"What did Tarn say to you this morning?" Yavi whispered.

"Not much," Dyna said under her breath. "Benton hasn't been able to open my journal, but Tarn didn't force me to."

Yavi raised her eyebrows. "He's searched for Mount Ida for years. Now that he has your map, I wonder why he isn't forcing you..." She paused and grinned. "I know why."

"Why?"

"Because of the Seer's warning. He's treading carefully."

Dyna finally got to hear the full divination, but she didn't like the last line and she didn't like the way Yavi was looking at her as though it was inevitable. For her to think she would ever be capable of finding that frightening man remotely appealing was preposterous. The line was vague because it didn't name who could sway him. There were different kinds of love other than romantic love, like friendship and familial.

It could mean anything.

Dyna wished she could ask the Seer herself, but she lived in confinement within the Unseelie Court under the protection of the Night Queen. To use her services, one must pay with a gift, for the fae never gave anything for free.

"Yavi." Dyna leaned closer to her. "When Tarn visited the Seer in Arthal, what was his payment?"

She made sure no one was listening before saying, "Tarn gifted the Night Queen a rare and highly sought item. A dragon ring."

Dyna gaped. It reminded her of the enchanted sword Rawn was searching for, one that had been forged with the magic of dragon fire.

"They say there are five rings and they carry a dreadful power," Yavi continued. "They were lost or stolen over the ages, but find one and the courts would trade anything for them."

If they were so powerful, Dyna wondered why Tarn didn't keep it. "How did he end up with a dragon ring?"

"Two years ago, before I was taken, Tarn crossed paths with a fae traveling through the woods in a yellow caravan. Von said he had bright golden eyes that seemed to look right through him." Yavi shivered, and Dyna did, too. She had seen eyes like that before. "Tarn wasn't interested in the fae's offered wares at first until he spotted the ring among the trinkets. A lucky find, I suppose."

There was no such thing as luck.

"*Leoake,*" Dyna hissed, glaring down at the oak tree tattoo on her arm.

That conniving, scheming, dastardly Druid! How far did his hand reach through their lives? Better yet, what was he *planning*? Because Leoake was also a Seer and he could have granted Tarn a divination. Instead, he gave him a dragon ring, knowing what it would be used for.

"What is a Leoake?"

"It's nothing." Dyna frowned, an idea coming to her. "Do you know how I can contact the fae?"

Yavi's eyes widened. "I heard if you make a circle of stones in the forest and put an offering inside while calling on them, one would appear to make a deal with you. But I don't recommend it. They're not to be trusted."

That was true, and yet she was considering the option.

Dyna clipped a stem. "I might know of a way to break the veil."

Yavi's eyes widened further. "How—"

A shadow loomed over them, and they looked up at Novo with the afternoon sun obscured behind him. "How much longer?"

"With only the three of us working, it will take some time," Dyna said. "I need plenty for the captain's treatment to take. A week's worth, at the very least."

"Gather as much as you can. The camp is moving tonight."

Yavi stood. "Already?"

His gaze flickered to Dyna. "There is no reason to stay in Azure now."

She stilled. "What do you mean? Where are we going?"

He didn't answer.

"We're headed to a private port near Indigo Bay," Yavi said, worry on her face. "A place for those avoiding the Azure King's eye. Tarn's ship is there."

Dyna froze. *A ship.* Of course, he had a ship. How else would he have traveled overseas? It was how he would reach Mount Ida. Indigo Bay was north on the Saxe coast. Perhaps a week of travel away. Longer with a camp full of men. If Tarn got her on the ocean, then she'd be trapped by water, taken to the other side of the world. She may never see Cassiel again.

Dyna forced herself to breathe and think. This changed the plan.

"Finish up here," Novo said, turning away as Geon rejoined them. "I'm hungry and want to go back to camp."

"It would be quicker if you helped," Yavi said, but he ignored her and she scowled at his retreating back.

It wasn't until he reached the shadow lingering beneath a tree did Dyna notice the girl that had been in the mage's tent. Novo pinned her against the trunk, and they hungrily kissed.

"Oh, good Gods." Yavi quickly pulled Dyna away to where they couldn't see. "Those two have no shame."

She flushed. "Who are they?"

"They are both spies like Elon. Novo works for hire but Len...she's Tarn's property. He purchased her when she was a child. He raised her and trained her. She's favored. Novo should know better."

Dyna recalled how angry Novo had been when he had attacked Rawn in the woods. It seemed personal, and now she realized it was. Rawn had nearly killed her.

"That's all they do." Geon snorted. "They're like rabbits."

Dyna stifled a laugh.

"One day, that will be you when you find the lass you like," Yavi teased as they headed for the barrels to empty their baskets, and he reddened.

Dyna let them chat as she fell back. Right now, Novo was distracted, and that created an opportunity that couldn't be wasted. "We will cover more ground if we split up," she said, walking backward. "I will take the north end of the field. You two take the south."

They stared at her in confusion, but she didn't wait for their replies. She strode away and exhaled in relief when they didn't follow. Once she was sure no one was looking, she darted into the dense trees and kept going until she reached the veil. Quickly gathering stones, she formed them in a circle. Then she pulled out a roll of bread from her cloak and placed it inside. It wasn't much of an offering, though he might not mind.

"Azulo?" Dyna called hesitantly.

It was a gamble to call on Leoake's familiar, but she didn't want another geas, and the little fox owed her a favor. After the news of the ship, she was more desperate than ever.

"I call on a debt owed," she said more confidently. "Azulo, come to me."

Only windy silence answered back.

After a few minutes of nothing, Dyna's shoulders slumped. Perhaps she didn't do it right, or the fae didn't like being ordered around. She turned to go when something flickered in her peripherals.

A faint, warm glow seemed to pulse within the trees on the other side of the veil. Then it faded and from the bushes sauntered out a fox with aqua-blue fur and a diamond-shaped patch in a deeper shade of blue on its forehead. He sat on his haunches, wagging three fluffy tails. Azulo looked a little bigger than the last time she'd seen him.

Dyna smiled and moved as close as she dared to the veil. It crackled faintly between them. "Hello there, sweet one. Can you see me?"

A golden light flared out of him, making her yelp. It quickly faded, revealing a lad with furry blue ears. He looked about ten years old and wore only a pair of trousers. Bright cerulean hair fell around his cherubic face to his chin, and his forehead now bore a sapphire gem.

"Of course, I can see you, Mistress." He grinned, revealing a small pair of fangs. "I am glad to meet you again."

Her mouth fell open. "Azulo? I-I didn't know you could take human form."

"I'm fae." He shrugged as if that explained it.

"All right...well, thank you for coming. I was hoping to call on that favor," Dyna said sheepishly.

His smile brightened, and he puffed out his chest, wagging his tails. "I am at your service. Whatever you desire, your sweet one will provide. My thanks for saving me."

She laughed, finding him incredibly endearing. "My word. Then I am very grateful you've come to my aid. Sadly, I have been captured by a wicked man, and he's trapped me behind this veil."

Azulo frowned as he studied it, and swirling blue markings pulsed on his chest and shoulders.

"It's supposed to conceal the camp from outsiders, yet it doesn't seem to work on you."

"I can see spells." His aquamarine eyes dropped to the oak tree tattooed on Dyna's arm, then to her chest. "As I see the ones on you. Master's geas has bound you almost as tightly as the bond on your soul."

Dyna's heart leaped. "My bond is still intact? It's fully there?"

He nodded.

She covered her mouth at the confirmation and wetly laughed. It caused her tender chest to spasm, and for a moment, she couldn't breathe. If it affected her this much, Cassiel must be suffering far worse.

"I cannot stay long," Azulo said, pouting. "We fae have rules about debts, which allowed me to come, but I'm ordered to return quickly. Make your ask and be careful what you say, as I can only grant exactly that."

She was grateful for the warning. Leoake should learn from him. "Before I make my ask, do you have the ability to remove the veil?"

He shook his head. "The spell is tied to the one who placed it. It lives because the mage lives. Shall I kill him? That would set you free."

She flinched back, not expecting such a morbid suggestion to come from his sweet face. He said it so casually, as though taking a life was nothing. It served to show that no matter how innocent the fox-boy looked, the fae didn't think like humans.

"No, don't do that," Dyna said quickly. "The bangles, what can you tell me about their magic?"

He glanced down at her ankles and smirked. "Mere witch trinkets. Easy to break with my teeth. Easier with the key."

The key! Tarn had a ring full of them with red bloodstones that matched the Crystal Core. He had used one to remove her collar. That must be how he was keeping the slaves controlled.

All she needed was the key and the arrow. Then she'd be free.

"Then I will find a way to remove the veil and the bangles myself," Dyna said. "Perhaps you could escort me away instead? Once I'm free, the wicked man will come after me, so I will need a way to quickly escape. Could you take me to Cassiel the same way you arrived here?" She assumed he had used some sort of portal, the way fae liked to travel. "He's looking for me. He shouldn't be far."

Azulo canted his head a moment, then nodded. "When?"

Yavi's voice called for her in the distance.

"Tonight," Dyna whispered. "Meet me here when the sun sets."

"Tonight," Azulo agreed. "Make your ask then. Oh, and Master has a message for you. He says, 'Wine is preferable to water, clever mortal.'"

She frowned, not understanding what that meant. Why would she care about his drink preferences?

"Where did she go?" came Novo's angry voice.

Dyna whipped around at the approaching shapes in the trees. When she glanced at Azulo again, he was gone, and so was the bread. She ran back the way she came, only to crash into Novo. The others stood behind him.

He grabbed her shoulders. "What were you doing?"

"Nothing. I was merely searching for Phyllon roots. A soporific will do Elon well."

His dark eyes narrowed. He didn't believe her lie for a second. "No matter how much you search, lass, there's no way out."

Well, she never was much of a liar.

Dyna crossed her arms. "You're not a slave. You work for pay."

Novo arched an eyebrow as if to say what was her point.

"But you hate it, don't you? I've seen the way you constantly look at the sky. You don't like being in the veil, but you don't leave because of her." She nodded at Len. "None of us want to be here, so *why* do we let him keep us here?" They gawked at her, and she took their stunned silence as encouragement to continue. "If we can work together to take Tarn down, then—"

Len sprang and tackled her. Dyna's back collided with the ground, leaving her winded. She only saw a flash of steel before she felt the cold knife's edge at her throat.

"Urnians bleat about slavery in dis country," Len hissed in a thick, broken accent. "In mine, we be beaten. Starved and raped. We be mules. But Master saved me. He is good Master. If ye rebel, I vill gut ye like a fish, from yer nethers to yer neck before ye scream."

Dyna's heart pounded in her chest as they stared at each other. This close, she got a clear view of the gruesome scar in the shape of an X that had been burned on the young woman's cheek.

"Len." Novo gave her a languid smile. "Come, let's go get something to eat."

Len nimbly rose to her feet. The curved knife flipped in her agile fingers as she sheathed it in the scabbard strapped to her thigh. Then she strode away, heading back for the meadow. Yavi and Geon gave Dyna apologetic looks before following Len at Novo's order.

"Be careful what you say around here, lass." He helped Dyna to her feet. "Tarn may be a hard master, but he gave these people a place to belong. That is more than most of them have had."

Feeling foolish, Dyna rubbed the new bruise forming on the back of her head. Tarn was more favored than she thought. Len may be willing to serve him, but there were a few others who certainly weren't.

CHAPTER 8

Dynalya

It turned out Minotaurs were very good at cooking, or at least, Sorren was. The stuffy tent smelled of roasted boar, but he had been kind enough to make her a separate pot of pottage stew. Dyna stirred her bowl, savoring the diced carrots, onions, parsnips, mushrooms, leeks, and barley. The aromatic herbs of rosemary and thyme balanced out the rich flavors perfectly. But Yavi had taken one sniff of the food and turned a tad green. She excused herself and hadn't returned. Novo left her in Geon's care, but he could hardly guard her when he was busy obeying Sorren's barking orders as they served the men.

Dyna kept to her corner as she ate, secretly taking account of the steady stream of Raiders passing in and out of Sorren's tent. There were nearly two hundred men, all varying ages and races, and they had their own form of hierarchy. The Raiders, riddled with weapons, were the fighting force. Rarely did she glimpse the spies, and only when they wanted to be seen. Then there were the mages who provided the magic and healing. Each group had their own leader, and Von oversaw them all for his master.

When Dyna spotted Dalton at the end of the line, she sent him a timid smile and he returned a surprised one. As the line shortened, she sent him two more lingering glances. It paid off when the mage made his way to her after he was served.

"Evening. Eating alone?"

"I'm short on company," Dyna said, maybe too suggestively.

Dalton grinned. He sat next to her, setting down the tray holding three steaming plates and tankards of ale. "Then I will join you for a moment. My brother can eat his meat cold."

She forced herself to giggle at his joke.

He cut into his food. "You seem in better spirits."

"A meal will do that to you."

"Aye, that's true. Sorren's a grump, but he knows how to feed us."

She swallowed another spoonful. "I didn't get a chance to thank you for the royalrods. It's amazing that you could grow so many in mere minutes."

"It's nothing." Dalton shrugged, though she could tell he was pleased.

"I wouldn't call that nothing. Your brother likes to boast, but you were the one who filled the field. How did you do that?"

He traced a finger over the wood grain patterns on the table. "The earth has music for those who listen."

She smiled, liking how that sounded. "Did you tell your father?"

"He would care nothing about that. To him, Clay is the most powerful out of us both simply because he can communicate with the trees and move the earth."

"Why should plant life be less important? They are the source of medicine and food. Benton is wrong about you, Dal." She called him by his nickname for more familiarity. "I think you might be more powerful than your brother. If you set your mind to it, I bet you could split open the earth and move the trees themselves."

Dalton hummed, amusement playing on his mouth. "Why all the compliments, Dyna? I'm astonished you lured me over here after our encounter in Landcaster."

Clearly, manipulating others wasn't her strong suit.

"You were an arse."

"I was," he agreed. "That doesn't explain what you want with me."

Dyna ducked her head timidly. "Could...you teach me?"

"Ah, was that your plan? Win my favor in hopes I will teach you magic?"

Or so he thought.

Dyna nodded, hunching in her seat with visible embarrassment.

Dalton smirked and soaked up the leftover meat broth with some bread. "Allow me a moment to think." He pretended to frown at the roof thoughtfully as he chewed. "Mmm—*no*."

She pouted. "Why?"

"Several reasons. Your bangles have your Essence locked away, for one. Not to mention Tarn might murder me if my father doesn't first. You're a *girl*, and you cannot wield earth magic."

Dyna glowered. What is it with mages and their misogynistic ideals? "I can wield magic, and it has nothing to do with my gender. You can teach me other spells that don't pertain to one element."

"Is there one in particular you're referring to?"

"I...have trouble making a shield." Dyna winced because it was true. She hadn't mastered that spell yet, since it was the last one she had been trying to learn. Possibly because she at last sounded genuine, Dalton bought her excuse.

"You don't know how to make a shield?" He chuckled. "That is a preliminary spell. I learned that when I was six summers old."

"Well, since you're clearly advanced, I thought perhaps I could learn from you."

Truths within lies.

At Dalton's attention, it proved that was how real manipulation worked. The perfect balance of sympathy and suggestion to misdirect while truly getting what she wanted. Information. Dyna felt guilty about it, but squashed it. She needed to learn everything she could about the veil, and quickly. Tonight was her only chance to escape.

Dalton hesitated to answer, so she heavily sighed. "I knew I should have asked Clayton instead."

He scowled. "I won't teach you magic, Dyna. But I can show you how it's done by a true mage."

Thereafter, she spent the evening outside, oohing and aahing as a group of Raiders took turns throwing knives at Dalton or trying to land a punch. He deflected them all with a simple shield and it rippled gold on impact.

He may not have intended to teach her, however, she also learned by watching. Dyna studied his stance and the way his Essence moved. She was miffed that his bangles allowed him to use magic, unlike hers. He only couldn't use attack spells. But finally, she understood how to form a shield.

Now all she had to do was to get him to show her how the veil worked.

Geon slipped out of the cook's tent and sat beside her on the grass with two mugs of warm cider, offering her one. "Here, this will warm you up."

"Thank you." Dyna graciously accepted. The hot mug felt good against her stiff fingers.

When she first met Geon in Landcaster, he seemed older. Up close, she saw he was a year or two younger than her.

"You're welcome." He nudged her shoulder. "How is your head?"

She grimaced and rubbed the knot on the back of her skull. "It's fine."

"Len can be defensive of Tarn, but she did it for your sake, as well as his."

She frowned at that. How was that for her sake?

Geon sighed. "Back in Corron, I didn't need to warn you. I could have stalled until Elon arrived, but when you healed me, I saw your kindness. There is little of that left in this world." A small smile tugged at one end of his mouth as he watched Dalton cast out a flashy spell that had the Raiders cheering. "Dal can be a prick sometimes, but he's my best mate. And because of it, I know how easily he's led by a bonnie face."

His worried copper-colored eyes met hers, and she realized Geon had been listening to their conversation at dinner. And he was warning her again.

"I know you want to reunite with your friends, but don't use mine to do it. You will only get them killed. That is what happens here if you cross Tarn. Either you fight with him or die by him. There is no other option. So please, I beg you to leave Dal out of whatever you're planning."

Tricking and lying. It wasn't who she was. *Be smarter than them, and you will win*, Lucenna had said. That didn't mean be cruel. Because she would be lying to herself to believe that Dalton or others wouldn't have been punished if she managed to escape because of them. Knowing now that they could be killed made the guilt she'd been ignoring come flooding back.

Dyna wrapped her arms around her knees and laid her head over them. The brisk wind dried her wet eyes. All she wanted was to go home and hug her grandmother and Lyra. She missed North Star, the beautiful rolling hills, and the calmness of it all. She closed her eyes and pictured herself lying in the meadow surrounded by colorful wildflowers, inhaling the sweet floral scent of spring. Cassiel was there with her as they picked out shapes in the sky. He would have liked her village.

But none of that would ever happen if she was stuck here. Winter was coming. She had to reunite with him and Rawn and cross Troll Bridge before the snow came, or they would be stuck in Azure for another three months. Her one year before the Shadow's return was trickling away, and she was no closer to getting the Sōl Medallion. It seemed whatever she did, something was always in the way of reaching Mount Ida.

Tarn was merely another obstacle.

"Where are you from, Geon?" she asked.

He leaned back on his palms. "I'm from Tipton. It's a tiny town north of the Three Rivers. Have you been thereabouts?"

"I don't know much of Urn."

"Nor did I until I joined."

"You *joined* them?" It astounded her that someone would willingly relinquish their freedom.

Geon gave her an awkward shrug. "Aye. I was a starving waif with nowhere else to go. Von brought me to Master Tarn, and I entered his services as a

Raider, but I wasn't very good at it. It happens that I'm better off using a knife to cook. I may be a slave, but I have a family now."

He meant Yavi, Von, and Dalton. Perhaps including Sorren. They were his family. But the difference between his and hers was that they were together.

"They mean a lot to you," she said.

"They do."

"Because they are your home, and you would do anything to protect them. Even if that meant letting others suffer. I think you and I are the same in that regard."

Geon wore an expression that was a mixture of unease and new understanding. At that moment, she recognized they would both do what they had to for their family.

"I don't want anyone to die," Dyna murmured. "I will find a way out without implementing anyone, all right?"

They shared a long look. Before he could reply, Dalton trudged over to join them.

He rolled to the ground and laid his head on Geon's lap, wearing a tired grin. "Ugh, my power is nearly drained. I've even sprouted a sweat. Whose idea was this?"

Geon shoved him off. "Yours when you chose to flaunt your powers for a girl's attention."

"Did it work?"

"You were incredible," Dyna said brightly. "I could never hope to reach your caliber."

Dalton laughed and dragged an arm across his sweaty forehead. "I know she's inflating my ego, but I rather enjoy it, anyway."

"Yeah, yeah." Geon flicked his nose. "Because your head isn't big enough, eh?"

At the crunch of gravel approaching, they looked up to see Von. His gaze briefly met hers. "Is the Master's meal ready, lad?" he asked Geon.

"Aye, Commander. It should be now." He got up, and Von followed him into the cook's tent.

"Think you can manage a shield now?" Dalton wiggled his brows. "I saw you studying me."

She shrugged. "Perhaps. What kind of shield did you use?"

"A standard one. It defends against physical attacks."

"Ohhh," she emphasized her awe, pretending this was new to her. "There are different kinds?"

"Of course. There is an enchanted shield which is stronger and used as a defense against spells. Containment domes are fifty times stronger, and they work well to contain enemies or to protect yourself from them. They also conceal the presence of magic."

"Like the veil," she mentioned casually.

There was a change in Dalton's demeanor as he sat up. "No...veils are cloaking spells."

"I haven't seen one like that before." She looked up at the twilight sky where it rippled iridescently. Its magic constantly prickled against her senses. "It feels different."

"Well, that's due to the fact that it's created from the Spatial Gate."

Dyna's eyes widened again, and it was a genuine reaction. That meant the veil didn't simply stand over whatever area they chose, it *created* a pocket of space in which they hid the camp. It separated them from everything in the Mortal Realm. Which explained why they couldn't be found. That sounded very much like a shield to her. But it had to be portable to move with them.

The warding spell placed on her village was stationary and it hid them from outsiders, but it could be found if someone stumbled upon it.

"Is it a complicated spell?" she asked.

"Yes, and difficult to maintain. For most."

"Not for your father?"

Dalton snorted. "He was Grand Magus."

"But after so many years, it must cost him to maintain such a spell. Forgive me if I speak plainly." She lowered her voice. "But how does he maintain it and continue to cast magic? I imagine doing both must hurt."

It must have cost Benton to fight them at the grove while cloaking the camp at the same time. Unless he had to release it to use his magic.

"To hold the veil while performing spells is incredibly impressive," she pressed at his silence.

Dalton gave her a tight smile, neither agreeing nor denying. It only helped to support her suspicion. "I told you, he's powerful."

But using copious amounts of Essence could kill even the greatest mage. So how did Benton manage it on his own for so long?

"Could your brother cast one, too?" she asked.

"Clay can hardly cast a veil, let alone sustain it." He blanched at the slip of his tongue, but she pretended not to catch it while her mind was reeling.

That was how Benton did it.

He used his sons.

It made sense. A spell of that magnitude must need a powerful source— like their lifeforce. Now that she looked at him, Dalton looked very tired. He hadn't used enough magic to be spent. It was because his Essence was being used elsewhere.

"I think I have done enough dallying for one day." He stood. "I must head back."

"Must you? I wanted to see you make another shield."

Dalton chuckled uneasily. "It's probably best I don't."

"Why would it be so wrong to teach me magic?" She crossed her arms.

"There is an order to things, and allowing women any power will destroy our way of life."

It sounded as if he was repeating something that had been told to him.

"How did your mother feel about that?" she asked.

Shadows crossed Dalton's face as his eyes dropped to the ground. "I didn't know my mother."

"Because you were taken young?" Dyna couldn't help but feel sorry for him. She had lost her mother young, too.

"Before then...She was desolate."

Dyna frowned. "What is—"

They were interrupted by Geon and Von's return. Geon carried a silver tray loaded with covered plates. It was a fine setting, unlike the wooden bowls and mugs the Raiders used.

"Take it to the Master, lad. He's waiting."

Geon nodded and marched away, carefully balancing the tray.

"Any improvement in the captain's condition?" Von asked Dalton.

"Aye, Commander. Dyna's potion is working. And I believe they finished harvesting what they could of the flowers."

She nodded her confirmation. They had three barrels loaded in a wagon right beside Benton's tent, which was completely unnecessary. Good thing there were no other Herb Masters here. The mages served as Tarn's healers because of their magic, but they didn't have a vast knowledge of medicine.

"As you were. I want a full report on Elon's status within the hour."

"Aye, Commander." Dalton gave her a wink and sauntered off.

Von turned to her next. "Come. You will join Tarn for dinner. It isn't a request," he added at her expression. "He wishes to hear about your endeavors today."

Von continued, and Dyna followed without complaint. She had been waiting for this. The camp was buzzing as the men broke down the tents and loaded the wagons. They were moving tonight, and Azulo was waiting. Her chest tensed, sweat beading on her back. *Get the keys,* she chanted to herself.

They entered Tarn's tent as the Forewarning Crystal's light faded. Per usual, he was seated at the head of his table, idly flipping through a small book.

"Have a seat," he said without looking up.

Dyna skirted the table and chose the end again, the furthest seat away from him. Von took his post by the entrance. The soft clink of utensils was the only sound in the tent as Geon plated the food and served Tarn some wine.

"You've eaten." It wasn't a question. At her silence, his frosted stare flickered to hers. They reminded her of polished celestine, clear blue and hard as stone.

"Yes," she said when it was clear he expected her to answer him.

"Wine?"

"No, thank you."

"Pour her a drink." Tarn's eerie eyes remained locked on hers, intense and unwavering. "She's thirsty."

Dyna's heartbeat raced under his stare that seemed to dissect her. She forced herself to look away. Geon approached with a silver flagon and poured water into the equally fancy goblet already set for her as if they had expected her to sit there.

"I hear the healing was a success, and Elon is on his way to recovery. That deserves a toast." Tarn lifted his goblet. His sleeve lowered enough to reveal his cuff with three amber beads, each one containing black clovers. There was no need for them anymore. "To the Maiden and her invaluable expertise."

He waited for her compliance again. If he wanted her to play the obedient little lady, then she could put up with it for a few more minutes until she had her freedom. Dyna lifted her cup in a mock toast before taking a quick sip. Her mouth curled at the bitter taste. The storage barrels were probably full of sediment and growing moss.

"How long did you study to become a Herb Master?"

"All my life, it seems." She looked away from him, pretending to be bored as she let her gaze wander to his desk. It was cluttered with scrolls and ancient artifacts. The slaver's keys had to be there, buried beneath the missives somewhere. Was the arrowhead there too?

"A family trade, I assume," he said.

"Yes." She yawned and leaned back in her chair, sluggishly glancing at the charms and spells dangling from the roof.

The Crystal Core shone blood red in the candlelight. Once she found the keys, she would set everyone free. Yavi, the mages—Sorren. The Minotaur would probably rampage through the camp. It would make for a good distraction.

Removing the veil was going to take some stealthy maneuvering, but she may not need the arrowhead now that she knew how it worked. If only one of the mages lost their hold on the spell, it would fall. She could probably take down all three with the royalrods once she got near enough to set the barrels on fire. The toxic smoke would quickly overtake the air, trapped in a dome of their own making, leaving everyone desperate for air. Then they wouldn't have a choice but to drop the veil. But pulling it off without being caught, the thought only made her feel exhausted. She yawned again, and her eyes grew heavy.

"Tired?" The candlelight made Tarn's features sharper in the tent, highlighting the jagged scar on his face.

"It was a long day."

"I'm sure it was. You spent the better part of the afternoon picking royalrods." Tarn set his elbows on the table and linked his fingers. "Which was an interesting choice, given *goldenrods* would have been equally effective without the toxic properties. Not to mention, you insisted they harvest a year's worth when you truly only needed a few petals. Care to explain?"

Dyna stilled. Unease washed through her mind, and it tripled when she couldn't sit up. She felt weak and tired. Her head went cloudy, blurring her sight.

"What...did you...do?" she garbled. Jerking up, she knocked over her goblet, and the foul-tasting water spilled across the table.

The water.

He *drugged* her.

Leoake's sly voice whispered in her ear as if he stood over her shoulder. *Wine is preferable to water, clever mortal.*

She internally cursed that dastardly Druid and his vague warning.

Tarn closed the book in front of him, revealing her notebook. The one where she had filled the pages with notes on plants with their medicinal use as well as their poisonous properties.

"Hard as it may be to believe, I do, in fact, read." He came to sit on the edge of the table again as he watched her struggle to stay awake. "Whatever you planned with the royalrods, I suppose it had something to do with the veil. The kitchen lad tells me you're quite interested in it."

Geon didn't look at her as he ducked his head and slipped out of the tent. She should have known he would report her. She'd practically forced him to when she made it clear where her priorities lied.

Von merely watched her with a grim expression.

"You were very meticulous in your notes, Maiden. I learned all sorts of things. Like how the oil from Dreamshade leaves can induce heavy sleep. In the right doses, of course. Too much and one may never wake again." Tarn lifted her chin. "Did you think escaping me would be that easy?"

Dyna let out a choked whimper as her head lolled. Feeling was quickly leaving her body. All she kept making was mistake after mistake. There was nothing smart about this.

"It's unfortunate, but I can't risk leaving you awake when we move tonight."

The news made her want to scream in frustration. Only too late did she realize they traveled at night under the cover of darkness because they wouldn't have the protection of the veil. Whether she'd collected the items she needed, with the spell removed, she could have run to Azulo and been taken to Cassiel.

Now her only opportunity for freedom was lost.

"I think you forgot one important thing," Tarn told her, as her vision darkened. "It matters not whether the veil comes down. You were separately veiled the moment we took you. Because of it, you will never be found."

They cannot smell you, hear you, let alone touch you. Not even if you stood right in front of them.

All of her scheming was for nothing. Azulo had tried to tell her. The only way to remove the veil was to remove the one who placed it.

She keeled over, and a soft numbness cradled her body, with Tarn's ice-blue eyes following her into her dreams.

They were moving. At the steady stride and beat of hooves, she must be on a horse. The drug was keeping her immobile. Her cheeks were cold, but the rest of her was warm. Heat pressed into her back from whatever she leaned up against. Strong arms on either side of her kept her in the saddle.

Dyna pried her heavy eyes open a mere slit, but she couldn't perceive much through her blurry vision beside the darkness and still trees. The moonlight hardly reached them. Her eyes refused to stay open, and it was probably for the best.

"It's...dark," she whimpered, not caring who heard. "I need the light. Please."

Because when the darkness found her, so did the Shadow. Its misty claws would sink into her bones, and sometimes all she could do was lie there and scream until she couldn't anymore.

"Sleep, Maiden," Tarn's cool voice drifted above her head. "The only thing to fear in these woods is me."

That was supposed to comfort her? Strangely, it did.

There was something in his words. Not arrogance, but the simple fact that he was dangerous and anything that confronted them would be quickly dealt with. She felt the strength in his body pressed against her back and his conduct that asserted lethal power. Even without having seen him fight, she sensed he was a predator.

Tarn couldn't possibly defeat a demon, but at the moment, his presence seemed to diminish the Shadow's. Whether it was the thought or the gait of the horse, she sank back into a fitful sleep.

CHAPTER 9

Lucenna

Lucenna looked around her enchanted tent, at the piles of books and the crystal orb on her desk, her massive bed, at everything that filled up the space, and yet it felt so empty. She took a step, and her boot hit something. The wooden training ball bounced across the ground, bumping into her bedpost. With a flourish of purple mist, Lucenna recalled the ball, and it landed in her hand. She brushed her thumb over the smooth crescent sigil of House Astron embossed on the surface.

Was Dyna all right? Were those fools taking care of her? The earthy scent of rosemary drifting from the teacup steaming at her bedside table sent a guilty pang through her.

Gods. She shouldn't be moping. She chose this.

A pulse throbbed against her temple, and Lucenna sighed at her orb swirling with fog. She sat at her desk and tapped on the glass. Her brother's worried frown greeted her. He must have just woken because he was lying in bed, his long white hair strewn around his pillow.

"I know what you're going to say," she said.

Lucien rubbed the sleep from his lilac eyes and sat up to lean against his headboard. "Go back. We both know you regret leaving her. I can feel it."

She didn't have the energy to be annoyed at their twin link. "No. It's for the best."

"Was it?"

The candles flickered with purple flames, and the charms on the ceiling clinked softly in the stark silence. Lucenna had been traveling alone for years.

Why did she feel the loneliness so keenly after only spending one month with Dyna and the others?

"They have their own troubles, and I have mine," she snapped. "Involving myself with them led to Father catching wind of me again. It's best I travel on my own. I move faster, and I don't have to worry about anyone else. My mission hasn't been compromised. I have memorized the map, see?" She cast a projection of the map in the air. The lines pulsed purple, Mount Ida's island shining the brightest. "I can make my way there alone."

"But you don't have to be alone anymore, Lu."

Lucenna lowered her head and hid under the curtain of her white hair, so he wouldn't see her eyes welling. It was nice, she had to admit, having someone there when she woke. She missed their chatter and spending the days magic training with Dyna. Even missed arguing with the grumpy Celestial. She'd found a second family. Cousins.

But she had a mission to complete, and that couldn't happen if...

A tear spilled down and landed on the desk. "If Father found me while I was still with them...he would have taken her, too."

That was why she left. Because she was a coward. Her father was too powerful and if Dyna ended up siphoned like her mother, Lucenna would never forgive herself.

"There is strength in numbers—"

"Please, leave it be, Lucien," she said and wiped her cheek. "I don't wish to speak of it anymore. It's been days since we parted. They are most likely miles away by now. I'm leaving Azure, and that's final."

He sighed and settled back on his pillow. "When will you reach Indigo Bay?"

"Tomorrow."

She heard no one asked questions there. Gold was the only requirement, and Lucenna now had plenty of that. Once she boarded a ship and sailed away from this kingdom for good, she could return to traveling without worry of being found.

"Good. Father arrived in the Port of Azure yesterday, so you will evade him with plenty of time. Good luck. I am always here whenever you need me."

She gave him a wistful smile. "I know."

"Lu?" he said before she ended the call. "It wouldn't hurt to see how far they are."

Then the orb cleared, reflecting Lucenna's glower back at her. Nosy mage. Her brother was always—

A howl sounded outside. It sent a shock of goosebumps down her arms, and she whipped around to the tent entrance.

"Zev?" Lucenna sprinted outside into the cold night, but her heart sank at finding nothing but the quiet forest.

It must've been a figment of her imagination. She made it clear she didn't want to be followed, and Rawn was too much of a gentleman to go against her wishes.

But the howl came again. It sounded much closer, and different. She remembered Zev's having a deeper pitch. Lucenna stared at the trees, straining to listen beyond the wind. The moonlight didn't reach into the shadows.

She was struck with relief when a pair of yellow eyes appeared in the bushes. Until another set of yellow eyes slinked forward, then another, and another. Growls rumbled in the forest.

Lucenna scoffed a dry laugh at herself for getting her hopes up. They hadn't come.

It was only a pack of wild wolves.

"Scram before I set your tails on fire." Lucenna cast out a streak of purple lightning, and they scurried away yelping. Her long sigh swirled into the air.

Where were they now? Most likely avoiding the main roads with the bounties on all their heads. They would need a discreet way to leave Azure, too. She paused outside of her tent and looked back at the trees.

What if...what if they were also headed for Indigo Bay? If so, maybe she could meet them.

Lucenna ignored the inkling that they may not want to see her now and closed her eyes. She exhaled a low breath, letting her consciousness sink into the *Essentia Dimensio*. She landed in a pitch-black environment. It appeared empty, but its welcoming energy hummed through her being. Her Essence formed into a brilliant purple sphere that spiraled with lightning.

At the flick of her hand, the sphere whooshed high above into the empty blackness and burst into a shower of light. Vivid purple streaks shot out into the distance, expanding into a net as it searched the world for that green glow. But Lucenna's Essence dispersed the further it went until it completely faded away.

She snapped her eyes open with a gasp. It couldn't be. Dyna's Essence...it was nowhere to be found. Even if she was cloaked, Lucenna would have sensed her. But this feeling, this nothingness, it meant...

"No." She wouldn't believe it. Something must have happened.

Something was wrong.

Lucenna's mind raced with a million possibilities, ignoring the one she didn't want to accept. She looked to the north, where a ship waited a few miles away, then to the south, where she had abandoned Dyna—the same direction as her father.

Ever since she left the Magos Empire, the days had been tainted by risk and failure.

"I'm tired," Lucenna had said to her mother on another night like this when they were cold and starved and halfway across the world with no one to aid them. "I am tired of being afraid. Of constantly running and hiding. Of searching for something we may never find. Who are we to think we could change anything?"

Her mother had merely smiled at her with soft lilac eyes. "What are we fighting for if not for the future? It's in your blood. No matter the battle or who you face, you are a woman. And they will learn you are a force to be reckoned with."

Inhaling a deep breath, icy air filled Lucenna's lungs. The scent of fresh pine and soil layered the foundation of her decision. She waved a hand at her tent. It rose and spun in the air with fairy dust, shrinking as it flew into her satchel.

Then she strode into the forest and went south.

CHAPTER 10

Cassiel

Cassiel's wings were aching by the time they reached the forest outside
of the Port of Azure. They stopped in the exact spot they had last
spoken to Lucenna. Letting his wings rest inside his enchanted jacket,
he paced in the night as the wolf buried his nose in the grass to search for a
scent, and Rawn crouched to study the ground by moonlight. Cassiel couldn't
do more than wait, but after an hour of windy silence, he knew the truth.

"This is pointless," he said. "Her scent is gone."

And it meant Dyna was out of his reach.

His chest only caved in further, and he leaned on his knees, struggling to
breathe. She may live through a broken bond, but he wouldn't. No Celestial
could live with only half a soul. But instead of grief, only rage seared in his
veins. How dare they touch his mate? Something hot scorched his skin, and
the air warped as his vision shifted color.

Cassiel refused to die.

Tarn and everyone who served him, he would set every one of them
aflame. His sword seemed to vibrate at his waist with the need to avenge.
Someone was calling him, but he couldn't think past the roaring in his ears.
Everything inside of him was ablaze with an all-consuming decision to
obliterate everyone and everything that kept him from Dyna.

"They took her from me." His voice sounded strange to him, like a
monstrous beast speaking from his mouth. "They will all burn."

Blue flames surged from Cassiel's fists and flared up his arms.

Zev and Rawn jumped back with a startled shout.

The heat burning through his body vanished beneath Cassiel's shock. All three of them gaped at the fire dancing at his fingertips. They glowed vividly within the dark trees as though he held tendrils of fallen stars.

"*Elyōn*," he breathed. "What..."

"I thought I had seen you do that before. Is that not normal?" Zev asked, the cerulean firelight illuminating the astonishment on their faces.

He had to swallow before he could speak. "Nothing about this is normal. This shouldn't be possible..."

And why didn't it burn him? He felt the tremendous heat it expelled in the air, and so did the others by the way they stood far away from him. But in his hands, the scalding heat didn't seem to bother him. The flames swam through his fingers and up his wrists, merely hovering there as though...waiting for something. He stood stock still, not daring to move in case he made it worse.

They gawked at him. "Prince Cassiel..."

"What?"

"Your eyes are burning," Zev said. "With flames."

Then Cassiel noticed his vision was also cerulean. He tried to blink it away in a panic, and eventually his vision cleared. "What is happening? This is Seraph fire." He stared at his hands. "It's not supposed to be...free...in this manner."

"There is no record of it happening before?" Rawn asked.

The question distracted Cassiel enough that the flames died away. "Only once. Thousands of years ago, with the first Celestial king, but never since. Seraph fire is very rare and only wielded by weapon alone."

"Well, not at the moment," Zev said warily. "What does it mean?"

Cassiel groaned and roughly raked his hair out of his face. "I don't know, and I don't care to know. I cannot fathom anything past the fact that my hands were on fire, and it didn't harm me. At the moment, all I care about is Dyna."

By their wary expression, they clearly wanted to ask more about it, but whatever they saw on his face warded off their replies. Questions rattled in his mind, but he didn't have answers. It was a problem for later.

"What are we to do now?" he asked them. "We can't do this without Lucenna, and her scent is gone." Cassiel's eyes widened when a new concern hit him. "She may not be in Urn's Chip anymore."

"With the bounties on our heads, Lady Lucenna would not be able to board a ship."

Zev rubbed his face. "She can easily cast glamor to change her appearance and get past the guards."

Rawn shook his head. "She fears capture by her father, and she is now a fugitive of Azure. Highly populated areas carry a higher risk. I believe she would resort to what feels safe, and that is taking to the wilderness to avoid main roads as she had before. However, the kingdom is vast, and I must admit, I have little hope we will find her." He sighed. "This may be beyond us."

Cassiel felt as if he might spark fire again. They couldn't give up here. "I will fly above and search for her myself."

"You will only search aimlessly, Prince Cassiel. You are but one person."

"Then I will search the skies until I fall down dead!"

He was at his wit's end. The three of them were not enough, and they couldn't follow him into the sky.

His breath caught, and he looked up at the moon. There were others up there. The Valkyrie were out searching for him. Calling them was a risk, but he didn't care. For Dyna, he would do anything. Even if the cost was giving up his freedom...and his wings.

Cassiel removed his jacket.

"What are you doing?" Zev asked.

"I'm leaving to find reinforcements. The Valkyrie will be nearby."

"Is that a wise choice?" Rawn said.

"At the moment, it's the *only* choice." Cassiel folded his jacket and slipped it into his pack. "We need Lucenna to find Dyna, and we need help to find them both as soon as possible."

"But won't they force you to return to the Realms?" Zev asked.

"They will certainly try, but I will convince them to aid us in the search first. We were headed for Hermon Ridge before all of this happened. If we don't reunite our group and cross Troll Bridge before winter arrives, we will be stuck in Azure. And well, I will probably perish from the broken bond. So yes, I must do this."

Zev exchanged a look with Rawn. "Which way do you think they went?"

Cassiel studied the dark stretch of sky. "Most likely north. They will assume that is the direction I would take to avoid any towns and cities."

"Then we will head east."

"Why east?"

"We know Dyna is somewhere west," Rawn said. "Lucenna will not have returned south. East is the best direction."

"And Lord Norrlen said there are Lycans in the plains near Emberdin," Zev added. "They're called the Lupin Pack."

The news left Cassiel momentarily speechless. Zev shifted on his feet, optimism entering his expression. This was the first they were speaking about it, but he could tell how much it meant to know there were others like him.

"Wolves help wolves." Zev shrugged. "Perhaps it's the same for Lycans."

Cassiel nodded and clapped his shoulder. "I wish you luck."

"And to you."

Rawn mounted Fair. "God of Urn willing, this works, and we will be reunited soon."

Please, Cassiel sent a prayer to the Heavens. *Guide me back to her.*

He leaped into the icy air. Catching the wind, he rode it high into the misty clouds, chasing what he couldn't reach.

"I will find you," he whispered into the frozen void. And he swore some part of him heard her reply. *I'm waiting.*

Cassiel flew all night, searching high among the clouds for any sign of the fierce female warriors who may very well be his last hope. He kept his sword out, the cerulean flames trailing behind him like a flag. Every thirty miles, he would swoop down to set a tree aflame and leave behind a trail for those who recognized Seraph fire. But dawn arrived on the horizon, marking the end of his fruitless search. They must be further up north. He would have to travel on foot during the day to avoid being spotted by humans, then take to the skies again once it was dark.

The bitter air chilled his lungs, and he exhaled heavily with a curse. The action made his chest tighten with pain. It was telling him his body couldn't endure much longer this way, but he refused to stop. He would never stop searching for her.

Cassiel sank through the clouds to land—only to fall into a waiting net. It snatched him off his orbit and forced his wings against his back.

"There you are, little prince."

He barely caught a glimpse of familiar red feathers before he plummeted through the air. His vision spun with streaks of sky, clouds, and golden armor. It felt as if his insides shot up inside him at the fall.

"Sowmya!" he bellowed. "Release me this instant, or I will have you demoted!"

The lieutenant's chuckle blended with the roaring wind. They came to a short stop, and he was thrown from the net. Cassiel tucked his wings and rolled mid-air to catch the ground and rise on his feet.

He glared at the female. "Was the net necessary?"

Sowmya gave him a cool smirk. The morning light glinted on the golden scale mail armor, layering her shoulders and upper arms. On her plated chest was the embossed seal of Hermon Ridge: a *Hyalus* tree within a mountain. Her deep, wine-red wings fluttered as she removed her winged helmet, and tendrils of black hair tumbled around her dusky face, flushed pink from the cold. "We could not risk you escaping us a second time."

"You clearly followed my signal. I wanted to be found."

"Yes, Your Highness. We rather enjoyed putting out the fires you left behind for every citizen in Azure to see."

He stiffened at the curt voice and turned to face Yelrakel, Captain of the Valkyrie. Her gray gaze regarded him through her golden helmet molded into wings. She had always been like that with everyone. Eventually, he realized she was simply a stoic female who regarded her position very seriously. Her large, gray wings arched behind her in the mild breeze as she marched to him with the rest of her squadron. Each held a different weapon: flaming swords, spears, bows, and whips of fire.

She and Valkyrie clanked a fist over their hearts and lowered their heads to him in greeting. They were as unique to each other as the clouds in the sky, with a variety of skin tones, texture of feathers and hair, and eyes of every color.

Removing her helmet, wisps of dark red strands stuck to the sweat on Yelrakel's forehead. She glanced at his sword. "Your flame. It has been blessed."

"Yes."

"When did it change?"

"That is not important right now." He pressed on his dry eyes. "I spent all night searching for you."

"As have we." Her mouth pursed. "I'm sure you can imagine what I came to say."

Cassiel nodded stiffly. "Make the proclamation."

Yelrakel straightened her shoulders. "The High King summons Cassiel Soaraway to answer for his crimes regarding the events in the Port of Azure and other related offenses. He is called to Hermon Ridge, where the inquest is to be held."

He knew it was coming, but hearing the summons sank a chill down his back, and his wings shuddered. What he had done in the port couldn't be ignored. His father would exile him, if only to make him an example before anyone else broke Rael's Laws.

Still, Cassiel held his composure. "I acknowledge the order, and I will make my way there presently," he said. Yelrakel nodded and turned to lead her squad into the sky. "Once I have sorted a personal matter."

The captain jerked to a stop, and metal ground against metal as all the Valkyrie turned to stare at him.

"There is someone I must find, and I need your help."

She shook her head in disbelief. "Your Highness, the High King—"

He held up a hand. "I understand my position, Captain. No one in their right mind would risk offending my father further, but truly, I'm not in my right mind. Delaying my summons will not change the outcome we both know awaits me." He exhaled a low breath at her grim expression. "But I must do this. I must find her."

"Who?"

This was it. The moment he exposed the extent of his misdeeds. Giving divine blood to a human was the most severe crime for their kind. And the Valkyrie wouldn't go against his father's order...unless there was another to overrule it.

There was one clause Rael made sure to put within their laws that all Watchers had to obey as protectors of the Realms and the crown. The security of mates within the royal family overrode any order.

Dyna should be here, taking part in this decision, but finding her took precedence. It meant he needed to make the choice for both of them.

Cassiel steadied his resolve and spoke the pronouncement. "I am searching for Dynalya Astron. A human who not only holds immunity and amnesty in all four Celestial Realms, but who is now Princess Consort of Hilos. For she is my wife and True Bonded mate."

CHAPTER 11

Dynalya

Dyna blinked sleepily at the morning light filtering through the tent roof. Her mind was slow to recall the events of last night, but anger instantly cleared her mind. Her opportunity to escape had slipped out from under her, and Azulo most likely left when she didn't arrive.

Right now, all Dyna wanted was to slap two people.

She turned at the sound of soft humming coming next to her. Yavi was in the middle of washing her face. She wore only a thin chemise, and she pressed a hand over the small mound of her belly when she bent to reach into her chest of clothing.

Dyna's eyes widened, and she sat up. "You're with child."

Yavi jumped, letting out a high-pitched shriek. She rapidly held a dress over her body, gaping at Dyna in horror. Then she dropped on her cot and covered her face. "Oh, how could I have been so stupid?"

"Is Tarn...?"

"No!" Yavi recoiled with revulsion. "Von is the father."

Dyna's eyes widened further at the gold ring hanging from her neck. It was no wonder they spoke to each other unreservedly. They were life-mates.

"God of Urn." Yavi's trembling hands covered her face again. "Please, I beg you, don't reveal this to Tarn. I know you want your freedom, but please don't tell him. He would kill Von and my baby."

She sat next to her. "Yavi, of course I won't tell him."

"You wouldn't?" She looked at her worriedly with welling eyes. "Geon told me about..."

Dyna glowered. "I would never put a child at risk."

"Oh, thank you." Yavi hugged her tightly. She was shaking. "You don't know how cruel Tarn can be. I fear what that man would do if he ever found out I'm Von's wife."

Dyna didn't know what to think of it, either. Slaves were forbidden to have families. "Does he know?"

Yavi sniffed and wiped her eyes. "No."

"How far along are you?"

"I'm a little over three moons. I've been able to hide it with my clothes, and well, I make sure it's dark when we..." Yavi flushed. "I take care not to undress in front of him anymore as well."

Dyna squirmed. "Oh, right. How do you hide your other symptoms?" She recalled how Yavi turned green when she smelled the roasting meat. "He must have noticed your bouts of nausea and that you no longer have your menses."

"Von has been distracted with tracking you and serving his master's every whim." More tears gathered on Yavi's lashes, and she shook her head. "I can't bring myself to tell him. I don't know how he will react."

"You think he would betray you to Tarn?"

"I don't know." Yavi closed her eyes. "I once believed his love was unconditional, but I'm not so sure anymore. If I tell him about our baby, I'm afraid to be proven right."

Whatever Dyna's opinion of Von, if he was willing to risk marrying Yavi, then it had to be love. But this was a dire problem that would force him to choose either her or Tarn, and she didn't know which way he would bend.

"I am not his first priority." Yavi's lip quivered. "I know he loves me, and that used to be enough, but I think what we have won't last. He sleeps in another tent now to avoid any suspicions. It pains me to be away from him...especially knowing in the end I will have to leave him."

Dyna rubbed her back. She wanted to comfort her but didn't know how else she could help in this situation. They couldn't have a baby in a Raiders camp.

"I didn't know how I would escape until you came." Yavi wiped her face and took her hands. "It gave me hope because I knew you would get out, and I thought I could go with you."

Dyna hadn't exactly planned to bring anyone with her. She'd only meant to take down the veil, leaving everyone to run on their own. Evidently, her previous plan lacked proper preparation. But after learning this secret, she felt compelled to assure Yavi's escape for her child's sake.

"Geon is sorry about what happened," Yavi said. "He was worried about Dalton."

She knew that's why he did it, but she was still irritated.

"There will be another chance, Dyna. You will think of something."

If they also wanted to escape, then why was the planning only left to her? The first failure left her not knowing where to start.

"What do you think you will have?" she asked to change the subject.

"I'm hoping it's a boy. I would love to see a little Von with his somber frown." That drew a feeble smile out of Yavi, but it quickly dimmed. "My family lives in Wyndham. It's a city in the Kingdom of the United Crown. Before you arrived, my plan was to wait until Tarn's ship moored in Dwarf Shoe to make my way there." She glanced down at the slave bracelets on her ankles. "But now I have these."

The United Crown was on the other side of the country. Even if they got out, Dyna didn't know if Yavi would make it in time to deliver.

"Does anyone else know?" she asked.

"No—"

Both fell silent at the sound of footsteps approaching their tent.

Yavi turned to Dyna desperately and mouthed, *Please don't tell him!*

Von cleared his throat outside. "Yavi?"

"Yes?" she answered as she quickly put on her frock. It was a simple maroon one that left her white chemise sleeves uncovered. Dyna helped lace up the bodice, making sure it was loose enough to be comfortable.

"May I come in?"

"No," Yavi blurted, glancing at Dyna. She only wore undergarments and a camisole.

"All right."

"Pick something to wear," Yavi whispered, throwing a thick shawl on. "You can use the washcloth in the basin to clean yourself."

She arranged the garment strategically to hide any signs of pregnancy before going outside. Dyna sighed at the basin. She wished to bathe in a stream, regardless if it gave her frostbite. It had been days since she last properly washed.

"How is she?" Von asked quietly.

"Still asleep," Yavi replied curtly. "How much did he drug her? Wretched man."

Dyna quietly wrung out the soaked washcloth, wondering if they knew how thin the tent was. She quickly cleaned herself as best she could.

"Are you angry with me?" Von asked softly.

"You left me," her voice cracked. The pain was clear in her accusation.

"It was for your safety, love. I'm not fond of the arrangements either, but it's necessary. Don't you know I miss your warmth at night?"

There was a long pause. Dyna thought Yavi was embarrassed by Von's ardent confession as much as she was, but then she heard the soft sounds of kissing. Dyna flushed and busied herself with sorting through the clothing.

After a minute, he cleared his throat and said in a normal voice. "Wake the Maiden and bring her to Sorren. She will need to eat to recover."

"Yes, Master," Yavi said flirtatiously.

He chuckled quietly before his footsteps faded away.

When Yavi entered the tent, she wore a dreamy smile. "That man still knows how to make my heart dance." She noticed Dyna's beat red face and laughed. "Oh, did you hear us? I'm sorry!"

"I-It's all right."

Yavi floated over happily and sat on the cot beside her. "It's nice to confide in someone else with our secret. Geon and Sorren know about us, but I cannot discuss it with them. They wouldn't understand a woman's feelings."

Seeing Dyna was too flustered to pick something from the chest, Yavi pulled out a bronze-colored dress embroidered with golden threads on the collar and hem. Thick gold strings braided through the front from the breast to the waist, and the tapered sleeves ended at a point.

"This one." Yavi smoothed it down on her lap. It was very nice. "It's the dress I was captured in so long ago."

"I can't take that," Dyna said, feeling too guilty to remind her of her past.

Yavi gave her a sad smile. "It doesn't fit me anymore, and it would be a shame to let it rot in a box. Besides, I think it suits your complexion better than mine. Please take it."

Murmuring her thanks, she accepted the dress hesitantly and changed into it as Yavi folded the other clothing in the chest properly, humming to herself again.

"Yavi?" Dyna fidgeted with the lace on her neckline, feeling her cheeks burn hot.

"Hmm?"

"Can I ask you something?"

"Yes?"

"W-what's it like?"

A sly smile rose to Yavi's face. "What is *what* like?"

Dyna didn't dare say it. She busied herself tying the strings of the dress, blushing furiously at the thought of intimacy. "I mean, I am a Herb Master. I know how it works…"

Yavi laughed softly and came behind her to help brush out her hair. "Well, when the day comes that you first experience that with someone, you may be anxious and excited, maybe a little tingly all over. But when you come together with someone you love, it feels like magic."

Like magic...

"Now, are we referring to one of your Guardians? You mentioned someone the other night. What was his name?"

Her heart spasmed. "Cassiel."

"The Celestial?" Yavi's eyes widened. "I heard he is quite powerful and beautiful, too."

"He is..." Her vision blurred. "He has eyes like starlight and wings like the night..."

Speaking of him hurt. It was as if his absence had torn a piece of her away. The constant ache in her chest throbbed painfully.

Yavi brushed the hair from Dyna's temples and tucked it behind her ears. "I'm sorry they stole you away from him, Dyna. You didn't deserve that. But I believe you will see each other again. Have faith, all right?"

She had to keep fighting. "All right."

"Come, let's go find something for you to eat. It's mid-morning, so the men have cleared out of Sorren's tent by now."

They headed out together and were greeted by the bright sun. The weather was a little warmer today, and everyone was enjoying it. They passed a group of Raiders eating and lounging at a campfire, but their rowdy conversation quieted as all eyes fell on them.

"Avert your gaze," Yavi ordered.

They obeyed except for one. It was the same man who had leered at them on the first day Dyna arrived. He had oily black hair, peppered gray, and pitted scars on his face.

His dark eyes narrowed on Yavi as he came to stand in front of her. "Know your place, woman. I should tan your hide. You're in need of it."

Yavi lifted her chin. "Touch me, and you will regret it, Haran. Now step aside."

His lip curled into a sneer. "You shall refer to me as Lieutenant now. I was promoted this morning."

Yavi's confidence wavered at seeing this man didn't care who she was. She backed away slowly, shielding Dyna with her back. "Forgive me, Lieutenant. We will be on our way."

"I haven't dismissed you." Haran snatched Yavi's arm, making her wince under his tight grip.

Dyna clung to her other arm. "Let go!"

"Unhand me!" Yavi shouted at the same time. "I'm on an errand."

"I'm not done with you, woman." Haran's mouth twisted into a leering smile, and he yanked her to him. "I might take part in your comforts first."

The hair prickled on the back of Dyna's neck, and her heart raced with sudden panic. Yavi trembled against her, because they both knew what he intended by that statement.

"Don't be daft, Haran," said a man sitting by the campfire. He didn't look up as he worked on sharpening a rapier sword on a whetstone. "Leave her be."

"You shut your hole, Bouvier," Haran snarled. "You're a spy. You have no authority in what I do."

Another spy?

Dyna hadn't met this one yet. By his elegant gray tunic and fine brown boots, he clearly wasn't a Raider. Bouvier was an older man with graying hair and a mustache he kept short and neat, but by no means did he appear weak. He glanced at her and nodded.

What was that supposed to mean? Was it a greeting or reassurance?

Bouvier nudged the burly Raider beside him. A man with skin as dark as a summer night and dreads to his shoulder. "Speak some sense into him, Olsson."

Olsson grunted as he eyed Yavi and Dyna warily. He scratched at the scruff on his face before rising to his full height. He was massive. "Aye, Lieutenant Haran, it's best to send them on their way," he said, his voice gravely and deep.

"Why do you fear a woman?"

Yavi glared at him and said with as much confidence as she could muster. "Release me, or you will pay."

Haran laughed. "The only payment I seek is you beneath me."

She slapped him. He snarled and backhanded Yavi so hard the blow tossed her to the mud.

"Yavi!" Dyna dropped to her knees beside her. "Are you all right?"

Yavi gaped up at Haran, holding her cheek. She pulled back her trembling fingers, and they came away with bright red smears. Deafening silence fell around them. Olsson motioned at a young Raider, and he sprinted off through the tents.

Bouvier shook his head. "Decrepit lout. You've dug your grave."

Haran ignored him or perhaps didn't hear him. "Go on, call upon your master, woman. Commander Von will thank me for teaching you proper respect."

Haran raised his fist, and the rings on his thick fingers glinted in the sunlight. Yavi curled into a ball, protecting her stomach. *The baby!*

Dyna leaped in between them. The blow landed across her cheek, and she fell in a heap. Pain burst behind her eyes, her vision flashing white. She fought to breathe. To move. Throbbing rushed through her skull, and a piercing ring filled her ears as something warm and wet leaked down her chin.

Yavi's muffled words barely reached her. "You struck the Maiden!"

"It was her own doing for getting in the way. Now come with me." The Raider snatched Yavi's arm, and she screamed as he dragged her toward a tent. None of the other Raiders moved to stop him. They couldn't when he outranked them.

Dyna, I'll always protect you, but one day I might not be there... Zev prepared her for this. They all did. The only defense she had left was herself.

She pushed to her feet and stepped in his way. "Let her go."

"You'll have your turn." He tried to shove her aside, but she thrust her palm up against his elbow, breaking his hold, and yanked Yavi away from him.

"Either you stop, or I will make you stop. Your choice."

He sneered. "You think you can fight me, girl?"

Shifting her body into position, Dyna flipped the knife she had stolen from him in her hand. "I've been trained by a werewolf, a Celestial, and a sorceress. You tell me which one of us has the better chance of walking away."

His expression darkened. "Women these days don't know any respect."

He lunged, and Dyna rolled across the ground out of the way. Grabbing a handful of dirt, she hurled it at his face. Haran stumbled backward with a curse. He swung another fist. Dyna pivoted and slashed the knife across his side. Not deep, but enough to make him bleed. She slid on the ground and slashed through his ankle. Down he went. Before he could move, Dyna punched him straight in the throat.

Haran dropped to his hands and knees, face dark purple as he wheezed for air.

"Don't come near her again." Dyna led Yavi away as the Raiders hooted with laughter, but their amusement died away when a shadow fell over her. She looked up at Haran's blazing eyes.

"I'll carve the flesh off your face, then rut your corpse." He raised a knife, and she simply...froze.

"Stop!" Olsson shouted. He and Bouvier ran for him.

Why would these men choose to defend them now? The far thought faded to the back of Dyna's mind as the glinting blade came for her.

A dark shadow tore through them, and the knife was hurled aside. Von spun and delivered a kick to Haran's jaw, throwing him down. Behind him stood the young Raider, who had run off at Olsson's order.

Turning to Dyna, the commander's mouth thinned at the blood on her face. "It's all right now, lass." He slowly reached for the knife in her shaking hand and carefully pried it free. "You're safe."

He'd saved her life...again.

Dyna couldn't accept that. Why had she frozen?

She stepped back, and Von glanced past her to Yavi. His wide eyes landed on the bleeding welt on her cheek, the condition of her clothing, and the direction of the tracks in the mud. Every angle of his face grew taut and his gaze... the pure murder in it sank a chill through Dyna's chest.

"Why was this not stopped?" Von asked the Raiders, his voice eerily calm. They dropped their eyes. He looked down at Haran next. "You not only harmed the Maiden, but you also put your hands on my property."

Bouvier sheathed his sword and stepped away with Olsson, but they remained in the vicinity, watching, as was everyone else.

"Commander, the slave woman was defiant." Haran staggered to his feet, blinking furiously to focus. He sniffed at the blood leaking from his nose. "She's no one to give us orders. I had to reprimand her."

"By striking her and taking her to your tent next?" Quiet malice lurked in Von's voice.

The man swallowed. "N-no, Commander."

"No one has the right to put their hands on her. Not even you." Von grabbed Haran's arm and jerked it tight against the socket. "May this serve to remind you of your error in judgment."

Then he snapped it in half.

Dyna's stomach heaved in horror as the man writhed and screamed in agony. Bloody bone jutted from his skin.

But all eyes moved from Haran to the figure standing across the clearing.

The sight of Tarn made Dyna's heart jolt behind her ribs. The Raiders went still, a silence falling over them. The temperature dropped in the air as if frost had arrived with his presence. He seemed so otherworldly in the late morning. His white-blond hair was silver in the sunlight as his long coat billowed in the breeze.

"Disperse." Everyone scattered at Tarn's command.

It shocked her how swiftly they obeyed orders with absolute compliance. Then those cold eyes fell on her next. Yavi grabbed Dyna's hand, and they fled together for Sorren's tent, nearly crashing into him and Geon.

"What happened?" Sorren asked. "We heard screaming."

"Haran," Yavi whimpered.

"He did this to you?" Geon helped her sit at the serving table where Dalton was seated.

Dalton hurried over. "He hit you, too?"

Dyna nodded, wincing at the sting when she touched the cut. "It looks worse than it is. I'm fine."

"You're not. Here, let me fix it." Orange Essence glowed in his palm, and he laid it gently against her cheek.

The tension eased out of Dyna's body as warmth sank through her, banishing the pain. "This is the first time I've received Essence Healing. It feels nice."

Normally, she was the healer. Dalton smiled at her warmly. If he was still speaking to her, they must not have told him about her schemes.

Sorren's low growl rumbled in the tent. "Wait for that miscreant to come in here. I'll castrate him."

"No need," Yavi mumbled blankly. "Von got to him..."

The faint sound of Haran's screams reached their ears, and they all cringed. His reaction had startled Dyna, but it seemed they weren't very stunned.

"The commander is ruthless when he's angry," Dalton told her.

"But he's agreeable for the most part," Geon argued.

"Speak for yourself." Dalton withdrew his hand and winked. "There. Lovely as ever."

She tentatively touched her cheek, finding it flawless, not a hint of a scar. His abilities far surpassed hers. He even healed the bruises on her chest and neck.

"None of that coquetry," Geon said. "Yavi needs healing next."

"You were more fun as a Raider." The mage retorted and approached Yavi, but she shooed him away.

"I'm fine, Dal."

He hesitated. "Are you sure? It's going to swell terribly by tomorrow. The healing will only take a minute."

She shook her head.

"Come see me if you change your mind." Dalton lifted a tray with three bowls of porridge and left.

Sorren and Geon looked confused by the refusal, but Dyna knew why. Essence Healing revealed everything within the body, and Dalton would easily discover she was with child. But the blow had knocked her down, and any fall could be harmful to a pregnancy.

Dyna crouched by Yavi and whispered, "Are you all right?"

"I'm frightened." Her mouth trembled. "What if..."

"Eat something. If there is no movement by the end of tonight, or if you bleed, come to me." Dyna took a soaked cloth Sorren handed her and carefully cleaned the cut before applying some honey on it. She sent a prayer to the God of Urn that the little one was all right. She hated not having her magic. It was times like this when she needed it most.

The tent flaps parted with Von's entrance, and his eyes immediately fell on Yavi. Dyna stepped back as he hastened to her side. "Let me see your face."

She hid beneath her auburn hair. "Leave it."

"Yavi." Von's brisk voice left no doubt that it was an order. At her sigh, he crouched and gently turned her chin to him, examining the bloodied bruise now taking form. A growl ripped from his throat.

Yavi caught his hand before he could leave. "You have done enough."

Von's eyes were dark as a storm. "It's less than what he deserved. I punished him as is my right. If I didn't, the others would think they could strike you without consequence."

"Torture, killing—that isn't who you are. You're not your master. That's what I want you to remember. The man could barely stand after your kick, short of Dyna bloody throttling him."

Von glanced at her then, and his fury slowly fell into a faint smirk. "That was an impressive hook, lass." He rubbed his throat as if he felt the blow. He must have seen the end of the fight.

Sorren pointed his cleaver at her. "This wee human? I highly doubt it."

Dyna frowned. What was so hard to believe about that?

"She did." Yavi let out a shocked giggle. "She beat him in three moves."

"You can fight?" Geon gaped at her. "And you felled him in a dress? I wish I could have seen it."

Now that everything had calmed down, Dyna's anger came rushing back. She gritted her teeth and swung a fist at him.

"Woah!" Von yanked her back before the punch landed.

"Let me show you well I can fight! Release me, Von."

He chuckled and hauled her a few steps back so she couldn't reach him. "As amusing as that might be to see, take a breather, lass."

Geon winced sheepishly. "I'm sorry, Dyna. Your plan would have hurt several people. I had to stop you."

"Tarn drugged me!"

He sighed. "The alternative would have been burying my friend. He won't kill you. You're too valuable. We have all been commanded not to lay a hand on the Maiden. But Dalton? The rest of us? Tarn wouldn't hesitate for a moment to take our lives. Do you understand? Any misstep here is a death sentence."

"If that were true, then he wouldn't have an army," she shot back. "It's impossible not to make mistakes."

"You're right. Occasionally, Tarn finds it in himself to be lenient." Geon pulled up his tunic and turned, displaying the scarred stripes going down his spine. "This was my second chance. There won't be a third. But Haran, I bet he won't live to see tomorrow."

Dyna stopped struggling at the sight of his back. He'd been flogged. When Von was sure she wouldn't attack Geon, he let her go. A sort of heavy silence filled the tent.

"Who taught you how to hit like that?" Yavi asked after a long pause in an attempt to lighten the mood.

Dyna turned away so Von would fall out of her view. "My...cousin taught me."

The heavy silence doubled. She felt his unease as he went to sit with Yavi.

"I truly am sorry for what happened," Geon said softly. He took the wet cloth from her and folded it to the other side to wipe the dirt from her hands. "Forgive me?"

"Hardly."

"What if I bake you some fresh bread?"

She smirked at his pout. "Then I might consider it."

Their chuckles died away when the tent flaps parted again, and they all met Elon's indifferent gaze. By his black armor and the red hilt of a sword glinting beneath his cloak, the elf was back to work. And Dyna knew why he'd come.

Tarn had sent for her.

CHAPTER 12

Von

Von shielded his eyes from the bright sunlight streaming into Sorren's tent. Elon stood at the entrance, the bright sun gleaming behind his silhouette. He was always well informed of the activity in the camp. No doubt Bouvier had reported to him what had occurred. Elon's amber eyes fell on Dyna, communicating with nothing but a look.

She rose and walked outside.

"Commander." Elon glanced at him next, indicating he was summoned as well.

Beneath the table, Yavi squeezed his hand. Von curled his fingers around hers in reassurance. This wasn't to penalize him for the attack on the lieutenant. Tarn was most likely annoyed that he hadn't promptly returned.

They had been in the middle of discussing the mission to Beryl Coast before they were interrupted with the trouble regarding Dyna and Yavi. To find his wife beaten, he had thought of nothing else but unleashing his rage on Haran. But Von hadn't expected Tarn to follow. It was so unusual for him to leave his tent for any occurrence that held no importance to him.

Von followed Elon outside, and Dyna trailed after them.

"How are you fairing?" he asked as they walked through camp.

"Well enough." Elon's complexion hadn't fully regained its color, but he didn't show any sign of pain. He may be pushing through it because he worked for pay.

"Rest while you can," Von said. "We will leave soon."

Elon nodded. He led them past Tarn's tent to the wooded area behind it before slipping away. There, the Master sat on a boulder beneath the shadow of a tree with Len at his side. Haran kneeled in front of him, his head hanging low. The position drudged up an old memory that Von quickly shoved aside.

Well, he wasn't looking forward to this. He hoped Dyna had a strong stomach.

"Pardon the delay, Master." Von bowed. "I was seeing to the Maiden."

The excuse was partially true. Tarn wouldn't care about Yavi.

"Get rid of it," Tarn ordered, his attention moving on to Dyna.

She sucked in a sharp breath, and Von noticed then Haran was already dead.

His face was blue from the lack of air, his wide eyes bloodshot from ruptured vessels. A dark purple indentation marked his throat. Dyna's punch wasn't severe enough to break his windpipe. There was only one person Von knew who was capable of that attack.

He hooked his arms beneath Haran's armpits and dragged him away. Two Raiders walking by halted when they noticed their dead lieutenant. He beckoned them over.

"Bury him in the woods," Von said as he laid the body down. "Do it properly with the last rites of his beliefs. Then remind every Raider: touch the Maiden and consider your life forfeit."

When he returned, Tarn said, "Find another to fill the post. Be it a subservient one this time."

But there may not be another Raider willing to be lieutenant. Abenon had been mauled a month ago, and Haran held the position for less than a day.

"Why did you kill him?" Dyna asked, looking sick.

"For disobeying my command," Tarn said.

"He hit me, and I defended myself. He didn't need to die for it."

Von noticed she withheld the fact that he had saved her life. Nor would he mention it either, or she would end up a slave, too.

"Well, then. How did she fare?" Tarn asked him, noting her battered knuckles. "She was injured earlier."

"I believe Dalton tended to it," Von said, not expecting the question. "Otherwise, she held up her own during the confrontation."

"Well enough to be of any merit?"

Dyna glared at him.

"I would say so, Master. She's had some instruction, it would seem."

Tarn tilted his head. "If he had been anticipating that, things may have ended differently."

She frowned. "Are you saying it was luck?"

"I'm saying let's see how well you do against an opponent who is ready for you." Tarn glanced at Len, and she bowed in compliance at his silent order. "Go and see if you can learn something."

Von couldn't help staring at Tarn this time. This was the last thing he expected.

"You're going to have her train me?" Dyna asked, staring at him. "Why?"

Tarn came to stand in front of her. She planted her feet, though his proximity forced her to lean back to look up at him. Their height difference was substantial. "Consider it a privilege, Maiden. Inadequacy is unacceptable here. Strengthen your body as you have your knowledge, and perhaps the next Raider will think twice before touching what belongs to me."

A shocked scowl crossed her face, and she hissed. "I'm not property, Tarn. Least of all yours."

Len yanked her away before she could say more.

Von normally knew Tarn so well he could see through his subtle expressions and statements to his true intentions, but this left him confused. What was the purpose of teaching her how to fight when it could be a hindrance later?

Tarn turned to him. "Prepare whatever you need for the excursion to Beryl Coast."

Bouvier had arrived last night with new information regarding the ancient temple ruins there. A Relic Hunter was leading an excavation in search of a Sacred Scroll, so they were pressed for time.

"Yes, Master. However, I suggest giving the excavation two more days to dig. It will save us the effort of doing it ourselves. Then we will arrive to relieve them of the scroll."

Von said it for his team's sake. Elon was hardly back on his feet, and it took Bouvier nearly two weeks to ride back. They needed time to recover.

"Very well." Tarn went into his tent and sat at his table. "Meanwhile, send someone to investigate the grove for any signs of her Guardians. When he returns, take all the spies with you to the ruins. I don't want to risk losing this scroll."

Von didn't understand why they were still searching for the Scroll of the Unending. Tarn now had the map that would lead him straight to Mount Ida, where the Unending Tree grew. He also seemed to have lost interest in the Moonstone.

"What of the journal?"

"Benton insists Dyna's Essence is needed to open it," Von said. Which meant removing her bangles.

Tarn's jaw worked, his fingers drumming on the table. "She will join me for dinner at the end of the day."

Von bowed and stepped back outside. The frosty breeze cooled the sweat on his forehead, but it didn't carry away the cloud of confusion now circling his head.

What belongs to me...

A shudder passed through Von's chest. Was Tarn claiming ownership over Dyna as simple property, or was this part of the prediction of the Seer's divination? No. Tarn knew the warning.

Since they left Azurite, he had no interest in women and didn't seek any out. But Von sensed Tarn's attention on the Maiden was different. He was constantly making plans, and Von wasn't privy to all of them. Which only made his apprehension grow because he knew in the end, it would be Dyna who would suffer.

The poor girl had been through enough.

The Raiders passing by lowered their heads when they saw him and kept on their way. By now, news of what happened to Haran had spread through the camp. He reached Sorren's tent in time to see Yavi limp out. The sight of her beaten appearance made him wish Haran was alive simply so he could kill him again.

When no one was looking, Von lifted Yavi in his arms and carried her into the woods.

"What are you doing?" she asked. It was a tired question, more than a protesting one. Her arms wrapped around his neck. "Do you plan to carry me all the way to my tent? A convenient excuse, no doubt."

"Any excuse to spend time with my wife is a good excuse," Von said as he trekked along the perimeter of the veil.

Yavi rested her head on his shoulder. She said nothing, but he heard her crying softly.

"This shouldn't have happened to you," he said.

She shouldn't have been taken from her family in the first place. This wasn't the life Yavi was meant to live, even if it brought her to him. All he wanted was for her to be happy, and she would never have that here.

But he was a stone stuck in Tarn's foundation. Buried so far deep, there was no digging him out. *Alhaya*, she had said to him in a moment of anger, but it was true. He was eternally chained to him in ways far more dire than she knew. But he wouldn't let that be her fate, too.

Von's chest tightened at the thought of sending Yavi away. She cried every time they talked about it. He wished he could go with her, but walking away from his master would incur his wrath and that of the fates.

"What was your life like before me?" she asked softly. "Before Tarn. You've never truly spoken about it."

Von sighed at the thought of Troll Bridge. All he knew, who he once was, the life he had lived, it all ended in that place the day the Horde overran their town.

"Tarn has always been there," Von confessed. He ducked under a branch, careful to avoid Yavi getting swiped. "My father served his father, and I was expected to do the same."

"But you weren't a slave."

"No." Von looked out at the rows of tents past the trees. He hadn't been a life-servant then, but he had felt chained, nonetheless. "We were both squires training to be knights. It was a hard regiment, for our lives truly depended on how well we could swing a sword."

"Because of the trolls."

He nodded. The Bridge was harsh, and the winters were brutally cold, but it was also when the trolls would hibernate. As soon as the temperatures rose, so did their fear, because they knew the beasts would wake. "No matter how hard they trained us, many would die every year fighting back those beasts."

Von still remembered how his mother would weep at his bedside every night, praying to the God of Urn for his protection. And instead of being a grateful son, he would resent her for thinking that words would have any power to protect him from an existence they forced him into.

It was a life of constant fear.

"Every summer, the squadron would ride out on missions to try to find the source of the trolls. Where they lived, and how to kill them. We constantly failed to control their growing population. Every year our numbers dwindled."

They would trudge back to town covered in troll guts and blood, carrying the rotting bodies of their comrades. The stench was so embedded in his memory that it was something he would never forget.

"I had been so aggrieved for being forced to leave Old Tanzanite Keep to live in that wretched place," he said. "I hated how devoted my father and mother were to the Morken House. Hated their zealot beliefs of duty. Above all, I hated that I didn't have control over my life that could end at any moment."

Yet speaking about it now drudged up an odd nostalgia. A piece of him had remained in that place among the dead.

"One winter, Lord Morken finally had a thirty-foot wall built from lumber around the town, and at last, we felt somewhat safe," Von said. They reached the woods near their old tent, and he carefully set her down.

A breeze rolled through the trees, making them rattle and hiss. They stretched for the sky like brittle bones.

"But you weren't," Yavi whispered. The passing wind wove through her hair and lifted it against the sunlight, where it turned a shade he hadn't seen in a very long time. He was hit with the memory of a body on the ground, blood soaking through streams of golden brown curls. "Von?"

He flinched away from Yavi's touch on his arm. "Pardon, love. It's... hard to speak about."

She looked up at him forlornly. Would she think differently of him if she learned Azurite could have been safe if he had honored his duty instead of running from it?

Yavi embraced him, burying her face in his chest. "It must have been awful to witness everyone you know die. I'm sorry that happened to you."

He closed his eyes. Yavi tightened her arms around him, and at that moment, she was all that held him together. She suddenly jolted with a yelp. A shocked smile crossed her features, and her eyes welled as if she had received the best news.

"What is it?" he asked.

Yavi dropped her head against his chest. "I merely felt ... better. Thank the Gods you're still here with me."

Von kissed her temple and held her to him as they swayed to some unheard song. He felt her joy and her relief. Whatever had made her happy, he wanted to share that with her.

"I must return," he reluctantly said after a while.

She tightened her hold. "Stay."

"I must see to the preparations for Beryl Coast."

Yavi glowered up at him. "It will be another pointless mission, Von. You spend months chasing rumors that mostly turn out to be false leads. But why does he continue to hunt this scroll now that he has Dyna?"

Von couldn't answer because he didn't have one. He'd always sensed Tarn's plan went beyond simply being immortal.

"The Sacred Scrolls weren't meant for this." Yavi's face creased with sorrow, and he knew she was thinking of the life she had lived before, working as a linguist in the libraries. It had been a source of pride for her.

He tucked a lock of Yavi's soft hair behind her ear. "Do you hate me for taking you from your home?"

Tarn had ordered him to steal her away, and Von didn't give her a chance to say goodbye to her family. She refused to eat and cried for days, slowly withering away. It chiseled at his hardened heart as he tried to comfort her.

When he'd earned her first smile, Von had felt something warm lit up inside of his chest. It wasn't long before she had his heart.

"I used to wish my ancestors were never acolytes of the temples," Yavi murmured against his palm. "So it wouldn't have led to my slavery hundreds of years later, but then I wouldn't have met you." Her hazel eyes lifted to his. "You're my home now."

"And you're mine." Von lifted her face to him and kissed her. She tasted of honey and cinnamon. The wildflower scent of her hair made him feel like they were standing in a meadow instead of a barren forest. "I will never tire of kissing these lips," he breathed against her mouth. Trailing his nose along her cheek to her ear, Von slid a hand to the small of her back and pulled her closer. "Or the rest of you, for that matter."

Yavi gave him a sly smile. "I should hope not."

She slipped her hand in his and led him to the tent that had once been theirs. No one was around to see, but he tugged her to a stop.

"We can't. Dyna might return."

"She knows." Her words were a splash of freezing water.

"Yavi!" he whispered sharply under his breath, surveying their surroundings in case anyone heard.

She pulled him inside. "Don't worry. Dyna promised to keep our secret."

Von was past worried. He took her cousin's life. And Dyna now knew the one thing that could get them both killed.

CHAPTER 13

Dynalya

Dyna hit the ground with a breathless cry. She spat blood on the ground, holding her aching stomach. She wasn't sure if the spy was indeed teaching her or if this was a punishment for trying to escape. Len backed up so she could stand. Lights danced in Dyna's vision as she rose to her feet, swaying. She was grateful for the old leathers they gave her to change into. For once, she felt a little like her old self.

"I think she's had enough, Len." Novo lay in the grass nearby with his arms crossed behind his head, cavalier hat tipped over his eyes.

"No, I haven't," Dyna panted as she wiped her bloodied nose. Her body ached with the new bruises she felt forming, but her adrenaline was on a high. She wanted to hit and keep hitting. Needed to get out all the pressure painfully building in her chest. "Again."

Len threw a kick. Dyna dodged it and swung a fist for her kidney. But Len was too fast. She leaped in the air, catching Dyna around the neck with her legs, and flipped her. Her face smashed into the ground again. She lay there, gasping for the air that had been wrenched out of her. The dust stinging her eyes made them water.

"If you kill her, the Master will be angry," Novo chuckled. "Learn to pull your punches, love."

Len curled her lip and spat a word that could only have been an insult.

Dyna forced herself onto her knees. "What does that mean?"

"*Pathetic.* Slow like baby."

"I'd learn how to move faster if you taught me properly instead of merely thrashing me." Dyna pushed herself to stand, holding her glare. "Or is violence the only use you have for your master?"

Len bared her teeth in a hiss. Her boot shot out, and it snapped Dyna's head back, the taste of copper bursting in her mouth. If she fell, she never felt it. The next thing Dyna knew, Novo had one of her arms hanging over his shoulder as he half carried, half lugged her across camp, her feet dragging beneath her.

"You have a knack for provoking her, lass."

The buzz of muffled voices and movement swarmed around her as tents were broken down.

"It wasn't me," he announced to whoever must have questioned their appearance. "A casualty of Len's."

A chorus of chortles followed in their wake, making Dyna's throbbing face burn.

Novo helped her stumble into Tarn's tent. He was in a chair by his bed with a book. He hardly spared her battered face a glance before returning to reading. The dim candlelight cast half of his face in shadow, hiding most of his scar. Novo carefully placed her at his feet and backed out of the tent with a bow.

After flipping another page, Tarn closed his book. "Did you learn anything?"

"Only that you're a sadist," she growled weakly. Every part of her body ached.

The sharper pains throbbed in her jaw where the kick landed. She sucked in a sharp hiss through her teeth at what breathing did to her ribs. Nothing felt broken, but every agonizing movement sent tears to her eyes.

The smell of food coming from his table made the emptiness chew through her stomach, and her throat felt coated with sand. Heavy exhaustion was the most prevailing feeling. Every bit of strength was gone, like someone had pulled on the end of her thread and kept pulling until she was completely unraveled.

At least she was alive.

"The ability to endure pain is a warrior's true weapon," he said. "Master that, and nothing will ever hurt you."

"Is that what you call training? You knew she would beat me." Dyna sniffed, getting a whiff of the dry blood that coated her nostrils. "What happened to not allowing me to be touched?"

"Len only strikes with purpose."

"Is that what you taught her? You cannot answer everything with violence. It's senseless."

"Violence is the way of humanity, and with time, you will come to understand it's the only language it speaks." Tarn set the book on the bedside table, his wintery eyes holding hers. "I don't kill without a reason. Each death serves a purpose, like removing their nauseating existence. The problem with some people is that they're breathing."

She let out a disgusted scoff. "Are people so worthless that you don't care what lives you end?"

Tarn only looked amused by the question, as if her anger enticed him. The candlelight haloed his white-blond hair as he canted his head. "Only the strong rise above the weak, Maiden. And if they died, it's because they lacked the strength to live."

She limply shook her head. "Killing must come easy to you. Saving people, that is more difficult. The day you come across someone you wish to save and cannot is the day you will truly feel powerless."

His gaze became glacial, his expression turning sharp. She couldn't hold its intensity and dropped her eyes.

"Look at me." Tarn leaned forward, and his cold fingers took her chin, forcing her to meet those ice-blue orbs he had for eyes. She couldn't look at him without holding her breath or feeling goosebumps prickle her skin. And when he spoke, his voice sent a cascade of shudders down her spine. "You're so far out of your depth you fail to see what this world does to the weak. One day, it will crush you, and I wonder what that will do to your sweet, *innocent* heart."

Dyna's knees trembled where she knelt, her bruised hands curling into fists on the hard ground. He must enjoy this position of having her kneeling at his feet. "I question if you have a heart when your soul must be black with all the countless people you've killed."

"When someone attempts to take my life, I won't hesitate to take theirs. Survival demands more than blood. It demands souls." His thumb grazed the small split on her bottom lip, making her wince. "If you want to live, you must pay the price. And most do."

She yanked her chin away. "That's evil."

He straightened in his seat and picked up a goblet from the bedside table. "No one is ever purely evil, as no one is ever purely good. We all have darkness in our hearts, Maiden. Even you."

"I will *never* be like you."

"Because you think you would never take a life?" Tarn smirked, swishing the contents in his goblet before taking a drink. She swallowed back her thirst. "You pretend to be standing on some moral high ground from which you judge me, but the truth is when danger is put between yourself or another you care for, you will act. It's an instinct we all have, or did you forget our first meeting outside the grove when you lifted a sword and aimed at me?"

Dyna could only glare at him, even as the memory sprouted something cold in her chest.

"To protect your Guardians, your only thought was to stop me— permanently." He leaned forward until all she could do was stare into his pale eyes. "And the only way to do that was to *kill* me."

Dyna couldn't deny it. Couldn't pretend her only goal had been to run him through. Now the very thought of murdering anyone churned her stomach. She wasn't a killer, but she had wanted to end him out of sheer desperation.

To know she was capable of that frightened her.

Tarn crossed one leg over the other and propped his elbow on the armrest, leaning his chin against a fist. "You assess what I have done and paint me the villain. But when everything you treasure is stolen from you, your pure little Maiden heart will become cold and full of hatred. Revenge will be all you want, and the only thing that will ever bring you joy is watching your enemies corrode at your feet."

Behind him hung the flag with the Ice Phoenix crest. She knew nothing else about Tarn other than what he'd revealed and what she'd learned. He was a descendant of Jökull—and the Azure King's son. Now that she met the man everyone feared and studied the long scar across his face that was clearly intended to end his life, she suspected the King wanted him dead for more than what he had done.

"Is that your plan?" she asked. "To have Azure corrode at your feet?"

The candlelight illuminated half of Tarn's face as he looked up at the flag. "The phoenix is a curious creature. They are immortal only in the sense that when they die, it obtains new life by arising from the ashes of their predecessor. Years ago, my predecessor unintentionally brought about my existence. Unfortunately, he also saw that I was born simply to annihilate him and his reign. And from the ashes, I will bring forth mine."

A cold premonition settled on her skin. She wondered what King Lenneus had done to incur Tarn's wrath.

"Is it true what they say?" she dared to ask next. "Did you kill the Duke of Zircon?"

It was the reason for his bounty.

Tarn sat back in his seat, his eyes sharpening like icicles. A chill seemed to move in the air, making the hairs on the back of her neck rise. "Do you want the truth?"

She nodded, though her insides twisted.

"The duke's life was cut tragically short when I put my sword through his mouth, so the last thing he experienced was drowning in his own blood."

Dyna dropped back on her heels at the gruesome reply. "Why?"

"For the lies his mouth had spoken."

She recalled the rumor against Tarn's mother. The one of her being bedded by the Duke and it causing a strife with his father, Lord Morken, Earl of Old Tanzanite Keep. The only way the Azure King could appease the slight was to give him the land of Troll Bridge. And it led to the death of his whole town.

"What lies?" she whispered because he implied there was more than one.

A slight smirk turned up the corner of Tarn's mouth. He went to his table to serve himself more wine. "If you wish for me to share, then I expect an exchange. Why do you fear the dark?"

Dyna glowered at the question. She tried and failed to stand on her sore legs. He merely watched as she used the armrest of his chair to push herself to her feet. But her legs felt like soggy bread, and she stumbled into his chair. She wanted to get back up, yet the warm seat had her body sagging into it.

"You panicked the first night when the candles went out." He sat in the chair at his table. "Then in the woods, you begged for the light."

She raised a hand to her face. It shook from exhaustion and pain, but the old echo of fear stirred somewhere in her chest. He didn't need to know about her past. The man would probably find a way to use it against her. "I was merely startled to wake in a place I didn't recognize."

Tarn looked at her with his eerie gaze that said he didn't believe her.

She needed to evade his ire and try to escape this camp unscathed. The only way she would survive him was to keep her usefulness. He wanted her map, and she felt the demand hovering over her head. But if he found out the journal never had it in the first place, he would probably do away with her nauseating existence, too.

"Why am I here?" Dyna asked, bracing for his response. Her stomach promptly chose to let out a loud rumble, making her flush.

"Well, at the moment, to see you fed."

She salivated from the mention of food, but the distance between her and the table felt like a mile. Any attempt to walk would end with her sprawled on the ground and probably unconscious. The need for sleep was already sinking into her body.

"Then you can wash off the filth," Tarn added as he frowned at her appearance.

Then she noticed the edge of a wooden tub partially hidden by a privacy screen. Steam swirled on the surface. The very thought of taking a wonderfully hot bath had her aching body begging for it. But it also put her instantly on the defense.

"You drew me a bath?" she asked warily, not sure what he was planning now.

"After the day you've had, I think it was well earned, don't you? Plus, you're beginning to smell." At her glare, he arched an eyebrow. "I don't plan to be here while you bathe, if that's your concern. Unless you require assistance."

"No," Dyna growled.

Tarn might have smirked, but he turned away before she could see it. Was he teasing her? All of this unusual consideration made her suspicious, but she was too tired to dissect what it meant.

Tarn surprised her when he placed a cup of water and a plate with bread, cheese, and half a pear on the bedside table for her. Perhaps he wasn't as menacing as she thought. Then again, he most likely drugged the food, but Dyna didn't care. She downed the cool water, relishing as it slid down her throat. She hardly noted it didn't taste odd this time before tearing into the food. It didn't take more than two minutes to scarf it all down. By the end, her body sank into the backrest. She waited for him to command for the map, but Tarn wasn't paying attention.

He stared blankly at the journal on the table, his breathing a little uneven. The dim candlelight exposed the sweat on his forehead. She recognized the signs of dependence on remedies and the effects it created in the body. The bitter scent of herbs reached her nose before she heard the sound of more wine pouring.

Dyna wobbled to her feet. "I'll take that bath now, if you don't mind."

Tarn stepped out without further prompting. The food and desire to be clean provided enough strength to stagger to the tub. She confirmed he wasn't coming back before undressing. It took a couple of tries to get her shaky fingers to remove the straps of armor. Hissing through her teeth, Dyna carefully peeled it off, trying not to touch her wounds. She stepped into the water to find it perfectly hot and steaming. It wouldn't surprise her if it was enchanted as well. With a groan, she sank into its delightful warmth and laid her head back on the rim. It was an unexpected luxury out in the wilderness, but it made her want to cry from the much-needed relief it brought.

Her heavy eyes drooped, and her mind drifted. But real rest wouldn't come when the wards droned like a nest of hornets. Tarn had turned his tent into a fortress. For all his bravado, most of the spells were for his protection or used for that purpose, like Witch's Brew.

Once he had the Unending, he wouldn't need any of it.

CHAPTER 14

Zev

I t was the scent of blood that caught Zev's attention first. He stopped in his tracks, observing the plains of Emberdin. It was quiet, save for the chatter of wildlife and birds cawing overhead. The brown grass stretched wide into the horizon with a strip of gray mountains in the far distance. A gradient of rich blues blending into purple and pink painted the dawn sky as the sun began to wake. Rawn drew up short behind him as they studied their surroundings. Fair's hooves clomped on the ground restlessly, sensing what Zev had finally caught after two days of searching. He breathed in the crisp air, and it came to him again.

"I smell blood," he warned under his breath.

Lord Norrlen silently armed his bow.

Zev inhaled again and fell stock still. There were two traces, but beneath the metallic smell lingered a gentle but so penetratingly familiar scent. His wolf rose to attention. This feeling growing within him triggered an instinct— of like calling to like.

The scent of an Other.

A *female* Other.

There were various scents of more like him, but hers was fresh and so captivating that he struggled to focus. It carried on the wind, luring him across the plains. Zev forced himself to keep his pace slow instead of running to find her as his wolf demanded. The need was so strong every muscle in his body tightened with resistance not to chase it. He searched the tall grass for any movement. Rawn said the Lupin Pack was amiable, but even the most tolerant wolf didn't take kindly to strangers in their territory.

There was a barely audible crack of a branch. Both he and Rawn tensed. If it had been anyone else, they wouldn't have heard it. Zev's wolf eyes ignited as his claws grew.

They waited. Listening.

"Hello?" His voice carried over the plains into the windy silence.

There were no distinct landmarks here. Other than the sparse woods a half mile to the right, he only saw a large lump of a brown rock in the grass.

Except it wasn't a rock. It had fur.

Zev hurried to it, coming around to find a dead elk. It was gouged out by its throat, and lying beside it was the one he scented. A female white wolf. Bright red blood stood out against her coat, most of it gathered by her shoulder. She snarled and snapped her fangs, warning them to stay back.

But he simply stood there. Staring into those vivid blue eyes he had seen before.

"Zev," Rawn prompted him softly.

Right, she was injured and needed help, but at the moment, they were a threat. For a werewolf, or a Lycan rather—she was small. Half his size. Zev thought to make himself smaller and less threatening, but as soon as he crouched, she bolted.

"Wait," Zev called as he chased after her. "We mean you no harm!"

Even wounded, the white wolf sprinted across the plains for the trees. How frightened must she be to combat the pain like that? It would only make her injury worse.

Rawn told him to hold when they reached the woods, but Zev went in after her, anyway. He barely caught a glimpse of white disappearing past the bushes. He sped up, leaping across fallen logs. Crossing the bend, he saw her again as her body gracefully leaped across a ravine and missed the landing. The wolf went tumbling into the shallow creek below. She lay there among the rocks, panting. Her lips pulled against her teeth at his approach.

"It's all right. I'm here to help." He paused a few feet away from her, waiting for her reaction. She was too weak to do more than growl. "God of Urn, as my witness, I won't hurt you, little wolf." He slowly approached, making sure his claws were retracted. He left his neck exposed as a sign of good faith. "May I carry you out?"

She whined weakly, panting with shallow breaths. Zev gently lifted her body, careful of her injured shoulder. She keened and flailed. Either from pain or to escape him.

"You killed an elk all by yourself?" Zev asked to distract her. "That's impressive. At most, I have seen three fully grown males take one down. Never one."

She fell still at that, and her blue eyes regarded him.

"Many have fallen to their antlers, little wolf. You're lucky to be alive." He leaped up the ravine and landed on the ground above. Laying her back down, he studied the gash where she'd been impaled. "Aye, it seems you avoided the worst of it, but may I tend to your arm? If it isn't set before you heal, it will leave you with a permanent limp."

She already knew that, of course. Zev simply spoke in soft tones to keep her calm.

"You must change back," he said. She snarled, and he held up his hands. "Or not."

She probably felt safer as a wolf. Rawn strolled up from behind and handed him a waterskin.

"Are you thirsty?" Zev uncorked the top and offered it to her.

The white wolf only continued to stare at him, her nostrils flaring as she inhaled his scent. Her head tilted, and she sniffed further. She jerked her head back, as if confused. No, *shocked*.

"Here." Zev reached out to support her neck to help her drink.

But he and Rawn whipped around at the sound of running paws tearing up dirt. He rolled out of the way in time to miss the flash flying over his head. A massive white wolf landed in front of the female. Its fur bristled as it lowered into a threatening crouch and let out a deep, vicious growl.

Arctic wolves. Two of them.

And the new one was male. The wolf bared its sharp fangs, threatening to attack.

Keeping his head lowered and arms wide, Zev slowly backed up, and Rawn did the same. He took in a discreet sniff, and it told him two things. This wolf was an Alpha, and kin of the female. The male's eyes were different, however. One was yellow and the other blue.

"I only meant to help her," Zev said. "Nothing more."

The female whined, catching the male's attention. He circled her and chuffed at the wound angrily, then nuzzled her cheek. She must have communicated something to him through the Pack link because he spun his head around to Zev. His nostrils flared wide, and his fur receded to stand on two legs. The male stood a couple of inches shorter than him. Light blond hair fell above his unusual colored eyes. Less vivid, but one remained blue while the other settled to brown instead of yellow. He was perhaps a few years older than Zev. Body coiled with muscle and marked by the typical scars of a wolf.

101

On his shoulder, he bore black markings in twisting, angular patterns. It wasn't a Pack Mark Zev recognized.

After staring at him for a long minute, the male spoke with an unusual accent not heard in Azure. "My sister says you helped her."

Sister...

"But that isn't why you've come."

"My name is Zev Astron. This is my companion, Rawn Norrlen. It's a pleasure to meet you." They nodded in greeting, though both of them had noticed the large shapes slinking through the trees. "We're here searching for the Lupin Pack. For more of my kind."

"Your kind." The Alpha canted his head, eyebrows set low over his eyes. "We haven't seen your kind in many years."

Zev frowned in confusion. "Are you not Lycans?"

"Yes. I mean to say, your breed is uncommon. The last I have heard of your kind, they had all settled in the south, within Lykos Peak. You're far from home, Zev Astron."

The Alpha kept his eyes on him as more wolves prowled forward and surrounded them in a loose circle. Not quite a threat, but enough to warn that they were prepared to fight if need be. From scent alone, they were all ranked as lead warriors. He felt their stares as they sized him up.

Zev's wolf growled inside of him, not at all intimidated. Fair nickered, jerking on the reins. He settled with a soft murmur in Elvish from Rawn.

"Pardon," Zev said. "I'm not seeking to trespass on anyone's territory or position. Nor do I seek to recruit members for Lykos."

The Alpha studied him further, probably listening to his heart rate. "Good," he said once he decided Zev wasn't lying. "Lupin isn't in a position to lose anymore wolves."

Zev caught the strange wording. "You're not part of the Lupin Pack?"

"We're friends having come to visit." The Alpha accepted the bundle of clothing a gray wolf carried to him in its jaws. He slipped on a pair of trousers, then held out a tunic to the female. "I am Ronin. This is Lara."

She attempted to shift, but whined sharply when putting weight on her injured shoulder. Zev moved to help, earning Ronin's warning growl to stop. Lara shifted on her second attempt, and it cast her scent through the air. It swam through his senses, luring him in such a way, it made him take another step. Her brother viciously snarled, and the Pack formed a perimeter of protection around her.

Ronin blocked her out of view with his large body, his claws extending.

"Zev," Rawn warned under his breath. "Don't take another step."

But at the moment, Zev didn't care if he got bitten. He didn't know what this feeling was, but she'd triggered a primal instinct to get close enough to breathe her in. She inexplicably drew him, filling him with the need to…mark.

A burly male with dark reddish hair stepped in Zev's way and flashed his fangs in a feral growl. "Stand back, mutt."

The male expelled a territorial musk. The sign of one who had declared a female for himself and would kill anyone who challenged him.

It snapped Zev out of it. "Ah…sorry…" He flushed. "I didn't mean…"

Ronin nodded stiffly. "Unmated females can have that effect on males. They sometimes forget themselves, so I prefer they keep their distance from my sister."

"Aye." Zev swallowed, his face heating further. "Sorry."

He'd seen something similar happen in Lykos Peak. When an unmated female smelled so enticing, it drove the males mad. It would fade once she had been marked by her chosen mate.

Zev had no intention of doing anything.

It wasn't the fact that she was unmated that called his attention. There was something fascinating about Lara's specific scent that his wolf demanded to explore. It was something new, yet not as if he recognized it. Even though he'd never come across it before. He caught a glimpse of her glowing blue eyes past Ronin's shoulder and knew he had seen them.

In the void.

Nothing else of her was visible except her slender feet. She shook out the dark gray tunic Ronin handed her and slipped it on. Zev was suddenly aware she was very naked. He cleared his throat and moved several feet back.

"What kind of Lycan is he?" the burly male sniffed the air. "This breed, I cannot place it."

"You haven't met his kind before, Finn." Ronin slowly eased out of his tense crouch. "He's a rare breed. Lucanis."

The Pack growled low. Some were threatened, but others seemed intrigued. There were many breeds of werewolves, but Zev's previous Pack had only one.

Lara stared at him openly.

"Lucanis?" Finn circled Zev, sniffing him. They were more or less the same height. "You must be big, eh? My breed is *Ru*canis. The red wolves of the Northwest. I'm rather big myself, but I doubt you're as big as me. Shall we compare?"

The Alpha rolled his eyes. "Is that necessary?"

"I know you, Ronin. You want him on the line."

Ronin crossed his arms, eyeing him again as though to take his measure. "You must admit, he would do well. We don't have any Lucanis yet, and they are massive."

Zev glanced between them, trying to decipher what they meant.

Finn's large palm shoved Zev's shoulder, or attempted to. He didn't move an inch. "Shift."

Zev pushed his hand off. "I'm not sure what you're talking about, but I'm not a threat to you or whatever line you have. I'm not interested."

"I want to see your wolf." Finn's eyes flashed vivid green. "Show us the mighty Lucanis."

Zev's eyes flared yellow, his wolf rising to the challenge. But they didn't come here to make enemies. "I don't wish to fight."

A barking laugh boomed from Finn's chest, and he turned to the Pack. "I ask to see his wolf, and he immediately thinks of violence."

"It's not a challenge." Ronin's mouth hitched up on the ends. "But there is no reason to bend to my beta's demands."

Beta. Of course. Arrogant. Authoritative. It fit the mark.

They were both very young to hold such a prominent position. Zev should have noticed by the way Finn stood on Ronin's right as his second. On his left remained the gray wolf who had passed him the clothing earlier. That must be his delta.

"Where is your Pack Mark?" Finn asked him.

At the question, Zev inwardly braced. "I don't have one."

Every wolf present reacted to the news differently. Some with contempt, others with wariness or surprise.

"He's an omega," Finn announced, as if they hadn't heard him clearly.

He was a lone wolf.

Unwanted.

And the word was said with as much derision as when Zev was called the Other. But he understood their wariness. Omega wolves were outcasts for a reason.

"Why did your Pack not accept you?" Ronin asked. It was a personal question and one that needed addressing.

Zev exhaled a heavy breath. "Because I was different from them."

The Alpha only gave him an understanding look, and the wolves quieted. They knew what it was like to be cast out. "For being an Other?"

For being a monster, the Madness whispered in his thoughts. *For who should want a kin-slayer?*

Zev looked away and responded with a short nod, agreeing with them both.

If the Alpha knew how far gone he was, this Pack would cast him away as well. One look at Ronin was enough to prove he'd long regained control over his Other. No imprint of chains marked his body. No burns scarred his wrists from wearing silver manacles every full moon night for years. He only bore the scars of a wolf, not of shame.

And for once, Zev was grateful Cassiel had erased his scars. Because to get help, he would have to keep that secret.

A slip of movement drew his attention to Lara coming out from behind her brother. Zev's next breath stalled as he saw her. Her height reached Ronin's shoulder. Long white-blond hair fell around her shoulders in waves. Her blue wolf eyes stayed on his face, and he found himself memorizing hers. The elegant angles, skin the color of the moon, lips like petals. She was strong. It was clear in how she stood and in the lean muscle of her graceful form. The dark gray tunic she wore fell mid-thigh with the sleeves rolled up to her elbows. His gaze dropped to her feet, following the path of her long legs, up her arms, to the blood seeping through the fabric on her right shoulder, and rising again to the soft curves of her face.

Lara was beautiful.

He'd known she was since he saw her wolf. And not a scar to be seen.

They held the stare for a moment before she said, "I would like to see your wolf."

A faint accent tinged her words. But her voice—it reminded him of crisp nights and the rustle of a soft breeze. Of the free wild.

Zev stilled, stunned by the sound and her request. If they considered him a threat now, surely they would if he shifted. But she was watching him with those vibrant eyes. Waiting. And damn if his wolf didn't bristle with pride. They both knew his form was impressive.

Not looking away, he kicked off his boots and peeled away his tunic. She stared at the many scars marking his body. The sign of his chains was gone, but not of the violent life he lived. An omega was always challenged, and it had been marked on him by claws and fangs.

Her stare dragged over every inch of him as she studied each scar along his arms, chest, and ridges of his stomach. Then he removed his trousers next. The glide of her eyes slipped to his feet, and ever so slowly, made their way up to his face again.

Zev called on his wolf.

An ache passed through his body as his muscles rippled with the shift. His large paws hit the dirt, and he rose to his full height. The Pack snarled, some stepping back and others holding their ground. Their alarm barely registered when he was so focused on the sharp rise of Lara's chest. Her scent heightened in his senses, and her pupils dilated, mouth parting with a low breath.

"You're right," Lara told the beta. "He isn't as big as you. He's bigger."

The wolves barked with what could only be laughter.

Finn's mouth curled, and he crossed his arms. "He's dangerous."

But there was only a gleam in Ronin's odd eyes. "I'm willing to bet he is."

"Is that what you want in Lángshān?" Finn asked him.

Zev stiffened and shared a startled look with Rawn.

He quickly shifted back and stared at the Alpha. "You're the Garou Pack from Xián Jīng."

Zev and Rawn lingered by the tree line as the Pack worked on dismembering the elk for meat. Ronin had Lara pulled aside. She kept her head low as her brother lectured her on the reckless hunt. Zev tried not to listen, but his wolf was so highly aware of her that he couldn't help but catch their voices in the wind.

"What were you thinking?" Ronin growled.

"I was thinking about food. They haven't been able to hunt for weeks."

"I know that, Lara. We're leaving them our provisions, and I had the others out hunting."

She shook her head. "Dried meat and a few measly rabbits won't sustain them. I saw the elk, and I made a choice."

"A foolish one! Instead of calling me, you hunted on your own. You could have been killed. I agreed to bring you with us because you promised to stay out of danger. Not to get yourself skewered."

Lara's shoulders sank, the confidence seeping out of her demeanor beneath her brother's chastisement. It drew out a memory of the way Dyna deflated when Zev refused to let her learn how to use weapons. He had only wanted to protect his cousin, as Ronin wanted to protect his sister. But the hurt on Lara's face was a mirror reflection of how Dyna had looked. And it left behind a new weight of shame over his head.

Lara covered her wound, looking away from her brother. "I will live, Ronin. Which is more than the Lupin Pack could say if they don't have food."

The Alpha sighed heavily. "Half of their Pack is gone. I don't think the other half will make it through winter."

Zev straightened at the news. Lord Norrlen nodded that he heard as well.

She shook her head, sadness entering her eyes. "There is still hope for some. We can't leave them behind like this."

"We will do what we can for them. We take care of our own." Sighing, Ronin mussed her hair. "I'm sorry I yelled at you. Please don't give me cause to worry. We have lost enough."

She mumbled something in return.

He nodded. "Go help the Pack take the meat back to Lupin territory. But don't carry a lot with that wounded shoulder." Lara made a face and joined the others. Ronin glanced at him next. "Come with me."

He continued walking east, and Zev joined him. Rawn followed behind, leading Fair along.

"There seem to be various breeds among you," Zev commented. "In Lykos, there is only one."

"Lara and I are of the Arctic breed. My delta, Valto, over there, he is Canis." Ronin motioned at the gray wolf that had yet to shift. "The Garou Pack has nearly every breed." His odd eyes glanced at him. "Except for yours."

"Are you many in number?" Zev asked.

"I would say so. It wasn't always that way. It began with my father when he searched for other Lycan's, and he found them. Scattered lone wolves cast out for being half-breeds. He became Alpha when they gathered together as their own Pack. Every three years, he would travel across the country to visit the Packs in case another Lycan had been born. If they were rejected, we took them in. Now it's my turn to lead and to find more like us."

Something sank like a stone in Zev's stomach, and he came to find it was an odd mixture of dejection and resentment of having no one come searching for him. "I never knew there were others. I've always thought I was alone."

"You're a Lycan. You're not alone." Ronin searched his face with a knowing sympathy. "Thirty years ago, my father attempted to approach the Lykos Pack, but they're territorial purebloods. They nearly killed him for being a Lycan, so he never returned. But if I had known you were there, I would have gone for you, Zev. That is the Garou way."

They reached a small village in the forest. It was made up of burrows carved into trees. Zev halted at the sickly scent in the air. It smelled of waste and rot. The Lycans he could see didn't stir at their arrival. They lay in their fur beds, coughing, and retching.

"You came here searching for help," Ronin sighed. "But Lupin isn't in a place to give it."

Zev stared at them, alarmed. "This is distemper. It's a fatal disease for our kind if not treated."

"There is no treatment. We can only do what we can to keep them comfortable and wait to see if some are strong enough to survive. I wish I could bring them to my healer, but they cannot make the long journey with us to the west."

"So you will leave them here like this? Winter is coming."

"We will stay as long as we can, but I have little hope they will live another week."

Zev hated seeing this. To find there was more like him and left to die such a slow death.

The rest of Ronin's Pack arrived with the food, and they moved through the village, handing out meat and water to the ill. Lara passed by them, now fully dressed with the gray tunic tucked in a pair of black, form-fitting pants and knee-high black boots. Streams of sunlight seeped through the barren trees. He watched the light illuminate her long blond tresses that fell in soft waves along her back. She looked more ethereal than mortal this way.

"Don't get too close," Ronin warned her.

Lara ignored him. She gathered a sickly pup in her arms and helped him drink. The Alpha groaned under his breath in annoyance. He moved a step as if he might drag his sister away.

"Ronin," Zev caught his attention. "I came here searching for more Lycans in hopes they could help me track down a friend of ours. A sorceress. Like an enchantress," he amended at his confusion. "I believe she might have come in this direction, but I lost her scent. We need her magic to find my kin. One who is a powerful healer."

The news brought a stillness around them, and Zev felt several eyes fall on him.

"I don't mean to use that to influence you, but I think there was a reason I came to be here. I believe it wasn't simply to ask for help, but also to give it."

"You may be right." Ronin studied him for a long minute. "My sister saw you coming."

Zev furrowed his brow, not sure what he meant. He couldn't help glancing in her direction.

"Lara told me she had crossed through the moon mirror in her dreams. Have you heard of it?"

Zev shook his head, but the dark void of reflective water passed through his mind.

"A discussion for another day, perhaps. In this dream, a black wolf appeared. We didn't think much of it since they haven't been seen in many years." Ronin canted his head as he continued observing him. "Yet we crossed paths with you a few days later."

"I…I saw her in my dream as well," Zev said faintly. "A white wolf…with her eyes."

He had thought it was some fevered hallucination, but this proved it was much more. Something brought him to them. He didn't understand what it meant, but his wolf was still inside of him, listening.

"It's strange how the world works," Ronin said with a thoughtful smile. He motioned at the gray wolf, and it trotted over. "Valto had been northeast visiting another Pack before reuniting with us. I don't know about a sorceress, but he mentioned crossing paths with a witch."

The air stalled in Zev's lungs. "What did she look like?"

Valto's fur rippled and receded as he came to stand on two legs. He was a young man with dark skin and light brown eyes. "I didn't get a good look at her," he said, his voice tinged with another unfamiliar accent. "As soon as she noticed us, she threw out her spells."

"What color was her magic?" Zev asked urgently. "Was it purple?"

Valto's eyes widened. "Yes, how did you know?"

Zev let out a shocked laugh. Relief welled his vision. He turned to his friend, and Lord Norrlen's throat bobbed as he swallowed back his own emotion.

They had a lead.

CHAPTER 15

Dynalya

Dyna stared at the bow and quiver of arrows Len handed her, baffled to be trusted with a weapon. But after days of beatings, she wouldn't question it aloud. Len hissed some instruction at her before she wandered off with Novo. Dyna suspected target practice was meant to keep her busy while they went to frolic deep in the forest. Even Yavi and Von would end up taking their tent at night, forcing her to share quarters with Tarn.

She never asked to stay, and he never offered, but she would end up falling asleep in the chair by the brazier from sheer exhaustion. She waited for him to order someone to carry her out, yet she would wake in the same spot in an empty tent with a blanket over her shoulders.

Every time she stepped outside, they would always be in a new location. How did Tarn move the tent without disturbing her?

Dyna glowered at the tree thirty yards away where she'd cut an X. The bowstring creaked as she pulled it back and aimed. Snow flurries drifted down, her breath clouding in the air. It didn't stick to the ground yet. There was perhaps a week or two left before the gorge of Troll Bridge was filled with snow. She needed a new plan.

The arrow flew, but it skidded off the edge of the trunk and plunked to the ground. Dyna sighed. Would she ever get anything right?

She couldn't protect her family. She couldn't protect her friends. She couldn't shoot a damn arrow. They were only five days away from the port, and she wasn't any closer to finding another way to escape.

Dyna snatched another arrow, notching the bow. *Mind your sight,* a voice whispered through her memories. Her skin tingled as she imagined Cassiel beside her, his gentle hands adjusting her form. It made her vision well.

She pressed a fist against her chest. It still hurt, but knowing he was alive was all that kept her from falling apart. The ache was a constant burden she had learned to live with, but she could only imagine it was much worse for him.

"Feel the weight of the weapon."

Her back tensed at Von's sudden voice behind her.

"Not only the physical weight, but the weight of its meaning. Of the target you intend to hit. Once you understand that, you won't miss."

Target.

All she could see was the knife plunging into Zev's stomach, the black blood spilling from his mouth. The fury rising in her veins melted the weather's touch. There was only one target in her mind now.

Dyna pivoted on her heel and aimed. The string creaked as she held it taut, the arrow point lined up perfectly with Von's face where he stood a few yards away. His wide eyes fixed on her, a new acknowledgment entering them at the hatred he must see there. They looked at each other in silence, with nothing but the snow drift between them.

"Believe me, Commander," she said. "I know its weight well."

His expression fell to resignation, as if he'd been waiting for this. And he looked sad. Not by this moment, but because this was what his life made him. Her fingers trembled on the bowstring with the urge to shoot. It would be so simple to end him right here, where no one could see. The image of Zev sinking to his knees and keeling over repeated in her mind.

Her blood heated with rage.

Dyna swung to the right and released. She'd been off by inches, but Tarn caught the arrow and snapped it in half. He stood in the shadows of the evergreen trees with Dalton behind him. The young mage grimaced. After bowing to Tarn, he rushed away and Von's image vanished.

She clenched her teeth. "You were testing me."

Tarn strolled forward, flurries catching on his black coat. "I wonder, Maiden, would you have shot him?"

She had certainly considered it. Would she have killed Von? She was so furious and saddened by Zev's loss that the need for revenge might have won if she hadn't noticed Tarn first. That darkness was startling.

The real question was, would she have missed?

The touch of Tarn's stare lingered on her down-turned head as she gathered the fallen arrows into the quiver, leaving behind a tingle on her scalp. She roughly wiped an escaped tear from her cheek.

"Do you weep for the Lycan?"

Dyna threw down the bow and quiver. "His name was Zev!" she shouted, a sob catching in her throat. "He was my cousin, as close as a brother to me, and you killed him!"

Tarn idly studied her. "It seems you have forgotten I was not the one who stabbed him."

"Von may have held the knife, but you gave the order." She had pushed his loss from her mind to survive her time here, but Zev was gone. If she ever escaped, he wouldn't be there waiting for her. The thought carved a new hole in her chest, and Dyna felt like she couldn't breathe.

Muffling her cries, she crouched to pick up the fallen arrows. Dyna filled the hole of anguish and pain with snow, because if she revealed her weaknesses to this man, he would carve a deeper chasm until she broke in half, too.

"That which you feel right now—anger, sorrow, love—they are useless feelings that serve only to bind you. Thank the Gods he's dead, for now you have nothing left to lose."

Dyna snatched an arrow and lunged at him with a feral scream.

Tarn caught her throat. He shoved or lifted her, too fast for Dyna to know, and pinned her against a tree. Her heart thundered in her ears as he squeezed—not enough to cut off air, but enough to prove how easily he could snap her neck with little more than a flex of his hand. His eyes—they were like chips of ice.

Beneath them, she glimpsed a spark of something that sent frost crystalizing in her veins.

Pressed flush against her, his hard face was inches away, his chest rising and falling sharply with heavy breaths, or maybe it was hers. She was too aware of her feet dangling off the ground and the helplessness of her position. The arrow had fallen somewhere when his other hand had pinned her wrist above her head.

She was completely at his mercy.

Attacking him was stupid. She had gone briefly insane from her wrath, which instantly cooled to fear.

"You have little regard for your life," Tarn said, his voice deadly soft. "That will be the last attempt you make. Try it again, and I will punish you."

Dyna swallowed beneath his grip as she remembered Geon's scarred back. Any punishment Tarn gave would be cruel, but she had to question his restraint.

"Why haven't you killed me yet?" she faintly asked, feeling trapped against the wall of his chest and the rough surface of the tree pressing into her spine. He was the only thing holding her in place.

"I will." Tarn's hand slid lower on her throat, where his thumb found her racing pulse. "The moment you stop being useful."

Her heart raced as she waited for him to decide how useful she was. The only reason he had captured her was for her map. Yet why…?

Her legs floundered in the air, causing her bangles to clank lightly.

Then the answer came.

She scoffed. "I know why you don't have me open the journal. To do so, I would need my Essence, and I can't do that with these bangles on. You're not willing to take them off at the risk of giving me my magic back."

His jaw flexed. "You could tell me where it is." She opened her mouth to answer, but he shook his head. "I expect any location you give would be a lie unless you wish to disclose such information in my tent."

Where he could prove her claim against the runes.

At her glower, his mouth thinned. "Yes, I thought not."

Tarn could easily torture it out of her if he wished, so why the hesitation?

"Is it the divination that gives you pause?" Dyna asked. She felt the rise of his chest halt. "They told me what the Seer said. That I may be your undoing."

He didn't answer, but she saw the growing ire on his face.

"Perhaps I am the one with the power here," she said, feeling haughty. "You won't hurt me. Not until you know what that last line means."

There was only the wind and the silence as they stared at each other past the flurry of snow. A muscle flexed in his clenched jaw. He despised it, this small sliver of a hold she had over him. The spiteful satisfaction she felt from it made her smile.

He looked at her mouth, and for a frightful moment, her heart stopped. But there was only cold indifference in Tarn's gaze when it lifted to hers again.

"Do you know what true power is, Maiden? It's having control and influence over others. I can end your life or I can make you my perpetual slave, leaving you to never see your family again. I am the bow that directs the arrow's course of your life. That's power. And you lack it."

His icy grip squeezed her throat. She kicked and wheezed, her lungs burning for air. He held on long enough to make her fear for her life before letting go. Dyna collapsed to the ground. Tarn left her there, coughing and gasping, not bothering to see if she followed or not.

She touched her throbbing neck with trembling hands. Did he contemplate killing her or was that all to prove a point?

Slumping against the tree, Dyna buried her face over her knees and silently wept. She wanted to go home. She missed her village, its safety, and the idle peace of a simple life. Now she was across the country, lost and imprisoned by strangers because of fae prophecies. She laughed wetly at the ridiculousness of it.

What was she doing? She clenched her fists, biting back a scream. That man, the world, had her under their heel. Control over her life had been taken from her. She was trapped and smothered beneath the mercy of others. Her whole life had centered on not being strong enough.

But when would that stop being an excuse?

If you want to be a fighter, then be one.

When Len returned, they sparred. Dyna struck with all of her fury. Flesh against flesh. Bone against bone. Her body spasmed with every hit she took, but Dyna spat the blood from her mouth and pushed herself off the frozen ground again and again. She fought against the loss of Zev. Against the desperation to return to Cassiel. Against Tarn.

She beat her fists with the urge to stop being the one everyone stepped on.

Her opponent's leg shot out. Dyna pivoted, and the sweeping kick missed her by inches. Taking the opening, she swung, and the punch landed, throwing Len back.

She rubbed her jaw, staring at Dyna with mild surprise. *"Gasan,"* she said in what almost sounded like approval.

Dyna wiped the blood from her nose and lifted her fists, falling into position. She refused to be anyone's arrow.

This was where it ended.

Len nodded and motioned. "Again."

Dyna attacked with everything she had. She beat down the frail, naive girl that left North Star. Tore apart her weakness. Kicked down her failures. Punched through her fear. She shredded it all away until her flimsy shell crumbled into itself.

And with each strike that followed, that frail girl slowly began to perish.

CHAPTER 16

Dynalya

The next few days were the same. Dyna would wake, spar, or train with weapons until she could hardly move, then trudged back to camp before sundown. Tarn hadn't spoken to her since the incident in the woods. She had seen little of him, too. Whenever she reluctantly returned to his tent at night, he was never there. But she was getting stronger, and her endurance was growing.

Dyna was determined to stay awake tonight.

Her boots crunched over gravel as she strode through the camp alone. No one guarded her anymore, and the Raiders hardly stared. They thought she had accepted being trapped, but no matter how many times she failed, she wouldn't stop trying to find a way out.

Following the smell of food, Dyna made her way to Sorren's tent and was welcomed by warm laughter. Yavi and Geon were teasing him about something again.

"Aye, there she is!" Geon cheered when he saw her. "Look at her in all that leather. She looks like she could beat me senseless, and I might enjoy it."

Dyna snorted and slid into the chair next to Yavi.

"Is Len going easier on you?" Yavi asked.

She gave her a look.

With a soft laugh, Yavi tucked one of the loose strands that had escaped Dyna's braid behind her ear. "Well, you don't look as bad today. I think you have fewer bruises."

"Only because I learned how to duck," she said.

And Elon had given her an ointment to speed up the healing. Perhaps for the royalrod potion she had made for him. Now that she thought of it, what did Benton do with all the flowers they harvested?

"How are you feeling?" Dyna asked Yavi discreetly.

Happiness lit her face. "Every flutter is a joy."

"Good." She squeezed her hand.

Sorren grunted at Dyna in greeting and set a plate of food in front of her. The rich scent of wild rice with herbs, mushrooms, and carrots made her mouth water. One bite and the combined flavors melted on her tongue.

She gave the Minotaur a grateful smile. "It's delicious, Sorren. Thank you."

But he only gave her a stiff nod and lumbered away. He must be in a sour mood.

"So, Dyna, we're waiting to hear what your next strategy is," Yavi said excitedly at normal volume, prompting Sorren and Geon to glance at them. "We're running out of time. We'll be at the port in a couple of days."

The sudden attention left her startled. She hadn't expected her to bring it up in front of the others.

"They know," Yavi waved it away. "Geon swears not to interfere this time, or we will make him shovel horse dung every day for a month straight."

Dyna's eyes widened at her.

Yavi flushed. "They're coming, too. We're leaving together. All of us."

Geon nodded.

"So what's the plan, lass?" Sorren asked gruffly.

Dyna looked away from their waiting stares. "I...well..."

She didn't have a plan. Not yet. Her previous attempt had been disastrous because she hadn't thought things through properly. And now she had to implement everyone else in a new plan.

A rough growl rolled in Sorren's throat, and he continued chopping meat. "The way I see it, the lass may not want to leave. They're training her, and they don't guard her anymore. Clearly, Tarn means to give her a place among his inner circle. She looks like a spy now."

Dyna froze. Was that his plan? To make her into one of his spies?

Yavi's smile faded as they all glanced down at Dyna's black leather armor. "Tarn has shown her favor," she said in feeble defense. "That's a good thing. She's supposed to capture his heart and be his undoing."

Dyna gaped at her. "What?"

"Oh, aye," Sorren retorted. "The favor of his protection and the warmth of his bed is a grand thing."

Heat rushed to Dyna's face, and shock locked the breath in her lungs.

"Sorren!" Yavi gasped.

Geon's eyes bulged. "Oi, that's a bit much even for you, hairy lug."

"No, let him speak." Dyna stood, raising her chin. "Tell me exactly what I have done to deserve this scrutiny, Sorren? Much less your slight against my integrity? Since I have gotten here, I have been spelled, enslaved, drugged, beaten, terrorized, and rendered unconscious. That certainly sounds like a mighty *grand* thing."

Silence filled the tent.

"Yet Tarn was the only one who gave me a place to sleep in a camp full of men that would have their way with me if he didn't command otherwise. Because of it, you accuse me of consorting with the enemy. Would you prefer I be assaulted or left to freeze outside?" They lowered their gazes beneath her glare. Dyna exhaled a sharp breath. "I'm only trying to survive. Like all of you."

She strode back out into the brisk cold.

"Wait." Yavi hurried after her. "Dyna, we're sorry. Sorren didn't mean it. He's been trapped in his tent for the last three years. I think with all my talk of you bringing us freedom, he's merely impatient for it to happen."

"Yavi, I'm not your savior," she snapped. "I'm not here to make some divination come true. And I'm certainly not spending my nights attempting to make Tarn fall in love with me. I had no choice but to share his tent when yours was taken. Now I wonder if that was your plan in the first place."

Yavi's cheeks darkened, and she couldn't quite look at her.

Dyna let out an appalled scoff. From the moment she arrived, someone wanted something from her. It hurt to find her only friends here were no different.

"If you could merely steer him off his path, all of our lives could change."

"And you expect me to do that with *love*?" Dyna demanded. "That will never happen, Yavi. Ever. If you want freedom, then come up with a plan to save yourselves instead of using me to do it."

She stormed away before Yavi could say more.

Tents came down all around her, horses saddled and packed as the Raiders prepared for another trek through the night. She let her furious steps aimlessly move in no particular direction. They only wanted to be free. Dyna understood that. She simply didn't think they'd use her to get it. An unpleasant thought reminded her she had attempted to use Dalton for her freedom, too.

When had desperation taken over her decency? There were others here as trapped as she was.

You can't save everyone. Her vision brimmed with tears at the memory of Cassiel's voice.

"I can damn well try," Dyna whispered back.

At the sound of approaching footsteps, she glanced up to see Dalton coming. But he spotted her and quickly went in the opposite direction. Scowling, Dyna chased after him.

"Dalton!" She jerked on his shoulder, forcing him to spin around. He nearly dropped his staff. "Might you try apologizing instead of avoiding me?"

Sighing heavily, he rubbed his forehead. "I'm sorry, Dyna. I had to do it."

"Did you?"

"Yes, if I want to keep my neck intact," Dalton exasperated. "We all obey him in whatever he commands."

At the unease on his face, she reined in her anger and decided not to punch him. "How did you do that, anyway? I have seen illusion spells change appearances, but you projected Von's."

"It wasn't an illusion. I planted a vision of the commander in your mind and amplified what you felt about him. You did the rest."

He'd been in her head, sorting through every dark and secret thought she had. It left her feeling exposed and violated.

"Tarn asked you to show me Von?"

"He ordered me to show whoever you wanted to see dead." Dalton's brown eyes flickered to her uneasily. "Von wasn't the first choice, but I couldn't bring...*it*...out. After seeing how much it haunts your past, I couldn't do that to you."

What would she have done if she'd seen the Shadow there in the woods?

Inwardly, Dyna trembled at imagining those molten red eyes. Emotion swelled in her chest to be spared that terror. Her shaking hands reached out, and she tightly hugged the startled mage. She didn't know why she did it. Perhaps she merely needed the comfort of someone who knew her pain and was sorry for it.

"Thank you."

Dalton awkwardly patted her back. "Aye."

"But don't do that again." She shoved him off with a glower. "Or I will be the one you fear."

At that, he chuckled, eyeing her tight leathers. "I think that would be very unlikely. Not while you're dressed like that."

Rolling her eyes, they fell into step together. "How unusual that your father didn't insist on Clayton casting the vision since he deems him *so* powerful."

He also wouldn't have been as compassionate either.

Dalton smirked and bounced his staff against the ground, sparking the orange crystal to life. It glowed in the growing darkness as the sun set beyond the trees. "Visions are one thing I'm far more superior at than my brother."

"It's earth magic?"

"No, it's cognition magic. All guilds can use it. The mind is fragile and easily corrupted with the right spells."

Dyna wondered if it was like King Yoel's compulsion or the Shadow's trance. It drew a new vulnerability she didn't like. She had some practice protecting her mind when she made a shield for the bond and made sure to build hers now.

"Spells," she repeated. "Meaning, other than visions?"

"Illusions, dreams, emotions, memory, and hallucinations fall under it."

"Was this something you learned from your father?"

"I learned it on my own..." They reached an abandoned campfire and sat on a couple barrels left beside it. Dalton's gaze had gone distant to some memory. "I told you my mother was desolate."

Dyna nodded. She hadn't heard of that before.

"The Magos Empire can only function as long as we keep the laws," he said. "Those who defy them... are siphoned or made desolate. It's when a sorceress is trapped within their mind with a spell we call *halucinor*. It's a practice that came into law about twenty or so years ago."

"God of Urn, that's awful," Dyna said. "Your father did that to your mother? Why?"

"He caught her using magic. It would have brought shame to House Slater if anyone knew. Once I finished nursing, he locked my mother's mind away." Dalton's features creased with faint sorrow. "I could stand in front of her, and she wouldn't see me. Her eyes...they were empty. But I had to see if she was still there somewhere. I wanted to meet her."

"So you taught yourself cognition magic."

"I studied everything I could on the subject. Eventually, I managed to enter her mind through dream walking. It's the easiest spell. It allowed me to see what my mother was seeing as she dreamt."

Dream walking...

Dyna had experienced something similar. Sometimes during her nightmares, she seemed to stand outside of them as they happened.

"But at least my mother lived in a peaceful dreamland, and she was happy. I learned how to guide her dreams to her past, so she could relive good memories. I visited her when I could, even if she didn't know I was there." Dalton shrugged and forced a smile. "Well, I haven't seen her in years. Father said he released the spell, so I assume our family is caring for her now."

But Dyna could tell from his expression that deep down, he didn't believe it. Benton wouldn't care, and House Slater had no reason to take in an abandoned sorceress. Neither of them said such things aloud.

"How old were you when you were captured?" Dyna asked.

119

"I was eleven summers old. My brother was fourteen. If we hadn't gone to the Magai Tournament, I often wonder what would have come of our lives."

"What's that?"

"Once a year during the Summer Solstice, mages, fae, and elves from around the world come to Ledoga in the midwest for a tournament of magic. Clay was supposed to fight in the junior league," Dalton said.

"If I had ever arrived, I would have won."

They looked up at Clayton's presence, his eyes glowing faint yellow in the twilight.

"I have no doubt you would have." Benton stepped into the firelight. "We lived far different lives before all this. Yet here we are. Captured and bound to the scum we're forced to call Master."

"Not for long," Dyna said quietly, sensing the mage was also planning something. "You want out. So do I."

Benton smirked. "Good. Then we will sort something out and see what we can learn of your abilities."

What did he mean by that?

The old mage spared Dalton a long glance before heading to Sorren's tent with Clayton.

She narrowed her eyes. "Your father sent you to befriend me, didn't he? He wants to use me to escape."

Dalton shushed her, looking around, but no one heard. The camp was in an upheaval as the Raiders worked to break it down. He dropped his voice to a whisper. "Don't pretend you didn't do the same to extract information out of me."

She made a face at being caught.

"It's a good thing we want the same thing: to get out of here. You need to bring down the veil, which only we can do."

Dyna glanced at the bangles. "And you want out of your bindings, which I am the only one with access to Tarn's tent to get the keys."

Dalton nodded. "To get what we both want, we have to form an alliance. Are you with us?"

Mistrust was her first instinct, but hopefulness radiated from his expression as he waited for her answer. Dalton only wanted to go home to his mother. Dyna understood that more than anything. And this would be the closest she would get to another chance.

She nodded once. "Whatever plan we come up with, it has to include the others, too."

He grinned. "Agreed. Come on."

Dyna followed after a hesitant pause. "What did your father mean about my abilities?"

Dalton's steps crunched over gravel in the silence before he vaguely said. "You come from two bloodlines."

Azeran and Helia.

"Are you telling me I'm part sun and lunar sorceress?" she asked, her eyes widening.

"It's not a thing to be proud of. Any found with mixed bloodlines are siphoned."

She stared at him. "Why?"

"Because it goes against the Mage Code."

"I don't understand."

Dalton increased his pace. "It's not for women to know."

Dyna kicked his calf. His leg gave in, and he barely caught himself on his staff. "Don't speak down to me because I am a woman, Dal. I don't care what your father believes in or whatever Magos believes in. Tell me."

He glowered at her.

"If you want an alliance, then it starts with trust. Tell me the truth, or I will find my own way. But clearly, you need me, so speak." Dyna crossed her arms, and he groaned. "Why is it wrong? Does it truly dampen magic? If so, why would your father want to give me to your brother?"

Dalton's glower deepened.

"The Mage Code is slavery. You must see that in your predicament. I don't think you're accepting of how women are treated in the Magos Empire, much less of how your mother was treated." They stood in the night, studying each other. She was asking a lot of him, but she had to know. "Therefore, explain to me *why* would your father want me for his son when I don't have a lot of power?"

Huffing a curse, Dalton grabbed her arm and hauled her into their tent. "You want the truth?" he whispered sharply. "Dyna, you *are* powerful, and for the simple fact because you are a *woman*. Especially because you have mixed blood from two guilds. Part moon. Part sun."

In her shock, she couldn't reply.

Dalton leaned against the desk and crossed his arms. It was riddled with potions and herbs. She recognized Azeran's journal with the stack of books and the hindrance arrow among the clutter of trinkets. Beside the desk was a barrel of harvested royalrods.

His throat bobbed a few times before he said, "Sorceresses...are more powerful than mages. They simply don't know it."

Dyna kept still, repeating his words in her head several times to be sure she heard correctly. "Marrying outside the guilds doesn't dampen magic, does it?"

"It makes their magic more potent because they can influence more elements. Like a Transcendent."

Her mouth fell open. That's why she had green fire. Her Essence blast was powerful because it truly had the force of the sun. "So mages bind our magic through law or spell because they fear women being more powerful than them?"

He ducked his head. "I didn't make the laws."

"No, but you know what it means. Women are suffering for the pride of men. Mages are stealing their power, Dalton. They're dying!"

"Not all mages siphon," he said sheepishly. "Some give their wives or daughters jewelry to dampen their power. Some use spells like my father did. Your father did the same."

"He would never," she hissed.

Dalton blinked at her. "You…have a powerful spell put in place to block your magic. I sensed it in Landcaster. Didn't you know?"

"I learned of the barrier recently, but it wasn't my father who placed it." As Dyna said it, doubt clouded her mind. Was her father responsible?

"Regardless of who did it, the spell is weakening," Dalton said. "Such things cannot remain in place forever without constant restoration. Over the years, the spell weakens under the pressure of your magic as it builds and builds with no place to go." His expression tightened, and the crystals overhead flickered. "When the barrier breaks, Dyna, all of your pent-up Essence will explode. And God of Urn forbid anyone be around you when that happens."

CHAPTER 17

Von

Von didn't know why he prayed anymore. Whether it meant anything or if his plea even reached the God of Urn. Still, he remained kneeling, his head pressed to the ground. He asked for the same things. Forgiveness for what he had done, for what he would be made to do, and protection for the one he loved. But for all his begging, his soft words seemed to stay trapped within the quiet tent. No one was listening.

The brisk wind hit his back at the swish of the tent flap opening. "Oh, pardon."

Von sat back on his heels with a sigh. It was fruitless, anyway.

He stood and faced Dyna. "If you're searching for Yavi, she is with Sorren and Geon, helping them with the kitchen."

He glanced around to see what was left, but he was finished packing. Breaking down the tent was next.

Dyna still lingered behind him, and when their eyes met, she held his. They had avoided each other for the most part, unless required, but she didn't outright speak to him or look at him. Von had been relieved about it, not having the nerve to face her after what he had done to Zev.

The moonlight highlighted her silhouette, catching on her hard eyes as she studied him. She knew about his secret, and he had been waiting for the consequences to surface.

"Do you pray often?" Dyna asked, surprising him.

"Not as much as I should."

She looked different. The softness of her features was fading. He had seen a glimpse of it in the Port of Azure when she had raised a knife to protect the Celestial. Then again in the grove, when she swore to end her life for her Guardians. That sweet, innocent girl he first met in Landcaster was learning how dark the world was.

It saddened him.

"Was there something you wished to discuss?" he asked. "Or is this when you threaten me?"

No matter how good Dyna was, she was human, like everyone else. Von wouldn't blame her if she tried to use him as a way out of Tarn's clutches.

"What do you want from me in exchange?" Von pressed when she didn't answer. His throat bobbed with a thick swallow at her continued silence. "Dyna, for what it's worth, I'm sorry about your cousin. I don't take lives lightly, but each one I take is with the intention of preserving my own. I have someone to live for. When it comes to fighting to defend that, I will take down anything and anyone who stands in my way."

Unintentionally, his apology came out as a threat. He had no urge to harm Dyna, but he feared her now that she could hurt Yavi.

When she offered no reply, Von sighed and started breaking down the tent. Her presence lingered behind him as he worked.

"She cannot be here," Dyna finally said. "I know it's not my place to say it, but you won't be able to hide your relationship much longer."

Von fell still. That was the last thing he had expected her to say.

He glanced around them to make sure no one was nearby. "How did you come to find out?"

Her eyes flickered away briefly, and the color of her cheeks darkened. "I overheard you both one morning."

"Oh..."

They both stood around awkwardly, not sure what to say next. He continued working, and to his surprise, Dyna helped with the tarp.

He cleared his throat. "I plan to send her away. The timing must be right."

But the bangles would prove a problem. He had to get the slaver's key. He finished bringing down the tarp and stretched it out on the ground to roll it up.

"Do it soon," she said. "It's not safe for her here. What happened the other day proves it."

Von hadn't expected Dyna to care for Yavi after only knowing her for a few days, yet he could hear her genuine concern.

"I will," he promised. "Thank you...for coming to her aid."

He had yet to say it until now.

Dyna gave him a stiff nod and turned to go.

"Why didn't you shoot me?" Von blurted. She halted with her back to him.

He had been there in the woods, standing at a distance as Tarn had ordered. The rage he saw on her face, the deep anguish and hate, he expected her to kill the vision of him. Dyna had attacked the Master instead. That was something he killed for, however small the slight.

Yet as Tarn had held Dyna's life in his hands, he showed restraint.

She partially turned, glancing at Von over her shoulder. "You had sad eyes."

That's what saved him? Her sympathy?

Dalton's vision could only bring out how she perceived him, and she saw the burden he carried. He didn't know if that was a good thing or not.

Lost in thought, Von watched her head for Sorren's tent, where Geon and Yavi were loading crates into a wagon. They both yanked her into a tight hug between them. Sorren's large hand poked out of his tent, holding a sweet bun on a plate for her. It made Dyna laugh as Dalton ambled over to join them.

As much as she hated it here, the Maiden somehow made a spot for herself among them. She had a way of drawing people. Perhaps with that inherent kindness that was so rarely ever found, it made one want to protect it. Von felt it, too. He knew what his master was doing with that little test in the woods.

It's what Tarn did with everything that fell into his hands.

He broke them.

Olsson and a group of Raiders came to help Von finish rolling up the tarp. Soon everything was all loaded, and the camp was ready to move. He headed for his waiting horse, and Coal nickered in greeting. Once Tarn gave the signal, he led the procession of men and wagons into the woods. Von stayed near the back with Elon to keep an eye on the Minotaur.

But Sorren wasn't thinking about escaping. He was too distracted staring at the night sky speckled with stars, the moon glowing beyond the sparse clouds. The camp moving was the only time he was allowed outside. He hauled his wagon along, the weight nothing to his strength. Dalton, Yavi, Dyna, and Geon sat inside as they whispered among themselves. The young mage kept an orange sphere of light above their heads, and it cast a soft spectral light over the dark woods.

Clayton rode in a wagon in the middle of the procession with two Raiders sitting on either side of him. It was their usual arrangement. They were under strict orders to slit his throat if Benton tried anything. Von spotted the old mage up far front where Tarn kept him in his view.

"Did Novo and Len return?" Von asked Elon under his breath, knowing the elf could easily hear him.

"Yes," Elon replied. "No sign of her Guardians. They checked their last location and noted tracks headed northeast."

Von raised his brows at that news. He didn't expect them to yield so easily. However, they wouldn't have been able to search for her past the cloaking spell.

"The werewolf survived," Elon told him next. "They found paw prints. The Celestial must have healed him."

Von feigned disappointment, but inwardly he swam with relief. He would tell Dyna the good news as soon as he could privately pull her aside.

"How unfortunate," Von said lightly, then moved on from the topic. "Now that they are back, the spies will travel to Beryl Coast. Have them pack light. We will depart tomorrow night. As for command, while we're away, I have Olsson in mind to promote to lieutenant. The man is loyal and has been with us the longest."

And he knew how to keep his head. Olsson was a good fighter and naturally intimidating to others due to his large size, without having to threaten them. He understood how Von managed the camp at Tarn's behest and would follow those measures.

Elon nodded. "Wise choice."

After the trouble with Haran, Von didn't want to make another poor one.

The elf slightly tilted his head as he looked ahead, listening to something. "Tarn requests the Maiden's presence."

Requests. That was putting it kindly.

With the veil down, Tarn probably wanted to keep an eye on Dyna in case she got any ideas.

Von nodded and tugged on his reins to slow Coal down, leaving Elon to ride past him. He lined up beside the wagon to find Yavi and Geon had fallen asleep. Both leaned on each other's shoulders, sharing a blanket. She had seemed more tired these days.

Dyna and Dalton huddled in a corner, whispering. They quieted as soon as they noticed him.

"Hold," Von told Sorren, and the wagon came to a stop. He frowned at them. "What are you plotting?"

The spectral light gleamed in Dalton's eyes as his lips parted in a shrewd smile. "Only villainous schemes of grandeur."

"Don't joke about such things, lad. Come, Dyna. The Master calls."

She looked at him warily before she hesitantly rose and allowed him to help her climb onto Coal. She sat at his back and clutched the ends of his jacket. At the light prod of his heels, his horse eased into a slow trot along the procession. This was Von's way of delaying the inevitable, even if it was only by a few minutes. But it didn't ease her stiffness. Dyna's breathing grew heavier as they left behind the soft orange glow at their backs and entered the dark trees. The men were quiet as their boots crunched over leaves and the frozen ground. It accompanied the sound of creaking wheels and hooves with the rattle of dried branches. He thought Dyna's hands might be trembling.

"Are you cold?"

"No," she answered stiffly.

He couldn't see her face to know what she was feeling. It was so dark in the forest, with only the faint moonlight to light their way. Ah.

Von tugged off the crystal tied to his belt. Once whispering the word *lux*, he held the glowing crystal over his shoulder. "Here. Keep it."

There was a heavy pause, then it was gently pulled from his fingers. "Thank you," came her soft reply. Its idle light haloed behind him, lighting the ground as they moved.

"Try...try not to provoke him this time," Von said quietly. Tarn may not be so lenient again. "Do whatever he asks."

"Do you always do everything Tarn asks?"

Von was aware of every scar on his back for when he didn't. The most recent ones were added because of his failure to capture her in Corron. His life stopped being his a long time ago.

"It's the way of things here," he said.

"That doesn't mean it's the right way." There was a weight in her tone that made him think of everything he had done at Tarn's command.

But the Lycan lived. It was one life he didn't have to carry. Von opened his mouth to tell her the news—

"I admit, coercing you did cross my mind, but I think you have enough over your head." Dyna handed him the crystal back. "One day, perhaps very soon, you will have to decide for yourself, Von. And I pray for Yavi's sake you decide the right thing before it's too late."

The crystal's light vanished, plunging them into the dark. Flurries of snow flowed past them, the icy wind stinging his face. A flare of fire burst to life ahead, and Von's heart pitched. It was only a Raider lighting an oil lantern, but an awful shudder sank down his spine.

After leaving Dyna with Tarn, he rode back to check on his wife. Dalton had left to join his brother, and Geon was awake. Without being asked, the lad hopped out to take Coal. Von climbed into the wagon and gathered Yavi in his arms.

The Seer's divination repeated in his mind endlessly until he fell asleep and dreamed of flames consuming him whole.

CHAPTER 18

Lucenna

Lucenna's heart raced wildly as she ran through the dark woods. The faint moonlight formed sinister shadows in the barren trees. Her panting breaths shot white clouds in the frosty air. Curse her damn luck! A gust whooshed through the branches, causing them to rattle loudly. Fear prickled all over her body like needles. She felt his impending presence getting closer, and it terrified her to her core. She was invisible, but she left footprints in the mud.

"Lucenna..." a voice hissed.

She shrieked and threw a sphere of raw power behind her. The fiery glow briefly illuminated the laughing face of her pursuer as it flew past him, and he slipped into the shadows again.

"You cannot run from me, daughter."

Lucenna stumbled backward and tripped over a thick tree root. Landing hard on her side, rocks and broken branches stabbed her palms. She ignored the stinging pain and scrambled to her feet.

His cackle echoed in the woods as she spun in a circle, searching for him. A red light shone like a beacon in the night. The light grew brighter to reveal it came from a crystal resting within the weaving of a white staff. Holding it was Galvaston Astron, Head of the Lunar Guild.

Dark purple robes flared at his feet as he came forward. His white hair was kept short, and he had the same lilac eyes, his face sharp and severe. He hadn't changed since she'd seen him last. The same day she lost her mother.

Lucenna squeezed her trembling hands into fists. The brisk wind pressed against the sleek layer of sweat on her face and neck.

"At last, I have found you." Her father's mouth curled in a cold smile. "Or was it you wanted to be found? Your bounty led me to Azure, and you were foolish enough to get caught."

Lucenna glared at him. For all of her efforts to find Dyna, he caught up with her first. She should have known he could track her down even if she was cloaked.

His potent Essence hung like a heavy blanket in air, making it hard to breathe. "You have caused a lot of trouble for the family."

"You mean for you," she hissed.

Galvaston's jaw clenched tightly, and his eyes flickered with magic. "Mind how you speak to me, Lucenna. Don't make this difficult. It's time to return and fulfill your duty to the Magos Empire. It's a great honor. Your power and womb will bear the heirs to come."

Her magic crackled on her skin at his words. That's all they saw her as. Some broodmare to make little princelings, then they would drain her of her ability to Transcend. What honor was there in that?

"If I'm not mistaken, I thought you were fond of your betrothed."

Lucenna's expression softened at the mention of Prince Everest. She glanced down at her engagement ring. The pink diamond gleamed in the dim moonlight.

A satisfied smile rose on her father's face when he saw it. "Prince Everest is waiting for you, Lucenna. Once you're at his side, he will ascend to the throne."

She intended to return to Everest but not at the expense of her liberty and magic. She had a mission to complete first.

"Yes, and you would become Grand Magus on the Archmage's council, filling your coffers with the gold you sold me for." Electricity sparked at Lucenna's fingertips and coursed up her arms. "Unfortunately, I refuse to be your pedestal to power."

She flung out her hands, and streaks of lightning blasted through the air towards him. Galvaston snarled in shocked anger. He waved his staff, and her magic dissipated to nothing. She stilled at how easily he blocked the spell.

"How dare you use magic against a mage," he bellowed, as his eyes glowed brighter. "You have broken our most sacred law."

Damn their laws.

Galvaston struck the ground with his staff. Red lightning raced across the forest floor for her. She conjured a dome, and the spell clashed against the surface, flickering gold on impact. His expression wavered with surprise for only a second, but it was enough to remind her of one thing. She was an Astron. Rebelling was in her blood. And she would fight him with all she had.

Lucenna filled her hands with magic. "The day I return is the day I break the Mage Code. I will crush everything you stand for under my heel."

He bared his teeth.

"I will finish what Azeran started," she promised. "We will free all those oppressed in the Magos Empire, and any who should oppose us will fall. I have lived my life at the mercy of men. Never again."

His mouth curled, and they circled each other. "You're an imprudent girl with sacrilege ideals. Those zealots that call themselves the Liberation have poisoned your mind."

"They freed it with the truth." Lucenna willed her Essence to fill her. The surge of power charged through her veins, and her silhouette radiated vivid purple. "My magic is my own. And neither you nor the Archmage will take it from me."

Lucenna hurled a surge of power. It hit his shield with a might that pushed him back, his feet sliding across the mud until he caught himself with his staff.

"I see now. You're too far gone," Galvaston said coolly. "You leave me no choice. I will cleanse you, but you will still be useful to the prince."

Lucenna knew what spell he planned to use.

Lightning coiled around her body. "I would rather die than allow myself to become desolate."

Her magic tore through the air with every spell she could conjure. He effortlessly deflected her attacks with a wave of his staff, knocking them into the night sky, where they exploded in the clouds with a thunderous boom. A surge of purple crashed through the trees at her command, coming right for her father. It hit and exploded, shaking the earth. Lucenna slumped back, panting through a breath as smoke filtered through her vision. Did she get him?

A laugh answered. "If you think this is power, you don't know the meaning of it."

Her father strode out of the smoke, untouched. Not a single spell had gone past his shield. Lucenna shook her head, backing away. Her confidence was slipping away as fast as it arrived.

He waved his hand, and a sphere of light came for her like a meteor. It barreled into her chest, throwing her against a boulder. She wheezed for the air knocked out of her lungs. The smell of scorched leather burned her nose. Pain throbbed through her being that threatened to pull her under.

She couldn't fall here.

Lucenna tried to pull herself up on shaking arms, but the blow had left her stunned. Blood leaked from the back of her head, and her vision spun.

A glowing red mist snaked through the air before she could duck. It snatched her up, and it yanked her to her father. She hovered above him helplessly as his magic crawled over her head. Her fingers clawed desperately at it, but they went through.

"You never stood a chance against me," he said, sounding almost disappointed. "You abandoned your home and turned your back on the empire—all for what? Where is the Liberation now, Lucenna? Look at what following them got you!"

His magic infiltrated her mind. He was stealing away her will and locking it away. Lucien's panic flooded their link. He felt her begin to fade. She would lose her brother, and the people she fought for, and fail to avenge those she lost.

What are we fighting for if not for the future?

"You will submit," her father said. "Even if I have to hurt you."

Lucenna looked down at him through her blurred vision with a trembling hatred, and tears rolled down her cheeks. "You hurt me a long time ago..." she said through her clenched teeth. "...when you siphoned Mother."

Galvaston's eyes widened. "What?"

She may not be anywhere near as powerful as him, but she would make sure he felt her pain.

Her Essence had been slowly weaving its way inside of him unnoticed, waiting until it had completely invaded his skeleton. Lucenna twitched her finger. His rib audibly cracked and pierced his lung. At Galveston's cry, his hold on her vanished, and she dropped to the ground with a heavy thud.

His enraged eyes fixed on her. He easily wrenched her Essence out of him and his own pinned her against a tree.

"Foolish girl. You shouldn't use magic you hardly understand."

Lucenna shrieked when his Essence shot into her body and wove through bones like steel thread. Her forefinger twisted until it snapped completely backward. Lucenna screamed and writhed against the vice grip she couldn't see. It slowly crushed her until she was trembling on the ground.

He sighed and approached her. "It matters not how much you resist, daughter. Out here, you are alone." His staff waved over her face, the crystal pulsing red. "Now, it's time to come home—"

He cut off with a bellow. She stared at the arrow protruding from her father's thigh. Who shot that?

Another arrow whistled through the dark and hit his left leg next. He bit back a scream and staggered back as blood soaked his robes. His power over her vanished. Lucenna quickly scrambled to her feet and backed away, holding her injured hand to her chest. They wildly surveyed the trees.

Her father clenched his teeth and yanked out the arrows. "Who's there?"

A menacing growl responded in the woods to the right. Then a flutter of wings came from the left. Another arrow sliced through the air and shattered the staff's crystal. Darkness fell over them.

"The only one alone out here is *you*," said a familiar, harsh voice.

Lucenna stifled a strangled sound that was part laugh and part sob

They were here.

They came.

"Come out!" Galvaston shot out erratic streams of electricity.

They caught against bushes and trees, and the bright flames cast dancing shadows around them. He flinched at the loud howl ringing in the woods. It was followed by a chorus of wolf cries and snarls. Galvaston frantically searched the trees as he brandished his useless staff like a weapon.

Nervous laughter bubbled in Lucenna's throat at his fear. She had never seen him afraid before. He wasn't prepared to fight an unknown source, and mages had no combat training. There was never a need.

Across from her, an enormous black shape slipped forward into the moonlight. The wolf's muzzle wrinkled back over its glistening teeth, and another growl rolled through its massive chest. She knew those bright yellow eyes.

A winged figure stood within the trees on the opposite end of the forest with a flaming blue sword in his hand. She glanced at the branch above her head to spot another crouched form with an armed bow.

They were draped in shadow like sentinels of the night.

And they had Galvaston surrounded.

"Who are you?" he demanded, staggering back.

Lucenna smiled. "It's not them you should worry about."

She looked up at the moon as it rose above the clouds. She was born of the Lunar Guild. The moon was her strength. It recharged her magic, filling her with a surge of power, and static prickled the air. She let it build as she commanded it to brew a storm. The wind wailed, shaking the trees. Dark thunderclouds began to roll and rumble overhead. Galvaston gaped up at the sky, then at her.

Her Essence channels were fully open and roaring with the Essence boiling inside of her. It was too hot, the pressure unbearable, and the pain was tearing her apart. She shook from the effort it took to hold.

"What are you doing?" Galvaston cried out. "Stop! You will destroy us all, including yourself!"

She gave him a cruel smile. "You took away my Mother. I don't care if I go down as long as you go down with me."

Lucenna thrust out her arms with a scream, and purple light blazed through the forest. But he shouted a spell, and in a flash of embers and lightning, he shifted into a gray hawk. It shrieked angrily before it fled into the thunderstorm.

No... She tried to throw another spell, but her legs gave out and the world was tilting. Someone called her name. Then the darkness rushed to meet her.

CHAPTER 19

Dynalya

Dyna sat ramrod straight in the saddle, very aware of Tarn sitting behind her. His presence carried an ever-present chill. Yet while everything about him was cold, her back was warm. His body shielded her from the brisk wind and flurries swirling in the night. They had ridden enough ahead of the procession that it seemed they were the only ones moving through the still trees. She kept her eyes on the lantern floating through the dark. Tarn had commanded Benton to place it, but it couldn't have been for her.

Dyna didn't dare look at the shadows flickering in the corners of her sight. Her heart thudded behind her ribs. She regretted returning Von's crystal, but she had her opal knife again. Its reassuring weight was now strapped to her leg beneath her skirt. Moments ago, it had been tucked in the back of Von's belt. If Tarn tried putting his hands on her again, she would stab him.

"I understand now," he said. "You're not afraid of the dark. You're afraid of what it holds. It's more terrifying to think of what might be there than the dark itself."

The shadows seemed to grow around her with the lure of his voice. Dyna balled her hands, forcing them not to shake.

"The oldest emotion of mankind is fear. And the strongest kind is fear of the unknown. At the moment, its smell seeps from your pores. I wonder what terrors you have met in the dark, Maiden."

His frosted breath tickled her cheek, and she caught his scent, that reminded her of winter and spiced wine.

"And what is it that *you* fear?" she asked, ignoring his statement.

"Nothing. For I never allow such things to control me."

It was Dyna's turn to smirk. "Did you forget I'm a Herb Master, Tarn? I know what Witch's Brew is and how it works. It not only prevents sleep, it dampens your emotions. You're not one without feeling. You simply repress them. Why? So you won't feel guilty for all the lives you've taken?"

Only the clomp of hooves in the silence answered.

"You cannot hide from your humanity forever."

His low laugh made the hair rise on the back of her neck. "You're assuming I'm human."

"Even monsters sleep," Dyna shot back. Sooner or later, he would have to stop taking that potion.

"Hmm. You're far less intelligent than I thought. A person in my position cannot afford tedious things such as sleep."

Because it put him in a vulnerable position to have his throat slit. Of course, he would have that concern when the freedom of his men depended on his death.

"And I thought you weren't frightened of anything."

"Don't confuse precaution for fear," he said. "Take it as a lesson. Self-preservation should be your only priority, for regardless of who it is, even those closest to you can betray you."

It sounded as though he spoke from experience. But it reminded her of the mages and the delicate alliance they formed.

"The Raiders follow you out of fear for their lives and the life-debts you forced on them. True loyalty is earned by trust, kindness, and mercy. Which you have proven to have none." Dyna was shocked that she dared to say such a thing to him. She braced for Tarn's anger, but he only made a contemplative sound in the back of his throat.

"There are a few things I have an interest in, and the opinion of what others think of me isn't one of them. I'm not a good man. It's pointless to pretend otherwise. However you live your life, you'll always be the villain in someone else's story."

Was she the villain in his story? He had a goal, whatever it was, and she was an obstruction in the way of it, as he was in the way of hers.

"Most sail through life looking through a dirty spyglass at a perfect horizon," Tarn said. "While neglecting to notice the beasts lurking beneath the sea of iniquity. What they don't realize is that they were born with claws and fangs and a bloodthirsty instinct that's been quelled by the need to be virtuous for others. And it kills them. You're given only one life. To live is to see that you yourself are a beast."

It wasn't merely about being self-serving but about survival. Tarn was willing to do whatever was required to get what he wanted. His hands were red with blood, and it didn't bother him in the least because he accepted his darkness. It was a part of everyone, and Dyna couldn't deny it was in her as well.

"In the end, all that matters is that the men fall in line. They have seen what happens if they don't."

She smirked. "You want them to fear you. Am I to fear you, too?"

"It would be wise if you did. To see me as the evil you would paint me as." Tarn jerked the reins to lead his horse around a tree, and the force thrust her backward into his firm chest. "I don't need their trust. Only their obedience. And I expect yours."

She quickly straightened. "You expect too much. If you want the map, then set me free."

"How curious that you should bargain with me for something that is already mine. When I give my word, I keep it. I expect others to do the same."

Dyna made a face at him over her shoulder. "Are *you* judging *my* honor?"

His cool eyes narrowed. "Perhaps I should have Benton retrieve Mount Ida's location from you."

Her smirk dropped. She was acutely aware how easily the old mage could do it now that Dalton had told her about cognition magic.

"You have one day to decide."

He was still giving her a choice? It was more than she expected from him. Yet her anxiety grew with knowing they would reach the port tomorrow.

"Whatever you have in mind for me, it won't happen," she said. "I will never give in to you."

"Sweet little scarlet flower." He leaned in dangerously close, and his voice dropped low, each word a provocative promise. "You have no idea what I have in mind for you."

Dyna held perfectly still, ignoring the prickle of goosebumps that sprouted on her arms. What was he planning to do with her? She thought all he wanted was the map. Was there something more? The question sent cascades of shivers across her skin.

The rest of the night went by in silence. Exhaustion settled over her, but Dyna was determined not to sleep. Her dry eyes felt like they had been rubbed with cotton. She had to shake herself awake several times. It was an hour before dawn when they finally left the forest and entered another clearing. Raiders spread out to stake a spot in their new camping grounds. Tarn dismounted, and she yelped when he plucked her off the saddle like she weighed nothing. Her sore legs wobbled as soon as her feet landed on the ground.

After hours riding a horse, she was achy and numb. Dyna took a step, and her foot slid through a patch of moss. She should have gone sprawling in front of everyone, but Tarn's hand shot out and snatched the front of her cloak. He was completely composed as if catching her was purely reflex instead of intention. Tarn waited for her to get her bearings before letting go.

She brushed herself off. "I didn't think you were capable of chivalry."

Startling anger sharpened his features. The breath caught in Dyna's lungs at the frost emanating from his stare. Something about the word had infuriated him. His soul-numbing eyes released her from their hold when he faced the Raiders.

"Place the veil." Tarn's command rang out like steel, hard and effortlessly powerful.

Benton and his sons gathered in the center of the field and held hands in a circle. Their silhouettes glowed brightly with the color of their Essence. Red, orange, and yellow. It bled from them and swirled in the center of the circle, then shot up into the sky. The colors blended into a silvery white as it reached the peak and spread outward like a massive, translucent dome about half a mile in size, curving as it came down. As soon as it touched the ground, her prison would once again be in place.

Dyna tensed at the urge to dash for the strip of freedom that was quickly dwindling. But Tarn gave her a look that warned her not to attempt it. The opportunity to run vanished when the veil reached the ground and sealed them inside. Its power hummed in the air like static. Everything outside of the veil was blurred and dull, displaying they were in a separate realm now. Panic fluttered in her heart. She had to remind herself this was part of the plan.

They were almost there now.

"Good girl," Tarn said.

Dyna glared at him.

Von and Olsson barked orders at the Raiders to set up camp and dig the latrines. The spies slipped into the shadows to take the perimeter watch. Tarn reached into his coat and flung out a dash of gold pixie dust. From it appeared his tent in tiny form before it floated away, expanding as it went, and settled on the north end of the camp. She should have known that was how he moved it when he was so reliant on magic. Lucenna did the same with hers.

Dyna gaped at him in disbelief when she realized something. "D-did you shrink me inside every night while I slept? I'm not a fairy. You could have killed me!"

He tucked his hands in his coat and strode toward his tent. "It's magic. Don't question it."

The man had kept her in his pocket like some trinket!

She picked up a stone off the ground with every intention of throwing it at his head. But then she noticed Von watching halfway across the camp. He crossed his arms and frowned at her hand pointedly. Dyna grumbled, letting the stone drop by her feet, and followed after Tarn.

"Master, we should discuss the mission before I go," Von called as he approached.

Sighing loudly, Dyna blinked wearily as they waited. She wanted to lie down.

Tarn's pale eyes slid to her. "Go rest. I imagine your frail body needs sleep."

Dyna glowered at him, but didn't protest. She dragged her feet to the waiting black tent, and the dancing lights of the amethyst crystal greeted her at the entrance. As soon as the tent flap settled in place behind her, Dyna grinned. He bought her act and didn't think twice about letting her come in on her own. Who knew the habit of sharing his tent would give her an advantage after all?

Dyna sprang into action. There was perhaps a minute before Tarn returned. Barely any time to search for the keys—and something else that she needed for herself.

She ran down the length of his table, glancing at the mess of missives, scrolls, and books. One book was open to a page that made her halt. She stared down at a detailed illustration that seemed so real one could touch it.

The Lūna Medallion.

Dyna slumped in a chair by the brazier for warmth as she waited. Her head lolled against the headrest to paint herself the exhausted damsel, but it wasn't difficult to do when she hadn't slept for a day. Lazily, Dyna traced the path of the oak tree tattoo spanning her arm. She wished Leoake had placed his geas in a more conspicuous place. Her heavy eyes drooped closed, and she might have dozed off for a bit.

The sound of rushing steps and muffled curses alerted her awake. Dyna kept still, pretending to sleep as she listened to Tarn ransack through his desk for a minute before daring to peek through her lashes. He yanked off his coat and revealed his tunic sticking to the sweat on his back. His heavy breaths labored as he tossed aside books and quills. He searched for something. Dyna tensed in her seat. If he discovered what she took...

But she relaxed when he drew out a nearly empty glass vial. The black contents whirled as Tarn quickly dumped every drop he could into a goblet. He filled it with wine next and gulped it down to the dregs.

Are you aware of what that does to you? She wanted to ask. *Of the toll it takes?*

From his condition, he'd been using Witch's Brew longer than he should have. After a while, the body grew tolerant as well as addicted. He was drinking it every few hours now simply to stay awake, but no matter how strong the magic, no one could go forever without sleep.

Tarn tore off his soiled tunic, halting her next breath. It wasn't his partial nakedness that shocked her. Not even the rigid muscles of his tall frame. Many horrifying scars covered his body, as if some creature had chewed him up and spat him out. He cursed under his breath again and rummaged in a chest of clothing. The firelight from the brazier gave her a full view of the deep mutilations that lacerated his back. Not only made by teeth...but with a whip.

Thick scars crisscrossed down the length of his spine. They were long healed, at least externally, yet they were more terrible than all the rest. That sort of thing left a mark on more than the body, and it had a way of resurfacing again and again.

She would know.

"You don't drink Witch's Brew to avoid assassination," Dyna whispered. Tarn stiffened, and his cold, pale blue eyes met hers over his shoulder. The tent went cold at the warning on his face not to speak aloud what she'd discovered, but the words fell from her lips, anyway. "You're afraid to dream."

His face grew eerily still as he stared at her in silence. She expected him to deny it, but he didn't. Perhaps because she caught him by surprise, or because he knew she could see the truth. Perhaps he was contemplating killing her for unearthing this secret he couldn't expose.

Tarn slipped on a clean tunic and faced her, with the front still left undone. The mauled scars creasing through his hard chest and abdomen were glaring in the firelight. It cast shadows against his face, turning his cheekbones as sharp as two knife edges.

This may be the most valuable discovery she had unearthed about this man. A hint of humanity, magically hidden away. It astonished her he had such a personal vulnerability. Though Dyna's heart raced under his icy stare, she wanted to know more.

"What has the world stolen from you, Tarn?"

His jaw flexed. The burning wood popped, and embers swirled into the air between them.

"What secrets and fears lie hidden in your mind that you cannot bear to remember them? It must be dire enough to bury them with potions. I wonder what you would see if you were made to dream."

"Careful," Tarn said, lethally quiet. "Don't toy with me unless you're prepared for the consequences."

His voice was controlled, but it was easy to hear the anger beneath the surface.

Dyna hid her nerves behind an air of indifference. "What consequences might those be? You won't allow me any harm. The men know—"

The mood rune blazed at his back, outlining his silhouette in a menacing red hue. Her breath clouded in the tent as the temperature dropped with a chilling power. The depth of his gaze frosted over, and beneath the ice lurked something dark and dangerous—and God of Urn help her if it ever fully surfaced.

"They may not touch you, but I will do with you as I please," he said, and she had the phantom sensation of his fingers grasping her neck.

She swallowed. "All I mean is that I can help you."

Tarn braced his hands on the chair's armrests, trapping her in place with his piercing eyes. "Let me make one thing abundantly clear, Maiden. I'm not a tortured soul in need of saving, and I'm not known for mercy. Expect none from me."

The firelight dimmed, darkening the tent. Dyna shivered at the sudden cold pressing against her. The sound of a faint crackling drew her to glance down. Frost coated the armrest beneath his hands. It crawled over the wood with layers of ice, taking over the chair.

Tarn possessed magic.

Why had she not noticed before? The air had always grown cold in his presence. It wasn't because he unnerved her, but because he affected the temperature. He was a descendant of the Ice Phoenix, after all. But how far did his power go? No one had mentioned it to her, not even Yavi. Possibly no one knew. It would be like him to keep such secrets.

Right before the ice touched her, it halted and melted away. Tarn stood back. The fire flared to life, and the tent warmed once more.

"What was that?" she asked faintly.

"A hint of the consequences should you rouse my ire." Tarn went to the table and took his usual seat. As soon as he looked at the book left open, his jaw clenched. "You were snooping."

Dyna sat up with a shrug. "I wasn't the one who didn't put away his things. Now I know why you were looking for Lucenna, or her medallion, rather."

She came to stand beside him. "You want to open a portal to Mount Ida with the Moonstone. Well, she doesn't have it. It's on the island."

He closed the heavy cover, letting the book slam shut. "I suspected as much."

"So you have Von looking for this other Sacred Scroll." She pinned a page beneath her finger and rotated it toward her. "Will it tell you how to become immortal?"

The page nearly tore when he snatched it free. He put it away with the other gathered pages into a leather folder. "Among other things."

"Like the full power of the Unending?" Dyna guessed. She couldn't quite contain her amusement at seeing Tarn's eyes narrow. Cool, smooth victory flowed through her like crisp water. There had to be more to it, but the little knowledge she gained was a win that brought her that much closer to learning about his plans. "Jökull's power is on that treacherous island, but you don't know exactly where or *how* to get to it without that scroll."

"Your map will serve as a start." At his icy tone, her stomach dipped in warning. Better not push him any further.

Danger lurked in the shadows of the tent, and it suddenly urged her to leave. No matter his sharp beauty and splinter of humanity, every instinct told her this man was a slayer.

"Perhaps." She turned to go.

"Enjoy your last day of brashness. Tomorrow, you will give me what I want." His promise sank a shudder down her spine.

Unfortunately for him, she didn't plan to be here tomorrow.

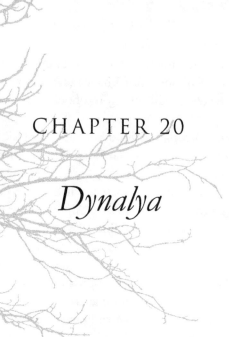

CHAPTER 20

Dynalya

That evening, Dyna slipped into the mage's tent. It was quiet inside, muffling the camp ruckus of voices and wagons being loaded. Dalton jumped up from his seat at the table and rushed forward, nearly tripping over his feet. His dark brown hair stood on end as if he'd been raking his fingers through it for hours.

He looked pale. "Do you have it?"

She nodded. "Are you all right?"

"No. I think I m-might vomit." He chuckled weakly, his fingers drumming against his staff. "This could end very badly."

Dyna laughed, even if her heart was pounding, too. "Have faith."

She wiped her clammy palms on her leg before reaching inside her cloak and pulling out a bronze ring holding a set of three matching keys. Each one had a red crystal at the top and sharp ridges. She had already taken hers off the ring.

Dalton's eyes lit up, and he reached for them. "If someone other than Tarn uses the slaver's keys, the Crystal Core will alert him. We need to be at the border before removing them."

She stepped out of his reach and tucked the keys away. "I know."

He glowered. "We had a deal."

"We agreed to use our advantages to escape, but I'm not oblivious, Dal. Where are your father and brother?"

They should be here to discuss any remaining details. But then again, they hadn't been part of the conversation when a plan was formed. Still, she didn't trust them.

"They are waiting for us at the veil," Dalton exasperated. "It wouldn't be discreet if all four of us went at the same time."

Dyna searched Dalton's face for any sign of treachery, but he genuinely looked nervous and excited to be free. "I will hold on to the keys to your freedom until you give me mine. I also want my journal back."

His glower turned into a sly smirk. "You're becoming more demanding. I like it."

Dyna rolled her eyes and followed him to his father's cluttered desk. He plucked Azeran's journal off the top of a stack of books and handed it to her.

"We wouldn't have any use for it, anyway."

Since they couldn't open it without her. Dyna tucked the journal safely into her enchanted satchel. She had recovered that from Yavi's tent earlier. Thanks to the stardust, she filled it with food, water, medicine, and as many essentials as she needed for travel, but their tent showed no signs of packing.

"What of your other things? Will you not pack?"

"It would only weigh us down." He looked around, and his brow tightened. "There is nothing we want from this place. Besides, it would be best if it didn't look like we were planning an escape if we failed."

Dyna sent a prayer to the God of Urn that they wouldn't.

She glanced back at the desk. "Then, if you don't want them, can I have the book you mentioned to me last night? The one on cognition magic."

Dalton shrugged. "Sure, take it. I don't need it anymore. I've long since memorized its pages. Planning on meddling with someone's mind?" he asked as she sorted through the tomes.

Only her own. She wanted to learn more magic, but she was interested in the barrier placed on her. With cognition magic, she may figure out how to remove it.

"I thought it might be an interesting subject to study." Dyna spotted a small leather-bound book with the title *Cognitive Arts*. She threw a quick glance at the other trinkets and found what she was truly looking for. The arrowhead with the hindrance rune carved on it. "Ah, here it is."

Snatching up the book, she feigned accidentally knocking over the stack. They bumped into the glass bottles full of powders and potions, sending them crashing to the floor.

"Oh, I'm sorry about that." Dyna rushed to clean up the glass, but Dalton waved her away.

"No worries, I got it."

While he was distracted, she tucked the arrowhead in her pocket. That morning, she had searched Tarn's tent for the dissipation arrowhead that broke spells but never found it. He probably kept it on his person, so this was her backup plan.

Once Dalton had dissolved what remained of the bottles to sand, he stood. "There."

"Ready?" she asked him.

He rubbed the back of his neck, and his throat bobbed. "I believe so. Everyone else knows what to do?"

"Yes. They will use their keys and run as soon as the veil is down."

"Gods, we're truly doing this."

She patted his arm. "You're going home, Dal."

That drew a bright smile on his face. They left the tent and went in opposite directions. Couldn't risk being seen leaving together. Her pulse drummed in her head with anticipation.

Dyna counted down as she crossed off each phase of her plan.

One...

She walked past the cook's tent, where a wagon was pushed into the entrance. Sorren was busy loading it with familiar barrels. A distinct floral scent floated on the evening wind as she passed by him. They shared a look, and she nodded.

"Hungry?" Sorren asked. He tossed her a small sack without waiting for a reply.

Dyna caught it and kept going. More tents dropped around her as the men continued working. She spotted Geon helping the younger Raiders gather the horses. She handed him a scarf from her satchel as she passed by.

Von came into view, where he worked on rolling up the tarp of his tent. Yavi stood behind him, holding onto the reins of a gray horse packed with bags.

"The Master is waiting for you, lass," Von said, glancing at fleetingly.

She caught his unease. Tarn expected the map. If Von was worried for her, he didn't need to be. He didn't know what was about to happen.

"I'm headed to him now. Here, I brought you something to eat." Dyna reached into the sack and handed Yavi a roll of bread.

Yavi's shaking fingers curled around the roll, cupping it close to her chest. "Thank you." Her hazel eyes misted, and she gave Dyna's hand a gentle squeeze. *Be safe*, it said.

"Of course. Take this. It's cold." Dyna handed her another scarf and carefully wrapped the thick wool around Yavi's neck, making sure to cover her nose. She squeezed her hand back. *And you.*

After sharing a look, they parted ways.

Two...

Dyna waited for a group of passing Raiders to block her from Von's view, then she pivoted and went east, putting Tarn's tent behind her. Tremors crawled all over her back as she picked up the pace. Checking that no one was watching her, she dashed into the growing shadows of the sparse forest.

No one gave chase.

The electrical hum of power in the air led her to the three mages waiting by the rippling veil. Her heartrate spiked as she looked beyond them to the faded realm almost within reach. The distant camp could somewhat be seen through the barren trees.

"Did anyone see you come here?" Benton asked. "Were you followed?"

"I wasn't seen." She moved, so the veil was at her back, putting the mages in front of her.

"Good." He watched her intently as Clayton moved to his flank. Tension lined their shoulders. "Hand over the keys."

She narrowed her eyes. "Drop the veil first, and I will toss them to you."

He scowled, and the crystal in his staff glowed. So did Clayton's.

Dalton stared back and forth between his family and her. "What are you doing?"

"What mages always do," she told him. "They never planned on letting me go."

"Is that true?"

"She's paranoid, Dal." Clayton's glowing eyes stayed on her as his fingers drummed against his staff. He looked like a cat waiting to spring the moment she blinked. "Dyna thinks everyone is after her."

"There is no time," Benton snapped. "Keys, Maiden."

"Not yet."

"Not yet? What are you waiting for?"

Dyna smiled.

There was a shout in the distance, and they looked up at the dark smoke swirling above the camp. It had the Raiders coughing and shouting. There was

145

another commotion as a stampede of their horses swarmed the camp. The chaos had all the men panicking.

Three.

"Catch." She threw the keys at Dalton.

Snatching the hindrance arrow from her pocket, Dyna slashed it down the veil. The cut glowed silver as it split like a tear. She leaped through and tumbled to the ground. The veil instantly repaired itself—as she hoped. The arrow couldn't break the powerful spell, but hindered it long enough to give her a chance. Whether it would work had been a gamble, and it paid off.

Now everything inside of the veil was dull and faded. But her chest still ached with the missing bond. The veil placed on her body had remained.

Dalton stared at her in dismay. "Dyna? I thought we were doing this together."

She looked away from him and quickly gathered stones. "I'm sorry, Dal. I never said we would leave here together."

Maybe it was selfish of her, but she had to think of herself now. She had to find Cassiel.

"You treacherous little wench," Benton coughed, his eyes watering from the toxic smoke. "What is this?"

"The royalrods…" Dalton covered his nose with his sleeve. "She had them set it on fire—"

They started wheezing. Benton cast a dome shield over them, and they sucked in clean air.

"It was my contingency plan in case the one we agreed on didn't follow through. And clearly, I needed it." She looked at Dalton. "Did you know?"

He blinked at her. "N-no, of course not."

"But you suspected they would try something, didn't you?" When he looked away, she scoffed. "I thought you were different, Dal."

Shame crossed his face. Dyna quickly formed a circle on the ground with the stones and laid down the open sack inside, revealing a cut of ham. She whispered to it under her breath.

"We had one chance to escape unawares, with as much of a head start as possible," Benton shouted at her. "Now the entire camp is alert!"

"They are momentarily blinded, so you won't get a better opportunity. You might want to drop the veil, and soon before you go blind from the fumes as well, Grand Magus. I did my part in getting you the slaver's keys. This is where our alliance ends."

A slithery grin crossed his face. "Did you think you were the only alliance I made?"

At the neigh of horses, Dyna whipped around to see armored men riding in from the southeast. The sunset gleamed on their dark blue armor, and on their chest shone the sigil of an interwoven seven-pointed star.

Azure Knights.

The veil dropped, and smoke wafted into the open sky. A gust blew it into Dyna's face, making her cough. The ground thundered beneath the beat of hooves as the knights swarmed the camp.

"You called them here?" she gasped.

"Many want Tarn dead. Including the King of Azure. I made sure they would be waiting," the old mage said. "You're right, Dyna. This is the *perfect* opportunity to wipe out his army. Thank you for inhibiting them."

The sounds of clashing swords and startled cries rang in the air. They would be slaughtered!

"You're coming with us." Clayton lunged for her.

"Clay!" Dalton yanked him out of the way of a blue explosion.

They all scrambled back as Azulo appeared from the trees with orbs of glowing aqua-blue magic hovering around him, to her utter relief.

"Azulo!" Dyna ran to him, but Benton hit her with a blast of his Essence and hauled her back.

"Make your ask, Dyna," Azulo said urgently. "I can't take you and stop them at the same time."

Her heart sank, and she shut her eyes. If they ran, that would set three mages on her tail, and she had no power to fight back. "Stop them."

Azulo's orbs shifted into massive drakes, and they attacked the mages. One landed on Benton, and he let her go. Dyna dove out of the way from the boulder Clayton threw. She landed heavily on her stomach.

Dyna gasped at the warmth of the bond sparking in her soul, and she looked down at her bloodied hand. The hindrance rune. It had impaled her palm when she fell. Tears sprang to her eyes as the bond shook with Cassiel's presence, but it vanished a second later when the veil on her body reformed itself. The arrowhead couldn't break that spell either.

Azulo crouched defensively in front of her, his shoulders and arms lighting up with spiraling blue symbols. He made a motion with his fingers, and his apparitions turned into roaring dragons that spat fire at them.

Benton countered with three roots that tore out of the ground and beat back the dragons. "Reform the veil!"

147

His sons clasped his shoulders, and the colors of their Essence shot into the sky. A new rippling dome formed over the camp again with them inside.

Benton sneered. "Run along, little girl. While you still can."

The veil reached the ground, and they vanished. There was no sign of the camp, nothing but the quiet plains in the late evening. No sounds of battle, no smells of the smoke, no sign whatsoever of the Raiders or knights. Her mind almost couldn't accept it existed, or that she had escaped such a prison. But she felt Benton's invisible glare burning into her skull.

"Thank you," she told Azulo. "I suppose we're even now."

He nodded, glaring where she imagined he could still see the mages. "Yes, but my magic is tied to the sun, Dyna. I can only hold them back until it sets."

The sun was sinking on the horizon. They were minutes from nightfall.

"Go. Now!"

Dyna fled.

CHAPTER 21

Lucenna

Lucenna woke to the annoying pulsing in her temples. Everything hurt, and her heavy body felt so cold. The relentless throbbing continued. Gods, all she wanted to do was sleep.

"He is calling again," an irritated voice said. "He won't stop until she answers."

"Her brother is concerned for her wellbeing," another replied quietly.

My brother? The thought cleared the fog of sleep.

Lucenna attempted to move, but she couldn't bring herself to yet. Her body was weak and unresponsive to her desired action. Her brow furrowed with annoyance. She concentrated on opening her eyes and managed to peek through her thick lashes, but instantly closed them at the firelight piercing her sight.

The pulsing in her temple fueled her irritation. Lucenna sent Lucien assurance through their link, letting him know she was alive. She must be alive by how much pain she was in. His relief hit her like a punch in the gut. She gasped, then coughed when the cold air caught in her lungs.

"My lady?"

"Has she at last awoken?"

Shadows stepped over her, shielding the campfire's bright light. Lucenna squinted through her lashes at the ones looking down at her. Slowly, her mind placed the faces of Rawn, Zev, and Cassiel.

Rawn kneeled by her side and laid a gentle hand on her forehead. "How are you faring? You have spent most of your Essence."

"What...happened?" Lucenna asked, her words raspy and faint. Her throat was incredibly dry, as if she had swallowed dust.

"You have been unconscious for a day," Cassiel said. "Night has fallen."

"What?" Her head spun when she tried to get up. "Why does this feel familiar?"

They had gone through this before.

Rawn placed his arm under her back and helped her sit. "At a leisurely pace now, my lady. Zev, will you fetch me the tea, please?"

Lucenna blinked her bleary eyes at their surroundings. They camped in a small clearing within the dense trees. Fair nickered as he grazed on a mound of grass by a set of shrubs. Sleeping mats and packs were set haphazardly around a small campfire. Lucenna focused on the soft crackle of the flames and scent of burning wood. It brought back a rush of memories, and she looked down at her bandaged hand, her broken finger throbbing.

"My father, he found me," Lucenna murmured, staring at the men. "You were there. Again."

They flinched when a spark flashed above her, and a piece of parchment fluttered down onto her lap. Lucenna frowned at Lucien's use of sending her a message through a small portal. He really must stop doing that. She picked up the parchment and squinted at the smudged writing.

If you are well enough to ignore me, you are well enough to speak to me. I must see you.

"Your brother has sent several messages," Cassiel said.

That's when Lucenna noticed a stack of torn parchment neatly piled beside her, along with her satchel.

Zev returned with a wooden cup of tea and handed it to her. Lucenna received it in her cold, feeble hands and breathed in the earthy scent of rosemary.

"Drink, my lady." Rawn said, "This will revitalize your Essence."

She carefully sipped the hot liquid, its wondrous heat soothing her sore throat. Fair nuzzled her cheek, and Lucenna stroked his nose. "I missed you too, handsome."

"Forgive us for going against your wishes." Rawn tipped his head in apology.

"If you hadn't, I would be on my way to the Magos Empire with my father. Thank you for coming to my aid."

"Think nothing of it, my lady. I wish we had arrived sooner. We were searching for you."

"You were?" Lucenna felt warmed by that. She was going to apologize for leaving in the first place, but then Cassiel interrupted.

"I saw your magic illuminate the sky. It's how we found you. Your father is a misogynistic clot."

She smirked. "That he is, and you certainly sent him off with his tail between his legs. I have never seen him so frightened in my entire life. It sounded as if the forest was filled with wolves."

"Zev made a few acquaintances," Rawn told her. "Prince Cassiel called in reinforcements, as well."

Following where he looked, Lucenna stiffened at those idling in the bushes. She could make out the large shapes of wolves on the left and the Valkyrie on the right. They had called in a full cavalry. All for her?

Lucenna peered up at them questioningly. Cassiel's complexion was pale, and the whites of his eyes were red from lack of sleep. Zev and Rawn were also run ragged, their clothing torn and dirty.

Dread sank in her when she noticed someone missing. "Where is Dyna?"

Rawn lowered his head with a heavy sigh. "A day after we parted, Tarn came for Lady Dyna. In the fray, we lost her to them."

Lucenna blanched at the news. "What do you mean? He has her?"

Vivid blue flames shot out of Cassiel's hands, making her recoil.

"Good Gods!" She gasped. "That's new."

"Why did you leave us?" he asked. "Tarn came himself this time with Von, a mage, and an elf. Both of which had powerful magic we could not withstand."

He didn't say it aloud, but she felt the words. *If you had been there, she wouldn't have been taken.*

Lucenna was too stunned by his anguished expression to argue against it. She hadn't been around to fight with them. She had run away because she felt she had to protect Dyna and herself. But in the end, Dyna was captured anyway.

"I'm sorry," Lucenna said faintly. "I..."

"Do not blame her for this," Rawn said. "It was not her doing."

Cassiel rubbed his face. "It's not her I blame."

"We tried to go after them, my lady, but the mage cloaked her with a veil."

It was no wonder why Lucenna couldn't sense Dyna. And now she understood why they searched for her, too. "You need a tracking spell."

"In Corron, you helped me find her once." Cassiel violently ripped out a cluster of feathers from his wing and thrust them at her. "We need you to do so again."

At her stare, he clenched his jaw.

"Is this not enough? How many would it take? I will rip them all out if you wish." His shadowed eyes were half-crazed and desperate.

She shook her head. "Stop, I don't want your feathers—"

"Lucenna," Zev finally spoke. His voice was hoarse and cracked with every word he spoke. "They *stuck* me with silver, and I was a useless mutt in the mud. She screamed for me while I was dying, and I couldn't do anything to save her. She doesn't know I'm alive. I don't even know if she's alive." He took her hands. "We will give you all the gold we have. Please. Help us."

Emotion welled in Lucenna's throat, her vision blurring at the sound of pain in his plea. He was unraveling. They both were.

"Pardon us," Rawn said. "For bringing this difficulty to you. We would not have come if the need not be so dire."

Wiping her eyes, Lucenna inhaled a deep breath and slowly let it out. "Of course, I will help find Dyna. I care about her too, you fools."

Zev and Cassiel sagged with relief, as if they feared she would deny them. All three gratefully thanked her, speaking over each other. Lucenna downed the rest of the tea and held out her hands. They all came forward, but Zev was the closest. He helped her stand. Her vision skewed slightly. Her legs gave out, but he quickly pulled her against his side.

"Thank you. Give me a moment to find my bearings."

The heat from his large frame seeped through her clothes. It was a werewolf trait, if she remembered correctly. She sighed happily as it banished the cold.

"Zev, you've all the comfort of a hearth," Lucenna told him. A faint shadow of amusement pulled at his dismal expression. "This mage you spoke of, what's his element?"

"Earth." Rawn's jaw clenched. So, he had been the mage's opponent.

Her mouth quirked. Earth mages thought they were more powerful because everything around them could be affected by their element. But it made them overconfident, and she enjoyed putting them in their place.

"I think I'm ready," Lucenna nodded. Zev stepped back but stayed near in case she needed him again.

"Will you be able to track her past the veil?" he asked.

"It will be difficult, but I will try."

She closed her eyes and breathed in slowly. Her consciousness slipped away into the dimension where Essence lived. Hers was faded and weak, but she was determined to continue. Lucenna cast it out. The purple light stretched thin as it searched for Dyna in the darkness, but it couldn't go far, and it snapped back.

Lucenna groaned, pressing a hand to her throbbing temple. "I can't."

"What does that mean?" Zev asked anxiously. "Are you saying...?"

"No, it's me," she said. "I haven't fully recovered. I don't have enough power."

Lucenna glanced at the feathers in Cassiel's fist. He held them out to her. She only took one and cupped it in her hands. A golden haze appeared around the long, black feather. Its magic fueled her Essence with a powerful surge.

She closed her eyes and found her renewed Essence blazing brightly in the *Essentia Dimensio*. It bolted forward with a will of its own, expanding her net with a force. There, in the darkness of her mind, was a green light in the far distance, but her spell bounced off the dark cloud that had it contained.

"He not only veiled Dyna's presence in this Realm, but he also has her hidden in a pocket within the Spatial Gate," she told them. "Whoever this Earth Mage is, he's formidable."

"Is she lost to us?" Rawn asked.

"If we hadn't met before, perhaps, but I can see her Essence." Lucenna furrowed her brow in concentration. "I only need to—"

The veil vanished. It was gone, blown out like a candle.

Cassiel gasped and clutched his chest. "Dyna..."

"What is it?" Zev demanded, grabbing his shoulders. "What's wrong?"

Dyna's green Essence brightened and Lucenna latched on before the veil slammed back into place.

Cassiel dropped to his knees, grunting in pain. "No! It had come back. I felt our bond for only a moment."

"She's alive?" Zev asked urgently.

"Yes...But the veil hid her again."

"One second was all I needed to get a firm lock on her," Lucenna smiled. "Whatever happened, or whatever she did, that one second was enough."

They all looked down at the ground as the tracking spell formed into an illuminated purple path of enchanted fire at her feet. It snaked across the forest floor into the woods.

"I'm going ahead," Cassiel said, casting off his coat.

"Wait." Lucenna grabbed his arm. "Dyna is three days west. If the tracking spell fades, keep going. The mage placed a second veil on her body, and something else has her magic locked away. Even if you arrive at her location, it may still be difficult to find her."

"Take this." Rawn whipped out a knife from his thigh holster. "It's enchanted with the same spell as my sword. Use it to cut through the spells trapping Lady Dyna."

Cassiel tucked the knife in his belt. Then his large black wings spread wide, and he soared into the sky. The Valkyrie flew after him. Zev shifted, landing on all four paws, and sprinted down the path. The forest rattled as the Pack of wolves followed.

Rawn nodded to her. "We are forever grateful, my lady. I believe it's here we part ways?"

Lucenna shifted on her feet. She had hoped they would invite her back into their company. But why would they when she willingly turned her back on them?

"If you don't mind, I would like to accompany you to make sure she is all right," she said.

Rawn smiled warmly. "You are more than welcome."

He quickly gathered their scattered belongings and fastened their packs to Fair's saddle as she tucked away her brother's messages. Lucenna took his outstretched hand and mounted behind him.

With an Elvish command, they raced down the fiery path.

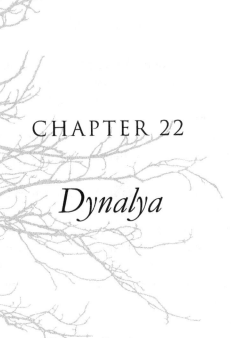

CHAPTER 22

Dynalya

Dyna's shadow stretched ahead of her as she leaped over boulders and ducked around trees. Sunset's golden light bathing the ground began to fade. Her heart raced with every labored breath as time chased her into the forest. Then she was plunged into twilight. Dyna stumbled against a tree, entering a short clearing on the edge of a cliff. Beyond, the ravine was dark and so far down it had to be about five hundred feet high.

Shakily, she searched through her satchel and drew out a slaver's key. She crouched and quickly fit the teeth into the tiny hole in her witch bangles. They fell away, and Essence immediately rushed into her veins. Her eyes misted as a familiar green glow filled her hands. But she couldn't celebrate that because her bond still hadn't returned.

Cassiel. She looked out at the horizon, wishing with all her heart to see his form flying against the moonlight. *Find me. Please find me.*

But Cassiel couldn't find her until she broke the spell. Dyna squeezed the arrowhead tight in her fist and kept running east. He had to be in that direction.

The forest grew darker with the coming nightfall. There was no time to be afraid. She focused on putting as much distance between her and the camp as possible. Moonlight formed a dim path on the ground, so she followed it. She was so focused on not acknowledging the dark that she didn't notice the waiting shadows until she came face to face with a group of Azure Knights.

Her boots scraped against the hard earth, stumbling to a stop in a glade. They looked imposing and vicious in their heavy blue armor. She panted heavy breaths as she spun around, looking for an opening to escape, but they had her surrounded. One stepped forward and removed his armored helmet. By the moonlight, She could partially distinguish a man's rough face with a beard and short dark hair.

He eyed her suspiciously. "What's this? You're not who we expected."

They must have been waiting here to finish whoever had escaped the assault.

"I think she's one of Tarn's spies sent to scout ahead," said another man, taking in her black leather armor. "She wears his colors."

Dyna shook her head as she discretely slipped the arrowhead in her satchel. "I'm not. I was his captive, and I only now made my escape."

"Something a spy would say."

"Kill her and be done with it," ordered the first knight. "You know our orders. No prisoners."

Her heart jolted.

"Wait, Captain, if she was in Tarn's camp, then she may have information for the King," said the knight beside him. "We should take her with us."

The captain's mouth curved in a lewd smile. "Hmm. Well, she is pretty. At the very least, she will provide entertainment. Bring her."

The knights lunged for her.

Dyna's hands lit with magic, and she flung a sphere of Essence at them. The blast threw them back, and they gaped at her. "I am not going anywhere with you," she hissed. "The next one who approaches me will lose a limb."

The men laughed. Each pressed on the Azure crests embossed on their chests, and their armor hummed with magic as golden light rippled over them. Of course, they had damn shields.

The captain sneered. "Tarn has witches among his spies now?"

"I told you, I'm not his spy."

"She's right." The sound of that voice, as frigid as winter, sank a frightful chill down Dyna's spine. "One of mine would have already slit your throats."

Knights yanked out their swords as they stared into the dark. Their feet shifted over the ground, the metal of their armor clinking.

Swallowing, Dyna slowly turned around and spotted the distinct black form lurking within the trees. Her heartbeat thundered in her ears, her legs locking in place. Her shaky breaths clouded in the air as the temperature dropped. Fear permeated the night, every instinct telling her to flee.

It stepped closer.

The tip of a steel blade came first, then boots, until Tarn fully emerged. His eyes eerily gleamed white in the moonlight spilling through the branches, shadows clinging to the planes of his face. He looked like Death itself, dressed in all black, his long coat fluttering in the breeze. And the scent of blood came with him. He held a sword, red dripping off the blade's edge. The pommel was embossed with a sigil she couldn't clearly see.

His gaze cut into hers, frigid with a quiet wrath that made her insides go cold.

Tarn walked past her and faced the knights. Fifteen men in all. He swiped a hand through the air, and their enchanted shields peeled off their bodies like tattered sheets, only to be absorbed by the glowing black clovers on his cuff.

"Let us skip pleasantries," Tarn said into the shocked quiet as he removed his coat. "We both know why you've come."

The Azure Knights breathed heavily, their breaths marking the air as they crouched into defense positions.

Tarn's sword whirled with a flick of his wrist. "Shall we?"

The captain put on his helmet. "In the name of His Highness, King Lenneus of Azure, I sentence you to death."

The men charged all at once with a battle cry. Tarn shoved her out of the way, and she caught herself on a tree. Their gleaming swords swept for him. He spun under the arc of a blade and slashed through a man's torso. His body pivoted as he cut through a knight's throat and dodged the whizzing blade of another. He moved so quickly, so deftly, Dyna stared with rapt horror as he hacked his way through the band of men simultaneously, countering every strike.

Red splattered on his face with each kill as he slayed them one by one. Blades missed him by inches. They never touched him. His movements were so precise and graceful. He moved with an elegance she had never seen. Something that only came with rigorous years of training.

Of killing.

Two knights charged for him, and Tarn stepped back at the right moment, so they struck each other. She shuddered at the sound of his low chuckle. He was toying with them.

This was nothing to him.

Ice sprouted from his hand, coating his blade. He surged forward and slashed down across a knight's chest, and in the same momentum, his sword swept up to cut the next. Clouds passed over the moon, and the darkness shrouded her vision. All she could see was the flash of steel and spurt of red with blood-curdling screams filling the forest.

Moonlight spilled back through the branches as Tarn struck the last man down. Turning, his attention fixed on her next. His predatory stare bore into her as if deciding where to stick his talons first. If Dyna wasn't leaning against a tree, her knees might have given out.

Tarn raised his sword above his head, and she scrambled back to run. He was going to kill her for escaping. She tried to cast a shield, but it sputtered in her shaking hands. He flung the weapon. It flew past her head, and she heard a cry. Dyna spun to see a hidden knight stumble forward with the sword through his chest.

She tripped out of the way before the man keeled on top of her. Tarn snatched her arm and hauled her to her feet.

"Did you think you could run and I wouldn't find you?" His icy voice froze her to the bone.

"I—"

Tarn wrenched her aside. Steel flashed from the corner of her sight as a spinning knife flew past, missing her completely, but he winced and glared down at the cut on his bicep. The wounded captain was still alive. Tarn ripped his sword from the dead knight's chest and went after him as he attempted to crawl away.

Dyna cried out. "No!"

Tarn thrust the blade into the back of the captain's neck. Her stomach heaved at the sound of the wet squelch when he jerked it free. She slapped a hand over her mouth, muffling a whimper. God of Urn. He'd murdered the man in cold blood. Without mercy or hesitation. Yet he'd also pulled her from the knife's path.

Tarn had saved her life.

Dyna saw the satisfaction on his face when they both realized it. She bolted.

Tarn caught her within three strides and hauled her around to face him. "You cannot escape me, Maiden. You now belong to me for the rest of your life."

"I will never be a thing you own!" Dyna punched and kicked, but it was like fighting an unmoving glacier. Any spells she tried were consumed by the clovers. Her fist grazed his chin, and his expression grew livid. Frost crept out from under his hold and crawled up her arm to her neck. It hurt terribly, and panic crystalized in her veins, but she merely glared up at him. "Go on, then. Kill me. Because I won't stop trying to get away from you."

A muscle in Tarn's jaw flexed as he regarded her coolly, then the frost melted away. He dragged her into the woods. "Perhaps I should thank you for running. It revealed rats invading my nest."

She dug in her feet, fighting every step. "You already had rats. Benton was the one who—"

Dyna stumbled when Tarn dropped to one knee mid-stride.

"What—" He cut off with a painful gasp. "What is this?"

158

His body curled forward, and he fell on his hands and knees as he heaved with heavy breaths. His fists shook on the ground, struggling to stay upright. Confused, she canted her head, listening to him wheeze for air.

What happened?

Dyna glanced at his bleeding arm. She crouched and carefully picked at his sleeve to inspect the lesion and found a murky green foam burbling from the swollen ridges. "You've been poisoned."

Tarn let out an indignant laugh. "Of course. That slithering prick would rather use such cowardly methods to get rid of me than to do it himself," he growled through his clenched teeth. His arms gave out, and he fell face down. With great effort, Tarn rolled onto his back. His lungs rattled with shallow breaths, and he hacked up blood. "Curse him to all Seven Hells."

She levitated the bloodied knife that cut him and lightly sniffed it, analyzing the distinct, sickly sweet scent. "Fengu," she concluded. "You've been poisoned with one of the most lethal venoms only found in Xián Jīng. I hear your lungs hemorrhaging from the inside as you fall into paralysis. You must feel the numbness settling. It will be a painful death by slow asphyxiation. I think you'll be dead in about five minutes."

Tarn's mouth pinched, and his sweaty complexion paled further. "How fortunate that you're here." He reached in his coat for the vial of Witch's Brew. Probably to dampen the fear that must be sprouting in him now. "Heal me."

Dyna snatched it away. "No."

Rage swam in his wide eyes. He snarled muddled words he could hardly form. "I saved your life. It belongs to me now. Obey my command."

"Slavery has been abolished in Azure, Tarn. I belong to no one, least of all you."

He grabbed her neck, but there was no strength in his shaking grip. "You will heal me or die with me."

"No, I won't." Dyna easily pushed it away and stood. She watched his chest spasm as he hacked out more blood. Not moments ago, Tarn had seemed like the most terrifying being, but now he'd been defeated by a mere nick. "Oh, how it must feel for the great Tarn to be so powerless. On the brink of the very death he sought to avoid."

"You're...relishing this... aren't you?"

Yes, a part of her was satisfied to see him suffer for once. Because, at the moment, he was the weak one.

"'Only the strong rise above the weak,'" Dyna quoted him, balancing the bloodied knife in her hand. "It was you who taught me the true meaning of power. Thank you for the lesson. I shall not forget it."

As much as the fury contorted his clammy face, a faint smirk rose to Tarn's mouth. "Then you may..." he rasped, "survive this world yet."

His pale eyes slid closed, and he stopped moving. Dyna counted the slight rise and fall of his chest. Each labored breath grew fainter and fainter. Seeing Tarn this way was strange. He looked so innocent and helpless. As though he hadn't recently slain everyone else lying in the glade. It was a trick of her compassion. She had borne witness to his cruelty. He killed so many people.

This was his fate.

Dyna's steps were soft in the quiet night as she walked away from the dying man. She had to continue with her journey and find Cassiel. But Tarn's fading life was a weight over her head. Herb Masters vowed to treat all, including the wicked. She argued no one would blame her if she omitted that vow this once.

Yet her feet stopped. Angry tears welled in Dyna's eyes as she warred with herself. The man hurt her. He killed Zev. He held her captive. Left to die there on the frozen ground was no more than he deserved. But if she took another step, it meant she was a beast like he claimed.

We all have darkness in our hearts, Maiden. Even you.

She should leave him.

Anyone else would.

Tarn laid waste to everything in his path because he believed it was the only way to live. Something had twisted him so terribly it scarred his body and his mind. But perhaps, he could see a new way...if given a chance.

Shaking her head, Dyna rushed back to Tarn's side and filled her hands with magic. "Don't make me regret this."

CHAPTER 23

Dynalya

The scent of flowers and wet earth drifted to Dyna's nose as she used a stone to crush purple petals, roots, and other herbs in a bowl. The wind eerily wailed outside of the hollowed-out redwood tree she had found. Its round walls curved to leave a narrow opening, and the top coned to a point like nature's version of a tent. It was big enough to fit them both.

Tarn was still unconscious. He lay awkwardly slumped against the inner back wall. She'd stuffed his coat under his back to keep his heart elevated. Her magic had stopped the venom from reaching his heart and repaired his lungs, but the wound still needed treatment. His body had to do the rest.

Sweat beaded on his flushed face and bare chest. She had cut off his tunic and removed his shoes in case his limbs swelled. Each breath was shallow and rapid, pulling against his ribs. Dyna touched his forehead, and her palm burned with his high fever.

She didn't think the man could be anything but cold.

Gathering the poultice in her gloved hand, Dyna applied it to the wound on his arm, then bandaged it. She'd been prepared with those this time. After tearing up his tunic, she soaked some strips in water and folded it on his forehead.

If he made it through the night, he would live.

The trees rattled outside, and flurries blew past the dark entrance. The moonlight hardly reached this part of the forest, forming strange shadows that seemed to move. No, nothing was out there.

Dyna shut her eyes and forced herself to take a breath. *It cannot hurt me. It cannot reach me. I am not alone.*

She huddled closer to Tarn. His presence helped, despite him being a step away from death. Her eyes stayed on the flame flickering in the center of the hollowed tree. She'd coaxed a small campfire with some flint and steel. It wasn't enough to drive away the dark or to keep her fully warm when the frigid wind slipped in through the entrance. She threw a blanket over Tarn and wrapped her cloak tightly around her shoulders.

No one had come looking for them yet. Maybe no one would. She had felt the seed of guilt plant itself when the knights rode into camp, and now it was growing into a weed with thorns. She couldn't have known that would happen.

God of Urn, what about Yavi, Geon, and Sorren? They were in the thick of it. Did they escape? What if they got hurt? As soon as the royalrods were lit, Sorren was supposed to break out of his bangles and grab the others.

And Von? How did he react?

No one knew what he would do if he knew about their plans. Yavi didn't want to risk it. So they decided not to tell him until it was time to run, and too late for him to alert Tarn. Dyna hoped he escaped with them.

If anyone survived the ambush, it was the spies. They certainly would come looking for their master. It was best to be gone before they did.

Dyna peered at Tarn. It was odd to see him finally sleeping. His body desperately needed it, and now he had no choice. She pressed two fingers to his wrist to measure his pulse. It was still too fast for her liking. Her attention drifted to his scars, and she couldn't help staring. There were so many. Jagged and puckered, and years old by their pallid color. The worst ones were the bites. They marked his chest and arms where teeth had sunk through. Something had tried to eat him alive.

A shudder traveled down her spine. What happened to him?

Well, there wasn't anything else to do now but wait. She took out some bread and cheese from her satchel to eat. The corner of Azeran's journal poked out of the top, but when she drew it out, it wasn't her journal at all. It was a preliminary book on earth magic. Dyna could have sworn she'd seen the Astron sigil on the cover before tucking it away. How did she mistake it…?

Dalton.

Dyna groaned. He must have cast some sort of illusion to make her see the journal. Stupid cognition magic. Her mental shields hadn't worked against him. But why did they want to keep her journal? They couldn't open it without her—and neither could Tarn.

That must be it. They didn't want to risk him getting the map and becoming immortal, because then they would never be free.

Not much good this magic book would be. She wasn't of the Earth Guild, or any guild for that matter, but it reminded her of what Dalton said about her lineage. Could she use sun magic, too? She'd unleashed green flames in the fjord. So perhaps...she could.

Dyna glanced at the small campfire and called on her Essence. It rushed through her veins, humming readily. Healing Tarn hadn't completely drained her, as it would have before. Maybe her barrier was starting to weaken. After being withheld for so long, her Essence pushed against the walls of her being, filling every crevice. And it wanted out.

She stared at the flames, concentrating on the intent as Lucenna taught her. Its heated energy wove through her magic, and she whispered the Magos word for fire. *"Ignis."*

The flames flared high.

Dyna yelped and jerked back from the heat. God of Urn. She did it.

But the amber beads on Tarn's cuff lit up, and the black clovers inside consumed her Essence from the air, leaving the fire to dwindle. She frowned. Right, he still had those. Their power prickled against her, hungry to ingest more of her magic.

Dyna carefully unbuckled his cuff and carried it outside. She buried it deep within the roots of the tree where she could no longer feel the clovers, then covered it up with some leaves. There. No need to leave him with a weapon he could use against her.

Satisfied, she went back to the campfire and played with the flames. They rose and fell at the wave of her fingers, following every silent command. Soon, the inside of the tree was completely warm. She grinned to herself, giddy with excitement. This opened a whole new side of magic for her. There was so much more she could learn. But her smile faded at the reminder she wouldn't be able to share it with Lucenna. Dyna hoped she was all right, wherever she was.

Sighing, she returned the useless earth magic book to her satchel, and it bumped up against the other one Dalton gave her. She pulled out the small leather-bound book. It was light in her hands, and shadows traced the stamped title, *Cognitive Arts*.

Now this magic she could use.

It may help her figure out how to remove whatever barrier contained her power. Dyna had studied enough magic books to pick up lessons quickly. She merely didn't have enough Essence to practice what she'd learned—until now.

And she had someone to practice on. Her eyes slowly slid over to her patient again. What hid in that mind?

Dyna spent the next hour reading by the firelight. Dalton said dream walking was the easiest, so she started there. From what the pages described, she could enter the dreams of another with her Essence and by opening her mind. That sounded fairly simple.

Tarn faintly moaned and jerked, making the compress slip off his forehead. His breathing quickened as his eyelids fluttered back and forth rapidly. He must be having a nightmare. She glanced at his scars again. A rough one.

His features pinched, and her curiosity grew. Dyna bit her lip, contemplating. Did she want to go rooting into Tarn's mind? There was no telling what she would see, but doing so might reveal who he was and what he was truly after.

Dyna slowly reached out, hesitating a few seconds before lightly placing a glowing hand on his arm. She closed her eyes and exhaled a few low breaths to clear her thoughts. This was how the book said to do it. To breathe in and out and...

She sank.

The first thing to hit her was the smell.

The stench of rot and blood flooded her nose. Then she felt the humid summer heat on her back. She was running. No. He was. She was experiencing everything as he saw it. Tarn's ragged breathing sounded loud as they ran together.

His steps clanked heavily, and a helmet obscured his vision. Trees whipped past them, and others in dark blue armor ran ahead. They...looked like Azure Knights.

The roar of beasts came from all around. Rampant fear wrenched through her body when an enormous shadow came bounding for them, shaking the earth. Tarn twisted with a cry and slashed his sword through gray flesh. A bellow followed, but he ran before she could see what it was.

"Fight, men!" someone shouted in the distance. "Hold the line! Courage!"

Screams of the dying and the horrifying roars muffled the command. Tarn stumbled through the trees, holding his wounded side. His shaking, gloved hand pulled away wet.

"Help me!" someone begged. "HELP—" The scream abruptly cut off with what could only be death.

Dyna whimpered as the ground shook and snarls closed in. Branches snapped as gray forms loped through the surrounding trees. The cries of neighing horses followed. They galloped past them with their riders or with empty saddles.

Everyone was fleeing.

A young knight caught up to Tarn and smiled in relief. "Captain—"

Something hit him, and his body collided with the ground in a wet crunch. Blood and sinew spurted from his dented helmet.

Dyna fell back on her hands and feet. She looked up in horror at the gigantic creature standing over her. It had thick limbs and a body covered in gray armored skin. Bone spines protruded from his shoulders and elbows. Stringy fur lining its torso, shoulders, and wide jaws to its pointed ears. It carried a severed leg in its three-fingered, clawed hand. The terrifying creature had only two holes for a nose above its bloodied mouth, and three completely black eyes.

A troll.

It focused on her. On Tarn. Her heart thundered in her chest, terror freezing her in place. Drool seeped through its sharp teeth. There was only one thing it wanted. To eat.

The troll lunged.

Dyna screamed, and something violently snatched her from the dream. Her back slammed into the hollowed tree with Tarn's arm pressed into her throat. His wild eyes didn't see her. They were completely lost and petrified.

"Tarn!" she shrieked, pushing against his taut hold. "Let me go!"

He pressed harder, and she kicked wildly, desperate for air. But whatever strength he'd found quickly vanished, and Tarn slumped against her. Dyna pushed him off, and he sprawled on the ground, his body heaving with rapid breaths. His pale eyes blinked weakly at their surroundings, then landed on her.

"You..." Tarn croaked. "You shouldn't have come back..."

"Then you'd be dead." Dyna grabbed the fallen blanket and put together a makeshift bed. She helped Tarn lay down on it and inwardly shivered at the feel of his rough scars. Those frightening beasts must have mauled him. Her heart was still pounding.

"Why are you looking at me like that?" he snarled.

Dyna looked away. "I saw it," she whispered. "Your dream. I saw what happened to you."

Tarn's breathing halted. She didn't dare meet his gaze, though she felt his stare clinging to her like frost.

"I don't want your consolation or your pity," he finally said. In the next second, the cognition magic book landed on the fire. "Stay out of where you're not wanted."

"No!" Dyna snatched the book and put out the flames. It was futile. Half of it was charred black, rendering the pages useless.

Tarn's heavy panting resonated in the hollow tree as he searched through the pockets of his coat. "Where is it?"

"It's gone."

"What do you mean?" he growled, though the frail sound held no bite. "Give it to me."

"Water first." Dyna pushed a waterskin to his mouth and forced the contents down his throat.

Tarn coughed forcefully, shoving her hand away. "Give me the vial!"

He was furious and desperate. Anything not to fall back into that nightmare. But she couldn't let him have it. His body needed rest to heal, and it was time he was weaned off the potion.

"I told you it's gone," she said. "You've had enough."

"I'm contemplating killing you right now..." he said, each word slurring. Tarn reached for her, but she easily pushed down his trembling hand. His eyes rolled, and he slumped back on the blanket. "You...the water..."

"Dreamshade oil. Tastes rather awful, doesn't it?" She stuffed his folded jacket under his head and dipped the compress in more water before placing it on his forehead.

He fought to stay awake, but it was a losing battle. "I will punish you for this..."

"Sleep, Tarn. You can thank me tomorrow for saving your life."

CHAPTER 24

Dynalya

Tarn had told her to stay out of his head, but Dyna woke to the sounds of another nightmare within the hour. After knowing what happened to him, she couldn't listen to him suffer through it. So Dyna sleepily moved to lie beside him and placed a hand on his clammy shoulder. With a trickle of her Essence, she slipped back into his unguarded mind. The smell of death and roars bombarded her again. She quickly pulled him out.

There was another side of dream walking that drew out memories of the past. She tried to guide him to a happy one, but it wasn't easy. They became drifting wisps of smoke as images and voices whisked past her, too fast to see.

Eventually, everything cleared, and she found herself in a stone corridor. Dyna searched for Tarn's tall form but found a thin, pale child instead. No more than four or five. His distinct white-blond hair fell in soft waves around his face. He wore a fine black dress coat and a satin cravat. A little lord in fine clothing.

This time, she wasn't standing in Tarn's place but was separate from the dream as she watched it happen. He lingered outside a door. A stripe of light landed on his cheek as he peered through the crack. The wailing of a baby and faint voices trickled into the hall. Dyna inched closer and peeked in, too.

A very beautiful woman lay in a large four-poster bed with her back resting against the pillows. Rivers of silky golden hair spilled down her shoulders. She hummed to the bundle in her arms, rocking it gently, her face so full of love. The cries quieted to gentle gurgles. Several women hovered around the bed to get a closer look at the newborn. They had blurred faces, as though someone erased them. Everyone was out of clarity and faded except for the mother.

"He is perfect, Gwenyth," said a faceless woman in a chair beside her. "What a handsome boy."

The other on her left agreed. "Lord Morken will be pleased to, at last, have a proper heir."

Lord Morken? They must be in Old Tanzanite Keep.

The women shushed whoever had spoken. The mother pretended she didn't hear, but her cheeks flushed as she rocked her baby. She looked up at the door, and Dyna gasped at the pale blue color of her eyes.

Gwenyth spotted the boy, and her lips formed a gentle smile. "Come here, little one."

Everyone turned to stare at him, and he hesitated.

"Come, Tarn."

His small hand pushed on the heavy wooden door, and he dutifully entered with a bowed head. She motioned for him to come closer, but his presence seemed to invite strain in the room. The women excused themselves and left as he approached the bed.

"I feared she would die during childbirth," the same insolent woman whispered as she passed by Dyna to enter the hall. "Giving birth to that other *tarnished* child nearly killed her."

Gwenyth's smile stayed in place, though Dyna knew both she and Tarn had heard. He looked up at his mother with matching eyes that already understood so much. At her prompting, he climbed onto the plush bed and peered down at what she held. The newborn had fine, downy hair and a rosy face.

"Say hello," Gwenyth said. "What shall we name him?"

He paused, then mumbled a suggestion.

"That's a mighty name for someone so small," she teased. "That's your choice?"

Tarn nodded.

"Then we'll call him Dale for short. Would you like to hold him?"

He blinked at her a moment, then looked down at his pale hands.

"It's all right. You won't hurt him." Gwenyth's tone was tender, but there was something on her face. Sadness and worry hid behind the smile. "Here."

She brought Tarn to sit beside her, and she gently laid the bundle in his arms. She kept a hand beneath the baby's head for support. The boy stared at him in quiet fascination.

"He's your wee brother, no matter what anyone says," she murmured. "You share blood, and that binds you for life. So you must always protect him, Tarn. He will need you."

The boy didn't answer, and Dyna thought his hands might be shaking.

His mother brushed the hair from his forehead, making him look at her. "This changes nothing. Old Tanzanite Keep is yours. It will always be yours by birthright, my little phoenix."

Dyna stiffened. She knew?

The door barreled open and a lord in dark blue armor entered. He was also clearly visible. The man was of average height but broad-shouldered, with blond hair and a bearded face that was once handsome in his youth. On his chest plate was the gold sigil of Azure. It had to be Lord Morken, Dyna guessed. A knight of the King and the Earl of this castle.

For a moment, he looked happy. His flushed face was lit with a wide smile, his hair windblown from probably having ridden home at the news of the birth. But his blue eyes landed on Tarn, and they hardened. All traces of his smile vanished into a scowl.

Gwenyth wrapped an arm protectively around the boy. "Dear—"

"I don't want him anywhere near my son."

"Don't say that, Thorne. He's yours, too."

"He is no son of mine. Get him out of my sight!"

Dark smoke swept the scene away, and Dyna was taken through brief flashes in Tarn's past. There were fleeting pleasant moments, each one ending badly. He was quiet and kept to himself, so he was chastised for being an odd, lazy child. The times he played with his younger brother ended with servants snatching Dale away out of fear he would hurt the heir. Then another baby was born a few years later. Gwenyth nearly died from the birth, and from then on, she was bedridden.

Lord Morken took out his anger on his sons as they grew. He cut them with his mouth and whipped them with the rod if they failed in their swordsmanship or schooling. Tarn tried to always push Dale out of the way or cover him with his body to take the brunt of the beatings.

He endured it all in silence.

Each time the smoke swept Dyna into another memory, its color darkened further and further.

Tarn was made to go to the finest schools and wear the finest clothes. He went through hard combat training since his childhood to one day be a knight. His peers were the children of knights who paid homage to the Lord of Old Tanzanite Keep.

Among them was Von.

Dyna nearly didn't recognize the short chubby boy. His father, Lord Conaghan, was Lord Morken's right-hand man. Therefore, Von became Tarn's companion out of decorum. He was a lively boy who made friends easily. He was always laughing and being rowdy during lessons. At prayer, he would whisper naughty jests to the other children and mocked the vows of chivalry they were made to recite. No one beat him. No bruises marked him. At social gatherings, Dyna stood with Tarn as they watched young Von be doted on by his mother and father.

Perhaps because he'd seen him do these things, Tarn grew a little bold. At twelve years old, he made the mistake of insulting his instructor during a lesson on Everfrost history. Which brought him to the frozen courtyard of the castle. Tarn stood barefoot, dressed in thin trousers and tunic. Snow caught on his lashes as he stared blankly at a fixed point ahead.

"When you step out that door, you're a representation of me and our House," Lord Morken said behind him. "We are knights. The pride of our king. Yet you have failed to uphold the conduct of a simple squire. I will make sure you never forget it again."

There was no rod in his hand this time, but a gruesome whip. Horror sank through Dyna. Lord Morken released the thick coil, and she and Tarn flinched when the leather slapped the ground. Dale wailed from the courtyard doors, begging their father not to hurt his brother before a servant pulled him away.

"Kneel."

Tarn unbuttoned his tunic and lowered to his knees. The fabric fell away, and Dyna's heart sank at the view of bruises and scars from previous beatings. His back was so thin, his spine jutted through his skin.

"What are the ten rules of chivalry, Tarn?"

His mouth trembled, but he held his head high and straightened his shoulders. "Honor." The whip cracked, tearing a laceration through his flesh. Tarn fell forward on his hands and knees. He clenched his teeth, biting back a cry. "Honesty."

It came for him again. The sound it made when it met his flesh was thunder in Dyna's ears. She covered her mouth and recoiled with each strike as her vision welled.

"Valor." *Crack.* "Loyalty." *Slash.* "Respect."

She covered her ears to dull the sound of his body tearing, but she couldn't look away.

"Truth!" Lord Morken bellowed when Tarn fell silent. He continued lashing each word into him. "Discipline. Humility. Duty!"

Stop, Dyna wept. *Stop it.*

But her pleas went unheard.

"What is the last one, boy? Speak!"

Tarn couldn't form words anymore. Pain had stolen his voice.

The last strike of the whip flattened him on the ground. Glistening blood seeped through the gashes, rolling down his back to paint the crevasses in the cobblestones red. Still, Tarn didn't make a sound. He lay there with his cheek pressed against the stone. His expression was blank, the last spark of life leaving his eyes. He had withdrawn into himself. Sealed away his emotions because it was the only way to endure.

"Never have I been so disgusted with you." Lord Morken tossed the bloodied whip aside. "Tarnished bastard."

He stormed back to the keep, leaving the beaten boy behind. Flurries drifted from the gray sky, falling over him like a soft blanket. Dyna cried because she knew this was the moment his soul broke. She kneeled by him, wishing to put the pieces back together, but it was too late. He had already lived this.

Here was the sincere truth of Tarn Morken, shredded and exposed beneath the snow. The beginning of the real story behind his mysterious legend. Frozen forever in a heart forged by cruelty and ice.

His bruised eyelids fluttered closed over his eyes, the color of winter. Frost sprouted from his fingertips, and it crackled as it spread across the ground. Then his brittle voice whispered the last rule of chivalry into the air.

"Justice."

Dyna jerked up from a dead sleep and gasped at the morning sun streaming into the hollowed tree. She was supposed to leave before dawn! She grabbed her satchel, but her hurry stalled when she saw Tarn. He never deserved such abuse. The brutality crushed him, and after that day, he changed. It molded him to show no pain. To feel nothing and care for nothing but becoming the perfect soldier.

Why did Lord Morken hate him so much? Was it all because of a rumor? She couldn't understand it.

Tarn was the son of the Azure King, but Dyna hadn't seen that discovery in his past yet. Regardless, rumors spread through court that Lord Afton was his real father, and the defamation only made Lord Morken furious that he'd been cheated out of a proper wife. Tarn was fourteen when the strife between their Houses started, and men were called to arms.

It ended when the King gifted Lord Morken the land of Troll Bridge. He was tasked with the honor of taking his peerage there to make a new settlement for Azure. But it was disguised exile, and everyone knew it. Old

Tanzanite Keep was left in the hands of a steward, to be inherited by Dale when he came of age. But she knew what became of Azurite.

Tarn's little brother never lived to see the day.

Dyna laid a hand over his forehead and smiled faintly. The fever was broken. His pulse had slowed almost to normal. She quickly cleaned his wound and applied more of the poultice before wrapping it in fresh dressings. She glanced up and jumped when she noticed Len and Elon standing at the entrance of the tree.

They hadn't made a sound.

Though she was glad they survived, she was also devastated. It was too late to run now.

"Maiden," came Elon's soft greeting. They took in Tarn's condition, and Len's livid eyes narrowed on her. Dyna quickly explained everything.

The elf studied her a moment before asking, "Will he live?"

She nodded.

"Wait here," Elon said to Len, then he slipped away into the morning as quickly as he appeared.

The spy didn't move from her spot as she stared at her for what seemed like hours. Len finally looked away when they heard Elon's return, accompanied by the clomp of hooves and the rattle of wheels. Taking advantage of the opening, Dyna slipped the hindrance arrow from her satchel to her boot before going outside.

Her heart sank to find Elon wasn't alone.

Von brought the horse-drawn wagon to a stop and climbed down from the driver's seat. His stony expression was shadowed with exhaustion. His torn, black uniform was covered in dried blood, half the knives missing from his bandoliers. Von didn't acknowledge her. He and Elon went into the tree and came out carrying Tarn between them.

His skin looked gray in the daylight. The signs of his strength and ferocity from last night had receded to the edges of his face. No one spoke as they carefully loaded him into the back of the wagon, and Len covered him with the blanket. The men climbed back into the driver's seat and looked at Dyna expectantly.

Tension clung to her like thick syrup. "I saved his life, Von. That should earn me my freedom."

He said nothing.

"Get in," Len hissed from behind her. "Before I cut out yer tongue."

Dyna considered using her magic, but she wasn't a match for them. She climbed into the wagon, and Len hopped in after her. Blinking back tears, she looked to the east as Cassiel fell out of her reach once more.

Flurries continued to flutter by as they rolled through the forest in silence. She prayed it wouldn't turn into snow. The sands of time were trickling by, and the chance to cross Troll Bridge was closing.

When they neared the camp, Len completely covered Tarn out of view with the blanket.

The veil was still in place.

She thought for sure the mages would have escaped, but Novo was there keeping a sword at Clayton's back. The young mage used his staff to hold a partial opening in the veil for them to enter. His irises flickered yellow, watching her coldly as they passed.

The camp was completely destroyed.

Half the tents were trampled, dying fires smoked on broken crates and wagons. There were bodies everywhere. Knights and Raider alike. Her stomach churned, and she looked away. Blood soaked the ground, squelching under the slow turn of the wheels. Olsson directed those still alive to line up fallen Raiders on one side of the camp.

So many dead.

Dyna searched for Geon, Sorren, Yavi, and Dalton. They were nowhere in sight, and the cook's tent was burned to ash. She pulled up her cloak, hiding from the survivors staring at them pass, their accusation digging into her back.

The wagon creaked to a stop in front of Tarn's tent. It was the only one that had taken no damage, probably because of the magic it bore. Von and Elon carried Tarn down with as much discretion as possible, using the wagon as coverage. Dyna sensed they didn't want anyone to see him in his current state.

Len jerked her chin, ordering her to follow. She entered behind them as they laid him on his untouched bed and covered him with the sheets. Elon stepped out, leaving her alone with Von.

He turned to face her, but his eyes still didn't meet hers.

"Von—"

He raised a hand. "Don't speak. Only listen. I lost eighty-three men last night. *Eighty-three.* And I nearly lost—" He bunched his fists. "Your plan didn't work. No one made it out."

Dyna gasped, imagining the worst.

Von finally looked at her. "They're alive. By the skin of their teeth. Yavi is so determined to believe that you're her hope it nearly took her from me."

She stared at him in disbelief and let out a sickened scoff. "You have some nerve. You killed my cousin and stole me away from my family. I've been drugged and beaten, collared like cattle, yet you think I'm wrong for wanting a life that is mine?"

So many emotions crossed Von's face: shock, shame, guilt, and a heavy sadness that startled her. He turned away and braced his arms against the back of a chair as though needing something to hold himself up.

"I never meant for anyone to get hurt," Dyna said. "I only wanted my freedom back, and so does Yavi. She has endured captivity for years, but if you think she has accepted it, then you don't know her at all."

After a drag of silence, he asked. "How did you save him? Fengu is fatal."

"Fortunately, I had the exact flower needed to counteract the poison. Royalrods."

He rubbed his face. "Of course. Well, now that the King is using Xián Jīng venom, I will need the antidote to always have on hand."

"Have the mages brew more of the potion I made for Elon. That will stop the poison if you can get it to him fast enough."

Von approached the bed and looked down at Tarn with an unreadable expression. "You could have run and left him for dead, lass. Yet you didn't. Why?"

Dyna thought about her reason for compassion, to not be like Tarn by saving lives instead. But in the end, she was partially responsible for the loss of many, and she didn't know how to accept that.

"Because I'm a stupid human," she muttered.

Von exhaled heavily, and it seemed to put his role back in place. "You are tasked with Tarn's recovery. You won't step out of this tent for anything. Whatever you need will be brought to you. No one will enter here while he sleeps, and you will speak to no one about this. When the Master wakes, he will decide your fate."

Dyna crossed her arms. "Fine. Then, as the Herb Master here, there are two things I require for his healing. It's non-negotiable."

Von waited for the answer.

"First, I keep my magic. I will need it to treat him. Since it will help instead of harm, the wards shouldn't attack me."

His mouth pursed, confirming this. "And second?"

"No more Witch's Brew."

CHAPTER 25

Dynalya

The enchanted tent must have been warded against sound because no one came running at Tarn's screams. But the amethyst crystal continuously spun, announcing that either Von or the spies stood guard outside. With his immunities compromised from the poison and the cleanse from Witch's Brew, Dyna couldn't risk giving Tarn more Dreamshade oil. The only way to quiet him was to put him in a deep catatonic sleep or direct his dreams.

Cognition magic came easily to her once she understood it. At any signs of a bad dream, she moved him to a memory he didn't mind. Mostly ones where he trained with Dale. She liked those. The mood was different with his brother, peaceful. Sometimes she would join in the training with them and learn a few things, too. She should get herself a sword.

Dyna reached for Tarn to remove him from this nightmare, but he woke and snatched her wrist, his bloodshot eyes furious.

A growl ripped from behind his clenched teeth. "Give me the potion."

She pulled her hand free. "No."

"Von!"

"No one is coming, Tarn. There will be no more Witch's Brew. Let it go."

He sat up, and she tried to push him to lie back down, but he grabbed her neck and strangled her. The Mood Rune blazed red, then flashed several colors as they struggled. Blue. Purple. Black. Rampant with every emotion he had contained until now. From his rage and anguish, she knew Tarn would kill her to stop the dreams.

Dyna's body lit up green with her magic.

His eyes widened. "Don't—"

She grabbed his face and put him to sleep. He fell on the bed, dragging her down with him, and the black smoke plunged her back into his memories. It wasn't by choice now.

As if he needed her to see.

The past brought her to a land covered in snow. Tarn was a young man now, about seventeen or eighteen, his body filled out with lean muscle. Features sharp in a way that made him striking, and his face bore no ugly scar yet. He helped his younger brother push a cart full of firewood through the thick slush from the barn to a courtyard she didn't recognize. The air here was colder, and the trees were pines. A massive manor cast shade over them. It looked newly built, with five floors high and towers on each corner like a crown.

They were now living on Troll Bridge.

"Stupid snow." Dale kicked at a mound blocking the wheel. He'd grown into a handsome teenager with pretty blue eyes and features that resembled his brother's, yet his father was in there, too. "It's always so cold here. Everything is covered in ice."

Tarn jerked the wheel free and pushed on. "In the ice we mold our truth, even whence hidden by the snow."

Dale huffed. "Did you read that in a book? Admit that you hate it here, too."

The courtyard doors opened, and a servant called them into the manor at their father's behest. Dale jogged ahead as Tarn took his time with the cart. Each step was slow, delaying whatever inevitable punishment was waiting for him. The scene changed to place Dyna in a grand hall she hadn't seen yet as Tarn entered. The stone walls were cruder than the ones of Old Tanzanite Keep, bearing the large flags with the crest of the Morken House: a circled frame with elegant lines, and a jagged snowflake sat in the center with twelve points.

Tarn bowed to Lord Morken and to Lord Conaghan. There was a third man there with a narrow face and sharp nose that reminded her of a hawk. His bald head shone beneath the tall windows of the hall. What caught her attention was the golden badge on his left lapel with the sigil of the Ice Phoenix.

Their muffled voices spoke of duty and the family line. Something Tarn had no interest in. He let them drone on, the words blending in a dull hum.

"Do you understand?" Lord Morken barked at him, his voice clearing.

Tarn lowered his head in compliance.

"Good. You will wed next winter once your estate has been built."

Wed?

Dyna felt Tarn's shock, though his indifferent expression didn't change. Lord Conaghan gave thanks for the honor, then excused himself.

"Garent shall see to the plot of land," Lord Morken said, glowering at the bald man. "I trust you will choose wisely."

"Of course, my lord." Garent glanced at Tarn before he bowed and also excused himself.

"I don't like that man. It's been four years, yet the King insists on having his viceroy decide where we build, who leads the troll assaults, and overseeing every decision I make. It's an insult." Lord Morken's glare turned to Tarn. "As for your bride, she is a plain girl. Scarred and by no means a picture of beauty, but from noble stock. The Conaghan House is an esteemed family."

Tarn said nothing. He was going to marry into the Conaghan family? Dyna didn't know anyone else part of that House other than...

Lord Morken scowled at his lack of response. "It's more than a bastard deserves."

As if giving him a wife he didn't want was a gift he should be grateful for.

Tarn didn't protest. He didn't make any comment on it at all. It was merely another punishment to have him marry someone Lord Morken considered of barely adequate caliber.

"You must have met the girl. She's Von's sister."

At that, surprise flickered crossed Tarn's features. Von had a sister?

The memory whisked them away outside on a spring day. Tarn stood on a tall hill with a view of Azurite. Behind him were the cornerstones of a new house for him and his bride. But the only thing he seemed interested in was the wooden wall that surrounded the entire circumference of the town. Dyna thought she heard the distant rumble of roars.

"The beasts are waking."

They turned to see Von climbing up the hill. He had also grown into himself. Taller and lean, his once jubilant face now a little harder from having lived in such a dangerous place.

"It's odd to see my mother and father excited about a wedding when I'm sick to my stomach of the Horde coming again. She says life must go on, and we must be proud of the one we were given." There was a sullenness to Von's words. He glowered at a field on the right side of the town that was filled with graves. "This isn't life. Since when is dying for lord and land a grand honor to be proud of?"

Tarn regarded him coolly.

Realizing he was speaking to his lord's son, Von flushed. "Disregard my ramblings. You know I never thought much of the vows they made us hold. We're not children anymore, Tarn. Now you're to wed. You must be *thrilled*."

"Indeed." The sarcasm in Tarn's voice was thick.

"Do you enjoy nothing else other than swinging a sword?"

At his narrow stare, Dyna didn't think Tarn was capable of finding anything a source of joy.

Von cleared his throat. "Well, I think you and my sister will get along fine. Aisling has this way about her that you can't help smiling around her. She might be the one to thaw that ice-cold heart of yours." He chuckled at Tarn's confused frown. "You don't remember? I introduced you to her at my squire ceremony."

"That was two years ago," he finally said.

"Ah, that is true. Then come meet your bride-to-be." Von led him down the hill to another smaller mansion below the rise. He waved to a young woman riding a beige horse in a fenced pasture. His sister's face was lit with a wide grin as she led the horse into a wild gallop. Her mauve dress and chestnut brown curls flared behind her.

"Aisling!" Von called through his cupped hands. "You're supposed to be inside tending to your embroidery, not riding."

She threw back her head and laughed freely. "Don't be so pompous, Von. Come ride with me!"

Tarn's expression was aloof, though he tracked her across the field.

"Later," Von said. "I want to introduce you to someone."

Pulling the reins, Aisling turned her horse around and rode back. When she saw Tarn, pink seeped through her sweaty face. The horse slowed to a canter and stopped before them. Her fingers drifted to the scar above her brow, and she subtly adjusted some strands of hair to cover it.

"Aisling, this is your betrothed," Von said, helping her dismount. "Tarn Morken."

"Yes, I know." A gentle smile rose to her lips. Her eyes were a warm honey that turned to gold in the sunlight. Lord Morken was blind, Dyna thought. Aisling was lovely. Taking the ends of her dress, she dipped in an elegant curtsey. "Hello, Tarn. It's a pleasure to meet you again."

The image of her faded, and Dyna found herself at the day of the wedding.

When Tarn took Aisling's hands during the handfasting, she gasped at his icy touch and flinched away. She didn't mean to, but shadows crossed Tarn's face, and he didn't touch her again.

In their new home, he arranged for them to sleep in separate rooms. He ignored her for the most part, spending his days training in the courtyard with a blade or strengthening his body with rigorous drills. Yet Aisling found a way to always be near her distant husband. She would sit beneath the shade of an apple tree with a book and peek at him past the pages with a light flush on her cheeks.

Neither of them had asked to be in this marriage, but something was blooming there, Dyna found. Perhaps not love from him, but every now and then, Tarn would watch her, too. Mostly when she was distracted with a book or happily humming to herself. His attention followed her as though she were a curious thing he didn't quite understand.

Aisling was always the same, even in the presence of his stiffness. Her smiles were endless, her happiness constant. When she laughed, there was something contagious about it that brought a smile to Dyna's lips. And she thought, almost to Tarn's. It drew him. That profound, untainted happiness that he never had. Found in a dark place where none was expected to be.

The memories continued to fade and solidify into others as they passed through the seasons. Pockets of time that held significance to Tarn. Her arm unintentionally brushing his in the garden without her flinching away. Aisling tending to his wounds after a summer troll attack. His eyes meeting hers across the dining table holding autumn's harvest. Sitting by the fireplace together as it snowed outside, listening to her read to him.

Then, one night in the hall leading to their chambers, Aisling wished him goodnight at his door. Tarn reached for her face, bathed in moonlight, but he hesitated to touch her with his cold hand. She cupped his palm to her cheek, and his forefinger landed over the tiny scar above her brow, slowly tracing it.

Neither spoke a word, at least not aloud.

He only gazed at her in silence. At last, accepting who she was to him or what she had become. Tarn pressed a light kiss to her mouth, tentatively at first, until Aisling's arms wove around his neck, kissing him back. In their time together, with nothing more than a smile, she had thawed a piece of him.

And maybe, Dyna thought, he wondered if this was joy.

Taking her waist, Tarn drew Aisling into the bedroom, leaving the door to close behind them. Then the memory spiraled away into a wisp of smoke, and it was no longer dark.

CHAPTER 26

Dynalya

With all good things, nothing lasts forever. Dyna saw the end come one humid summer day when Aisling sat beneath the apple tree reading in the shade, her pink dress spread on the grass. Tarn's sword sliced through the air as he sparred with Dale. They halted at the sound of a horn blaring through the air.

The world seemed to still as they stood there, listening with dread. A second horn blew, and Dale visibly paled. Then came a third. Aisling covered her mouth, her eyes growing wide.

Tarn rushed to her. "You need to get inside."

"They couldn't have gotten through our wall!" Dale exclaimed.

"Wood is not stone," Tarn said. "Go back to the manor and bar the doors. You know what to do."

His younger brother hid his fear behind a stiff nod and sprinted back home.

A knight in blue armor came galloping into the courtyard next and yanked on the reins. "Captain, the trolls have breached the gates."

"I know. Have the men meet me out front."

Tarn had his armor on within minutes. His heavy steps thudded in the hall of his estate as he headed for the front door. Aisling stood there with her servants, tears glistening on her lashes. He briefly paused before her, his hand coming to rest on her stomach. Dyna's eyes widened to find it was very round and heavy with child.

A sense of foreboding fell over her.

"Come back to me," Aisling whispered, brushing his cheek.

Something crossed his pale eyes. Words he couldn't say, but they were there on his face.

"On your life," was all Tarn said to his servants. The cold command made clear what would happen if his wife were harmed.

Everyone dutifully bowed.

"We will barricade the doors," the manservant said, hand resting on the hilt of his sheathed sword. "She will be safe, my lord."

Sparing her one more glance, Tarn swept out of the house and marched outside to his waiting men on horseback. Their faces were grim and full of dread.

Tarn put on his helmet and mounted his horse. "Where is Von?"

He wasn't among the men.

"He must already be down there, Captain."

"Then he honors the call. Today you are Knights of Azure, and they will know our names. Go with your god."

"And may he receive me!" The men hollered in a cheer.

The earth rumbled as they charged down the hill. Screams echoed in the distance, and smoke spiraled into the sky. Dyna ran out of the house with Aisling, and they looked down at the turmoil below the rise. Trolls swarmed the town, snatching up those attempting to flee. Lord Morken's dual swords severed through each one that came his way, moving with a swift agility. But the knights scattered as they tried to fight for their lives. The massive Horde poured through the broken gates like a gray sea of death.

And Tarn led his small unit of men straight to it.

The dream smoke came for Dyna and dropped her into the middle of the chaos. Trolls roared as they ran past her, ferociously smashing through knights. Their screams rang in the air as they were torn apart. Some fought desperately, but the weight of their armor slowed them down. They couldn't move as fast as the beasts. Couldn't outrun them if they fell off their horses.

They were being slaughtered.

Dyna ducked out of the way of a falling troll and shrieked at the swipe of Tarn's sword going over her head. He shoved the blade through a troll's neck and spun away to fight another. A knight fell at her feet, the man's terrified eyes now empty of life. She scrambled away, her shoes and hands slipping through the bloodied mud.

"Forward, men!" Lord Morken shouted to anyone who listened. "Kill the wretched beasts!"

A piercing sound reached her ears, and Dyna turned to see a bald man huddled under the broken gates, blowing on a thin whistle.

It was Garent, the King's viceroy.

Trolls bellowed at the sound, and more of them charged into the town. He was calling them!

Tarn realized this at the same time Lord Morken did. Both cut their way through the Horde for him. When the viceroy saw them coming, he dropped the whistle and ran. Tarn flung a knife, and it stabbed the man's leg, knocking him down.

Lord Morken threw himself at Garent and rammed fists into his face. "Why!"

"I was ordered to." Garent cowed, looking past him to Tarn. "He wasn't supposed to survive this place. None of you were. Then he begot an heir. It had to be done to protect the throne."

Lord Morken dropped him, turning to gape at Tarn.

He stared back at them, too startled as Dyna was, both of them coming to a horrible understanding.

"King Lenneus..." Lord Morken said as he stood, leaving the viceroy to escape. "You're *his* bastard."

The roar of the trolls dulled to a hum beneath the craze in his wild eyes. He picked up his swords and stalked toward Tarn. "Now I finally understand why you were a curse on our lives. He won't stop trying to kill us until you're dead. For your family, you have to die!"

Lord Morken bellowed and swung. Dyna cried out as the blades came for Tarn's head. He parried with his sword, but he retreated instead of advancing, scared and confused. Lord Morken bellowed and brought down his blades, breaking Tarn's sword in half. His next swing sliced through Tarn's side.

He fell to the mud, scrambling back. "Father, please."

Lord Morken's mouth twisted with disgust. "You were never my son."

Tarn looked up at the man who beat and molded who he was from his own hatred and finally accepted that truth.

Lord Morken raised his sword for the final blow, and Tarn threw out his hands. Streams of ice shot out and pierced through his armor like massive spears protruding out of his back.

The Lord gaped down at himself. Blood spurted from his mouth and he fell heavily to his knees. "This...is why he wants you gone..." He let out a wet, bitter laugh. "You're...the next Ice Phoenix."

Then he dropped dead in the mud. Tarn stared at Lord Morken, then at his trembling hands, too numb to notice the shadow of a troll falling over him.

Tarn! Dyna screamed.

Throwing himself out of the way, he grabbed Lord Morken's sword and shoved the blade through its jaws. Tarn staggered to his feet, tripping as he stumbled away from the beast.

"Captain!" A knight grabbed his arm and hauled him to the gates.

"What are you doing?"

"Getting out of here. Azurite is lost, sir!"

"Stop, go back!" Tarn turned to see more trolls storming through the town. "No—"

A stampede of knights and beasts thrust him through the gates and regurgitated him outside into the forest. The men ran for their lives all around him, forgetting the town they swore to protect. Panic and survival were all that drove them now.

Lord Conaghan shouted in the distance for the men to hold the line.

Groaning in pain, Tarn's gloved hand pulled away wet from his wounded side. Someone's scream for help abruptly cut off and Dyna knew she'd seen this part of his past. Tarn ran with the heavy sword, not knowing which direction was home. She gagged on the smell of rotting flesh in the summer heat and the swamp stench of the trolls.

A knight caught up to Tarn, only to be crushed by a troll's massive fist.

Tarn fell back, scrambling to get away from the enormous creature. Its three-fingered clawed hand snatched him from the ground. He cried out and struck the creature, but the sword bounced off the bone plates of its body. He couldn't reach the only soft spot beneath their jaws. The troll's teeth crunched through Tarn's armor and he screamed, blood spraying free. Two more trolls came, each fighting to get a bite of him.

Dyna stifled a whimper as they began to eat him alive.

Von sprinted out of the trees. He leaped up and drove his knives into the troll's eyes. Down it went, tearing Tarn from the hold of the others. Von moved deftly in no armor, evading the trolls trying to grab him. He tossed out more knives, each one perfectly hitting their eyes. They bellowed from the pain, left blinded. He quickly slit their throats, then ran to Tarn.

Von..." He lay there, shaking as he bled out. "You saved me..."

"I relieve you of your debt." Von shoved a red capsule into his mouth. *Yunnan*, Dyna recognized. Xián Jīng medicine to halt internal hemorrhaging and to ease pain. He quickly dumped a special powder over Tarn's wounds, and it stopped the bleeding. Von forced him to sit. "You have to get up, mate. We can't stay here."

"Aisling." Tarn collapsed against him, his eyes rolling. "Aisling."

Von hauled him to his feet. "If you want to see her again, you need to move!"

Once Tarn got his bearings, they fought their way desperately through the Horde. They rounded up the remaining knights and worked as a team to kill the trolls one by one. For every felled beast, they lost men until it was only them standing in the forest of bodies in the sunset, every part of them layered in sludge, blood, and troll guts. They leaned against each other, dragging their feet.

"Keep moving," Von panted. "Once we reach Azurite, we will be safe."

"The trolls got through. They breached the gates."

Von jerked to a stop. "What do you mean? How?"

"You didn't know?" Tarn glanced down at Von's torn clothing. "You're not wearing armor, and you weren't with the unit. Where were you when the horns rang?"

He looked away from him.

Tarn glared at him sharply. "You were deserting."

"Look around you!" Von waved at the dead. "That could have been me or you lying there. I never asked to be a knight. I don't want it. I want a life that is mine!"

Dyna sighed sadly, realizing why Von had reacted the way he did when she said the same thing.

"So you turned your back on your vow to the God of Urn and left your post on the wall." Tarn straightened. "How long had you left the gates unguarded before you heard the call?"

"What are you saying?"

"How long?" Tarn shouted, grabbing his tunic.

"I don't know. Fifteen minutes perhaps?" Von stared back at him, shaking his head. "I ran back as soon as I heard. Tarn, I had locked the gates behind me. I swear I did."

But all the Azure King needed was an opportunity.

The town wall came into view. Tarn dashed for it, and they followed. When they crossed the gates, Von slowed in distraught horror at the burning houses, bodies scattered everywhere. Even from the bottom, Dyna could see Tarn's estate engulfed in a plume of fire. Black smoke billowed out of the broken windows, spanning the sky.

Tarn sprinted up the hill to it. His manservant lay in the grass, ripped in two. A choked sound left his throat when he saw the broken door splintered from the frame.

Dread built in Dyna's chest. *Don't go.*

Tarn tripped up the stone steps to the broken doorway and stopped short. She didn't need to see his face to know what he saw. He fell against the wall, no longer able to hold himself up. The ceiling groaned as fire roared over it.

Dyna slowly came up behind him as he sank into a pool of blood gleaming orange. It soaked through the floorboard, coating his pants.

Aisling lay there in the hall. Her beautiful, golden brown curls splayed around her head, painted red. Her stomach...was torn open. Tarn's shaking hands reached for her still face, hovering over her empty eyes. Dyna heard his screams, though he never made a sound. It was his soul crying out as the last of it died inside.

Von ran through the doorway. "Did you find her? Is she..." He froze. "Aisling..."

"You did this," Tarn croaked shakily, his fingers curling through the thick blood. "You did this. *You.*"

Von shook his head, choking on a sob. He covered his face as his body shook. "I'm sorry," he wept. "I'm so sorry."

"They are all dead because of you!" But the look contorting Tarn's face. It was shock. Devastation. Loss. Guilt. He hardly noticed Von there. He wasn't speaking to him.

Von staggered outside and dropped to the muddy hill. His body bowed with wretched sobs as he looked out at the town rendered a mass grave. Buildings were torn down. Bodies left ravaged to pieces. His home below the rise was a torch of flame. It was all gone.

Everyone was dead.

He threw back his head and screamed at the hazy sky. His screams tore at Dyna's heart. Each one echoed through the air, choked with smoke. She cried with him, wishing to take away the agony engulfing him. Tears left paths on his face stained with dried blood and mud. When Von could scream no more, he curled on the ground.

"Please...please..." His hoarse voice weakly begged the God of Urn to forgive him as the sun sank on the horizon. Rain clouds rolled overhead and thunder rumbled in the distance.

Dyna gasped at the sight of a troll bumbling through the town. There was still one left. Panic shot through her when it spotted Von and charged. She reached for him but her hands went through him, because this was only a memory.

Von, get up! She shouted.

He watched it come, not bothering to move. The brokenness on his face reminded her of Zev, and she knew, after everything, Von didn't care to live anymore. The beast snatched his limp body in the air and opened its jaws, reflecting another moment of her past like this.

Von!

Steel slashed through the troll's arm. Blood spurted, and Von hit the ground with the bloodied limb. The troll's pained roar ripped through Dyna's ears. Tarn leaped into the air and swept Lord Morken's sword through its neck. Off came the head, wetly plopping on the ground. He snapped out a kick at the headless troll and sent it tumbling over the hill.

"You have no right to throw away your life," Tarn said, his voice layered with ice. "It belongs to me now. No Gods will hear you, Von. The fates have forsaken you. There is only one penance for your sins. From this day forward, you will serve with your life in payment for what you have taken from me, as the holy law demands. Until that debt is paid."

Von stared up at him, his breaths trembling. Wobbling onto his knees, he closed his wet eyes in acceptance and bowed.

"Yes...Master."

CHAPTER 27

Dynalya

Dyna left the dream with tears streaming down her face. When she first met Von in Landcaster, she thought he looked like a kind man who was a little tired and a little sad. Even when he stole her away the first time, those opinions didn't change. Not until he killed her cousin. Then she hated him and wanted him to suffer painfully, violently. Wanted him to feel the tearing in her heart when Zev fell. Yet when she had pointed an arrow at him, that shadow of sadness remained.

It had imprisoned him as much as his duty.

Maybe everyone was imprisoned by something. She was trapped by her fears. Tarn was hiding from his grief. And Von was chained to his guilt. He carried all the blame, forged it into manacles, and bound himself to them all these years.

Tarn's eyes fluttered open and found hers. He may not have sensed her presence in his dreams, but her wet cheeks gave it away, and he knew what she saw. Dyna wiped her face. For a while, they simply sat there together in his tent, breathing in the herbs of the charms above and listening to the gentle crackle of wood burning in the brazier. The air filled with the many things that went unsaid. Perhaps he was plotting her death for disobeying him, or because she could make him her slave, too.

Dyna broke the silence when she dipped a fresh cloth into a bowl of water. It trickled as she wrung it out and wiped the sweat from his forehead. "I relieve you of your debt."

He snatched the cloth. "I have no debts."

She rolled her eyes at his indignant tone. Of course, he couldn't be bothered to show any gratitude, regardless of her saving his life. "Even if I were so inclined to make you my life-servant, I don't believe you would allow someone to have such power over you."

Not after what he endured under Lord Morken. He had enough of others controlling his life.

"In that, you are correct." He glowered. "Only you would save your enemy."

"You're not my enemy, Tarn."

He was struck silent by this, searching her face for the lie he assumed she spoke. She hummed when the truth rune lit up blue.

"We shall see," he said.

Sighing, Dyna reached for the bandage on his arm, but he winced and lurched away. She gave him a look. "I need to change the dressings."

"Then be careful." Tarn gritted his teeth as she untied it and pulled the old poultice off to reveal the wound. While swelling had significantly lessened, it now oozed a foul puss, which she expected. The healing needed a little more help. "Why does it look that way? You call yourself a Herb Master?"

"Cease your fussing." Her nose twitched at the sharp vinegary smell of disinfectant ointment as she poured it on a clean bandage. "Only a child mewls from such a little cut."

"First you defy me, then you insult me. Many have died for far less."

"For someone who is infamous for taking lives, your threats seem to fall short." She pressed the bandage on the injury, probably harder than she needed to, and wrapped it around his arm, yanking the knot tight enough to make him hiss a curse.

Tarn snatched her wrist and wrenched her so hard she nearly fell on him. "For someone against violence, you seem to enjoy inflicting pain."

She glared. "Perhaps only against you." But her anger switched to regret at remembering the lashing he received as a child. Most of his life was made up of pain inflicted on him. Dyna shrank back in her chair and lowered her head. "I'm sorry."

"Don't do that," Tarn said icily. "I don't want your pity."

"It's not pity." Dyna couldn't bring herself to look at him past the red curtain of her hair. Everything she'd seen had been so personal and horrible. She couldn't help feeling sympathy for him.

He exhaled heavily and sat up in his bed. "I told you not to pry where you didn't belong."

"At first, I did pry," she admitted. "But after seeing...I couldn't stand leaving you to experience it again. Guiding your dreams to the better parts of your past was the only way to pull you from the nightmare."

"How naïve of you to think it wasn't all a nightmare."

The tendrils of his memories had been swathed in dark smoke, but there had been light moments too. Beautiful instances trapped between the stroke of a hand and the glow of a smile, moments where he had received something genuine and precious as her love. How devastating it must have been to at last find a sliver of joy, only for it to be cruelly torn away.

Fifteen years later, that wound was still unbearable.

"So you became addicted to Witch's Brew to forget," she murmured. "All this hate you have, your grief and pain, it's like mold. You have left it to grow in the edges of your being, not realizing it's taken over you. Ignoring it will only make you ill." She tangled her fingers together on her lap, her breath clouding in the tent as the temperature dropped with his anger, but she kept talking. "You rebuke those who follow you for their mistakes because you see your reflection. Von is kept around as a source for you to punish. You chose him to blame for everything wrong in your life, but I think we both know the one who you truly blame is yourself."

"You think you know me after seeing a few memories?"

"I know the pain you carry." Dyna met his frosted eyes. "Because I lived it when I saw my family killed, too." She was cursed to experience that day in her dreams over and over, as though it was the only time her mind didn't have the strength to forget. "I am sorry for those you lost...but emotions aren't a weakness. It's part of being human and we cannot hide from that."

Tarn's mouth twisted in a sneer. "Is that so? Then what of you? I watched how you reacted at the mention of your cousin. Your grief reared its head only to be cut down by you, so don't pretend to judge how I deal with mine."

Her eyes welled at realizing he spoke the truth.

Grief took different forms. Sometimes it moved through you. Sometimes it got stuck.

Hers had been buried. Her grief for Zev, her father, her mother, and Thane had been locked away to rot, because facing it would hurt much more. Their loss had carved a hole in her, and she felt its vacancy when she was reminded of them. A sound of laughter. The smell of lavender. The dust of magic books. Every moment had left her immobilized, so she had to bury it. Maybe she didn't know how to grieve, or she did and she hid it because then she would never be able to get up.

The tears Dyna fought spilled. The reason she was stuck on that snowy hill was because she never let herself move on.

"I wish I could forget, too," she whispered. "But you cannot erase your past...as I cannot erase mine."

Tarn looked away from her. "Enough talk, Maiden. Get out."

With a heavy sigh, she stood. "Call me Dyna."

Dyna was glad to finally breathe in the fresh air. She found Len standing guard outside of the tent. Once telling her Tarn was awake, the spy smiled and ran in. Dyna continued on in search of Yavi, but she wasn't around. None of the Raiders would speak to her, so it took stopping by the mage's tent to get answers. Novo was their assigned guard, and he refused to let her see Dalton.

"No one is to speak to them until Tarn decides their fate," he said. "They are traitors, lass. He isn't a man who forgives that."

She recalled the viceroy's treachery and knew where Tarn's lack of tolerance came from. But violence shouldn't be answered with more violence.

When she asked for Yavi, Novo pointed her toward another large tent across the camp. It was big enough to fit a Minotaur, and Dyna was glad to find them all inside. Sorren sat on the ground, his arms and ankles chained to the support pole. Yavi and Geon sat with him, both bruised and wrapped in bandages. When they looked up, they ran to hug her.

"God of Urn, are you all right?" Dyna asked worriedly, looking them over. "What happened?"

Geon sighed and rubbed the back of his head. "The plan worked at first and Sorren came for us, but it went south when...we told Von what was happening."

Yavi covered her mouth with a trembling hand as she cried. Her voice was small and broken. "He...he chose Tarn."

Dyna embraced her tightly. Yavi broke down and sobbed, her body wracking with them. She was grieving. To her, this was the end of their marriage.

"He didn't choose Tarn over you." Dyna took her face. "I know it's hard to understand, Yavi, but Von's doing this because he feels he has to. You need to ask him how he became a slave."

Odd that she was the one defending him now, but nothing was as simple as it seemed.

"I know how." Yavi moved out of her hold. "He saved that man's life when he should have let him die!"

Geon wrapped an arm around her shoulders, gently shushing her. "There wasn't time to argue with him. As soon as the Azure Knights infiltrated the camp, Von left to lead the battle. We tried to fight our way out, but there were too many knights, and they had Sorren surrounded."

The Minotaur growled. "We nearly made it until they knocked me down. When I woke, I had these back on." He beat his chained hands against the ground, making the brass bangles clank against his hooves.

"I tried to help, but one nearly got my head," Geon said. "Then Yavi…"

They all looked at her. Yavi wept as she shakily lifted her skirts. Dyna's eyes first snagged on the slave bangles she still wore, then she noticed her skin. From her left foot to her thigh, her leg was warped and waxy with fresh scars.

"A burning wagon pinned me down," Yavi said. "Von got me out, but not before this. Dalton had to heal me…" She looked at Dyna, fear entering her expression as she touched her belly. "He knows."

Dyna gasped.

Dalton would have discovered the pregnancy as soon as his Essence moved through her body.

"He won't say anything," Geon insisted, taking Yavi's hand. They must know now, too. "He wouldn't do that."

Sorren's growl rumbled through the tent. "You think he won't? Their heads are due to be removed, lad. They will do anything to secure their lives. We'll probably die next."

"What are they being held for?" Dyna asked. "Only for dropping the veil?"

Geon nodded. "Von suspects Benton somehow called the Azure Knights here, but they are blaming you."

Which didn't surprise her. The old mage would use anyone or thing to preserve his life, but if Dalton had told him about Yavi's baby, he wouldn't have wasted any time to expose it either.

"Dal hasn't said anything yet," Dyna told them. "So we need to give him a reason to keep your secret."

"How?" Yavi asked.

"By finding a way to save their necks. Also, Von hasn't disclosed your attempted escape yet, and I don't think he will." She kept it to herself that his master had been unconscious the whole time. "Tarn is distracted by the current state of the camp."

A commotion came from outside, and they all looked at her grimly.

"Sounds like he is very undistracted now," Sorren said. "Careful where you meddle, lass. Once you start pointing fingers, they point right back."

"Then I will make sure they point only at me."

As the Maiden, she had some leverage. Albeit a tiny one.

Dyna rushed outside and saw the Raiders surrounding something. She sprinted to them and pushed her way through the wall of bodies. Her blood ran cold to find the mages kneeling in the center with Tarn standing before them. He was still pale, but dressed and clean. And in his hand, he held Lord Morken's sword.

She leaped in between them, throwing out her arms. "Stop."

"Move her," he commanded with idle boredom.

Von stepped forward, but Dyna lit her hands with green flames, halting him in place. Gasp and murmurs surged from the crowd.

"I will knock you across the clearing, Commander." She waited for him to understand she meant it before addressing Tarn. "Don't you tire of death? You cannot kill everything in your sight."

His eyes narrowed. "Careful. At the moment, you're the only thing in my sight."

But the mild threat hardly phased her.

"They don't deserve to die," Dyna said aloud. She shot the mages a warning look over her shoulder. Benton and Clayton glared at her, but Dalton seemed to understand the message she tried to convey. "I was the one who lit the royalrods on fire, and I forced Benton to drop the veil by threatening his son. I held him at knifepoint."

The Raiders snickered at that.

"It's true." She drew the opal knife from the sheath on the back of her belt with her magic and levitated it in the air for everyone to see.

Von patted his bandoliers, realizing it was missing. "When did she…?"

"Which son?" Tarn asked icily.

"Me," Dalton said, his expression now completely neutral. He pointed at the long red scab on his throat. It must have happened during the skirmish. "She cut me good."

Tarn pointed the sword at him. "You expect me to believe she overpowered you?"

Dyna expertly flipped the knife, making it whirl in her hand. "I told you I wouldn't stop trying to get away, even if that means I have to draw a little blood."

But Tarn didn't look away from the mages. He gripped the sword's hilt tightly. Dyna glanced at Von, silently begging him to help her.

"They fought with us during the attack, Master," the commander said after a pause. "And healed the wounded. Our losses could have been much greater without them. We still have a use for their magic."

Tarn's wintry eyes met hers. "Do we?"

Now that her magic was free, wielding as she did, proved she knew more spells than she pretended. And he held a great interest in that.

Dyna would worry about it later. Holding Tarn's gaze, she inched forward and gently laid her hand over his, making him lower the sword until the tip hit the dirt.

Under her breath, she whispered. "Reason and compassion outweigh violence. This is where gaining their true loyalty starts. With mercy."

Everyone's attention clung to them, waiting for his decision.

She huffed. "Please, Tarn."

As he scanned her face, one end of his mouth hitched. "For you, Dynalya, with pleasure."

CHAPTER 28

Dynalya

To Dyna's surprise, he truly pardoned the mages. Sorren's kitchen was set up in the new tent, and no one else mentioned a word of escape or betrayal. Raiders were chatting again at campfires as they ate a fresh meal, and the tension in the camp seemed to ease. Still, Dyna didn't trust this new passivity yet.

She lingered outside, waiting for Tarn's next move. He *did* say he would punish her. Regardless, she had to celebrate the significant victory of staying his hand. Now Dalton wouldn't have a reason to reveal Yavi's secret, and they could form another plan.

Her knife bounced off the frozen earth, skittering away. With a sigh, Dyna picked it up and tried again. It flew past, missing her target by several inches. She glowered at the charred stump of wood. How did he make it look so effortless?

"The hilt is too weighty for throwing," Von said, appearing at her side. "Try this one instead."

He pulled out a slender knife from his bandolier and handed it to her. It was a flat, solid piece of dark steel. Rough, black cloth wrapped around the thin handle and the pommel was replaced with a simple ring.

"Release with a smooth motion when you throw. Don't flick your wrist or it will spin excessively." Von took out three more, whirling them by the rings in his fingers. She studied his perfect stance and how he grabbed the blade side instead of the hilt. He tossed them one after the other in rapid succession.

Each flawlessly hit the target with low *thunks*. "With time, you will come to calculate the rotation and distance of the target."

Dyna nodded and copied as he had done. The knife missed, but this time, it pierced the dirt. Von handed her two more. She hit the stump on the second try.

"Not bad, but not good enough to subdue a mage." Von tucked her opal knife back in his belt. Only now, she realized he had swiped it back from her. Well, it seemed they drew the line at leaving her with a weapon. "For whatever reason, Tarn accepted your story."

That didn't mean he had believed it.

"Thank you for helping to spare their lives."

"That's important to you, isn't it? To save the lives of your men after all the ones that were lost in Azurite." She searched his startled expression as he tensed. "I saw what happened in your past through Tarn. Magic, if you will. That wasn't your fault, Von. I know you felt it was, but it had nothing to do with duty."

"It had everything to do with it," he said sharply. "I was never supposed to leave the gates unguarded. It was my fault the trolls came."

He truly believed it. Had Tarn bothered to tell him about the viceroy? But after so many years of holding on to the blame, Dyna didn't know if he could forgive himself.

Von rubbed his face. "Every time I consider I can be free, more people die."

Like during the skirmish. He must have almost escaped with Yavi until he saw the knights cutting down his men. No wonder he stayed.

"You think if you turn your back on your vow of a life-servant that history will repeat itself?"

"I know it will." Von then told her the Seer's divination about Yavi. Goosebumps prickled down Dyna's arms at the eerie words. "Fire nearly took her from me the other night. It was my last warning."

Now she finally understood. Von was staying because he believed breaking his holy vow again would result in taking Yavi's life. But there was more than one way to die, and lying to each other did them no favors.

"You need to tell her about this," Dyna said. "About everything. There is much you both need to discuss, but hiding it is only causing you both pain. You're losing her, Von."

His expression flooded with misery. "I know."

It seemed he wanted to say more, but a group of rowdy Raiders passing by interrupted them. They quieted at the sight of her. At the sudden tension, magic crackled on the surface of her skin. Whatever the men saw on her face convinced them to move on.

Von stared at her. "Your eyes are glowing, lass."

She blinked repeatedly and took a breath to calm her Essence. Was that new? "Sorry."

He glanced down at her feet and she knew what he was thinking.

"I won't wear the bangles."

"Aye, well, the keys conveniently went missing the day you attempted an escape." He crossed his arms. "Do you have something to do with that?"

"They might be somewhere out in the woods." Better to let him think she'd lost all the keys.

"Hmm."

Von made no further comment on it and he escorted her back to Tarn's empty tent. She sat at the end of the dining table as she stared up at the large flag with the Ice Phoenix crest. So many secrets must be hidden behind it. She glanced at the history book left for her. It was opened to the portrait of King Lenneus. He had light blue eyes, pale blond hair to his shoulders, and sharp features with a familiar severe beauty. She flipped more pages back to the kings before him. For the past five hundred years, they all had the same face, and went into seclusion after forty years of their reign. The queens were documented to have died in odd accidents, all after giving birth to the next heir.

But there had never been an heir.

Until now.

The amethyst crystal spun, and a brief draft brushed against her legs. She didn't turn around.

"All the kingdoms have their secrets," Tarn said, his low voice raising the hair on her neck. "This one is Azure's."

"Is he immortal?" Dyna whispered.

Tarn sat across from her. "His life was endless like the fae, but no, not immortal."

"You said *was*," Dyna repeated when her mind caught up. "But he could be, right? King Lenneus, or whatever his true name is, must also search for the Tree of the Unending. He planned to become immortal and rule forever—but he never planned for you." She closed the book with the sigil of an interwoven, seven-pointed star.

"They say Sunnëva left the phoenix's power for her children to inherit and that it was lost when they passed away, but it never was," Tarn said. "Jökull's abilities could only be passed down to those who shared the blood of the Ice Phoenix and the Morkhàn clan."

He laid his hand flat on the tabletop, and frost spread from his palm, coating the surface.

"That man didn't know who my mother was the night he took her." His fingers curled, making the ice crack. "He'd been too drunk off his wits at some ball in his castle to recognize the heiress of Old Tanzanite Keep. All he saw was a woman who dared refuse him. Lord Afton lured her to a dark room, held her down and muffled her cries, while the King had his way with her."

Dyna looked away from the intensity of his vivid eyes. The temperature in the tent dropped further, making her breath cloud.

"It wasn't until I was born that he realized the consequences of what he'd done. There can only be one living descendant from both bloodlines to claim the inheritance of the Ice Phoenix."

She recalled the day in the courtyard when he'd sent ice crawling over the cobblestone.

"You took it from King Lenneus," she realized. "And his long life. That's why he wants you dead."

"Well, according to Lord Afton's testimony, before I split his jaw open."

As much as the image made her stomach churn, she couldn't blame Tarn for what he had done. Lord Afton and the Azure King were responsible for the outcome of his life. From enduring Lord Morken's hatred to the loss of his wife.

Dyna sat up straight as she realized something. "Lord Morken ... and your mother are from the same House?"

"The Morken family has always governed Old Tanzanite Keep and they would never allow another House to lay claim over it. Women have no rights to property in Azure. As her father's only heir, my mother was forced to marry a distant Morken cousin. Somehow, Thorne was the best choice."

His expression remained stoic, but Dyna heard the coldness frosting over each word. "So if you die, the King will recover Jökull's abilities. That's why you seek Mount Ida, because he is very determined to kill you." She shook her head. "Immortality isn't invincibility."

He'd dedicated his life to becoming undying because both of his fathers had tried to kill him. He was nearly eaten alive and witnessed everyone he knew torn apart. He spent years making the kingdom tremble at the sound of his name, but truly it was he who was terrified.

Tarn leaned back in his seat and crossed one leg over the other. "I don't seek it out of fear," he said, as though he could read her mind. "I descend from a *god*. My one sole purpose is to inherit what is mine, including the throne of Azure. Once I am immortal, I will become the next Ice Phoenix, and return for Lenneus's head. He will raise an army against me, of course, but by the end, I will have cleansed this land of his scourge, and bury it in ice and snow until nothing remains. Then I will rule over his ashes with none to defy me."

Her eyes widened and her body went cold.

He intended to return Azure to the Everfrost.

"You would destroy the entire kingdom to kill one man?" She could see from his expression, Tarn didn't care who suffered, as long as he got the single thing he cared about most. Revenge. "That would make you a monster."

"Sometimes, to defeat a monster, you must become one." He stood to grab his goblet from the bedside table. It stunned her when he poured himself water instead of wine. "We all have one in us, clawing to get out."

"Even me?"

Tarn faced her and the air thinned as those ice-blue eyes seemed to see past everything to the depths of her being. "Especially you. I saw her out there when you came at me with the arrow and when you considered letting me die. She was there, looking back at me. And you know what I thought? Should you ever let her out, she would be glorious."

Dyna could picture it. She swathed in a menacing green light, stepping out of the darkness like a wraith. A creature that laid waste to everything in its wake.

She shuddered and looked away. "I suppose you're right. I could easily become a monster, too. It's what happens in our lives that can influence which way we fall, but you are *choosing* to be one. This path you're walking will only lead to your destruction and everyone who follows you. Half your men are dead. The rest will follow if you don't stop."

"I already know what must be done." He returned to the table. "It begins with Mount Ida. Your Essence is free, and I'm allowing you to keep it, granted you cooperate."

She glowered at him, knowing exactly what he wanted.

"Regarding that, where are my black clovers?"

Her glower switched to an innocent pout, and she shrugged. "Perhaps they've been claimed by the forest somewhere."

Tarn pressed on his forehead. "You have exhausted my patience, Dyna."

"And mine has reached its limit." She tried not to react to his use of her name. It was the second time he had called her by it, and that gave her a small hope they could find common ground after all.

"I'm beginning to find you rather tiresome. You, of all people, know what I'm capable of, yet you're so determined to incur my wrath." But the threat didn't match Tarn's idle tone.

"I think you would go farther if you requested things differently." She crossed her arms. "How about you learn to make friends instead of enemies?"

He arched an eyebrow. "You want to be my...*friend?*"

She flushed at the way he put it. Like she was a silly girl with childish notions.

"Well, come now, friends tell all their secrets." His mouth curled on one end as he watched her squirm. He was teasing her, which was so bizarre. "Why are you going to Mount Ida?"

Well, she knew enough about him, so she traced the grooves on the tabletop as she told him her story. He listened without interrupting, his attention never leaving her face as she described the Shadow demon coming to her village on the winter solstice, and how it tore through the villagers like paper. Her throat dried as the back of her eyes stung, but she kept her voice steady when she spoke of her family's death.

Dyna wiped a stray tear. "I hid, listening to it prowl in the dark as it hunted me. Whenever night falls…"

"You feel it there."

She nodded. "The only way to destroy it is with the Sōl Medallion."

"Destroying a Shadow demon," Tarn mused. "That's a lofty goal, if not incredibly stupid."

Dyna then regretted telling him anything. "You don't know how far I will go to protect my family."

"Those who protect the weak die."

"You protected me," she reminded him. He could say it was to retrieve an asset, but they both knew he saved her life out there in the woods. "And I returned the favor. Not many would have done the same, mind you. Whether that was the right choice, I have not yet decided."

They stared at each other past the flames flickering on the candelabra placed between them. "The way I see it, if you hunt the Shadow, the only place you will go is through Death's Gate," Tarn said, completely ignoring her statement. "Unless…"

"Unless?"

He took a drink. "You join me."

For a moment, she was too stunned to reply. Von entered and set their evening meal on the table without a word. After tasting a serving of the roasted chicken, greens, and rice, he served them and left.

Dyna deliberated for a moment, then picked up her plate and came to sit next to Tarn. "Are you asking me or telling me? Because I won't be your slave or your spy. And I won't be part of any destruction. If you want my help, then give up your vendetta against the Azure King. You can have a life of wonder instead of death." She hesitated before hovering her hand over his bandaged arm. He watched in silence as the green light of her Essence drifted down and healed him, hardly leaving behind a scar. "If you give it a chance, I can show you."

He gave a contemplative hum. "Are you trying to charm me?"

"Is it working?"

"Hardly." Tarn picked up his fork and dinner knife to cut into his chicken. "You reproach my ways, yet I think you understand them clearly. I find it amusing that here we are, discussing it like civilized people, when several days ago you were ready to skewer me outside the grove."

Dyna frowned at him dully and ate some rice. "To defend my mate, yes, I would have killed you."

He paused. "Mate?"

"I'm bonded to Cassiel." The sound of his name sent a throb through her heart, and the rune for truth glowed blue.

Tarn rested his chin on a fist. "Interesting. The divination named you the Maiden."

"Yes, and?"

"Have you consummated your marriage?"

Dyna's face flamed at the personal question.

"Ah, fair virgin you still are. What husband doesn't bed his wife? Does he not know where to put it?"

She stared at him, speechless.

He noticed her expression and cleared his throat. "I've angered you. Pardon. That was unbecoming of me to say."

Taken aback by the unexpected apology, Dyna's anger deflated. "Careful, Tarn. You nearly sound like a decent person."

"Hmm. We can't have that." He took a bite of food. It may have been the first time she had seen him eat, too. His appetite was returning now that he was off the potion. "I do wonder, if you should lose your maidenhead, will the divination no longer come to pass?"

"I hardly think the fates care about my virginity," Dyna huffed.

"Should we put it to the test?"

Her eyes bulged at the suggestive joke that she would have never expected from him. "Tarn, simply because I won't kill you, it doesn't mean I won't stab you."

His mouth twitched in a slight smirk. "Well, now I understand your reaction when Benton first placed the veil on you. It separated you from each other and it hurt."

She pressed a fist to her chest. It still did.

"Tell me, how is it you became blood bonded?"

Dyna didn't want to answer, but his intent gaze didn't leave room to deny him. She shifted in her chair. "It simply came to be."

"It was a marriage of convenience, then."

"In what manner?"

"Well, you're no ordinary woman, Dynalya Astron. You carry the blood of a mage. The only map in existence to Mount Ida is bound to your very Essence. You are a mighty convenience."

"Cassiel doesn't care for magic and riches."

Tarn leaned forward. "Then what does he care about?"

Dyna didn't know the answer. What did Cassiel care about? He was searching for his mother. That was his purpose on this quest, but what would happen at the end of it? What would the Realms say about their marriage? From what she knew of Celestial history and humans, their reaction wouldn't be a good one. She was no one of note to marry a prince. It was a worry in the back of Dyna's mind. A fear that it would end up tearing them apart.

"What is the meaning of your expression?" Tarn asked, amused. "You seem distressed. Did you not hear his passionate proclamation to never cease searching for you? Might that not be your answer?"

Dyna looked away to the hot coals glowing in the brazier.

"Love is such a sordid feeling and a waste of time. It's not worth the tears." Tarn poured himself more water, then poured a cup for her. "Take my advice. Don't allow yourself to be encumbered by something so mawkish as romantic attachments."

She waited until her misted sight cleared to look at him again. "Is that what you tell yourself when you think of Aisling?"

His amusement faded, and the change in mood marked the end of their conversation. They said no more, and after their meal, Dyna eventually drifted off to sleep where she was. At some point, she heard his quiet voice speaking to Von.

"She no longer cowers in fear of me." She felt Tarn's stare linger on her sleeping form curled in the chair before his presence stirred the cool air with his passing. "Not that it would matter in the end."

When she sleepily peeked through her lashes, he was gone.

201

CHAPTER 29

Dynalya

The next evening, Dyna curiously studied the runes burned into Tarn's tent, the charms on the roof, and all the artifacts strewn about. Each one was different, created and left behind by different hands.

"You have been all over the world," she said, picking up a small polished statue of a water dragon made of jade.

"You cannot understand the world unless you see it," Tarn replied absentmindedly from his spot at the head of the table. A crease formed in between his pale brows as he read a document. "Put that down."

"Because it's valuable?"

"Because it's cursed."

Dyna quickly returned it to his desk and continued perusing his clutter. Among the artifacts was a small chest stamped with the sigil of Xián Jīng. It was gilded with decorative corners and sealed shut with a golden clasp. "What is the purpose of carrying all these things? Do they have some use, or are you secretly a hoarder?"

"Don't touch that," he said without looking up.

Dyna's fingers halted an inch away from it, and she folded her arms behind her back. "Why? What's inside of your fancy box?"

"The past and the future."

She glowered at his sarcastic response. Did he have to be evasive about everything? Tarn reached for the goblet that was usually at his side and grabbed only air.

Dyna hid a smile and went for the decanter on the sideboard. "I'll get you some wine."

She'd successfully nursed him free of the foul drug, but he could still have a drink. "How do you feel now that your mind is free of Witch's Brew? If you have trouble with insomnia, I have something for that and it smells much more pleasant than bitter herbs."

Tarn was too absorbed in what he was reading to answer. Coming on his right side, she poured while trying to catch a peek at what had his rapt attention.

Tarn covered up the document. "Do you mind?"

"Still not the trusting sort," Dyna teased.

Instead of sitting at the end as she usually did, she sat beside him. Now that they were cordial, she had to convince him to let her go. She saved his life. He owed her that much.

"And you trust too easily." There was a nuance in Tarn's tone that made her smile waver. He sorted through the missives on the table. "Have you thought of my offer?"

"Is that what you call it?"

"Once I have the Unending, slaying a demon will be nothing," Tarn said, his pale eyes meeting hers. "By my side, you will achieve everything you desire. All you have to do is pledge your loyalty to me. This is me *asking*. In case it escapes your attention, I never do. By all means, think it over, but I won't ask twice."

Dyna frowned. "Is that the scope of your proposal? *Asking* me to join you? Therefore, I should be grateful and serve you loyally as you pursue your wicked cause?" She had changed out of her black leathers into a blue dress to display that she wouldn't become another spy. "I thought after last night you would give up this vendetta."

His face hardened. "Then you're shortsighted. I will destroy Azure and render the entire Jökull and Morken line to nothing until I'm the only one left standing."

A scatter of chills shot through her chest. She should have realized that would be part of his plan. By ending those family lines, there would be no other Ice Phoenix. No one left to steal that inheritance from him as he had stolen it from the Azure King.

"Then you will have a kingdom of bone and ice."

"So be it," he said tightly. "I'm offering you what you've never dreamed of, Dyna. An abundance of wealth and power. Protection. Nothing would ever threaten you again." As he spoke, something unexpected entered his gaze.

She slowly shook her head. "I don't need that. Gold and power don't sway me. And I think we both know I can protect myself."

His brief annoyance eased into a smirk, and he steepled his fingers. "Do you refuse me because of your Celestial? Bring him too, if you want. He could be useful."

Dyna stood in angry incredulity, and her hands flickered green at the ravaging protectiveness she felt for her mate. The wards hummed. "I refuse you because I won't support the destruction of an entire kingdom. Regardless of what you offer me."

Tarn studied her face and whatever her expression showed. "Then it will be at your peril."

"Is that it, then? If I'm not with you, then I'm against you?"

A pause as he considered her words. "Whether you go to the island or stay on this land, without me, I don't see you surviving." Then, to her horror, Tarn brought his goblet closer as he drew out a vial of Witch's Brew from his coat pocket.

"You don't need that anymore!" Dyna slapped it from his hand, accidentally knocking over the cup. He snatched up the papers before they were soaked.

Tarn turned to her, his brow lowering over his cooling eyes. It sent a faint quiver down her spine, and it shocked her to realize she hadn't felt it in days. When had she become so comfortable with him?

He set the documents on his chair and took a step forward. She forced herself not to move, refusing to give him any more gain. But Tarn hadn't done it to frighten her, though his next movement did.

"I will play no more games with you." He held out his hand. "Join me. Together, we would leave a mark on history."

There was no doubt what kind of history he would bring.

She stared at Tarn's open palm, at the long elegant fingers that swiftly ended lives. Ones that were once wrapped around her throat. They were pointing at her now. Not in threat, but in invitation. A small action that carried a great significance. It was something she had never thought to receive from him.

Not in this way, with this offer.

Her mouth trembled to realize what he was truly asking. This was him removing a small piece of his armor. Taking his hand meant he was giving her a chance to gain his trust, and with it, she would gain a powerful ally instead of an enemy. She could see how far she could go with that type of power, but the cost was climbing another mountain of bones and losing herself.

As much as she had hated Tarn and feared him still, some part of her liked that he reached out to her. Relieved that he was capable of it. But more lingered under his ask, something that had surfaced unbeknownst to either of them until that instant. Suddenly there, or perhaps slowly growing in the shadows of their encounters, but neither dared to admit it…because they both knew the truth before she ever opened her mouth to respond.

It had never been a question.

Her heart. Her soul. Her body.

They would always—*always*—choose Cassiel.

Dyna met his gaze and hardened hers. "No."

There was a pause as her definitive reply fluttered in the quiet tent. Tarn's fingers curled into a loose fist, and he dropped his hand. Something flickered in his expression. It was fleeting, too quick for her to know if she truly saw it. Then his eyes fixed on a spot behind her head.

"Thank you," he said. "For reminding me why we're here. Somewhere amongst our days together, we have both briefly forgotten it. This has gone on long enough. We will arrive at the port come dawn. It's time you open the journal and give me the map."

She sighed, tired of this old discussion. "I won't."

"You won't, or you can't?"

Dyna held quiet, her pulse speeding. The truth rune was at her back.

His eyes dropped to her, a knowing in them. "Answer."

"I said I'd come with you willingly. I didn't say I'd give you my map."

"It was never in the journal to begin with, was it?" At her silence, Tarn's chest rose with a low breath, passing audibly through his teeth, but he didn't look angry, which put her on edge. He scoffed a dry laugh and rubbed his jaw as if it impressed him. "Ah. You're capable of being clever, after all. Therein lies your predicament."

"Mine?" She crossed her arms, feeling a little smug for outsmarting him. "I'm hardly concerned."

"You should be. I agreed to spare your pathetic Guardians, provided you give me what I want."

Dyna's smirk dropped at the threat. "That's not what I said—"

The mood rune behind him burned red. Anger wasn't the right word. He was furious.

Her breath caught at Tarn's icy grip wrapping around her arm. Yet he didn't squeeze hard enough to hurt, and his calm expression didn't change. "Regardless of what you said, the exchange was implied. I'm not in the business of kindness, but I will give you one last chance."

I won't ask twice. Yet he had for her.

Perhaps she should have given him something, but Dyna had found her bravery and was holding to it. "Whether it's today or tomorrow, the fact remains. I will not yield."

"You will." Tarn grabbed the back of her neck and yanked her to him, close enough to see the deep darkness beneath the frost in his eyes. "Even if it's not by choice."

Then his mouth was on hers.

Dyna squirmed and pushed against his vice hold, squealing in horror against his lips. It was a kiss like winter's breath, cold and hard, coating her in frost. In it, she felt his dismissal. Of her and any influence she might have had over him. Of any human decency that may have been cultivating in his conscience. The person Tarn could have been was gone and buried beneath the snow a long time ago.

Left to die a lonely death.

Dyna broke his hold and shoved him back with an angry gasp. "What are you doing?" she shrieked.

He exhaled a husky scoff and laughed. "I was merely testing the parameters of this prophecy. Clearly, you didn't enjoy that, and neither did I. You leave much to be desired."

Dyna drew back her hand and slapped him sharply across the face.

It snapped his head to the side. He stood there a moment, stunned.

She wiped her cold mouth, but it didn't remove her shame. "That is the last time you ever do that."

Tarn worked his jaw, her handprint pink and stark against his pale skin. "Yes, it will be."

Whatever reservations he might have briefly had for her faded beneath the frigidity of his stare. The first version of him she'd met outside of Willows Grove returned. No...he'd always been there. She simply allowed herself to forget it.

"Truth be told, I never needed the map," Tarn said. "I only needed you. The map, or the key rather, is right here." He tapped her temple. "I merely have to retrieve it."

She recoiled. "You wouldn't."

Above their heads, the Forewarning Crystal spun for a moment. Brisk wind blew in from outside as Von, Novo, and Len entered and stood at attention. There was a resignation on their faces, and no one looked at her.

He'd known.

When Tarn had made his offer, it had been another test. Not for her—but for himself. To see if he could truly not be swayed by her. Even with that rare hint of hope she had caught in his gaze, he knew she would refuse him.

And he had planned for it.

Panic bubbled up her throat. "Please, don't do this. I know you don't want to do this."

"You have wasted your energy in trying to change me, Maiden. I'm not someone to share your emotional scars with. I'm not your friend."

Maiden.

The disparity was a line in the sand.

Dyna clenched her shaking fists, wanting to ram them in Tarn's face. Disbelief warred within her chest. She saw him for who he was in the past while forgetting who he had become now.

"Oh." His mouth curved with mock sympathy at the bitter tears welling in her eyes. "I told you who I was, and you chose not to believe me. I can hardly be blamed for your disappointment."

There was no kindness on Tarn's face. He was choosing to be her enemy. He chose it when she didn't take his hand, or maybe when he'd almost died for her sake, nearly meeting his undoing.

They were always going to end up here.

Dyna filled her hands with magic, and the wards instantly knocked her down. She screamed into the rug as magic speared into her like a thousand bolts of lightning. The pain rendered her immobile, leaving her gasping for air.

"I am the rightful King of Azure," he said above her. "And I will have what's mine."

New slave bangles clamped around her ankles, stealing away her Essence again. Novo and Len hauled her up and dragged her for the entrance.

"Tarn!" she shouted at his back. "It doesn't have to be this way!"

He ignored her, pouring more wine into his stupid goblet.

"If you do this, I will fight you," she swore. "I will do everything I need to stop you."

"You have neither the will nor the means to fight me," he said with a sigh. As if he was tired of her childishness, for she understood nothing at all. "You have overplayed your hand. I've always had the power here. You were foolish enough to think otherwise—little colt."

Dyna froze.

Tell me, how do you tame a wild horse?

It all began with building trust. Instead of crushing her spirit, he altered between placid and the perfect amount of pressure. Everything he had said and done had a purpose. He desensitized her to his presence. Trained her with his ways.

This whole time, Tarn had been taming her.

He told her he would, yet she had been completely blind to every step he took in their interactions, making her think she was gaining leverage against him when she earned his confidence. Until he fit her with the bit and bridle.

The truth of how seamlessly he had manipulated her was a blow. It landed somewhere in her chest, leaving her winded. Dyna could only stare at his back blankly as they led her away.

Tarn so easily defeated her.

But it wasn't a victory he enjoyed. Not when he couldn't look at her now.

Tarn only kissed her to see if he cared. He was doing this now—because he did.

"I know the truth," she said faintly when they reached the threshold. "I'm a weakness. And you hate that you have one."

Tarn stiffened.

There was a shift in his shoulders, a turn to his head, but they pulled her outside, and the tent flaps settled in place, concealing him from view.

CHAPTER 30

Dynalya

With each step of her dragging feet, Dyna felt the saddle tighten on her back. Len and Novo forced her along the muddied path. No one spoke as Von led them away from Tarn's tent. The air was heavy with the thoughts she could sense from them and her own growing fear.

When Benton's tent came into view, her heart rate spiked. "Please, Von. If he gets the Unending, we're all finished. Every life within these shores will be wiped out."

The commander's pace remained steadily onward.

"Is this what you want?" she asked him. "You know what he plans and what this will mean for Azure. Help me stop him."

"Kata," Len hissed in her language, telling her to be silent.

"He serves the Master, lass," Novo said under his breath. "His hands are tied."

"No, they aren't." Dyna kicked out, nearly catching Von's leg, but they hauled her back. "You fear the consequences of disobeying the holy law? The only law is the one of the soul. You know what this is doing to you, but do you know what will happen if you don't fight? Yavi will die."

Von whipped around, his expression warning her to shut her mouth.

But Dyna picked at that wound, knowing it was her only chance. "She will, Von. And not because of the fates or some judgment of the Heavens, but because you're holding on to some belief that this is right. He made you believe that you owe him something. You *don't*. Tarn stole your will, and he will steal her from you, too."

His expression wavered, fear flickering behind the anger.

Benton peered out of his tent. "Ah, you're here. Good. Bring her in."

The interruption was enough to settle Von's manacles back in place.

She thrashed, digging her feet into the ground. "Stop this."

"*You* can stop this, Dyna." He exhaled heavily. "Merely tell him what he wants to know. Where is Mount Ida?"

"You know I can't tell him."

A somberness fell over Von, and he moved back for Novo and Len to drag her forward. She screamed at him, and his features creased as he watched her be taken. He knew it was wrong, but he had been chained to Tarn for too long.

Well, she wouldn't take this.

Dyna elbowed Len in the face and punched Novo in the kidney. He released her with a curse. But she only made it two steps before Benton snapped his fingers. Her limbs locked in place and her mouth sealed shut as his red Essence carried her inside the tent and deposited her in a chair. Dyna tried to fight against his power, but she couldn't move.

Clayton and Dalton lingered in the shadowy corner of the tent, silently watching.

Von followed them in and stood by the entrance. "You're only to extract the location of Mount Ida from her mind. Nothing else. She isn't to be harmed."

"Yes, yes, I know." Benton waved him away as he flipped through his grimoire.

"Painless, Benton."

"Of course." He smiled at her over his shoulder, but it was unkind and scheming. "I'm not a barbarian."

Dyna shook her head at Von, her bravery draining away. Pure panic was taking its place. She was helpless. Restrained. At the mercy of a mage that saw her as an object and not a person.

"I will be right here," he said.

The reassurance did nothing to quell her fear. Sweat trickled down her neck, the thud of her heart pounding loud in her ears. She tried to think of a way out, but nothing came to her.

Why had she come back?

She had escaped. Her plan had worked. If only she had spared no sympathy for that man, she would have reunited with Cassiel. He would have found her by now. She knew it. A piece of her shriveled up and died to know her freedom had been right there within reach.

If only she had let Tarn die.

For once, Dyna wished she had been heartless enough to let him suffer an agonizing death. A dark thought wanted that now. But she had saved him because she wanted to believe he might have been someone worth saving. And he betrayed her.

I can hardly be to blame...

No, she was.

The amethyst crystal above their heads spun, and a soft voice called from outside.

Von swept the tent flaps aside to reveal Elon. "What is it?"

"A word, Commander."

Dyna shook her head, silently begging. She was more afraid to be left alone with Benton than anyone else in this camp.

"I will be right back," Von promised, glaring at the old mage. "Don't begin the spell until I return."

Benton waved him away in annoyance. "Make it quick then. I don't seek to earn more of the Master's displeasure."

Von shot her one last look and stepped outside. The tent flap settled in place behind him, and Dyna dropped her head. Tears dripped onto her lap.

"There, there." Benton tsked, lifting her chin. "No need to cry, child. I will never let Tarn get what he wants. That man deserves much, but not that."

She blinked through her blurry vision, staring up at him in confusion.

At the flick of Benton's finger, his magic released her. "We're leaving this place."

"You're setting me free?" she asked once will returned to her body.

"Unfortunately, you're too valuable. The perfect token to escape this place and return to where we belong."

Clayton's eyes glowed faint yellow, wearing the same slithering smile as his father. Dalton couldn't look at her. He stared at his feet, fidgeting with his staff.

"I helped you!" Dyna shouted. "This is how you repay me?"

Benton shrugged. "You have our many thanks."

"What are you going to do to me?"

"Your family is gone, but if you could see them again, would you want to?" he asked. "I can give you that."

She shook. "How?"

"Through a deep and everlasting dream. And I promise it will be painless."

A horrible feeling sank in her stomach when she realized what he was about to do.

"Father." Dalton took a step. "We shouldn't do this. It isn't right."

"Quiet." Clayton shoved him back.

"It needs to be done, son. This is the only way we stop being slaves." Benton looked back at her. "I will do what I must to stop Tarn from becoming immortal. With your mind gone, no one can ever reveal Azeran's map. Don't pretend this isn't what you wanted."

"I would never show it to him," she said.

"After what you pulled, I cannot take that chance."

This couldn't be happening. She had to think of a way out.

You haven't the means nor the will to fight me.

It had always come down to that. Her ability. Her will. In everything she faced, she always felt weak and too scared to act. It had gotten her here. It wasn't a question of good against evil anymore. But what she was willing to do—to survive.

"What if...I choose to go with you?" Dyna asked. "That's what you want, isn't it? To bring me to Magos. My Astron lineage will restore your position with House Slater."

A new path formed before her. The steps needed to cross it would carry a heavy cost. There was no debate anymore. Knowing what awaited, the choice had already been made. She straightened in the chair. Tarn's last words continued circling in her head, each one fortifying her decision.

You haven't the means...

"Would you come willingly?" Clayton asked.

Dalton shook his head at her, his brown eyes distraught.

Aware of the crystals above, Dyna nodded without speaking.

"Stop." Dalton rushed forward. "Father, please don't do this!"

...nor the will...

Clayton hit his back with a flare of yellow magic, knocking him down. Dalton rolled over and punched his brother with a glowing fist. The tent filled with the sounds of their curses and blows.

"You would submit?" Benton pressed.

Swallowing, Dyna nodded again. Her heart pounded, and her legs braced.

...to fight me.

The old mage gave her a mocking chuckle. "Did you truly think I would believe that?"

Dyna glared up at him. *"No."*

She snatched the hindrance arrow from her boot and shoved it into his throat. Benton stared at her, choked sounds escaping his open mouth. Dark blood gushed out of the wound and his lips, coating her hand red. There was so much blood. Benton crumpled to the ground. Gasping, Dyna leaped out of her chair, stumbling away from what she'd done.

She...she killed him.

The stain of that settled over her as it marred an integral part of her being.

The veils were gone—both of them. They vanished off the camp and from her body at the same time. It struck her all at once.

Freedom. The bond. *Cassiel.*

He was near.

She felt his shock and his sheer relief that made her want to weep. The bond sparked in her chest like a small bud of warmth.

Dalton stumbled forward with a strangled sound, holding out his shaking hands at his father on the ground. Clayton bellowed a scream that was a mix of fury and anguish. He threw a spell, and Dyna dove for the exit, landing outside.

Meet me at the cliff! She sent through the bond, praying he was coming from that direction.

She scrambled to her feet when Clayton stormed out of the tent. He tossed a blast of yellow Essence for her head. She threw herself out of the way. It missed her by inches, its heat searing her skin. The spell hit the ground with a *boom* so powerful that it shook the earth, tossing debris into the air.

Dyna scrambled to her feet as the earth opened out from under her. A scream tore from her throat. "Von!"

He was her enemy.

The one to deliver her here.

But in that last cry of desperation, she called his name. Because she knew, in her heart, he was the only one who could help her now.

Von caught her hand before she fell into the hole and hauled her back onto solid ground. Elon was close behind, but before either could ask what happened, a force blew out, skittering magic through the air. It hit them all, slamming her body into the dirt. Sharp rocks bit into her chin, dust coating her teeth. Clayton pinned her with his magic, and she screamed, clawing at the ground as he dragged her back to him. He threw himself on top of her, and his hot hands clamped around her head, yellow light flaring.

"Get off me!" She threw her head back and smashed it into his nose.

Clayton's hold slipped. Dyna rolled away from him and swung her boot into his jaw, knocking him back. She looked past him to Dalton. He held his father's limp body in his lap. Tears streamed down his face as he looked at her, his face full of heartbreak and questioning why.

Heavy breaths shuddered out of her lungs, and her mouth trembled. "I-I'm—"

"She killed my father!" Clayton shouted, the accusation punching her in the stomach. "The veil is down!"

Von's wide eyes fixed on her, where he and Elon were rising to their feet. Raiders gathered behind them at the commotion.

Dyna bolted for the forest. On her third breath, she heard them give chase. The camp was a blur of tents and shouting voices. She sprinted past the perimeter and cut into the forest. Her lungs burned for air.

Don't stop! She bit back a sob at the sound of Cassiel's rich voice in her mind. *Run! Keep running!*

Her legs pumped as she sprinted as fast as she could. The enchanted bangles beat against her ankles with every step. She couldn't think about that now. Branches whipped at her face as she tore through the bushes. Her heartbeat thudded in her ears, urging her onward. She ran and ran through the dense trees, leaping over logs and dodging low branches. The voices were closer. Her fear doubled at the sound of neighing horses joining the hunt.

Dyna surged out of the forest onto the flat, rocky clearing, ending in a cliff with a five-hundred-foot drop. But the dark sky was empty. It held nothing but the moon obscured by clouds. She whimpered and whipped around as the Raiders came up behind her. They had her surrounded with no place to go. The men parted as Tarn rode forward on his horse. He dismounted, with Von and Clayton coming up behind him.

Dynalya.

She looked out deep into the forested ravine and spotted figures with colorful wings headed in her direction. Moonlight glinted on their golden-scaled armor. The white flame of their weapons glowed brightly in the night. The Valkyrie. But she focused on the one dressed in black, his ebony wings flaring behind him. The sight broke through her adrenaline, and she let out a relieved cry.

"Jump!" she heard his shout in the distance.

"Stop her," Tarn commanded.

Flaming spears and arrows zipped past her head, swiftly taking down Raiders like tumbling pillars. Von yanked his master out of range from the attack and used his body to shield him. That one small action bought her an opening.

Von looked back at her over his shoulder and mouthed one word: *Go.*

Dyna didn't hesitate. She sprinted for the edge and leaped. Her arms and legs whirled through the air in a groundless run. Cassiel soared toward her, and she reached for him. Their fingers swiped past each other, missing by centimeters. And she plummeted against the roaring wind, her red hair trailing after her.

Cassiel's frightened shout reverberated through them both.

His beautiful large wings tucked against his back, and he dove, speeding against the roaring wind. Their hands strained to reach each other. All she could think about was that this was how they had met. With a cliff and the open sky.

Cassiel latched on to her hands and wrenched her tight against him. His wings snapped open right before they hit the ground, and they soared into the sky. The Valkyrie circled to join their flank.

Passing the cliff where the Raiders stood on the edge, she met Tarn's cold gaze.

Let me go, she prayed. *Please, let me go.*

His silhouette grew smaller and smaller as he watched them fly away into the night. Then the man who had kept her captive turned and strolled back to the woods. Tears welled in her eyes.

She was free.

Dyna looked at her bonded. "Cassiel." His name caught in her throat as she sobbed. The bond continued to weave itself together piece by piece, at last falling into place. Filling her with all the emotions. His thoughts. His touch. The relief. The joy. So overwhelming, she wept into his chest, clutching him tightly. "Cassiel."

His own eyes shone wet as he held her close. *"Lev sheli—"*

A blow crashed into her back. Yellow light swarmed her body, and pain cleaved through her skull, stealing her breath.

Cassiel screamed her name. The impact sent them careening through the air. The wind slashed at them, and she didn't know if they were falling.

Clayton struck her with a spell. She recognized his magic. This was his revenge for his father. To leave her a broken shell after she had finally reunited with her mate.

Dyna tried to fight the mage. To keep him out of her head. She tried so hard to build her mental shield—but he was in.

His magic slithered through her very being, immobilizing her body as he invaded her mind and buried all of her in a dark corner of her consciousness. She tumbled through a chasm, leaving the sky and the moonlight above to fade further and further.

Cassiel's cry followed her into the darkness as the last spark of magic swept her away.

CHAPTER 31

Cassiel

They fell like stars from the sky. Cassiel fought against the wind to open his wings as the ground rushed to meet them. He righted himself in time to skate over the trees, but it was too late to climb the air. He had seconds to shield Dyna with his body and wings and roll so he would hit the ground first before they crashed. The collision snapped several bones. He must have gone unconscious for a few seconds because the next thing he knew, Sowmya was shaking him awake. Cassiel breathed through the pain as his blood worked to heal him. Valkyrie landed in the distance, the sound of beating hooves nearing. A black form appeared in his blurred vision, whining and nudging to get through his wings.

"Oh, Gods. Dyna." Cassiel jerked up and let his wings fall away to reveal her still body in his arms.

The clouds parted, and moonlight fell over Dyna as everyone gathered around her. She was covered with scratches and bruises. Her dress was torn and caked with dried blood. But her eyes—once bright green and full of life— were vacant. She stared past him to the sky. At nothing.

It flooded Cassiel with fear. "Dyna?"

Zev keened, nuzzling her cheek. She didn't stir.

"Shield us," Rawn said.

Lucenna cast out a cloaking spell that rippled through the air.

Cassiel held her bruised face in his shaking hands. She was ice cold, but he felt the faint pulse in her wrists. The newly reformed bond was still there, so why wasn't she? "Dyna?"

Zev shifted. "What happened? Something struck you, and you fell out of the sky!"

"They struck *her*." He patted her cheek. "Dyna!"

There was no sign that she had heard them. Her blank face made his insides twist. Normally, the bond thrummed with her emotions and thoughts, but now it was quiet, her consciousness far away and out of his reach. He didn't understand.

The bindings on her ankles matched the collar Tarn had first put on her. Maybe that was it. Taking out Rawn's enchanted knife, he hacked them off. The bangles fell to the ground, but still nothing.

"Dyna?" Cassiel called shakily. "Can you hear me?"

"I stayed," Zev said, taking her other hand. "I stayed. I'm here."

She didn't react to them at all. Every part of him was shivering.

Zev shook her. "Dyna!"

Rawn grabbed his arm. "Cease."

"Why does she look like that?" he demanded. "What's wrong with her?"

Rawn observed her catatonic state, sadly shaking his head. "I do not know. Her eyes, they are..."

"Empty," Lucenna gasped.

"They hit her with a spell," Cassiel said, punching the ground. This couldn't be. He had found her and lost her in the same moment. "They did this to her."

"She's desolate," Lucenna said. "A wicked practice the mages do to their rebellious wives or daughters to expunge their minds of memory and personality. Nothing but a shell to do with what they please. Dyna is alive, but only just."

Cassiel wanted to scream. He couldn't stand the sight of his bonded this way. There was no recognition in her. Nothing.

He gently gathered Dyna in his arms, feeling like he was dying all over again. Her features fell out of focus because his vision blurred. He thought of the way her smile lit up when she saw something new. Of her laughter when he said something unintentionally funny. Of the feel of her hand always reaching out to take his. Of the soft, genuine moments where she had knocked down his walls. Was all of that lost?

There was no hiding the pain splintering through him. He didn't care to. He could only sit there, holding his broken mate and fighting to breathe. Because for the last few months, she had given air to his lungs. Dyna had been a spark of light in his darkness, but he had been afraid to want it, because he knew if he lost it, there would be no repairing the pieces.

"Is that it then?" Zev asked, his voice breaking. "She's gone?"

"No," Lucenna said. "She is in there somewhere."

Her words were like a blow to his stomach. It dislodged the lump in his throat, and he and Zev sucked in a breath.

Cassiel looked up at her. "Can you fix this?"

Lucenna fidgeted with her hands. "N-no, yes, I mean, I know there is a spell to reverse it, but only a skilled mage can perform such complex cognition magic."

He leaped to his feet, cradling Dyna to him, because now that there was hope of a cure, he wouldn't stop to get it. "If there is a way, then you must undo it."

"You know nothing of magic, Cassiel. I cannot simply *undo* such a spell."

Rawn placed a hand on his shoulder, walking past him to Lucenna. "You are a powerful sorceress, my lady. If anyone should have the power to heal Lady Dyna, I believe it to be you."

She sighed. "I don't know if I can do it."

"Please," Zev said. "You have to try."

Looking down at Dyna somberly, Lucenna inhaled and nodded. She opened her satchel and flicked her hand. The tent swirled out into the air, spinning as it grew and landed a few feet away. "Bring her."

"Form a perimeter and keep watch," Cassiel said to Yelrakel, his next words a near growl. "If anyone tries to come near, kill them."

The Valkyrie bowed.

He headed for Lucenna's small tent and was reminded of how big it was when he entered. The candles were lit with purple flames, and crystals dangling from the ceiling offered soft light. One end held the kitchen area with a dining table. The other side was a desk with books and scrolls and her orb resting on a brass metal stand. The air seemed to crackle at the faint touch of magic, and it smelled the same as before, like sage, cinnamon, and lavender.

Ignoring the mess of clothing and books in random stacks placed around the tent, Cassiel laid Dyna on the four-poster bed as Zev and Rawn entered behind him.

Lucenna began flipping through some thick tomes. With each book she went through, she grew more anxious.

"What are you searching for?" Cassiel asked.

"For a record of the spell I need." She dropped her head in her hands, fingers pulling at her hair. "But I don't have a cognition magic book."

A heavy dread fell over them at the understanding that she couldn't help them.

Cassiel glanced at the orb. "Wait, your brother. Might he know something?"

Lucien had helped Dyna before when she'd been wounded by the grindylows. It had been a blow to his pride, but right now, Cassiel felt his desperation climbing. He would grovel to the mage if that's what it took to get Dyna back.

"Gods, you're right." Lucenna sat straight and concentrated on the crystal ball. It fogged with white smoke and cleared as his image materialized.

Cassiel and the others came to stand behind her. It was about time they met him. Lucien was a male version of his twin sister. Long silver-white hair was braided from his handsome face, and lilac eyes lined in pale white lashes regarded her. He was dressed in fine deep blue robes with his white-wood staff resting against the wall behind him.

"Lucenna?" He straightened when he noticed them. "Who—"

"These are the travel companions I spoke of before. We reunited again, but that isn't important right now." Lucenna waved it away when he tried to ask more. "I will properly introduce you later, Lucien. Right now, I need your help. Dyna has been placed under the *halucinor* spell and I don't know how to reverse it."

Lucenna had spoken so fast her words blended together, and Cassiel hardly understood what she said.

Lucien blinked at her for a moment to make sense of it, and his eyes widened. "How did that happen?"

"There's no time to explain. Can you help me?"

"To reform her mind, you will need a vast amount of Essence. It takes years to perfect such a delicate process, which is why most don't bother with it." The mage looked at something below out of sight as he shuffled through pages. He must be sitting at his desk, too. He stood and went out of view briefly, then returned with a thick book. He set it down below and rapidly flipped through more pages. "Not even I have performed a reversal before. It's very difficult to do, Lu. You might inadvertently hurt her."

Lucenna groaned and kneaded her temples.

Cassiel didn't like the doubt between them. They had to try everything they could to save Dyna. He finally found her. He wouldn't let anyone give up.

He removed the previously plucked feathers out of his pocket. "These enhance magic. Can they be of any use?"

"He's a Celestial?" Lucien at them, and his sister nodded. "With those, you can perform an *animus* healing spell."

"What is that?" Zev asked. "What is wrong with the other spell?"

"Lucenna isn't advanced enough to cast a reformation," Lucien said. "However, Celestial feathers have natural curative traces in them. In the past, we used them to cast powerful healing spells."

"But *animus* is for concussions," Lucenna said.

"Precisely. Right now, Dyna's mind is broken. An *animus* spell heals brain injuries as well as reconstructs fragments of broken memory."

"Lady Dyna's injury was caused by magic, not blunt force," Rawn mentioned. "Will the spell still perform the same?"

"I honestly don't know, but it's our best option."

Taking a breath, Lucenna stood. "I'll do it."

"Only use one feather," Lucien warned. "Those are very powerful and could do more harm than good."

Cassiel frowned. He handed her one and put away the rest. Wouldn't more power be a good thing? His feathers broke down Dyna's barrier, so they should break whatever spell was on her now.

"I would like to witness, if that's all right," Lucien said.

"Allow me." Rawn lifted the orb, and they all went to stand by the bedside together.

Lucenna sat on the bed and rested Dyna's head on her lap. The black feather glowed gold, then dissolved in her hands before she laid them over Dyna's temples. She closed her eyes and remained motionless. No one spoke. They held their breath in anticipation. After a few minutes of nothing happening, Cassiel's irritation and worry increased. He was about to speak when a bright white light streamed from beneath Lucenna's hands. It came over Dyna's head, spreading to her body.

"Good," Lucien murmured. "It's working."

Cassiel held his breath. But the light stopped growing, and it flickered in and out like his hope. He held her limp hand in his. *Come on, Dyna.*

But Lucenna shook her head. "She's...she's lost in here. It's so dark and cold. It's snowing...there is something else here...something bad."

Cassiel stilled, and he looked back at Zev. They both knew what that meant. Dyna was wandering through her past.

"Careful," Lucien said. "You are in a memory. Don't get lost as well. She's there. Find her. Guide her back."

Worry creased Lucenna's face, and the light dimmed.

No. It had to work. Cassiel's chest tightened as the light flickered. He pressed a fist over his heart. The bond was still intact, but it was weakening. Everything was tilting again.

Lucenna's breath hitched. "She's hiding from something. She's so scared."

He felt despicable helplessness, knowing how terrified Dyna was, and he couldn't reach her. He wished to tear into her mind if only to pull her out himself.

"Lucien, I don't know if I can—"

"Don't you dare give up," Cassiel snapped. "Bring her back!"

Halfway gone by madness and desperation, he snatched the rest of the feathers and pressed them over Dyna's forehead. The tent burst with a blinding white light as they dissolved into gold dust. The air grew thick with a wild charge, and he felt it crawl along his skin, raising every hair on end.

Everyone was shouting and moving and grabbing him.

"Prince Cassiel! Move back!"

"What have you done?"

"Lucenna! Stop! That's too much!"

Cassiel ignored them all and shoved off whoever was trying to drag him away. He took her face. "Come back to me, Dyna. Come back!"

Her eyes snapped open. There were no pupils. No irises. Only glowing orbs of vivid green.

The white light over her body flared to blinding, making Cassiel shield his eyes. The heat coming off the spell forced him to step back. It grew immense, and it burned against his face. His wonder replaced itself with fear. A powerful wind roared around them, and the pages and books and any loose item in the tent spun in the crackling air.

"What is happening?" His voice was lost to the wind. He felt something building and bursting, and—

A blast exploded past them like a sharp wave.

It ripped away the world and hurled Cassiel backward, but he never hit the ground. He seemed to sink through it and simply kept falling and falling.

CHAPTER 32

Cassiel

Nine years ago

C assiel stood on his balcony, watching the snowstorm whip through the kingdom of Hilos. The moon was full, shining proudly for the winter solstice night. The bitter wind bit his cheeks and left his wings stiff, but Cassiel cared not. He watched the entrance gates to the castle as he had every night for the past four years. Waiting. Hoping to glimpse a familiar silhouette in the moonlight.

"She is not coming back."

Cassiel whipped around and caught the shape of another, watching him from the pitch-black doorway to his bedroom. They slinked forward, and the silvery glow of the night caught on the silks of her gown before illuminating the Queen's face. The sharp points of her golden crown glinted, white wings glimmering behind her. Aversion simmered in her cool glare as she looked down her nose at him.

Propriety demanded that he bow, but Cassiel glared up at Queen Mirah with as much defiance as he could muster at ten winters old. Though the twitch of his black wings gave away how much she intimidated him.

Her mouth thinned. "Petulant little brat."

He gave his back to her and stared into the storm, but ignoring her never worked. She would leave once she finished reminding him of his place. As if he could ever forget.

"Your mother has abandoned you." Mirah came to stand beside him.

"She has gone to Mount Ida."

"Is that what you believe? Your mother fed you a tale of magic and adventure. She could not bring herself to admit she wanted nothing to do with her cursed child. Half-Celestial. Half-human. You were not meant to exist, and it disgusted her."

It's not true, he told himself. She promised to return.

Queen Mirah leaned down close as she looked over his shoulder at the winter storm. "Your mother returned home to her kind."

Cassiel looked up at her. "To Carthage?"

"That is where your mother is from, but no, not there. Before she sullied these halls, she lived in a village called North Star." The Queen pointed a sharp finger out into the night. "It lies not too far from here. A short flight indeed."

Shock and doubt clashed together, sending small prickles sinking through him. Had his mother truly been so close?

"She has family," Mirah continued, syrupy sweet, though it still carried that cold draft that coursed down his back. "*Your* family."

Cassiel slowly walked out onto the balcony, staring into the snow, wishing to catch sight of her.

"Go to her. There is nothing for you here now."

But...but he did have someone here.

"I have Father," he said, but his voice came out small. Unsure. After tonight, he didn't know if he had a father anymore.

"How long did you wait in the dining room until you realized he wasn't coming?" Mirah asked with mocking sympathy. "He no longer cares about you, Cassiel. Why remain where you are not wanted?"

The back of his eyes stung. Cassiel hadn't realized he was crying until he flinched when she brushed a tear from his cheek.

"The best thing for everyone is for you to leave and never come back. Same as your mother did." She turned away with a soft swish of her gown and headed for the door.

Cassiel spun around. "North Star—" But he cut off, not wanting to beg her for any more information.

As if she read his thoughts, a slow smile rose on the Queen's face. "The village is secure in the mountains. Spelled to be hidden away, safe and protected...except on a night when the moon is full. Like tonight. It's a populace of humans and mages who keep secrets of their own. A perfect place for you to live safely with your mother. But alas, you did not hear this from me..."

Then she slipped into the hall. Cassiel looked down at the silver flute in his hand. He had nothing here anymore.

He threw open the doors to his wardrobe and tossed a handful of clothing into a rucksack, then slung on a thick black coat lined in fur he pulled out of a drawer, not bothering to close them again. Grabbing his sheathed sword resting against his bedpost, he tossed his silver circlet on the bed.

The wind blew in from the balcony where a new future waited.

Cassiel didn't let himself think. Didn't let doubt or question stop him because if he did, his courage would falter.

So he ran out of the balcony and leaped. His wings snapped open and caught the rampant wind. It pushed and tugged at him wildly, snow whipping into his eyes. Cassiel forced his wings to beat again against the freezing storm and push north.

But no matter how fast he flew, worry followed him. What was he doing? He was still half Celestial. It had been ingrained in him to never leave Hilos. Cassiel stopped and hovered in the storm as he looked back at the castle. It rose as a sharp white peak, needle points poking into the sky shrouded in a veil of snow. It was quiet. No patrols were out. No one cared to stop him. Candlelight flickered at the windows of the King's study.

His father had forgotten him. So why should he stay?

Cassiel continued and flew as fast as he could over the forest of Hilos, urged by the thought of seeing his mother again. He passed by the towering *Hyalus* tree glowing in the night. It marked that he was nearly at the border of their territory. The bitter wind left him numb, but he didn't stop. The flight seemed endless, and he wondered if he had gone in the right direction when he spotted the glow of firelight in the distance. Torches.

Cassiel smiled and picked up speed. But what he had thought were torches was a village on fire. He could hear the screams as people ran in all directions. The white plane of snow was stained with splatters of blood. A black shape burst in and out of existence, moving too fast for his eyes, as it cut down any movement in its path. It snatched a child out of a cottage and raised it in the air. It was a black creature made of smoke and darkness, with eyes so red he could see them from the sky.

A Shadow demon.

Cassiel watched in horror as it swallowed the child whole.

Every bone within him turned to ice, his mind repeating the horrible image. He struggled to move past that until Cassiel realized he was watching the demon eat child after child. Some villagers gathered and fought, throwing every spell they could at it.

Cassiel's shaking hand went to his sword. Celestials could fight demons, a frail thought surfaced, but fear downed it out. He had to find his mother. But where? Mirah hadn't told him how to find her!

The Queen...had she planned this? His mother was never here, was she?

There was a shout, and the Shadow cut through a group of villagers, their bodies falling into pieces. But a woman threw up a spell that fell over the demon, trapping it in a gold dome. A man raised his hands as he chanted a spell, and his green magic darkened as a glowing red line split the ground at his feet. It expanded, then rose, forming into an immense black gate with sharp pickets. It was made completely of bone and smoke.

The Gates of the Netherworld.

Cassiel's stomach heaved, and terror gripped him as its foul presence filled the atmosphere. These people meddled in black magic. He couldn't stay here. Cassiel's wings spasmed painfully from the cold. They would freeze soon if he didn't get out of the snowstorm, but he didn't have the strength to fly back to Hilos.

In the distance was another light within the mountains, a familiar soft glow he recognized. Cassiel flew for it and found a white tree glowing in the night among the pine trees. This *Hyalus* was smaller than the one in Hilos, but its light would ward off any demons for the night.

He landed in the thick snow before the glowing trunk. He rested against the tree, panting. "I need your shelter, please."

To his absolute gratitude, the tree roots groaned and opened, creating a burrow at the base of the tree.

"Thank you," Cassiel gasped and crawled inside. It offered steady light within. He watched the storm, hearing the faint screams carried on the wind. He closed his eyes and clamped his hands over his ears. His sword seemed to hum at his waist, as if it detected the one thing it was meant to destroy, but Cassiel didn't leave his hiding spot. He couldn't fight a demon. Not with his Nephilim blood that lacked any divinity.

Cassiel didn't know how long he had hidden in the burrow when he heard the snap of branches, then a scream outside in the forest. He flattened himself in the burrow, fearing the Shadow had come this way. Peering out into the snow whipping past, he saw nothing until a hand seemed to pop out of the ground. It was a little girl covered in blood. She dragged herself out of what must be a gulley she had fallen in. An attempt to stand on an injured ankle sent her sprawling in the snow. She couldn't walk. Her red hair shone like streams of flames under the moon as she crawled her way to the *Hyalus*. It was the only thing that could protect her.

Cassiel moved to help, but the law to never reveal himself to humans made him hesitate. It was wrong. How could he leave her out there?

A growl rumbled in the night. Behind her rose the immense shape of the Shadow within the forest and its eyes glowed red.

Cassiel froze, his soul internally screaming. He didn't know why it cried out, but he couldn't let the demon have her. He grabbed onto the roots of the tree, hauling himself outside as the Shadow pounced. "No!"

The *Hyalus* burst with white light, flaring so blindly the Shadow screamed and whipped away.

Cassiel scrambled out of the burrow into the tree's glow and held out a hand to the girl. She accepted it and the moment their skin touched, an electric shock went through his body. It shot through his heart, heat swarming his chest in a way that left him gasping.

"Get in!" Cassiel yanked her into the burrow.

They fell inside together. Her wide green eyes fixed on him, shivering uncontrollably. She was in a thin nightgown, barefoot, and nothing more. Her complexion was as white as death, and her lips a purplish blue. She wrapped her thin arms around herself and curled into a ball, silently crying. Snow and blood stained her face and clothing, but she didn't appear harmed. Only shaken.

He reached into his pack and pulled out an extra tunic. "Here."

She blinked at the offer, tears on her face. She reached for it and her fingers brushed against his. A zap of energy hit them both again, and they flinched apart. Her wide eyes looked at him, really looked at him, and widened further. She looked past him to his wings, and her little body sagged.

"Seraphim," she whispered.

"What? No, I—" Cassiel scrambled to get away from her, but the girl collapsed on his lap and her arms latched around him.

"Am I dead, too?" she cried. "Did I never leave the forest?"

She must think he came to bring her to Heaven's Gate.

He sighed. "You are not dead."

She looked up at him with welled eyes. So pretty and sad. So human. Cassiel hesitated and brushed away the tears from her cheeks. Again, that energy clashed against his skin, and he saw a flash of color. She held his hand and his eyes drooped closed. A sort of second sight revealed the dancing green color of this girl's soul. It was warm. Welcoming like a place he belonged. And somehow, everything seemed to align as if at last he had found his home. One he had to protect.

Then he finally understood exactly what that meant.

Cassiel opened his eyes and looked down at the small girl that stared at him in wonder, like she felt the same. Her trembling hand reached up to him, her fingers brushing his cheek. His skin tingled under her touch.

"What is your name?" he whispered.

"Dynalya..." The name of a flower that matched the shade of her hair.

His arms tightened around her shoulders, bringing his wings forward for warmth. "My name is Cassiel and I will keep you safe, Dynalya."

A tear spilled down her temple. "I'm scared."

He didn't know how else to make her feel better, but there was only one thing that helped him. "Do you like music?"

She nodded. Cassiel took out his silver flute and played her his mother's song. The gentle notes filled the tree's burrow. Dynalya's eyes closed, tears clinging to her lashes as she listened.

But it ended with a horrifying shriek outside.

The Shadow was back.

Dynalya whimpered and burrowed into him. This time, Cassiel didn't hesitate. His terror was still there, but it dimmed beneath his need to shield, the need to answer a calling the moment he saw her soul.

"It's all right," he promised her. "I am here."

She looked up at him again with eyes full of trust and he couldn't help smiling. No one had ever looked at him like that before. Like he was needed.

"Stay here."

Taking up his divine weapon, he crawled out of the burrow back out into the storm. He walked across the snow to face the large black mass that slipped out of the trees. It stopped at the tree line when it spotted him, eyes molten red.

He had already lost his mother. He wouldn't lose this.

Cassiel drew out his sword and white flames burst to life along the blade, illuminating the night. "I am Cassiel Soaraway," he called to the Shadow demon. "And by the power of *Elyōn*, you will not touch my *mate*."

CHAPTER 33

Cassiel

Cassiel woke up with a start. He blinked up at the dawn sky where he lay on the hard ground. Dazed, it took a second for his mind to comprehend...that hadn't been a dream. It was a memory. The *Hyalus*. Dyna. He'd been there that night when the Shadow came. Why had he not remembered until now? The dream had been so vivid he could still hear her cries.

A devastated scream pierced his ears and he jerked up, shoving off the large piece of tarp that had been on top of him. He blinked against the bright morning sun glaring down. Pieces of a tent lay shredded around him with torn scrolls, books, wood, and clothing.

Cassiel searched for the source of the sound, and his heart leaped when he saw her. The morning sun haloed around Dyna's fiery red hair. The light caught the tears glistening on her cheeks. Her wide eyes were crazed as she looked around them. The bodies were everywhere, of their friends, the Valkyrie, and the wolves.

The blast must have knocked them all out.

Cassiel scrambled to his feet, and her frightened stare snapped to him.

He inhaled a shuddering breath at the life he saw in her eyes. At the recognition. His vision blurred, and a sob caught in his throat. She glowed as though she wasn't real, as though she had gone far beyond any place he could follow.

Cassiel still wasn't sure if he was fully awake. He only knew that he needed to hold her. But she looked so frightened, he thought she might bolt if he moved.

"Dyna..." he called softly.

Her face crumbled, and she let out a cry. Then she ran for him. He sprinted to meet her. She threw herself into his arms and their bodies crashed. Their bond slammed through his being in one stride like the rapid flame of a matchstick, knocking the breath out of him. He clamped his arms around her, holding her to him.

"Are you real?" she asked. "Are you truly here? If this is a dream, I don't wish to wake."

Cassiel reveled in the sound of her voice. "I'm here."

He set her feet down, and his whole body curled over hers, wrapping her in the shelter of his wings. Her trembling hands clung to his back as she melted into him, as if they needed to be submerged in each other. After going so long without her, he couldn't accept having any space between them.

"I'm here," he murmured again. "I'm real."

She buried her face in his chest as he held her tightly against him while the sobs shook her body. "You found me."

"Always." He cradled her face, pressing his forehead to hers. That well that he thought would always remain dry was so full, spilling endlessly with the tears he couldn't stop. "Even if my body was broken, I would crawl my way to you. And if I was no longer part of this realm, I would have found a way. I will always come for you."

The emptiness that had carved out his soul filled overwhelmingly with home. Dyna righted the axis of his world at last. Cassiel brushed her matted hair away from her bruised face, her shoulders, needing to feel her, to check that she was physically whole. She was finally in front of him. Safe and warm. He kissed her temple and kissed away the tears from both cheeks, her nose, her jaw.

And the bond hummed with his heartbeat. *There you are, lev sheli.*

Dyna held onto his arms as she wept. *My soul missed you.*

I'm sorry for making you wait. He pressed his mouth against hers, awakening her Essence with the feel of his flame as it burned through them both.

Her heart called to him, so Cassiel yielded and pulled her close. He kissed her slow and gentle, treasuring every touch of her soft lips when he nearly would have never felt them again. And it was as perfect as the first time. Dyna sighed against his mouth as he slid his hands into her hair. Her arms wrapped around his neck and she rose on her toes to kiss him back. The bond burned between them, sparking with a magic all their own.

A distant sound tugged at his attention. Cassiel tried to ignore it, but then he heard a groan and scuffs in the dirt. Reluctantly, he let her go and turned to see everyone slowly waking. Zev got to his feet first, his green eyes locking on her.

Then Dyna saw him.

Her mouth fell open, lips shaking with a silent cry. Her eyes welled with fresh tears as she took in his tall frame standing against the sunrise. Familiar and warm.

Alive.

"Zev..." Dyna walked two stumbling steps before her legs gave out, and she fell to her knees.

Sobs wracked her entire body. A ball of emotion welled in Cassiel's chest at the feel of her overwhelming relief and joy. Zev lowered beside Dyna and wrapped her in those strong arms that always made her feel safe. His shoulders shook as he wept with her.

Lucenna helped Rawn limp over to them, their own eyes misting, too.

"You did it," Cassiel said. "You brought her back."

She smiled. "We all did."

He knew it wasn't over. Many more things were coming their way, along with a formidable enemy that would inevitably return. But they were finally reunited. So for now, at least at this moment, everything was right.

CHAPTER 34

Von

Von looked away as Novo slammed his fist into Clayton's face. The young mage only gave them a bloody grin and spat at the ground.

"What did you do to Dyna?" Von demanded.

"Her mind is expunged. Wiped clean, so she may never reveal the map to your master." For someone beaten up and tied to a tree, the mage had the nerve to be smug.

Raiders were gathered around to stand witness. Tarn stood aside as the spy beat the mage further.

"Enough." Von grabbed Novo's wrist. He was only a lad.

Clayton laughed and wiped the blood from his torn lip on his sleeve. "It's useless to have me beaten, Tarn." He boldly met his stare. "Release us, and I will undo the spell, then cast another to track her for you, but I have served you far enough. I'm trading the Maiden for our freedom."

When Dyna dropped out of the sky, Von had felt his body go cold. Her prince fell with her into the ravine, and there was no sight of them again. He feared they didn't survive. But they found no bodies when they went searching.

"Is she alive?" Von asked.

Clayton sneered. "Not for long. Not without me."

He shook his head. The mage wouldn't admit to it if she was dead. Not knowing what happened to her was the only thing keeping him alive right now.

This never should have happened. Why did he leave her out of his sight? He gave his word that Dyna would be safe.

"You need me," Clayton retorted at Tarn. "If you want the Maiden found, you will set us free. I'll bow to you no more."

Tarn said nothing. By his lack of response and expression, the verdict was clear.

"You and your father have broken your servant's oath and defied the Master's order, Clayton." Von rubbed his face. "Unfortunately, you won't be the only one who will suffer the repercussions."

The Raiders parted for Elon and Len, who dragged Dalton forward. At the sight of his young brother beaten bloody, Clayton fought against his restraints. "Leave him. He did nothing!"

Geon and Yavi rushed forward, but Olsson held them back. The lad looked at Von, silently begging for his friend. His stomach sank. Everyone knew their fates had already been decided.

"How did Dyna get the arrow?" Tarn asked him.

Dalton lowered his head. "I-I don't know, Master. It was left on my father's desk. It seemed such an inconsequential trinket. I didn't know she would..." His mouth quivered, and he looked at his shocked brother. "I'm sorry."

"Stop talking," Clayton growled at him. "Don't tell them anything."

"How did the first veil come down?" Tarn asked next.

Dalton sealed his mouth shut, but Novo whipped out a knife to his brother's neck and he revealed it all.

"Kneel," Tarn commanded when he finished. Elon pressed on Dalton's shoulder, forcing him to bend to his knees.

"My father only wanted to regain our freedom," Dalton mumbled, his hands shaking on the ground. "Why do I have to die for that?"

The question broke something in Von. If only he hadn't stepped out of the mage's tent.

All Benton wanted was to be free. What he had done was to serve that purpose, but why had the old mage thought there wouldn't be repercussions for his defiance? He served Tarn for five years. In that time, he learned the extent their master was capable of when angry. Benton thought his magic made him indispensable. He had been wrong—and his sons would pay for it.

"Don't do this," Clayton begged. His hands sparked with magic, but the bindings zapped him. "Leave him alone!"

Tarn's stare remained on Clayton. A hush fell, everyone surely feeling the same fear at the chill stirring in the air.

"I can undo the spell," the mage repeated, now earnest. "You only need to release us!"

232

At his silence, Clayton tried another spell, and the black clover bracelet on Tarn's wrist immediately absorbed it. He had found it that morning when stopping by the hollowed-out tree.

The mage screamed as his Essence was stolen, and the witch bangles punished him with electrical shocks for using attack magic. Clayton was powerless to fight back. When he realized he never had the advantage, his face filled with fear. "Master, please spare my brother. Dal wasn't part of our plans. It was only a moment of madness. I can help you find the Maiden."

"Is she *alive*?" Von pressed.

"I don't know." The uncertainty in Clayton's voice left no room for hope. The weight of Dyna's death fell on his shoulders. It was his fault again. He got her killed.

Tarn's sword rang as he drew it free.

"Wait! Wait! I know where Mt. Ida is!" Clayton shouted.

Everyone else stilled at the news. Von's heart picked up speed because he could tell it wasn't a lie. In his last desperate attempt to save them, Clayton was willing to tell Tarn whatever he wished to know.

"I saw it when I was in her mind. It's…" He trailed off, glancing at everyone intently listening.

Von motioned for them to step back at a distance where they couldn't hear. Tarn crouched in front of the mage and dipped his chin, indicating he should continue.

Clayton's throat bobbed. "It's within the Leviathan Ocean. About twelve hundred knots west off the coast…yonder what sailors call the Heartless Boneyard."

That place was a death trap for ships, riddled with the bones of human and sea beast alike. No one has ever crossed it alive. No wonder the island went undiscovered.

Tarn stood.

Clayton smiled up at him shakily. "Forgive me, Master. I should never have defied you. It won't happen again."

"No," Tarn said. "It won't."

The sword swept through the air. Blood splattered across the frozen dirt at Von's feet. Clayton's body jerked, his eyes stretching wide. Red streamed from the slit in his throat.

"Dal—" He reached out for his younger brother, a wet gurgle leaving him. His body swayed, then he slumped against the tree, his blank eyes staring at nothing.

Dalton's mouth gaped in a silent cry. His trembling fingers hovered over Clayton's face, his expression forever fixed in shock. "Dyna…she was under his *halucinor* spell. Her life was tied to him." He whimpered, pure anguish overtaking him. "Now she's surely dead, too."

Tarn's expression froze a moment before his mask fell back into place. If he ever cared about Dyna, he had erased it with Witch's Brew. "Then there is no one left to stop me."

Von closed his eyes.

He failed her.

Now the divination was lost, and next the world.

Dalton wrapped his arms around himself, rocking back and forth. Orange sparked around his body and the air crackled with static. Von stepped back, the hair rising on his neck. The lad let out a broken cry, and the wail reverberated through the camp.

The next moments were a blur.

Dalton's cry turned into a scream of rage. Orange light shot out of him. It blasted Von away and everyone else standing near him. The witch bangles punished him with electricity, but he bore the pain. His eyes glowed with pure hatred at the man that killed his brother.

"Don't do it, boy!" Von shouted at him, but he knew Dalton had made his choice.

Dalton yanked a slaver's key from his robes and unlocked them. His silhouette blazed vivid orange.

His magic was free.

The Raiders charged for him, taking out their weapons. Dalton clenched his fists and whipped up his arms. Jagged mounds of rocks burst from the ground and hurtled toward them, crushing in faces and chests. Spearing his fingers into the dirt, the ground let out a horrendous groan, then it rumbled violently. A deep crevice split the ground and fractured through the camp like a snake. Several Raiders fell in screaming, swallowed by the earth before they could escape.

Von slid on a slant of loose rock, aiming to take him next. He threw himself and caught the edge of the crevice. His fingers clawed desperately for flat land, his feet searching for purchase on the rock face. Elon and Olsson seized his arms and hauled him back up to safety. There wasn't time to thank them.

They ran south with the fleeing Raiders. The direction was taking Von away from Tarn. It went against his duty, but instinct and fear for Yavi put her first.

Tents collapsed all around them, as wood support beams snapped in half. A stampede of their horses crushed any that had fallen in the mayhem. Confused and frightened Raiders trampled and shoved each other to get away. A fire roared as it burned through an overturned, broken barrel of ale outside of the Sorren's tent. The confined Minotaur tried to fight back the flames with a blanket, but he was quickly losing.

"Help him!" He told Olsson and Elon as he sprinted past.

Von braced himself to stay erect as he ran through the quake. He found Yavi and Geon outside of her tent, supporting each other. Relief rocked through Von's heart as he sprinted for her. She cried out when she spotted him. Geon let her go, and she threw herself at Von, sobbing against his chest. He could breathe now. It was enough to know she was safe. The support beam of Yavi's tent cracked loudly. It was going to come down next.

"Both of you, flee this place!"

"What do you mean?" she cried. "You're coming with us, aren't you?"

Von cupped her cheek. "I must go back."

"Dalton doesn't know what he is doing," Geon told him. "Please."

Von couldn't answer him. "Go. I leave her to you."

"No! You don't need to go back for him!" Yavi clung to his coat. "Von, please stay with me!"

He kissed her passionately, and when he felt Yavi's arms relax around him, he broke out of her hold. "I'm sorry."

He sprinted back to his master. He must uphold his sworn duty to Tarn and die with him if that was the debt the God of Urn demanded.

"Von!" Yavi's cry followed him.

He returned to the clearing to see Dalton had collapsed the crevice into a profound hole. It surrounded the tree where Tarn stood among its roots, holding onto the trunk. That saved him only because Dalton couldn't bring himself to harm the ancient tree. It held strong, its thick deep roots emerging from the rock face. The glowing mage continued screaming through his brandish of power while he commanded the roots next. They snaked up, alive and quick as tentacles for Tarn. He leaped out of the way for a branch, dodging the roots whipping through the air.

Von sprinted up behind Dalton. Snatching a dagger from the sheath at his hip, he beat the hilt against his head. Dalton fell limp, falling face first on the ground. The quaking ceased, and all fell still. After a minute of quiet, Tarn climbed down the tree. He used the extending roots to cross the crevice onto solid ground.

His unfeeling eyes fixed on Dalton.

There was no saving the boy. Tarn would kill him as heartlessly as his brother, if not worse. Von had enough of seeing others cut down. He was tired of the blood and the death.

Dalton had been bound to this life since he was a child, and it wasn't fair. It never was. He hadn't gone out of his way to offer any kindness to him, but now that it was too late, Von wished he had taken the time to do so. Maybe things might have turned out differently.

He crouched down beside Dalton and made the mage sit to look at him. Tears welled in his faintly glowing eyes.

"Are you going to kill me now?" Dalton asked, his voice so sad and tired.

Von rested his hands on the lad's shoulders. "I'm sorry for the childhood stolen from you, and for the ill done against your family," he said softly. "That's finished. I liberate you of your servitude, Dalton Slater of the Earth Guild. You will be a slave no more."

The young mage closed his eyes, and for the first time since they met, he gave Von a genuine smile. "I...I will see my mother again?"

His vision blurred.

"Yes..." Von pulled him into his arms, hugging his quivering form. After a pause, Dalton embraced him in return and clutched his jacket with trembling fists.

"You're free," Von whispered, and he snapped Dalton's neck.

The crunch of breaking bone rang through his ears. It was quick and painless. Gone in an instant. Von held the limp lad to his chest as he felt the murder damn him further. It was the first and last kindness he could offer.

Over his shoulder, Tarn fixed his icy gaze on him next.

This was it for him, too.

He accepted his fate.

His actions brought these deaths and nearly took the life of his master. He couldn't have missed that Von had left him to find Yavi first. Dying was his befitting punishment. But Tarn didn't take his life. He didn't speak. Didn't condemn him.

Tarn simply strode away.

But it wasn't a relief. It merely meant the guillotine hovered above his neck, and he was left with the unease of never knowing when it would fall.

A cold breeze pushed against Von as he watched Tarn lead the procession of Raiders into the dense woods. Sorren trailed at the end of the line with a wagon carrying what remained of their camp gear. Elon walked behind him, keeping a hand on the hold of his sword should the Minotaur act out of place.

"Where are Geon and Yavi?" Von asked when they passed him.

"They are paying their respects." Sorren eyed Von down his long snout and nodded behind him. "As should you."

He spotted their shadows lingering near the far edge of the camp by three graves under Dalton's tree. It was the only ones Von had dug because he couldn't leave them to the crows. The other Raiders who perished, and most of the bodies left by the skirmish, had been claimed by the earth.

Geon sat before the tree with his head bowed. Yavi stood behind him, her arms wrapped around herself. Von didn't know how to face them, but he couldn't leave before he at least said he was sorry.

He walked around the massive chasm to reach them. "Lad—"

Geon jerked to his feet and walked away from him. Von sighed as he watched him go.

"Are we simply to leave them here?" Yavi asked, not looking at him.

"There is nothing more we can do for them."

"This isn't right..." Yavi pressed the heels of her palms against her eyes, her cheeks wet with tears. "I was so sure that Dyna would be the end of Tarn. I believed it. She was..."

Her hope for freedom.

"It was unfair of me to put so much on her, but now she is gone, and so are they. I'm so sick of seeing lives cut short. Of losing the only family we have for *that* man." Yavi finally looked at him, her eyes sharp and angry. Accusing. "None of us had a chance to say goodbye to Dal."

Before you broke him. She didn't need to say it, but Von heard it all the same.

It had been the quickest way to end his life without unnecessary suffering. He wished he could have done more, but all he could offer was to spare him a horrid death. "You can say it now."

"He is no longer here to hear it."

Von reached for her, but Yavi tore her arm out of his grasp. He glanced down at her clenched fists. "I didn't mean for any of this to happen."

The harsh wind blew against them, rattling the dry leaves still clinging to the trees. It swept through her auburn hair and it clung to her wet lashes. Yavi's gaze drew inward as her expression went numb.

"You will be headed to the port with the others. I have a task in Beryl Coast," he said. "I don't know how long I will be gone. A fortnight, at the very least, if not longer. Will you allow me to embrace you before I go?"

Their mission had been delayed, but Tarn made it clear they were to depart at once. This was the last shred of a second they had left.

When Yavi didn't leave, Von took a step forward hesitantly and gathered her in his arms. She was stiff as a rod.

"Why did you go to him?" Yavi asked faintly, no more fight in her words. As if it was a question she had asked herself over and over, and this was merely an echo. "Yet again, you chose the Master over your life with me. I see now ... you will *never* choose me."

She stepped out of his arms and followed the procession of Raiders.

Von had once asked himself why the God of Urn had made him a slave, but he had always known the answer. He deserved it.

He failed and failed and continuously failed. His whole life was constructed of failures, and he knew nothing else. There was no end to it. Everything he ever wanted was slipping through his fingers. He felt it as he watched Yavi walk away from him once again.

Crows cawed loudly as they picked at the bloated flesh of the bodies left behind. Both Raider and knight. He memorized their faces along with all the others that had died in the quake. Their spirits were there in the campgrounds with him, their cries haunting the wind. The sound joined the screams and roars of trolls in his mind.

Remorse strangled him as tight as a noose. So many lives were lost because of him.

Von kneeled down by ashes of the old campfire surrounded by charred stone. He gathered a handful of twigs and leaves and tossed them in. From his pocket, he pulled out flint and steel and beat them together until a spark caught. He blew on the smoking leaves gently, coaxing a small flame to grow. It was probably pointless, but it was all Von could offer to the lives lost here. One last vigil to guide them through the Gates.

Standing, he looked upon the graves of House Slater one last time. "May you leave the Mortal Gate with no burden to bind you," he murmured. "May you cross Death's Gate with all faults forgiven. May you pass through the Time Gate with the wisdom of the age. May you pass through the expanse of the Spatial Gate's wonder. May you pass through Life's Gate as you did at the beginning. May you arrive at Heaven's Gate at the end. May the God of Urn receive your souls."

As Von walked away, he felt their judgment fall on him, and the weight of it grew heavier and heavier with each step.

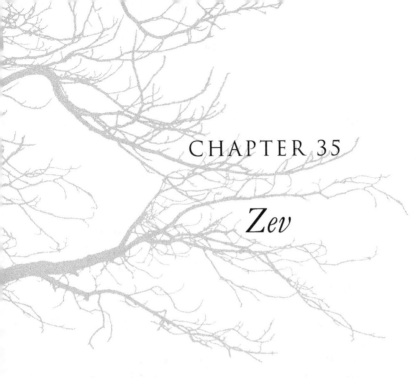

CHAPTER 35

Zev

Zev could count on one hand how many miracles he had witnessed in his life. Right now, it was seeing Dyna alive and well and with them again. Her laughter at something Lucenna said rang within the woods they traveled through. Since her return, Dyna stayed beside him or Cassiel as though she needed it. Neither of them felt the need to part from her side, either.

"You're staying," Dyna said to Lucenna as she healed her broken finger. "I will hear no argument against it."

The sorceress shrugged. "Well, I suppose if you simply must have me around, I have a moral obligation to comply."

Rawn chuckled, sharing a look with Zev. They both knew she wanted to stay, and he was glad she did.

If it wasn't for Lucenna's quick thinking of forming a shield a split second before Dyna exploded with magic, they might not have all survived. They had yet to fully understand what happened. Some of the spell had struck him, and it led to vivid dreams of his past that Zev didn't want to think about.

Dyna didn't have all of her memories back yet. Lucenna assured them they would return in a few days. But he was more worried about Tarn.

They felt an earthquake the day after they reunited with Dyna, and Lucenna said there'd been magic in it. Whatever it was, they moved fast and covered lots of ground. Especially after Dyna revealed what the man was after.

The Seer's divination was one of the freshest memories she had, and they fell in quiet shock as she recited it to them. At the description of each of them joining her side, it confirmed they truly were her Guardians, including Lucenna.

"In Corron, you saved my life when I tumbled down the hill and stopped my descent," Dyna told her. "I would have broken my neck if I reached the bottom. Then you helped me find my magic."

"For all of us to meet, as the Seer predicted, I think much more will come of it." Rawn looked worried, if not a little curious. "I expect two more will join our company soon."

"Someone with a familiar face and a creature with the strength of ten. You say Princess Keenali is the fifth?" Zev frowned thoughtfully as he recalled the dark-skinned fairy with yellow butterfly wings. Well, she had been strong.

Dyna smiled. "Keena meets all the signs. I felt a connection to her as I did with all of you, and she saved my life."

"The Morphos Court happens to be in the northwest, not too far from Troll Bridge," Rawn mentioned.

Her face lit up. "Then we will pay her a visit once we cross."

"What about the familiar face?" Lucenna asked. "Would it be someone familiar to us or to Tarn?"

Cassiel shrugged. "I would think familiar to Tarn, since the foretelling was for him."

"Only time will tell," Dyna whispered. Her expression was the same when the Druid had said her Guardians would reunite with her on their own. Did she know who the sixth one was?

It would be someone wanting revenge, and a man like Tarn must have a lot of enemies. Whoever they were, Zev hoped they would be his downfall. He didn't want it to be Dyna.

"Does Tarn have a love-mate?" Lucenna asked when they fell quiet. Because they must all be thinking about the same thing.

Dyna shook her head. "Not anymore. His wife passed away a long time ago."

Which was strange to hear. Tarn didn't seem capable of caring for anyone, let alone having a wife, not after seeing those cold eyes. It made Zev feel sick to think that such a murderous man could end up falling for his cousin.

"Then what else could the last line mean?" Lucenna asked.

"Love would be thy undoing," Rawn repeated thoughtfully. "Prophecies have a tendency not to be forthright, as they can hold many meanings. That line does not explicitly name who he will love. Naturally, one assumes it's the Maiden, but it could refer to someone he has loved in the past or does currently. Family, for example, or friends."

Dyna nodded. "I thought the same...but all of his family is dead, and he has no friends. Tarn won't allow himself to form an attachment to anyone, not even me."

Cassiel's expression hardened. "It matters not. Next time he comes, I will finish him."

There was an oath in that threat that Zev would gladly support.

The Captain of the Valkyrie swooped down and bowed to Cassiel and Dyna. "We found a place for you to camp further north, Your Highness. We will keep watch in the skies tonight. The Lycans are marking a perimeter."

"Thank you, Captain."

They had a small force watching over Dyna now. The Valkyrie protected her by law, and the wolves by kinship. It made Zev feel so much better about her safety. But he knew it wouldn't last for long.

They came out of the forest and entered a meadow. A little beyond the way was a small creek. The evening sun was beginning to lower in the sky in the distance above the trees. Cassiel and Dyna strolled ahead to the water, hand in hand. Zev frowned as he watched them go.

Rawn came to stand beside him. "I know their union was unexpected, but they are True Bonded," he said, as if Zev wasn't reminded every time he looked at her glowing skin. "There is not much that can be done."

"You knew about them, didn't you?"

He flushed. "I may have overheard more than I should have."

"They're bonded?" Lucenna asked in surprise. "How? When? An exchange of blood means they are married."

"She didn't exactly consent to it," Zev growled.

"Well, she doesn't look disappointed." Lucenna grinned when Cassiel wrapped Dyna in his wings, his eyes never leaving hers. "He looks at her like she is the only one that exists in his world. It's the very picture of devotion. I don't doubt for one second his feelings for her are genuine, Zev. Why does it bother you so much?"

Zev couldn't bring himself to answer.

He left Rawn and Lucenna to set up camp as they idly chatted about stopping in the next town to replenish provisions. He headed for the creek, not sure how to address what he needed to say, but felt he had to.

When Zev approached, Cassiel glanced at Dyna and she nodded before he walked past him, leaving them alone.

Zev stared at her, recalling something he had heard about True Bonded mates. "Can you ... speak to each other mentally?"

She smiled. "Yes."

"What did he say?"

"That he would be nearby."

Zev glanced over his shoulder. Cassiel was speaking to Rawn, though his attention stayed on her.

"He mentioned you were still angry with him." Dyna sat down by the bank. "Are you angry with me as well?"

Zev frowned and sat beside her. "Why would I be?"

"If I hadn't gotten myself injured trying to chain the Other instead of fleeing, Cassiel wouldn't have had to heal me. Then when he told me the truth, I asked him to keep it a secret from you. So I deserve your anger as much as him, right?"

The question made him see he had focused all of his resentment on Cassiel for the bond when it had been an accident. He could claim it was wrong because of where they both came from, but that was only a small part of it.

"No..." Zev finally replied. "I am not angry with you." He looked away to the far end of the creek, watching the water flow by. "Do you remember the Shadow?"

"The most significant memories returned first," she faintly said.

"Do you...wish it was something you could forget?"

When he looked back at Dyna, she had her eyes closed. Even so, he could tell she looked sad. "I think I did at some point, but recently I learned memory is the core of who we are, and to erase it would leave us blind."

It made Zev think of his father, and the day he wished to erase. "When I found you half frozen in the snow, heart and mind nearly broken beyond repair, I swore to myself I wouldn't let anything hurt you ever again. You needed me then, but I needed you, too," he admitted. "I needed a reason to live, and I put that burden on you. Becoming your protector became a part of who I am, and now it's hard to let it go."

He had placed the value of his worth on her to find some purpose to stay alive and combat his Madness. But by taking up that role, he didn't let her grow, so he could be the one she relied on.

How was that fair? When grief had drowned her, she never made him her raft.

"I asked you once what you wanted of me. Do you remember what you said?"

Dyna's green eyes misted, and she nodded.

"You told me to fight for myself." A lump formed in Zev's throat. He had been so distraught that day to have his purpose taken away. It had left him feeling so lost.

He still felt that way a little.

Dyna hugged his arm, pressing her forehead against his shoulder. "I know it hurts right now, but whatever you face, good or bad, all of it passes in time. Sometimes life seems like a hopeless and endless storm, but the clouds will part. Don't give up. Keep going. Keep living. Whatever hardships come, continue onward, even if your path veers in a direction you didn't expect. Everything will be all right. *Live.* And one day, you will create your own happiness." His skin grew wet with Dyna's spilled tears. "That is what I should have told you at the grove."

Zev kept his sight on the horizon as his vision blurred. He could see it. A new future forming ahead of him. All it took was the courage to follow it.

"When I was dying, I realized you were right. No one else can live my life for me. I'm fighting to breathe every day, but it's getting a little easier. One day, I will learn how to fight for myself, too."

He glanced at the forest where he could distinguish the white form of a wolf passing through the bushes. His own wolf stirred at her faint scent carried on the wind.

"This thing between you and Cassiel, the True Bond...has it changed you?"

"It has." A smile lit Dyna's face as she wiped her eyes. "I have a connection to him that is unlike anything I have experienced before. His mere presence puts me at ease. The second I see him, I can only describe it as this warm light filling my heart. I feel complete with him. He's the other half of my soul."

Her confession stumped him, and Zev forgot what he was going to say. He hadn't thought her affections reached that far. As he watched her fondly gaze at Cassiel fly in graceful arcs among the clouds, he knew Dyna's heart was no longer hers.

"Please don't tell me I shouldn't feel this way, or that the Realms will contest our marriage. I already know that. It doesn't change how I feel."

"All right." Zev wrapped an arm around her shoulders. "I won't."

They sat quietly, listening to the flow of the creek pass them by as the sky shifted into the blue shade of twilight. He didn't know when Dyna became a lady. She had grown on this journey and it made him a bit sad because she was no longer that little girl before the darkness had changed their lives. But he was also proud.

She glanced at the wolves, watching them. "You've made friends."

"They're Lycans," he said, and Dyna gaped at him. "I asked them to help me find you. They're the Garou Pack from the west. They're a good one, I think."

A relieved smile crossed her face, emotion contorting her features. "Zev."

"I don't know what will come of it, but it helps to know I'm not alone. Seeing my kind in a Pack, it..."

"Gives you hope."

"Something like that. But they are here now because they also need help. Another Pack further southeast is ill with distemper."

She gasped and leaped to her feet. "You should have told me sooner!"

Once he introduced her to Ronin, Dyna walked off with his Pack as she started listing ingredients she would need, asking how many were sick to estimate the quantity of medicine. They wrote everything down, and the wolves set out to search for the specified plants needed. It wasn't a cure, but it would ease the pain and strengthen their immunities to combat the virus.

Cassiel flew down and landed next to him, some distance away from the others. They watched Dyna together, simply passing the time as night arrived.

"I don't like you right now," Zev eventually said.

"I know."

"But regardless of how the bond came to be, the fates decided she was meant for you, it seems. I really can't imagine why."

Cassiel smirked. "Because I'm a handsome prince? What else would she deserve?"

"A less arrogant one would have been kind," Zev retorted. But his start of a smile faded and so did Cassiel's because this was serious. They were talking about her future. "I listened to Dyna cry every night for a year when she lost her family. She did her best to stitch her life back together after the Shadow shredded it apart, always smiling for everyone when I could see the sadness she tried to hide beneath it. That night had left cracks in her heart. I did all I could to make sure nothing ever broke her again." They faced each other. "I watched her grow into the woman she is now. All I want is for her to be happy. I want to believe she will be happy at your side, but I fear your people will not accept her. That this fragile union will fall apart, and it will be another thing that breaks her. Can you tell me she won't suffer?"

Cassiel gripped his hands together, his shoulders dipping. "I wish I could promise you that."

Zev knew as much, but to hear it still made his heart sink.

"To be a Nephilim is to be scorned," Cassiel said. "The Realms have never looked favorably upon me and I, too, fear that will fall upon her. Regardless of what happens or what they say, I can promise you one thing." His expression hardened and a faint blue glow flickered in his eyes. "I will protect her with everything I have. She will always come first in all that I do, even at the expense of myself. I will shield her with my very life until my dying breath."

Zev didn't know what the future held for them or what would come from their bond, but there was nothing more reverent than that promise. All of his opposition bled out of him, because he knew Cassiel would sacrifice everything to keep her safe. He couldn't ask more than that.

At his silence, Cassiel heaved a breath. "Must I beg for her hand?"

Zev barked a laugh. He would never prostrate—

His laughter died when Cassiel lowered himself on his knees and deferentially bowed. He stared at him, too shocked to speak for a moment. "You would beg for her?"

"For her, *yes*," Cassiel answered without hesitation, and his expression carried nothing but the truth.

"Good. Then she's your living calamity now." Zev clapped Cassiel's shoulder, squeezing hard enough to make him wince. "As for my promise to you, if anything happens to my sweet cousin, I will rip out your heart."

"Fair enough."

Chuckling, Zev helped him up, and they made their way back together. "Oh, and I won't consider this a marriage until there is a proper wedding. Until then, if you attempt anything past holding her hand..."

"Allow me to guess. You will rip out my heart." Cassiel's smirk wavered as he watched Dyna laughing with Lucenna. "If the worst ever befell her, I would no longer have a heart for you to take. For it would be the end of me."

Zev recalled how he fell out of the sky when the bond broke. His scream that rang through the woods was the most horrific sound to tear through his ears. A shudder sank through his chest.

It was the sound of a soul shattering.

CHAPTER 36

Dynalya

D yna waved goodbye to the Garou Pack as they prepared to depart, now that they had the medicine needed. Zev followed them to the woods to give his thanks to the Alpha and the pretty sister he couldn't stop staring at. She would have to ask him about her later.

He eventually rejoined all of them by the campfire as they listened to Lucenna's story about facing off with her father. She described to her how Zev, Rawn, and Cassiel had frightened him so terribly, he forgot he was a powerful mage. The firelight glowed against their faces as they laughed. They looked so at peace she wished to preserve this moment in a box and carry it with her.

Zev's grin faded when he noticed her getting teary. "What is it? What's wrong?"

She laughed and wiped her eyes. "Absolutely nothing. I'm simply happy to be with all of you again. The day I started my journey to Mount Ida, I didn't know any of this would happen. I never imagined meeting any of you or the things we would go through. Thank you for being with me."

She met Cassiel's gaze where he lounged on the grass next to her. He gave her a fond smile that left her a little breathless. She had the sudden urge to kiss him.

He reached across the grass at the same time she did and they linked hands. The electric current of his touch seeped into her chest, but it built in a rapid spark. A green flash shot out of her fingertips and zapped him, making them flinch apart.

He winced. "Ow. What was that?"

"I-I don't know. I'm sorry." She reached for him worriedly, but another current sparked, making him yelp.

Zev poked her arm next, and she zapped him, too. Dyna stared down at herself. What was happening? She felt her Essence humming as though it had been charged and little green flashes crackled along her skin.

"Must be the spell," Lucenna said. "Sometimes remnants can remain after powerful magic is used. It should cease by tomorrow." She gave them a sly smile. "Until then…"

"No touching," Zev growled at Cassiel.

The bond thrummed with strong protest from both ends. She had only had him back one day, and now this?

Sighing, Dyna looked up at the clouds overtaking the night sky and let out a long exhale that fogged in the frosty air. "Winter is coming. We need to leave Azure before the first snowfall, and head to the nearest port. It's not only about reaching Mount Ida within the year anymore. We can't let Tarn become immortal."

"Then we must reach the island first," Rawn said, and they all nodded in agreement.

Lucenna's smile turned wicked. "I am looking forward to meeting this Tarn."

They all looked equally eager for a rematch. Now that Dyna knew about his past, and what she was up against, she felt more prepared to face him again.

"How long until we reach Troll Bridge?" She turned to her mate. He knew the way, and they needed his uncle's permission to cross it.

"Perhaps not long," Cassiel said, but there was something disquieting in his silver eyes as they landed on the large alps coated in white caps of snow in the distance. "Before then, to Hermon Ridge first."

Dyna felt his unease before he swiftly pushed aside the emotion. He was quiet throughout dinner, then eventually wandered off on a walk alone.

She waited until everyone was asleep before searching for him. The bond easily led her to a tall crag where he sat, looking at the mountains. She stood there a moment, admiring him beneath the moonlight as the wind ruffled his inky hair and feathers.

He noticed her and leaped down. "Dyna."

She unfolded the blanket she'd been holding. "Sit with me?"

Cassiel understood what she wanted without needing to say it. He sat and his silver eyes churned with starlight as she approached him, never looking away. Laying the blanket between his legs and against his chest, she sat there, then covered herself completely with the ends. His arms and wings came around her. His body sagged against her back, and his forehead rested on her covered shoulder. She leaned into him and closed her eyes.

"Thank you," he murmured, his breath tickling her neck. "I needed this."

She did too. As if something inside of her didn't feel right without physically touching him. "I know it isn't the same..."

"Forgive me. You have been through enough without my selfish need to be near you." He gently squeezed her. *After suffering your absence, I cannot bear to be apart from you in any way. I may kiss you now and damn the consequences.*

She felt a little breathless again. "You say that now...But it will pass."

"Thank the Gods for that. But how are you feeling? We haven't had a moment to talk about what happened...while we were apart."

She had only told them bits and pieces of her time in Tarn's camp. Some memories were fuzzy, and she didn't fully recall all she'd seen during dream walking. But a lot happened while she'd been captive, and some of it weighed heavily on her heart. She told Cassiel everything from the moment she arrived to the moment Tarn kissed her.

Dyna felt it when he stopped breathing. The bond went silent with his shield falling in place, and she knew he was hiding from her.

He must feel so betrayed.

She blinked back tears. "I'm sorry. Are you angry?"

Cassiel hid most of it, but the emotion was so potent she felt it hovering behind the shield like the heat of a fire. "Not with you. That man will die for taking you from me. Learning how he made you suffer only assures it will be a painful death."

The quiet wrath in those words made her skin prickle with goosebumps...because it reminded her of Tarn. Of his own frightening violence and the claim that everyone was a monster.

Even her.

"I should have let him die," she whispered. "Why didn't I let him die?"

"That's not who you are. There is nothing wrong with that. It simply means you have a better heart than most of us."

"That's not true..." She closed her eyes. "You haven't asked me how I escaped."

"Do you wish to tell me?"

She had to swallow before she could say it. "The veils..."

Cassiel didn't reply, but he put it together without her having to speak it aloud. She had explained how the spells were powered and by who.

"At that moment, I chose myself. But sometimes, I hear the sounds Benton made when he...and Dalton's face..." Her voice caught as everything she had kept buried about that moment surfaced. "I feel his blood on my hand. I remember the smell. There was so much of it."

Cassiel tightened his embrace, enveloping her in a protective hold. "You did what needed to be done."

"I don't want to be a killer..."

It was so easy to cross that line. But maybe it wasn't as simple as good and bad when they lived in a world layered in shades of gray.

"I will be the one who kills for you," Cassiel said. "I will guard every part of you, Dyna, including your soul."

"And what of yours?"

"It only lives because you live. When you were taken, I felt as if I was dying. I would have if Lord Norrlen did not convince me you were alive."

"It hurt," she said faintly. "The moment the veil was cast, I thought...you were dead. The pain almost made my heart stop."

Cassiel's forehead rested on her shoulder. "This is what it means to be True Bonded. It has fused our souls to the point we cannot live without each other. I feared it. To be so attached to you that the loss of you would be the loss of me. You never asked for this. That choice was taken from you, and I will never stop being sorry for it."

The words were soft but carried weight. Dyna pulled away to look at him.

His dark lashes lowered, obscuring his eyes. "Things have changed. They *are* changing. I have little hope that our bond will last..."

She waited, knowing this was what had troubled him.

The dread in his eyes made her alarm climb. "The High King has summoned me to answer for what occurred in the Port of Azure."

Then her heart truly stopped.

"I broke the Accords..." he said. "I was pardoned once, but I cannot hope for a second. The trial is to be held in Hermon as soon as my father arrives."

Her hands started shaking. "You will be exiled?"

"I don't know. There is a high chance that might happen. And if it does..." His wings shuddered.

She looked at the beautiful black feathers, and she wanted to scream. If he was exiled, they would take his wings and, with them, his divine blood. It meant their bond would be severed.

Permanently.

Her tears spilled. "No..."

Cassiel reached for her wet cheek but stopped himself. "I would do it again, *lev sheli*. No matter what happens, I will never regret saving your life. I only cannot stand the thought of losing all memory of you."

Dyna was hit with pain so powerful her body spasmed. With every exile, King Yoel used his power of compulsion to make them forget who they were. He would erase her from Cassiel's mind.

"I barely found you," she choked on a sob. "Don't tell me we will lose each other again."

Her lungs constricted. She couldn't breathe. Cassiel grabbed the blanket's ends and pulled her back to him. He squeezed her tight until the wave of panic ebbed.

"Don't go. We will cross the Bridge without them knowing and leave Urn." But Dyna knew it was a measly plan.

"I cannot escape my father. The Valkyrie will ensure I return to Hermon Ridge either by choice or by force."

They looked up at the warrior females circling the sky above them. They remained at a respectful distance, but their alert attention was always on Cassiel.

"But you sacrificed yourself to save your wife. That has to count for something." Dyna felt a shift in him. A pause in his breath, the stilling of his hands on the small of her waist.

A rough sound rolled in the back of Cassiel's throat. "Say that again."

The vibration of his low words felt like the phantom caress of his fingers on her skin. His hands slid up her covered arms to her neck, the heat of his palm leaking through the fabric. The way he looked at her made her pulse speed.

"Your wife," she breathed.

He leaned in close, his mouth inches from hers. She felt the heat coming off them and the energy of the bond hovering on her lips. Gods, she may dissolve if she didn't kiss him soon.

"Every part of me at this moment is burning, Dynalya," he said. "So much that it may not be a good thing."

The fervor vanished with her confusion.

"I have something to show you." Cassiel shifted back and lifted his hand. For a moment, nothing happened. Then a bloom of cerulean flames danced at his fingertips.

She flinched back. "God of Urn. Is that Seraph fire?"

He nodded. "My sword was not the only thing affected that day. They seem to come at random. I cannot control it."

"How? Why?"

"I don't know. I suppose my father will. All I know is that untamed Seraph flames are dangerous, and it might be another cause of what keeps us apart. I'm afraid I might hurt you."

The flames were small but conducted a startling heat against her face. She had seen how powerful Seraph fire was when the Valkyrie had rendered people to instant ash with it.

Cassiel saw her expression, and he lowered his hand. "I frightened you—"

"No," she said firmly. "And I will never be, Cassiel. We will figure this out as we have everything else. At the moment, saving you from exile takes priority."

He raised his eyebrows, and a small smile appeared. "You may not have been raised a noble, but you certainly know how to give a command, Princess."

The title didn't seem to be hers, or if it ever truly would be. Not when what they had now hung so delicately in the balance.

But a question had been in the back of her mind since he first mentioned taking them to Hermon Ridge. How would they present themselves at court? Did she want that?

"Let's not get ahead of ourselves," she said.

"Dyna." He frowned, seeing right through her brittle bravery. "I care not what the Realms say. I am yours, and you are mine."

To hear that made her want to weep again.

The truth was, she felt unfitting. Cassiel wasn't merely a highborn. He was a prince of a long-standing kingdom. They hadn't had time to talk about their relationship since the willow. They were bonded, but until recently, it had only been in name. What they had now was something new and wonderful and so fragile. They had leaped so many steps ahead she found herself tripping and didn't know where she would land. But she couldn't ignore the glaring truth.

King Yoel could separate them if he so wished.

"Do you truly believe he would take away your memories?" Dyna asked.

Cassiel looked away. "He may have already."

She listened in quiet shock as he told her about his dream. But none of it sounded right. "That can't be. You weren't there. I remember running to the *Hyalus*...and it took my hand..." Her eyes widened. "It cast out a brilliant light that kept the Shadow at bay. Then..."

Then everything else was fuzzy.

But that was due to hiding in the burrow all night, leaving her delirious and freezing.

"Altering memories is one of the High King's abilities," Cassiel said. "My previous memory of that night was completely different. I had flown out into the storm to find my mother, but the cold numbed my wings, and I fell out of the sky. I broke several bones." His brow creased. "He sent me away to live in Hermon after that."

All Dyna remembered was her own father saying farewell and walking through the Gates. Perhaps it wasn't Yoel. Her father might have put a barrier on her. He very well could have used cognition magic to change what they saw that night, too.

Cassiel sighed. "We won't know the truth until we can speak with him. If I'm even permitted the chance. I deliberately disobeyed him when I joined you instead of going to Hermon as he ordered. I have traded my feathers, and we bonded because I broke the first law in giving you my blood."

"But no one other than us knows about our bond yet..." Dyna stilled when she remembered something. "Earlier today, the Valkyrie bowed to me."

He looked shamefaced. "I had to disclose our marriage to have them aid me in your search. Being part of the royal family provides certain protections, but they know nothing of how it came to be."

Dyna understood why he did it, though a minor part of her was bothered. Not by what he had to reveal, but because she had no choice in the matter. From being held captive, her magic taken, trapped in her mind, all of it left her feeling so powerless that she needed to have control over her life.

"From now on, everything regarding us will be decided by us," Cassiel said.

"Thank you." She slumped at the relief it brought her to regain a bit more of what she had lost. But she had so much more to lose. "I think we should keep the bond a secret."

He stilled. "What?"

Her chest tightened, but she continued. "We will say the disaster in the Port of Azure was because of the wanted notices. You were captured by a poacher seeking to earn his fortune, and he discovered what you were."

Lying wasn't something she condoned, but she was desperate, and it was the plan that made the most sense to her.

"It will work. Your father will see your innocence, and your sentencing will be reduced. When the court has settled in time, we can later disclose our bond as something that came to be."

Cassiel didn't seem convinced. "I'm required to speak the truth before the court."

"It's the truth. We're simply omitting some of it."

His eyes roved over her face. "Why do you want to do this?"

"It's my turn to protect you." Dyna clenched her fists, and her skin glowed green with her riled magic at the thought of anyone hurting him. "This is my fault, Cassiel. Tarn wouldn't have known about you if he hadn't come after me. If I hadn't gotten hurt, we never would have bonded. If I hadn't done something thoughtless, you never would have traded yourself. I dragged you into this mess because I'm a stupid human."

Cassiel chuckled. "You are a smart one, too. Occasionally."

She glowered at him playfully through her misted vision.

"Come." He stood. "There is something you need."

Confused, Dyna got to her feet. Her heart skipped a beat when he slipped off his long jacket.

His silver eyes slid to her slyly. *My lovely, sweet Dynalya.* He draped the jacket over her shoulders and held her gaze as he fastened each button, making sure she was covered. *Whatever are you thinking?*

She flushed at his smirk and hooked her arms around his neck. "Only of possibilities."

Flashing a grin, Cassiel swept her into his arms, and they both looked up at the stars. "Don't let go," he said in her ear.

They shot into the sky with a flutter of wings. The land quickly fell beneath them as they rose high into the night. She leaned her head on his shoulder, simply enjoying this moment. It was exactly what she needed.

They had been together only a short while, but she couldn't imagine not having him in her life when he had become an integral part of it. Even if King Yoel erased Cassiel from her mind, her soul and heart would feel his absence so keenly she would know something was missing.

The tears she'd been holding back fell. *If the worst comes to pass, please don't forget about me.*

I could never, lev sheli.

Dyna made a promise to herself that nothing and no one would sever their bond. She would fiercely protect it, as Cassiel had protected her because it was theirs. And nothing would take it from them.

PART II: POWER

CHAPTER 37

Cassiel

Since the magical explosion, Cassiel's dreams have been strange. He blinked up at the dawn sky, streaked pink and orange, where Dyna was suspended several feet high above him in the frigid morning air. Her arms hovered at her sides, locks of bright red hair flowing around her head like a wreath of flame. Sleepily, he lifted a hand for her, wondering how she got up there.

The ground felt cold and hard beneath his back. Rays of the sun peeked over the trees and glimmered on the frost coating the grass in the clearing. Every inhale chilled his throat and lungs.

Finding this dream rather vivid, Cassiel frowned and sat up.

Everyone else was sleeping around the dead campfire, except for Lord Norrlen. The tips of his nose and pointed ears were flushed pink from the cold, and disheveled blond hair fell in a tangled array down his shoulders. And his wide eyes were pinned on Dyna.

Cassiel blinked up at her with a new awareness. "This is not a dream, is it?"

Rawn slowly shook his head. "I'm afraid not. Lady Dyna is in the sky."

Cassiel jumped to his feet so fast, blood rushed to his head.

Rawn leaped over the campfire's ashes and covered his mouth before he could shout. "Be silent," he whispered. "If this is what I suspect, then you mustn't wake her."

Cassiel shoved his hand away. "What do you mean? What is happening?"

"I believe Lady Dyna is experiencing what may be the Rising."

He gaped at him.

The Rising was the awakening of power in mages. How can that be when Dyna said she hardly had any magic?

But he had seen her do amazing things with Essence Healing, and she was also a descendant of Azeran. A shudder crawled down Cassiel's back when he recalled the massive wave of fire she released at the fjord, and then the explosion when they broke the spell...

They both looked at Lucenna.

"I shall wake her before Zev," Rawn whispered, eyeing the wolf. "He may not take too kindly to seeing his cousin on the brink of the Heavens. Please remain calm. There is no need for alarm." He gave him a look, warning him to be still, then crouched by Lucenna. "My lady."

Her brow scrunched, and she groaned, burrowing further within the blankets. "Leave me be," she grumbled, her voice thick with sleep.

"My lady," Rawn whispered again, tugging on the blankets. "I'm afraid I must insist."

Lucenna lifted her head, and she glared at him through narrow slits. "Why do you wake me at such an ungodly hour?"

"Pardon me, but you must see this."

She sleepily looked at where he pointed and shot up straight, now fully awake. "God of Urn!"

Her shout woke Zev. Cassiel and the others froze as the wolf yawned and stretched, shaking out his flank.

"Good morrow, Zev," Rawn whispered to him. "Please do well to remain calm."

The wolf cocked his head questioningly at them before he followed their stare up to Dyna. Zev rapidly shifted to his nude form, rising on his feet. His sharp canine teeth were visible in his gaping mouth.

"Why is she up there?" he exclaimed.

"Quiet!" Lucenna whispered, hiding behind her hands. "Get dressed."

Zev hastily yanked on dark brown trousers and a tunic. "Why is she in the air? Get her down!"

Cassiel crouched in preparation to fly.

"No." Rawn caught his shoulder. "She could fall."

"I will catch her."

Lucenna shook her head. "You cannot touch her."

"What do you mean?" Cassiel's head snapped around to her.

"You may have guessed what this is," she said to Rawn.

He nodded but didn't look overly concerned, so Cassiel took a breath to sort himself.

"I have only seen the Rising Sleep happen with children in the Magos Empire when their magic awakens," Lucenna said. "I thought Dyna didn't have enough magic to experience it."

"Perhaps this is associated with the spell," Rawn mused, coming to the same conclusion as Cassiel.

"This is why she's different. Whenever we touch her, we are struck with her Essence," Cassiel said, frowning at Lucenna. "It's clearly not due to the remnants of a spell gone awry."

Lucenna rose to her feet and crossed her arms over her black dress. "Do you mean the spell that went awry because of you? It wasn't supposed to react in that manner."

Did he do this then? Because of his feathers?

"Something must have happened," Zev said. "It cannot be a coincidence."

Cassiel exhaled sharply through his nose and pressed on his forehead. "Whatever occurred, that magic affected our minds."

It uncovered the dream of the *Hyalus* tree.

Your bond was awoken the moment she first touched you, the Druid had said. Cassiel thought Leoake lied, but he and Dyna met as children. It was a memory buried so deep he may not have ever remembered if not for the spell.

"I had sensed a barrier containing Dyna's magic," Lucenna told them and glanced at Cassiel. "It only lowered when she used your feathers."

Rawn thoughtfully watched her in the air. "Could it be that when you reversed the spell on her mind, you may have removed whatever barrier contained her power?"

"I think you're right. It's not there anymore. I will have to ask Lucien about this. He will know what to do."

"How do we get her down?" Cassiel asked.

"We wait for her to descend. No one can touch her in that state." Lucenna picked up a pebble from the grass and threw it at Dyna. It hit an invisible surface and burst with a bright spark, a golden ripple revealing the transparent dome that surrounded her body. "That confirms it. Dyna's magic has been released. The sphere is a self-defense apparatus that protects her while she is vulnerable. Don't worry. She will come down on her own. If you startle her awake, she will drop. Attempt to catch her and she will strike you with a volt of raw Essence so potent it may kill you. So be patient and wait while I contact my brother."

Rawn nodded, silently ordering them to obey. Then he followed her to a heap of large rocks with the view of the Hermon Ridge Mountains at their backs. The orb in Lucenna's hands glowed bright white before she spoke to it animatedly. She held it above her head so Lucien could see.

Cassiel wished he knew what they were saying. Zev watched them intently, the distance not a hindrance to his keen hearing.

Sitting back down, Cassiel remained on watch in case Dyna should fall. It seemed like hours before she began to descend. Zev whistled. Rawn and Lucenna rushed to join as she came to rest on the ground.

Dyna's bright green eyes fluttered open sleepily, then they widened in surprise to find them all staring at her. "What's wrong?"

Cassiel and Zev glanced at each other, then at Rawn, and they all looked at Lucenna.

She glowered at them. "It's nothing to fret over. It will cease once Dyna adjusts."

"Adjust to what?" Dyna asked, sitting up.

"You were ... floating a moment ago," Cassiel told her.

Zev pointed up at the sky. "Up there."

"While you slept," Rawn added.

Dyna's eyes widened further. "What?"

"Stop it, you're frightening her." Lucenna glowered at them, then gave her a little smile. "Turns out you have plenty of magic in you, after all. You're in the Rising."

Dyna stared at her mutely. Her shock and bewilderment roiled through the bond, followed by a wave of overwhelming weight.

Breathe. Cassiel told her. *I know it's a lot to be told first thing, but you must breathe.*

She nodded and inhaled a shaky breath.

Good. Once more.

Dyna inhaled and exhaled another breath before she could speak. "But how can this be?" she asked Lucenna. "I'm past the normal age of magic development."

"We think your full power was released when I reversed the spell. Your barrier is gone."

The explosion... Dyna looked up at him. *He said it would happen when my barrier broke.*

Who?

"I agree," a voice called, and they glanced at the orb resting in the crook of Lucenna's arm.

"Oh, good morrow Lucien," Dyna said with an embarrassed smile. "I'm sorry to further burden you with my never-ending dilemmas."

"It's no trouble at all, Dyna. This is a rather curious situation, but it's you that I'm concerned about," the mage replied. "Your magic has surfaced, and it can be dangerous. The Rising happens during childhood because magic is diminutive at the age of five, which makes it the perfect time to train and harness it as your Essence grows. But it's been growing within you untamed. You must work hard to control it."

"I don't understand what this means," she said, her voice small. "Am I not the same anymore?"

Cassiel crouched next to her. "You are Dynalya Astron. Nothing about that has changed."

That seemed to ease the apprehension building in the bond. Instinctively, they reached for each other, but the moment their skin touched, a spark of energy struck him.

Dyna sighed. "I'm sorry."

"It's not your fault." He glowered at Lucenna over his shoulder.

Lucenna smirked. "The currents are her raw magic, Cassiel. I didn't give it to her. I simply gave her access to it."

"And the sorceress grants her sorcery..." Rawn murmured under his breath. "It's all coming to pass."

"Ah, that explains the shocks of power you mentioned the other day," Lucien said. "I should have realized what was happening."

"Don't worry," Lucenna told her. "Your magic will settle once you learn to manage it. Come along, I think we have much to discuss. Now the real lessons begin."

Lucenna led her back to the rocks to sit. Dyna held the crystal orb and nodded to whatever Lucien was saying.

Groaning, Cassiel rubbed his temples. What more could befall her? All he wanted was to bring joy back to her life.

"Your Highness." The sunlight graced Yelrakel's golden armor as she landed and bowed. "I must fly ahead to announce your impending arrival. Lieutenant Sowmya and a small party will stay behind to escort you."

"There is no need, Captain. We will make our way there."

"I'm afraid I must insist." Because she couldn't risk him running off again.

Cassiel glanced at Dyna and he smiled faintly. "Very well. We will stop by the town of Hallow's Nest on our way to the mountain. Meet us on the ledge in four days with what we discussed."

She nodded. "I will. However, there is a concern I must bring to your attention."

By the look on her face, Cassiel knew he wouldn't like it in the least.

CHAPTER 38

Dynalya

D yna looked down upon the town of Hallow's Nest. It was set on a lowland near the Hermon River, surrounded by rolling hills and fir trees. The morning sun hid behind gray clouds, and the cold left a dewy gleam on every blade of grass. They had traveled for three days to reach the town and needed to stop to rest and restock their provisions before making the trek to Hermon Ridge. The mountains rose just beyond the town like stone giants dressed in snow. God of Urn willing, their stay would be short, and they'd cross Troll Bridge soon. Dyna felt a tingle of anticipation and some restlessness.

Lucenna grumbled tiredly. "Suppose we could find a tavern here? I miss sleeping in a bed."

"There is only one lodging house in town," Cassiel said, frowning. "But I have little hope we will find any rooms now."

For a small town, it was teeming with people. A steady stream of them traveled on the main road.

"Best we head in," Rawn said. He took the lead, with Zev and Lucenna following him.

The tall, wet grass stuck to Dyna's boots and legs as they made their way down the short hill. It settled a cold in her bones that made her shiver.

"Here." Cassiel lifted her on Fair's back, but nearly lost his hold when her fingers accidentally brushed his exposed wrist.

"I'm sorry," she said again for what seemed like the twentieth time that morning.

Right when Dyna thought things may be normal for her, something new always came along. Well, nothing had been normal for her since she lost her family. This was merely another thing she had to withstand.

"I'm fine, *lev sheli.*" He tugged his coat sleeve, so it came over his leather gloves.

They had all taken to wearing gloves and keeping a subtle distance, which she pretended not to notice. Not that she could blame them.

Feeling her dejection, Cassiel reached out. "Dyna—"

Don't. She leaned back in the saddle.

Her magic would only hurt him again. She felt it there, hovering on the surface, free and ready where it had once been a task to produce a trickle.

He dropped his hand. "I hate this."

"I know." She hated it, too.

"How fortunate that Fair is immune." Cassiel gathered the reins, giving the horse a pat. "I am not envious at all."

That at least made her smile. Rawn's horse was the only one not affected by the currents that had taken over her body.

"That's because Fair is special, aren't you?" she stroked his white mane. "Elvish horses are accustomed to magic, I suppose."

Fair nickered in response, bobbing his head.

Her unrestrained power felt so strange. She compared it to suddenly being given a vast inheritance and not knowing how to take care of it. Lucenna continued to train her, but that didn't stop her from hovering in the air at night while she slept.

Fair straightened out once they reached the base of the hill, and Cassiel led them to the others waiting by the entrance to town. They all pulled up their hoods before going in. If luck was on their side, there wouldn't be any bounty hunters this far up north.

Hallow's Nest was a homey town that resembled Landcaster. It had similar charming wattle and daub structures with steep roofs that lined the roads. Townsfolk went in and out of many small shops either selling clothing or goods. Wagons with the last of fall's harvest rattled past them as they rolled over the uneven cobblestone.

Dyna could tell the difference between locals and those merely passing through. The travelers were unusually beautiful with perfect blond hair and blue eyes, and they wore fine robes of a distinct style that she had only seen in one place.

Many of them shot long side glances at her mate. Very few stiffly dipped their chins in a subtle nod.

Cassiel...

263

You noticed them.

It was hard not to, despite their wings being hidden within their enchanted clothing. *Are they...?*

Yes.

Her cousin noticed too, by the way he sniffed the air. "Why is this town full of Celestials?" Zev whispered under his breath, alerting the others.

Rawn glanced at a pair of them with warmer skin tones, who cast them narrowed looks. "Some have arrived from every corner, it seems."

"It's that time of year." Cassiel ignored those who acknowledged him, though she could sense he wasn't happy about their presence. "They have come for the Festival of Light. It's a holiday we hold at the beginning of winter. Every year, it's hosted by a different Lord and all the Realms arrive to celebrate. Unfortunately, it's my uncle's turn."

Dyna's stomach sank. That meant nearly every Celestial from Hilos and the Four Realms will be in Hermon Ridge when they arrived.

Yelrakel warned me before she left, Cassiel told her through the bond. *It's supposed to be a time of peace for my people. Let's pray they remember that.*

But her apprehension only doubled.

"We will go ahead to reserve our lodging before there are no rooms to be let," he said aloud to the others.

Rawn nodded. "I suppose now would be a good time to restock our provisions."

"And a tent, *please*," Lucenna groaned. Out of all of her possessions, only her bag and orb had survived the spell's blast.

Leaving Fair with Rawn, they parted ways. She and Zev went with Cassiel as he led them to a three-story house with several windows on the outskirts of town. The hope of finding a place to stay dwindled when they found the front door open with a line of waiting Celestials.

"That looks promising," Zev rumbled.

Everyone turned to look at Cassiel. In a blink, he became that stoic prince she remembered. Royalty shone in the way he held himself, the sun somehow seeming to grace every fine line of his elegant jacket. His expression was cold and severe, one that exuded authority and expected compliance.

All stepped aside.

Cassiel strode onward. Dyna and Zev closely followed. She felt every eye watching as they made their way inside. The old woman at the counter noting down guests greeted Cassiel with warm familiarity, but informed them that the last rooms were taken by the two males standing at the front of the line.

They were pale-skinned Celestials with long, braided blond hair. Embroidered on the corner hem of their light purple tunics was the silver emblem of a shield wreathed in flame. It was a new sigil she hadn't seen before.

Cassiel fixed his cool gaze on them. They stiffly bowed their heads and left the lodging house.

"I will take their rooms, Yara," he told the old woman. To the other Celestials, he said sharply, "This lodging house is full. Find somewhere else to stay for the night."

The majority departed at his command. A few of the pale ones lingered, holding his stare as if to defy him. They wore a darker shade of purple and more weapons. Tension filled the silence as Cassiel turned to face them.

Sowmya and five Valkyrie appeared from the tree branches outside. They landed in the shadows of the forest and drew their weapons. The Celestials grudgingly moved on and the road emptied.

"I thought they were going to fight you for it," Zev chuckled once they secured their belongings and went back outside.

"I'm sure they considered it," Cassiel said. He nodded to the Valkyrie, and they returned to the trees, vanishing behind the leaves. They hid so well, Dyna sometimes forgot they were around. "The males of Skath like to resolve nearly everything with a challenge."

"Skath?" she repeated. It was frozen land far northwest on her map. "Another Realm is hidden there?"

"Yes. Skath has frigid temperatures year round, and it's inhibited by large carnivorous beasts. Humans stay away, therefore, it's a good place to hide a Realm. Like the land, the Celestials that live there are harsh and quick to violence. They even created a steel that deflects divine fire, and they use it for their shields. Lord Hallel oversees that Realm now."

"Who lorded over it before?" Zev asked.

"He usurped it from his eldest brother during a challenge. Slew him, quite savagely, and took everything he owned."

God of Urn.

"It's the only time the death of a Celestial is permitted without the authority of the High King."

Zev shrugged. "It happens among the Packs too when an Alpha's position is weakened. Have any of the Lords attempted to challenge your father?"

"It's not permitted. During the First Age, our people once lived together under the rule of the first High King. But he left no heirs, so at the end of his reign, his three generals fought amongst themselves over who should take the throne. They had barely survived the recent war against demons. To avoid another, three Realms were established and given independence with the promise that whoever wears the crown is never to be challenged."

"And your uncle now lords over the fourth Realm," Dyna said. "Each has their own Watchers as well?"

"Of course, and their own armies."

"Where are the other two located?" Zev tilted his head, alert to the nearby sounds of the surrounding land. He glanced up at the tree canopy, perhaps listening to the Valkyrie following. "If I may ask."

Cassiel parted aside the thick shrubbery and revealed an open clearing. He motioned for them to step through. They left the path, and he led them to a nearby shallow stream where he crouched to refill their waterskins. "Lord Gadriel lords over the first Realm, the floating islands of Nazar. They lie above the Vale of the Elves. Hidden for the most part within the towering clouds."

The revelation left her in awe. Dyna would have to look over the map again, but she was sure Nazar wasn't noted. Azeran's map would only show places he had visited or knew of two hundred and fifty years ago. It was outdated, but whenever they discovered a new place, it would appear on the page by some embedded spell. "I didn't know Urn had floating islands."

"I heard there are many in Arthal," Zev said.

"With four Realms, how do you know who is from where?" Dyna asked.

"Celestials take pride in their territories. During gatherings, they will dress according to their flag colors and the shades represent their class. The darker the color, the higher their status of nobility." Cassiel picked up a stick and drew a rough symbol of a sun fanned by six wings. "The emblem of Nazar. Their color is yellow." Next, he drew another of a pair of open wings with two crossed swords at the center. "The second Realm of Edym lies within the desert of Harromog Modos. Their color is red. It's ruled by Lord Raziel, grandfather to my brothers and sister."

That meant he was the father of the High Queen. Dyna remembered her striking beauty and locks like a river of sunlight. They had briefly met Cassiel's family in Hilos. She forgot the names of his youngest sister and brother, but Malakel she remembered clearly.

Cassiel drew the fire shield symbol. "Skath is the third and their color is purple." He outlined Hermon's sigil of a tree within a mountain next. "My uncle's color is blue." And above the four, he drew the crowned fire sword for Hilos. "As you know, Hilos is white, and it stands above all."

"Hmm. I think it's risky to have the Realms separate from the main kingdom," Zev said. "Any of them could one day decide to challenge your father or break away all together."

Cassiel frowned at the sigils in the mud. "The only one I would wager having the capability to challenge Hilos would be Edym, but I don't believe Lord Raziel would break the peace."

"Because he is the Queen's father?" Dyna asked.

"Because his grandson will one day take the throne."

To think Malakel would be king made her worry, Cassiel too, by the way his expression creased.

"Do you have more family?" Dyna asked to change the subject.

His mouth pursed with dull annoyance. "I have a cousin. My uncle's son. He lives in Hermon." Cassiel put away their waterskins, and they headed back for the road. "Before you ask, no. Asiel is not a half-breed. My uncle was married when he defected from Hilos. His wife did not agree with his views but joined him in Hermon Ridge out of obligation to their union. After several centuries of suffering her scorn, Lord Jophiel agreed to release her once she provided him with an heir. And she did. Within hours of the birth, she dropped their baby in his arms and left for another Realm."

"I thought Celestials didn't have annulments," Zev said.

"Marriage contractually cannot end, but they can reject a bond. It's rarely done because when Celestials love, it's profound. They also loathe with equal intensity. To have reached that point, the bond..." A look crossed Cassiel's face, and she wondered if he was thinking of King Yoel and Queen Mirah. "It's left to wither and crack, abandoned between two doors closed shut against each other. They will always know where the other is, but it ruined the vows they made along with their affections."

To have love die like that sounded very sad to Dyna, more so to be left behind by a parent. "Her son must be devastated."

"Don't waste your sympathy on Asiel. He could not care less about his mother."

She caught the detest in her mate's tone. "You haven't mentioned a cousin until now."

Cassiel's jaw clenched as he glowered at the road ahead. "He's not worth the breath to mention."

The activity of the town picked up as more Celestials arrived by the hour. Dyna followed Cassiel and Zev along the merchant stalls, perusing their wares. Rawn and Lucenna were ahead, bargaining over the cost of a tent.

"How about some gloves?" Cassiel asked her, holding up a leather pair. "To ward off the cold."

Zev leaned down to whisper in her ear, "And to keep you from zapping everyone. Him in particular."

Rolling her eyes playfully at him, Dyna conceded and wandered to the stall beside it, selling brooches. She was admiring one fashioned into a green leaf veined in silver when a prickle of awareness touched her back. Dyna glanced across the busy street and froze when she spotted Von.

The thick crowd swarmed around them as they stared at one another.

At first, she thought he had tracked her down, but his eyes were wide, as though he couldn't quite believe she was there.

Dyna went straight to him. Von reversed several steps, nearly stumbling, into a shadowy alley between two shops. He threw out his hands in a motion to make her stop. The lump in his neck bobbed several times, trying to come up with words he couldn't speak. Up close, he appeared weary, his complexion ashen. Purple shadows sunk in the circles around his eyes, and a beard was overtaking his gaunt face.

Guilt.

Dyna could see it weighing him down heavily. She moved a step, but Von quickly backed up several more. He looked anxious and confused by her presence. Dyna realized the last time they were together, he had seen her fall from the sky.

Oh. He thought she had died, and that it was his fault.

"Von, it's all right," she said softly. "I'm all right. I am alive."

His broad shoulders rose with a sharp breath, his eyes growing glassy. "How?" he finally croaked.

"Lucenna reversed the spell."

A weak laugh left him, and he rubbed his face. "Oh...of course..."

Dyna felt the roiling energy of Cassiel's presence before she saw him. A flash of black struck Von and his body crashed at the end of the alley, hitting the cobblestone hard enough to break something.

Cassiel came to stand beside her. He unsheathed his weapon as a snarling wolf flanked Dyna's other side. Across the alley, Rawn and Lucenna came up behind Von, armed with bow and magic. They had him trapped.

"I made you a promise of what I would do if she was harmed," Cassiel said. His sword crackled in the wind, blue flames licking along the blade. "There is only one thing I want to know. How quickly do you wish to burn?"

She shuddered at the quiet malice in his voice.

Von slowly righted himself off the ground. He didn't brace himself to fight or grab one of the many knives strapped to bandoliers hidden under his tattered black cloak.

Dyna reached for Cassiel's hand but stopped, feeling electric currents hovering at her fingertips.

Von wiped the blood from his mouth and grunted painfully as he stumbled to his feet. "They truly are your Guardians."

She hadn't grown accustomed to calling them that, but she could see it now in their love and need to protect her. And they did so fiercely.

The wolf stalked forward, growling and snapping his teeth.

"Stay, Zev," Dyna said calmly. He stopped between her and Von, his fur standing on end.

Von's mouth curved with a hint of a smile that didn't fully form. "I'm glad to see you alive." He glanced at Cassiel. "Thank you."

"Don't thank me when it was you who nearly took his life. Now I intend to take yours."

"There is no need for this," she said. "Von isn't a threat."

How can you say that after he kidnapped you twice and nearly killed Zev? Cassiel asked without looking away from him.

"Because he…" Dyna looked at Von and some unspoken emotion swelled in her chest. Even when she had been angry with him, she never felt unsafe. "He protected me while I was in Tarn's camp."

Von's throat constricted, and he shook his head. "I didn't…"

Dyna saw the misery in his eyes. A bad person wouldn't have cared. "Clayton acted on his own accord. I don't hold you responsible for that. You saved my life twice, and you helped me escape. If it wasn't for you, I would still be captive. Or dead."

She felt how the revelation shocked the others. Enough to make them lower their weapons, and Zev stopped growling.

Except her mate.

"That does not erase his deeds," Cassiel said through his teeth. "The best thing for us would be to remove him from the opposition. Permanently."

Dyna had a choice here, to either capture Von or let him go. Her Guardians would take him down, kill him if she wanted them to. He was the commander. A key component to Tarn's little army. It would be beneficial to remove him.

"You're right not to trust me, but I don't mean to stay," Von told her earnestly, because he must sense what she was thinking. "I was only passing through Hallow's Nest on my way to another city. But I have to go back, Dyna."

Because Yavi needed him…and so did their unborn child. Did he know yet?

Von reached into his pack, and they immediately armed themselves again. He only pulled out a familiar black book. On top, he added her opal knife. "These belong to you."

"Stay there," Cassiel snarled when he tried to hand them to her.

Dyna cast out her magic and gently took the items from Von. Her eyes watered at the familiar weight of Azeran's journal falling into her hands. She traced the crescent wrapped in vines on the cover. "Thank you."

"Take it as my sign of good will." And possibly a bribe, because Von knew he didn't have the advantage here.

If she let him go, there was no guarantee tomorrow he wouldn't be their enemy, but at the moment, she didn't see one.

"Let him go," Dyna said, holding his gaze. "I owe him a debt."

Rawn and Lucenna stepped aside and came to stand with her.

"Will you tell your master she is alive?" Rawn asked him.

"I won't mention her unless he asks. So please do your best to stay out of his way and out of sight."

"I won't allow Tarn to reach Mount Ida," she said. "I mean to stop him, Von."

A soft sigh left him, and one end of his mouth curved. It wasn't a full smile or a real one. It was tired and sad, but a little hopeful. "Then I wish you luck."

"Wait," Dyna called hesitantly when he turned. "Dalton…"

Von stopped with his back to her.

She swallowed to say the words, her fingers tangling together. "He must hate me…for what I did. Please tell him…" Her voice shook. "Please tell him I'm sorry."

His silence was heavy. "I'm afraid I won't be able to pass on your message, lass. The lad is no longer with us…He's free."

Then Von slipped out of the alley into the sun, falling out of sight.

It was the best news she could have received. It made Dyna so happy to know Dalton was on his way home and would see his mother again.

Cassiel sheathed his sword, extinguishing the flames. "We should not allow him to leave."

"I believe he told the truth," Rawn said. "He will not disclose her survival until his obligation as a life-servant requires him to speak of it."

Lucenna frowned. "How is that helpful? He will inform Tarn eventually."

Dyna wasn't worried about that. Knowing Tarn, he would find out one way or another.

They returned to the main road and headed to the lodging house for the evening. She could feel the bond jumble with Cassiel's anger and his need to go after Von.

"Are those for me?" Dyna asked, nodding to the small gloves he'd tucked in his belt.

"Oh, yes." He stopped to pull them out for her.

They were made of a soft leather that matched the color of her boots and reached all the way to her elbows. As soon as she had them on, Cassiel cradled her hand in his palm as he took a deep breath, and she felt the bond settle.

"Your sword needs a new name," Dyna said softly, glancing at the golden wings of the hilt at his hip. "It's no longer a simple divine sword now."

His mouth quirked. He saw through her attempt to distract him further. They linked fingers and continued. "Any suggestions? Or shall we keep to tradition and name it blue fire sword?"

Dyna laughed. "Hmm. I think it should be something to honor its new status. Seraph fire is a grand thing, is it not?"

"It's only given by *Elyōn*," Cassiel said, and they both looked up at the Heavens. "Then it shall be named *Esh Shamayim*. Fire extracted from the skies."

"That's beautiful." Dyna repeated the foreign words and made him smile at her shoddy pronunciation. "I like it."

CHAPTER 39

Von

Von left Hallow's Nest behind him with a weight over his head. He had to lie. No, he *chose* to lie. Because telling Dyna the truth would do nothing but hurt her, and he knew it would remind them both of what she had told him before.

Killing seems all you're good for.

And it was true.

When he was a mile down the road, Elon surfaced from the shadows of the trees, silent as a ghost. Their horses were with him. Von patted Coal's gray neck and mounted without a word. Clicking his tongue, they cantered onward.

Dyna was alive, but his relief tangled with worry. Tarn thought she was dead, and it had to stay that way.

"The others?" he asked when Novo, Len, and Bouvier had yet to join them.

"I sent them ahead to scout for any concerns, Commander," Elon said.

Like the Azure knights.

"They will meet us in Tanner's Cove."

That was a few days from Beryl Coast. They were close. As long as things went smoothly, they should return to Indigo Bay within two weeks. But there was always something around the corner.

Once they crossed the bridge over the Hermon River, Von tugged on his reins and led them off the main road into the woodlands. They rode through the day into the evening in silence. Elon didn't care for conversation, which Von was thankful for, consumed as he was by his thoughts.

As the miles grew between him and Yavi, the more he missed her. The way she had looked at him with such disgust and disappointment plagued him every time he closed his eyes. Leaving on his mission may be what they needed to give her some time away from him, but all he wanted was to go back and fall on his knees at her feet.

The low sun streamed in at their backs, stretching their shadows across the ground. A gust of wind tugged at his hair, carrying the scent of pine and coming frost. It would be another cold night.

"Commander!" Elon shouted. He flicked out his sword and blocked a whirling blade coming for Von's back.

He turned at the neigh of horses and cursed to see a group of men riding for them through the woods. Their navy blue coats flared behind them like sails, black masks covering the bottom halves of their faces.

The Skelling Mercenaries had found him.

"Go!" Von barked.

They kicked their heels and galloped as fast as they could. The last time Von faced two of them, he barely escaped. The odds against thirty were far less survivable. They raced out of the woodland into a wide clearing. The beat of hooves racing after them quickly caught up.

Elon hissed a word in Elvish. Blue magic cleaved through the air, but it bounced off the golden shields that flickered around each man. They must have charms against magic.

Damn.

"Don't waste your power," Von said. They raced across the clearing and soon a looming forest appeared ahead. The twisted trees were dense and dark.

They could lose them in there.

"Those are the Black Woods," Elon warned him.

"I know. Don't stop. That's an order!"

The men raced after them, shouting calls to each other. More knives came, and arrows too. They ducked, and Elon cast out a shield. The forest grew nearer. But right when they reached the tree line, Coal reared with a wild neigh. His horse had never done it before, so Von wasn't prepared to hold on. The reins slipped from his hands and he fell to the ground. He rolled away from stomping hooves before he was trampled. Elon fought to control his horse too, but it refused to go forward. He leaped off, and both horses rode away, leaving them behind.

Cursing his wretched luck, Von ran into the forest. He was plunged into brisk shadow and he felt an eerie dread crawl over him, but the threat at their backs wasn't any better. They ran and kept running until they found a dry, shallow gulley. Leaping in, they dove under the roots of a rotting tree. Shouting voices slipped through the shrubbery, the squelch of boots in the mud following.

"Spread out! They can't have gone far."

Von recognized that commanding voice. Waiting for them to pass, he risked peering above the lip of the gulley and looked through the thorny bushes. Two mercenaries stood nearby, one with blond hair and the other with dark brown curls falling over an eye patch. Klyde and Eagon. They were strapped with weapons, and each bore a white emblem spread across the back of their coats. A bird's skull pointed downward, piercing an upside down crescent.

A shout of alarm came from further ahead, and the mercenaries dashed for the sound. A massive ogre came tearing from the bushes. It was green and thorny, about fifteen feet tall. And a mercenary hung from its jaws. Its dull teeth bit down, and blood gushed out of the screaming man. The sight of it made Von recall memories that left him immobile.

The captured mercenary shoved his blade into the creature's eye, and it dropped him.

"Bring it down," Klyde barked. "Formation: High Cross."

Grappling hooks shot from the harnesses of three mercenaries, piercing the trees. The iron cables yanked the men into the air toward the ogre. Two whizzed past each other in the path of an X and they sliced through the creature's thick arms with a swipe of their blades. The third mercenary zoomed up and severed the head clean off. They landed in a flawless crouch as the beast toppled backward, falling dead.

It was over in three perfectly calculated moves. Von had never seen such a thing, let alone the harness contraptions they used. Klyde and Eagon had observed it with mild interest, as if this was an everyday occurrence.

A mercenary with a crop of messy orange curls ran over to the wounded man and yanked out a roll of bandages from his utility belt.

"Olyver," Klyde called to him.

"Deep lacerations to the torso and hip, Captain," the mercenary replied in a thick brogue accent, pressing on the wounds. "Aye, and his leg is broken, too. We need to take Sigrid to the nearest healer before the wounds fester."

"Tanzanite Keep is the best option," Eagon said, his voice muffled behind his black mask. "Hallow's Nest is unlikely to have a Herb Master."

Klyde cursed.

"He may survive the journey home, but do you want to risk it?"

Where was home? Their northern accent was clearly from Old Tanzanite Keep, but they didn't seem to live there.

"You know I won't," Klyde said. "Cam, Alasdair—accompany Olyver and Sigrid to the city, then make your way back to Skelling. The rest will stay and smoke out the spies. I know they're here."

Von ducked down further.

The named mercenaries quickly had the wounded man on a horse, and they rode out of the Black Woods. The others waited for their next command. A distant, frightening screech came from within the trees.

Eagon let out a heavy sigh. "Gale will finish me if these woods don't first. We shouldn't have come here."

Klyde chuckled. "There is no glory in cowardice, mate. Besides, what's an ogre or two?"

"Sometimes I wonder if you struck your head too many times. Do you fear anything at all?"

"Aye, I fear passing through the Gates alone. Which is why you're here."

Eagon sighed. "If we stay any longer, we'll die."

"Then we die with glory."

It was the hissing Von heard first, before the horrid acrid smell. Branches snapped, and the bushes rattled as two hulking serpentine beasts came slithering through the dark forest.

Basilisks.

They surrounded the mercenaries.

Klyde grinned sheepishly at Eagon's glare. "All right, I know we're in a bind, but never fear. I have a grand plan." He reached for the crossed swords at his back, each pommel adorned with a polished blue skull. "There is a wee chance we might die, but if we live to tell the tale, it will be the best one yet. You're with me, aye?"

"No, not aye."

"Good. Glad to hear you've got my back, mate."

"I said *not* aye," Eagon grumbled. He armed himself and they ran to meet the creatures.

The smallest Basilisk lunged for them first. They jumped out of the way in opposite directions, dodging the fangs by inches. It spun for the other mercenaries. Rolling to his feet, Klyde shot a grappling hook above him. It launched him into the air. He landed on the creature and shoved his blades into its skull. It screeched, flailing to throw him off. Klyde jammed them in further and twisted. That sent them crashing as it dropped.

Von jerked when he saw the larger one descending on him.

"Captain!" Eagon threw a knife.

It sliced through the Basilisk's eye, earning Klyde a split second to duck before it caught him.

He sheathed his swords and kept running. "Give me a line!"

Eagon whipped out two throwing stars from his coat made of red metal. He tossed them at the trees ahead of Klyde and they landed on two trunks ten feet in the air, equally spaced apart. They glowed red and a beam of light formed between them in a line, releasing a crackle of magic in the air.

Klyde sprinted for it with the Basilisk on his tail. It rapidly slithered after him, opening its wide jaws. Von stopped breathing because he knew the man was dead now.

He ran through the trees with the glowing line above him and shot another hook into the canopy. It yanked him into the air, in the path of those teeth. The Basilisk lunged for him—hurtling right through the line. It slit through its neck, spraying out blood and sinew like rain. The head slid off the creature and it collapsed to the ground with a wet thud.

Klyde landed in a crouch. "I wasn't sure if that would work."

Von was still shocked it did. Elon stood quietly beside him, also watching.

"Ready to leave?" Eagon asked, flicking something slimy off his shoulder.

"Go ahead without me."

"Klyde."

He walked away.

"Mate."

"No," Klyde snarled, all humor gone from his face. He removed his mask, revealing the thick scruff on his jaw. "Von is here. I have him cornered, Eagon."

"He went through the Black Woods. No one makes it out alive, and we certainly won't if we continue. If you tell the men to march on, we will follow you, Captain." He lowered his mask, his one eye on him. "I'm asking you not to get me killed for your vendetta."

Von had wronged many people in his life, but he didn't know what he had done to this man. Not once did he remember crossing swords with Klyde before their first meeting. And yet...there was something about his face that was familiar. The only thing he did fully recognize was the dual blade technique he fought with.

Klyde roughly rubbed his face. "Then we'll go around."

"That will add days to our travel. We have to go back. If we delay anymore, we risk being barred from home until spring. You know I can't do that."

Klyde stared into the woods, his fists clenching.

"Von isn't Tarn, mate," Eagon said. "I know what this means to you. He will answer for his deeds when the time comes, but that day is not today."

Von slunk back down in his hiding spot, staring at the dry creek bed. Who was he to Tarn?

Eagon's counsel seemed to have worked because the men cleared out of the Black Woods. Dirt shifted overhead and Von stilled at the sound of boots pausing by where he hid.

Klyde's voice dropped low, as if he was speaking only for him. "I will hunt you like an animal. There is no sanctuary in which you can hide from me."

The pure loathing in that oath rose the hair on Von's neck. He hid there with Elon for the rest of the night, wondering what he could have done to earn the hatred of a man he had never met.

CHAPTER 40

Lucenna

Magic was like lightning. The spark before the storm that could be both beautiful and so incredibly dangerous. Lucenna felt power crackling in the air, but it wasn't hers. She lowered her hairbrush and looked into the mirror set on the vanity within their lodging room. Through the reflection, she saw Dyna sitting on the edge of their shared bed, gazing outside at the night sky. The moonlight shone over her troubled features.

"What are you thinking about?" Lucenna asked her.

"Many things. Worries and questions. Some have answers, others perhaps not. If I were to sleep, would the ceiling stop me from floating away or would my magic make a hole in the roof?"

Lucenna came to sit beside her. Dyna scooted over, careful that their arms didn't accidentally touch past her gloves. "You won't float away."

"What did Lucien have to say about what I told you?"

She glanced at her satchel hanging from the chair. Her brother had only been mildly surprised to hear the truth about their people. That sorceresses were more powerful than mages, and it was the reason the Empire sought to control them. Lucien had suspected it, and Dalton only confirmed it. He was more startled by the fact that the union of a mage and sorceress from different Guilds didn't dampen magic. It wasn't permitted, so no one could have known mixing their blood meant they could use more elements.

Only the Archmage's family was allowed, since a Transcendent sorceress could be born of any Guild. So they could claim the ability to transcend the elements was passed down through the bloodline. It had always been about control.

All the lies made Lucenna want to destroy something.

"It's valuable information for the Liberation," she said. "There is talk of secretly teaching more sorceresses to use magic. But we lack information on mixed bloodlines. The Empire never pardons those who defy the law of marrying outside of their Guilds, and any children are quickly dealt with."

Dyna lowered her head.

"I have to believe there are some out there in hiding, or concealing the truth of who they are. But this news makes a significant difference, Dyna." Lucenna laid a hand over hers. "It means we have a real fighting chance."

They weren't as weak as the mages made them believe. That could be the very thing to draw more to their cause.

"Part moon, part sun, they called me," Dyna murmured. "It's why my Essence burns like fire."

Now it all made sense. The blast at the fjord had nearly destroyed it. That type of power could be detrimental at the hands of someone untrained.

"I don't have much experience with Sun Guild magic, but I can teach you other things. Let's hold a small lesson before we sleep." Lucenna laid face up on the bed and motioned for her to do the same. "I will teach you impressions. It's a fun spell. I want you to cast a small stream of your Essence and send it forth to float in the air."

Dyna lifted her hand, and Lucenna felt how the power in her blood easily surfaced to her fingertips. Green light flared to life in her palm. What had once felt so trying had become effortless. Her magic seemed almost eager to be used. Her brow tightened, and a small green globe of light gently rose in the air above them.

"Good. Give it a shape. Any one."

Dyna bit her lip as she concentrated, and the ball of light molded into the shape of a wolf. She went a step further and made it run as if it was crossing a vast meadow.

Lucenna smiled. "Excellent. Now speak to me."

Dyna blinked. "What?"

The image winked away.

"You already know magic is ruled by will and intent. Now you must learn to maintain your spells amid any distraction."

She brought it forth again, and this time her Essence formed into a prancing horse that looked a lot like Fair.

"A child mage is more dangerous than an adult one," Lucenna said. "They haven't learned how to control their Essence, and they are easily susceptible to their emotions. At the moment, that's you, so for the sake of others and yourself, you must always remain calm."

The prancing horse flickered. But it regained its light and reformed into a bird. Lucenna cast out her Essence and created small purple clouds through which the green bird flew. Miniscule flashes of lightning flickered above it.

"Add another impression," Lucenna instructed.

With the gentle wave of her hand, Dyna easily created a larger bird. A phoenix this time. "I feel so much power inside of me," she said, watching the birds fly together. "I'm afraid I won't be able to handle it. That I will...hurt someone. Again."

Lucenna looked at her. She had sensed a change in Dyna, suspecting it had something to do with more than magic.

"I killed the Earth mage," Dyna confessed quietly. "To break his spell and escape."

The birds faded, and the impression took the shape of a miniature version of Dyna sitting in a chair, looking up at an old man in long robes, right before she struck him in the neck. The moment repeated itself over and over.

"Do you feel guilty?" Lucenna asked, watching the rest of the scene unfold with the Raiders chasing her right before she leaped off a cliff.

"I do...for taking him away from those who loved him, but not for having done it." Dyna closed her eyes. "I fear killing people will be something I do without thought. I don't want that." Her voice dropped. "I don't want to be like...him."

The impressions changed to the image of a man. He stood facing away from them, but there was something ominous from only having a view of his back. *Tarn*, Lucenna guessed. Either Dyna didn't want to see his face, or she didn't fully remember it yet.

"You're not like him." Lucenna waved a hand and purple clouds swept Tarn away, leaving their Essence to swirl like smoke. "Levitate that candle douter while creating another impression."

Dyna flicked her fingers, and the long brass handle with a bell end lifted into the air. She created several impressions of forest sprites that flew around the douter, some sitting on it. Her magic was advancing nicely. She would acclimate to her full power in no time if she remained at this calm pace, but life was never still.

"You're not like him simply because you worry about taking lives," Lucenna told her. "That separates you both."

"I want to use my magic to help people."

"You will. Did you know that Essence takes on the color of your aura?"

Dyna nodded.

"Occasionally, it can change, but mostly, it remains the color presented when you first use magic. Green represents healing and compassion. It means you have a kind heart."

Dyna gave her a watery smile. "Azeran's Essence was purple, too. It means power and foresight."

"Exactly." Lucenna winked. "So take my word for it. You will do great things."

"If I...ever lose control..."

"I will be right there to stop you," she promised. "All right, focus. Keep levitating more objects while maintaining your impressions against mine."

With a flick of her hand, Dyna added a book to the air. Lucenna created an image of a wave washing away the sprites. Frowning, Dyna added a boot to the other objects and created a ship on the waves. Lucenna countered with a hurricane that sank the ship, swallowing the green light whole. Then she aimed a rain of purple arrows at her face. Gasping, Dyna threw out her hands. All the floating objects crashed on the ground as a golden light covered her. The impressions bounced off the surface, dissolving away.

"You made a shield." Lucenna laughed. "Well done."

Dyna flushed. "I dropped the spell."

"You did, but you also protected yourself, and that's the most important thing." She might have boasted about ending whatever enemy crossed her path, but Lucenna didn't enjoy killing. It was simply what she had to do to survive, because the world wasn't a kind place.

Sighing, Dyna rested back on the pillow, looking less weighted. "Where do you find the strength to be this strong?"

"We are women. The strength finds us."

Dyna smiled at that. Then her gaze went distant, and she nodded as if responding to someone. She was communicating with Cassiel, Lucenna guessed. Dyna had told her about their True Bond and how deeply it connected them. He must have been startled by the crash.

Zev, too, when his fist beat on the door next. "Dyna? What happened?"

"I'm all right, Zev," she called. "Only a little magic practice."

After a pause, he spoke, sounding much more relieved. "Might we save that for tomorrow morning? *Outdoors?*"

"She's fine, overprotective grumps!" Lucenna said loud enough for all three of them to hear in the room next door. "Sorry to disturb you. We will keep it down."

They used their magic to return the objects to their rightful places and settled in bed again.

Lucenna rolled over to face her and said quietly, "Are you all right? Having all this magic at your fingertips so suddenly must be a lot."

"It is," Dyna whispered back. "I wish the zapping would stop."

"Because you want to kiss Cassiel?"

She flushed. "Am I that obvious?"

Lucenna snickered. "Yes."

Dyna's blush sank down her neck, and she groaned, pulling a pillow over her face. "I know our marriage is unconventional, and the desire for it to go well is irrational, Zev thinks so, but I…"

Lucenna glanced at her hand lying flat on her pillow. Candlelight flickered over the pink diamond of her engagement ring. "You can't help who you love."

"Tell me about him," she said. "I can't quite recall his name."

"I've been betrothed to Everest since birth, but I didn't meet him until I was fourteen summers old." An image of his smile came to her, the sound of his soft laughter. "He's tall with amazing cheekbones. He has waves of dark brown hair, and eyes like soft amber. I was convinced he was the most handsome prince. He was kind to me…"

Dyna looked at her worriedly. "But?"

Lucenna shook her head and lowered her hand, twisting the ring around her finger. "My mother didn't trust him. She made me promise not to tell Everest we were practicing magic in secret."

Lucenna had found herself on the verge of confessing to him several times. She wanted to trust that he would understand, but witnessing the siphoned executions of sorceresses kept her from revealing it.

"Not once was he cruel to me during our courtship, yet I lied to him every day. About who I was and what I believed in. When he gave me this ring as a testament of his love, I felt awful because I knew the day we were to wed was the day I would betray him. But when he caught me escaping, he only smiled and promised to find me. That was four years ago. I was eighteen the last time I saw him."

Lucenna had held on to that promise over the years. It must have meant he supported her choice and would join her once the search for her ended, but she didn't think he would take this long. Sometimes, she wondered if he had changed his mind about her. After all the trouble she caused, he may no longer want her.

"He must truly care for you to let you go," Dyna told her. "He never knew about your plan to overthrow the Archmage and break the Mage Code?"

She couldn't help but think Everest knew she was hiding something from him, but he never forced her to tell him. "He surely knows now."

"You haven't spoken to him since?"

Lucenna's brow furrowed as she thought of all the times her brother avoided speaking of Everest or simply told her they had to keep communication limited between only them. "Lucien won't allow it. They were once very close friends, but they've grown distant. He said it was to keep me safe."

Dyna laid a gloved hand over hers. "And how do you feel about Prince Everest?"

"I'm grateful to him."

"Yes, but how do you *feel*? Do you...love him?"

Lucenna continued twisting the little shackle around her finger. It had been so long since they spoke. His voice didn't sound the same in her mind. Memories of him lost their color and sharpness over time, as if she was forgetting him.

Could she call what she felt for him love? When she was younger, it had felt like it, and they had acted on it, but what had she ever known about that?

Dyna canted her head when she didn't answer. "Who do you think about when you look up at the stars?"

The word must have triggered something in her mind because Lucenna had no business recalling the face of that soldier she met in the port. It wasn't someone she thought to recall ever again, or his name. But it came to her anyway, as clear as his smile when he said it.

Klyde.

If I'm so blessed, may you whisper it to the stars when you think of me.

She scoffed, muttering to herself. "Pompous man."

"What?"

"Nothing." Lucenna shoved the intrusive thoughts away and changed the subject. "Have all your memories returned?"

Dyna shrugged. "For the most part. But ever since I woke, I...I don't feel truly myself. Having my mind invaded and broken has left me with the fear of something like that reoccurring." She looked out the window. "I despise feeling so helpless and unprotected against magic."

Lucenna nodded. "I understand what it feels like being at the mercy of someone else's power. We can't stop someone from trying to use magic on us, but we can prepare ourselves to fight against it. I can teach you how to protect your mind."

"Really? Is it a complicated spell?"

"Not for this." Sitting up, Lucenna called her satchel to the bed. She took out a small pouch smelling strongly of herbs and gave Dyna a sly smile. "Much can be done with something as little as sage."

CHAPTER 41

Dynalya

I f Dyna could name one simple joy in life, it would be this moment with Cassiel's gloved hand in hers. They were on their third day hiking up the low pass of Hermon Ridge. The afternoon sun lay hidden behind a thick veil of clouds. Misty fog hovered over the pine trees, thickening as they rose higher. They reached a flattened terrain on the edge of the ridge. If not for the fog, she might have glimpsed Hallow's Nest far in the distance.

"Here?" she asked. Sowmya and the others had flown ahead yesterday, saying they would meet them at the ledge.

Cassiel nodded. "The Valkyrie will arrive shortly to escort us the rest of the way."

Zev shared a frown with Rawn. "I thought they had left to announce our arrival, so the Watchers didn't kill us on sight."

"That as well."

"How will they escort us?" Dyna asked him. "Are they to carry us?"

A mischievous grin played on Cassiel's lips. "Something of the sorts."

Lucenna shook her head at that and waved her hands to ward off the offending suggestion. "No, thank you. I will walk."

He snorted. "My, this is a day to remember. Are you afraid of heights?"

She huffed, her mouth pinching. "I wasn't born with wings, so I won't be flown anywhere. My feet stay on the ground."

"Hermon Ridge is the highest mountain in Azure. The climb is long, grueling, and highly dangerous. I don't recommend it."

Lucenna sat on a log and crossed her arms and legs. "Then I will wait right here in our new tent."

"If you stay behind, you will pass up the chance to see a Celestial Realm," Dyna said. "If it's anything like Hilos, it will be a marvel."

"It's much more beautiful than Hilos," her mate told her.

Rawn cleared his throat. "Pardon, Prince Cassiel. What will happen to Fair?"

"That has all been sorted, Lord Norrlen. I have secured a ride for all of us to make it up the mountain." Cassiel searched the sky, and he nodded. "And it has arrived."

They all looked up, and from the clouds appeared the Valkyrie, riding a herd of white horses—with massive white *wings*. Dyna's mouth fell open as they watched them gallop through the air. At the tail end were six more of the winged horses pulling a large carriage.

"G-god of Urn..." Zev sputtered next to her.

Lucenna slowly stood, her eyes bulging wide. "Are those...?"

"Pegasus," Rawn said.

Their hooves beat on the ground as the herd landed in the ledge's clearing. The Valkyrie dismounted, their golden armor glinting in the light. One approached them and removed her helmet, revealing a new female Dyna hadn't met yet. Her dark blond hair stuck to the sweat on her flushed face. Her honeyed brown wings brushed the ground as she bowed low to Cassiel—and Dyna noticed—to her.

"We have arrived, Your Highness. With everything you have requested. The herd only needs an hour's rest before we prepare to fly to Hermon Ridge."

"Thank you, Lieutenant Janel."

"I don't see the captain or Lieutenant Sowmya among you," Dyna said.

"They have resumed their duties, my lady." She bowed again before moving on to give orders. The Valkyrie led the winged creatures to the pool of water for a drink.

"There are three factions of the Valkyrie," Cassiel explained at her confusion. "The Castle Guard, the Watchers, and the Legion. Yelrakel oversees it all, and any additional missions granted by the Lord of Hermon Ridge."

Like hunting down a runaway prince, Dyna mused.

"As her second, Sowmya is Head of the Castle Guard, and will now oversee the safety procedures of the castle with Hermon's many guests. Since Janel leads the Watchers, she's here to escort us to Hermon."

"Are there no males among them?"

"Within the Valkyrie, no. The males belong to a different faction."

She found that all very interesting, but at the moment, she couldn't stop looking at the beautiful creatures. "You never told us the Realms kept Pegasi. I didn't know they still existed."

"It's a well-kept secret," Cassiel said. "They're sensitive creatures and require special care for survival. The last that remain live only in Hermon, as they can fly freely in the mountain fog without being spotted."

It must be why they had to climb a part of the range before the Valkyrie could meet them.

"Unfortunately, their wings are too sensitive to cold. Because of it, they cannot fly for four months out of the year due to the frigid temperatures. My uncle is considering having them migrate to another Realm. Perhaps Nazar or Hilos with more tepid weather."

Did that mean his wings were also as sensitive?

"But why would Celestials want Pegasi when you have wings of your own?" Zev asked him.

"For the same reason others use horses. To travel fast."

"How fast?" Dyna asked next, wringing her hands.

"The hike that would take us weeks on foot will only take them half a day." He smirked at Lucenna. "I had them bring a carriage as a precaution. I take it you and Zev would prefer it?"

She glowered back. "Yes, thank you. Who knew you were so considerate?"

Zev rubbed the back of his head. "Aye, as amazing as it would be to fly, I don't think they would want me riding them."

"There is a trailer compartment for Fair, Lord Norrlen." Cassiel led him to the back half of the carriage to reveal a separate section with double-doors. It had ample space inside to fit a horse, and they had layered it with hay. "He will be safe inside."

"Thank you, Prince Cassiel," Rawn said, visibly relieved.

You thought of everything, Dyna said through the bond.

He took her hand, their gloved fingers intertwining. *Want to see them up close?*

They left the others to arrange their belongings in the carriage. He led her to the nearest creature with a velvety white hide and long, sleek feathers. Sunlight shone over its silky mane as it nickered at her approach. It had pink skin around its muzzle and pale blue eyes that tracked her movement. In comparison, Fair had gray tones to his nose and brown eyes.

"Can I?" Dyna asked.

Cassiel gently laid her hand on the Pegasus's neck. It whinnied faintly, eyeing her as its ears twitched. He crooned soothingly in his language as they continued to stroke its mane.

"What did you tell him?"

His mouth quirked in a faint smile. "Are you nervous?"

"A little," she admitted. "I have flown with you, but I imagine this will be different."

"It certainly will be. I still remember my first time riding one. For you, it may feel as if you have wings of your own."

"I've always wondered what that felt like," she said, moving on to pet another. "Could you tell me?"

"Tell you what?"

"What does it feel like to fly?"

Cassiel looked up at the sky and the light caught the silver in his eyes, making them gleam. "It feels like catching the wind, and nothing else can touch you."

The way he spoke about it made her smile.

The hour went by quickly. Lucenna and Zev settled in the carriage after they placed Fair inside the back. Rawn chose to ride a Pegasus. It was an opportunity he couldn't decline, he told them. The Valkyrie mounted, and Cassiel and Dyna took the two in the middle of the procession. He added his jacket over her cloak and a scarf around her neck before helping her mount. Cassiel fastened her into the saddle with special-made belts that assured she wouldn't fall.

Still, her heart was racing.

Cassiel mounted the Pegasus beside her. "It's all right. I will be with you the whole way."

The wind picked up, tousling his clothing and hair. He looked ahead at the edge of the cliff with giddy anticipation.

Dyna widened her eyes. "No."

Cassiel grinned. "Yes."

She wasn't ready, but they were already moving. The Valkyrie led the gallop—right off the ledge.

"Wait. Wait. Waaaaa—" Dyna broke off in a shriek as her Pegasus leaped off the cliff into the fog.

Roaring wind rushed to meet her as they dove. The fog cleared, and she found herself falling headfirst down the high ravine. Screaming, Dyna squeezed her eyes shut, fingers clutching the reins for dear life. The wind pulled at her clothing and hair. If not for the harness, it would have pulled her off, too. Her Pegasus straightened out, and she felt the cool mist of water on her skin.

Cassiel whooped beside her, laughing. "Dyna," he called above the wind. "You're missing the best part. Look!"

She shook her head.

"Dynalya Astron, open your eyes this instant!"

She peeked. The herd flew across the shimmering river. The ravine narrowed and Dyna instinctively yanked on the reins, and they banked to the right, then to the left as they followed the current of the river.

"Well done!" Cassiel called above the wind. "Trust your instincts. Feel how the Pegasus moves. Lean with the turns and lead."

It felt about the same as riding a horse, only the ground was the air, and there was no limit to how high they could go.

As if the Pegasus understood, its wings beat, and the ground grew more distant beneath them, trees becoming a carpet of dark green. She was flying. Dyna laughed and held out her arms, her heart fully elated as they soared.

This isn't so bad, she sent out the thought. *I thought you promised me fast.*

He flashed her a wicked grin. *Hold on tight.*

Cassiel said a command in his language, and the herd of Pegasi ascended with a burst of speed for the Heavens. Their pearlescent wings caught the wind and hurtled them straight up the mountain's slope with an inconceivable speed. Dyna clutched the reins as the raging wind threatened to uproot her from the saddle.

They leveled out with the herd for a moment before diving again for the earth. Dyna grinned and yanked on the reins. Her Pegasus zoomed over the trees and spun through the air at her lead as they rode for the horizon. Cassiel cheered her on, watching her go.

The wind was hers at this moment. Dyna caught it, and she was riding it for all it was worth. She was weightless. Every worry, every fear, and doubt were left behind as they soared for the freedom of the sky.

Cassiel drew up beside her, nodding for her to follow. He rose higher, and she went after him, leaving the herd to fall behind. They raced through the sky together, arcing and whirling. The horizon stretched out as far as they could see, washed out by greens and blues. She could barely distinguish the faint gray silhouette of the Zafiro Mountains.

One day, she would see North Star again.

"Are you all right?" Cassiel called.

Dyna nodded, flashing him a big smile. "I have never been more all right than right now."

A soft look crossed his face, and she felt the bond thrum. They rose higher still, and Dyna knew where he was taking her. Their Pegasus worked harder as they fought against gravity. She looked up at the rapidly incoming ceiling of clouds and closed her eyes.

The icy mist brushed her face, coating her skin. Then they broke through and entered another land of clouds. It was ever-changing, moving like fluffy white waves. The sun gleamed in the clear blue sky. It was as magnificent as the first time, leaving her breathless. Cassiel sailed her along the plane, and she reached down to run her fingers through the clouds.

They returned to the herd and flew through the day. When the temperature dropped and evening arrived, they began to descend.

We are almost there, Cassiel said.

They passed through the misty veil, heading for a vast crop of tall redwoods. The Pegasi flew them over the canopy, and she spotted houses built into the trees. Several rope bridges were suspended between them, some spiraling down the trunks. Celestials flew among the branches, all with various shades of wings; some had rich auburn feathers with black streaks, others grayish blue, some bright red, and light brown with dark brown stripes or yellow with white undertones. Their hair and eyes too were anything but the typical blond and blue.

This was why Cassiel felt so at home here.

Beyond it rose the peak of the Hermon Mountains, layered in snow. Within the rocky slope was a great stone castle built into the cliff. It had enormous round towers and sharp pointed roofs, with blue flags flickering in the wind. Several large, open balconies decorated along the side of the castle, high and low, with many stone bridges between the landings.

Smaller trees grew along the ridges in the cliff, and next to the castle poured a grand waterfall into a crystal pool far below. The water roared as it cascaded down and cast a light mist in the air. Beside it stood an immense stone monument of a Celestial shaped into the cliff. A crown was carved on top of the face, set with a stern glower and beard. The statue held out an arm, palm open against the horizon as if to ward off whatever threat may want to come from beyond. The other arm held up a sword, ready to strike. The carving of its large bare feet rested on the ground against the ridge.

King Rael, Cassiel told her. *My grandfather.*

They circled the castle, high above the rooftops, giving them a wide view of the kingdom. At the zenith of the mountain grew a familiar white tree with sprawling branches. Sunlight glittered off the iridescent leaves that looked like glass. A *Hyalus* tree.

You have one here, too? she asked.

Every Realm has one.

Janel steered the herd to a wide, hexagonal platform extending on the south end of the mountainside. It was connected to a stone bridge that led to the castle. Hooves beat on the surface as they landed. Zev and Lucenna stepped out of the carriage as Rawn dismounted. Like Dyna, all of their mouths were slackened as they gawked at the beauty of this place.

Cassiel turned to them. "Welcome to Hermon Ridge."

CHAPTER 42

Dynalya

"It's breathtaking," Dyna said as Cassiel released the belts and helped her down the Pegasus.

"It is, isn't it?"

"Aye," Zev agreed, his mouth still gaping open. "It rivals your father's castle."

"It appears as though we are on the edge of the Heavens," Rawn said. "I must write about this to my wife. She very well may not believe me."

"I thought the ride here was the greatest experience of my life," Lucenna said, her wide eyes taking it all in. "I have changed my mind."

More Valkyrie had flown in to join them. Dyna recognized the Lieutenant at the removal of her helmet. Her eyes, as dark as cloves, focused on Cassiel as she came forward, powerful wine-red wings looming behind her. "Little prince."

Cassiel arched an eyebrow at her. "We are the same height now, Sowmya."

"I'm sure I'm an inch taller," she teased, but she looked uneasy. Her voice lowered. "We have not disclosed your bond as you asked. That is a private matter to be discussed with Lord Jophiel and the High King."

"Thank you." He squeezed Dyna's hand gently before letting go. They would bide their time and wouldn't reveal their secret marriage until his sentencing was sorted, but a tightening formed in her chest.

Cassiel hesitated before asking, "How did he take the news about the port?"

By his grimace, Dyna guessed he meant his uncle. Cassiel hadn't spoken much of Lord Jophiel. From the little he mentioned, it was clear how much he respected him.

"I wish you all the best," Sowmya said, giving him a playful frown, but it faded when she glanced at Dyna and the others again. "However, I'm concerned this may not be the best time to bring outsiders here."

Heat rose off Cassiel as his expression hardened.

The lieutenant inclined her head. "Pardon, Your Highness. I merely mean we have guests from every Realm in attendance, and not all share our views. Other than them, there is also the concern of—"

"Leave Asiel to me," Cassiel said, his tone darkening.

Dyna caught Zev and Rawn's cross expressions at the mention of the prince. She had the sense she was missing something.

"If any of you see him lurking around, make sure that he stays away from Dynalya. All in my company are under my protection and will be respected as my honored guests."

The Valkyrie bowed deeply.

"Has the High King arrived?"

"Not yet." Sowmya straightened from her bow. There was a pause before she said, "A representative has arrived in his stead."

The reply was too careful, and it made Dyna grow wary. But she sensed Cassiel was relieved, even if there was a hint of irritation beneath it.

Is that a good thing? She asked him through the bond.

It means my uncle will pass my sentencing.

That may be in their favor. Cassiel was much closer to Lord Jophiel than his father.

Sowmya seemed to want to say something more, but turned away and headed for the bridge. "Please accompany me to the castle. You are to present yourself immediately upon arrival. Leave everything. The belongings of your companions will be placed in the guest wing, and the horse will be taken to our stables."

Only six Valkyries accompanied them. Half flew back to their posts in the trees, and the other half led the Pegasus away.

Zev reached for her, and his finger brushed the exposed skin past her glove. He winced, his green eyes flashing to a glowing yellow.

Dyna sighed. "I'm sorry, Zev."

"It's all right. I think it's a good thing that you can do that, leastways while we're here."

"What do you mean?"

"Never mind."

Dyna frowned at her cousin. Were they aware of something she wasn't? She caught Lucenna's eye, and the sorceress only shook her head.

"I will fly ahead to announce your arrival, Little Prince," Sowmya said. Her red wings flared open, and she soared into the sky. She flew for the castle and landed on an open platform, disappearing from view.

Why does she call you 'Little Prince' Dyna asked.

His mouth twitched. *She has always done so. I was ten years old when I came to live here. Compared to her height at the time, I was little.*

They followed him to the stone bridge leading up to the castle. It was suspended hundreds of feet high in the air with no banisters. Lucenna clutched Zev's arm, looking a little pale.

Dyna looked out at the many homes residing high up in the redwood trees. They were beautiful, intricate wooden houses. People with no wings crossed the roped bridges suspended between them.

"Humans," Zev said, following her gaze.

Rawn and Lucenna were watching, too.

"My father withheld some truth of what happened during the destruction of Gamor," Cassiel said beside her. "The reason Lord Jophiel left Hilos was to save the half-breed children he was ordered to slaughter. He brought them here, and they became the first citizens of Hermon."

"But those humans appear young," Dyna said. "They aren't the ones that arrived with the Decimation survivors, are they?"

"No. Occasionally, a Celestial who has been out traveling Urn will return with a human love-mate. In some rare instances, humans wander into our territory, and they can never leave to preserve the secret of our existence here. They live here with us and most eventually marry. My uncle prefers to avoid bloodshed when possible."

Dyna smiled at Zev, and he affectionately patted her back. Maybe everything would be all right.

They arrived in front of two tall round towers with a set of wrought-iron gates and a lifted drawbridge.

Once the Valkyrie guarding the towers saw Cassiel, the drawbridge groaned and creaked loudly as it slowly made its descent. They flew out to unlock the iron gates as the drawbridge landed down with a heavy thud. The castle loomed above them, casting them in a shadow of its outline. The sunset beyond streaked the sky in blue, purple, and bright orange.

Dyna glanced at Cassiel, and he nodded encouragingly. But a nervous worry lingered on the edges of their bond. One they both tried to ignore.

They crossed into a vast stone courtyard leading to the castle's massive stone entryway. A new arrival waited by the entrance. A Celestial female with a striking beauty that made Dyna's mind stall. Her honey hair fell in rivers down her shoulders. It framed the perfect complexion of her face and slender frame.

Her pink lips split into a stunning smile. "Prince Cassiel," she called. "You have returned."

He nodded politely. "Lady Sarrai, you look well."

"I'm perfectly well now that you have returned to us safely."

Each step she made was done with effortless grace. Thin gold chains adorning her arms glittered in the light. The layers of her sapphire dress flowed like the petals of a tulip. A delicate layer of tulle hung over it with the bodice embroidered elegantly in golden floral designs. Dyna thought Lady Sarrai was a pureblood until she saw her wings. They were the deep gray of early dawn and glimmered as if coated in a fine diamond dust.

"Oh, how I have missed you." Sarrai threw her arms around him in an embrace.

Cassiel stiffened. Dyna stiffened too, and something that felt like protectiveness flickered in her chest.

"I have not been gone too long." Stepping out of her arms, Cassiel cleared his throat and glanced at Dyna and the others. "Everyone, please allow me to introduce Sarrai Nephele of Nazar, one of the few I call a friend. We both were raised here in Hermon together. Lady Sarrai, these are my travel companions—"

"Forgive me, but we should save introductions when we are not outside in such a dreadful cold," Sarrai said as she slipped her hand in the crook of Cassiel's arm. Gold bracelets glinted at her wrists with delicate chains attached to her rings. "Come. They are waiting for us."

Sarrai urged him along into the towering entryway without giving them a passing glance. Dyna exchanged a look with the others. It was as if they were invisible…or merely not worth the acknowledgment.

They followed them onto a stone overpass suspended above a garden below. Fountains rose on either side of it, with bushes of colorful flowers and shrubbery trimmed neatly. The overpass led them to another set of doors, where two male castle guards stood watch. They wore plated blue armor with a golden crest of a *Hyalus* tree within a mountain on the breastplates.

They tensed at their arrival, and their dark eyes watched Dyna and her friends closely as they approached. The guards bowed to Cassiel, then opened the doors to reveal a vast stone hallway with a long blue and gold rug running down the entire length of it. Torches lit the way, and on the walls hung grand golden frames of life-size paintings.

They were portraits of pureblooded Celestials.

All wore crowns.

"King *Kāhssiel*," Cassiel told them when they stopped in front of the first one. "The first to rule Hilos. My namesake."

Dyna hadn't known they named him after the first king. The male in the painting had familiar features passed onto his descendants. Now that she looked at him beside Cassiel, she found they had a striking resemblance. The same chin, same nose, same steel eyes. Every feature was a near match, as though this was what Cassiel would have looked like if he had been born a pureblood.

He pointed out the portrait of his grandfather. King Rael stood sternly with a thick gray beard. The old king matched the monument carved into the cliff side. The following portrait was of a beautiful Celestial female with a golden crown, who Dyna guessed must be Cassiel's grandmother, Queen Sapphira. It was followed by a portrait of another Celestial king, this one with strong traces of King Rael in his features.

"King Yoel," she heard Zev whisper under his breath to Rawn. "His father."

Cassiel ignored that portrait completely and stopped in front of another next to it with Sarrai.

"This one is my favorite painting," she said to him. "Lord Jophiel looks so dignified, does he not?"

"He does."

Lord Jophiel also shared similar features with his brother and father. In the portrait, he was young and handsome with a square jaw. A gold crown sat over his long blond hair, just above his striking gaze.

"We should not dally," Sarrai said with a sigh, sounding reluctant. Cassiel continued with her down the hallway, where more castle guards waited. Dyna knew they were old friends, but the sight of them together made her ache a little.

Yet that wasn't what truly bothered her. The anxiety she had been hiding grew in her chest with every step she took. This plan would never work. Why did she suggest it? Magic sparked at her fingertips. They should turn back.

They had to leave. Dyna scanned the area for a quick escape. But then Cassiel was there.

His gloved hands came over her face. *Lev sheli.*

She shook her head mutely. Her stomach churned. God of Urn, she was going to spew. *I can't go in there. Please, let's go.*

It will be all right. We will do it together.

Hearing that eased her heart a little. Her eyes held his, and she forced herself to take a breath. Cassiel's hand held her gloved one, sending her a wave of assurance. But Dyna met Sarrai's narrow stare, and she tugged her hand free.

His brow furrowed. *Are you ready?*

She shook her head again. *Are you?*

No, but as long as you are with me, I can face anything.

Then so could she.

The guards opened the doors for them, and finally they reached the throne room, where the Lord of Hermon Ridge waited.

CHAPTER 43

Cassiel

As much as Cassiel was glad to be in the one place he had considered home for most of his life, tension stiffened his wings with the urge to fly away. He lifted his shield to keep Dyna from feeling it, but he couldn't truly hide it. Dread had hovered over him since they reached the town, but his uncle was a fair and just Lord. Cassiel put his faith in that.

"His Royal Highness, Prince Cassiel Soaraway of Hilos!" The herald's announcement echoed loudly in the throne room. "In the company of Her Grace, Lady Sarrai and honored guests!"

Sarrai linked her arm through his, resting her hand on the crook of his elbow. It seemed to tremble, but that was probably him. He would rather have Dyna with him, but decorum required he go in with Sarrai first.

Taking a steadying breath, he led the way inside. The throne room was absolutely quiet. His anxiety grew with each step as their footfalls echoed on the polished stone.

Candles flickered from the golden chandeliers above them and on iron stands throughout. The throne room had two levels. They entered on the main floor, and the second held a gallery with several rows for seating. It was full of Celestial nobles, dignitaries, court advisors, and aristocrats. Every eye was like pins on his back. The castle guards stood on the lower level, lining the walls.

Cassiel strode down the blue rug across the enormous room to a series of tall white marble steps. Sowmya and some of the Valkyrie stood guard at the base. He let his eyes trail up the elevated set of stairs. Light poured in from the tall, high windows, crowning the massive gold throne constructed of wings that held court at the front.

It was an imposing chair. One demanding quiet obedience.

Then his eyes landed on the one who sat there. His mind struggled to make sense of it, because it was the last person he had expected to see.

Zev whispered a curse under his breath behind him at the same time Dyna's shock hit him like a cold splash of water.

Malakel appeared the same as the last time he'd seen him in Hilos. His perfect, long blond hair was held back by the golden circlet on his brow. Lavish white robes trimmed in gold flowed down to his feet. His pearlescent wings shone under the evening light. His eyes, like sapphires, cold and sharp, tracked their approach.

"Ah. The Black Hearted Prince at last graces us with his presence." Malakel's cool voice drifted down to them.

Cassiel clenched his jaw at the stupid moniker the Realms secretly called him behind his back. But why was he here? His steps slowed to a stop in the middle of the room when he didn't spot his uncle anywhere.

Sarrai clutched his sleeve tightly and her startled gaze darted at their audience as if this wasn't what she had expected, but she quickly schooled her expression. She curtsied and Cassiel bowed. He heard the soft rustle of clothing as the others behind him did the same. His wings twitched with his growing unease, but he forced himself to remain composed.

"Your Majesty, I was not aware court had been called," Sarrai said as she straightened.

"When did you need to be made aware of anything?" came Malakel's curt response, his stare fixed on Cassiel.

Sarrai flushed pink, though her outward poise didn't change.

"I'm pleased to see you," Cassiel lied. He straightened his shoulders, folding his arms behind his back. He shot Sowmya and Sarrai a sidelong glance for not warning him. "I hope the journey found you well, brother."

"Forgive me," Sarrai whispered under her breath, keeping her face pointed forward. "He arrived a week ago. Lord Jophiel departed the same day. Prince Malakel commanded that none should reveal it to you."

Of course. He wanted him caught off guard. This was all to show his superiority. Well, Cassiel was used to it. He merely needed to remain composed and let Malakel have his enjoyment at his expense. Then they could rest and wait until his uncle's return.

"You have done your part in escorting him here. Take your leave," Malakel dismissed her. "Court is now in session and Cassiel will be tried."

A shocked murmur passed through the room.

Cassiel stared at him, his pulse jumping. It had to be some sort of jest. "This isn't sanctioned. Court cannot be held without—"

Malakel held up a hand, cutting him off. "The High King and the Lord of Hermon Ridge are dealing with other concerns. I speak for him in his absence. There is no need to draw out the inevitable. The entirety of the Realms knows what you have done, Cassiel."

Dyna's shield crumbled, and her panic swarmed through him. *Cassiel,* her voice broke in his mind.

Stay calm.

He was also speaking to himself. His thoughts raced to find a way to escape the situation unscathed. With his uncle, they had a chance, but he knew from the dark look on his brother's face that the possibility was fading.

Cassiel stepped forward. "Malakel—"

"Kneel."

Two Royal Guards, in white with the sigil of Hilos on their chests, appeared from the shadows. They forced Cassiel to his knees and chained him to the thick steel links fused into the floor. His face heated with indignation, drowning out his apprehension. This was familiar. His fingers curled against the cold, hard floor. This he could understand.

Withstanding his brother's humiliations was a common occurrence. It was merely to remind him of his place, that was all. He need only tolerate it, and it would be over.

"This is where you meet my eyes," Malakel told him. Then he leaned back in the throne, projecting his voice through the room. "Cassiel Soaraway, you stand accused of several offenses. Breaking the Accords, disobeying the High King, exposing our people and giving your blood to humans. How do you plead?"

Merely bear it, Cassiel chanted to himself. *Bear it.*

"Well, Nephilim? I asked you a question."

"I will not plead to you," he snapped. "Unchain me. You have no right."

"I have every right." A cold smile curved Malakel's mouth, and Cassiel had a unnerving suspicion this wasn't another one of his cruel amusements.

"Where is Lord Jophiel?" he asked, sweat slicking his back. "Does he know about this?"

"Who do you think gave me the authority to oversee Hermon?" Malakel leaned forward, his blue eyes hard as stones. "I told you once. You may have escaped punishment the first time, but I will not allow a second. I know you hoped our uncle would spare you, but *nothing* will."

A chill skittered down his spine, and static stirred in the air, prickling the hair on Cassiel's scalp. He glanced at Dyna over his shoulder. She had her eyes shut. Her fists shook at her sides, sparking green. Zev took her cloak and pulled her to him. Rawn and Lucenna quickly blocked her from view of the court.

The pressure of her Essence pressed into his back. She was losing hold of her magic, and her fear was bleeding into him. *Cassiel!*

It will be all right.

It was a lie. They both knew it.

"There were extenuating circumstances!" Dyna burst out, rushing to his side. "It wasn't his fault."

"We can explain," Zev started.

Rawn said at the same time, "If I may beg on the indulgences of Your Majesty—"

"Outsiders don't speak in this court," Malakel thundered. "You will cease to interrupt or I will have you chained beside him. Now half-breed, answer. How do you plead to the charges?"

Every Realm was in attendance, and Cassiel finally saw what this was. Malakel would use this opportunity to make him an example, and to get rid of him for good.

"Guilty," Cassiel said blankly, too stunned to do anything else.

Dyna trembled next to him. He could feel her fighting to control her Essence. It crackled on her skin, sprouting a sweat on her face from the effort. Tears gathered on her lashes as she looked at him.

"Say it again so the court may bear witness," Malakel commanded.

Cassiel held her gaze. "I don't deny the charges."

"Well, at least he is honest. We have lost much to humans. Many lives were sacrificed to attain the concealment and protection of the Realms. I will not see it destroyed."

The dignitaries rumbled, voices rising and falling in a buzz of responses. And most sounded angry. There would be no support for him here.

The room was spinning. He made himself take a breath, but he knew what was going to happen and he wasn't ready for it.

"Cassiel."

He blinked up at Malakel. There was no kindness on his brother's face. There never had been.

"The court hereby acknowledges your guilt of breaking Rael's sacred laws. It thus follows without question, such a crime cannot go unpunished. Therefore, with the will and authority of the Heavens, I have passed judgment." He motioned. "Executioners, come forward."

"What?" Dyna gasped.

Sarrai covered her mouth.

"You cannot execute him on false charges!" Zev shouted.

"The charges are not false when he has confessed." Malakel crossed one leg over the other. "But alas, this isn't an execution. Don't think me cruel." He chuckled heartlessly. "It's an exile."

Four males dressed in black approached.

Two of them seized Cassiel's wings and yanked them out to expose the margins where it met the shoulder blade. The fear he'd been holding back barreled over him like a mudslide. He fought against his restraints, but the chains held him tight.

"Stop this, please!" Dyna cried.

"No! Release me!" Sarrai kicked and flailed as she was dragged away. "You cannot do this!"

Cassiel wrenched against the chains, shouting curses at his brother, who merely sneered at him. His friends moved to defend him, but Hilos guards drew their weapons, forcing them back. Dyna dodged and rushed to the dais. He shouted at her to stop. The guards wouldn't hesitate to cut her down! Sowmya whipped out her glaive and Seraph fire swiveled around the blade as she used it to defend his mate. The Valkyrie also drew their weapons and shielded her from any guards that tried to stop her.

Malakel's stare landed on Dyna when she reached the steps. "It was me!" Her cry echoed in the room for everyone to hear. "It was my fault. It never would have happened if not for me. I'm the one who should be punished!"

The room erupted with the shouts of nobles agreeing and disagreeing on the matter.

Dyna, don't interfere!

The guards took a step forward, earning Zev's growl. The Valkyrie braced to fight.

"Stand back," Cassiel shouted at the guards. "Don't touch her!"

Magic hummed in Lucenna's hands, getting ready to attack if they so much as got near her. Rawn called for Dyna to return to them, but she stayed on the steps, staring up at the prince.

"It was my doing," she said. "Not his."

Malakel indolently flicked his hand. The room settled, and the guards stepped back. Cassiel didn't like the way he was looking at her. Like she was merely an insect, he would take pleasure in crushing under his boot.

"Don't worry, human. Your immunity will be removed, along with him."

At the dark promise, Cassiel yanked on the chains, straining to get to her. "Malakel! I don't care what you do to me. Let them go!"

Malakel only smiled that same smile. The one that promised pain.

Cassiel realized the same time Dyna did that they were trapped. She stumbled, her knees cracking against the steps. Her body shook as flickers of green magic flashed around her. It burned through the bond, on the verge of bursting out of her control.

Breathe, he told her.

"How can you shear your own brother?" she asked. "This cannot be right."

"I am the heir of Hilos, son of the Heavens. I carry the authority of its sacred will." Malakel raised his chin, looking down at him without an ounce of compassion. Nothing short of cruel satisfaction. His sentencing resonated for all to hear, "Cassiel Soaraway is forthwith exiled from the Realms. Loss of the wings is loss of divinity, and with it the blessing of *Elyōn*. His name will be stricken from all records of history, never to be spoken again. His soul will forever be marked with disgrace, and at death, he will be turned away from the Gates of our ancestors. So be our sacred law."

Dyna whipped around, her teary eyes finding his. "No!" Her cry echoed in the throne room.

From the edges of his sight, the two remaining Celestials in black removed their swords of white flame and his wings were stretched out.

They would be severed clean through.

Cassiel tried to give her a smile, but it couldn't disguise the fear and misery consuming him at the perpetual devastation of what they would both lose. She ran for him, holding out a hand. But he was too far out of reach.

Look away, lev sheli. Close your eyes.

Cassiel lifted his shield, if only to protect her from the pain. Their bond pulled taut between them like a glowing silver strand.

His heart came to a stop, his breath gone.

He heard nothing, felt nothing.

Not the cold floor beneath him, not the searing power in his veins, not the shouts of everyone around him. All else faded except for the beautiful woman who chose him.

It was the cruelest fate to find the one he wanted a future with—only to lose her like this.

Malakel signaled, and the executioners raised their weapons. The rays of the setting sun spilling through the large windows bathed the flickering flames bright red.

Please. Don't look.

The divine swords came down.

Dyna's scream shredded through his heart.

Green light ripped through the throne room with a roar. The force hurled everything and everyone away. Cassiel jerked to a stop against the chains. Shattered glass blasted through the air, and fractures split through the stone walls. Voices cried out. Magic wrenched through the room in a massive storm.

The mountain violently shook from the fury of Dyna's might, and her glowing form lifted off the ground as she rose above the chaos. Her body radiated green like a menacing star. Her eyes had become two glowing torches as they fixed on Malakel.

He cowered by the throne, gaping up at her in horror.

Cassiel shouted over the storm for her to stop, but Dyna didn't hear him. She raised her hands, her Essence burning vividly. Magic bled through her fingers and spiraled up her arms as it grew brighter and brighter.

It was the same spell of the fjord.

She was going to kill Malakel.

Dynalya! Cassiel's voice rang in her mind, clear and true. *Look at me!*

The spell halted at her fingertips, and her glowing eyes snapped to him. Their bond was still there, like a warm glow in his chest.

Fully intact.

A sob broke out of her, and Cassiel sagged at the sheer relief. *I'm right here—*

Purple lightning flashed in his vision. Cassiel felt the blow at the same time it struck Dyna's chest and her magic disintegrated.

Then his mate dropped from the air with nothing to catch her.

CHAPTER 44

Cassiel

assiel didn't care how much it would hurt to touch her. He wouldn't let her fall. Seraph fire flared at his wrists, and the manacles snapped. He dove and caught Dyna from the sky, but no flashes of magic struck him. He brushed the hair from her face. She was fine. Only unconscious.

He flew down and landed as his companions picked themselves up.

Lucenna gave him an apologetic wince. "I had to. I swore I'd stop her."

"You did the only thing any of us could do," Cassiel said. Zev crowded him, looking down at Dyna worriedly. "She's all right."

"Lady Dyna...her power..." Rawn looked around.

Crushed rock littered the ground. Torn tapestries hung from the broken windows. The throne room was destroyed. Movement shuffled everywhere as the Celestials stood from wherever they had hidden. Some were healing from injuries, but nothing serious—

His eyes caught on the black scorch marks on the rug where the executioners had once stood. Their swords never touched him. His pulse beat wildly as he searched the room for the males in black garb, but Cassiel knew he wouldn't find them.

There was nothing left of them to find.

"She didn't know what she was doing," Lucenna said. "Her magic reacted to her emotions. She didn't mean to do it."

Zev looked at the scorched rug, and his yellow eyes widened. "Did she...?"

Rawn rubbed his jaw. "God of Urn."

"She is safe," Cassiel murmured, wrapping his wings around Dyna. "That is the only thing I care about right now."

He also tried not to acknowledge the fact that his flame had burned through iron chains.

"How about them?" Lucenna said under her breath. "They will care a great deal."

The entire room was staring at them.

At her.

"You have brought a witch to Hermon Ridge." Malakel rose to his feet, a snarl twisting his mouth. "There is no end to your treachery."

Cassiel's jaw clenched. "She isn't a witch."

"You would stand there with that lie on your tongue when we all bore witness to her sorcery? She murdered two Celestials! Nothing will pardon you from this, Nephilim. *Nothing.* Your life is now forfeit, including hers."

Hilos guards rushed through the throne room, lining up before the dais, and they drew their swords. Sowmya and the Valkyrie drew out their weapons—against the guards.

A burning heat curled in Cassiel's chest. Zev, Rawn and Lucenna flanked him, arming themselves with their choice of weapon. Claw, sword, and magic. *Esh Shamayim* hummed at his hip with the call of his fire. His veins burned with a fathomless need to *protect* what was *his.*

Suddenly, nothing mattered to him. Not the Realms. Not the judgment of the crown or the state of his future. He would throw it all away, and they would fight their way out of here because *no one* would touch his mate.

Cassiel met his brother's cold eyes with the steel of his own. "Attempt it, and I will truly show you the depths of my treachery."

The golden doors of the throne room slammed open with a deafening *boom.*

A unit of Valkyrie swept into the room in a steady march of gold, Captain Yelrakel in the lead. They stopped mid center, and their armor clanked heavily as they stood sharply at attention.

And behind them entered Lord Jophiel.

His dark blue robes fluttered around his legs with each purposeful stride. The fading light caught the ends of his circlet shaped like wings. He stopped in the center of his throne room and took in the destruction with an idle expression. No shock. No break in his regal pose. Lord Jophiel's deep blue eyes circled the room in one sweeping arc, then they landed on Dyna in Cassiel's arms before rising to his face.

Cassiel bowed, as deep as he could go while holding her. He heard the rustle around the room as everyone present did the same.

He swallowed, ignoring the flush of his cheeks and the shame weighing on his head. "My lord, I humbly beg—"

"Court is adjourned," Lord Jophiel announced, the command echoing in the room. He had a modulated voice, but there was no pleasantry in it. "Disperse at once. All those involved, in the council chambers. Now."

Lord Jophiel strode past him without sparing a glance. "Noemi."

A petite female with dark, curly hair stepped forward out of the crowd gathered by the doors. Her small wings were shaded deep russet to sunset orange. They tucked tightly behind her back as she curtsied, her light blue servant robes pooling around her feet.

"See to Prince Cassiel's guests." Lord Jophiel continued on with Yelrakel at his side. His pearlescent wings passed through another hidden doorway next to the dais, and he fell out of view.

The nobles muttered among themselves as they began leaving through the exits.

Noemi approached Cassiel, keeping her head lowered. "May I take her, Your Highness?"

Cassiel hesitated to let Dyna go, though he knew his uncle was waiting for him.

"I will take her." Lucenna stepped forward and lifted Dyna in a purple mist. She looked at Zev and Rawn. "Go with him. He will need allies in there. So will she."

They all glanced at Dyna's sleeping face. Whatever was said in that council room would affect her, too.

Lucenna let the small female lead her away. Cassiel glanced at the Valkyrie, and his gaze landed on Janel. The female bowed her head at his silent order and the warriors escorted his mate to safety.

He watched them go until they passed through the main doors. Every part of him wanted to go after her. When Dyna woke, she would be so confused and upset by what she'd done. He wanted to be there to assure her it wasn't her fault.

Sowmya moved to her place beside him. "Come along, Your Highness."

Sighing, Cassiel made himself turn and follow, with Zev and Rawn trailing behind him. The best thing he could do for Dyna now was to make sure the consequences fell only on him.

They left the throne room through the same door his uncle had exited and entered outside. He strode along the stone path past the gardens to another vacant hall. Their footsteps echoed in the silence.

"How concerned should we be?" Zev asked when they reached a tall dark door at the end of the hall.

"Very." Cassiel straightened his back, looking directly ahead. "Do me a favor. Unless addressed, please don't say anything."

Fates would be decided in that room. There was no telling which way they would fall. The only thing he cared about was keeping harm from Dyna. He would take it all.

The two Valkyrie standing guard outside of the room grabbed the heavy brass handles and opened the doors. They entered the large council chamber. It was a bland room with simple stone walls. The only decorative element was the large blue tapestry with a sigil of Hermon Ridge in the center. A long wooden table took up the majority of the space.

Malakel was seated in a chair, along with Sarrai. Yelrakel and Sowmya stood guard in opposite corners. His uncle leaned against the windows, looking out at the sunset falling over his Realm.

"I must admit," Lord Jophiel began. "When the High King called me away to meet him on a dire matter, I did not expect to come across the threat of war." He turned with a heavy sigh. His hardened expression worn for the court fell away, and all that was left was exhaustion. "What have you done, Cassiel?"

The heavy disappointment in the question made him lower his eyes. Cassiel had expected to be shouted at, though his uncle never once had before. Somehow, the soft tone in which he spoke was worse.

"He has doomed us all," Malakel said.

"Was that question intended for you?" Lord Jophiel's eyes cut sharply to his brother, making him stiffen. "Then you will *not* speak. Sit in silence and wait your turn to be addressed."

Zev muffled a faint cough.

"It pleases me you are well, Cassiel," Lord Jophiel continued. "We have much to discuss regarding your whereabouts since you departed from my Realm. Imagine my concern when I received the King's first inquiry about how well his son arrived. You led your father to believe that you were here with me."

Cassiel's face heated.

"The trip from Hilos to Hermon Ridge takes about a week by night flight, but as a month passed with no word from you, I was beginning to worry. Then we received news of a bounty placed on your head. On the High King's command, I dispatched the Valkyrie to investigate and to aid you at whatever cost."

The sound of distant screams and the smell of ash reached him. They had slaughtered the citizens of Azure. That had been the cost.

"Yet when they arrived, you evaded them. Now the very poacher that held you captive has attempted various times to cross into my territory. The Valkyrie have killed several of his men at the border, but *he* slips away each time."

The weight of disgrace fell over Cassiel, and he bowed his head. "Forgive me, my lord. It was not my intention—"

"Your actions don't match your intentions," his uncle said sternly. "I have taught you better and expect more from you. Each time you travel between the Realms, discretion is your responsibility—the safety of your kin depends on it. A prince must have more sensibility, Cassiel. Our laws are in place for a reason, and all must abide by them. Royals most of all."

He bore the chastisement, knowing he deserved it.

The hunts have started again because of his actions. Shame and guilt settled heavily in his stomach.

Lord Jophiel exhaled sharply and motioned to the chairs. "Sit. Your guests, as well. I will hear from you exactly what occurred in the Port of Azure, and the events that led you there."

Taking their seats, he told his uncle a vague version of the story. While being very careful not to mention why he had exposed himself, the map to Mount Ida, or his accidental bond. That would probably save him now, pardon him even, but they had agreed to keep it a secret. He didn't know how his uncle or his father would react to learning he accidentally bonded with someone not chosen by the court.

With a non-Celestial.

He could only assume it would mean his exile, or worse. Much worse. But he wouldn't think of that now.

"So, you disobeyed your father, and traveled across the kingdom with strangers, knowing it would put the Realms in jeopardy," his uncle concluded dryly. "I fail to comprehend how you came to conclude this was the correct path."

Beside him, Zev worked his jaw but remained quiet. Rawn's neutral expression didn't change, either.

"There were extenuating circumstances," Cassiel offered lamely.

"Oh, yes, of that I'm quite sure. Let us pretend you have told me everything," he said coolly, and turned to Malakel. "Now we shall discuss why you held court without my presence."

Malakel cleared his throat. "As you know, I was here in Father's stead. When Cassiel arrived, I intended for him to be properly punished."

"Punished?" Lord Jophiel glanced at Sowmya.

She inclined her head. "Prince Malakel ordered for the exile of Prince Cassiel."

The look he fixed on Malakel would make any sane person run. "With what authority did you pass a sentencing?"

Malakel shifted in his seat. "I am the heir apparent, Uncle. The future of Hilos. You will do well to refer to me with due reverence. I have every authority to—"

Lord Jophiel slammed his hand on the table, making everyone flinch. "You are a prince without a reign," he said tightly. "You don't lord over any Realm, and you have *no* authority over mine. The only one to pass judgment in my court besides me is the High King—a title you have yet to hold. If you wish to dispute that, might I suggest you speak about it with your father? I imagine he will have much to say about the unauthorized exiling of a prince."

Malakel shrunk in his chair.

Lord Jophiel removed his circlet and rubbed his temples. "What occurred in the throne room?"

"The girl…" Sarrai mumbled, keeping her head lowered.

Cassiel tensed.

"She's a witch." Malakel sneered at him. This was what he had been waiting for. Another opportunity to attack him. "She unleashed her magic and slew the executioners. Then she tried to kill me."

Lord Jophiel's head whipped to Cassiel. "What?"

"He brought evil sorcery here, Uncle. She must be dealt with."

Fire lit inside of Cassiel's veins at the threat. It burned through him as his heart pounded in his ears with a sudden impulse to eliminate his brother.

Zev grabbed his arm under the table, squeezing hard enough to get his attention. Cassiel glanced down at his lap where his clenched fists flickered with flame. Fortunately, they were hidden from everyone else's view.

He forced himself to breathe deeply and send the flames away. "My Lord, if I may explain."

His uncle waved exasperatingly. "Please. For I'm clearly missing something."

"Dynalya Astron is a sorceress of House Astron," Cassiel said. His uncle straightened in his chair at her name. "She is still learning how to control her magic. She didn't mean any harm."

"She killed two and nearly killed your brother. That is a very grave offense, Cassiel."

"She stopped the exile. She saved me."

"Yes." Lord Jophiel narrowed his eyes. "To a dire extent. Why? Your answer will include what actually happened in Azure this time."

Cassiel couldn't fully answer without exposing the truth. "There was some trouble in the port. The poacher captured Dyna due to a bounty placed on her head. I thought if I could simply trade myself for her freedom, I could find a way to escape...and the rest, you know."

Lord Jophiel's eyes widened. "You sacrificed yourself for a human?"

"With the help of *that* human, we rescued him," Zev said defiantly. "Why should her race be questioned?"

"We came to his aid, Your Majesty," Rawn said placatingly, giving Zev a look to comport himself. "We would not leave him in the hands of a poacher."

"Pardon," Cassiel interjected. "May I introduce Zev Astron of Lykos Peak and General Rawn Norrlen of Greenwood. As you must gather, this is Jophiel Soaraway, the High King's brother, and Lord of Hermon Ridge."

Rawn dipped his chin. "Your servant, Lord Jophiel."

"And yours."

"Dyna may not be a Celestial, but she is a person," Cassiel said. "Someone important to all of us. I'm sorry, my lord. But I could not stand by while she was to be killed or hurt. Even if the greater good or the law demanded it."

Lord Jophiel stared at him for a long stretch of a moment as something crossed his face. "Choices are difficult for princes and kings. Sometimes, one must choose the path that will save the most lives while sacrificing a few. It's a dark day indeed when a monarch sacrifices the most lives to save one."

Cassiel thought of the people that were slaughtered in the market because of him. He carried the loss of those lives and he couldn't walk away from it. They came here searching and hoping for a chance to be spared, but he broke the law, people died.

The heat in his veins settled down, and the bond quivered when Cassiel acknowledged the thought he had tried to ignore. He couldn't run from that, no matter how much he wished for it.

Standing, Cassiel came around the table to kneel before his uncle. "I will not beg for your forgiveness, for I know I don't deserve it, but I will beg you to pardon Dynalya on her behalf. My actions are my own, and I will accept any punishment you see fit." He closed his eyes. "Even if it requires the loss of my wings."

Zev's chair jerked back. "Cassiel!"

"I only ask that she and my companions be safely escorted from Hermon." Because in the end, he could accept whatever came as long as his mate was safe.

A long drag of silence filled the room.

Then a soft touch on his shoulder. "Stand, Cassiel. Your verdict is for the High King to decide, but I can assure you, there will be no exile."

The breath he had been holding shuddered out of him.

But Cassiel couldn't feel any relief. His wings wouldn't be sheared, but that didn't mean he wouldn't escape some sort of penalty.

"What news of my father?" he asked hesitantly.

"He is preoccupied with other government matters. Your summons is delayed until further notice."

Cassiel resisted rolling his eyes. Rael's Laws were broken, yet his father couldn't be bothered with his own sentencing. It's not as if he ever arrived when it counted.

Lord Jophiel's expression became serious. "We did, however, discuss your future, Cassiel. And the role you must fulfill for the Realms. The High King and I both acknowledge you are more comfortable here than in Hilos, and given recent events, it's clear you need something to dedicate your life to. After five hundred years, I'm also ready for a new course. So, I'm stepping down from my position as Lord of Hermon Ridge, and I have chosen its inheritor."

Cassiel wasn't sure why everyone in the room was staring at him. Then it hit him. "*Me?* You want me to assume lordship over Hermon Ridge? But Asiel is your heir."

Lord Jophiel frowned. "My son, as you can see from his lack of presence here, cares nothing about politics. He has long proved he is not capable and has no interest in overseeing this Realm. Therefore, he has been disavowed. I have chosen you to take my place, Cassiel."

He could only stand there mutely, too shocked to make sense of this.

"You cannot be serious," Malakel said. "He is a Nephilim."

"Did you forget who lives in Hermon?" his uncle said sharply.

Sound rushed through Cassiel's thoughts like a loud wind. He couldn't be Lord of Hermon Ridge. His father must have abandoned his plan to make him High King, thank *Elyōn*, but Lord of the Realm was nearly as bad.

"The charge of overseeing a Realm is a great one, Cassiel. One you should not do alone."

Dread sank through him. *No.*

"Your father must have discussed this with you already." Lord Jophiel saw the startled look frozen on his face and gave him an apologetic smile. "It's not a punishment, but a new chapter in your life. I think you would find much joy in companionship."

He shook his head. "My lord—"

"This is an order given by the High King, and you will *not* defy him. Your engagement is set, and the bride selected. I assure you, it's an auspicious match." Lord Jophiel held out a hand to Sarrai, and she took his palm, a smile lighting her face as she stood.

Cassiel's mouth opened and closed, trying to form words, but he was too stunned to speak, as was everyone else in the room. His chest was tight, the air too thick to breathe.

Lord Jophiel joined their hands together. "Cassiel, with my blessing, you will marry Sarrai at the peak of the Festival of Light."

CHAPTER 45

Dynalya

God of Urn, everything hurt. Dyna's body felt achy, and her veins throbbed. Muffled voices filtered through the hum in her ears.

"These will be your chambers during your stay, my lady," someone said. "I'm the stewardess of this castle. You may call me Madam Kahna, and this is Noemi. We will see to whatever you require."

"Thank you," came Lucenna's soft reply.

Dyna forced her heavy eyes to open. She laid in an unfamiliar bed. Lucenna stood at the door, speaking to a dainty, orange-winged female. Beside her stood an older female, her expression stern. Gray streaks wove among the brown braids, holding back her hair in a bun, her wings matching in color. Both wore light blue robes that flowed to their feet, long sleeves trimmed silver, with a silver pin of a tree at their necks.

"You will be called shortly for dinner," the eldest said stiffly. "There is a bathing room through that door. Please wash up and dress appropriately for dinner with his lordship."

Both curtsied before retreating.

Lucenna shut the door. She smiled with relief when she noticed her and came to sit beside her. "Oh good. You're awake. Are you all right?"

Dyna sat up, pressing a hand to her heart. "Why does my chest hurt? Where are we?"

The chamber was large and rounded in a circle, the floors and walls constructed of a smooth stone with gilded gold designs along the decorative columns. On the left of the room rested two large canopy beds made of redwood. Sheer tulle hung across the posts of both beds with white satin bedding and pillows.

On the opposite wall, flames crackled in the grand fireplace. Her mind flashed with the image of the divine swords held above black wings.

"Cassiel!" Dyna gasped and stumbled to her feet.

Lucenna caught her arm. "He's all right, Dyna. You stopped the exile."

"What?" She blinked at her a moment, her mind slowly working to understand that and the fact that Lucenna was holding her arm. Skin against skin. "The zaps…they're gone."

"When I placed you in the bed, you didn't rise. Either you passed through the Rising, or you expelled so much power, there wasn't enough to make you hover."

"What do you mean?" Dyna stepped away. "What happened?"

The look that entered Lucenna's eyes made her heart drop. She already knew what Lucenna didn't want to say, but she had to hear it.

Dyna looked to the open terrace with a view of the tree line outside. "Did I…hurt someone?" At her silence, she whispered, "How…many? How many people did I…?"

"Two lost their lives." Lucenna's voice sounded far away.

Two.

She was saying something else, but Dyna couldn't hear her clearly anymore. A piercing sound rang in her ears, muffling all else. The room was tilting.

"Dyna." Lucenna grabbed her shoulders and gave her a shake. "Take a breath."

She was. She was breathing while others weren't. That was her doing. Hers. She had wanted the barrier gone, wanted power, well now she had it.

Desperate for air, Dyna rushed for the veranda and pushed through the doors and ran into the brisk air. Her boots caught the floor, and she fell against the banister. It was an accident. She didn't mean to do it. She didn't mean to.

Breathe…

Lucenna was there, but Dyna pushed her hands away. Everything was closing in on her and green light flashed at her fingertips again. Her mind was tunneling, her vision darkening. Control. She needed control. To focus on something else.

Anything else.

The sound of distant laughter reached them. She glanced down through her blurred vision at the stone bridge way suspended between two sections of the castle. Ladies in fine dresses walked arm in and arm, their wings fluttering behind them.

"A wedding!" One mused excitedly. "And an ascension, all during the festival. Can you imagine?"

"It will be the grandest event held in Hermon Ridge," said the other. "Lord Jophiel will spare no expense in assuring only the best is prepared for Prince Cassiel's wedding."

Her breath caught. What—

"As he should. Lady Sarrai is the jewel of the north. Who else could possibly belong at his side? Their union will do well for the Realm."

"It's a splendid match, indeed." The ladies passed under the veranda, their voices fading away.

Her mind went still for a moment. It was quiet. So quiet.

"Dyna…"

All of her attention then focused on her friend's face. On the shock woven in Lucenna's features, the worry. It could only mean that Dyna's mind wasn't playing tricks on her. She'd heard correctly.

Something happened while she was unconscious. Cassiel went from nearly exiled to engaged to another. Whatever chance she had of being accepted as Cassiel's mate vanished when she attacked them with her magic. Even if that didn't happen, being removed for another…made sense.

Who else could possibly belong at his side?

A vicious twisting started in Dyna's gut and spread to her lungs, her throat constricting. The sensation swarmed through her being so painfully that she thought something had splintered somewhere inside, like a piece of her had fallen out of place.

"May I ask why such an adorable creature looks as if her world has ended?" a male voice asked.

Dyna looked up, blankly staring at the pureblooded Celestial standing on the banister. The setting sun radiated behind the young male as if he had walked out of Heaven's Gate. Locks of gold hair fell around the angles of his face. He wore silky robes as white as the wings on his back.

As the sun faded, the last streams of light haloed him, glinting off the gold circlet on his brow. He tilted his head at her curiously. One edge of his mouth curved in a soft smile. "Dynalya Astron, I presume."

She stood upright and dipped in a curtsey. "An honor to meet you…Prince Asiel."

There was no questioning it. The family resemblance was obvious. She stepped back as he landed on the terrace.

Lucenna hissed something under her breath. Asiel ignored her, his blue eyes on Dyna's face.

"The honor is mine." He bent in a courtly bow, and his eyes flickered to her hand. "You are bleeding."

She glanced down at her scraped knuckles, blood seeping from the torn skin. It must have happened when she tripped into the banister.

Asiel brought a finger to his mouth and bit it until he drew blood. He reached for her hand, but she stepped away from him, shocked. "I can heal you," he said, his smile a little too kind. "With a drop of my blood, your lovely skin will repair instantly, without a scar."

"Thank you, Your Highness, but I must respectfully decline," she said firmly.

Why was he here? This was wholly inappropriate, especially to offer such a thing. He knew the laws.

Asiel canted his head. "You don't wish to be healed?"

"Not by you." Dyna winced at how rude that sounded. "I mean, you cannot give me your blood. It's illegal."

And Cassiel had told her she couldn't take blood from another Celestial. Ever. Doing so would defile their bond.

"Very well. Tell me what caused these tears?"

"It's nothing important. Might I ask why you have come?"

"To our chambers, no less," Lucenna added behind her.

"Whatever it was, it must have been very important for you to cry." The prince said, disregarding both of their comments. He reached out to wipe a stray tear from her cheek.

Dyna swerved her head back, and he raised his eyebrows at the reaction. That was twice he had attempted to touch her and she couldn't help but suspect he was trying to Soul Search.

"You have heard of me, and only bad things, it seems." He tutted. "Pity. I would have enjoyed getting to know you without reservations."

"No, Cassiel...speaks very highly of you." She winced at the badly told lie.

Asiel chuckled. "It's kind of you to say so. It must be something you do, putting yourself before others. The way you did when you stopped my cousin's exile."

"You were there," Dyna said, realizing she had seen him before. "In the throne room."

He'd been the one holding Sarrai back during the sentencing.

"I make it my business to know who enters my kingdom, my dear." Prince Asiel tilted his head as he studied both of them with delight. "And I see two fair maidens. The God of Urn surely bestows upon me."

Lucenna placed herself in front of her. "Cassiel warned us about you," she hissed. "I think you should leave."

He had? Dyna didn't know anything about any warning, only that he wasn't fond of him.

Prince Asiel leaned his head back and laughed. "My cousin has a talent for overreacting and spinning tales. Though I don't have the faintest clue what he has spun this time, I assure you it's false."

Lucenna conjured a crackling purple orb in her hand, and it filled the air with menacing static. "Leave."

"Well, I best be on my way, then." Prince Asiel grinned further. With a flap of his wings, he rose into the twilight sky. "It was a pleasure to meet you, Dynalya. A beautiful name for a beautiful flower. I hope you have thorns. You will need them."

Then he lowered in a courtly bow and flew away. The warning lingered with Dyna, and she looked down at her hands that still looked too soft. Despite her killing two Celestials, he only saw a helpless female.

Sweet little scarlet flower...

Dyna ground her teeth. That's what they all saw.

Lucenna waited until he was completely out of sight before extinguishing her magic.

She frowned. "You threatened the Lord's son."

"I don't care. Cassiel doesn't want him lurking around you."

"Why?"

"Because he is a rake. He makes a sport out of seducing virgins. Primarily, human ones."

If Dyna wasn't so taken aback by the other news she heard, she might have been more shocked or perhaps laughed. Instead, she merely gazed down at the far treetops below. Lucenna came to stand by her as they watched the Celestials fluttering about, lighting torches outside of their homes for the incoming night.

"When I saw humans living here, I dared to hope," Dyna whispered. "That everything would be all right."

But that spark had died as quickly as it had formed. The thought of being allowed to stay with him seemed so impossible now.

"And why shouldn't it be?" Lucenna asked her. "What we heard could be a mere rumor. Even if there is some truth to it, you haven't given Cassiel a chance to explain. Assume nothing until you have spoken to him first." Lucenna brushed her messy hair aside. "I have seen the way he looks at you, Dyna. You're his *bonded*. His life-mate. His *wife*, should you need clearer words. I would be very remiss to believe he would so easily cast you aside for another."

I care not what the Realms say. I am yours and you are mine.

316

That's what he told her, and she believed him.

It was easy to feel insecure when comparing herself next to the beauty of Sarrai, yet the thought of anyone else attempting to take him from her made flashes of magic coil through her fingers.

"Dyna." Lucenna looked at her worriedly. "Come, it's too cold to linger outside." She led her back to the doors. "How do you feel now? Is your power spent?"

Her Essence felt strong, nowhere near dwindling. "It's perfect. Only my body feels tired. Does this mean I passed the Rising?"

Lucenna winked at her. "Yes. You're acclimating."

"But I lost control."

"Your magic unleashed to protect Cassiel. I think you have a hold of your power. It's your emotions that need to be tamed."

"How bad was it?" Dyna asked. "The throne room..."

Lucenna cringed. "Um, well, it's demolished. You turned into this green deity of terror that had Prince Malakel cowering. I had to strike you to make you stop."

Oh, that explained why her chest was sore.

Dyna finally remembered what she did in the throne room and what it had been like to wield so much power. It scared her. She was grateful Lucenna kept her word, because she would have killed Malakel. She had wanted blood, wanted to draw out her claws and make him pay.

I could easily become a monster, too.

Should you ever let her out, she would be glorious.

A shudder went through her.

"Honestly, you were a little frightening," Lucenna said as they entered their room. "Remind me to never stand between you and the grumpy prince."

But they paused when they found the Celestial with orange wings waiting.

She curtsied. "My lady, I'm here to help you dress for this evening's dinner with our Lord." She motioned to the dresses laid out on the beds. "I have prepared the bathing room."

"Ah, perfect," Lucenna said. "I would love to have a hot bath."

Noemi smiled shyly, her brown eyes soft and bright. Her wings trailed after her as she headed for another door. "If you will come this way, my lady."

They entered a stone room with a large, full bath built into the floor. Steam hovered on the surface. They undressed and slipped in. Noemi poured floral smelling oils and soaps into the water and worked on washing their hair.

"Thank you, Noemi," Dyna said as a gentle stream of warm water slid through her scalp and soothed her sore body.

"Of course, my lady."

"Is it odd to have us here?" Lucenna asked on the other side of the massive bath as she scrubbed her arms with a washcloth. "Must not be every day you serve non-Celestials."

"No, not very odd at all," came her cheerful reply. Noemi ran her fingers through Dyna's hair and murmured in soft awe in the language of the heavens.

Dyna smiled tiredly. "What did you say?"

"Oh, pardon. I was admiring your hair, my lady. I have never seen such a color."

"I was thinking the same of your wings. They remind me of sunsets and the orange poppies dancing in the meadow outside of my village in the summer."

It reminded her of home and made her a little nostalgic.

The servant stopped to stare at her for a moment, and her eyes seemed to water before she grabbed a brush and slid it through Dyna's hair.

"Did I say something wrong?"

"No." Noemi sniffed, giving her a tearful smile. She spoke a soft reply in her language and this time Dyna understood the *thank you* from the tone.

"I wish I could speak your language. It sounds lovely."

"I will teach you, my lady. What do you wish to learn?"

Dyna thought of Cassiel, hearing his voice when he spoke in his language. She fought the knot forming in her throat and reminded herself she made a promise about their bond. And she was going to keep it. "Well, there is one thing..."

CHAPTER 46

Cassiel

Cassiel left the castle behind and flew high into the darkening sky, needing air to clear his head. He soared higher until he rose past the waterfall for King Rael's monument and landed on the fingertips of the extended stone hand. Night had fallen, and tiny spots of torch flames flickered among the trees and along the castle walls. The faint moonlight struggled to shine through the thick storm clouds, inviting the scent of rain.

His wings sagged at his back with the heavy weight of his imminent title.

And his engagement to another who wasn't meant to be his.

At the announcement, Cassiel didn't say anything. Not when he felt Zev's eyes burrowing holes in his face, nor when Malakel laughed, or when Sarrai wore her courtly smile. Lord Jophiel excused them with a note they would discuss more about it at dinner, and Cassiel flew away without a word.

The lordship, the engagement that he would never accept—none of that mattered to him right now. It's what came after that frightened him.

He had hoped that by remaining an unimportant prince with no standing in court, they could be together without garnering very much attention. That he could hide Dyna away safely from anything that could harm her, but now... things were different.

As his mate, Dyna would be placed under the scrutiny of the court, and it would only lead to her suffering. That had been one of his fears when they first bonded. It was her choice to stay, but if she chose not to be with him anymore...he would understand.

The thought compressed his lungs, making it hard to breathe. His fists clenched until his nails pierced his palms and drew blood. He sighed, watching the tiny cuts heal in seconds.

He shouldn't have returned here.

Clouds gathered over the castle, and a soft rumble of thunder rolled overhead. Cassiel looked down at the Realm that would be forced upon him. The icy wind blew against his hair and face, doing little to ease the tension in his head.

Cassiel pulled on the delicate chain around his neck until he freed the sapphire ring from out of his coat. It was his mothers, but lately he had imagined it on a different finger.

He cursed under his breath. "Damn it all."

"Who are you speaking to?"

Cassiel inwardly flinched at the unexpected voice. By its mocking tone, he knew who stood behind him.

"How are you doing this fine evening, cousin? I have missed your sour complexion. I feared the festival would be a dismal affair, but after today, it seems we are in for some splendid amusement."

"Asiel, never a pleasure," Cassiel replied dully. "Now piss off."

Asiel never liked him, and the feeling was mutual. "Oh, is the little prince feeling sorry for himself? Did another usurp your birthright, as well?"

Cassiel stiffened. He hadn't thought about how Lord Jophiel's son would feel about all of this. He turned in the direction of his cousin's voice. Asiel leaned against the monument, partially hidden in the shadows. Moonlight graced the edges of his wings.

"Why are you brooding over your new prerogative? I understand that you are to be married soon. Permit me to tender my congratulations."

"You must know I did not plan this," Cassiel said. "I never wanted Hermon Ridge. I don't want any of it."

"You don't want it? Yet it was given to you, regardless." A coolness laced Asiel's idle tone. "Well, you can have it. I decided I'm not angry with you since you brought me such a lovely consolation gift, after all. I don't think I have bedded a redhead before."

Cassiel clenched his teeth with the sudden fury rolling through him. "What did you say?"

"Oh, did you not bring Dyna for me?" he asked with mock innocence.

"If you so much as touch her—"

"Too late. She hurt herself, and well, I could not stand by without providing her with my aid."

Cassiel froze. "What did you do?"

More thunder rolled, a flash of lightning briefly illuminating Asiel's face in the dark before the storm clouds hid it once more. "I'm sure you have imagined it. She was not at all surprised when I healed her with my blood."

His stomach dropped, but any doubt immediately cleared away. He would have felt it if their bond had been defiled. Dyna would never...

"You still reveal everything on that face of yours." Asiel laughed and stepped out of the shadows with a smug smile. He was only trying to get a rise out of him.

Yet it didn't stop the flames from beginning to coalesce in his veins. "This is your only warning," he said, each word low and rough. "Stay away from her."

Asiel's smile sharpened. "Why? I enjoy meeting maidens. A pure maiden, all the more."

He was burning now, quite ready to burst.

"Speak to her again, and I will break you in half." His voice came out like a growl from the depths of the Netherworld. Dark, and cold, and promising death, because it was the truth. He wouldn't hesitate to remove anyone who harmed her. "She is not another one of your conquests."

Surprise swept across Asiel's face, and maybe a little wariness, before a smirk hid it. "Then who is Dynalya Astron? After what she did to save you, I wager she is someone very special."

Cassiel studied his expression, trying to decide if he should break one of his wings and shove him off the monument.

"I confess, I did lie," Asiel said, moving around him. "Dyna was indeed wounded, and I offered to heal her, but she so adamantly refused. She was quite tenacious on the subject, as if the very thought offended her. I cannot help but suspect that she has already taken the blood of another. Yours perhaps?"

"No." But he had denied it too quickly.

Asiel answered with a gloating grin. "I hope you did not think that sounded at all convincing." Tension wove between them as they stood beneath the coming storm. "What will Father think when he finds out that his precious nephew broke another one of our sacred laws by freely giving away his blood, and to a human, no less?"

Cassiel worked his jaw. His cousin would have mentioned their bond if he really knew about it. All he had were suspicions. "Dyna aided me because I did the same for her. I saved her life with my blood. When Lord Jophiel learns of it, it will be because I'm the one to tell him. Not because you are threatening me."

Asiel paused. "Very well," he said cheerfully and turned away, losing interest.

That had been too easy. Where was he going with this?

"You are a prince, Asiel. Your actions reflect upon your father. Show him respect in that regard."

Asiel sneered at that. "When have I ever played the role of a dutiful son? The only one he expects that from is you."

There was some intent in there, something bitter and accusing. Cassiel supposed he may deserve Asiel's anger for losing his inheritance, but he wouldn't let him take it out on Dyna.

"I meant what I said. Stay away from her."

"Now, why would I do that?" Asiel laughed. His wings lifted him into the sky, his smile anything but kind. "Don't you see? I like pretty things I cannot have."

The sky was flashing with streaks of lightning by the time Cassiel arrived in the guest wing of the castle. He flew into a private garden with an open veranda that led to the rooms on one end, and the main corridor into the castle on the other. Stone braziers in each corner lit the space with warm firelight.

Zev and Rawn waited there, seated on the edge of a flowing fountain.

"Why didn't you refuse?" Zev demanded as soon as he landed.

"I could hardly get my thoughts in order, let alone speak a coherent sentence," Cassiel said. "Even if I had, I could not outright decline the engagement. I was not given much of a choice."

"There is always a choice, and I wouldn't have chosen to stand there like a fool."

Rawn moved between them. "My friend, please do not judge that which you do not understand. Cassiel is royalty. He must abide by certain propriety."

Zev growled, his eyes flashing yellow. "Unless my memory serves me ill, you're bonded to Dyna. You cannot marry another."

"Perhaps it does serve you ill," Cassiel snapped back. "I made a promise to always protect her, and that is what I'm doing."

"How is this protecting her? Confess to your uncle and that will put an end to your engagement," Zev said. "Better yet, why are we arguing about this? We should leave now while no one is watching."

"You don't understand. This is a command from the High King. His word is law." Cassiel sighed. He had broken too many rules already. "Running would dishonor my House and belittle everything Lord Jophiel has done for me. I hold him in the highest regard. Don't ask me to insult him."

This was a delicate matter, and he had to approach it carefully to avoid any backlash falling on Dyna.

Zev exhaled sharply. "This is what I feared, Cassiel. That she would be hurt and cast aside. You're willing to simply accept this?"

He glared at him, his tone hardening. "I never said that, nor do I plan to cast her aside."

"Then why didn't you tell him?"

"Because I gave Dyna my word that everything regarding us will be decided by *us*. No one else." He had felt how important choice was to her, and he would have to be reduced to a wretched thing first before he ever took that from her again. "If I had revealed that she is my bonded, not only would I have broken my word, I would have to explain that I healed her. Which is another law I have broken. As a result, two things would happen. Either my certain exile or… Dyna would be forced to become Lady of Hermon Ridge."

They stared at him.

"You do not wish for that?" Rawn asked.

Cassiel wasn't willing to say the court would strongly contest against a human holding such a position. He hated to think about that. "It does not matter what I wish for, Lord Norrlen. The only thing that matters is what she wants."

He turned to the veranda, where he felt her presence in the hall before she stepped out. Her cream gown fluttered in the wind, soft curls falling around her face. She was so beautiful it left him breathless. Always had. Even in the dark of night, there was something indescribable about her that brought out the light like his very own sun.

But the bond on her end was silent, and it made him ache. For a second, he was afraid of what she would say, but then her eyes welled, and he was done worrying about everything else.

"Only we will decide what happens next," he said, holding her gaze. "Together."

CHAPTER 47

Dynalya

Every facet of Dyna's attention was on him. She was hardly aware of Lucenna and Noemi beside her, or of Zev and Rawn. She only saw him. Lightning flashed overhead, catching the silver of Cassiel's eyes. He looked different within the backdrop of the castle, as though coming here had changed him. More ethereal. More striking. His clothing was sleek and elegant as his wings. Locks swept across his forehead, and she had the urge to run her fingers through them. Every inch of her being begged to get closer. To touch him and feel the energy of their bond flow between them.

"Noemi, please excuse me with Lord Jophiel," Cassiel said, not looking away from her. "I'm afraid Dynalya and I will not make it to dinner."

After a pause, the air shifted around her, and the soft footsteps of everyone faded away. Once they were alone, Dyna took a breath and walked down the steps into the garden, drawn to him by some unspoken beckoning.

Cassiel's eyes followed her until she stopped five feet away from him. Afraid to get too close, and afraid of what he would say. His shield was down, and it would have been easy to read him if she dropped hers, but a part of her was still holding back.

A small frown pulled at his lips. He gently prodded her end of the bond, asking to feel her. She shook her head. She didn't want him to see the ugliness inside.

"I heard..." she murmured. "About you and Sarrai..."

His wings unfurled as he stepped forward. "Dyna." Her name on his lips was an acknowledgment, an apology, and a reverence. "You are right to feel slighted. I'm sorry you learned of that before I could speak to you."

So it was true.

What was there to speak about if it was an order from his father? If Yoel learned of their bond, would he release Cassiel from the engagement?

"Tell me your thoughts." His voice was low, strained. "What are you thinking?"

Burning rushed up her nose and her eyes stung. "I knew whatever happened when we arrived would be difficult ... but this...it's a lot."

He reached for her, but his hand dropped. "Do you wish...for me to release you?"

The question was a fist around her heart.

But that wasn't his intention. He couldn't feel anything from her right now or perceive anything but the brokenness she couldn't keep from her face. His question sounded brittle. Vulnerable. She sensed it hurt him to ask it, but this was his attempt to give her a choice—and the chance to fight for him. He would never force her to accept being his and the burdens that came with their bond.

Dyna didn't care about any of that. Her reason dwindled to simply feeling unworthy and having no right to protest the engagement.

"I know none of this is what we hoped for." Cassiel moved a step closer. "My sentencing is yet to be decided, but they mean to make me Lord of Hermon. A life by my side would be harder. Unkinder."

Because they wouldn't easily accept her as their Lady. They would scorn her, and she knew it.

The wind picked up and blew against them as a soft mist fell.

"I once told you I couldn't free you from the bond," he said softly. "But Dyna, if you tell me this isn't what you want...then..."

He would release her.

Never had she desired to be released. Not even when she learned their bond was created by accident. Every shred of her soul wanted this—*him*. But from the uncertainty of his expression, he didn't want her to accept him simply because of their bond. Cassiel wanted her to *choose* to be his. To say it aloud. Because she wasn't the only one with insecurities. Which only made her want to laugh at how silly it all was.

The first time she ever laid eyes on him, she knew in her soul that her life would never be the same. That everything she knew about love and fate would change. It didn't matter that she was human, and it didn't matter that she was frightened of what the future may bring. Any risk was worth the mere chance that he could be her forever.

Dyna exhaled a sharp breath. "No."

"No?"

"No, I don't want to be released. No, I won't be cast aside for another. No, I won't let any person, thing, or law come between us. You belong to me and only me."

Cassiel inhaled faintly, his mouth parting. "Could you repeat that? I don't think I heard you clearly the first time."

"You belong to—"

He surged forward, and his mouth crashed into hers. An electrifying current tingled through her lips on contact. She threw her arms around his neck, rising on her toes, melting into the devouring kiss. His body sagged against her with relief, because for once, nothing was keeping them apart. His hands roamed to her waist and up her back, pulling her tight against him.

"I cannot describe to you how much I desired to hear that," Cassiel said when they finally stopped for air. He brushed her cheek. "And I can finally touch you."

She smiled. "I passed through the Rising."

"Thank *Elyōn*. It drove me mad to see you cry." Cassiel gently pressed his mouth to the corner of her lashes, kissing away the last of her tears. "Every part of me missed touching you." His mouth swept from her cheek to the shell of her ear. "To feel you. To taste your lips."

She shuddered, and her skin pebbled at his breath coasting over her neck. Cassiel's hands traveled down her spine to her waist, pressing their bodies closer together.

"The bond," he begged. "Please drop your shield. Let me in."

She sensed it left a big gaping void in his chest, a wall that kept away her soul, her presence, her voice, and it reminded him too much of the time they were apart.

Inhaling a shaky breath, Dyna let her shield fall. All of her self-doubts and insecurities, her guilt for what she had done, unleashed every chaotic feeling in their raw force, and he winced.

Cassiel shook his head as if it made no sense to him. "Did you truly believe, after all that we have been through, that I would not choose you?"

It took her a moment to confess. "A hidden part of me feared that I didn't fit by your side, but today…when you were on your knees…" She closed her eyes. "I couldn't let them hurt you. I'm sorry I killed them. I'm so sorry. But I couldn't let go."

He looked at her as if nothing else existed at that moment. "Should our positions have been reversed, I would have done the same without a second thought. That day beneath the willow, I did not mean we should attempt marriage or that I'm not sure of how I felt. I certainly did not mean I would attempt it with another if you denied me. All that I am is bound to you."

She had to remind herself to breathe because he had a way of making her stop.

Cassiel gathered her locks, tousling in the wind, and curled them over his fingers, bringing them to his lips. It was done in such a reverent way it made her heart slow. "*At haor sheli*...that is who you are to me. It means 'you are my light', referring to the first rays of the sunrise as it spreads across the horizon, fading all that was dark away. Dynalya, you are my dawn. Without you, there is no sun."

Her face crumbled as the tears she couldn't hold back spilled down her face. He held her to him, his wings gently enveloping her in warmth as if she was treasured. Loved.

That was what he was telling her in so many words.

"I expected our lives together would hold its challenges," he murmured. "That it would require many things I was not prepared for. But what I am prepared for is to fight for it because I want a life with you. I *choose* you. I chose you from the moment you first smiled at me. Never should you ever doubt that."

She buried her face in his chest. "Forgive me. I needed to hear it."

"Stupid human." Cassiel sighed. "I regret not speaking plainly from the onset. I shall do so now." He lifted her chin, so she looked at him. His thumb lightly caressed her cheek, tracing her jaw. "*Lev sheli,* I was yours long before I ever realized it, and yours I shall remain. *Ani ohev otach.*"

Dyna didn't need to understand his ardent words to know what he had confessed. The distance between them vanished as he drew her to him, his lips taking hers. His tender kiss worshiped every part of her mouth. Heat stroked down her spine, spreading in her chest.

Whatever happened from here on out or the hardships they faced, he was hers and nothing, absolutely nothing, would ever change that.

CHAPTER 48

Dynalya

They spent the evening together in the garden until they were caught in the pouring rain. Dyna laughed as they ran for the veranda's cover. Hands linked, he led her in the opposite direction of the grand hall to the north wing. The storm blew through the open corridors, causing the torches to flicker.

She had to rush to keep up with him, not because he was walking quickly, but because one of his long strides equaled three of hers. "Wait, where are we going?"

"To see my uncle."

Her eyes widened, sensing exactly why, and she tugged him to a stop. "Now?"

"I intend to make my intentions clear. To him, to my father, and to the Realms," Cassiel said, water dripping down his face.

They were soaked through. He removed his jacket, bringing it around her shoulders. He brushed the wet strands from her temples and smoothed down her hair. The way he was looking at her was making her pulse dance again, banishing the chill of her wet clothes. Dyna didn't think she would ever get used to it.

"Will you come with me?" he asked.

"Always," Dyna said, because she wanted everyone to know he was hers, too.

A smile lit his face, and it made her heart glow.

She was nervous about what Lord Jophiel would say and about what would happen from here on out, but Dyna wouldn't retreat anymore. Not when it came to what she wanted.

The soft patter of rain followed them as their footsteps squeaked on the marble floors. They eventually reached a door carved with the sigil of Hermon. After knocking three times, Cassiel led her into a large, quiet room. It was narrow, its size more measured in its length. The two opposing walls were filled with endless books and artifacts. Through an archway was the end of the room. The entire back wall was constructed of floor-to-ceiling windows with the storm brewing outside. From there, a spiral staircase led to an open veranda that circled the entire room with more bookshelves.

The room was dark with the chandeliers left unlit. The domed ceiling was made of glass, while the rest was painted with images she couldn't quite distinguish. Cassiel led her deeper inside and their soft footsteps carried in the quiet study. They passed a seating area with a couch and chairs, lamps resting on the side tables, heading to the soft glow of light at the end of the room. There, the tables were littered with more artifacts and scattered books left open. A sheet covered something wide and flat on a podium.

By the tall windows stood a male Celestial in navy robes with long blond hair flowing to his back, the tips of his white wings brushing the floor. He was motionless as he watched the storm. From the circlet on his brow, Dyna guessed this was his uncle.

"My lord." Cassiel bowed elaborately, and she did the same.

"Your father and I had a falling out some five hundred years ago when I broke away from Hilos," Lord Jophiel said as lightning flashed across the sky. "When I finally returned, it was on a day like this. A storm blew through the kingdom, and on the eve of your father's wedding, no less. What came with it changed his life. I wonder if another storm will do the same for yours. Change is inevitable, Cassiel. In time you will see it's for the better."

The ominous statement sent a nervous current through Dyna. What was that supposed to mean?

Cassiel's hand traveled to the small of her back, and a soothing warmth passed through his palm. That one touch was enough to steady her. "Forgive me for missing dinner. I needed some time."

"I suppose the news was startling enough to make you forget your manners," Lord Jophiel mused, his tone thoughtful. "If you have come to dissuade me, my hands are tied. I cannot countermand your father. I know you don't wish for lordship and all that it entails. It's a grand responsibility no one is truly prepared for, but I know you can do it."

"I understand," Cassiel said. "How quickly am I to assume your position?"

"As quickly as you desire. Today even."

"Perfect. I accept. However, I require one leisure year before fulfilling my duty."

At this, the Lord of Hermon Ridge turned to face them. He looked nearly the same as his portrait in the hall. His handsome face was free of any facial hair. He had strong cheekbones and a firm mouth. He was over five centuries old, but didn't appear much older than his nephew. Celestials were slow to age, yet Dyna wondered why the High King had looked about twenty-five years older than his brother when they couldn't have been too far apart in age.

Lord Jophiel's startled gaze landed on her face, then where Cassiel's hand still held her. She had the urge to pull away, but he gripped her waist firm. She felt no nerves from him. No twitch in his wings. Only confidence and assurance.

"The Lords pay homage to the High King," Cassiel said. "They answer his call and abide by the laws, but they rule their Realms outside of his influence, as is their right. As Lord of Hermon Ridge, I choose who I will spend my life with—and I have chosen."

Lord Jophiel's eyes widened, bouncing between them both. "Cassiel, the engagement was a royal decree. A command by your father."

"He may be the High King, but he does not command my heart. If he cannot accept that, then I relinquish the lordship."

They both gaped at him.

You would...give it up? she asked.

Cassiel wove his fingers through hers and brought her hand to his lips. *To be Lord is a grand thing, but it's nothing compared to you.*

Her heart did a little flip at the declaration.

Cassiel looked at his uncle again. "Forgive me, but I won't marry Lady Sarrai. I cannot when I am already bonded. I would like to properly introduce you to my mate, Dynalya Astron."

Lord Jophiel looked as if he'd been struck, his eyes widening further. "You have bonded?"

"Our blood is one," Cassiel said firmly. "And before you question it, or suggest something unmentionable to break it, what we have is a True Bond. It cannot be broken without breaking us both." His tone grew hard, edging on a cold warning. "And I hope you can understand I will do *whatever* is necessary to prevent that."

Silence filled the study with nothing but the sound of rain. A tremble went through Dyna at how quickly he went from affectionate to menacing. She kept her head lowered in the long stretch of silence.

Lord Jophiel let out a puff of air. "By the grace of *Elyōn*, Cassiel. The last thing I expected was this news, let alone to have you threaten me over it."

"Pardon me, Uncle. I did not intend it to be a threat."

"Yes, you did." His eyes flickered back and forth between them. "Quite frankly, many things now make much more sense."

Not sure what that meant, she exchanged a confused frown with Cassiel.

"I'm referring to you revealing yourself to save her, and she destroying the throne room to save you. It's what True Bonded mates do. They protect each other." Lord Jophiel's brow creased with concern as he looked at them. "Unreservedly. Your grandfather was True Bonded himself."

By his uneasy expression, he seemed to recall what King Rael did to avenge the death of his wife. Theirs had been a tale of tragedy that ended with an entire city destroyed. After what Dyna did to protect her mate, she feared what she would do at the loss of him, too.

"Well, come here, my dear." Lord Jophiel held out a hand to her. "I must greet my nephew's wife."

When they came to him, Dyna had prepared for the worst. Perhaps shouting, anger, or calling for the guards to take her away. Anything but the unexpected kindness on his face.

At her hesitation, Cassiel sent encouragement through the bond. Dyna gathered her wet skirts and went to take his uncle's hand, lowering into a curtsey.

"It's an honor to meet you, my lord." She felt that familiar electrical charge when her skin met his, letting her know he was Soul Searching.

"I see. You both certainly are of one soul. How did this come to be? I would appreciate the full story, Cassiel." He frowned at him. "At the news of your capture, I feared something terrible had happened to you. I was ready to bring the Legion upon the Port of Azure. Don't make me go through such a thing again."

Cassiel smiled faintly. "Please don't start a war on my behalf. My one life is not worth the loss of many more."

"What did you do to have a bounty placed on your head?" he continued sternly.

Cassiel hesitated to answer.

"Does it have to do with Mount Ida?" Lord Jophiel asked next. They both froze in surprise and he glowered. "Do you not trust me, Cassiel?"

"Of course, Uncle."

"When your father first told me you were returning to Hermon, he shared with me how you broke Rael's Law when you spared a human in his territory." Lord Jophiel glanced at her. "He also mentioned her werewolf cousin, and how they had a map to Mount Ida in their possession. When you did not arrive, I had my suspicions. Now you are here with a curious group of people and bonded. I assume you were on your way to Mount Ida, but with the bounties, you can no longer board a ship in Azure. Therefore, you have come to me, so I may allow you to cross Troll Bridge. Am I correct?"

Dyna's shock welded with Cassiel's at how deftly he figured it out. "Yes."

"*Why* do you have a bounty?" Lord Jophiel asked again, the sternness returning to his face. "It's about time you tell me the full story of your harrowing journey."

He motioned for them to take a seat on one of the sofas, and he did the same. They told him everything. How they had bonded and the remaining details of what had happened in the port, then of her capture and escape. By the end, Lord Jophiel was kneading his temples.

"If Father knew what I planned, he never would have allowed it. I have to go to Mount Ida. I have to find her." Some of Cassiel's emotions slipped through the bond, and she saw flashes of a woman with black hair.

"This is a lot to take to mind." Lord Jophiel sighed. "We will discuss that later. You gave your blood to a human, Cassiel. That alone would have exiled you. It resulted in a True Bond, which was fate, if not a miracle. For it's the only thing that will spare you." He gave him a disapproving look. "This is quite a mess. One I must inform your father of straightaway. There may still be repercussions for it."

Cassiel nodded stiffly. "I understand."

"I know my brother. Whether he approves or not, I don't believe Yoel will attempt to separate you. Nonetheless, this does change things."

"You mean I may no longer be considered to lord over Hermon Ridge?" her mate asked, a tad hopeful.

"I mean, this will change how you are both perceived by the Realms. The union of your father and mother caused great controversy, and she had only been a mistress."

A knot grew in Dyna's chest and a muscle flexed in Cassiel's tight jaw. His mother wasn't spared from the prejudice of his people, and neither would she. But she already knew that, and it didn't change her mind. They would withstand anything to be together and she decided then she would not be afraid.

"You are the first prince to marry a human. I cannot pretend the courts will find it favorable. It will be something you both will have to be primed to expect. As for the lordship, your ascension has not changed, at least on my part. In the end, it will be your father's decision. Nevertheless, there is one thing I am certain of."

She held her breath.

"There must be a wedding."

"A wedding?" Dyna shrunk in her seat. She could withstand the disdain of court, beatings, captivity, even leaping off a cliff, but dressing up in a white gown and getting married before the entire Celestial population made her want to run and hide.

Cassiel's mouth quirked at her reaction. "Is that necessary, Uncle?"

"Well, I'm assuming you did not perform the Bonding Rites or had any witnesses to your blood exchange."

They shook their heads.

"There is an order to things that you skipped, Cassiel. The High King is meant to choose the mates of the royal family, and there are rituals that must be completed to sanction a bonding. Well, what's done is done. For your marriage to be legally valid and presented to the court, you must be handfasted before *Elyōn*. All traditions must be honored."

Lord Jophiel lifted a hand when he tried to argue. "The Realms will not be denied this. During the wedding, Dynalya will be properly announced as Princess Consort of Hilos. Not only will it authorize the title she now holds, it's also the security needed to fortify her place as your lawfully wedded wife. This is for her sake, as well."

Cassiel's amused voice floated into her thoughts. *What do you think, lev sheli? Shall I force you to marry me again?*

Dyna laughed weakly at his jest. Anxiety droned in her like a hive of bees, but she understood why this had to be done. She also wanted to earn the court's acceptance, so if that included some grand ceremony, then that's what they would have. *I think I might faint.*

He cracked a smile and tucked a loose strand behind her ear. *Zev did say he expected a proper wedding. It's no less than what you deserve.*

But one worry they both had surfaced in the bond.

We're short on time, Cassiel. We didn't intend to stay much longer than tonight.

It will most likely be held at the peak of the festival, he said. *Which is in three days. After that, we leave.*

Three days.

It still felt too long, with winter's arrival hanging over their heads. If it snowed, they couldn't cross Troll Bridge.

They looked back at Lord Jophiel to find him staring at them. "Forgive me for asking this, but have you...consummated your marriage?"

Heat rushed through Dyna's cheeks.

Cassiel shifted in his seat, clearing his throat. "No, Uncle. Of course not."

"Good. There are steps you must take to establish your bond properly before you can...enjoy each other."

God of Urn. The conversation had taken an awkward turn. She didn't want to talk about this with his uncle, or even *think* of it yet. They were barely exploring their relationship.

"You mentioned she was taken and you could not find her. A True Bond cannot be hidden after it's fully formed. Once joined, no spell could ever hide her from you again." Lord Jophiel canted his head as he studied them further. "Yet I see your bond is nearly complete. Take care not to reveal your mind-speak in the presence of others. It's a rare ability and a good defense to have. It loses its value if many know about it."

Dyna glanced at Cassiel. *Perhaps you should tell him about your other ability.*

He nodded. "There is something I must show you, Uncle. Well, uh, during the confrontation with Tarn, something strange happened. My sword was...blessed."

An oddly careful expression formed on Lord Jophiel's face. "I see. Well, I would not find that strange, given the circumstances."

Cassiel looked away, and she felt a tiny trickle of his shame. He didn't confess the reason he shouldn't have Seraph fire was because he killed people. It was supposed to only go to those with a pure soul. He thought of himself as some mistake, but that wasn't true. He only looked like a star to her.

Dyna brushed his arm, encouraging him to continue.

"That's not all." Standing, Cassiel backed up several steps and held out his hand. At first nothing happened, but he glanced at her, and flames burst to life in his palm.

Lord Jophiel jerked back in his chair, exclaiming something under his breath in their language.

"Uncle?"

He quickly composed himself. "Ah...I'm sorry, my dear." He smiled at her apologetically. "Would you mind giving us the room for a moment?"

Dyna rose to her feet. "Yes, of course."

"She can hear anything you will tell me," Cassiel argued.

"It's all right," she said, then in the bond she added, *We can discuss it later.*

He frowned. *Wait in my chamber. It's at the end of the second hall on the right. The door will have the sigil of Hilos.*

Dyna curtsied. "Thank you for your kindness, Lord Jophiel. It's an honor to meet the person who raised Cassiel."

He stood to bow in return. "A pleasure, my lady."

She left the study feeling relieved that Cassiel's uncle was on their side. It was more than she'd hoped for.

After several steps, Dyna came before a set of wide, double doors with the mark of gilded wings expanding from a crowned sword lit aflame. The sigil of Hilos. Going in, she first entered a drawing room with paneled walls and plush seating for guests. The room felt cold, with no signs of ever being in use. Dyna followed the low firelight to the open doors leading to the bedroom where the hearth was lit, providing the space with gentle warmth.

Cassiel's room was elaborate, like the rest of the castle, with the walls adorned with carved moldings and gold, fine stone floors, and opulent furniture. But it held only what was necessary. A large bed rested between two windows, an armoire, seating by the hearth. Another doorway led, she guessed, to a private bathing area.

Dyna sat on a settee to wait. But after an hour, she was feeling sleepy. The sound of soft footsteps echoed out in the hall, and Dyna rushed to open the door. She froze, and so did Prince Asiel when he spotted her.

He chuckled, glancing around the empty corridor. They were alone. "Well, this is unexpected. It's an oddly late hour to be leaving a male's room unescorted."

A blush rose to Dyna's face. She wasn't sure if she should reveal the nature of their relationship yet. "I came by to see if Cassiel was here, but he isn't, so I will be on my way."

Asiel blocked her from leaving. "Why did you come to see him?"

"Nothing of concern."

"Oh, but I'm very concerned."

She glowered at his teasing. "Do you always take this much interest in everyone you meet?"

A sly smile curved his mouth as he stepped closer, cornering her against the door. "Only in those who I find rather interesting—"

He was ripped away from her in a flash of black. She hardly had time to register Cassiel's presence before he twisted Asiel's arm behind his back and slammed his face into the wall, the heavy thud echoing in the quiet corridor.

Asiel gave a short laugh, the sound muffled with half his mouth constrained against the stone. "Easy there, cousin."

"I warned you," Cassiel seethed, the low snarl rising the hair on Dyna's neck. He looked ready to dislocate his arm.

Asiel winced at the added pressure. "I was only speaking to her."

"Might I remove your tongue, so that will no longer be your excuse?"

"My word, I did not know you had it in you to be so violent. You are quite territorial over this human, and one I caught shamelessly leaving your room. Who is she to you?"

There was no hesitation.

Cassiel clenched his teeth and growled one definitive word that made his claim inherently clear. *"Mine."*

The sound of it reverberated through the bond, the possessiveness sending pleasant shivers through her body.

Asiel's smirk faded into shock.

"This is the last time you approach her without invitation. I will not be so kind again." Cassiel yanked him off the wall and shoved him away, making him stumble a few steps. "Now go."

Then he took her hand and led her in the opposite direction. Asiel was left to stare after them with a dumbfounded look on his face.

"You staked your claim in front of your cousin," Dyna commented neutrally. She wasn't upset by it. If anything, it sent a little thrill through her, but she also didn't mind watching him squirm a bit.

Cassiel sensed it, and his smirk grew challenging. "I plan to proclaim it before the entire Realm, *lev sheli.*"

She sleepily smiled at that and yawned. "You were gone awhile."

"Yes, pardon." His face creased, and a trickle of his concern slipped through the bond. "He gave me much to think about. Would you mind if we discuss it later? I think we should save the rest of this conversation for the morning."

After another yawn, she said, "I think you're right."

He drew her into an embrace. "Get your rest. Tomorrow will change everything."

CHAPTER 49

Von

Beryl Coast rested on a rocky rise, resembling a jagged tooth against the storm clouds. A deluge beat down on the steep roofs as wind blew mercilessly from the east. It tugged at Von's thick cloak as he and Elon observed the quiet city, torch fires flickering from the outside walls. It was too dark to see anything past the rain, but he could smell the ocean in the air. Their horses nickered restlessly. Von had found them a day after escaping the Black Woods.

Len, Novo, and Bouvier rode out of the dark to join them. At Von's nod, they followed the road into the city. They kept their heads low against the rainfall until they reached the entrance. The drunk guards manning the gates looked the other way when Bouvier tossed them a bag of coins, and they cantered in.

Oil lamp posts lined the dark, empty streets. All doors and shutters were closed against the storm.

Von signaled Bouvier to take the lead since he knew the city. The quicker they were finished here, the better. The trip back to Indigo Bay where Tarn's ship was docked would take them a little less than a fortnight, if it didn't snow first. They had to set sail for Dwarf Shoe before the Sax Sea froze.

Von was impatient to see Yavi again, and to bring her the good news that Dyna had survived. If she even allowed him to speak to her.

The clomp of hooves beat on cobblestone as they rode through the quiet streets. Bouvier eventually stopped in front of an old tavern. It was a modest building of three floors, with a crooked roof, and wedged between two tall structures. But the windows were lit and voices filtered from inside. Above it was a wooden carved sign reading *The Wench's Hole.*

"This is a good place to lodge for the night, Commander," Bouvier said, raking his wet hair over his head. "We won't find another place tonight."

Von glanced at the others and met their weary faces flushed, and wet from the cold. They were visibly exhausted. After days of traveling, they deserved the rest.

He nodded reluctantly, and they dismounted.

A young boy stepped out of the stable beside the tavern. He pipped from behind layers of scarves and an oversized cloak, "I'll take your horses, sirs."

"There's a good lad." Von tossed the boy a russet.

They handed him their reins before going inside. It was warm, with ambient lighting coming from the lanterns hanging from the bare beams on the ceiling. Patrons filled nearly every table, laughing and talking over hot meals. Most stole glances at them from the corner of their peripherals.

Len's dark eyes examined the room beneath her hood, as did Elon, perhaps listening to every sound. They were staking the area. Novo hurried off to speak to the tavern keeper with Len.

Removing his cloak, Von sat at a dirty table, with Elon and Bouvier following him. "Where's the location?"

The older spy had been scouting the area for weeks now, carefully noting the progress of the excavation of the ruins—an ancient temple dedicated to the worship of Jökull. It was the reason they were so sure it held the Scroll of the Unending.

Bouvier laid out a map of northern Azure on the table. They leaned over it to study the roads, and he pointed out a dirt path leading out of the city. "The temple lies fifteen miles east, less than an hour's ride by horse."

"And the asset?" Von asked.

"The Relic Hunter on site was close to discovering the location of the scroll. He would have stopped the excavation in this weather."

"How many are on site?"

"He only had three people on his team. One historian and two ex-soldiers that used to serve in the Azure army as hired protection. No one we can't handle." Bouvier folded the map and returned it to his coat. "If they found the scroll and left, it should be easy to track them."

Von rubbed the scruff on his jaw. It sounded like an easy score. They could probably do this without spilling any blood as well if they snuck in without being noticed. "Good. We'll set out in the morning."

Novo returned and removed his cavalier hat as he handed them keys. "You're on the second floor, Commander. I ordered meals for us as well."

Von brushed his thumb over the numbers embossed on the iron key. But he noticed they were short one. "Where's Len's key?"

"Right, you're on the third floor," he said, casually sliding a key across the table to her.

Len's quick fingers slipped it under her cloak. She leaned back in her seat, her expression fixed with careful disinterest.

Bouvier snorted. "And where are you staying, lad?"

Novo fluttered his lashes. "Shall I spend the night with you, love?"

"You're not pretty enough."

"After a few pints, you may change your mind and think me a pretty wench with a hole."

Bouvier threw a stale piece of bread at his head, making Len snicker.

A barmaid came by and poured them some ale, then she returned with steaming bowls of mutton stew and bread. Von ignored their ongoing banter as he ate, enjoying the warmth the food brought to his bones. But every once in a while, he caught Novo and Len exchanging lingering looks across the table, and he wasn't sure if it meant anything until they finished eating. Elon silently departed for his room first, then Bouvier. When Len stood to leave, Novo's heated stare followed her all the way to the stairs.

Best to nip that now.

Von set down his mug. "Watch yourself."

Novo glanced at him and grinned. "Commander, we have been love-mates nearly as long as you have been with Yavi." Chuckling at his staggered expression, he crossed his feet up on the table. "You forget that I'm a spy. It does me good to know everyone's secrets."

Von narrowed his eyes. "What do you mean by that?"

"It isn't a threat. I simply thought you would sympathize with my situation. I'm mad for her, and I'm willing to risk my neck to be with her."

The barefaced honesty caught Von off guard. "You need to improve your discretion. You're too conspicuous."

Instead, he should've told him that to court Len was to court Death. She was the only one Tarn showed any favor to.

Novo shrugged. "Bouvier suspects, but he doesn't care. I have saved his life twice already. He's in my debt. Captain won't say anything either."

Von's mug halted halfway to his mouth. "Elon knows?"

"Aye, he's got good ears, Commander." Novo grinned sheepishly. "Len can be a bit loud."

Von groaned in disgust and waved him off. "Keep that to yourself. How do you know he won't say anything?"

"Elon knows what it's like to be with someone he shouldn't."

"What do you mean?"

"You haven't figured out why he joined Tarn, yet?" Novo smirked. "His Red Highland tattoo was burned off. That only happens when an elf has committed treason against his kingdom. If his crime was spying for Greenwood, Elon would have lost his head. Instead, he was exiled. The only reason for that is because he loved a Green Elf."

Von sat up straight in his chair. He'd always wondered what had happened to make Elon leave his homeland.

"Captain immediately deposits his earnings after he's paid. Where did you think the money was going? He could only be sending it to his family."

Von had noticed whenever they were in a town, Elon would stop by the banks, but he hadn't given it much thought. The exile must have stripped him of his wealth, so he came into Tarn's service nearly two years ago to earn a living. The elf was always quiet and kept to himself. Von knew nothing about him, let alone that he had a family, yet Novo figured him out simply by watching him.

"Elon knows about you and Yavi, too."

Von nearly spat out his ale. "What?"

Novo chuckled and leaned back in his chair. "He's our leader for a reason, Commander. I believe he has known since last winter. If Elon was going to report it to Tarn, he would have done so by now."

All this time, Von thought he had been careful. He felt like an idiot. Now two of Tarn's spies knew along with Sorren, Geon and Dyna. His secret was fast losing its undisclosed value.

And it put Yavi in danger.

He eyed the young spy warily, not sure if he could trust him. But Novo only looked happy to discuss his own secret.

"I've been saving my earnings to buy Len's freedom," Novo said as he flipped a coin in his hand. "Tarn bought her for a thousand gold pieces. I have nearly fifty thousand. Once we return from this mission, I'm going to make him an offer."

Again, Von gawked at him in bewilderment. Why had it not occurred to him to buy their freedom? Probably because Tarn would never allow him to go. But Novo worked for pay and could leave when he wished. Would Tarn let him buy Len and walk away freely?

Von didn't think so, but he didn't want to damper the confidence radiating off the young man. Novo was happy with Len and didn't care what others thought of it. It made him yearn for Yavi. How much he desired to go back to how things were between them, but all of that was slipping through his fingers faster than he could grasp it.

Maybe it was the drink, but he felt so despicable for loving her and making her suffer as his wife. It was his fault for reaching for something he never once deserved.

Von poured himself more ale. "You're living in a dream, Novo. Created by a faulty wish."

"What else is there to strive for in life but wishes and dreams? I, for one, mean to have mine fulfilled." Novo grinned and stood. "Well, if you'll excuse me, my lady is waiting."

Von had made a wish on the stars once. It had yet to be answered, and he didn't think it ever would be.

Looking at the young man before him, so hopelessly in love, worry and dread rooted in his chest that they wouldn't have a happy ending, either.

Von was aware of the thick scars covering his back, a sign of his many failures. But defiance received another sort of punishment. He sighed into his mug, and the froth swirled with the image of Dalton.

"Don't underestimate him," he said. "Tarn can be merciless when angered."

"Aye, Commander." The low light from the lantern glinted off Novo's dark eyes. "The same could be said of you."

Especially when it came to his wife.

Von continued drinking long after the spy was gone. He drowned himself with the memory of how Yavi's skin felt in his hands, her lips on his, and her hazel eyes gazing back at him. He craved to inhale the scent of her soft curls when they brushed against his face.

Gods, he needed to sober up. Von trudged outside into the cold rain. It felt good against his flushed face. He leaned against the tavern and breathed in the fresh air until he felt his mind clear. Their marriage was unraveling because of who he was and the decisions he had made. But he couldn't wait around for a wish anymore.

He needed to tell her the truth.

A distant rumble of galloping horses cut into Von's thoughts. Glancing up the road, he spotted a unit of armed men riding in his direction. He withdrew into the shadows of the tavern's alleyway and let the dark envelop him. The men galloped past. Dim moonlight glinted over their armor, highlighting the kingdom's sigil on their shoulders.

There could only be two reasons for the Azure Knights' arrival. Either they somehow tracked them down—or the Azure King also had business in Beryl Coast.

CHAPTER 50

Zev

When the sun peeked over the horizon, a knock came at the door. Zev was already awake, sitting by the fire because he hadn't slept. Couldn't bring himself to when he was so wrought with worry. He glanced across the room to where Lord Norrlen stood on the balcony, nursing a cup of tea. They both shared a wary look.

"It's us," came Lucenna's soft voice.

Zev rushed to the door and yanked it open. The sorceress was there, but she wasn't with Dyna, nor was she alone. Cassiel blended within the shadows of the hall, dressed in black robes with tapered sleeves that came to a point at his middle fingers. His trousers were black, as were his boots, as if he cared for no other color today.

Zev had nothing kind to say to him. "I don't want to see you if—"

"You know, I'm quite tired of you growling at me." Cassiel strode in and shut the door.

"Where is Dyna?" Zev asked Lucenna.

"She is still sleeping." Her lilac eyes flickered to Cassiel. "He called on me before dawn. Said it was important, and to dress like a murderess. His words."

She wore tight, black leather and heeled boots, accentuating her every curve. Her eyes were rimmed with black kohl, lips painted dark red, and she'd braided her silvery white hair into a high tail. Knives glinted at the sheathes strapped to her thighs.

She looked striking, if not deadly. But why?

Cassiel came to stand in the middle of the room. "All you need to know is that Dyna and I have told my uncle about everything. Today, he has called parliament, so I may declare her before I do so publicly at court."

They all fell in shocked silence. Zev dropped to sit on the edge of his bed. God of Urn, it was happening. She would be acknowledged. The tight knot of worry around his chest loosened with his exhale.

"Dyna is now part of the royal family by marriage," Cassiel continued, looking at him. "By this time tomorrow, all of Hermon will know it, and soon the news will spread throughout the Realms. Our marriage will be a contentious issue, especially regarding her race." He sighed and flicked a hand. "But I am now Lord of Hermon Ridge, and that ascension will also be made known today. Another thing that won't be taken well."

It's what Zev wanted, for Dyna to be given her place, but now to hear how serious it was, he suddenly felt on edge. The knot tightened again.

"There is much stacked against you," Lord Norrlen agreed.

Lucenna leaned against the wall, crossing her arms. "You need supporters. I have seen the nobles at court and how they survive on power and favor. Without that, it will be very difficult for you both."

Cassiel nodded. "Which is why I will need to create that illusion for her until real support in court can be made."

Zev's eyes bled to yellow. His wolf paced inside of him, sensing the battle that was coming. He was more than eager to fight when it came to protecting his cousin's happiness. "And how do you plan to do that?"

"By making you Alpha."

The Hermon castle shook as the massive stone doors to the war room banged open from a sheer gust of electrifying magic. Cassiel strolled in with his wings arched like veils of black smoke behind him. Zev's paws clicked against the stone floor, flanked by Rawn and Lucenna at his sides. Court nobles quickly moved out of their way as they strode through the room. The guards standing in the corners stiffened and reached for their hilts.

Nobles filled every seat at the long meeting table. Some purebloods, most of them Nephilim. The room was so crowded with legislators they filled the alcoves and the gallery. Every one of them gawked at Cassiel and his looming entourage.

Long black robes billowed at his feet as he marched forward in the silence and came to the front of the table where his uncle waited. He slid into the head seat and leaned back, lounging on the armrest. Baffled murmurs buzzed in the room by the statement that action made.

Zev and the others took their places on either side of him. The beating hearts of everyone in attendance resonated in his ears, and he smelled their nervous sweat. The war room was the perfect meeting place, as they were in a sense at war. Cassiel had to fight for his position. And he could only do so with the best at his side.

Cassiel crossed his ankles up on the table, contemplating his people with mild interest. "Are your legs broken, or have you forgotten how to bow before a prince of Hilos?"

It was a casual question, but his dark smile could only be a threat. The room shifted with the rustle of wings as everyone reluctantly lowered into stiff bows.

"That's better."

A silence settled over the still room as everyone stared back at them.

"What is the meaning of this?" one of the pureblooded nobles demanded. His short hair was combed out of his squared features. By the splendor of his dark golden robes, he was high ranking. On his shoulder was the sigil of a sun fanned by six wings. "Who are they? Why are they here? This is highly unusual, Lord Jophiel."

"These are unusual times, Lord Gadriel," Cassiel replied instead. "Please take your seats."

If Zev recalled correctly, Lord Gadriel lorded over the floating islands of Nazar.

The rustle of fabric and perfumed scents filtered through the room as they were seated. He studied everyone, listening to their faint whispers and beating hearts, as he knew Rawn was, too. He kept track of every movement and noted the sigils they wore.

Even without them, it was easy to tell who belonged to which Realm. The Celestials of Edym were tanned, so exposed to the sun as they were, and they dressed in various shades of red. The Celestials of Skath were pale with lighter features, wearing purple clothing lined with fur. Those from Nazar wore yellow tunics, and those of Hilos were in long white robes embroidered with gold. But they were all the same, with blond hair, blue eyes, and pearlescent wings.

The citizens of Hermon had a variety of skin tones, from pale to dark brown, hair in all colors and textures, wings with vibrant patterns and shades. They were dressed in blue.

"I have called this meeting today to make an official announcement before the court." Lord Jophiel's voice projected in the room. "I have stepped down as Lord of Hermon Ridge, and Cassiel ascended last night."

The nobles responded with more shocked murmurs. Zev growled at the racial slurs secretly hissed by the purebloods about the dark prince.

"Asiel is the rightful inheritor of Hermon Ridge," Lord Gadriel said. "You would slight your own son?"

"Where is my son?" Lord Jophiel asked. "Do you see him? Because I do not. If Asiel had shown the slightest interest in matters of state, he would be in my seat now. Who better to take my place than someone elected by the High King? It is done."

"Then he is to wed Sarrai. You gave your word she would be the mate of the next Lord of Hermon. For that reason, she was raised here."

Zev flattened his ears. Over his dead body would he ever allow that to happen.

Resting his elbow on the armrest, Cassiel laid his chin over his curled fingers. "Odd. I was under the impression you abandoned your niece in Hermon because you didn't want to endure the shame of a Nephilim in your court."

The Lord of Nazar flushed red. Cassiel's uncle shot him a warning look. But this was good information, Zev mused. Lord Gadriel was insisting on this union because he stood to gain leverage here.

"As for Sarrai's hand, it's an honor to receive such a generous proposal." Cassiel brushed a speck of dust off his knee. "Unfortunately, I must decline. I already have my bride."

Zev tensed at the sudden return of shocked quiet blanketing the room again.

"To whom are you promised that we have not received any word?" asked the pale Celestial standing beside Lord Gadriel. He was tall, and well-built—a warrior, if Zev ever knew one. Deep purple robes stretched across his broad chest. The sigil of a fire shield was embroidered over his heart.

Cassiel crossed one leg over the other. "Lord Hallel, you have come far from the Realm of Skath."

He was giving them names and locations, Zev realized, of those he most noted as a concern. Hallel was a considerable one since he'd deposed his brother to rule over his Realm.

Cassiel's gaze traveled over everyone, waiting for an answer. "If you must know, my chosen is Dynalya Astron."

They blinked at him, confused.

His mouth hitched in a smirk. "The young woman who leveled the throne room yesterday. I intend to marry her before the court, and she will become the next Lady of Hermon Ridge."

The pureblooded Celestials jumped to their feet, shouting in outrage. They demanded Lord Jophiel reverse the ascension, and for Cassiel to be exiled for breaking the law. They threw out insults, each one stabbing Zev's ears like knives. Lord Gadriel suggested the human should be done away with.

Zev's snarl ripped through the room, instantly silencing them.

"There, there." Cassiel petted his fur, reminding him to keep his wolf calm. "I'm sure Lord Gadriel did not mean to threaten your cousin."

Zev snapped his teeth, taking a threatening step forward. The closest Celestials to him gasped and jumped out of their seats. The tempo of all their thrumming hearts climbed along with the scent of their fear. Only one heartbeat was steady. It belonged to a Celestial in dark red robes who lingered in a shadowy corner. He was partially hidden behind the wings of two guards in white. That must be the Lord of Edym.

Lowering his legs, Cassiel sat up straight and rested his hands on the table. "Oh, where are my manners? I neglected to explain the presence of my companions. This is Zev Astron, Alpha of the largest werewolf Pack in Urn." The lie was delivered with smooth idleness. "If you find his family name familiar, it is. You see, Dynalya is most certainly a noble, as she is the descendant of Azeran of House Astron, one of the most revered names in the Magos Empire. Who currently rule the Lunar Guild. Her other cousin, Lucenna Astron, is also present."

Lucenna's eyes glowed soft purple, electricity crackling around her.

"Some of you may not recognize him, but you have heard of him." Cassiel nodded to the elf in black armor standing beside him. "May I present Lord Rawn Norrlen, renowned warrior of the Greenwood Kingdom, general of its armies. These are the head leaders of Dynalya's guard, gentlemen. Each of them would defend her with a might to rival the Realms. Speak against me, I may forgive you, but if anyone else in this room wishes ill will against her again, I promise it will be the last words you speak before you meet the Gods." Cassiel's smile sharpened. "Now, who will escort you through the Gates depends on which one of us is the fastest. Venture a guess on who that would be."

All eyes landed on Zev. Well, at least they were smart.

He released a deep menacing growl that promised however fast they ran, he would rip into them before they could scream.

CHAPTER 51

Cassiel

Hermon's war room fell intensely quiet with shock and ire at Cassiel's declaration. They glanced between him and the Guardians, a new acknowledgment and wariness lining their stoic expressions. Their judgment fell on him, yet it carried no weight. Not anymore.

Damn the lot of them.

"Sniveling bastard." The sharp voice cracked in the silence like a whip. Every head turned toward the entrance, and the gathered Celestials bowed before the Crown Prince of Hilos.

Cassiel ground his teeth as he locked eyes with his brother. He forced himself to stay lax, to keep his expression neutral, though his insides burned with the effort.

"You intend to make *her* the next Lady?" Malakel said with disgust. "That position is for nobility. Not for decrepit creatures and common whores. To suggest it is to spit on our traditions. This repugnance is intolerable. After what she did—"

"It matters not what she did," Cassiel said, his voice deepening with the rise of his flame. It churned inside of him, unrelenting against his skin. "I am now Lord of Hermon Ridge. No traditions or judgements will sway my decision. Speak another slight against her, and you will experience the *meaning* of intolerable."

The very clear threat thickened the tension in the room, and the nobles glanced between them, waiting for Malakel's reply.

His brother curled his lip. "You are a stain upon our House and Father's reign. You dare destroy everything we stand for to save that worthless human?"

At the surge of his anger, power blazed in Cassiel's veins. Tendrils of flames unfurled from his hands on the table and snaked up his arms. Chairs screeched, and the council gasped as the fire demolished the table runner, and anything in its path, bathing the walls in a frightful blue hue.

He coolly met his brother's startled eyes and snarled, "Don't underestimate the things I would do for my *wife*."

New whispers passed among the gentry. He only caught a few words.

Fire wielder...

Cursed power...

Ravager king...

Cassiel held his brother's stare, though in the back of his mind he was stunned by how easily he summoned the flames. He called them back, and they faded away. Everyone gawked at him.

"Prince Cassiel has been blessed with Seraph fire," Lord Jophiel announced carefully as he took his seat again. "The likes of which we have not seen in many centuries, but blessed all the same."

More mutters filtered all around. Too low for Cassiel to hear this time, but most likely unkind by the way Zev's ears flattened against his head. They continued staring at him and he felt their shock like prickles on his scalp.

The silence was broken by Lord Gadriel. "You called her wife..." His eyes widened. "Have you bonded?"

Cassiel leaned back in his seat and crossed a leg over the other. "We have."

Outrage responded at the unsanctioned bonding.

"The union between Hermon and Nazar has been planned since Sarrai's infancy!" Lord Gadriel thundered at his uncle. "It cannot be prevented by someone of inferior birth. They must annul. Immediately."

Cassiel smoothed out his sleeve. "Your demand is denied."

Lord Hallel snickered, earning a cold glare from Lord Gadriel. The one thing Gadriel hated as much as Nephilims was the Lord of Skath. Cassiel paid no attention to the old feud. They were present merely out of privilege for their class. They had no say in his decisions. But he had to get a hold of his temper if he was going to win over his council.

"An annulment is not possible," Lord Jophiel said. "Dynalya is his True Bonded, the most sacred and protected union under Rael's Law. As you all well know. Because of it, the High King has granted them a special dispensation in regards to their unplanned bond and the events at the port."

Cassiel stilled at the news. His uncle must have spoken to his father after their discussion last night.

The nobles ruptured with anger, calling it nepotism. Which was preposterous because when had his father ever shown him favor? The King was merely applying the laws...or biding his time until he arrived to separate them himself.

The thought made Cassiel's insides burn again.

"But she's not like us," a Celestial with dark skin and braided black hair said. "What would a blood bond ever mean to a *human*?"

"And some of you are half-breeds." Cassiel steepled his fingers, pinning the council beneath his cool stare. "Is your blood less filthy than hers?"

They stared at his hands, flickering with flame. His anger was making his blood boil, and it showed. He went along with it, pretending it was intentional.

"When were they ever meant to be our equals?" someone muttered, the owner of the voice lost in the crowd.

Others agreed, but there were significantly fewer protests than before. Either because of his intimidating companions or his display of Seraph fire.

"The majority in this room have a human father or mother," Cassiel said. "Some of you have had a human love-mate at some point in your long lives. Yet you see yourselves better than them? This Realm was founded on acceptance. Created specifically for those without a place, for those who did not reject anyone different from us. Was that something you merely told yourselves, or have you changed your minds now that a human has gained status above you? We know the air of superiority the other Realms pretend to hold, but I expected more from Hermon." He didn't care that he was insulting the Lords to their faces. His focus was on his own council. "What disturbs me most is not your lack of respect for my standing, not even your contempt for my mate, but your utter hypocrisy."

The council shifted in their seats, dropping their eyes.

"You expect parliament to accept her when she is responsible for the exposure of our kind?" Malakel demanded.

"The High King is now in the Blue Capitol attending to that concern," Lord Jophiel said. "He has the matter in hand."

Cassiel's eyes snapped to his uncle. This was the first he was hearing of it.

"You mean Father is cleaning up *his* mess." Malakel shook his head and addressed the room. "You have a right to be offended by his choice of bride. Your new Lord knows what our people have suffered and yet he would stoop so low as to marry one of *their* kind. One who is wholly beneath his station. A lowborn who brings no dowry, no titles, no land. *Nothing*."

"I have no need of it," Cassiel said through his clenched teeth. He was losing his composure. His brother knew exactly where to push.

Malakel sneered. "Yet what can be expected from the Black Hearted Prince?"

Cassiel used to despise being called that until he found his heart truly was black. It sat within the hollow of his chest, thrumming with something dark and scorching.

"This is not the first time he broke a law for her," Malakel told them. "She trespassed into Hilos, by which we know the punishment is death. Yet he spared her."

The room rumbled with voices, or maybe it was Cassiel because something loud was rushing in his head.

Lord Jophiel stood. "Malakel—"

"And none of us have forgotten what she did in the throne room. She is no mere human when she has the craft and wears curses on her arm."

"It's a geas," Cassiel growled, his hands clenching.

"No difference."

"What about the guards she killed?" someone asked.

"As they were involved in the unauthorized exiling of a prince, their deaths were warranted," Lord Jophiel said.

Malakel let out a scoff. "Of course, how suitable. Once again, he is to be pardoned for his crimes. It's not right, Uncle. Now we are to allow a witch to walk freely where she could harm another one of us? Nothing was left of those guards. Their bodies will never be recovered by *Elyōn*. We cannot leave such evil power unchecked."

Zev, Lucenna, and Rawn braced beside Cassiel as he stood. His body shook as fire seared him from inside. It pushed against his being with a maddening instinct coming alive. One that demanded to protect—and destroy.

"To marry *it* is an affront against your country and your class. An insult to all those who died at the hands of *them*. This only proves you are not sane of mind, Cassiel. She bewitched you, so I will do what you are incapable of doing. What should have been done the moment her filthy blood met yours." Malakel motioned at his guards. "Bring her."

Seraph fire ruptured out of him.

It ravaged through the war room, and the nobles cried out, leaping back to escape. With a flap of his wings, Cassiel landed on the table and walked down the center, each step leaving behind a wreath of flame.

They tried it his uncle's way, but he never cared for politics. Dyna was his, and no law nor Realm would take her from him. Any to attempt it would be swiftly incinerated, and he felt no remorse at the thought. No hesitation. Some primal instinct called for destruction as his fire roared through the room, primed to consume them whole.

Cassiel? Dyna's frightened voice rang in his head. *Cassiel!*

He gasped sharply, and the fire died.

Everyone gaped at him with horror and fear, and something that might have been...awe. He locked eyes with Dyna, where she stood at the entrance of the war room. She only wore a gold nightgown, her robe hanging haphazardly on her shoulders as if she'd run out of bed to find him. Her startled emerald eyes searched his face as the bond buzzed with her alarm.

He caught his reflection in the windows and met a creature of annihilation, with flames for eyes. Apprehension fell over him. Not of his power—he had a startling hold over that. It was his endless rage that startled him.

The need to end without thought.

The eyes of every male fell on her body, and Cassiel's snarl ripped through the air. They all looked away, but Lord Hallel met his glare with a goading smile. He liked to fight, and Cassiel was furious enough to meet that challenge. Fortunately for him, his priority was his mate. Sowmya and Janel were with Dyna, but he didn't want her anywhere near this place.

"Escort her away from here," Cassiel whispered under his breath. "She is not safe."

Rawn and Zev marched through the scorched room for the doors, Lucenna following on their heels. Dyna went with them at their prompting, but her worried eyes stayed on him until she fell out of view. He would find her as soon as he finished here.

Cassiel looked down his nose at his people. "If you wish to continue breathing, I advise you to weigh your next words carefully." No one dared to speak. "Allow me to make certain things clear. Dynalya Astron will be crowned Princess Consort of Hilos. The title was hers the moment we bonded, and she *will* be your Lady. Nothing will change that, nor will any threat against her be forgiven. If that is something you cannot accept, then I will fill my council with those who can."

There was a brief pause as they absorbed his meaning. He had no problem taking away their titles if need be. The one thing the gentry valued was their place in court. The air shifted as everyone in attendance bowed, some now deeper than others. Besides Malakel, the only ones to remain standing were the Lords. They were on equal standing as him, but their hard expressions may as well have been a show of defiance.

"This meeting is adjourned. Take your leave." At his command, the room quickly emptied. Cassiel met his uncle's disapproving look and sat on the edge of the table with a sigh. "I lost my temper."

"I see that." Lord Jophiel frowned at the blackened walls. "When I advised a show of force, I did not mean with fire. A good leader must be respected, not feared."

"I know...Regretting your decision yet?"

"No. I do, however, wish you would stop destroying rooms in the castle. Well, I suppose now they will be remade befitting their new Lord and Lady. I will see to it, along with everything else needed for the wedding."

Cassiel didn't have a chance to mention that at the meeting. Oh well. Wayward tongues would do the work. Everyone would know about them soon and could assume it meant there would be a public ceremony.

"You did not tell me my father was in Azure."

"It's the business of kings, Cassiel. Don't concern yourself with it."

That must mean he was conferring with the Azure King over what happened in the port. The Accords were broken on both ends. If it couldn't be resolved, then it could become a dire situation.

"You spoke to him, then?" Cassiel rubbed the back of his neck. "Did he look angry?"

His uncle crossed his arms. "Do you truly want me to answer?"

"I suppose not."

"Well, the hard part is done for today. Go and prepare for the Bonding Rites."

Cassiel made a face. He had skipped that part of his studies. "I take it those are the traditions you mentioned."

"Really, Cassiel, you should know all of this. You have two days to complete the rites before the ceremony. Madam Kahna will inform you of the process."

Cassiel nodded and sighed again. "Thank you. Truly."

"Of course. It's not every day my nephew is to be married. I think you will come to enjoy some of our traditions," Lord Jophiel winked and left him to take in his destruction.

He needed to learn how to control this power before it hurt the one person he cared for the most. Perhaps they should have waited until his return from Mount Ida to announce the ascension. But it was best to establish his position now and build a new court for the future. He didn't know what it would bring, only that he could no longer float through life without a plan.

Because now Dyna was a part of it.

Cassiel strode out of the room in search of her to apologize. She must have been frightened to see him that way.

"Well, that was certainly an interesting turn of events." At the voice, Cassiel turned to see Lord Raziel idling outside the door to the war room.

He wore traditional Celestial robes in deep auburn, trimmed in gold. Long blond hair framed his face, set with cool blue eyes. He was the oldest Lord among them. Older than the High King even though he didn't look a day over thirty. A gold pin of open wings with two crossed swords rested at the neck of his robe.

The most unnerving thing about him was the resemblance of his sharp features. Lord Raziel looked more like Malakel's elder brother than his grandfather.

As he neared, the feather tips of his pure white wings brushed the floor. "Much was revealed today that many did not expect. A Nephilim Lord is a historical event, let alone his unusual mate." Lord Raziel's expression remained indifferent, his tone casual, but Cassiel knew an insult when he heard one. "Though all of it was overshadowed by your revealed abilities. I can hear the walls whispering already."

Oh, he knew they were. He was used to being the topic of discussion, and this would be no different. It was best to ignore all of it.

"Do you know what they are saying?"

Cassiel folded his arms behind his back, schooling his expression. "I care nothing for court gossip."

"Nonetheless, you do care about appearances, at the very least when it comes to your human."

Fire swarmed in his stomach, but Cassiel kept himself unruffled as he scrutinized every word.

"Your *princess* has no real political standing or a drop of royal blood, but you have given her an illusion of power by arriving with assumed supporters. And now that everyone has seen the might of the new Lord of Hermon Ridge, most will hesitate to touch her, or challenge you for your Realm."

It wasn't surprising that he saw through his strategy. Raziel expanded his territory, power, and army through sheer astuteness.

Cassiel frowned with disinterest. "Is there a point to this conversation?"

"I merely wished to commend you."

"On what?"

"On understanding the rules of kingdoms and thrones. Now they know you will not hesitate to decimate those who would stand in your way."

Recalling the flames raging through the council room, Cassiel clenched his jaw. "That is not the way I will oversee this Realm."

"Then perhaps I overestimated you, youngling." Lord Raziel turned away, leaving the last of his voice to echo in the cold hall. "Power is not only taken by force, it must be held by force. For what monarchy isn't founded on blood and war?"

CHAPTER 52

Dynalya

D yna gathered the hem of her nightgown as she rushed down the
hallway, searching for any familiarity. All the halls looked the same.
She tried to connect with Cassiel, but he'd lifted a shield on his end
of the bond. It had been since she walked in, seeing him within a sea of Seraph
fire. A shiver passed through her. He must have looked terrifying to them. To
her, he'd looked like an enthralling being from another world. But how did he
do that?

They didn't know the full extent of his abilities yet, and she could only
imagine they would continue to grow. It made her worry about him.

"My lady." Noemi hurried after her. "We must get you dressed."

"Not until I find Cassiel first." They had led her away from the war room,
but she tried to go back and lost the way.

"He will come find you when he is ready," Lucenna said. She, Rawn, and
Zev had been following her around like her own personal guards. Which
might not have been necessary when Sowmya and Janel marched after her,
the clank of their armor apparent with every step.

All of it made Dyna feel suffocated.

She halted in the open hallway, facing another garden. "What happened?
Why did he attack them?"

"My lady, we should escort you back to your room," Rawn said. The black
wolf beside him chuffed in agreement, making Noemi flinch back. "It's best to
remain out of sight until Prince Cassiel returns."

None of them wanted to answer her questions. It could only mean whatever happened wasn't good. When Noemi came to wake her that morning to dress for the day, she'd felt Cassiel's sudden mind-numbing fury and ran to find him.

Breathing heavily, Dyna gripped the stone banister facing the garden. It was starting. The conflict of their union. She knew it would come, but she wasn't ready for it.

"I will take it from here," Lucenna whispered to the others. "She needs some space."

Zev's wet nose nudged her palm, then he and Rawn strode down a different hall.

Closing her eyes, Dyna reached through the bond, but his shield was still in place. It was best to give him time.

He would come to her, eventually.

"You shouldn't be seen like this," Lucenna told her. "You have an image to uphold."

Sighing, Dyna continued down the corridor in the opposite direction. She heard voices and came around the corner to find an angry male in golden robes speaking to Sarrai in harsh whispers. She kept her head respectfully lowered; body perfectly poised. But her cheeks were flushed pink, and her lashes were wet.

The male spotted them, his eyes pinning on Dyna. His mouth twisted in a glower of disgust. He marched away. Sarrai noticed her next and her flushed face tensed with anger.

It wasn't midday, yet the news of their marriage was spreading through the castle like wildfire. Sarrai must feel as humiliated as Dyna had when she learned of Cassiel's engagement to another.

"Lady Sarrai," Dyna took a hesitant step. "I'm very—"

Sarrai's elegant skirts twirled as she strolled away. A flock of ladies came out of a corridor to join her, and Sarrai said something that made them glance at Dyna. One look at her disheveled appearance, and they burst into a fit of mocking titters.

Noemi spread open her orange wings, blocking her from view. "My lady, please come this way." She led them away down more hallways until they came before a set of golden doors. Sowmya and Janel took their posts on either side of them.

"Where are we?" Dyna asked. "Whose room is this?"

"Yours, my lady." Noemi smiled and led her inside, past the drawing room, to the bedchamber.

Kahna was there with other servants prepping the room, opening the curtains, and straightening the sheets. It looked similar to Cassiel's, but with softer colors in warm shades of taupe, white, and gold. Chandeliers hung from the high ceiling, and a plush carpet lined the area beneath her massive bed adorned in several white lace pillows.

They bowed at her arrival.

"Welcome, my lady," Kahna said curtly. "These are your chambers until you are wed, and your ladies-in-waiting will see to your every need." Her eyes flickered to Noemi. "Where are the others?"

The dainty Celestial flushed, her orange wings twitching at her back. "They...are tending Lady Sarrai, madam."

Kahna's mouth pursed. No one else wanted to serve her, but Dyna didn't mind. She didn't grow up with servants, and all of this was too excessive for her, anyway.

"It's fine," Dyna said. "I don't need a lady's maid."

They looked at her as if she had two heads.

"Unacceptable," Kahna said sharply. "As the mate of Prince Cassiel, our Lord, your status is that of Lady, and soon to be crowned Princess. You must be dressed and treated according to your station. In the eyes of the court, prepare yourself to be judged on everything from your appearance to your conduct." Her eyes traveled over Dyna's messy hair, clothes, then to her bare feet, and her mouth pursed with disapproval. "I see you are in dire need of tending." She clapped her hands. "Get to work!"

The servants sprang into action. They brought in piles of gowns, carts of shoes, chests with jewelry, and other shiny things. She was plopped into a velvet chair before the vanity. They were a whirlwind as they brushed, washed, prodded, and trimmed her into perfection. They had her in a dress in less than an hour and were now working on her hair. Lucenna watched it all from the couch by the hearth, trying not to snicker.

"Find this funny, do you?" Dyna huffed.

"Shoulders up and back straight." The madam jabbed her spine with a sharp finger, making her sit ramrod straight. "Your posture is appalling. Were you not schooled in the etiquette and manners of a proper lady?"

"Apparently not..." Dyna muttered.

Kahna's mouth pursed again. "We must prepare you quickly, then. You will have much to learn. Lessons in how you must hold yourself at court, the workings of the Realms, and the Bonding Rites. The rites are your priority for the next two days, as they are very important. It's to prepare your souls and bodies for a perpetual life of marriage."

"I think she means sex," Lucenna whispered loudly.

A rush of heat flooded Dyna's face, and a glance at the mirror showed Noemi and the other servant girls blushing, too.

Kahna glowered at Lucenna. "She is, in part, correct, my lady. Preparation for your consummation comes with the Rite of the Flesh. As Noemi will be your lady's maid, she will explain what each rite entails."

Noemi smiled shyly at Dyna as she pinned up a section of her red hair.

"There will be a banquet tonight for the Festival of Light and to celebrate Prince Cassiel's ascension. You must attend and be properly presented before the Realms. We will return later to help you into an evening gown, my lady." Kahna's sharp eyes slid to Lucenna. "Does your companion need to be escorted back to her room?"

"She will be staying with me in my chambers," Dyna said. "Please bring her belongings."

The servants gaped.

"My lady, I'm afraid that is not fitting—"

"It's not up for discussion," she said firmly. "Thank you, madam."

Everything was happening so quickly. Dyna needed one thing to be her decision. Her new chambers were enormous, and she couldn't be alone at night. She needed a familiar face around her right now.

Kahna looked as if she had swallowed a spoonful of lemon juice. She bowed stiffly and left the room with the other servants.

"She wasn't happy," Lucenna said.

Dyna sighed. "I don't think she was happy with me to begin with. They aren't pleased that Cassiel chose a human for a mate."

They had all expected a Celestial, who was a picture of elegance, confidence, and grace. Someone like Sarrai.

"Madam Kahna has always been stern, especially regarding decorum," Noemi said. "It's how she runs the castle promptly, but don't take her manner at heart. And my lady, truth be told, your union is a symbol of hope for many of us who wish to coexist with humans. We simply aren't nattering about it in the halls."

"Even if most of them are miffed about it, they can sod off," Lucenna said. "No one can change the fact that you two are bonded."

She went to Dyna's new massive bed and propped herself up against the mounds of silk pillows. With a flick of her wrist, a small table with a pot of tea and pastries floated to her. Then she grinned at them mischievously. "All right, Noemi. I want all the explicit details of the Bonding Rites. Tell us everything, starting with the *Rite of the Flesh*."

"Oh, you!" Dyna threw a hairpin at her.

Laughing, Lucenna patted the bedding. "Come, come, both of you. Now we can talk freely without the overbearing madam."

Dyna hooked her arm with Noemi's, and they went to lounge on the bed.

Lucenna levitated a cup of steaming tea to the both of them. "So?"

Noemi hid a grin behind her cup. "Well...there are three rites, and they serve to align you mind, body, and soul with your chosen. Only a fourth of love-mates make it through the rites."

Dyna's brows tugged up. "Only a fourth?"

"When faced with forever, the rites put much in perspective. Your case is unusual as you have already bonded, and you are True Bonded at that. It means you are a perfect match. Nonetheless, preparing for your wedding night is the third rite and the most important step."

Lucenna wiggled her eyebrows. "Because she is to learn about Celestial pleasures?"

Dyna's face flamed. *God of Urn.*

They hadn't talked about that yet. A flutter went through her stomach at the thought of being that close to Cassiel, that exposed.

"Oh, no." Noemi flushed with a shy laugh. "That part is left up to them to learn together. I'm referring to everything before. The Rite of the Flesh begins on the night prior to the wedding. My lady will be brought to a sacred pool where only females are allowed. There, she will perform a ritual of purification. She will submerge into the waters and cleanse away any impurities that ails her and come away renewed, so she may join her husband with a pure body."

Lucenna arched an eyebrow at that. "Hmm. And what of Cassiel?"

"The prince will also go through the rite in a different form, where he will prepare a special paint."

Dyna and Lucenna shared a confused look. "Paint?"

"It's a private ritual only males can attend. Prince Cassiel will make the paint that is meant for only himself and his bride. On your wedding night, he will use it to paint his matrimonial vows on your body, and you will paint yours on his."

Dyna's heart lodged in her throat. They were going to do what? She stirred her tea nervously, her mind in a sudden whirl.

Lucenna's grin grew cheeky. "And they will do this...*naked*?"

Her tea spoon went flying across the room. "Oh, good Gods!"

Lucenna burst into a fit of laughter, and heat flooded Dyna's cheeks. The memory of Cassiel's defined bare chest and arms crossed her mind, and she swallowed. The thought of freely touching him made her heart hitch with nerves, but also with alluring curiosity.

Noemi stifled a giggle behind her hand. "Well, it will be their choice, even though that's the purpose of it, I suppose. The paint will fade away, but the vows are permanent. And when they join, their promises will be sealed in their bond."

Lucenna hummed and popped a small cake in her mouth. "That all sounds intriguing," she said, as Dyna took a sip of her tea. "But I hope she isn't expected to produce an heir soon."

The scalding liquid lodged in her throat, and she coughed violently. "I—we—I can't–t–there will be no heirs right now!" She quickly set her teacup down, and it clattered loudly on the saucer, nearly dropping it.

She didn't even know if Cassiel wanted children. God of Urn, she wasn't ready to speak about it, let alone know if she wanted them, too.

"Oh, well, we have a contraception that works very well, should you prefer," Noemi said. "We use the seeds of the hallow lily, and it prevents conception for a year. It essentially causes one to be infertile. Very beneficial, and no chance of any surprise little ones, unlike the herbal tea that does not always work. The best part is you will have no monthly menses."

"Oh, really?" Dyna's eyes widened in interest at this new flower she didn't know about.

"One year without bleeding?" Lucenna said, looking equally excited about that.

"It works for males as well, but we hardly use the seed since it takes years for us to conceive, considering we live so long. Chances of pregnancy averages once in a hundred years or so."

"Was King Yoel an exception?" Dyna asked. He had four children, and all were close in age.

"Well, occasionally, there is a period when a male may be overly...fertile."

Dyna squirmed. She couldn't risk a pregnancy while on this journey. "I will take the contraception, thank you."

"Me too," Lucenna chimed in. She grinned when they looked at her. "I may not have a love-mate, but I can do without the bleeding and bloating."

Noemi laughed. "I will see about securing the seeds for you both."

"What about the other two rites?" Dyna asked.

"The first is the Rite of the Mind, in which you share your most intimate thoughts. The second is the Rite of the Soul, where the couple will Soul Search and see into each other's hearts."

Dyna canted her head. "Is that the purpose of Soul Searching?"

"Originally, it was intended to see into the hearts of humans, to measure if they were good people and worthy of *Elyōn's* aid. Now we use it to see if our hearts are aligned with each other. It's a little different for those with a human mate since you cannot Soul Search. The alternative is to braid your handfasting sash together with special ribbons. If your hearts are aligned, the ribbons will stay white. If not, they will blacken."

She didn't know there was so much to the culture of Cassiel's people, especially with marriage. It was all so fascinating.

"There are other traditions during the ceremony," Noemi added.

Somehow, that only made Dyna more nervous, but also excited and a little sad. She was getting married. She was already married, but this would be a grand wedding her grandmother and sister wouldn't be able to attend. What would they think once they learned her husband was a Celestial Prince?

"You will begin the rites tomorrow, so your wedding will fall on the third day of the Festival of Light."

"Why must it be during the festival?" Dyna asked.

"It's not a requirement, but it's believed marriages during this time are sanctified, for the Festival of Light is when the Realms come together for seven nights to honor *Elyōn*. There is food and music, and presents we call light gifts. Tonight is the blessing when the *Hyalus* tree is lit. It all has a special meaning."

Dyna glanced at the silver candelabra on the windowsill. It was in the shape of a tree with seven branches, and each had a candle. "It's a long-standing tradition?"

"Oh, yes. It was established during the first generation of the Forsaken when King *Kāhssiel* ruled. He was the first king of Hilos and a great ruler..." Noemi trailed off, her smile wavering.

"But?" Dyna pressed, picking up on the subtle reluctance.

"Forgive me, my lady." She shot out of bed. "I'm lazing about when I should be working. I will be back this evening to help you dress for the banquet."

Noemi dipped in a quick curtsey and rushed out of the room as if she couldn't escape fast enough. Dyna frowned, wondering what had spooked her so much to avoid telling them more about the first king.

CHAPTER 53

Rawn

The land of Hermon was beautiful, with breathtaking mountain ranges that made Rawn want to weep when he first saw them. He never thought he would see a Celestial Realm in his lifetime, and had wished to paint the view of it for his wife. But every hour he spent here diminished that wonder with each hissing whisper floating through the castle. Such dreadful bigotry the purebloods spoke of each other were like nails in his ears. The only thing that helped muffled the voices was standing outside with the rush of the wind.

"I need you both to be my ears tonight," Cassiel said.

Rawn glanced over his shoulder from the balcony. The prince stood before a floor-length mirror as his valets dressed him in navy robes for tonight's banquet. He had traded the intimidating glower he wore in the war room for a grimace of worry.

"Take everything you heard this morning seriously."

"Was she threatened again?" Zev asked, his voice bordering on a growl.

He'd been washed and shaven, against his will, if asked. He constantly tugged at the collar of his dark gray tunic. The lavish fabric must feel strange and too delicate for his rough skin and claws.

"Not outright." Cassiel frowned. "But I don't trust the Lords, and I don't trust Malakel. I cannot help feeling on edge."

From the whispers Rawn had been catching all day, the concern was valid. An icy gust blew against him, fluttering the ends of his formal, olive-colored jacket.

"Lucenna is keeping guard," Zev said, "Not to mention the Valkyrie."

Cassiel rubbed the tension gathering on his face. "This must all be a lot for Dyna. I did not have a moment to find her before Madam Kahna cornered me."

Rawn and Zev had caught up with him when the stewardess made him sit through a lesson on the Bonding Rites. His complexion was a little green.

Zev smirked. "Are you going to be sick? You look more frightened of the rites than facing off with your people."

Cassiel glared at him as a valet placed a silver circlet on his head. "Addressing parliament is not the same as cutting out a piece of my rib and burning the bone to make sacred paint. Did you miss that part?"

Zev scrunched his face. "Your customs are strange."

"No, they are *different*," Rawn corrected as he reentered the room. He offered the valets an apologetic smile when they glowered at Zev. "I find taking a piece of the rib closest to the heart sets the moral principle of marriage. To sacrifice one's flesh signifies loving your mate and protecting her with your body and soul. The act of the vows is performed in such a way that visibly displays this promise of love and unity. It's a beautiful tradition."

Rawn looked outside again at the endless horizon in the south, where he had left a piece of himself behind. The elves had different traditions for marriage, but they held the same meaning. He bound himself to his wife, and every part of his being craved to return to her.

"That will do, Aharon," Cassiel told the male with blueish-gray wings. The other two valets were twins with matching brown hair and feathers. They bowed and left the room.

Cassiel sighed at his reflection in the mirror. "I don't know if I did the right thing today. Now I fear I might have placed a target on Dyna's back."

"You mean because of the rumors?" Zev asked.

Rawn had caught the whispers in the alcoves and secret corners. While the castle residents were taken back by his human mate, the principal topic of discussion was Cassiel's ability to wield Seraph fire. Only one person has ever had that ability, and they were convinced it meant his return.

"They are calling you the reincarnation of King *Kāhssiel*," Rawn said.

Cassiel rolled his eyes. "It's all court blather."

It must not be the first time he had to endure gossip-mongering, but Rawn had seen how damaging it could be at court. He had gone through the same with his wife, but they had made it work—until he was forced to leave her. Being here reminded him of too many things he would rather forget.

"Your enemies will use what they can to disparage your position in hopes of removing you," Rawn said. "You did well to defend Lady Dynalya. She is your wife, and the Realms must know it. You are overwhelmed, understandably so. This is a new responsibility over your heads, and your support is marginal, but this is where you begin to build your life."

He could see Cassiel's worry. Heard it in his irregular breathing, the shift of his feet, and his elevated heart rate. Zev heard it, too. He glanced worriedly at Rawn.

"We will protect her, Prince Cassiel. Enjoy your evening with Lady Dynalya. Zev and I will be watching and listening."

Zev nodded, crossing his arms.

"Thank you." Cassiel sighed. "I confess, I don't exactly know what I'm doing."

"Presently, your position is vulnerable as you transition into your new station as Lord," Rawn told him. "You must establish power and find backing from the other nobles." He cleared his throat. "Preferably without coercion."

Cassiel grimaced and looked down at his hands worriedly.

They had yet to really discuss what happened in the war room, but Rawn felt a sense of trepidation. Cassiel's power was growing exponentially in a precarious way, and he had revealed that to a crowd full of nobles with their own objectives. Instead of helping their cause, they may have made it worse.

This could end very poorly.

"Can he do that in three days?" Zev asked. "This place makes my wolf antsy. The sooner we can go, the better."

Rawn had to agree. He was impatient to leave, now more than ever. Winter was imminent. It lingered in the air, and he sensed the approaching snowfall. His worry spiked at the thought of being stuck in Azure until winter ended.

He laid a hand over his front pocket, where he felt the last letter he wrote to his wife.

The chance to mail it to her hadn't arrived yet, and there would be none until they crossed Troll Bridge. He had never missed a month of sending her a letter. Merely thinking of how his wife was handling it formed a knot in his throat.

He had spent far too much time away from home. Every day out here kept him from it. He felt his resolve grow weary under a growing desperation to see his family again.

Cassiel nodded. "As soon as Dyna and I are wed, we leave. I have informed my uncle that I require a year before officially taking his place."

That settled Rawn, and he tucked away his frustration. He could withstand a few more days.

However, would they allow him to leave? Lord Jophiel knew about their plans for Mount Ida, and he surely passed on that news to the High King. What did Cassiel's father think of all this?

On their way to the main hall, several Celestials and servants passed them in the corridors. They either stared at their prince or quickly walked past. Cassiel ignored it. He strode purposefully onwards, his expression perfectly cool and indifferent. Either he was practiced at pretending not to care, or he truly didn't.

The faint whispers drifting in the halls filled Rawn's ears with a constant hum.

"...bonded with a human..."

"...wields Seraph fire..."

"...rotten black heart..."

"...the first king returns..."

There were conflicting opinions about who the first king was. Some seemed to hold King *Kāhssiel* in esteem, but all of their tones held a connotation that implied there was some dark history behind it.

"She will soon die," a male voice hissed faintly. *"We will wait for the right moment."*

Rawn and Zev whipped around in the direction of the voice but saw no one in the empty corridor. Rawn listened carefully past the sound of their beating hearts and breathing, reaching for the barest whisper.

"What is it?" Cassiel asked warily.

Zev's eyes bled to yellow, and his claws extended. "A threat," he growled under his breath.

Rawn reached for his sword as footsteps drew closer from an opposing hall leading into the corridor. The last person he expected to see was Lady Sarrai. She came around the corner with Lord Gadriel at her side. Both froze at the sight of them. Though it may have been due to the way Rawn and Zev looked poised to attack.

"Lady Sarrai," Cassiel greeted in his measured manner, indicating they should stand down. "Lord Gadriel. Are you joining us for dinner this evening?"

Rawn and Zev straightened.

Lady Sarrai composed her expression and only acknowledged Cassiel. "It's the first day of the festival," she answered with a gentle smile. "You know it's my favorite."

Lord Gadriel, however, continued studying them with cold eyes. Rawn read the tension in his body, but he was not interested in any confrontation. "Don't dally here," he told her curtly as he stepped back.

Rawn couldn't be certain if he was the one who spoke, but it seemed likely. The Lord headed for an opening in the banister with nothing but open air over the mountain. His massive wings extended, and he leaped into the sky.

"Walk with me?" Lady Sarrai asked.

"Of course." Cassiel took her extended hand and placed it on his curved arm as he escorted her.

Rawn nodded for Zev to let them walk several steps ahead. Enough for an illusion of privacy, though he was listening very carefully to her voice and heart rate. There was no mistaking what he had heard.

"I have been meaning to speak to you," Cassiel said. "To apologize for how you came to learn about my bonded. It seems gossip has a way of getting ahead of me before I have the chance to explain myself."

"They are saying she enchanted you into marrying her."

He hummed. "Don't tell me you believe in such things."

"Are you with her of your own free will?"

"I am."

They stopped a short distance from the banquet hall, teaming with a medley of voices. At the sound of soft footsteps, Rawn noticed Lady Dyna coming down an opposite corridor behind Sarrai, accompanied by Lucenna and two Valkyrie warriors.

She paused at noticing them together and lingered back.

"If that is so, then why did you bond so suddenly without the proper rites and your father's permission?" Sarrai asked. "Without acknowledgement of the court?"

Rawn glanced at Zev, and he winced.

"I regret the way our bonding was done," Cassiel said, holding Dyna's gaze past Sarrai's shoulder. "For I wish I could have properly courted her in the way she deserved. But in any other fate, the result would have been the same. She is who I choose. It was not due to enchantment or any outlandish schemes. She simply saw me for who I am rather than what I was made to believe. That was enough."

So many emotions crossed Lady Dyna's face, and all of them made Rawn secretly smile. Whatever misgivings she may have had or feared of the other woman evaporated in that instant.

"I see..."

Cassiel's attention dropped back to Lady Sarrai.

"Your eyes." She smiled in a way that looked a little sad. "They once bore trapped stars, but now they are shining in someone else's sky."

Lady Sarrai bowed to him in a curtsey and glided into the banquet. A simple ending to an engagement that didn't fully take root. But Rawn couldn't forget she may not be as innocent as she appeared.

"Prince Cassiel—"

Cassiel shook his head. "Whatever you heard, tell me later," he said under his breath. "I'm sure you will hear more tonight."

Rawn read the request in his expression. He didn't want his mate to worry, so he was keeping this from her.

Cassiel went to Dyna and pulled her into a recessed alcove in the corridor, partially hidden by a column. He leaned his forehead against hers as she closed her eyes. They were most likely speaking to each other in private.

Rawn and Zev gave them space and joined Lucenna by the entryway. Her lilac gown flowed freely around her legs with each step, attached by the fabric of braided satin around her neck. They had woven her silvery white hair in an elaborate design that pulled it away from her face.

She let out a huff of air. "It's starting to seem like we have enemies everywhere, don't we?"

"We may know of one," Zev growled. "Lord Gadriel might be planning to go after Dyna."

Lucenna's mouth curled. "I knew I didn't like him."

"As uncle of Lady Sarrai, he stands to lose sway here," Rawn said quietly.

"No wonder he was angry she wouldn't become Lady of Hermon Ridge," Lucenna whispered back. "Nobles are all the same. They only care about power and will do nearly anything to keep it."

Rawn had dealt with his fair share of that in his youth and was glad it was over. "Zev and I will monitor the banqueting room as we keep an eye on Lord Gadriel."

"And anyone else who may be trouble," Zev added. "You stay by Dyna's side tonight."

Lucenna nodded, and they ended their discussion when Cassiel and Dyna rejoined them hand in hand. Her gown was a dark shade of sapphire, flowing around her in soft waves of tulle and satin. The bodice was embroidered with silver flowers and leaves, each centered with pearls, glittering with every movement she made. Her shoulders and back were left bare, with puffed sleeves hanging low on her arms.

"Lady Dyna, you look lovely," Rawn said with a gallant bow.

Zev grinned and did the same. "Like royalty."

"Stop teasing me, Zev." Dyna flushed. "Merely tell me I look absurd."

"Nothing about you is short of divine." Cassiel tucked a loose curl behind her ear. "Shall we?"

That brought a shy smile to her lips, and she nodded. Rawn was happy to see it, if not a little forlorn. It reminded him of what he had been missing for the last twenty years.

"So, Cassiel," Lucenna commented casually as he led them to the hall. "I heard about certain activities that involve paint."

He stayed facing forward, but the back of his neck turned bright red, matching the color rising to Dyna's cheeks. "Piss off, Lucenna."

"What?" She snickered. "I think it will make for a most *exciting* first night together."

"I don't want to hear about this," Zev grumbled.

The sorceress let her teasing fall away as they entered the great hall. It was full of Celestials from every Realm. Each wall bore a tapestry displaying their sigil and colors. Rawn's senses were instantly overwhelmed with smells and sounds as voices flooded his ears. Picking out any sign of danger was going to try his abilities tonight.

CHAPTER 54

Zev

Zev barely listened to the conversation between Rawn and Lord Jophiel about the winter traditions of Greenwood. He studied everyone in attendance at the banquet. Cassiel was seated at the head of the long redwood table, dressed as the very embodiment of royalty. It had been some time since Zev had seen him in such finery. Dyna was seated on his right with Lucenna, and Lord Jophiel on his left, followed by Rawn and Zev as honored guests. The chattering nobles seated further along the table shot looks at Cassiel, and many of them were unpleasant.

It reminded Zev of the time he sat at King Yoel's table, which now seemed like ages ago. The great hall had immense marbled walls gilded in veins of gold. Several large golden chandeliers hung from the ceiling with flickering candles. Plates and cups made of crystal and a variety of in-season fruits and vegetables filled the table. No meat, as usual, but in Hermon Ridge they allowed cooked food. And there were tiered platters full of pastries dusted with sugar and berries. He secretly chuckled at the pure bliss on Lucenna's face when she bit into one.

Many servants moved about the room, serving food and drink. Several guards and Valkyrie watched quietly from their posts on each wall and entryway. A female Celestial played a big golden harp in the corner, harmonizing with a sweet melody in the language of the Heavens. The music didn't help Zev's unease.

He picked at every voice, searching for any threat against his cousin, but all the noise was making his head spin.

The tenor of Malakel's voice floated to him. Zev glanced at where he stood with Lord Hallel and Lord Raziel on the far end of the room, each nursing a drink as they held some conversation not clear enough to catch. Lord Gadriel sat with Lady Sarrai at the center of the table, also whispering among themselves.

His wolf growled quietly inside of him. He knew the Celestials wouldn't readily accept Dyna, but would they stoop so low as to kill her? With how much they hated humans, he wouldn't put it past them.

Sorting through the voices, Zev focused on Lord Gadriel's conversation with Sarrai.

"How is my mother?" she asked.

"She is well."

"I'm pleased to hear so." Sarrai pushed a fork through her food restlessly. "I have been thinking, my lord. When you return to Nazar, could I … accompany you and stay awhile? Only for a few days. I would like to visit her—"

"Your place is here," Lord Gadriel said sharply, and she shrank from the rancor in his next response. "With your *kind*."

Sarrai tried to keep her expression indifferent, but Zev read the hurt welling in her eyes and the flush in her cheeks.

"I did not invest in your future to have it deposed by some human. Do your duty and honor the great name that you bear. The day you are permitted to enter my Realm is when you become worthy of it."

A low, piercing hum cut off Zev's concentration. He locked eyes with Prince Asiel, where he sat at the opposite end of the table. A subtle smirk rested on his face as his finger slowly circled the edge of a glass of water. The sound was lost in the room, but it was loud in Zev's ears. He knew it bothered Rawn by the way he stiffened beside him.

Was Asiel another threat they should look out for?

The prince glanced at Dyna, and his smirk grew. Cassiel had made it very clear that Asiel targeted human girls for his enjoyment. Zev would bite off one of his limbs if he ever came near her. Asiel's finger halted at the unexpected color change of his irises.

"If I may, there was one thing we wished to ask, Lord Jophiel," Rawn said, drawing Zev's attention.

"Ah, yes." Cassiel lowered his voice so only they could hear. "We need to cross Troll Bridge as soon as possible, Uncle. I was hoping you would grant us passage."

All of them leaned forward in their seats to hear his reply.

A guarded expression crossed Lord Jophiel's face as he looked at his nephew. They held a long stare, and Zev heard Cassiel's pulse climb. Earlier that afternoon, he had finally shared his reason to go to Mount Ida. From the way Dyna's green eyes bounced between Cassiel and Lord Jophiel worriedly, she already knew about his missing mother.

"Do you know why It's called Troll Bridge?" Lord Jophiel finally asked them. "It's an isthmus that bridges Azure to the rest of Urn, and it's quite beautiful with oceans on both coasts. However, it's *infested* with trolls."

"They are aware," Cassiel said.

Lord Jophiel nodded and leaned back in his chair. "Then you know how perilous it is. They are thoughtless creatures, but deadly in a frenzied Horde. Azure gave up colonizing the land because of it. Please know you would take a monumental risk going there."

"Is it impossible to cross it alive?" Lucenna asked.

"Well, I did not say that." Everyone stilled, hearing something in his tone. Lord Jophiel glanced at Cassiel. "There are other people there now. They have taken up residence on the Bridge and built a stronghold."

Zev and Rawn exchanged startled looks.

"Who are they?" Cassiel asked.

"They are sellswords. Expert killers. They would have to be to survive in such a place. They keep to themselves and only ever fight for whoever pays them the most gold. Their town is self-sustaining, with no king to rule them, and they want it to remain that way. I have met their leader and have agreed to keep their existence undisclosed from Azure. They do the same for Hermon, and keep the trolls from migrating into the ridge."

Cassiel gaped at him. "They know about us?"

"Yes. It's a secret only known by the High King, the Lords, and the Valkyrie. It's time you know things of this nature now that you are Lord of the Realm."

"Are they agreeable men?"

"I would say so. However, they can be hostile when the safety of their town is threatened."

"If you don't mind, could you inquire if their leader would consider escorting us to the end of their territory?" Rawn asked next. "Payment is not an issue. Our only intention is to cross Troll Bridge to the west. We have no interest in disturbing their anonymity."

"I have not been in contact with them for a few years now. We only know they are there for the lack of trolls. I could send a message, but that would require consent from the High King first." Lord Jophiel frowned at Cassiel. "I will not bar them from going, and as Lord, I cannot truly deny you. But we both know the one who you must seek permission from is not me."

Cassiel's expression grew serious. "I understand. Thank you, Uncle."

Ultimately, it would be King Yoel's decision, but knowing Cassiel, Zev didn't think he would wait to get his answer.

Rawn locked eyes with him, then the rest of them, and each nodded in agreement. They all had a reason to reach Mount Ida. Crossing Troll Bridge was the next step. "We are grateful to you, Lord Jophiel."

"Of course." Worry crossed his face. "Another concern, if you have not reached the end before the first snowfall, you will be detained on the Bridge until the snow melts."

"For that very reason, we must not delay."

Lord Jophiel's eyes flickered between him and his nephew. "I understand your urgency, but I do hope you will consider staying until the wedding."

"Of course," Rawn replied with a polite smile, but Zev sensed his impatience. Every delayed day was an added risk.

"My lord?" They looked up at Lady Sarrai's arrival. She smiled at Lord Jophiel. "It's time for the blessing."

"Ah, yes." He stood and climbed the steps of a short empty stage that had been purposely cleared. On the back wall was a massive window covered by a heavy, velvet blue curtain with thick, golden tassels. He faced the room, and everyone quickly quieted, all attention falling on him.

"This is the most significant part of the year," Lord Jophiel began, his modulated voice projecting clearly. "It's a time when whatever our strife, the Realms come together to celebrate the miracle of light. We all know the story of our ancestors, but we will share it with our guests today. During the First Age, our people lived beneath the dominion of the God of Shadows. But King *Kāhssiel* rose up and led a bloody war against his army of demons that lasted for decades. In the coldest winter the earth had ever seen...the sun *vanished*. Left in endless darkness, our people feared we had been abandoned. No matter how much they begged the skies, their prayers were unanswered." Lord Jophiel paused, emotion crossing his face. "The war was brutal, and the chances of victory faded with every death. When all seemed lost, a great white tree sprouted in the middle of the battlefield. It glowed brightly with a light so pure, our people knew it was a sign that *Elyōn* was still with us."

A moving quiet filled the room, and in this moment, there was no plotting. No anger or scheming. But remembrance. A deep meaning for the Celestials that even Zev felt.

"The impact of such a miracle stirred their souls and renewed their faith. The *Hyalus* tree provided light in that final battle for seven straight days until King *Kāhssiel* vanquished the army of the God of Shadows. At the end of his dark reign, the sun, at last, returned. It was not the light that saved them from our enemies. Nor did it help them win the war. It was the *message* that we had not been abandoned that gave them the courage to fight on. And that is something worth celebrating."

The crowd applauded, their cheers filling the room.

"The sun is about to set, and we need someone to lift the curtain for *Elyōn's* blessing over the Realms," Lord Jophiel said. Lady Sarrai stood straighter, smiling up at him expectantly. But his gaze wandered past her and landed on Dyna. He held out a hand to her. "Who better than the new Lady of Hermon Ridge? Come, my dear, and you too, Cassiel."

The room was quiet, their shock sticking to Zev's skin.

Dyna looked terrified. She shook her head pleadingly at Cassiel. He grinned and laced his fingers through hers. They must have shared a brief conversation because she exhaled a low breath, and he led her up the steps. After a moment, everyone stood from their seats and packed around the stage to see.

Which put several bodies between them and the ones they were supposed to guard. Zev glanced at Rawn and Lucenna as they all came to the same realization. They hurried through the throng in opposite directions, listening to the whispers and watching for movements.

"...look at her up there..."

"...our ancestors would weep with shame..."

"...wingless and ugly..."

"...that should be Lady Sarrai's place..."

"...provincial in every way..."

Their hissed words made Zev's teeth grind. He itched to take a bite out of each of them, but he kept moving, supervising his cousin and the crowd.

"...no doubt she sought an advantageous match with the prince..."

"...of common stock..."

"...a scullery maid, if I ever saw one..."

"...she's enough to whet the appetite..."

He growled, turning to search for the male who said that. A hush went through the crowd as the servants snuffed all the candles except for one candelabrum on the table. Zev anxiously glanced at Dyna, but for once, she didn't look afraid of the dark. She and Cassiel each took the thick tassels on either side of the velvet curtains and pulled, exposing a massive window. Beyond it, in the far distance, was the summit of the Hermon Mountains, capped with snow. Within the range grew a *Hyalus* tree with sprawling branches.

The last of the fading sunset washed its silvery trunk and transparent leaves in a golden orange. Twilight arrived as the sun dropped behind the ridge. A glow started at the roots of the tree first, then it shot up the trunk to the branches, and the leaves burst with blazing light. A cheer of awe filled the room. The *Hyalus* glowed so radiantly it was as if the God of Urn had planted it from the seed of a star.

It was the first time Zev had seen it so radiant.

The light shot through the leaves, and they floated away into the night sky like a thousand wishes. Glittering blessings from the God of Urn.

"Her filth must not be permitted to defile the Realms."

Zev whipped his head around. It was the same hissing voice from before. Rawn stopped on the other end of the crowd, catching it, too. Zev searched for Lord Gadriel, but he was gone. So was Lady Sarrai.

"Their scourge must be cleansed," the voice continued. *"Their souls ripped away from existence."*

He was running now, hunting for whoever was speaking. Faces were shadowed. Bodies too cramped together. Zev wove his way through them, searching the obscure alcoves.

"If he awakens, his power will be the end of us all."

"The lords are missing," Rawn said urgently, appearing beside him.

"And so are the princes."

Asiel and Malakel were nowhere in sight. Who was it then? Who was speaking? Zev spun in place, his eyes bouncing off hundreds of faces. His heartbeat raced, sweat sprouting on his back. His distress was so great the room felt like it was closing in on him.

"Extinguish her and the Nephilim. Immediately."

A horrible chill sank through Zev's body. "They're a target!" he shouted at Lucenna and Sowmya. "Get them out of here!"

The Valkyrie stormed the stage, startling Cassiel and Dyna. They dropped the tassels, and the curtain fell over the window at the same time the candlelight was snuffed out, plunging them in pitch black darkness.

Then the screaming began.

CHAPTER 55

Dynalya

Dyna's bedroom was dreadfully quiet compared to the rush in her head. She sat on the end of the bed, restlessly picking at the hole torn in the hem of her dress. Cassiel sat in a chair across from her, leaning forward with his head against his linked hands as his anxiety and anger slammed into her in droves. To the point that she had to raise her shield to make sense of her own convoluted emotions.

Someone had tried to kill her tonight.

"This is unacceptable," her mate snarled. "I want them gone."

Lord Jophiel sighed and rubbed his face. "Cassiel, this is an occasion of union for the Realms. You cannot cast out the Lords, especially when you are transitioning to power. It will reflect unfavorably upon you. There is unrest and we must not make it worse."

"One of them, if not all, is conspiring against us, yet we are expected to continue with our rites as if nothing is happening? As if she is not in danger? Whoever they are, they don't care about the festival. They tried to assassinate her during tonight's blessing. They might have reached her if not for Zev's warning and the crowd causing a panic. Who is to say they will not attempt it again at our wedding, or the next opportunity that arises?"

Lord Jophiel looked at her worriedly, then at her friends standing quietly by the bed. None had left her side since Sowmya yanked her off the stage and flew her to safety. Now several Valkyrie were posted outside of her door and balcony.

"Tell me again what you heard," Lord Jophiel said.

Zev softly repeated the awful words and Dyna's vision blurred. Lucenna stopped her trembling hand from unraveling the tulle any further. They truly hated her. No one wanted her with Cassiel. So much so they would rather see her dead.

His regret and dejection filtered through the bond. He wanted to come to her, but she already felt crowded and overwhelmed. *I'm so sorry, lev sheli.*

Dyna shook her head, not wanting to look at him. She was still angry that he hid the first sign of a threat from her. She didn't want to be coddled.

You cannot keep these things from me, Cassiel. We spoke of this.

Forgive me. I wished for tonight to be perfect. I did not want you to be troubled by their prejudice. I...

He didn't want her to live the life his mother did.

Of course, that was his worry. She could feel it coiling in her chest. It convulsed so wildly, and she saw his fists spark.

She shouldn't have been up on that stage.

You had every right to be there, Cassiel said tightly through the bond. *How quickly our people have forgotten that we did not win the war against demons alone. The humans joined our ranks, and they fought with us side by side.*

But that was before humans had turned on them.

"Only one person was speaking?" Lord Jophiel asked, looking pensive.

Rawn nodded. "A male."

"But clearly they were speaking to someone," Cassiel said. "We don't know how many are involved."

"Or if it's a real plot to assassinate you both." His uncle frowned. "They sound like an extremist spouting drivel."

"From my experience, extremists can be very dangerous," Rawn said. "They truly believe their radical views are correct, and they will work to bring such fundamental changes to fruition in their society, through whatever revolution they deem necessary."

"What did they mean by 'if he awakens, his power will destroy us all'?" Lucenna asked.

Dyna had caught that, too.

Lord Jophiel gave Cassiel a sidelong look. "They were referring to your Seraph fire. The only Celestial to have the power to wield it freely was King *Kāhssiel.* He was a Seraph when he fell to earth, and one of the original warriors of *Elyōn.* Through him, we established Hilos and had an age of peace. But he later turned that same fire on his own people."

Cassiel exhaled heavily and pinched the bridge of his nose. "And I did the same...in the war room."

The image of his bright cerulean flames spiraling around him surfaced in Dyna's memories. He must have looked so menacing to his people with his eyes like torch fires, expression stone cold—and murderous.

"No wonder some of them are convinced he has returned." Zev groaned and leaned his head back, rubbing his neck. "Gods, Cassiel."

Now Dyna understood why Noemi had avoided speaking about the first king. They feared King *Kāhssiel* had been reborn. Which was ridiculous, but such a rumor had now grown grave. Perhaps they weren't simply targeting her because she was human, but because she was also his weakness.

"They threatened Dyna." His silver eyes met hers across the room. *And all I could think about was extinguishing them all...*

"You could not help but want to protect your mate, Cassiel. It's natural, especially with a True Bond," Lord Jophiel said. "Seraph fire is meant to eliminate any danger, and that purpose will have some effect on your instincts and emotions, but you must have discipline. I will assign someone to help you train your fire."

He nodded grimly. "Yes, Uncle. Thank you."

"It's the least I could do. I wish we knew more. Nothing about the voice was recognizable? Nazar and Skath have a slight inflection."

Zev and Rawn shook their heads.

Lord Jophiel sighed. "Then we don't know for certain if it was the Lords, so we cannot make any unfounded accusations. There were hundreds of Celestials present. It could have been anyone."

Unless...the assailant suspected they were listening and purposely changed their voice to mask it.

Dyna thought of Asiel and his sly smile that seemed to scheme. Could it be his voice they heard? Some part of the prince must feel slighted to lose his place as heir of Hermon Ridge. Sarrai lost her place to her. Either of them could be involved. But it seemed too obvious.

Cassiel scowled. "Then what are we to do?"

"Nothing," Dyna said. Her voice came out faint, but everyone stared at her. "We will do *nothing*," she repeated firmly and stood. "Whether the threat was real or not, they will tread carefully now. Perhaps it was purely a test of our defenses, and we revealed ourselves. They know my Guardians are listening and watching. If there is another attempt, it will be better crafted." Magic crackled around her hands, surging with her intent. "And I will be waiting."

No one would be allowed to intimidate her. She had already decided to fight for their future, and she'd learned that sometimes you needed to get your hands bloody to survive. So if anyone came after her or her mate, she would not hesitate to take them down.

Cassiel came to her side. His warm hand cupped her cheek, and her skin tingled with the energy of his touch. *Valiant little warrior.* His rich voice curled through her mind, his silver eyes gleaming like sharp blades. *I care not who it is. Whoever comes after you will burn, even if that means I turn on them all.*

With Cassiel's words circling her mind, Dyna got little sleep. He wanted to protect her, but she had to protect him, too, and his soul counted in that. She couldn't stand by while he only grew more paranoid for her safety and ended up doing something he would regret. It didn't serve her to wait around for her assailant, not when there were too many suspects on the table.

She had to clear them out.

When morning came, Dyna set out to find Lady Sarrai before she had to meet Cassiel to perform their rites.

She followed the sound of quiet footsteps and paws clicking against the ground as Zev and Lucenna guided her through the winding corridors of the castle. They were under an invisibility spell to make her appear less protected, if that could be possible with the two warrior females on her heels.

Cassiel insisted Sowmya and Janel keep her guarded since the Valkyrie were the only ones he trusted to abide by Rael's Laws. Rawn left to accompany him through the Rite of the Flesh, in case he heard anything else. Each of them was instructed to stay out of sight until the assailant made their move.

Eventually, Zev brought her through an archway that led outside to a vast garden full of trees and shrubs. She caught the sounds of voices next and took the gravel path to find Lady Sarrai…and Prince Asiel.

Sarrai had her back to him, body poised as she fixed her eyes on a tree in the distance. "Why did you do that?"

His blue eyes were vulnerable and open in a way Dyna hadn't seen before. "You know why," he said. "I will always come to you when you need me."

Her mouth trembled, and tears gathered on her lashes, but her voice remained steady. "Please go, Asiel."

Many raw emotions crossed his face before a smirk fell back in place, and he took a step away from her. "We both wear masks in this place, Sarrai, but I see right through yours as you do mine. If being Lady of the Realm is what you desire, then I will see that you have it, if only to be worthy of your gaze." Asiel's wings spread wide and he leaped into the sky.

As soon as he was gone, Sarrai's face crumbled. She dropped onto a stone bench and shook with quiet sobs.

"Stay back," Dyna whispered to Zev and Lucenna. "Both of you. Whatever happens, don't reveal yourselves."

The air stirred and dents formed in the gravel with their silent retreat. She glanced at the Valkyrie, and they moved to guard the entrance of the archway.

Only then did Dyna approach. "Sarrai?"

Gasping, Sarrai's head snapped up, and anger sparked in her wet eyes. "You ruined everything."

The weight of that accusation hit her in the chest. It reflected the one she held all of her life since the night the Shadow came.

"Why did you have to come here?" Sarrai asked through her tears. "It's not right. You are not worthy of the position you hold! No one wants you here. You are not needed. You are not welcome," she sobbed. "You don't belong!"

But there was no hatred behind those words. No disgust. Only misery.

"It's true," Dyna replied softly. "You're right. I don't belong here."

It was the last thing Sarrai must have expected her to say because she stopped yelling.

"But you're not really speaking to me, are you?" Dyna sat beside her and looked out at the garden. Last night, Zev told her what Lord Gadriel had said to her during the banquet. "Sometimes our hate stems from things we hate about ourselves. You call me unworthy, because that is how purebloods make you feel. Unwanted. Unwelcomed. Unneeded."

Sarrai looked away.

"Does Lord Gadriel make you feel less than because your wings are a different color than his?" Dyna let out a scoff. "It's so absurd, really. When I first saw you, I felt so terribly inferior. I envied your beauty and elegance, how you drew every eye in the room you entered. The Celestials in this Realm call you the jewel of the north. If your uncle refuses to see that, it merely means he's blind."

Sarrai's eyes lifted back to her, so many emotions crossing her face. Surprise. Sadness. Hurt.

Cassiel wasn't the only one cast out for his differences. How many more of his kind had been censured by those with narrowed views?

Dyna sighed up at the warm sunlight falling over them. "Your value doesn't decrease because others refuse to see it. Don't confuse someone's inability to love you as a measure of your worth. That is their failing, not yours."

The tears delicately balancing on Sarrai's lashes spilled. She closed her eyes and exhaled a long shaky breath, as if releasing a weight. "I decided I don't care if he accepts me anymore. My whole life, I prepared for the position you now have. I was meant to be Lady of Hermon Ridge. It needed to be me, so I could see my mother. So I..."

"So you could be with Asiel?" Dyna guessed. "Your hand was promised to the next Lord, and he was the one you awaited to marry."

Sarrai flushed, ducking under her hair. Dyna finally realized the one who she wanted had never been Cassiel. Sarrai was in love with Asiel, and from the look on his face it was clear he held affections for her, too.

"If I may be honest, I wouldn't have foreseen this," Dyna said. "I was told he was a...rake."

"Many believe it." Sarrai laughed wetly and wiped her cheek. "When I arrived to live here, I was seven summers old, and so very aware I had been abandoned for being different. Asiel never judged me for it. He accepted me for me and I had never had that, not even with my mother. Then Cassiel arrived, and we got along well, being two Nephilim cast out for what we were."

"But *they* didn't get along," Dyna said.

"Asiel wasn't cruel like his brothers, but he liked to bait him. I think he couldn't help it. His father's love and attention went to his cousin, and he didn't want to share mine. I didn't understand that at the time, so Asiel distanced himself. When we became older, he pretended to entertain human girls to provoke me. The more he did it, the more attention I gave to Cassiel. A stupid game of jealousy we played with one another. Nonetheless, his dalliances and disrespect to the court created a persona Asiel didn't care to correct."

Dyna supposed that explained why the prince pretended to have an interest in her. It was to aggravate Cassiel out of spite, but Asiel stopped when he found out they were bonded.

"Does he care?" she asked. "About Hermon Ridge?"

"He would gladly have you think otherwise, but if you look close enough, you will find he's always there, tucked away in the crowd."

As he had been during the summons.

"When Cassiel was called back to Hilos, I think Asiel could finally breathe," Sarrai said. "And so could I. It was as though whatever had taken up so much air between us was gone and we could rekindle our friendship...which turned into more than either of us imagined."

"But Cassiel returned, inadvertently taking away Asiel's position, and it broke you two apart." Dyna sighed, now seeing the truth. Cassiel didn't know about any of this. "You need titles to be together?"

Sarrai shook her head with a hopeless shrug. "He is a pureblooded prince. I am a Nephilim. The bastard daughter that resulted from a forbidden tryst. Such a union would never be accepted. Not without a political alliance."

"Well, the same was said about us."

She gave her a look. "Was there not an attempt on your life last night?"

"Yet here I am," Dyna said. "I don't care if they don't accept me either, Sarrai. The only thing I care about is being with him. Everything else we will face together. Life will never be easy, but don't let that stop you from what you want. Even if it seems impossible to reach. For what good are wings without the courage to fly?"

Sarrai gazed at her for a moment, a kindling of hope entering her eyes, but it faded as quickly as it appeared. A gray feather slipped from her wing and fluttered through the air before the wind carried it away. "Sometimes, no matter how much we want something, the right thing is to let go. I know my place, as I know our union cannot be possible. Asiel refuses to accept that, the way Cassiel cannot." Her blue eyes met hers. "Having no love makes one so fiercely defensive once love is finally given. The need to protect that is soul consuming. Both of you are from different worlds. Can you keep your life a secret and abandon your family for him? Can you withstand everything that will come for being his wife?"

The question made Dyna's heart pitch. She couldn't pretend it wouldn't be hard. It already was. But she wouldn't change a thing. Although, weathering hardships wasn't what worried her.

She rose. "Being with Cassiel is worth anything, no matter what may come. For the only thing I cannot withstand is losing him. The rest I will gladly bear."

Sarrai looked down at her lap.

Excusing herself, Dyna walked down the path for the castle, feeling lighter now that she crossed at least one name off their list of suspects. That left the Lords and Prince Malakel. Asiel was a possibility, but she had her doubts now.

Footsteps crunched over the gravel beside her, and then the clank of armor as the Valkyrie followed once she crossed the archway. Zev affectionately nuzzled her shoulder, and Dyna felt warmed by his approval. Perhaps being Lady wouldn't be so awful.

Rounding the corner, she collided with someone and was immediately shoved off. Zev caught her fall before she went sprawling.

Prince Malakel scowled down at her, and for once, Dyna recognized the look of revulsion. She lifted her shield on the bond so Cassiel wouldn't be alerted. They didn't need another reason to cause more conflict when his position in court was so delicate.

She straightened and folded her hands at her waist, awaiting Malakel's derision.

He scoffed with disgust at the shimmery streams of her sky-blue dress. "Look at you. The sight of you trudging through these halls as if you mean something is sickening. If it had been up to me, you would have been buried beneath the trees in Hilos."

Her pulse pounded from the venom in his words. She gave a very subtle motion of her fingers, warning her Guardians not to react. This was good. Let him speak his hate, all the better to rule him out.

Dyna gave him a tight smile. "How fortunate that it wasn't up to you." She paused deliberately before adding, "Your Highness."

Malakel's nostrils flared, his mouth curling. "When you stand in my presence, I expect you to bow."

He certainly had some nerve. She regretted not throwing that fig at his face in Hilos. Her hands clenched with the desire to throw something else at him now.

She lifted her chin. "Bowing condones respect, which I have none for you." Gathering her skirts, Dyna tried to step around him, but he moved in her way.

"You will go when I allow you to go, witch," he snarled, and her hackles rose at the insult. "I know you bewitched him. It was not with your countenance, for you lack beauty there. It was your curses and enchantments that twisted his sanity. You must weave them so deftly that they are beautiful to the ear, infinitely profound. Poison laced in sugar for a prince with a black heart made of stone, so starved of affection. It would take such spells to become enamored with a common thing like you."

Static crackled in the air as Dyna struggled to steadily breathe. She wanted to remind him what she could truly do with her enchantments, but the tension growing from Lucenna and Zev fighting to restrain themselves made her rein it back. *Stay calm.*

"That Nephilim has always been a blight to the Soaraway House," Malakel continued. "Mixing his blood with yours was a great disgrace, as was his birth, but I rejoice in the fact that his line will end with him. Think nothing of a future. Dare not dream of bearing children. If you defy this, I will make sure your life is a short one."

Air trapped between her lips at his pretentious audacity. Her magic roiled again with the urge to strike him. Clenching her jaw, she willed it to settle. After spending weeks with a man who instilled true fear, Malakel's attempt at intimidation was a joke.

"You think threatening me makes you better than him, does it?" Dyna said flatly. "Being a pureblood isn't interesting or special. That belief is as pointless as the air of bigotry you breathe. The only reason you step on Cassiel is to feed your idea of superiority—but it's a lie. Because the truth is, he has always been your better."

Astonishment flashed across Malakel's face, and his mouth opened and closed repeatedly with a response he struggled to form.

"No." She lifted a hand. "I'm speaking, and you will listen. While I respect your ability to talk on and on, my patience does have a limit. You have insulted me in every possible way, and I won't hear it. *You* are the one mistaken if you think you will have any influence over the kind of marriage I have with *my* husband."

His face flooded red, and he said through his teeth, "I beg your pardon?"

"You're more than welcome to beg for it."

He thrust her backward into the wall, pinning her there by her shoulder. A growl ripped through the corridor and the Valkyrie instantly drew their weapons.

"It would be wise of you to stand down," Dyna said. She was looking at Malakel, but she was speaking to her Guardians.

She gripped Zev's furry scruff tightly. His powerful form was vibrating and if Malakel didn't release her, he would lunge at any second. Lucenna's magic was static against her cheek at how close the sorceress was.

Both were ready to kill him.

Malakel didn't have an inkling of the danger he was truly in.

"You dare draw your weapon against me?" he thundered at Sowmya. "I am your crown prince!"

"This is Hermon Ridge," Dyna said. "Where I outrank you. Right now, you're in violation of Rael's Law in harming the True Bonded of a Prince of Hilos, the mate of their Lord. They're bound to defend me, regardless of the threat. Now *remove* your hand from me, sir."

His chest heaved with loud breaths, eyes burning with fury. He dug his fingers into her so tight, her collarbone felt as if it would snap.

"Malakel."

He stiffened, and they glanced at the pureblooded Celestial standing a few feet away. The wind tugged at his long hair, rippling across his deep red robes. Behind him stood two male guards in white. His dark blue eyes, flecked with a lighter blue, were stoic, calculating, and intelligent in the way they took in the scene before him.

"Do not diminish the prestige House Welkin holds," he said, his voice as elegant as it was cold.

Dyna glanced at the gold pin at the center of his collar. It was shaped into opened wings with two crossed swords in the middle. Lord Raziel of Edym, she guessed. Welkin must be his family name. The resemblance between them was glaring.

The prince stepped back with a bow of his head. "Pardon me, Grandfather."

The Valkyrie eased out of their positions. Dyna adjusted her dress in place to hide the welt she knew would form. Hot pain throbbed over her collarbone.

"See that it does not happen again." Lord Raziel didn't spare her a glance as he passed with his guards. A faint citrus scent trailed after him.

Malakel maintained his neutral expression after he was gone. "It's beneath me to waste time on your inane existence. I will find it in my mercy to allow Cassiel to live his short, pitiful life with you." At her confusion, he smirked. "Did you not know? A union between a human and Celestial hardly lasts. The bond is too fragile when one of you is mortal. I may not need to lift a finger. In fifty years or so, you will pass through the Gates, and Cassiel will simply perish on his own, as do all those with a broken True Bond."

Dyna's chest heaved with a shallow breath. Somehow, she hadn't stopped to think about how much time she would have with Cassiel. Her lifespan was hardly anything compared to his.

"So, in the face of things, you are nothing." Malakel chuckled as he walked backward in the direction Lord Raziel had gone. "In time, you will be little more than an afterthought. If you even survive that long. That Nephilim ruins everything he touches. You fool yourself if you think he will not ruin you, too."

He could spout whatever nonsense he wanted. Her trust in Cassiel could no longer be shaken. Nevertheless, she wouldn't let him have the last word.

"I wouldn't be so sure about the future, Prince Malakel." Dyna strode away, letting her voice carry in the corridor. "Life tends to hold surprises."

CHAPTER 56

Dynalya

When the hour came to begin the rites, Dyna followed the beacon of the bond to a room where the Captain of the Valkyrie stood guard. As the new Lord of Hermon, it was her duty to protect Cassiel now. "Good morrow, Captain."

"My Lady." Yelrakel opened the door for her and bowed as she entered.

It was a simple stone room with an interior balcony framed with arched columns and a balustrade. Beyond it was the view of frosted trees and Rael's statue. The sound of rushing water from the cascades reached her, as did the warmth of the roaring fireplace in the corner.

"Ah, you have arrived. Perfect," Lord Jophiel greeted her with a kind nod. "Now we can begin."

Cassiel sat at a round stone table. He looked a little pale, his forehead damp with sweat. But his eyes lit up when she entered.

"Are you all right?" she asked worriedly. "You look ill."

"I'm fine. I passed through my purification ritual." Cassiel's hand drifted to his ribs and she felt an echo of his pain in the bond. "It's a step I would gladly do again," he said when sensing her alarm. Taking her hand, he pressed his mouth to her palm. His reverent voice coiled through her mind. *Flesh of my flesh. Bone of my bone.*

Dyna didn't quite understand what he meant, but the glow in her chest was thrumming.

Lord Jophiel cleared his throat, reminding them of his presence. "In this room, you shall perform the Rite of the Mind and the Rite of the Soul."

Cassiel tensed, making his uncle chuckle.

"It's a painless rite, at least physically." He motioned to the table. It held a basket with white ribbons and a page of parchment written with some script. "These are the handfast ribbons. You will braid your sash with three strands as you ask each other the list of questions on this page. I admit, they are difficult things to ask, but the purpose is to be fully open with one another, so you may enter your marriage without reservations." He pointed to the brass bell hanging above their heads. "The bell will ring if one of you withholds honesty."

It was embossed with lettering she didn't understand. It reminded her of Tarn's truth rune in his tent. That one was made to catch hidden lies. This one was made to catch hidden truths.

"The room is warded to suppress sound, so no other will hear. Your companions and the Valkyrie will stand guard outside. Take your time and come out when you are ready." Lord Jophiel excused himself thereafter.

Dyna bit her lip as they both looked around the room. Nerves danced along the bond, and she wasn't sure if it was all hers or both of theirs.

Cassiel took the page. "Shall we sit over there? It will be much more comfortable."

He motioned to the blue velvet divan facing the open balcony. Dyna nodded. Taking the basket, she went to sit. There was a folded blanket waiting, which he draped over her lap and settled beside her. She pulled out the silky ribbons. They were pure white, shimmering beneath the sunlight.

Cassiel rested his elbows on his knees as he read over the page. One edge of his mouth curved. "Well, this seems more like an interrogation than a rite."

Dyna fidgeted with the ribbons as she tied three strands together on one end. "Is it that terrible?"

"The worst. We may not be able to look at one another after this."

Oh dear. Would it be too late to skip this part? She couldn't see how it should be necessary.

At Cassiel's grin, Dyna swatted his arm. "You're teasing me."

"I could feel you ready to leap out of your skin." He turned his body to face her, and leaned against the backrest. His knee rested against hers, warm and comforting. His relaxed position and half smile put her at ease. "Shall we take turns holding the sash while the other braids?"

Dyna handed him the tied end of it and glanced at the page. It only contained three questions. "These aren't difficult." She gathered the three ribbons and began weaving them together. "The first one is to share a struggle of the present. Well, I'm struggling with controlling my magic."

The bell chimed with a gentle, tinkling sound.

Dyna frowned. "It's true."

It chimed again.

"I think we are meant to discuss more personal thoughts we would not dare share with another," Cassiel said. "The internal dark corners we may sometimes be ashamed of."

Only a fourth of engagements made it through the rites, and now Dyna saw why. Answering the list of questions would require her to peel away all manner of armor. She would be raw and exposed, left at the mercy of hope that the one to see her heart could accept it as it was. Except there was no reason why she should be afraid of that with him.

"I…pretend not to hear what they say about me," Dyna said to the ribbons. They slid against her fingers as she continued weaving them together, the hissed voices repeating in her mind. "It would be a lie to say the words don't hurt, but what I fear the most is that one day you may believe them, and leave me behind because of it."

Dyna felt Cassiel's gaze on her, but she couldn't bring herself to look at him. She was secure in their affections, but Sarrai's comment had stirred the worry that he may think she was better off not in his life.

He lifted her chin so his stormy eyes could meet hers. "Dyna, when you were taken from me, I was half out of my mind. Leave you? That will *never* happen." There was a finality to his statement that was both commanding and assuring. "Tell me what you heard and from who, so I may remove their ability to speak—or breathe, depending on what was said."

Dyna rolled her eyes playfully. "We can't solve everything with murder, Cassiel."

"I wholly disagree." He handed her the tied end of the sash and gathered the ribbons. It was nearly a foot long now. She watched his fingers braid the loose ends deftly. "I want names."

She didn't think he was joking, and it worried her.

"I don't know who they are, and even if I did, I wouldn't tell you." What she'd heard were mostly things whispered in the hall and in the commons area.

Filthy human.

Murderous witch.

Geas cursed.

The speaker always vanished around a corner before she got a good look at them. During the banquet, someone said she should be made a courtesan rather than a wife. She realized too late that the memory had slipped past her shield, and Cassiel stilled. She caught the sharp edge in his features as he looked out at Hermon Ridge.

"My mother..." His voice came out low. Strained. "She used to love coming here. Before she left, we would visit every summer when my father was too busy tending to the Realms. Then I realized Hermon became her sanctuary, for no one here knew she was the High King's courtesan. She had asked my uncle to introduce her as my servant." A bitter laugh escaped him and his face creased. "Because then she could avoid the court's prejudice by appearing below them."

That made Dyna so sad her eyes watered. How much his mother must have suffered.

"Hilos broke her. I could not protect my mother from it then, but I will be damned if I let that happen now." Cassiel turned to her. "I struggle with the fear that I will not be enough to protect you. That if I look away for one moment, you will be taken from me. Either by their hatred or some other tragedy I cannot prevent." He cradled her hand with the geas and his brow tightened as he ran his fingers over the oak tree. "Every time I see this, I'm reminded of Leoake's warning. I cannot shake the feeling that I may be taking you to your death. After experiencing the likeness of a broken bond, I know I could never survive losing you."

"Nor could I," she murmured. "But you're not taking me to my death, Cassiel. I am choosing to go to Mount Ida."

But speaking of it reminded her of what Malakel said. Any day could be the end, and what they had would vanish. It wasn't enough to simply fight for what she wanted, but to also live for it.

"Hmm..." Crossing her arms, Dyna tapped her chin as she pretended to think very deeply.

"What?"

"I'm trying to imagine what Lord Norrlen would say at this moment. He always has the perfect wisdom to share when I'm in my doubts."

Cassiel's mouth hitched. "Shall I ask him to step in?"

"No. I think I got it. Fear is like the sea. If we let ourselves sink in it, we will drown. No one knows how long they have or the hardships to come. All we can do is spend our days treasuring each moment."

A smile spread across his face. "Not bad."

"Thank you. Next question."

"What secret do you hold from the past?" he read.

"Would you like to go first?" she asked.

Cassiel shrugged. "None come to mind. I don't have any secrets that you don't know of."

The bell chimed, proving that to be false. Dyna smirked.

"What? No. I..." Cassiel frowned at the bell in confusion for a second, then he shifted on the divan and tugged at his collar.

Dyna grinned and inched closer. "You have one. Tell me."

"It's more of a...humiliating secret." He cleared his throat, pink coloring his cheeks. "Please don't hold it against me."

"This is us being open and honest with each other. Nothing you say will upset me."

"Well...you remember the inn we stayed at in Corron? The morning after?"

"Yes." She flushed. How could she forget?

His knee bounced nervously. "With your body pressed against mine, I woke...aroused. It was startling and unexpected, so I..."

Bolted.

Dyna stared at him a moment, then she covered her mouth before she burst into a fit of giggles. "Oh, dear. Now I completely understand everything."

Cassiel rubbed the back of his neck. "It's a natural part of the body."

"It is." Fighting to hold back a grin, Dyna patted his restless knee. "You're right. Was it startling because I'm human?"

His dark lashes lifted as his silver eyes met hers with a sudden intensity, her pulse skipped a beat. "Because it had been the first time I ever desired anyone."

Dyna swallowed, feeling the heat rise to her face. He had never been attracted to another before her?

Cassiel handed her the ribbons. They had a good length going. "Your turn."

She chuckled weakly, suddenly too shy to look at him. "Well, in regards to Corron, I suppose my one secret was also of that night."

This caught his attention, and he straightened. "Oh?"

"You were rightly drunk and...*hot.*" Dyna bit her lip. "You removed your clothes."

His eyes widened. "What?"

"Your tunic, I mean. I could see...everything." Her fingers lost track of the braid as she recalled his beautifully sculpted body. "I liked seeing it," she admitted. "And then, when you were asleep, I touched your...wings."

Cassiel sucked in a dramatic gasp. "Dynalya Astron, I am appalled."

She covered her face. "I'm sorry!"

He laughed and pulled down her hands. "Silly girl. I suppose it was my doing for indecently stripping in front of you and leaving myself to be violated."

She groaned, covering her face again.

"Dyna." At the rumble in his tone, she peeked at him between her fingers. "You may look all you wish."

Her heart did a little flip at the sly look in his eyes.

"There, we easily finished that question, didn't we?" he said.

A chiming responded.

She hummed. "Do you have anything else to confess?"

"No...?"

The bell protested again.

"Ah..." His throat bobbed. "Well..."

At his palpable hesitation, Dyna peered into the bond and caught a quick memory of her breasts in his mind. "Cassiel!"

"You were injured, so I had to remove your dress to treat your wound. I swear before *Elyōn* that is all." He looked genuinely apologetic.

Dyna shook her head and laughed. "Deviant." She glanced at the page for the next question as he took the sash again. "What do you hope for in the future?"

"The future?" Cassiel's brow furrowed thoughtfully.

He fell quiet for a long moment, leaving her to worry. "Do you see a future with me?"

Cassiel brushed the hair from her eyes. "*Lev sheli*, I have seen it since the moment beneath the willow. I don't know what kind of life we will have once we return from Mount Ida, but I see you in it."

Her heart warmed, and she grew timid at how easily he said such things. Before, he was never so open, but now it was as if he wanted to share everything he thought. It was a new side of honesty she hadn't expected from him.

"I suppose I also may not have allowed myself to think of tomorrow when I'm worried about today." He looked out at Hermon again. "I am meant to oversee this Realm, but I don't have the support I need to do that. The Lords hold me in no regard, as I did not plan to one day stand among them. I don't know how to find the right connections or how to be a Lord. This may be beyond me."

She wasn't the only one left floundering with their new responsibilities. They may have been approaching things the wrong way.

"Looking for support among the Lords may not be the right step," Dyna said. "At least, not yet. Hermon is in transition with a new leader and things may feel uncertain for them. Our first objective should be finding support among the citizens of your Realm."

Cassiel gave her a thoughtful smile as he considered that. "I think you are right. I should make a foothold here first, before anything else. And you? What do you hope for in the future?"

He had too many worries about the present, but she had started thinking ahead. After this morning, it was a pressing concern at the forefront of her mind. It doubled after hearing what he feared.

Suddenly feeling the urge to move around, Dyna got to her feet and paced on the balcony. "I don't know what the future holds for us either, Cassiel. I left North Star hoping I would survive long enough to complete my mission. My hope for the future was to destroy the Shadow, save my sister, my village, and myself. But—but now..."

"But now?"

"Now my future isn't only mine anymore." Dyna threw up her hands as she pivoted on her heel, words spilling out faster than she could stop them. "I'm unexpectedly responsible for a Realm full of Celestials. Half of which would rather see me dead or gone. I'm expected to consummate and birth heirs." Her face heated. "We hardly adjusted to being bonded. I-I'm not prepared for the thought of children. Yet Malakel had the nerve to say he wouldn't permit us to have them. As if he would have any right to decide—"

Cassiel grabbed her shoulders and made her stop. "He said what?"

She scowled at the wall behind him. "That your line would end with you."

The threat part she omitted because Cassiel wouldn't take it well. She could already feel his anger simmering in the bond.

"It doesn't matter what he thinks." She lowered her head, something shaking in her chest. "But do you...want them?"

"No," Cassiel admitted, and her heart unexpectedly sank. That feeling finally answered how she truly felt about the subject. "After the life I lived, despised for being a half-breed, I did not want to father a child only to suffer my same fate. I had no plan to bond. No plan to live outside of futile nothingness. Then you came, and I wished for more."

He held her face, once again making her meet his eyes. Their color was the gray before dawn, sometimes turning white when the light hit them. It reminded her of new days, of waiting for something good to happen.

"Like you, I have yet to prepare for more than what we have right now. Do I want children? Not at the moment. We are still learning who we are together and apart. The future brings endless possibilities. If one day we want to take that step, it will be something *we* decide. No other will have a say in it."

That was all it took to settle her. The possibility of one day made her ridiculously happy. The only hope she had for the future was to embrace whatever came with him at her side.

"Good." Dyna hid her face against his shoulder. "Then...I'll be sure to take the...contraceptive."

Cassiel's fingers slowly traced the line of her spine. "So," he purred in her ear. "You have been thinking about *that, lev sheli?*"

"No," she said defensively. Her cheeks flamed when the bell chimed, and he chuckled.

"When did you speak to Malakel?"

"Before I came here..."

The teasing faded from his expression. "What else did he say?"

"Nothing at all true." She squeezed her eyes shut when another chime rang. "Some of it was lies, bell."

Cassiel led her to sit on the divan. He crouched in front of her and waited patiently for her to speak.

Dyna gathered the handfast ribbons, weaving them through the final span. "He said...that in the face of things, our union didn't matter because my lifespan was short, and I would pass away in due time." The back of her eyes stung. "And you would be left behind to perish from the broken bond. To think you would die because of me. I can't bear it, Cassiel. I can't."

Sighing, he rested his forehead against hers. She felt his next words like a soft breath of air against her cheek. "Walking this world for an endless age alone will never outweigh one lifetime with you. And if a mortal life is all we have, then I will spend an eternity searching for you in the next one."

It was devastating, the things he did to her heart. If he was attempting to make her cry again, he succeeded. A small laugh bubbled out of her when Cassiel licked away a tear from her cheek.

Dyna lifted their handfast sash to show it was perfectly white. "Our hearts are aligned."

"I never had any doubt." The back of his fingers brushed her jaw before letting his hand drop on her shoulder. A sharp throb of pain there made her hiss. Her shield slipped enough for him to feel it and his eyes widened. "What happened?"

"Nothing."

The bell chimed.

His eyes sharpened, and his tone grew lethal. "Dyna."

"It's nothing—"

Cassiel tugged down her sleeve, exposing her shoulder, and the large red welt that marked her pale skin. A stillness fell over him. Something dark and dangerous coursed through his features.

"Who hurt you?" The question was a growl, raspy and thick.

She didn't dare answer, but she saw the moment it came to him. His irises spiraled into vibrant blue, burning with a vast and menacing wrath that rose the hairs on the back of her neck. Seraph fire sprouted in his hands, then in a wreath around his feet. The stone beneath his boots blackened and began to crack. Her heart beat wildly at the pure rage teeming in the bond and it sent a shiver through her.

"Malakel." His voice. It was something feral. So foreign it was unlike anything she had heard from him before.

Dyna shrieked at the combustion of blue flames erupting out of him. It roared through the balcony like a tidal wave. The heat ripped through the air, scorching everything it touched. Cassiel didn't notice. Standing, he marched for the balustrade.

"Cassiel, wait!" Dyna ran to him.

He leaped into the skies at the same moment she threw out her hand. Her fingers went right through the wisps of flames trailing behind his feet. It should have melted her flesh, but it only felt like a gentle brush of warmth. In her shock, she reacted too late to stop him.

Cassiel's wings carried him away.

And he was headed directly for his brother.

CHAPTER 57

Cassiel

C assiel tore through the sky with only one intention in his mind. He circled around the castle for the grand hall and crashed through the windows. Glass rained and screams rang out as hundreds of startled faces gaped up at him. His vision flooded blue, firelight bathing the room in the same color. Celestials scattered out of the way. He found Malakel standing below him. Cassiel dove and slammed into him, flying backward onto the dining table. The momentum slid them down the length, dishes crashing and food flying everywhere.

They came to a stop halfway with Cassiel's opal knife at Malakel's throat.

"Cassiel!" his uncle shouted. "Stop! What are you doing?"

He shook with the restraint it took not to drive the edge into his brother's neck. All eyes were on them. Malakel's Royal Guard swarmed the table and yanked out their divine swords. Valkyrie stormed forward and crouched with their weapons to defend their Lord. The room was intensely still, waiting for his next move.

Someone called his name, but it was muffled beneath the crackle of his flames licking along his arms, inching for his brother.

"Go on, Cassiel," Malakel muttered low enough for only him to hear. "Show them who you are."

Rage seared through his very being. He should. He should feed him to the flames and watch him turn to ash. Fire flared at his back and people cried out. The guards withdrew several steps backward, no one daring to touch him. The air warped and wood crackled, the smell of food burning rushed up his nose.

The force of his contained power felt like it may demolish him, as though he were trapped under the pressure of its weight.

"You will not murder your brother in cold blood," Jophiel bellowed from a few feet away. "Release him!"

His chest heaved, and fire ravaged down the table. No one would command him anymore. After everything Malakel had done, he deserved to bleed out on this table.

Someone neared.

He snarled at the intruder, but it wavered when he saw her.

"Cassiel." The sound of her soft voice dulled everything else.

Dyna walked toward him, and others shouted at her to stop. She came anyway, each step even and purposeful. She stepped into the cloak of his roaring flame, and horror rocked through him. But his mate only smiled as she cupped his cheek. It was cool and striking against the heat scorching the rest of him.

"It's all right. You can let go," she said in soothing tones. "*Ata hakohav sheli.* Your light is only for me."

The bond vibrated and softly glowed in his chest.

He couldn't quite breathe at seeing her touch his fire. The cerulean flames licked around her skin, as though to caress her dotingly. Everyone stood frozen still, their wide eyes fixed on them. A low exhale slipped from his lips as everything in him calmed. The fire died away, leaving behind tendrils of smoke. Cassiel let her take the knife from him.

"Come with me."

He moved with her inviting tug on his sleeve and slid off the table. The fury that had burned through him dimmed until Malakel opened his mouth.

"The witch truly has you by the—"

Dyna moved so fast Cassiel didn't see when she threw her fist until it connected with his brother's face. The blow pitched Malakel back into the glass littered table. That strike was a thing of beauty. She had amazing form.

"I am not a witch," Dyna hissed.

Malakel touched his bleeding lip and snarled, leaping up to go after her.

Cassiel stepped in his way and grabbed the front of his robes. "I have endured the blows of your disdain," he growled low. "But she will never endure the same. Touch her again, and *I will burn you alive.*"

Malakel gritted his teeth, his fists shaking as if he wanted to test that threat. The flash of blue in Cassiel's eyes was enough to make him flinch back.

He faced his court, and they cowed against the walls, gaping at him as if he were a monster. Perhaps he was. If he wouldn't have their support, then it was all the better that they feared him.

Cassiel's stare swept over each of them as his voice carried through the room. "If anyone else has something to say about my mate, you can say it to me."

Cassiel couldn't be around anyone. He commanded Sowmya and their friends not to leave Dyna out of their sight. Then he flew through the broken windows again. He needed air. His heart was pounding, and his blood boiled. It felt as if his fire would make his body implode. Was this how it would be? Setting everything on fire with every spark of his fury?

He didn't want that.

Cassiel cursed at himself for putting Dyna in danger. She could have been killed because he was overcome with anger, and it would have been his fault.

The thought created an unbearable pressure in his body. Seraph fire expanded inside of him, pushing against his being with the need to burn. Holding it in felt like it was tearing him apart.

He didn't know how much more he could take.

"My Lord."

Cassiel spun around and scowled at Yelrakel. She shouldn't follow him when he could explode at any second. "Leave me."

"I cannot," she said firmly. "You will come with me."

He clenched his teeth. "Are you giving me a command?"

"My Lord, you destroyed the grand hall and set it on fire. Someone could have been gravely injured. Including My Lady."

Cassiel's scowl dropped. "I…"

"You did not intend it, I know, but next time you lose your temper, someone may end up dead. I wish to prevent this from happening again." Her eyes narrowed on his sweaty face. "And I can see you are ready to implode under the might of this power you do not understand. If you wish to learn how to wield your flame correctly, then please come with me."

It's what he desperately needed, someone to show him what to do because he couldn't go on like this anymore.

He followed the captain through the sky to the back of the castle. They landed in the barracks where the Valkyrie roomed. Several females walked about in various activities. Some were in the open courtyard, going through rounds of sparring, combat training, or polishing armor.

They bowed as Cassiel approached.

"Valkyrie," Yelrakel called. "Line up."

The females quickly moved to put on their golden armor. In minutes, they were gathered with shields and winged helmets, standing in perfect formation.

"*Elyōn* deemed me worthy enough to bless my sword." The captain rested a hand on her hilt. "The weapon serves as a proper conduit to direct the flame. However, that is not the same at the hands of a being who can wield Seraph fire with every thought and chaotic feeling. Like you, King *Kāhssiel* had trouble controlling his power. He would incinerate everything around him with the switch of his mood, which, as you have seen, is quite disastrous. He also learned his power needed to be expelled, or it would tear at his being. The first Valkyrie served him long ago, and their armor was made with sacred metal that could withstand his flame, so he would not harm them in battle. Otherwise, anyone who got too close was annihilated."

By some miracle, Dyna had touched him with her bare hands. Was that a one-time thing, or was she somehow immune?

"My Lady is special, it would seem," Yelrakel said, sensing his thoughts. "But others are not. For the good of this Realm, you must learn how to focus your power with more finesse and direction. I will train you as the first king was trained."

The sound of metal grated as the females crouched in formation and drew their divine swords. They were looking right at *him*.

Cassiel widened his eyes. "And how was he trained?"

Yelrakel bowed deeply. "With brute force."

She stepped backward and thrust her boot into his back, sending him stumbling into the courtyard.

And the Valkyrie attacked.

Cassiel was tired, beaten, clothes torn and filthy, but he hadn't felt this great since before Dyna had been taken. His mind was at ease, his fire a small cinder in his chest. He spent hours training with the Valkyrie. If that could be what it was called. After seeing they wouldn't hold back and his fire couldn't harm them, he unleashed all he had. They trounced him for the most part.

Yelrakel barked orders at him until he figured out how to coordinate and strategize his attacks. The flame came easier than he thought it would. Once he stopped second-guessing himself, his Seraph fire moved around him with an odd familiarity, as if by some unexpected instinct.

Cassiel circled the castle in the blue hour of the evening, soaring over the canopy of treetops. The bond brought him to the balcony outside of Dyna's chambers. He spotted her through the glass doors, sitting by the hearth with Lucenna as they drank tea.

He landed and entered the room.

"Make it a quick visit," Lucenna said with a small smirk as she rose. "The stewardess will be back soon for your Rite of the Flesh. She may faint if she catches you two unescorted."

Pink colored Dyna's face, and Cassiel gave her a look. With a quiet snicker, Lucenna slipped out the door. The woman found enjoyment in making them squirm.

He nodded to Sowmya, and the lieutenant bowed to them before leaving through the balcony. Her wine-red wings carried her away, where she joined Yelrakel waiting in the sky. The two Valkyrie shared a kiss and flew away together.

"I didn't know they were love-mates," Dyna said curiously.

He leaned against the wall by the large window facing the kingdom. "They have been lovers longer than I have been alive. Yelrakel is not one to display her affections publicly, and Sowmya holds regard as her subordinate while they are on duty, so it may not be obvious to others."

"I see." She went to him. "Are you all right? You silenced the bond."

Cassiel chuckled sheepishly. "I didn't want you to feel me being felled by a group of females. Yelrakel had me train my fire until all I could produce was smoke." The light mood faded a little at the mention of his new abilities. He cupped her cold hands in his and the heat constantly living inside of him sent out a soft warmth. Her knuckles were battered. "Forgive me. When I saw what he did to you..." He closed his eyes as his stomach pitched at how close he almost lost everything. "I could have hurt you."

"You didn't."

"How?"

She shook her head. "I don't know. Perhaps because we're True Bonded or because I'm part sun sorceress. Your Seraph fire is hot enough to disintegrate everything it touches, but to me, it feels warm and gentle. I think even in your madness, it would never hurt me, Cassiel."

He looked down at their joined hands and allowed a small petal of flame to dance over the back of his knuckles. It cast a blue glow against her face. She ran her fingers through it, and his breath hitched. The sensation it created was like feeling her caress the most sensitive parts of his body.

You truly were made for me, weren't you?

Her lips curved. "Well, after today, I doubt anyone will argue against our union now. All of Hermon Ridge has newfound respect and a healthy dose of fear for their Lord."

"Good." It was about time they regarded him seriously. He cut his finger and brushed a drop of his blood over her torn skin, and they watched it heal. He healed her bruised shoulder next. "You have not lit the candles," he commented.

She glanced at the *Hyalus* candelabra resting on her windowsill. "I must light them?"

"Of course. It's an important part of the festival. The candles are to be displayed on the windowsill to brighten up the night, the way *Elyōn's* light aided us in banishing the darkness from the earth."

A sad smile rose to her lips as she gazed at it. "My bedroom in North Star is full of candles. On the floor, my desk, nearly every flat surface. Every night, I would light them out of fear, but one day I wish to light them as a symbol of banishing my darkness."

He really wanted that for her. To leave behind the shadows that had plagued her past and step into the light as she had helped him do. "Now would be the perfect time to start."

Taking the center candle, Dyna lit it with the fire from the hearth, and they took turns lighting the wicks until all seven candles illuminated the room.

"Watch," he said, nodding to the window.

They waited for a moment, and then one tiny window in the distance glowed. Then another on the right within the trees. And another in a castle tower. Soon, windows all throughout the kingdom lit up with candlelight. It flickered like hundreds of fireflies in reverence to the God of Urn. The happiness that settled on Dyna's features made the bond vibrate in his chest.

Cassiel reached into his jacket pocket. "I meant to give you your light gift earlier, before everything happened." He held up a delicate silver chain and from it dangled an iridescent gemstone. As the last of the twilight faded, it glowed as bright as pure starlight. "It's infused with the magic of the *Hyalus* tree, so it may always light your way."

He had sworn to never leave her in the dark, and now, wherever she was, he would keep that promise.

"Cassiel." Emotion crossed her face. "It's beautiful, thank you."

"May I?"

Dyna turned around, and he gently swept her hair over her shoulder. The soft curve of her exposed neck in the firelight sent a current through him. Carefully, he brought the chain around. She seemed to tense slightly at how close he stood. Her honeysuckle scent drifted to him, and he couldn't resist breathing it in to imprint it in his memory. Goosebumps prickled where his low exhale stroked her. He gently laid the clasped necklace at her nape and the back of his fingers grazed her soft skin, shooting electric tingles down his arm.

They were still. Trapped in this breath of a moment, and he wondered if she could feel what she did to him. The want and yearnings, the desire to bind himself further to the one who had his heart and soul. The bond hummed between them.

"This is one of three gifts," he said faintly. "The other two I will give to you in time."

"To say I haven't had a chance to prepare a light gift for you sounds like a poor excuse now," came her soft reply.

He never needed one when she stood right here.

Not able to resist any further, Cassiel brushed his mouth on the curve of her neck. Dyna's breath caught. He pressed a kiss over her fluttering pulse and gradually traveled up her neck to the lobe of her ear. *You are my gift.*

Dyna turned to face him, her eyes shy but equally burning. A renewed heat worked its way through him, but it was due to another flame. He glided his hand down her arm, reveling in the feel of her skin. His fingers traced the edge of her hand to her pinky, each stroke sending a current of energy through his body.

That was all he would dare to touch, no matter how much he longed to bring her to his bed and make their bond complete. His heart pounded, and so did hers, as they became increasingly aware of how alone they were with nothing but the quiet crackle of the hearth. Craving scorched in his being to feel every soft curve of her, but there were steps to take, and he would always honor her first.

"I must go," he whispered.

Dyna didn't move until he walked backward onto the balcony and rose into the air with a flap of his wings. The wind wove through her hair, tugging the ends of her dress as she followed him to the banister.

Cassiel took her hand and kissed it. "Good night, *lev sheli*. By this time tomorrow, we will be wed."

Then no one could ever dispute their relationship. She would be his by law and by right.

"Good night," she said softly.

But he couldn't make himself go quite yet. "Can you say it again?" he asked. "What you said to me in the hall?"

Dyna smiled, the beauty of it timid and sweet. *"Ata hakohav sheli."*

A quiver rolled through him. Like the first time, those words did something to his being. "Where did you learn that?"

"My lady's maid has been teaching me your language. Did I say it correctly?"

"Yes." He murmured, some part of him still not sure if this was his reality. "You did."

He trailed his fingers across her cheek, needing to touch her one more time before soaring into the sky.

I mean it. Her voice wove through his mind. *You're my starlight.*

And you are my dawn.

A smile remained on his face as he flew all the way up the castle to his balcony and strolled through his dark bedroom. It dropped when Cassiel sensed he wasn't alone. He whipped around, but the intruder was already coming at him. They grabbed his wrist, and the ember in his chest vanished. He gaped at his uncle standing partially in the shadows, the other half of his grim face lit by moonlight.

"I'm sorry," he said solemnly.

Cassiel glanced down at the brass cuff he now wore. He felt his flame trapped behind an invisible barrier with no way to escape. "What is this? What have you done?"

"Seraph fire is dangerous, Cassiel. In the wrong hands, it becomes a destructive power, and you have proven you are not ready for it."

He stared at him, shaking his head in disbelief. No. His uncle couldn't be the one planning against them.

"Not you..." Cassiel said. "Don't tell me it's you."

Lord Jophiel lowered his head. "I wish I did not have to be the one," he said, regret in his voice. "But you have left us no choice. For the good of the Realms, you must wear this bangle...by order of the High King."

CHAPTER 58

Von

They waited until the cover of darkness to sneak up on the Azure Knights. Von slinked forward in the dark and paused behind a tree at the edge of the forest. Several blue tents with the Azure sigil had set up camp outside of the temple ruins in the distance, confirming what he feared.

They had also come for the scroll.

The ruins stood on a platform of stone. Broken steps covered in ice led to a set of crumbling pillars that barely held up the arched stone roof. Torch fires lit the campsite, but everything was unusually quiet. It set Von on edge. He raised his fist over his shoulder, warning his team to remain hidden.

Von listened, waiting for any sound. He couldn't hear anything besides the wind beating against the tents. He glanced up at the tree where Elon hid. The elf landed nimbly on his feet beside him without making a sound.

"There is only one," Elon said, his voice barely a whisper.

A faint cry drifted to them. It came again, falling into a painful moan.

"Stay back," Von said into the darkness at the others.

Drawing out two knives, he slinked into the camp with Elon, keeping to the shadows, and watching every corner for movement until they came upon the first body of a knight. The man lay sprawled on the ground as if he had merely tripped in a drunken stupor. Frost clung to his lashes and brows, but it wasn't the cold that killed him.

A throwing star protruded from the back of his neck, leaving a dark pool of blood to crystalize beneath him.

They continued and found more dead around the ashes of a campfire that had long gone out. Others were killed in their beds or on watch.

"Someone beat us here," Von said.

Elon took the red hilt of his sword, soundlessly drawing the blade free. They continued to the center of camp and came upon the source of the sounds. An older man, beaten bloody, was tied to a post with a gag over his mouth, his head hanging to his chest.

"The Relic Hunter," Elon concluded.

"The knights must have done this," Von said. "But it looks like another party ambushed them, as well."

"They have been dead for hours. Whoever dealt with them, likely left with the prize. No one else is here but us."

Von cursed. If the scroll was gone, then they had to track down whoever took it, or he would be finished. Tarn warned he wouldn't accept another failure.

He signaled for the others. Three forms slinked out from the darkness. Len slung her bow and quiver on her shoulder, and Bouvier sheathed his rapier.

Lowering his mask, Novo let out a low whistle as he observed all the bodies scattered through the camp. "Aye, I think we lost this one, mates. But they left behind the old bugger." He nudged the Relic Hunter's boot, and the man groaned again.

"Untie him and get him warm," Von ordered. "He may know something useful."

Bouvier and Novo worked on getting the rope loose. Once the knots were off, the man slumped against them.

His bruised eyelids fluttered. "The scroll..."

Von crouched down to his level. "Is it gone?"

"Don't let him...have it..."

"Who?"

"The King..."

It was clear the King of Azure had something to do with this when the knights had ridden through the city, but why would he want the Scroll of the Unending? Was he also searching for immortality, or was this done to impede Tarn? Von didn't know the full extent of his master's plans besides becoming eternally powerful and overthrowing King Lenneus, but he sensed more was afoot.

"What are you saying, old man?" Novo asked as he searched his pockets. "Do you have it? Where did you put it?"

"Stop." Von caught Novo's arm. The Relic Hunter was too weak and frozen to the bone. Unhooking his waterskin, Von helped him drink. The man coughed, and his lungs wheezed for air in a way that said he didn't have long. "What happened here?"

"Do you serve...?"

"We don't serve the Azure King."

The Relic Hunter's mouth twitched in what may have been a relieved smile. "He sent me...here to find the scroll...then he sent them when we did..." His bloodshot eyes rolled to the dead. "To kill me and the others...but...I...hid it..."

Von stilled, not sure if he heard him right. He patted the man's face when his eyes drifted closed. "Where, sir? Where did you hide it?"

"Where the phoenix rises..." the man said faintly. "Destroy...you must destroy it..." Then his chest fell still, and he didn't move anymore.

Von pressed his fingers to the man's throat. No pulse.

"He's dead," Novo sighed and got to his feet. "With his injuries and the weather, the old man's heart couldn't take it."

"What does the Azure King want with the scroll?" Bouvier asked.

"If I know anything, nothing good. But it may still be here." Von stood and spun his knives between his fingers as he studied the ruins. A place dedicated to the worship of Jökull, the God of Death.

"Have you been inside?" he asked Bouvier.

"Aye, Commander. There's not much there. Only an effigy."

"Of the Ice Phoenix," Von guessed. "The old man must have hidden the scroll there before they grabbed him. All right, move quickly and set up a perimeter. I'll take point—"

Novo dropped.

He hit the ground flat on his back, his blank eyes staring up at the starry sky. From his left temple protruded a throwing star. Von stood there, his slow mind struggling to accept the suddenness of his death.

"Novo," Bouvier breathed in disbelief.

Len screamed.

More throwing stars zipped through the air. Von tackled Len down as one whipped past her face. Elon and Bouvier dove to the ground, scrambling to hide behind the tents. Von spotted movement on top of the temple.

"Roof!" he shouted.

Elon snatched Len's fallen bow and shot off a series of arrows. Their attacker ducked. She fought against Von's grasp to get to Novo, screaming and screaming.

"He's gone, Len!" Von struggled to hold her as she writhed wildly to free herself. "Now isn't the time to grieve for him. We're under attack!"

She threw her head back into his face. Von released her at the flash of pain watering his eyes. Using the cover of Elon's arrows, she sprinted for the temple.

"Len, stop!" Von shouted.

"She's going after him," Bouvier exclaimed.

Len evaded the rain of throwing stars as she dashed up the steps. The onslaught stopped when she made it inside. There was no telling how many they were up against. Von grabbed a torch and chased after her with the others. He heard steel clashing as they ran up the steps. Inside, they found her fighting a dark shape in the faint moonlight.

Von tossed the torch over a dried bush, and it blazed with fire. It lit the temple walls and fell over the massive statue of a towering bird at the front.

There was no one else here but Len and their assailant.

By his distinct features, the man wasn't from Azure. He wore a black robe fashioned into the style of Xián Jīng. His long black hair was tied back in a high tail on top of his head. His curved knives effortlessly deflected Len's with lightning speed.

She fought with anger and unfocused aggression. Her moves were reckless, only aimed at killing instead of defense. The man delivered a powerful kick that sent her reeling into a pile of broken stones. He focused his black eyes on the rest of them next.

Elon threw out a streak of blue lightning, but the man ducked and the spell hit the walls. The temple groaned and shook violently, threatening to bring the roof down.

"No magic," Von ordered. "Len, stand down."

They didn't know who this man was or what his abilities were yet. This wasn't how they faced their opponents.

But she got to her feet and readied her karambit knives, baring her teeth. He killed her love-mate. By the rabid craze on her face, nothing Von said would stop her now.

The man didn't even look at Len, as though she was not a real threat. He swiftly took out another throwing star and tossed it at her. She dodged and leaped at the man. His body whirled in a spin kick. It caught her chest in mid-air, throwing her back. Len's head bashed against a broken pillar, and she crumpled to the ground.

She didn't move again.

Von's knives shook in his hands at the fury building inside of him. Last night, Novo had been full of life and hope for his future with Len. And in a blink, it was gone. He pinned his eyes on the man who stole it away from them.

Elon shot more arrows. Metal rang out as the man knocked them out of the air with his knives and threw another in return. It split the bow's limb in half. Elon dropped it and whipped out his sword. He and Bouvier attacked. The man easily fought with his two opponents, a knife in each hand. His moves were swift and meticulous. The type of skill that could only be instilled in him from birth.

Von had only seen one person move that way before.

The Wraith.

"Fall back!" Von shouted.

"The bastard's mine," Bouvier growled. He raised his arms to swing his rapier sword, but the assassin twisted out of the way and spun a knife in his palm, plunging it into Bouvier's heart.

A cry tore from Von's throat. "No!"

Elon let out an enraged snarl through his teeth. The man leaped back, and he gave chase.

Von ran to Bouvier and caught him as he fell. Blood gargled from his mouth, gasping for air. His frightened eyes looked up at Von.

"C-commander..." His trembling fingers gripped his forearm.

"You'll be all right," Von murmured. "Let it pass. Let it pass."

The spy exhaled one last shaky breath as blood dripped from his mouth. Von couldn't do anything but watch the life drain out of his eyes.

Gently closing them, Von laid him down and rose to his feet. He turned to the sound of metal clashing against metal and focused all of his rage on the man. He looked back at him, and a cold smile curved his mouth.

But in the light, Von saw it wasn't the same man responsible for Tarn's scar. The Wraith was already dead, he recalled, and this was merely another Xián Jing assassin paid to retrieve the same thing they were after.

"You're going to pay for their deaths," Von promised as he joined Elon's side.

The man's black eyes gleamed with excitement as they circled him slowly. He took the long grip of his sword and pulled it free. It was slender, fashioned with a curved, single-edged blade and a squared guard. A thin ray of firelight danced on its edge as he moved into a crouched stance.

The corner of a rolled-up parchment peeked out of the assassin's robes.

The Sacred Scroll

Von glanced at the phoenix effigy. The stones had been disturbed between its taloned feet. The Relic Hunter had been left alive merely so he could learn where to find the scroll.

"Who sent you?" Von demanded.

He only smiled darkly and beckoned them with his fingers.

405

"I'll take the right," Von whispered, picking up Bouvier's rapier. It was going to take both of them to end their opponent.

Elon's eyes narrowed. "Swiftly now, Commander."

They attacked at the same time. Yet the man deflected every hit, meeting them move for move with incredible agility. The clash of their swords rang in the temple as they fought to gain advantage. It was like fighting a ghost.

He darted out of the way, and Von's knife only caught air. Backing away, the assassin looked down at his robe. He smirked, as if intrigued that he was almost cut. This was a game to him. Some sort of sick enjoyment.

Von parried his next attack, but missed the knife slicing through his thigh. He bit back a hiss, faltering. Elon pushed him out of the way of the blade coming for his head.

Von hit the ground and rolled around in time to see the assassin slash him across the stomach. "Elon!"

He threw a knife, piercing the assassin's shoulder. Elon snatched their opponent's weapon at the same time and swung. Their opponent pivoted from the blow but a splinter too late. The blade caught the edge of his waist.

He backed away with a hiss. He scowled down at the blood soaking his clothing, then started walking backward.

That little cut was enough to make him retreat?

"You're not going anywhere!" Von rapidly whipped out two more knives.

The assassin ran out of the temple and he chased after him. A line of throwing stars came spiraling through the night for his face. Cursing, Von ducked out of the way. By the time he got to the steps, the assassin was galloping away on a stolen horse.

Damn their rotten luck.

He spun around and ran back to Elon.

"I'm all right. He barely nicked me." Elon grunted as he yanked open his thick leather armor to reveal the shallow slice across his abdomen. "My armor stopped the worst of it."

"Thank the God of Urn."

Elon winced and sat on a broken pillar with his help. "I thought I was headed for Death's Gate."

"You nearly were." Von ripped off the edge of his shirt and pressed it to the wound.

"You must have concluded what I did about that man. He was no ordinary adversary."

Von scowled in the direction he went. "Why did he come all the way from Xián Jīng for a Sacred Scroll? Someone must have sent him."

"Tarn won't be pleased."

"This isn't over." Von got to his feet with a snarl. "We're getting that scroll, and I'm going to kill that man."

"Commander, I won't be coming with you." Elon's brow pinched as he looked out at their dead companions. "I don't want to end up like them. My mate has been waiting for me in Dwarf Shoe for far too long. He never would have known what happened to me if I died."

It was the most the elf had spoken of his private life, or in general, for that matter.

"I tire of death, but I will do what is necessary to go home." Elon seemed to tense for a moment, waiting for his response. He was essentially abandoning Tarn's service, and that one statement made clear his intentions if someone stood in his way.

Von held out a hand to help him stand. "I'm not one to detain you from returning to your family, Elon."

It's not as if he could, anyway.

Elon looked relieved he wouldn't have to kill him, and he picked up his fallen sword, sliding it in place. "Can I ask for you to report that I fell here?"

"Aye. It's going to be a quiet trip back to Indigo Bay."

"You could come with me."

"I can't."

Elon nodded. "Because of your wife?"

Von groaned. "How long did you know?"

"From the beginning."

"Why didn't you report it to Tarn?"

"Because I respect your character, Von," Elon said, calling him informally by his name for the first time. "You're a good man. I pray one day you will also walk away from this." He looked around at the spies and a despondency crossed his expression, showing how much he cared for his team. "I will help you bury them."

"No, you should go," Von said, his throat catching. It seemed all he did these days was dig graves. "I will take care of this."

The elf sighed heavily. "Best of luck to you."

"And to you, my friend."

Elon's mouth curved in a faint smile and he headed for the temple entryway. As Von watched him go, he couldn't help but feel a little envious of his freedom to walk away from this life. Now he had to go back and report everyone's deaths and the failed mission. Tarn would probably kill him, but Von had to go back.

He had to go back to Yavi—

Elon's sudden gasp echoed through the temple, and he stumbled to his knees.

"Elon?" Von ran to him.

He caught Elon before he slumped over and helped him lie back. Elon gripped his stomach, gasping in pain. A green liquid foamed from the wound as though something foul oozed inside. A sheen of sweat sprouted on his ashen face and he wheezed for air. His eyes squinted at the temple's ceiling.

"I can't move." Elon grated out. "His sword...it was..."

"Laced with poison," Von said in shock. "That's why he ran. You cut him with it."

"Good," Elon said through a painful breath. His skin lost color by the second.

"What poison did he use?" Von exclaimed. "Tell me what to do! I can find a Herb Master in the city, or I'll catch the assassin. He will have the antidote."

"No..." Elon's pained expression became anguished. His breath came out low and shallow. It cost him a great effort to fill his lungs. "It's too late. I can't...feel my body."

Von shook his head. He glanced at Len and Bouvier a few paces away. Novo was dead outside. Coldness sunk in his bones, and the familiar weight of guilt fell heavily over his shoulders. So many kept dying for Tarn's pursuit.

How many more would he have to grieve before this ended?

"Sylar..." Elon whispered, his face grimacing with pain and sorrow. "Little Step city..."

Von clenched his jaw, fighting back the despair wrapping around his throat. "I'll find him, my friend. I swear on my life."

A broken smile touched Elon's lips. His amber eyes slipped closed, and he fell still. Von stared at the unmoving elf through his misted vision. Of all of Tarn's Raiders, he never thought this warrior would die before him. Dark green froth continued to burble from Elon's wound.

And Von's mind went still with one thought.

Fengu venom.

CHAPTER 59

Dynalya

"**G**ood morning!"

Dyna blinked sleepily at the chirpy voice and barely noticed Noemi floating through the room before she yanked open the heavy drapes. Bright morning sun streamed into the windows and burned her eyes. She moaned, hiding her face in the pillows. The lump sleeping next to Dyna cursed when Noemi yanked back the blankets.

"Time to wake up. We have a grand day ahead of us!"

"Leave me or I will throw you off the balcony," Lucenna hissed.

"I will merely fly back," Noemi replied cheerfully.

"Please rise, my lady." At the sound of that stern voice, Dyna and Lucenna sat up to meet Madam Kahna's pinched expression. "There is much to do before the wedding tonight."

Right. Time to make their marriage official before the eyes of the court.

Servants strolled in through the door with carts of tea, bread, and an assortment of fruits. Others came in with carts of shoes and dresses.

"There is more I must do?" Dyna asked. "I thought I completed the Bonding Rites."

Yesterday evening, she had gone through the Rite of the Flesh.

The cold water had sluiced off her body when she stepped out of the sacred pool within a cave buried deep below the castle. Several female Celestials had been in attendance, each of them dressed in simple white robes. Including Lady Sarrai. Their voices wove together in their language as they said the prayer for purification to wash away all of Dyna's impurities.

Well, after submerging herself seven times, she had to be clean. Her skin felt fresh and her hair silky. It fell around her shoulders in soft, red waves.

"You did, my lady. You are cleansed and may join with your mate as you please."

Dyna flushed at how freely they spoke about that around here. As a Herb Master, she learned everything there was to know about intimacy, but reading about it and performing it were two different things. Lucenna peeked at her behind her pillow and smirked. Dyna shot her a glower.

"Now we must prepare you for the day." Kahna nodded to the servants. "We have brought you some food to break your fast."

"Could I meet Cassiel for breakfast?" Dyna asked.

"I'm afraid not, my lady. The Prince must also prepare for the wedding. You will see him when it's time to handfast before *Elyōn*."

She pouted and tugged on the bond. Cassiel answered right away. *Lev sheli? Madam Kahna has come to torture me.*

Only a little. He replied, amusement in his voice. *She means to pamper my bride and ensure every eye will be on you.*

Dyna groaned. She rather crawl back into bed and sleep a little more. *I'm considering marrying my pillow instead.* The sound of his warm chuckle made her smile. *I will see you tonight.*

I will be waiting.

With a tired sigh, she got out of bed. Her body felt sluggish from their late night magic lessons, since she hadn't been able to sleep. It didn't help. She was kept up due to nerves about today and the thousand other thoughts that kept turning in her head. Like about their future as Lord and Lady and whether Cassiel would be allowed to cross Troll Bridge, so he could find his mother.

Why did she leave her family behind?

Cassiel said it was to find a way to preserve her lifetime, but it didn't seem right, somehow. Dyna sensed it was something else. Something much more significant that warranted risking her life and leaving her son. Maybe Lord Jophiel would know something.

She ate some fruit and cheese as they worked on her hair and lathered her skin with sweet smelling oils. Lucenna seemed to be enjoying herself, but Dyna still couldn't get used to being waited on hand and foot, and constantly bowed to. There were several ladies-in-waiting to help this time. She often caught them staring at her.

Apparently, walking through Seraph fire was rarer than wielding it.

"My lady, here is the contraceptive you requested," Noemi whispered when Kahna was distracted. She handed Dyna a small glass vial with brown kernels inside that resembled apple seeds. "Take one seed for every year you wish to be infertile. They are instantly effective. You may have one more bleed, but it will be faint and last only a day."

Who knew how long it would be before the topic of growing a family came up again, or what their future would hold, but for now, she and Lucenna took one. The seeds had a waxy coating and didn't taste like anything.

The rest of the morning was spent weaving fine silver strands through her hair. Dyna was made to sit still through it as she fought to stay awake. She groaned at the faint ache in her head and body. Learning how to levitate herself with her Essence took a toll.

"I need tea," she mumbled, pressing on her temples.

"Already done." Lucenna poured her a cup, and the scent of rosemary drifted in the air. "You know, there are other much more *satisfying* ways to replenish your Essence." A slow grin took over her face. "Quicker than rosemary tea, if you gather my meaning."

Dyna flushed bright red. "Y-yes, I'm aware of that method."

Azeran had detailed all the methods mages could revitalize magic, and intimacy had been one of them. Something about there being an exchange of life force during the act.

"And I'm sure your Celestial wouldn't mind in the least." Lucenna winked, making her redden further.

A knock came at the door, and Kahna opened it to reveal another servant.

She curtsied. "Lord Jophiel sends his compliments, and he apologizes for the interruption. If My Lady can spare a moment, he asks that you join him for tea."

This could be a good opportunity to ask him about Cassiel's mother.

Dyna glanced at Kahna, and the stewardess pursed her lips. "I suppose we can spare an hour."

"With pleasure, I will join him directly," Dyna answered the servant.

The ladies quickly dressed her in a fine gold gown for the meeting, then the Valkyrie escorted her and Lucenna to Lord Jophiel's office. It was a good thing Sowmya knew the way, because she was still learning the halls.

When Dyna recognized the corridor, she stopped. "I will be fine from here."

Sowmya and Janel bowed before taking their posts at the end of the corridor.

"Then I will go to the ballroom and see how it's coming along," Lucenna said. "Shall we meet in your rooms later?"

Dyna nodded. Taking a deep breath, she glided down the corridor with her hands folded at her waist, as Noemi had taught her. When she reached Lord Jophiel's office, the door was slightly ajar. She raised a hand to knock.

"Have you done what I asked?"

She froze at the sound of King Yoel's voice coming from inside.

"Yes," Lord Jophiel replied, his tone tired.

"This is necessary, brother. I do what I must not, only for my son, but for our people. We have both known this was coming since that night. Cassiel is the future of Hilos."

She covered her mouth.

King Yoel had never changed his mind.

He still planned to make Cassiel High King.

Dyna tensed at the sudden feeling of a presence. She glanced over her shoulder and found Prince Malakel standing a couple of feet behind her. He stared at the door. The expression on his face...it was the last thing she expected to see. Instead of anger, the prince looked lost. Like everything he had known had been erased. Malakel turned away, his white wings hanging low. He quickly vanished down the corridor.

"Forgive me, but do you think our people are ready to have him as their King?" Lord Jophiel asked. "They were not prepared at the beginning. How could they be now?"

There was a long pause, and Dyna pressed her ear closer to the crack, straining to hear King Yoel's answer.

"I wish we had more time to prepare him and the Realms, but time is always short, Jophiel. It passes quickly, and it cares not if you are ready for it. Once they found each other, it was inevitable. Nothing can interrupt what must happen tonight."

What did that mean? What was happening tonight?

Other than their wedding...

"The rites are finished, and the paint prepared. Their bond will be complete. I have spoken about it with Cassiel."

They were speaking of the consummation. Why was that so important to everyone?

"Good."

"Will you arrive for the ceremony?"

King Yoel was quiet before saying, "I'm afraid not. I have more to do here."

"What am I to tell him about Mount Ida? He's requested to cross Troll Bridge."

Dyna held her breath to hear his reply. Would King Yoel stop Cassiel from continuing on their journey? After what happened in the port, it was very likely.

But Dyna didn't hear his answer. She pressed closer to the door, and it loudly creaked open under her weight. Lord Jophiel looked up from where he stood before a podium by the back windows. On it rested a wide silver plate that glowed brightly, its light illuminating his startled expression for a short moment before it faded away.

Dyna's face flamed hot. "Um...pardon. You...called for me?"

Lord Jophiel straightened with a bemused frown. "Yes, but I meant to meet you in the drawing room of my chambers, my lady. Not here."

"Oh, I'm terribly sorry. I assumed—I-I will excuse myself."

"It's fine. You are here now." He motioned for her to join him.

Dyna's gown rustled as she slowly came closer. Lord Jophiel studied her face, and she did her best to compose herself, but she couldn't quite hide how flustered she was.

"I trust what you overheard will stay in this room."

She nodded.

"Between us," he clarified. She glanced around the office but didn't see the High King. "We intended to disclose the news after some time, but I imagine it's good news for you, nonetheless."

"For me?" She frowned, unsure of his meaning. "Because...it means I am to be Queen?"

"Is that what you desire?"

He was asking about more than simply wanting the throne. Many suspected she, a common girl with no background, planned to tie herself to a prince. Spelled her way into his heart by some evil magic.

"I never desired it," Dyna replied coolly. She motioned at her regal clothing, then the kingdom. "Nor any of this. In my village, everything we own is earned by our hands. I never cared for wealth or status, and I certainly don't care for your implication. I'm intelligent enough to make my own way. All I ever desired from Cassiel was to be by his side."

To say such a thing aloud, it hummed in the bond.

A soft smile rose on Lord Jophiel's face. "Forgive me, I had to ask. Merely to prove this union was beyond any doubt. We have much to lose and cannot leave anything to chance."

Then she noticed the truth bell hanging from the domed glass ceiling. Lord Jophiel was testing her? Not only him. He said *we*.

Dyna spun round, searching the gallery for any hidden, winged forms. "King Yoel?"

"He isn't here," Lord Jophiel said.

"I heard his voice."

"We spoke through the water mirror."

413

She glanced at the wide, flat bowl on the podium and inched closer to see it. The outside was silver and scalloped like a seashell. The inside was lined with iridescent mother-of-pearl. It held clear water and nothing more.

"It works similar to orbs, but with magic of its own. I'm a collector of such things." Lord Jophiel looked out at his office, and she followed his gaze to the many items on display and the power she could feel from them. "Every piece has a past, such as the necklace you wear."

Dyna brushed her fingers over the crystal resting on her chest.

"It once belonged to the first High Queen of Hilos, then it was passed down to each one thereafter. It belonged to my mother for some time before it was given to Cassiel's mother. Now it's yours." His expression was neutral, but she wasn't sure if he approved of her wearing it. "The smith who created that necklace was also the one who made this." He motioned at the pearlescent plate.

"You use it to communicate with the High King?"

"Yes, for short amounts of time, and only when necessary. It could be used as a tool to spy on others. However, others can spy back."

She studied it curiously. "This is the only one?"

"There are four magic mirrors in all, so you never know who is watching." He looked down at his reflection in the water. "The sun mirror was once in Arthal with the fae before it was lost. It required blood to see what will be. The moon mirror requires tears to see what once was. The water mirror requires salt to see what is present."

Dyna was detecting a pattern. Each mirror represented an element. "Is there an earth mirror?"

He nodded. "It's in the possession of the Archmage."

"What does it do?"

"Not even I know the answer."

Dyna looked into the water mirror, intrigued by this new magic. "If I may ask, could I...?"

"Of course." Lord Jophiel took something from the table behind him and held out a small wooden bowl of salt. "Sprinkle some inside and stir the water as you think of who you want to see. There must be a mirror or source of reflection nearby, like a window or water. Those proficient in magic may see you, regardless if you do not intend it."

Dyna did as he instructed and circled her fingers through the water. Rings spread through the surface as it clouded. She thought of her cottage and she received a dim image of Lyra sitting at her desk. A soft gasp left her and emotion welled in her chest as she saw her little sister's tawny eyes reflected in the sunlight, the delicate heart-shaped face that was all their mother. Her red tresses were braided back into a coronet.

"Where are you, Dyna?" Lyra whispered, her eyes welling. "Please, come home."

Dyna's eyes watered too as the image vanished. She wished to appear before her sister now and hug her tight, but she couldn't, not yet. Not until her journey was over, but people stood in her way.

With a stir of the water, she spied on Tarn next. Instead of his tent, he was in a room she didn't recognize, sitting in a wingback chair by a fireplace.

But then Tarn's glacial gaze flickered up—right at her.

Dyna jumped back with a gasp, and the image quickly faded. Her skin prickled with goosebumps.

God of Urn, he didn't see her, did he? The man still frightened her, and she stupidly forgot he had magic.

But if those with magic could see her, then there was someone she wished to speak with. Lord Jophiel must have seen something on her face because he extended the salt bowl to her again.

"Whatever is said stays in this room?" she asked him.

He nodded.

Dyna sprinkled in more salt, and the whirling water settled on an image of a woodland. She glared at the green-haired fae sitting on the edge of a creek with a blue fox on his lap. He played a lilting tune on a pan flute. It was a hypnotic sound, alluring and beautiful that seemed to pull her closer and closer to the mirror. The spell ended when the song did.

Leoake's gold eyes blinked at her like a sleepy cat, and he grinned. "Well, hello there."

"You can see me?"

"Hear you, too. So can others if you're not careful, clever mortal." He chuckled. "And we both know what happens when you don't heed my warnings."

She worked her jaw, wishing she could reach in the mirror and strangle him. He intentionally sent her a vague message that didn't help her at all.

"Then I will make this quick." Dyna held up her cursed hand with the tattoo of an oak tree. "Remove it."

The dastardly Druid responded with a jeering laugh. "I cannot remove the geas until our deal is complete."

"A deal you trapped me in."

"Is it a trap if you willingly walk into it?"

Dyna groaned through a sharp breath, gripping the edge of the podium. She hated that the geas was a source of fear for Cassiel and judgment from others. She wanted it gone. "You could at least change the appearance or make it more discreet," she said tightly. "It's dreadful, and I don't want it to be the first thing everyone judges me for."

"Hmm." Leoake strolled alongside the bank, his hair perfectly matching his dark green jacket embroidered with golden oak leaves. He gave her a smile as sharp as his pointed ears. "Very well. I'm feeling generous today. Take it as my wedding gift."

Sunlight glinted on his many rings as he snapped his fingers. The geas tingled, then the canopy of the tree began to fade until it disappeared from her skin, as if wiped away by an invisible cloth.

"Where did it go?"

He winked. "An answer to be revealed when you're both discovering other things about each other tonight."

"Leoake!"

"Worry not, my dear. He will be pleased." With a mischievous laugh, the Druid sauntered away from the creek. Azulo yipped at her before the water mirror cleared.

Face burning, Dyna didn't dare look at Lord Jophiel. "I must return, my lord."

He cleared his throat. "Right, of course."

She dipped in a curtsey and hurried for the door, but halted when she remembered her reason for coming. "Can the mirror find anyone? Perhaps it can find—"

Lord Jophiel shook his head despondently, knowing what she would ask.

Dyna's heart sank. "Do you mean she is...?"

"All I know is the water mirror cannot locate her. It means she is no longer in this realm, or she is cloaked. Either way, Cassiel's mother is lost to us."

Mount Ida was smothered with magic. The island itself couldn't be found without a map. Maybe his mother made it and it hid her now, too.

"Were you friends?" she asked.

A sad fondness settled on his face. "We were, a long time ago."

"Why did she leave?"

Lord Jophiel glanced fleetingly at the bell. "Perhaps in search of a future."

Dyna didn't understand what that meant, but he most likely wouldn't tell her more.

"Oh, I nearly forgot the reason I called on you." Lord Jophiel walked down the step to the table with the seating chairs. On it rested a small ornate jewelry box made of pink pearl and gilded with flowers and vines. "I have a light gift for you."

She paused in surprise, not expecting this. Noemi had told her light gifts were usually from close family or lovers.

He opened the small box and presented it to her. "It would greatly honor me if you would wear them tonight."

Laying on a velvet cushion rested a pair of dangly sapphire earrings. They were beautiful. It left her speechless.

"Before you say you cannot possibly accept it, I will beg you to allow me this." To give her such an extravagant gift, it must mean he considered her family now.

She accepted the jewelry box carefully, feeling the weight of it in her hands. It was probably worth a fortune in itself. "Thank you, Lord Jophiel. These have been a trying few days. Your kindness and welcome have truly meant a lot to me."

"I admit, I was not sure what to expect once meeting you, but after what I witnessed yesterday, it could only mean you are his match. The Realm sees it as well," Lord Jophiel said, looking out at the mountains. "When he first came here, Cassiel's spirit was broken. Seeing his kind living freely in Hermon slowly brought him back to life. He grew strong, if only to spite those who had wronged him. Anger and hate followed him like a shadow, but when I saw how he regarded you, those shadows had diminished." Lord Jophiel looked at her warmly. "I have never been more astounded than when I saw him truly smile at declaring you as his. You have brought him joy, Dynalya. It is I who must thank you."

His gentle praise snipped the final threads of her insecurities. She had changed Cassiel's life as much as he had changed hers.

"I think you did a great deal for him as well, Lord Jophiel. He greatly admires you. To Cassiel, you're like a father."

An emotion crossed his face that she couldn't read, and he lowered his head. "And he is like a son to me. Cassiel is not happy with me at the moment, and that is understandable, but I will always do what's best for his well-being, even if he does not agree with my methods."

Dyna's brow furrowed.

At her visible confusion, Lord Jophiel cleared his throat. "Ah. He did not tell you."

"Tell me what?"

"Cassiel is to wear a bangle for the time being."

She recoiled. "You put a witch's bangle on him?"

"I'm very sorry. It's entirely a precaution." Lord Jophiel linked his hands behind his back. "I fear for your future here and for Cassiel's. He cannot attack his people when they disagree with him, or destroy rooms at the spark of a temper. It's not done. Diplomacy is how we manage. We have all Four Realms in attendance today for the wedding, and I cannot risk something happening."

She shook her head at the sudden turn in conversation. "Therefore, your best judgment is to take away his defenses when our lives are currently in danger?"

"The ballroom will be full of Valkyrie. They will protect you, my lady. I promise this is only temporary. I will take it off myself once he learns control."

Dyna? Cassiel's alarmed voice blared in her head at the emotions and magic roiling through her. *Breathe, lev sheli.*

She forced herself to fill her lungs with air and release it slowly. Lord Jophiel backed away from her as green light tinted the room. She glanced past him to her reflection in the window. Her eyes were glowing a menacing green. Her body trembled from the memory of having her magic locked away while trapped in Tarn's camp.

How can he do that to you?

It was a command from my father, apparently.

That reminded her of what she had overheard earlier. *"Have you done what I asked?"*

Dyna composed herself. "I will take my leave," she said before they thought to put one on her as well.

Lord Jophiel nodded, watching her carefully.

She left the office with a churning in her stomach. If it was King Yoel's command, she couldn't do anything about it, despite her wanting to rip it off Cassiel this instant.

There was no contesting a King.

CHAPTER 60

Cassiel

Cassiel's heartbeat thudded loudly in his ears. It drowned out the soft hum of the hundreds of Celestials in the ballroom as they waited for the bride to arrive. He ignored all the eyes he felt watching him from where he stood within the platform set in the center of the floor. Four columns wrapped in blue flowers and sheets of white tulle rose on each corner of it. He kept his hands folded together, so he wouldn't fidget with his black brocade jacket. It was fitted from his shoulders to the waist, with an elegance suited to his lean physique. Instead of the traditional white robes, he had chosen a modern look for the ceremony, but now it felt too tight and hot.

Yet he could be dressed in mud and still feel like a thousand bats were rampaging in his stomach. Why was he so nervous?

The last rays of light spilling through the massive windows at Cassiel's back faded as the sun set beyond the mountain, and soft music began to play.

It was time.

He looked up at the double doors on the second-floor entryway. The Valkyrie stationed there bowed and opened them. And then he saw her.

His heartbeat slowed.

And his next breath stalled.

A hush fell over the room. It had to be Dyna's beauty that silenced them, because she seemed to glow as though she had walked through the Seven Gates to find him.

Dyna's white gown glittered like streams of moonlight beneath the chandeliers. The bodice accentuated every curve in embroidered silk and trimmed in silver. Her shoulders were bare, with only sheer sleeves on her arms ending at points over her hands. A veil covered her head, falling down her back to look like small wings.

Emotion constricted Cassiel's throat. For a moment, he forgot how to breathe.

His bride.

His mate.

His.

Dyna froze on the top step. Her nerves prickled against him, and he could feel her heart pounding.

Look at me, he sent through the bond. *Only me.*

She did, then her shoulders straightened, and after a pause, she slowly climbed down the steps. Every eye followed her descent to the first floor. Zev and Lucenna waited at the bottom. They escorted her across the long red carpet leading to the platform. Dyna reached it and he took her trembling hands. Her gaze met his through the veil, and Cassiel was mesmerized all over again.

He gently squeezed her fingers. "You look like a dream."

The smile that earned him stole whatever was left of him. She possessed it all.

The music quieted as Lord Jophiel climbed the steps of the platform and stood before them. "We have gathered here today to celebrate the union of two souls," he announced to the court. "Two souls cut from the same cloth of stars by *Elyōn* himself. Dynalya Astron and Cassiel Soaraway…" He looked at them. "Do you choose to bind yourselves to one another from this day until your last day?"

She nodded.

You must say it aloud, Cassiel sent into her thoughts.

"Oh, right, yes, I accept," Dyna stuttered, and he was sure she was blushing terribly under the veil.

Cassiel fought a smile as he said aloud, "I choose to bind myself from this day until my last."

Lord Jophiel nodded. "Present the sash and the rings."

Dyna removed the braided ribbons from some hidden pocket of her dress and gave it to Lord Jophiel. He nodded to Cassiel next.

Taking her hand again, Cassiel slipped his mother's ring on her finger. *"Harey at mekudeshet li be tabaat zot,"* he said and translated for her. *You are now blessed to me by this ring.*

The sapphire stone glinted under the candlelight, the silver band woven around it delicately. A trickle of her surprise traveled down the bond. She shakily took the other gold ring waiting in his palm and slipped it on his finger as she repeated the same words. Lord Jophiel motioned for them to kneel together. Then he wrapped the sash around their linked hands.

Laying his palm over their bound hands, his uncle spoke the prayer for the God of Life to consecrate this union, binding them to one another eternally. A servant brought a small wooden table to put between them, and Lord Jophiel laid out a scroll on top of it. It was filled with script. A contract of marriage.

He pulled out a knife.

This is the bonding part, Cassiel said, sensing her unease increase.

Dyna opened her hand. Lord Jophiel drew the knife across her palm, then Cassiel's, and pressed them together. "With your joined blood, *Elyōn* binds thee as one."

Light burst from their joined hands in a brilliant ray. Electrical warmth flooded his body, and he heard Dyna's soft gasp as she felt the same. The rapid tempo of her heart thumped in his chest where his heartbeat matched hers. Soft currents of pleasure rushed through his body, nearly toppling him.

The crowd awed loudly.

"It's a sign that means you are True Bonded," Lord Jophiel whispered to them.

And it was witnessed before all to see. Now no one could question their bond. To do so would be to question their maker.

Dyna breathed heavily, turning to him. *This is what you felt...the first time?*

It was stronger by threefold.

This time, it was milder since they were already bonded.

Lord Jophiel held their hands over the scroll and a few drops of their blood pattered onto the page before their cuts healed. He unbound the sash and handed Cassiel a quill. He signed his name in a swirl of ink on the contract, then Dyna signed hers below his.

"The bride and groom may kiss to seal their oath," Lord Jophiel announced.

Cassiel reached for her veil and lifted it off her head. Her bright green eyes met his. The bond drummed with her pulse and awareness of everyone watching.

Cassiel leaned closer. *All I see is you...*

Dyna's eyes fluttered closed, and he pressed a kiss to her lips. The tension eased out of her body as she leaned into him. Someone came forward and placed something cold and heavy on his head. He straightened to see his uncle do the same to her. Dyna reached up, her fingers brushing the edges of the sapphire jewels, and the silver points now circling her head.

A crown.

She gaped at him. Cassiel shot her a smile and bowed his head, motioning for her to do the same.

Lord Jophiel's voice carried in the room, "Prince Cassiel Soaraway, son of the High King, rise."

He stood.

"Dynalya Soaraway of House Astron, rise now as Princess Consort of Hilos and the Four Celestial Realms."

Cassiel helped Dyna stand on her wobbly legs. She was trembling. He brushed his fingers over the small of her back, and she straightened as if his touch was enough to draw out the bravery he knew she held.

"I present before the Realms, the Lord and Lady of Hermon Ridge."

Together, they faced their court. A room packed with Celestials, half-breeds, and purebloods alike. Dyna's hand tightened in his, and he braced for their public rebuttal.

There was a still pause.

Then the ballroom was a flutter of wings and gowns—as the court deeply bowed as one. Music thrummed through the room, signaling the end of the ceremony, and blue and white petals floated down like a sprinkle of snow. Lord Jophiel smiled at them and stepped down from the platform as two servants came forward. One removed the table, and the other wiped the dried blood off their hands with a damp cloth before quickly leaving.

Cassiel took her hand and bowed to kiss the back of it. "May I have this dance?"

Dyna stepped forward as he slid a hand to her waist and led her into a sway. She stole glances at the still court. It was customary for everyone to join in the bride and groom's first dance, but no one moved yet. None of it mattered. The only thing that mattered was in his arms right now.

Cassiel pulled her flush against him, drawing a small gasp from her. "Eyes on me, Princess," he whispered in her ear.

Her cheeks pinked, but she curled her hand over his, and her anxiety melted away. He held her close as they moved to the music. Zev led Lucenna to the dance floor, and Rawn accompanied a Celestial female. The show of support meant a lot to him. They weren't alone. That indication soon led to the citizens of Hermon to join them. Then the ballroom was a sway of bodies and colorful wings.

The majority from the other Realms remained idling by the walls and the galleries in a sea of white feathers. He didn't bother to look for the one person he knew wouldn't be there. His kind was with him, and that held more meaning than anything else.

Dyna's eyebrows furrowed when she sensed his thoughts. *Your father would have come if he could.*

It's all right. Gracing me with his presence was never something he cared to do.

Cassiel told himself he didn't care, but his stomach pitched a little at recalling the last time he had waited for his father to make an appearance. He stopped expecting him to arrive a long time ago.

They danced through a few more songs before Cassiel led her off the platform. They walked the red carpet to the dais that held a single grand throne of gold with red velvet upholstery. They passed it to the massive windows that overlooked the mountain range. He moved them so they were partially hidden behind the drapes for a shred of privacy.

Dyna exhaled a heavy breath and leaned against the wall by the window. She reached up and removed her silver crown—a tiara rather—staring as it glinted in the silvery light streaming from the *Hyalus* tree outside. Every sharp point was embedded with jewels, encrusted with diamonds and large sapphires. The largest of them was at the center. Only the best, all for her.

"God of Urn."

"It's your second light gift," Cassiel said. "In case it escaped your memory, I did say I would give you a crown."

"As many as I wish," she replied faintly. "So laden with jewels, I would hardly be able to lift my head. I see you kept your word."

He pretended to look hurt. "You don't like it?"

Her wide eyes flicked up to him. "No, it's not that...I was jesting when I said..."

"I was not. This is the first of many."

"But I...I can't take this. It's too much." He sensed she worried how this would be perceived by those who accused her of landing an auspicious marriage for wealth.

"Well, if you don't want it..." Cassiel reached for the crown.

"No." She held it to her chest. "I'm a princess now, and it's mine."

He grinned. "Then you do like it?"

"I do." Dyna rose on her toes and kissed his cheek. "Thank you. If you ever decide to give me another, could it have fewer jewels? Even if it's fashioned from wood, I would be pleased."

"And have others think I'm snubbing you? I would never, stupid human." He took the tiara and placed it back on her head.

It fit her perfectly. As though she had been born royalty.

Dyna smiled at the Hermon mountains where the *Hyalus* glowed brightly in the night. Its light highlighted the joy on her soft face. "To think this all started with a tree. I was determined to reach the light in the distance, because

423

I knew somehow that was where I needed to go. And there you were, standing on the edge of it. I don't remember it yet, but the feeling I felt then is what I feel now when I am with you. Warm and safe...and home. When we met again years later, and I heard your song, I think a part of me remembered that feeling and I had to follow it." She turned to look up at him. "It wasn't your music that called out to me that day. You did."

The sound of those words fell over him like a soft veil he didn't want to let go of. Since that winter night by the tree, the impression of something was left behind. An echo of her cadence. He had strained to listen to the notes he couldn't fully grasp, tried to turn it into a song that failed to form. It plagued him, and it only faded when she reappeared again.

Cassiel cupped her cheek, brushing his thumb over the softness of her skin. *All my life, I had been searching for something, never knowing what it was...until now. My soul was waiting for you.*

It was strange how fate worked. Where such small unintentional actions could lead to something that changed the path of the future. He hadn't been living before this, because now he could finally breathe.

He brought her mouth to his as they swayed together to the soft music. Songs came and went, time leisurely passing them by as they kissed. He was simply content to exist in this moment.

Dyna's fingers played with a lock of his hair at the nape of his neck and she hummed. *They cut your hair.*

His valets had sheared a few inches off that morning. *The occasion called for it, I suppose. Not to your preference?*

Her green eyes glittered under the chandeliers as she smiled. *I may be partial to its previous length.*

Then I won't cut it again.

Perhaps I should cut mine to my chin. She laughed at his glower.

Don't you dare. He adored her long hair.

Someone cleared their throat. "Pardon the intrusion, Prince Cassiel."

"Intrusion not accepted," he said, gently running his fingers through Dyna's silken locks.

"Shall we return later?" A female voice snickered. "He's so absorbed by his bride his eyes haven't left her once. As if he's afraid she might disappear if he looks away."

That made Cassiel's stomach pitch.

At Dyna's shy smile, they glanced at their friends standing at the foot of the dais.

"Congratulations, Lord and Lady," Lucenna bowed elaborately. "May the fates and the Gods bless this auspicious union for as long as you live."

Cassiel should be annoyed at her teasing, but her earlier comment left its weight.

"There have been no whisperings today," Rawn said, reading his worry. "It appears any scheming has stalled for tonight or ended all together now that you are publicly bound."

Even so, Cassiel wouldn't risk leaving his guard down. He tensed when Dyna left his side to hug Lucenna and Zev. He followed, keeping watch on the surrounding crowd.

Sowmya and Yelrakel stood on opposite ends of the dais. The Valkyrie were on guard in every corner of the ballroom, and along the walls, and the galleries above. It would take a foolish person to attempt anything now.

"We came to see if you were hungry," Zev said. "Dinner is served."

Half of the court continued dancing while the other half drifted toward the tables with piles of food. His growing unease made his stomach churn.

"I think I will skip dinner," Cassiel said.

"Then shall we escort Lady Dyna to the table?" Rawn asked.

His chest tightened at the thought, even if she would only be across the room. He glanced at the crowd again. Some were watching, but only out of curiosity. Still, he couldn't help fearing something lurked in the corners, waiting for an opportunity to cut her from his life.

His seraph fire roiled behind the barrier, and suddenly Cassiel was grateful the bangle was forced on him. He wasn't ready for such power when it convulsed every time his instincts sparked with a consuming need to protect his mate.

Dyna's hand slipped into his. "I will stay here."

She had seen right through him, but he wouldn't let her go hungry for it.

I'm fine, really. She insisted before he called for a servant to bring a table.

Sighing, he said to the others, "Thank you for keeping watch this evening. The Valkyrie are on duty should you wish to go enjoy yourselves."

Rawn laid an arm across his chest and bowed. Zev and Lucenna did the same. "It's an honor, Prince Cassiel. We will remain on guard as well. Any threat that should present itself..."

"Will be dealt with," Zev growled.

That assurance was enough to settle his worry. This was their wedding. He didn't want it soured by the thought of what if. Right now, she was safe with him. No one was coming for them, at least not tonight.

Once their friends departed, Cassiel sat in his throne and pulled Dyna onto his lap. "Are you happy?"

"I am." She laid a hand on his cheek. "More than I can describe." But she glanced at the sapphire ring on her finger, and her smile wavered. "This..."

"It's the ring my father gave to my mother when they were wed in spirit, since he was bonded to another." Cassiel held her hand, grazing his thumb over it. "She asked me to keep it for her the night she left. She said if I became a man before her return, then I was to give it to the one who became my reason for living." He met her soft gaze. "It belongs to you now, *lev sheli.*"

Dyna blinked back the wetness in her eyes, and red locks slipped down her shoulders at the solemn tilt of her head. "This ring represents hope and a promise between you and your mother. We don't know what happened to her, and we won't until we reach Mount Ida. You deserve to have that closure first before parting with it. I don't mind waiting."

"I thought you might say that, and it's all right. This one is borrowed." Cassiel motioned at the gold band he wore. "Lent to me by Lord Norrlen. It's merely symbolism. I will hold on to the ring for as long as you wish, but it's yours, Dyna. If you want it."

"There is only one thing I want." She tugged on his collar, inviting. It was all the encouragement he needed.

He slipped his hand to her nape and lost himself in a kiss, in the dancing storm of her soul. He let himself fall through it as he had on that full moon night some months ago, knowing that was where he would always find himself, too.

CHAPTER 61

Dynalya

The wedding showed no signs of stopping by the time Dyna and Cassiel were called away to perform their vows. She was brought to her chambers first, so her ladies could help her change into a lacy nightgown with thin straps. It was beautifully designed, but hardly modest. It left her back bare, falling low on her spine, the front accentuating her chest. The floor-length mirror displayed the shadows outlining her curves. Not much was hidden in the low light.

She clutched her trembling hands together.

Lucenna adjusted the jeweled headpiece that held back Dyna's hair. "I was a little scared, too, the first time, but when it's with someone you love, there's no reason to be."

"I don't think I'm afraid," she said. "It merely feels like I'm standing on the edge of a cliff again and searching for the courage to jump."

"Again?"

Dyna laughed weakly. "I have fallen off my fair share of cliffs."

This was different, though. They would paint on each other's bodies. Her heart rate fluttered wildly to picture it. To have Cassiel's warm hands touching her without constraints...and what it could lead to.

Nothing can interrupt what must happen tonight, King Yoel had said.

She was expected to lie with her husband. Dyna wanted to, but the idea of it being an expectation, of anyone having a say in what she did with her body, robbed her of the elation that should be there. Instead, she was tense and nervous and frustrated.

"It's time," Kahna said, a lantern in her hand.

Dyna swallowed and nodded.

In the drawing room, Kahna pressed on a carved leaf in the decorative molding, and a section of the wall popped open like a door. It led to a dark corridor that only held bland stone.

"That's been there the whole time?" Dyna asked.

"Not many know about them, Your Highness. Prince Cassiel gathered you may prefer discretion."

Her thoughts stalled with the sudden change in address. "Ah, yes. Thank you."

The last thing she wanted was to go inside of the dark space, but she also didn't want to trudge through the castle halls in her nightgown either.

The thought of seeing him eased some of her tension, and Dyna took a deep breath.

Lucenna entered the dark hall and scouted the space. At her confirmation that it was secure, Dyna went in after the stewardess. The lantern's light bobbed with their silent walk, though Dyna's necklace radiated bright enough to illuminate the space. She was brought to what turned out to be another door flush against the wall. Kahna pressed on some part of the moldings, and the door opened. She entered the drawing room of Cassiel's chambers.

Lucenna gave her an encouraging smile. "Would you like me to wait in the corridor in case...?"

"N-no. That's all right."

"Then I will return to the festivities with Zev and Rawn. A swarm of Valkyrie are standing guard outside the main door and on the roof. At a respectable distance, of course. Well, enjoy." With a last playful wink, Lucenna closed the hidden door, and it vanished seamlessly into the wall.

She sensed Cassiel was in the other room, and that he was equally aware of her presence. A tremble trickled through her chest, and Dyna closed her eyes, searching for valor. After another breath, she slowly pushed open the door and entered his bedroom.

Cassiel glanced up from where he stood by the bedside table and went still. His grip on the bowl he held tightened. His mouth parted, and his gaze rove over her slowly, dropping to her bare feet, over her the nightgown, and back to her face.

"*Elyōn...azor li,*" he said under his breath.

The heated whisper sounded like a prayer that begged for help, and it sent a rush of heat to her face.

Cassiel's black trousers ended at his calves, and he'd rolled his unbuttoned white tunic to his elbows. Her eyes traveled from his broad shoulders to his chiseled chest and kept going down, taking in the lines of his sculpted abdomen.

Putting the bowl down on the table, Cassiel's bare feet leisurely made their way across the room to her. She watched him come, her heart thrumming with something like panic.

He stopped.

"Dynalya." Her name fell softly between them. Cassiel searched her eyes, perhaps gauging her reaction to him, before taking the last step. He lifted her hand and pressed his lips to her fingers. "You don't have to do anything you don't wish to do."

"But—"

"No one will decide the makings of our marriage bed. The only permission I require is yours."

The breath that had been trapped in Dyna's lungs released in a low exhale.

He trailed his fingers down her cheek, and the stiffness in her shoulders melted away. "We will never do anything you are not ready for."

Dyna dropped her head on his chest, closing the space between them. She held onto his presence, the solidity giving her a foundation to stand on. Her relief couldn't be hidden in the bond.

"A lot has happened so fast. I...I need a moment to breathe. Would you be disappointed if we didn't...?"

"No," he answered without hesitation. "We came together in a way neither of us planned, missing too many steps I should have taken." Cassiel leaned in closer, his nose grazing hers. "You deserve a mate who fully knows your heart until you are willing to let me know your body."

His rich voice vibrated in her ear, sending an electrifying hum through her that turned into a sinking heat as it lowered into her stomach. Simply putting the power in her hands...it made her earlier nerves vanish as a new sensation filled her. One that heated her skin and thumbed her pulse with a different rhythm.

He trailed his hand from her shoulder to her elbow. "Your geas."

She glanced down at where he stroked her skin free of any marks. "I had it moved."

The path of his hand paused, and she knew he was trying to guess where it was now. "Would you like to hold our vows?"

It meant he would see her bare, touch her, and make promises they would carry for the rest of their lives. For that, she was ready. Dyna swallowed and nodded.

"Shall I go first?" he asked.

She nodded again, highly aware of the course of his fingers leisurely traveling to her wrist, caressing gentle circles in her palm. Every stroke left behind tingles shooting up her arm.

"All right," Cassiel murmured. Their fingers wove together, and he walked backward, leading her to the bowl on his bedside table. It contained a black solution she assumed must be the paint and a brush. "Where should I start, Princess?"

It was odd to hear the title, as warm as it was. Like a heavy coat she wasn't accustomed to yet. His breath feathered down her neck as he pulled her closer. She tried not to think about how much she could feel the strength of his body against hers, but her mind was turning foggy as she admired the defined planes of his chest and torso up close. He hummed in question, and she realized she hadn't answered him yet.

Her voice came out breathy and unsure. "Leg?"

The drift of his hand paused, and he looked down at her thighs. He seemed to stare at something with a sudden intensity that she gasped when he lowered to the ground.

"Cassiel, you're a prince. You must never kneel."

His silver eyes looked up at her as if she was the beginning and end of his every thought. "I will always kneel for you."

The ardent heat behind that affirmation made her heart skip a beat.

He motioned for her to sit on the cushioned stool next to him. His attention slid down again to what had been his focus before. He took the hem of her nightgown and slid it up her leg. She tried not to flush at the reveal of the ugly scar on her knee left behind by the grindylows. Her stomach jumped when the golden chain of the garter on her upper thigh was unveiled. Her lady's maid insisted she wore it.

By the way Cassiel's eyes seemed to flame, Dyna wasn't sure if that was a good thing.

The chains glinted as his thumb slid beneath the garter, pulling it taught. Little cascades of shivers went down her leg. Then, ever so *slowly*, he dragged the garter down. The feel of the fabric, the coolness of the chains, and his touch trailing after it like fire were doing odd things to her breathing. Every part of her was aware of him. The way he touched her was so gentle, like she was something easily broken, something so delicate. Cassiel's other hand rested on the back of her leg for support. His palm was hot, almost scorching, sending an indescribable heat flooding through her body.

Gathering... somewhere new.

Cassiel was so close his nose grazed her leg as he seemed to inhale her scent. He was enraptured by what he was doing, completely entranced. Not daring to move, Dyna's chest rose and fell with shallow inhalations. The garter dropped to her ankle, and he gently lifted her leg to slide it off. Resting her foot on his knee, Cassiel pressed a kiss to her inner thigh, and Dyna thought she might lose her ability to breathe.

The sensation left behind an imprint.

An invisible, heated mark created by his mouth.

"Hold here, please," Cassiel said softly, lifting the hem to the crease of her thigh. He brought the bowl to rest beside him and lifted the brush. At the first cool touch of the paint, she jumped. The brush moved smoothly in his hand as he drew swirly strokes in a language she didn't understand. He was the artist, and she was the canvas. Each stroke was beautiful, coursing down her thigh, over her knee, to the end of her ankle.

His gaze lifted to meet hers, and he translated the vow in a soft murmur through her mind. *From now and through the ages, I will forever be yours until I fade among the stars.*

Emotion swelled through her. The vow settled on the bond, weaving through her like a thread.

Dipping the brush in the bowl of paint again, Cassiel stood. She shivered from the cool touch of the soft, wet bristles gliding down her shoulder. His touch held a power that kept her grounded without having to speak.

Cassiel continued painting, translating every vow for her.

On her left arm: *I will have nor hold no other but you.*

On her right leg: *I will live each day worthy of you.*

Her vision blurred.

Cassiel gently painted on the side of her throat to her collarbone. *Every part of me, all that I have and will ever gain, belongs to you.*

He took her chin, thumb brushing her lips. "Two more vows, *lev sheli.* Where shall I put them?"

"What does *lev sheli* mean?" she asked faintly.

His expression softened, and he pressed a kiss to her temple. "My heart."

That soft confession sent tears spilling down her cheeks. A gentle swipe of his fingertip carried them away.

Cassiel was her husband. Her love. She trusted him with her heart, her mind, and her body. There was nothing more for her to fear tonight.

Dyna stood and lifted her nightgown over her head, bringing the silky fabric to cover her chest. Her skin pebbled in the cool air. She wore what barely counted as undergarments. Lacy white fabric that covered enough. Cassiel kept his eyes locked on her face. Wrapping her arms around herself, securing the disheveled nightgown in place, she turned around.

He was so close, the warmth coming off his body pressed against her bare back.

"You surprise me at every turn." The hoarse sound of his voice made her stomach tighten. "But then, you always have."

Dyna stood completely still. Then she felt the first stroke at her nape. Instead of a brush, he painted with his fingers. The impression of his touch was different, measured, and tender, exploring her skin. She followed the path of every unhurried caress, traveling down her back in winding trails.

When he reached the end of her spine, Cassiel softly blew on the wet paint to dry it, making her shiver. "*Eheye lach magen kol od nishmati beapi.* I will be your shield for as long as I live and breathe."

Dyna released a shallow exhale and faced him again. His silvery eyes held hers a moment before dipping to her feet. They slowly traveled from her ankles to her thighs, studying the curves and shadows. With a ragged breath, his fiery stare raked over her undergarments to her navel, then...up. Heat flared in his eyes. It was a look she'd seen only once before—in the Moors, when he'd been drunk with desire.

He found where the geas was placed.

The elaborate design of an oak tree spanned her ribs beneath her left breast. Cassiel's warm hand curled over it as he continued his perusal along the swells of her cleavage, across the scars on her collarbone, and finally to her face. His expression softened as he reached for her cheek, his thumb leaving a featherlight trail along her jaw.

Her heart hummed with his warmth, his strength, his breath falling on her skin. The depth of his gaze, how much adoration lived in them—it made her feel alive.

"Lay back for me," he murmured.

Dyna glanced at the bed behind him, and her blood swirled. A flush heated her face, spreading down her neck. She sat on the edge of the bed and lay flat on her back with her feet on the floor.

Cassiel placed a sheet over her from the waist down. The dignity and care of that action swelled another ball of emotion in her chest. He placed the bowl beside her, and she tracked the movement of his fingers as they dipped inside the black paint. He leaned a little over her, seeming to contemplate where to place his final vow.

His proximity was hard to ignore, and every nerve tensed with anticipation. She jolted at the first glide of his fingertip at the top center of her torso. This time it felt twice as intense, the touch somehow branding her skin.

His other hand came to rest on her hip, sending electrical shocks through all the nerve endings in her body. Her eyes briefly fluttered closed at the sensation. The temperature of her body rose a few degrees with each stroke. He gently drew on her stomach, completely engrossed by what he was doing. She remained frozen in place, aware of how the contact against her skin awakened little fires all across her body.

But this promise was different.

It was protective, possessive, and consuming.

His fingers inched past her navel, and a riot of warm sensations sprouted in her stomach, heat sinking to startling places. Her lips parted in a shaky breath. Their eyes locked, and the silver in his irises turned darker. His breathing was heavier, and a blush rushed to her face when she realized he felt her excitement.

He leaned over her with his hand bracing beside her head, caging her with his body. He was so close his breath fanned through her hair.

"Dyna…" his velvety voice said into her ear. "Everything I do, no matter how painful, will always be to protect you."

Every word of that vow seemed to sear itself into her soul.

She could hardly form a thought to reply. Her pulse sped as his lips brushed over her shoulder, insufferably light. Every worshipful press of his mouth was like a spell.

A flicker of magic meant to dissolve her.

As if it cost a great effort, Cassiel dragged himself away, leaving cool air to replace him. He placed the bowl on the bedside table. By the stiffness entering his shoulders, the mood had shifted.

Did she do something wrong?

Dyna sat up as he retrieved her nightgown. Without looking at her, Cassiel slipped it back over her head, and the hem settled on her waist.

A soft crinkle came from her pocket with the slip of scroll where she had written her vows in the Celestial language with Noemi's help. But they now seemed weak and trivial compared to his profound promises.

He stood, and Dyna caught his wrist, her feet landing on the plush carpet as she rose. She placed a hand on the broad stretch of muscle on his chest. She glanced up to find his dark lashes closed, casting soft shadows over the planes of his cheeks. In the dim light, she studied the alluring silhouette of his features. Heat hovered off him, and she wasn't sure if it was his contained fire or her proximity that affected him.

Cassiel.

A quiver traveled down her spine to her toes when his heavy-lidded eyes met hers. They burned with the same heat inside of her now. She glanced at Cassiel's mouth, and her lips ached for his.

She leaned in, but he stepped back, and that one little movement surprisingly stung.

"We should continue before the paint dries," he said.

"Right." Her body cooled, and all the previous heat rushed to her face. She'd gotten caught up in the moment without thinking that perhaps he wasn't—

"No." By Cassiel's frown, he had caught her complex emotions flickering through the bond before she could hide them. "My sweet fate, do you realize how much power you have over me?"

Dyna was the one who felt helpless when it came to him. He held some sort of force that drew her in.

She fell still when he leaned over her. She stopped breathing as his nose drifted over the sensitive skin of her chest, never touching, yet an electric charge followed the trail.

"Gods, your scent." Cassiel lifted his head, and his mouth hovered over hers.

She waited for the kiss, internally begged for it, but his nose brushed faintly over her cheek to her earlobe. Her breath caught as he glided down her neck to her fluttering pulse, and his tongue flicked over it, as if he couldn't resist a taste. A soft whimper escaped her. From his throat rolled a low rumble that vibrated all the way to her center.

"I worship every single part of you, Dynalya. Don't you ever think for one moment I don't want you."

His shield on the bond dropped, and she was hit with his nerves, his desire, and his blush-inducing need to touch her—*everywhere.*

"If I kiss you right now, I may not be able to stop."

"Perhaps I don't want you to stop," Dyna breathlessly admitted.

His eyes heated, his dilated pupils absorbing the silver. The hesitation was so thick she felt when it snapped.

"Sod it." Cassiel grabbed her waist and hauled her to him. She barely had a moment to gasp before his mouth crashed into hers.

CHAPTER 62

Cassiel

Cassiel could do nothing but surrender to her. To the rhythm of her heartbeat and the warmth of her skin. To her lips. Each kiss was yearning. Layered in adoration. Dyna kissed him as though he was the air she needed, and she couldn't go another moment without it. His entire body bowed over his mate with some indescribable need to envelop himself around her.

His legs nearly buckled when she finally touched him, too. The muscles of his back constricted as her hands slowly explored the span of it. A soft groan rumbled in his throat at the light scrape of her nails. Dyna's fingers continued their perusal until she reached the crease of his shoulder blades where they met his wings.

Cassiel lurched. He caught her arms, staring at her for a stunned moment. "You…" came his panting response. He swallowed and pinned her wrists to her sides. "You should not do that."

"Did I hurt you?"

"Um, no. My wings are merely very … sensitive."

"Oh." Dyna glanced down. "*Oh.*" She reddened and ducked her head. "I'm sorry."

"Don't be. You are the only one who makes me feel things I thought I was incapable of or too broken to feel." Cassiel rubbed the back of his neck. "But perhaps we should finish our vows before we get carried away again."

A shy smile graced her face. At the flick of Dyna's hand, a green mist lifted the bowl off the nightstand and brought it to hover next to them. The black paint inside glistened beneath its light.

She bit her lip. "No looking until I'm finished."

Cassiel closed his eyes. "Yes, Princess."

A perceptible pause followed. Then came a soft crinkle of paper and another minute of silence that he nearly peeked. The bond vibrated with her nerves. He understood how she felt. To be able to touch her freely had been nerve-wracking.

Cassiel tensed with anticipation as he tried to guess where she might start. He nearly jumped at the first stroke of her cool, wet fingers on his chest. All of his attention locked on the shapes that left blazing trails behind. He was secretly pleased she didn't bother with the brush. It felt more meaningful somehow. To mark him with her touch the way his touch had marked her.

"Why did you think you were incapable of...arousal?" came her tentative question.

It wasn't the personal nature of it that made him hesitate to reply. It was the answer. Being open didn't come easy, but Dyna had a way of disarming him.

"I suppose I thought it merely unlikely," he said finally. "Females didn't entice me, not that any found me suitable. I had no interest in love-mates. I saw what such ill-advised vulnerability did to my father and mother, and its result. I did not want that."

His life presented love as a fantasy. A delusion. He never wanted to be deceived by it.

"What changed?"

Cassiel exhaled a low breath. "You."

Her fingers paused above his shoulder.

"I...tried to hate you," he confessed. "I *wanted* to hate you. I thought if I was cruel and made you despise me as I was used to, I could ignore what you were doing to me."

He regretted those moments. When his lashing tongue hurt her out of cowardice, to avoid being the one hurt first. Not seeing her face now made it easier to tell her the truth. That aversion was all he knew most of his life.

"I did not know what it was. This new feeling. It felt a little like fear and helplessness. Like falling out of the sky. Mixed with a longing to have you simply look at me. Your acknowledgement somehow became what I craved. Whenever you did, it was like regaining something that was missing. Something I had lost. I was torn between the need to escape you, and guard you, and every passing day, I became more and more powerless to resist it."

He opened his eyes and met those emerald pools looking back at him in the way she always did. Like he was something important. *Someone.* To her. It meant so much to have her see him for who he was, that he didn't know how he would react if one day she didn't. But the worst thing? Would be if she suddenly saw him the way he saw himself.

A mistake.

To want something so desperately the way he wanted her was terrifying, because it left him with a question if this could be permitted. Could he take it? Was this truly meant for someone like him? The more he envisioned a life with her, the more he feared losing it. Feared that the world would change its mind and take her away.

"I'm...still afraid," Cassiel admitted. He lightly stroked the back of his hand down her jaw to her chin. "I believed for the longest time I was never meant to be happy. I somehow managed to find a sliver of it, and the thought of having it taken from me..." His voice dropped to a whisper. "It makes something dark and cold like ice weave through the flames that burn for you."

His Seraph fire—it only surfaced when he wanted to protect her. The brass bangle hanging from his wrist glinted in the low light. It had a tight hold on his power, but Cassiel suspected it wouldn't be able to hold him back when it came to her.

"Translate for me," Dyna said, and she crumpled up the scrap of paper she held. "I will fill our days together with the joy that is meant only for us."

Cassiel exhaled a shaky breath, the back of his throat tightening. He formed the ancient literatures in her mind and Dyna's fingertips continued their course down his arm.

He glanced at where she had previously written *I will love you* on his chest. She amended it with another promise. *I will love you through whatever darkness may come, through the ice, and through the flame.*

Cassiel stilled.

She loved him? She...loved him.

It shouldn't be a question after everything Dyna had done, and every declaration she had made. Yet to hear her voice give shape to the letters, it made his soul quiver. The back of his eyes stung as something lodged in his throat. He hadn't heard those words from anyone—in years. So much so that he doubted such a thing could be real.

Until he, at last, understood how it felt. To want to see someone, to be with them, and share every thought and mood with them, to have and to hold, to dream with, to *wish* with, and to want them with you every step through life.

That was right here.

His eyes fluttered closed as an electrical hum sank down his body when her fingers swept the last stroke down his abdomen, so close to his navel.

On his left arm she wrote, *Even when the world crumbles and we fade among the cosmos, I will still be yours.*

She lowered to her knees at his feet, and his next thoughts stalled. Heat whirled through his veins at the adoration in her gaze. She held onto the back of his thigh for support as she painted over his legs with a vow that echoed her confession beneath the willow. *My heart will always be filled with none other than you.*

Every single word imprinted itself on his soul. With each light stroke of her fingers, his mind hummed with flashes of hers, the greens and golds making him sigh. He could lose himself there forever if she let him. Dive in so deep, he would never want to leave.

Dyna stood and reached for his tunic with her trembling hands. The soft white fabric slid down his shoulders until it fluttered to their feet. She took her time admiring him, and air passed shallowly through his teeth at the desire on her face. Never had anyone looked at him like that before.

With want.

But his growing haze vanished when she went behind him. Cassiel stiffened and tucked his wings against his back. Not with her proximity, but with sudden self-consciousness.

"If I were to pick my favorite feature about you, aside from your eyes, it would be your wings," Dyna said. "When you wrap me with them, it's like an embrace of midnight. They are perfect, *kohav.*"

Star, she called him.

Something shifted inside of him again, as she made another fissure in the rock he carried within his hollow chest and chipped it away. So many rotten pieces had fallen, it left the softest parts uncovered.

Parts he didn't know he had.

Cassiel listened to the soft crackle in the hearth, breathed in the burning wood to steady himself. "I spent all my life wishing they were white."

"White is boring." She pressed a kiss on the left wing, then his right. Another shudder went through them, and his wings relaxed, exposing his back again. At the show of his trust, a sudden protectiveness flooded through the bond with that same dark coldness he had described, but it came from Dyna. Her next vow fell like embers off her tongue. "I will protect every part of you with all that I am and avenge every wrong done against you."

Her fingers marked the ardent vow down his spine, and he thought of the fearsome goddess who had obliterated the throne room on his behalf.

"I may be a healer, but nothing will stop me from protecting those I love."

Something thickened in his throat to hear her say that.

Dyna came around and her misted eyes looked up at him. "I will never let anyone take these away." She stroked his wing, gliding her fingers down the shimmering black feathers. He quaked at the sensation tingling through his body, and it gathered in places he tried to ignore. "Or make you feel less than for it." She stroked the other and his head fell back with a groan. "What does it feel like when I touch you?"

"It feels..." Cassiel cut off with a choked moan when she traced the margins, meeting his shoulder blades. He caught her waist. "Don't tempt me, *lev sheli*. If you continue to do that, you will be responsible for what happens. I have only so much restraint."

And every passing second was proving harder to keep it in place.

Her every touch was delicious, agonizing torture.

As if Dyna sensed it, she closed the inch gap between them, bringing her body flushed against his. Then she rose on her toes and her lips brushed his neck. Flames licked at where she touched.

He gripped her hips. "Can you...do that again?"

She kissed the same spot, and the flames shot through him.

Cassiel devoured her mouth as if it was the first time. Her arms snaked around his neck and wove her fingers through his hair. She rose on her toes to kiss along his jaw to his ear. A scatter of new sensations sank deep, sparking an instinct to throw her on the bed and claim her. A rumble rolled through his chest in warning. He pressed her tightly against him, where he could no longer hide his want. She slid her hands down his torso, trailing over the mounds of muscle stretching across his abdomen, and landed on the waistband of his trousers hanging low on his hips.

Cassiel's hands halted on her waist. "What are you doing?" he asked tentatively.

"Exploring?"

He chuckled airily in surprise. "What happened to the Dyna who feared walking into my room not an hour ago?"

"She grew a little brave." Dyna slowly traced the arch of his exposed hipbone, causing the surrounding muscle to constrict. "And curious."

Swallowing against the tightness in his throat, Cassiel searched her eyes. They gleamed in the darkness with a flare that had his pulse racing under her fingertips. The bond danced between them, throbbing in a way that demanded to fulfill the last step that would seal their union completely. Her earlier anxiety had faded to a dim memory and his was quickly following.

Being wanted, standing in this room half unclothed, all of it was still dreamlike to him, yet there was nowhere else he could imagine being than right here.

"I don't mean to confuse you with my earlier misgivings, but...I want to see you. To know you," she said quietly. "And to have you know me."

Cassiel held perfectly still, struggling to hold on to the restraint he swore to maintain, but she was making it *increasingly* difficult with the way she was looking at him. He gave his word they wouldn't do anything she wasn't ready for. That it would be her decision.

And she was telling him she was making one now.

"To know you..." His hands drifted up her shoulders to her face. Dyna's eyes fluttered closed as he leaned in close and breathed in her honeysuckle scent he couldn't get enough of. He trailed his mouth across her cheek, faint as a whisper. "I would need to learn what pleases you," Cassiel said, his lips so close to hers. "To learn what makes your body...sing."

The pleasant sting of her nails dug into his forearms, as if Dyna needed something to keep her standing. She was trembling.

He lifted her hand and kissed the inside of her wrist. "You have all the power here."

"I've never...I don't...know where to start." She weakly laughed, and he sensed her embarrassment at her inexperience. "Have you...?"

"You are my first in everything, Dyna. I suppose we will learn together."

Cassiel lifted her chin to him and lightly traced her lips with his once, twice, in the way that made her pulse dance. Then he sealed her mouth with a kiss. It wasn't long before their slow kisses grew hungrier and heated.

He walked backward, leading her away from the bed. A deliberate decision, he sensed, she was both relieved and disappointed by. He sat on the couch by the hearth pulled her onto his lap. They were a tangle of limbs and fabric and exposed skin. Her shy touches grew bolder with each one of his, and he no longer stopped her from exploring every part of him. His heart hammered as a languid heat climbed in his body with every press of her mouth. Dyna's red hair curtained around their faces, veiling them together in this moment made for them.

The room was a fog of intimate caresses and demolishing kisses. Their touches became a competition of reactions, creating sounds he never thought to make or to draw out of her. He felt every shattering feeling she did, and it hummed through the bond with wild currents. All so overwhelming, he reminded himself to breathe. But he had long stopped fighting the effect she had on him.

Tonight, he would only touch. Only savor and tease his desires.

Completely surrendering to the new discoveries, he found in the sensation of his mate. Her body felt so soft and warm. He slid his hands up her thighs beneath her nightgown and chased the music of her soft whimpers. When Cassiel found exactly what pleased her, it sparked a sensation that felt a little like taking to the skies. Each stroke of his fingers left him drunk on every cry and twitch on her face.

He lived for it. Breathed it. Because in this moment, he saw how much this wonder of a person became the center of his existence. Then Dyna took him in her hands, rendering him completely at her mercy. Cassiel succumbed to the pleasure that carried them higher and higher until they were both gone.

CHAPTER 63

Dynalya

Dyna smiled drowsily at the moonlight streaming past the curtains. She was sleepy, but she wanted to wait for Cassiel to return with the food they both desperately needed. Pushing off the blanket, she rose off the couch and stretched, shaking herself awake. She glanced at her reflection in the mirror by the wardrobe. Red tresses fell in messy waves around Dyna's face. Her skin was flushed, and lips were swollen. The evidence of everywhere Cassiel had been.

Clutching her wrinkled nightgown, Dyna closed her eyes, still feeling the phantom caress of his hands and lips. She traced the black trails left behind by his vows. Some were beginning to fade and would be gone by morning. Invisible, but always present in their bond. Permanently sealed once she was ready to join herself to him.

Dyna blushed at how little her nightgown hid. He wouldn't mind if she borrowed some clothes. From the wardrobe, she pulled out trousers and a tunic. The soft sound of a door creaked open in the drawing room by the time she finished dressing.

"Was there anything left?" Dyna teased as she fastened the waistband.

There had been piles of food at the wedding, but hundreds of guests. The kitchens were closed now, and the servants would have long retired for the night, so expectations were low.

She folded up the long sleeves as he entered behind her. "Please tell me you at least brought some bread."

He didn't answer.

The hairs stood on the back of her neck at the missing roiling energy that belonged to her mate. Dyna fell completely still, facing the balcony where moonlight glinted over the polished stone floors.

Cassiel, she called through the bond.

Patience, lev sheli. She could hear the smile and warmth in his voice. *I reached the kitchen, but no one is here. Who thought it was a great idea to put it so deep in the castle? I had to descend three levels of stairs.*

Dyna filled her hands with magic, but a cold blade met her throat.

"If you struggle or shout for help, I will plunge this knife through your skull," a rough voice snarled in her ear. "Your death will break him first. When he is writhing on the ground, I will hack off his head and throw him off the side of the mountain, where his filthy blood will be buried beneath the snow."

Horror rocked through her at the vivid picture that was created in her mind. Whoever stood behind her wasn't someone she had met or heard before, but his hatred was real. Dyna could feel exactly what he thought of Cassiel and the half-breeds.

But his rough voice didn't match the hiss Zev described the night of the festival. There had to be more people involved. The only way he could have snuck into their room past the Valkyrie was because he had help.

This was her chance to find out who was behind the plot. She wasn't the main target, otherwise he would have killed her already.

"I won't struggle," Dyna said.

The assailant wrapped black fabric over her eyes, tying it around her head. His large hand grabbed her arm next and slapped something cold on her wrist. Essence vanished from her veins and she bit back a gasp at the witch's bangle.

After quickly tying her hands together, he yanked, and she tripped blindly over her bare feet as he half dragged her across the room at a quick pace. The warmth of the hearth faded when they reached the drawing room. He moved past the main door, and she knew where they were going before he shoved her into the hidden corridor. Her feet landed on the gritty stone floor.

I found some bread, Cassiel said, sounding rather proud of himself.

Dyna coughed on the dusty air, catching in her throat. *Cassiel, please stay calm.* His contentment instantly switched to alarm at her cautious tone. *When you return, I won't be here. They've come for me.*

His panic barreled through her, and she sensed he was running. *I'm coming! It's all right. I'm choosing to go. I will find out who is behind this.*

What? Dyna, no!

Be prepared for anything. She threw up her shield and layered it with steel.

Cassiel banged against it, and the castle seemed to shake with his full fury. His Seraph fire convulsed through the bond. It was clawing its way out, and nothing would hold him back.

"He's coming," she said. "Take me where you planned and quickly, before he finds you."

The assailant pulled her through another doorway. The stuffy corridor was replaced with fresh air and an icy breeze slipping through her clothing. He hooked her under his arm and she heard the beat of wings. The whoosh of wind stole her into the air. Dyna dug her fingers into the assailant's clothing, clinging on for dear life. The bitter air pricked at her like a thousand needles. She wasn't properly dressed for the weather. It was so cold it stole away all of her body heat, and she was beginning to go numb.

How far was he taking her?

The answer came when he let go and she fell through the air. Dyna's shriek cut off when she landed on the frozen rocky ground, and pain throbbed against her scraped palms and knees.

"Where are we?" another voice sobbed. "Who are you?"

Dyna pushed off the ground and sat back on her heels. "Sarrai?"

The celestial female cried harder. "Why are we here? Did you do this?"

"Where are you?" Dyna stretched out her bound hands and searched blindly for her. Why was she here?

"I can't see," Sarrai cried. "Why is this happening?"

"Come to me. Follow my voice."

"Silence," the assailant barked behind her.

Across from Dyna came the soft scuff of boots. Someone else was here.

"My uncle is Gadriel Nephele, the Lord of Nazar," Sarrai hissed. "He will not stand for this. You will be punished if you—Don't touch me! Let me go!"

The sounds of a struggle filled the cave, feet wildly kicking at the ground. There came a sharp snap and an excruciating scream that pierced Dyna's ears.

"Sarrai!" Something hit the rock wall beside her and a dusting of snow dropped on top of her head. "Sarrai?" She reached out and felt a leg. Sarrai quietly sobbed. "I'm here. It will be all right. They will come for us."

"No one is coming ... My uncle must be the one behind this. He must want to be rid of me..." she cried weakly. "I didn't tell him..."

Dyna moved closer to her, feeling her shoulder. "Tell him what?"

"Asiel...I didn't tell him I love him...but now I am surely unwanted..."

Then her fingers found bloodied feathers and broken bones. "Why?" She screamed at whoever brought them here, trembling with anger. "Merely because she is different? Well, we all bleed the same color." Dyna looked out at where she guessed they stood. "Remove these bindings and let me show you."

Someone moved closer and a faint citrus scent drifted in her nose.

"That's enough."

Dyna stiffened at the sound of that voice. She should have known.

"Leave us," he ordered.

Footsteps retreated, then she heard the flap of wings fading away. The blindfold was removed, and Dyna met Malakel's sneer. He was the one behind everything? No, not completely. Otherwise, they would have recognized his voice.

His mouth curled with disgust at the paint on her neck. "What is it like to bed a Nephilim?"

Dyna spat in his face. If he wanted to be revolting, then she would give it right back. Malakel reeled back with a curse. She checked on Sarrai, but she wasn't moving.

"Lady Sarrai?" Dyna searched for a pulse and exhaled in relief when she found it.

Sarrai's lashes fluttered weakly. One of her gray wings was broken at the arch. She must have fainted from the pain. All she wore was a nightgown. Her skin was pale, body frozen to the touch.

Dyna looked out at where they were. At first, she saw nothing but snow and wind, until she noticed the white glow of the *Hyalus* tree far below. They were in a shallow cave on the side of the Hermon Mountains.

"You are vile." Malakel wiped his cheek with a handkerchief. "Like him."

"You call *me* vile? Look at what they did to her!"

He hardly spared Sarrai a glance. "She will heal."

"Why did you bring her here? What do you want with us?"

"From you? Nothing but Cassiel's downfall." Malakel leaned against the rock wall opposite of her and crossed his arms. Instead of his usual silk robes, he wore grand armor trimmed in gold with a gilded sword at his hip. Beneath his arm, he held a helmet molded with the shape of wings on the sides. "We both heard the same thing outside that door," he said, each word cutting. "I will not allow him to take my throne. He has stolen enough."

Gods, with everything that happened in the day, she had forgotten about Malakel.

Dyna shook her head. "Cassiel doesn't want to be king. If you would only talk to him—"

"You don't reason with abominations. You eliminate them." He narrowed his eyes at her hatefully. "This was probably your plan from the beginning, wasn't it, witch? Why have a prince when you can have a king?"

Before she could reply, another Celestial dropped from the sky and landed on the ledge outside of the cave. Snowflakes coated his blond hair and armor.

Asiel's wide eyes locked on her. "What is this?"

"This is bait." Malakel straightened. "How else did you expect to get him here?"

Asiel stormed toward them. "I didn't agree to this! Cassiel would have answered the challenge without the abduction of his mate." He spotted Sarrai's unconscious form and his chest heaved at the sight of her bloody feathers. "What have you done?"

"I said they are *bait*. You don't want Hermon. You want *her*. Near and dear as she is to you. Well, you cannot have one without the other. Did you truly think I would trust you to go through with our plan without the proper motivation?"

Sarrai moaned weakly as Dyna worked to reset her wing. The bone struggled to heal. Those cretins nearly snapped it off.

Malakel twirled a knife in his hand. "Challenge Cassiel and retake the Realm. I will take everything else. Defy me and I will defile Sarrai's blood by mixing it with this witch. Then you will never have her." He shrugged. "She is beneath you, anyway, cousin. Better to find yourself a pureblooded female instead."

Asiel was shaking. There was nothing but pure wrath etching his face. Dyna had only seen that look on one other person.

"You're not very smart," she said, scooting out of the way. "Or you would know better than to harm someone's mate."

Asiel threw himself at Malakel with a roar.

The princes crashed into the wall. Asiel drove his fist into him with a blind rage before Malakel kicked him off. They drew their flaming swords and took their fight to the skies.

Sarrai's wings twitched under Dyna's grip. The flesh was working hard to reattach itself. She tore a strip off her tunic and tied it around the wing for better support.

"Asiel?" Sarrai's lashes fluttered weakly.

"He's here," Dyna said. "They came."

In the distance, a blaze as bright as a blue sun cleaved through the vast night with the speed of a comet, turning everything in its path to ash.

Malakel saw him coming.

He disarmed Asiel with one skilled move and slashed through his stomach with the next. White feathers trailed after him as he plummeted from the air and crashed outside the cave. Dyna ran out to Asiel. Smoke spiraled from his torso, scorched black. He was unconscious and terribly wounded, but his blood was already working to heal him.

"I challenge you, Cassiel Soaraway!" Malakel's voice boomed in the night.

The blue comet halted.

Her mate was unrecognizable. He hovered among the stars as a creature of pure flame with molten blue eyes. Embers drifted off him with every flap of his wings. Cassiel's face didn't betray a hint of emotion, while his writhing fury coated the air.

He only came for one thing.

To kill the one who abducted her, and he had his target.

"I challenge you for everything you own," Malakel said. "Including your life."

CHAPTER 64

Cassiel

Cassiel landed on the mountain with a scatter of cerulean flames. The last of the witch's bangle crumbled off his wrist as he withdrew his Seraph fire, and it vanished, leaving his black clothing untouched. He completely ignored Malakel and strode to his mate. Dyna looked up at him from where she knelt by Asiel.

"He will live," she said.

Stupid human.

The only one he cared about right now was her. He spotted a few scratches, and her lack of shoes, but she was otherwise unhurt. His chest heaved with a deep breath he needed to hold himself back from snapping. His heart still hadn't calmed from the moment he realized she was taken. No, she *chose* to put herself in harm's way.

"Are you all right?" Cassiel asked once he got a hold of himself. Dyna nodded and took his offered hand. He wrapped her in a cloak of his fire to warm her body until she stopped shivering. *Do we need to discuss your tendency for recklessness, lev sheli?*

A faint smile touched her lips. *I came to find out who our enemies are.*

Yes, well, she certainly did that.

His thoughts stalled when he saw the brass bangle on Dyna's wrist. Sickness rolled in his stomach. It matched the one that had been placed on him. He would think about that later. Cassiel pinched the bangle between his fingers and it turned black with a coil of blue flame before collapsing in his palm. Dyna gasped softly.

Apparently, ensorcelled trinkets couldn't hold him back anymore.

"Did you hear me, Cassiel?"

He idly glanced at Malakel over his shoulder. "I heard you quite clearly—as did all the Realms."

Dyna looked past him at the hundreds of dots of color hovering by the castle. Some in white, others in blue, or gold. They were the Celestials Cassiel had woken when he tore through the corridors on a rampage, and others he had called. The tiny purple glow of Lucenna's power showed where she stood on a balcony with Zev and Rawn.

He had ordered no one to interfere.

If Malakel hadn't shouted for a challenge, Cassiel would have disintegrated him within seconds. He was infuriated enough to do it, but the law was the law. He couldn't back down from a challenge when so many were watching. Forfeiting was the same as defeat.

Not even his uncle could stop it.

Lord Jophiel and Lord Gadriel flew in front of the gathered crowd, with the Valkyrie keeping anyone from getting close. Malakel had also called his own witnesses. Celestials in purple and red stood by the *Hyalus* tree below, Lord Raziel and Lord Hallel with them.

Everyone silently watched.

It didn't shock him to find they supported Malakel. Lord Gadriel was most likely on his side, as well.

But why do this?

This is what Malakel wanted, Dyna said through the bond. *A grand audience to watch him overthrow you.*

That had always been him. Someone who demanded everyone's full attention. *Then I shall not disappoint him.*

Removing his jacket, Cassiel passed it to Dyna for her to wear. Instead, she covered Sarrai with it and levitated Asiel to lie next to her. "I've got them. We will be fine here."

He drew *Esh Shamayim* free from its sheath. The cerulean flames coating the blade danced in his vision as he walked to the edge of the landing and faced his opponent.

"What is the purpose of this challenge, Malakel?" Cassiel called up to him, because he had yet to understand. "Is your hate for me so deep that you must deny me any peace, or do you merely seek any excuse to get rid of me?"

Malakel sneered. "The plan was always to get rid of you."

It shouldn't have hurt the way it did, not after living for years with his brother's spite, but to hear there wasn't even a shred of care sent a bitter pang through his chest. Despite everything, Cassiel still searched his face for some wavering. For some strand of what bonded them as family.

But it had never been there.

How different would their relationship be if he had been born a pureblood?

"I'm not without decency," Malakel said, his white wings fluttering in the wind. "I would have allowed you to live with your little witch, but the moment you came after my throne, it accelerated your removal."

Cassiel stared at him, dumbfounded. "What?"

Dyna's voice drifted in his mind. *Your father...he still plans to make you High King.*

The news gripped his lungs. That can't be right. He was made the Lord of Hermon Ridge.

"I always knew Father favored you," Malakel continued. "I endured your presence long enough. All will bear witness to your defeat tonight. The prize will be everything you own. Your wings. Your title. Your place in the Realms. I will erase you and reclaim everything you stole from me."

Erase.

As if he were a blight to remove.

Fire crackled around Cassiel's fists, licking along his arms. This challenge called for them both to put it all on the line. Losing meant losing Dyna, and that was one thing he would never allow. "Those are the terms you are prepared to gamble?"

Malakel put on his helmet, looking at him with eyes like shards. "Yes."

That sealed their fates.

Whatever came of this night, Cassiel sensed it would change something for the Soaraway House, and it was out of his hands.

Exhaling, Cassiel spread his black wings. "I accept."

He leaped into the skies. His fire gave him speed and their swords clashed. Cassiel invaded Malakel's airspace, thrusting them through the sky.

"I question why you thought it would be a splendid idea to challenge me knowing what power I have now," he snarled.

Malakel only laughed. He head-butted Cassiel in the face, throwing him off. "I have trained all my life for the throne," he said. "How to rule. How to fight. How to strategize." He reached over his shoulder for what Cassiel had first thought was wing armor until the moonlight glinted off the sharp edge of a Skath shield. "It's you who underestimates me."

White flames spread across its surface, glowing brightly in the night. It was made of the most powerful steel of the Heavens, the same one used for the Valkyrie armor—and Cassiel realized—so was Malakel's armor.

It was the one thing his power couldn't penetrate.

Malakel came prepared for battle. Cassiel had arrived with nothing but his anger, but it cooled at seeing this would be a true fight.

He soared up into the Heavens. Malakel chased him among the clouds, and he spun, throwing out a ball of fire. Malakel dodged it and they came at each other, blade against blade. They fought and parried blows, fire roaring as it swiped inches from taking out their throats. Black and white feathers scattered through the sky with every ruthless attack.

Cassiel pivoted around and slashed, his sword clashing against Malakel's shield. He threw himself back to avoid the blade thrusting for his chest. He met him hit for hit, white fire against blue. But Malakel was faster, more experienced. He moved with a lethal dexterity that beat against him.

Perhaps it was his determination to win that gave him the upper hand, or Cassiel's own hesitation. Because as much as he despised Malakel, he was still holding on to some fiber that told him this was his brother.

Cassiel parried the next attack and called on his flame, throwing a volley of fire. Malakel flew out of the way. He hurled another fireball, and Malakel deflected it with his shield. The fireball ricocheted, colliding into the mountainside.

Cracked rocks and snow came barreling down—burying the cave.

Dyna! He bellowed through the bond.

I'm here! We're all right. Green magic blasted a hole through the snow. Asiel appeared there, helping Sarrai and Dyna climb out of the opening.

Dyna looked up. *Cassiel!*

He whipped around—

Malakel's sword slashed through him. The blow sent him plummeting back to earth, and he slammed onto the mountain's ledge, his body rolling until his back crashed against a rock wall. Bones snapped and white-hot pain burst through his wings, spearing his back. He must have blacked out a second or two. Cassiel couldn't move. His vision dimmed. Smoke wafted from his burned stomach. His wings—they were broken.

Without them, he couldn't heal.

He barely heard Dyna's cries through the ringing in his ears. All of his strength had drained out of him. His hands sparked uselessly with his power. She stumbled for him, whimpering from the agony impaling her, too.

Malakel landed and strode over with a cold smirk that held only victory. He crouched in front of him and jerked up his chin, forcing Cassiel to look at him through the fog dimming his mind. "It's finished."

Sharp pain burst in Cassiel's chest with startling intensity, stealing the air from his lungs. Dyna's scream echoed over the mountain. The sound sent a cascade of shivers through his body. The taste of copper rushed up his throat and coated his mouth. He choked on it, and red splattered on Malakel's armor. Stunned and confused, Cassiel glanced down at the knife hilt sticking out of his chest.

"Since the moment you were born, you took from me," his brother said stoically. "My birthright. My father."

Cassiel couldn't think clearly to respond. How could he accuse him of taking something he never had?

"Now it's my turn to take from you."

Dyna reached them and Malakel's hand shot out. He shoved her clear off the mountain's ledge. There was no time to scream. No time for nothing as her eyes met his for the briefest of seconds—then she dropped from his view.

Cassiel threw himself after her.

The icy wind ripped painfully at his broken wings. All he saw was Dyna dropping through the sky. If they died now, they would go together, because he couldn't do it.

He couldn't imagine tomorrow if she wasn't in it.

But his mate didn't look afraid. She only looked at him with faith and fortitude—because this was not their end.

Cassiel's fire ripped out of him and rageful power swelled through his veins with a will that refused to let her die. His speed increased as he dove for Dyna. Green light spiraled from her hands. It shot out like leashes of light around his body and she yanked herself to him. Cassiel caught her with a grunt.

Blue flames flared at his back and they came to an abrupt stop midair. Divine blood seeped through broken bones, numbing his pain to a duller ache as it wove his muscle and tissues. His fire wrapped around the blade in his chest and disintegrated it to nothing.

Dyna awed at that, and she ran her fingers through the flame. Then her eyes widened when they landed on something past his shoulder. "Cassiel..." she breathed. "You have fire wings..."

He turned his head to look at them. His glowing wings were now encompassed with Seraph fire. They flapped gracefully, sparking embers into the night. He would process that later. There was something he had to finish first.

Cassiel flew her to the ground coated in snow. *Wait here.*

Sowmya and Yelrakel were on their way to get her.

Dyna nodded, her eyes flickering with magic. Every aspect of her was as strong and fierce as he knew her to be. *Go. Do what must be done.*

She was the light to his darkness, the one who chose compassion over violence, but not now. Not when it came to protecting what they had. Because their future, their lives together, that was worth spilling blood to defend.

With another flap of his wings, Cassiel shot through the sky and back up the mountain. Adrenaline induced wrath burned through his being as he remembered every torment he sustained in Hilos. Malakel was the one who took from him. His childhood. His sense of self-worth.

And he nearly took his mate.

All of his pent-up hate and anger fueled his speed to the ledge. Malakel reeled back in disbelief to see him. Cassiel snatched him into the air and continued flying high into the atmosphere. Malakel shouted and tried to break free, but he had an iron grip on him.

"There's something you should know," Cassiel said when they reached the brink of the world. "You missed my heart."

He slammed his flaming fist into Malakel's stomach, and the sky exploded with a supernova of light.

CHAPTER 65

Dynalya

The soft lilting of a gentle melody drifted to Dyna from outside. Cassiel sat on the banister of the open balcony as he played his silver flute. The sheer curtains fluttered in the mild wind, framing him in the golden light of morning. The beautiful notes fell and rose in a sweet call. It was the same song he played the day they met in the forest of Hilos, but it tugged at the hazy memories hidden within the recesses of her mind. She predicted which note would fade before he brought the melody to its end.

"I know I've heard that song before," Dyna sighed sleepily from his bed. She stretched on the silk sheets, her face pressed against the pillows. The bedding was so warm and soft, she didn't want to get up yet.

The sunlight caught Cassiel's eyes as he looked at her. "You have."

Another gust of wind tugged at his clothing, ruffling black locks across his forehead. Rising to stand, his bare feet padded softly on the floor as he came back inside. He stopped by the bed and regarded at her with a half-smile.

"What?" she asked.

"Nothing. I simply like the view of you in my bed."

Dyna flushed. They'd gone no further last night, not that either of them was anything less than exhausted after the debacle.

The mattress shifted under Cassiel's weight as he sat beside her. "I played that song for you when we found each other at the *Hyalus* tree. You were afraid, and I thought it might calm you."

Neither of them knew why they didn't remember that moment, nor why he had suddenly recovered it when Lucenna's spell hit him. Dyna suspected there was more to their past that they had yet to discover.

"Could you play it for me again?"

He did, and she closed her eyes, letting the melody sink into her. It tugged at her mind again, flashing colors and something that may have been a voice singing along. It faded as quickly as it surfaced.

The frustration it left behind made her stomach cramp, but Dyna let it go. They didn't need anything else added to the inevitable matter waiting for them today. They both avoided talking about it, and she wasn't in a hurry to. For now, she was content to pretend it was a perfect morning.

"I'm glad to see you play again," she said, smiling at him softly. "I can hear how much you enjoy it."

Cassiel balanced the flute in his palm, sunlight catching on the vine embellishments decorating it. "From the moment I was born, everything was decided for me, down to who I was made to be. There was no other choice. No other fate. But music? That could be anything I wanted it to be. I could change the notes, control the pitch, and weave them into a new song. It gave me something in a world where I had little of anything that I could consider mine."

To hear that while knowing what Malakel had said to him last night saddened her. She wished to remove every spiteful word, every hurt and wrong they nailed into his heart. He was hers now, and she would take as long as needed to pull every single nail out.

"The music you make is yours," Dyna said, covering his hand with hers. "As am I. No one will take that from you."

His expression softened. She sat up with every intention of hugging her mate, but something wet slid between her thighs. Dyna froze for a second before peeking under the blanket. Oh no. She quickly yanked it back down.

"Umm...do you mind stepping out for a moment?"

Cassiel's brow furrowed. "Why? What's wrong?"

"Nothing," she said too quickly.

His expression grew concerned, and he pulled back the blanket. Her face heated at the reveal of the red stains on her nightgown and the bedding.

"I'm sorry. I forgot there would be..." Dyna cut off, too mortified to speak. She was warned the contraceptive may cause an early menses.

Cassiel tucked the blanket around her waist and pressed a kiss to her forehead. "You have nothing to be sorry for, *lev sheli*. Don't be embarrassed in front of me."

A knock came at the door in the drawing room. Cassiel went to answer. His faint voice drifted to her as he spoke with someone before returning with two female servants. Her heart skipped several beats when Cassiel lifted her in his arms, keeping the blanket around her body. His hands were warm around her back and knees, his forearms tight and strong. She slipped her arms around his neck and sank against his chest. Black feathers enveloped her like a cloak and hid her from view.

"Tell my uncle it's done," he said to the servants coolly. "Take the sheets to him as proof if he wishes. Then call for Dynalya's lady's maid to attend her."

"Yes, Your Highness," came their dutiful replies.

Cassiel carried her away as she heard the servants make for the bed, and brought her into the bathing room. It was large, made of white marbled walls with tall windows providing a view of Hermon. Levers hung from the braided rope above the wide bath in the center. It was already filled and steaming.

"I prepared it earlier." Cassiel put her down and reached for the glass bottles resting on a wooden bench beside it. He dispensed soaps that released a sweet floral scent and it turned the water milky as bubbles gathered on the surface. He respectfully looked away as she peeled off the soiled nightgown, then helped her step in. She settled on the stone seating that circled the circumference of the large bath. The water ended a little above her chest and hid the rest of her from view. Dyna dipped under, letting the water come over her head before sitting up again.

"Can I get you anything?" he asked, watching her with an unreadable expression. She shook her head. "I will wait for you in the drawing room."

Dyna caught his hand. "Thank you."

"You don't need to thank me for something so little."

"For now. For lying."

The servants were clearly going to report that they'd consummated. The entire castle probably knew by now.

Cassiel brushed a wet lock of hair from her cheek. "Neither I nor anyone else will ever force you into my bed. *But...*" His voice dropped to a soft purr. "You are always welcome to it."

Dyna's eyes flickered up and met his. There wasn't anything stopping them other than her own timid nerves. A warm electrical current flushed through her body at remembering the way he touched her after their vows.

Could she still be shy after that?

She sensed Cassiel knew where her thoughts had gone because his eyes grew heated. His eyes dropped to her mouth, and the bond stirred with something that made her heart rate increase.

He leaned in but stopped. "I should go."

"Don't go," Dyna whispered. She didn't want to be away from him yet.

Cassiel's dark lashes lowered for a moment, and his chest rose with a shallow breath. He rolled up his sleeves, and she watched his arms flex with his movements. Taking a washcloth on the bench, he dipped it in the water, and it trickled as he lifted it.

Those silver eyes held hers as he said, "May I?"

Her pulse skipped a beat at his lidded gaze and the intent of his question. Sweeping her hair aside, Dyna turned around and Cassiel sat behind her. All of her attention focused on the path of the washcloth as he slowly ran it across her shoulders. Warm water sluiced down her back in winding trails. His breath coasted over her wet skin, causing her pulse to skip and rise.

"Every moment I spend in your presence seeks to undo my every good intention," he said in her ear. "I'm clinging to the barest thread of my control."

The first press of his mouth on her neck sent a cascade of tingles through her body. Her toes curled in the water as the kisses continued down her shoulder, each one lingering longer than the last. She sighed at the delightful sensations flooding through her from the soft pressure of his lips, the tickle of his hair against her cheek, and the warmth of his chest cradling her.

Cassiel's fingers wove through her hair and gently tugged to expose more of her neck as his mouth stroked back up her throat to her ear. Every touch of his lips left behind a trail of fire. It sent her careening, and Dyna felt as if she was falling.

A sound rumbled through him that was part growl and part moan. *I was raised to be a prince with honor, Dynalya. I wish to match your pace, but having you like this, I can no longer ignore what you do to me.*

Cassiel yanked her around, sloshing water out of the tub. He silenced her gasp by capturing her lips. He kissed her hungrily, as if he couldn't go one more minute without it. Each one was savoring, and soft, and so profound she lost herself in it. His arms pulled her flush against him, heated palms sliding over her wet back. She clung to him, her fingers bunching his hair.

The thin fabric of his wet tunic brushed against the sensitive parts of her flesh. Heat coiled to her stomach, sinking low. Dyna wanted his touch there and everywhere else it had been last night. Her heart was racing with so many emotions she could hardly breathe.

Somewhere in the distance came a quiet knock. A low groan rumbled in Cassiel's throat and it vibrated against their mouths.

He tried to ignore it, but she sensed his attention reluctantly shifting.

The knock came again, more insistent.

Cassiel released a frustrated sigh and dropped his forehead against hers. "If they call me away for a matter of little importance, I will set something on fire."

She offered him a quick consolation kiss. "We have things to attend to."

He rose to his feet. All heat vanished from his expression, now set in stone. Cassiel made for the door, but his quiet voice still reached her. "I should have killed him."

His power had ripped through the Heavens last night, with a might that would have disintegrated anyone in its path. Initially, what saved Malakel was his armor. He had dropped back to earth unconscious. Cassiel could have taken his life, but the challenge was won, so he chose to walk away.

Dyna quickly finished washing and climbed out of the bath. She wrapped a thick white towel around herself and entered the bedroom as he returned with Noemi.

"My lady," she dipped in a deferential curtsy.

"Good morrow," Dyna greeted, then glanced at him.

He nodded. "It's time."

For them to call forth their court and deal with the outcome of yesterday.

"Come, my lady. I have brought some of your things." Noemi's orange wings fluttered as she led her to the drawing room, where it had been set up with clothing, shoes, and jewelry. Among them was her crown. "I know you prefer lighter colors, but I thought this one might be more fitting today."

Her lady's maid held up a long, shimmering black dress with a plunging neckline. It had subtle details of lace with a dark blue flowered pattern. Appearing before the court in Cassiel's color stated she stood with him.

A united front.

"Yes, you're perfectly right." Dyna ran her hand over the glittering fabric. The sapphire ring she still wore shone in the light. "Thank you, Noemi, for being so kind and thoughtful."

She beamed. "It's my pleasure, my lady."

"If it's not too much trouble, could you do me one more favor?"

CHAPTER 66

Dynalya

A s Lord and Lady of Hermon Ridge, Dyna would need to get used to addressing the court. It didn't mean she wasn't nervous. Her lady's maid had her dressed and ready by the time Sowmya let in her Guardians. They had dressed in black leathered armor, poised for their roles. Dyna rose from the vanity and folded her hands together at her waist, the sheer, tapered sleeves ending at her middle fingers.

All three took one look at her and bowed.

She chuckled. "Stop that."

Zev straightened with an awed expression on his face. "You look..." He sniffed, and the tension she hadn't noticed in his shoulders eased. "You're not mated."

Dyna blushed at the open statement. "We...uh...didn't."

"But the maids confirmed you did?" Lucenna whispered.

"I had my bleed."

She grinned. "Ah. Me, too. It's very light. It's wonderful."

"How are you, my lady?" Rawn asked, searching her face worriedly.

It had given them a scare to see her fall off the mountain, but Dyna hadn't felt fear at that moment. It wasn't because it was another instance she was falling through the air or because she had her magic. It was merely because Cassiel had been there. She simply knew he would catch her. Whether they would land or fall had not mattered.

"I'm all right," she assured them.

They looked her over again, as if needing to confirm for themselves. She had survived unscathed, for the most part. Any bruises and cuts had been healed by her mate.

Cassiel stepped into the room, dressed in black finery that shone of royalty with a matching crown in place. "Good, you are all here—"

She heard his audible inhale when he saw her. His silver eyes roved over her sapphire crown, slowly taking in the dress that enveloped her like the midnight sky. The pure adoration lifting to his face was so intimate, so potent, it made the others respectfully leave the room.

Cassiel lifted her hand and pressed a kiss on the back of her fingers. *You look like a Queen.*

Then whatever had been stirring in her settled with only his presence and the touch of starlight in his eyes. He was her balance. Her equilibrium in every way. The everlasting night, who had named her his dawn.

Dyna bowed her head, hair falling down her arms in red waves. His surprise fluttered in the bond. He would never ask her to bow to him, but she held such regard for her mate it was her way of showing it.

She felt the warmth of his affection as his thumb brushed over the sapphire ring on her finger. After today, she planned to give it back, at least until she could rightfully wear it.

Are you all right? Dyna asked through the bond, because she could feel the disquiet he had been trying to bury all morning.

Cassiel looked down at their joined hands. *Perhaps it had been foolish, but a part of me had hoped it was misplaced anger or merely disgust. That one day my brother could accept me. Last night proved I will never be part of the family.*

Dyna squeezed his hand. *You're a part of mine.*

He glanced at where their friends now waited in the hall, and emotion traversed his face. His throat bobbed a moment before he nodded. "Shall we?"

"Lead the way, Your Highness." Linking her arm through Cassiel's, he escorted her into the hall. Her Guardians moved to guard their backs, then the Valkyrie moved up front, and led them through the winding corridors to a section of the castle she hadn't seen yet. They came to a quiet foyer before a set of doors.

This was the first court they called into session. It was the beginning of what would pave their future with Hermon Ridge, and perhaps the Realms.

Dyna straightened her shoulders and composed her face into a cool, unfeeling mask. The Valkyrie opened the doors.

It opened to the high dais of the throne room.

Debris littered the marbled floors, and cracks splintered the walls, but the gallery and the alcoves were full of waiting Celestials. The buzz of voices quieted as they walked in together, arm in arm. Her Guardians entered but stayed behind within the shadowed corners. The Valkyrie lined the dais and the steps, standing at attention in their golden scaled armor. At the end of the steps to the right was Lord Jophiel, Asiel, and Lady Sarrai.

Cassiel brought her before the throne with another of equal size beside it. Inwardly, she smiled. Even in that, he beheld her.

The herald at the bottom of the steps announced them. "Presenting before the court, the Lord and Lady of Hermon Ridge: Prince Cassiel Soaraway and Dynalya Soaraway of House Astron, Princess Consort of Hilos."

They looked out at the crowd, and they all bowed. Cassiel and Dyna took their seats. Lord Jophiel tried to catch his eye, but her mate looked straight ahead.

"Bring in the prisoner," Cassiel ordered. He sounded deceptively calm, yet Dyna was so in tuned with him she heard the switch in his voice. It was the cold, authoritative demeanor he used with others.

The Black Hearted Prince.

A loud groan broke the silence as the large main doors opened. It was followed by the rattle of chains as the Valkyrie ushered Prince Malakel down the scorched runner to the foot of the stairs. His clothing was ragged and torn, face and hair smeared with soot. Yet he stood straight and regal with an insolent curl of his lip.

"I will only say this once." Cassiel leaned back in his seat, his command filling the throne room. "On your knees."

Fury twisted Malakel's face. From the bob in his throat, he was aware of every eye on him. Gritting his teeth, he stiffly lowered himself to the ground.

"This is where *your* eyes meet *mine*," Cassiel told him. Then he spoke aloud for all to hear, his words carrying in the silence. "Malakel Soaraway, the court witnessed the challenge you called upon their Lord, as they witnessed the kidnapping of their Lady and of Lady Sarrai. For all your efforts, you lost. Now your future is mine to decree."

"It's not." Malakel sneered. "You should have killed me during the challenge, Cassiel. Now you have lost any right to take my life."

"But I do have rights to other things," he replied, his gaze as sharp as steel. Malakel's sneer faded. "Unlike my own sentencing, I will give you a chance to stay my hand if you do one simple thing. Beg."

Malakel bared his teeth. "I will never beg to you."

"Not me." His head tilted in her direction, giving Dyna a tingle of surprise. "To her. It is she to whom you will plead."

"To a human?"

A coil of flame wove through Cassiel's fingers. "To my *wife*."

"I don't recognize her, nor you. Neither do the Realms. They will never accept you in place of me. Defeating me does not change who you are, Nephilim."

An ominous glow seeped into Cassiel's eyes. The room darkened with the dimming of the chandeliers, and a tremendous heat filled the air, sprouting a sweat on Dyna's back. Malakel lifted his chin, though he couldn't quite keep the fear hovering in the angles of his stiff body. She laid a hand over Cassiel's fist gripping the armrest. It shook with his restraint.

"You will," he said. "If you ever wish to fly again."

Malakel's jaw clenched, the twitch of his wings giving away his unease. He dipped his head a smidge of an inch. "I...beg...your *forgiveness*...my lady."

Every harsh word was forced and spiteful.

None of it was genuine in the least.

Dyna's magic hummed beneath her skin with the urge to terminate. He tried to kill them. He nearly succeeded. Perhaps they should take his wings as punishment, or take something more. But executing him would only prove she wasn't much different from him. Responding to violence with violence wasn't right. It couldn't be. As rulers of this Realm, they had to be wise, and dealing with a prince of Hilos required finesse.

Malakel moved to stand.

"Remain where you are," Dyna commanded. He glowered at her in disbelief, his mouth opening to respond. "And you will kindly remain silent."

The prince was so shocked his teeth snapped shut.

She glanced at Cassiel. *Do you mind if I...?*

A pleased smirk tugged at the corners of his lips. *By all means, Princess. You never have to ask.*

Dyna rose and moved to the front of the dais. "I am not a Celestial," she said aloud for all to hear. "I'm young and I don't know much about life, but I do know about humans. We feel and love, and fight, and hope, as you do. Much could grow between us and Celestials if given the chance. I would like to be the first to take part in that." She looked at the one in chains. "I forgive you for your wrongs against me, Prince Malakel. I wish you no ill will today."

He stared at her mutely. Confused by her words, or perhaps not expecting them. Whatever he was thinking, she hoped it would, in some small way, make a difference.

Cassiel came to stand beside her. "Dynalya is kind in her verdict. I, too, will enact mine. Malakel Soaraway, I hereby strip you of your title, your lands, and every asset of your wealth. You are forthwith banished to Edym. Never to step foot in Hilos or the other Realms again."

Malakel gawked at him as gasps and murmurs filled the room. Dyna was careful not to show any shock on her face. They hadn't spoken much of what the decision would be regarding Malakel, but when Cassiel asked her about it, she left the decision to him.

This was between brothers.

Secretly, she was satisfied with the verdict. It was about time Malakel received his comeuppance.

"You came after my mate, and for that, I will make you suffer as only I can," Cassiel told him.

"You have no authority to banish me!" Malakel shouted.

"Be grateful I'm not choosing to exile you instead. It was you who set the terms. Now you will reap them." Cassiel led her away.

"You cur!" Malakel leaped up, and the Valkyrie stepped in his way, crossing their spears. "Look at me, as I swear this to you now."

They turned, meeting his odious glare.

"One way or another, you will pay dearly for this, Cassiel. And I swear to all the Gods—" Malakel's eyes cut to her with a profound abhorrence she felt all the way to her bones. "It will shatter the very depths of your soul."

His pledge physically struck Dyna's chest as though his hatred marked her with a vile curse.

Cassiel leveled Malakel with a look that made the hair rise on her neck. Any hesitations he had for his brother died at that moment.

Along with another piece of himself.

A vengeful blue flame blazed in Cassiel's eyes as clouds passed over the sun, casting the throne room in shadow. "She has forgiven you because she has a good heart, but your torment ensured a long time ago that I would not. I warned you what would happen if you touched her again."

Dyna softly gasped when she felt his decision.

Wildfire sprouted from Cassiel's feet and shot down the steps faster than she could object, cresting over Malakel in a bright blue wave. The throne room erupted with screams. Lord Jophiel flew up the steps, shouting at Cassiel to stop, but he lifted a wall of Seraph fire that kept him and everyone else at bay.

The prince writhed on the ground as the inferno climbed over his left wing. The feathers curled, quickly turning black. Dyna's stomach churned at the horrible smell and the agonizing screams ripping into her ears. Cassiel watched it intently, his features hard and cruel.

Dyna took his face. His brightly glowing eyes met hers, and behind the fury was the depth of his misery. She felt the poisonous hatred sowing in Cassiel's heart and she didn't want that fusing to his soul. *Let him go, kohav.*

His fire wrapped around her like a gentle veil, cool to the touch. It didn't burn, and she knew it never would. *He hurt you.*

This isn't who you are. Killing him would only bring you pain in the end. Don't let this be another mark on your soul.

Cassiel closed his eyes, and the flames died away. Malakel shuddered on the floor as smoke spiraled from his left wing, completely charred black. Only his ragged breathing could be heard in the hushed quiet.

"You live by her mercy," Cassiel said. "Remember that."

"Guards, take Malakel to the infirmary!" Lord Jophiel thundered. He turned to them and said tightly under his breath, "In the council room. Now."

They followed his uncle; Sarrai, Asiel, and her Guardians trailing behind. The Valkyrie moved to their posts outside another set of doors and let them in the room.

As soon as they were seated, Lord Jophiel whirled around. "You cannot kill a Prince of Hilos!"

"Well, fortunately for him, he lives," her mate said, his tone deathlike.

"Seraph fire burns faster than divine blood can withstand. The healers will have no choice but to put him into a deep sleep to heal. The damage was so extensive he may never wake."

"I don't care," Cassiel said through his teeth, and Dyna felt the heat rising in the room.

"This is not the conduct of a Lord. If you had killed him—"

"He nearly killed my wife!" Cassiel roared, startling them all. "Then he threatened her life *again*. He deserves nothing more than to burn for it."

Lord Jophiel shook his head, staring at him as if he was afraid. "You have changed. I don't recognize you right now."

There was only anger on Cassiel's face, but Dyna felt the twinge of gaining his uncle's disappointment. "You are right. I did change," he said in a calmer tone. "I am her damned husband, and I will do what is necessary to keep her safe."

"You took one of his wings, Cassiel." Lord Jophiel rubbed his forehead. "You burned half of his body. Only your father may exile a royal."

"I did not exile him. He is banished to the Realm of Edym, and is merely no longer welcome to the others."

Dyna quirked her brows. *You sent him to the desert?*

The unbearable heat will do him some good.

Edym was also ruled by Malakel's grandfather. In that alone, Cassiel had shown some leniency.

Asiel scoffed. "Truthfully, Father, I intended to rip him apart, too. When I saw what he'd done to my mate, I cared not who he was."

Lord Jophiel's wide eyes flickered to his son and Sarrai. "What?"

Sarrai ducked her head, shrinking back. Dyna held her hand and gently squeezed it under the table in reassurance. She was Lady now and would make sure nothing befell them for simply loving each other.

"Why did you think I was there?" Asiel asked him. "If not to win back my bride?"

No one else reacted to the revelation. Dyna had already told them everything that had happened.

"Since when did this...?" His father could only blink at him, stunned. "I never suspected. You didn't show any interest in her or Hermon."

"How could I?" Asiel's eyes lowered to the table. "When you had chosen another to replace me?"

Lord Jophiel stared at his son, a pained look crossing his features. He sighed heavily and rubbed his face. "I have failed you both in so many ways. But I will not allow you to destroy yourselves. Asiel, we will speak about this later. Cassiel, be angry if you must. You have a right to be, but you cannot let that rule you. A Lord, much less a King, cannot afford to make such mistakes. Malakel will not go quietly, nor the High Queen. Prepare yourself. There will be consequences for this."

Cassiel's eyes flamed again, casting the room with eerie light. "Come what may, I will feel no remorse for what I did. Today marks the last day I show any leniency—regardless of who it is. And trust me, what you witnessed is the least of what I will do. All threats against my wife will be completely eliminated. No law will supersede that. No status or standing. For she is the only thing that matters to me. She is above everything. *Always.*"

Dyna's heart lodged in her throat, her next breath stalling as she stared at him. He meant every word.

Lord Jophiel's startled gaze flickered at the blue spark flashing in Cassiel's fist on the table. Then he stared at her next with a new understanding, one that she had slowly come to realize herself. When it came to her, nothing, absolutely *nothing*, would stop Cassiel from protecting her. He would no longer hold himself back anymore.

His power now made him unstoppable. Unchecked.

A shiver traveled down her spine at what that could mean.

"He is your brother. However much you hate him, he is still your kin."

"Our shared blood meant nothing to him. Long has it stopped meaning anything to me." Cassiel stood. "Thank you, Uncle, for your kindness and hospitality. Forgive me for disappointing you. I hope to do better once I return."

Lord Jophiel froze. "Return?"

465

"I'm afraid it's time we leave Hermon Ridge and continue on our journey."

Relief lifted the apprehension from the last four days off Dyna's shoulders. She was more than ready to go. By the expressions of the others, so were they.

"But you must greet your father. I received word that he is on his way."

Surprise swept through the bond, though Cassiel's expression didn't change.

"Then please excuse me with the High King," he said with every authority of a Lord, stunning his uncle—and her. "Regrettably, we cannot stay. Enough time has been spent here, and the first snow is imminent. We are departing today. I will leave arrangements in my absence. Be well, Uncle."

They bowed, and Cassiel hurried for the door, pulling her along. Now that they knew King Yoel was coming, he was anxious to leave and so was she.

"Running changes nothing." Lord Jophiel's statement stopped them in place with their backs to him. Cassiel's jaw clenched, and she felt his dread climb. "Because you know what this means. Out of respect for your troubles last night, I deferred to speak about this, but it cannot be ignored. Whether you recognize it or not, the law does. Thus, from today, you own everything Malakel had—including his inheritance. Notwithstanding validation from the High King, you are now the crown prince and the heir apparent to the throne of Hilos."

CHAPTER 67

Cassiel

"Are you certain about this?" Asiel asked him. He leaned against the wall, his arms and legs crossed. "I thought we detested one another." Cassiel stuffed the last of his clothing in his pack. "I detested your determination to get under my skin." Now knowing what had kept a wedge between them, he felt guilt for taking the affection of a father he had so desperately needed to survive. "If you can hold that stubborn habit for years, I think you can be Lord Protector of Hermon Ridge while I'm gone."

It was Dyna's idea, and he felt it was a good one. Asiel liked to pretend he didn't care about his home, but Cassiel always knew he did. Giving him the position will put someone in place he trusted to take care of the Realm as it should be.

"Can I ask you a question without you unleashing your fire on me?"

Cassiel strapped the belt of his sword in place around his waist. "Depends on the nature of the question."

"Why a human?"

He arched an eyebrow at Asiel pointedly. "Why do you love a half-breed? The fact that she is human is irrelevant. I am hers, and she is mine. There is no life without her in it."

Oddly, his cousin had nothing to retort. He only looked at him with an unreadable expression.

"You didn't hesitate," Asiel said. "When she fell. Your wings were broken, but you threw yourself after her anyway, even if it meant certain death. It was then I understood you would do anything for her. Does that include letting go?" He looked away to the balcony, where they could hear Dyna and Sarrai's distant voices coming from the courtyard below. "Could you let her go if it was for the best?"

Cassiel searched his face, seeing the desolation there. "Asiel, when I made you Lord Protector, I also named you my heir. Hermon will be yours again. I have spoken with Lord Gadriel on your behalf, and he has agreed to allow Sarrai to marry you at the next Festival of Light."

Asiel's head whipped to him. "What?"

"You have your bride."

His cousin stood there mutely for a moment, his throat constricting. "I won't thank you for returning what's mine."

"Don't. Merely be glad you did not challenge me for it. You would have lost."

Asiel scoffed at that, and his smirk edged on a smile. The wall that had formed between them through years of misunderstanding and rivalry would come down someday. It started by returning everything. Including his surrogate father. The loss made him sad, but Lord Jophiel had done more than enough for him, and he would always be thankful for that.

"Cassiel, I thought about it, and I don't believe Malakel was the only one there that night," Asiel said. "He could not have carried them both to the mountain on his own."

"I know." There was more to this, and until they could uncover it, he wouldn't bring Dyna back here.

"That is why you are truly leaving, isn't it?"

"We have other reasons to go. Don't allow any of Malakel's party to leave until you know who helped him."

"I will investigate, if only to make them answer for what they did to Sarrai. Entrust it to me." Asiel bowed, astonishing Cassiel.

Dyna had been right. Support from his court started here. Finding it in his cousin was the last place he would have expected, but his mate had been right about that, too. Would she ever stop surprising him?

Asiel turned to go, but he paused. "Be cautious, cousin. One forgets how easily we can lose the most precious things. I sense your reign, and that of your future Queen will stir the skies, and it will bring a great storm that will be felt throughout the Realms."

Cassiel let him leave without responding. The evening rays streamed in through the windows, falling over his mother's flute left on the bed. The throne may have passed to him by default, but he didn't plan on ever ruling. Dyna was too bright for his world. He wouldn't allow anything that would snuff out her light.

Tucking the flute in his pack, Cassiel strode out of his room. The bond pulsed with Dyna's call. He tugged on it in response to let her know he was coming. The day was ending, but they all agreed not to spend another night here. The Valkyrie were waiting to escort them to the bottom of the mountain on the Pegasi, and his uncle had disclosed a passage that was safe to cross Troll Bridge part of the way. After that, they would be on their own.

"Prince Cassiel."

Cassiel exhaled a sigh and turned to the form idling in the shadows of the hall.

"I commend you on surviving the trials of court. When one finds themselves in such an incredible position, it's certainly fascinating to see how it will all play out."

"And you will be watching, I'm sure."

Lord Raziel stepped into view. Cassiel braced himself for his next response. He must not be happy that his grandson was overthrown. It was a blow for House Welkin's reputation.

"Of course. It's not every day a Nephilim falls in line for the throne. Your father must be very proud." The Lord of Edym tilted his head in a slight nod of acknowledgment, something sparking in his stoic blue eyes. "Long may he reign."

His white wings flared open, and Lord Raziel flew away into the clear skies.

Cassiel raised his hand against the sunlight as he joined his waiting companions. He forgot all else when he met Dyna's radiant smile and took her outstretched hand. If a storm was coming, all he could do was prepare for the rain.

PART III: SOULS

CHAPTER 68

Rawn

R awn had the impression of fingertips on his cheek as a soft voice called his name. A warm summer breeze coasted over him, carrying the sweet scent of Dynalyas from the garden. He buried his face in her lap, refusing to rise. He would stay here a while longer. Only a little longer.

"Rawn," Aerina called again, and her lips brushed his forehead. "You must wake now, love. Please, Rawn. Wake up."

Wake up!

He gasped, and his frosted lashes snapped open. The remnants of his dream faded beneath the piercing ring in his ears, muffling the screams in the distance. The frozen lake he laid on burned his face and numbed his limbs. It vibrated beneath him with heavy, lumbering footsteps. Purple, green, and blue lights flashed around him. Something cracked and snapped. He sucked in a breath and his ribs constricted painfully where he'd been struck. Fair let out a shrill neigh, tugging at his cloak.

"Rawn!" Lucenna's cry cleared the haze, and the roar of trolls rattled in his skull.

Rawn snatched his fallen bow off the ground, rolling to his knees. Hissing through the pain, he drew back the bowstring and lined his sight on the target. Wind and icy rain blew between him and the incoming troll. The massive creature had to be at least twelve feet tall, gray body covered in plated bone and fur. It chased after Dyna and Cassiel as they ran across the frozen lake. Rawn shot the arrow, followed by two others. They whistled through the air and bounced off the creature's plated chest.

"Aim for the eyes!" Dyna shouted.

Rawn whipped out another arrow, and his arm trembled with the pain ripping at his ribs. He exhaled a low breath, letting everything fade to the background of his awareness, and released. The arrow skewered the troll's third eye. Dark gray blood spurted from its unsightly face, the creature bellowing in pain. It toppled and hit the ice, only for more trolls to come lumbering after it. One opened its gaping mouth full of jagged teeth and roared. Rawn winced at the deafening sound echoing through the forest.

Beside him, Lucenna filled her hands with crackling purple magic. "These damn things keep coming."

She cast bolts of lightning at beast after beast. Cassiel yanked Dyna out of the way and threw a blue fireball, blasting the head off a troll's shoulders. Her arms were alight with magic as she defended his back. Zev leaped onto another of the massive beasts and sank his teeth around its jugular.

It was the only soft spot on their bodies beside their eyes.

Rawn kept shooting, magic raging all around. There were too many. Killing merely one demanded all of their might. He reached for another arrow and grabbed only air. His quiver was empty.

The small Horde would reach them soon. He heard a cracking sound again and glanced down at the frozen lake. The ice was fracturing. It bore too much weight.

Lucenna cursed and filled her hands with Essence, building it into a large sphere. "Essence blast," she said. "I will blow a hole through them."

"Hold."

"You want me to stop?" she exclaimed.

"Yes. Get to land!" Rawn yelled at the others.

Cassiel snatched Dyna in his arms and flew the rest of the way, the black wolf sprinting after them. His wings couldn't keep them airborne much longer, and they crash landed on the hard ground next to him.

"Now!" Rawn shouted. "Break the ice!"

Lucenna hurled the crackling sphere, and it struck the center of the lake with a *boom*. Cracks spread like webs through the ice beneath the trolls' feet and they dropped through the dark depths with infuriated bellows, leaving all to fall still.

They dropped on the bank from relief and exhaustion. None of their weapons worked on those massive creatures. Their plated skin was too thick. Fire helped, but it cost all their power to burn through their thick hides, and they had been fighting since morning to survive the Bridge. They were spent.

"If we don't find shelter by nightfall, I don't know if we will make it," Lucenna said, panting. A layer of sweat beaded her pale complexion.

Zev growled in agreement.

Cassiel helped Dyna stand. "I will fly ahead."

"You can't," she said, her breath clouding in the frosty air. "Your wings."

Cassiel grimaced as he stretched them out, but Rawn saw the stiffness. Like the Pegasi, he couldn't fly in these frigid temperatures. It was so cold, Rawn's enchanted cloak couldn't completely keep it out. Withholding a shudder, he took Fair's reins and nodded for them to keep going.

This was only day one, and they still had three more to go. He was beginning to worry they may not reach the other end.

Rawn shoved that thought aside. He had to make it. Aerina was waiting for him.

He lifted a hand to his chest. The old letter he had yet to mail her rested in his pocket like a weathered treasure. Worn on the edges from time, but it was the most valuable thing he owned.

He had to let her know he was still alive.

He had to cross Troll Bridge.

The sooner he reached Mount Ida, the sooner he could return to his homeland. After twenty long years, he had enough. He couldn't go another season without seeing his family again.

"Are you all right, Lord Norrlen?" Dyna asked him worriedly. "You took a heavy blow."

Rawn pressed on his aching ribs where a troll's fist had hit him. The blow had been so hard it threw him across the lake. "Yes, my lady." He heaved a breath, his lungs struggling to intake the bitter air. "Thank you."

"I don't like the way you're breathing. I need to examine you once we—"

A distant roar echoed through the barren trees.

"Go!"

They sprinted through the forest. The icy rain and wind mercilessly beat against them, half blinding him. Rawn's heart thudded in his chest as he ran, the ground shaking with the incoming Horde. They needed a plan.

The sound of trolls roaring, their running steps and heavy breaths, was all he heard, so when he noticed the sound of water, it was too late. They skid to a stop at a bluff, where it dropped into a waterfall. Fair neighed wildly, backing away from the edge.

Cassiel cursed. "Do we jump?"

"To the Seven Gates with that," Lucenna hissed. "I'm not jumping."

Rawn shook his head. "We will not."

The bluff wasn't too high, but the edge of the riverbank was frozen. The water would numb them in minutes. They couldn't risk that.

"Here, we fight." He drew his sword. "Attack in pairs as you strike and defend. Get them over the ledge if you must. Whatever you do, hold your ground."

Lucenna turned to face the forest, her body crackling with magic. Cassiel did the same, and Dyna's hands blazed green. Zev crouched low, releasing a deep snarl.

The trees rattled, and branches snapped. Rawn mounted Fair, and they rode ahead, leading the attack. When the first troll stormed out of the forest, he let a knife fly, and it impaled its throat. Galloping past, he swept his sword for the next beast.

Currents of magic and fire exploded around him. A black wolf dashed alongside him and sprang on the troll that nearly swiped at him. Cassiel flew ahead and slammed his flaming sword down through the thick skull of another.

Trolls swarmed out of the balding trees. His ears rang with the cries of his companions and raving roars. The Horde cut through them, separating them in different directions. His blade slashed and speared as he fought.

They were everywhere.

It reminded him of the Grindylows, and he felt a shiver brush his spine. The sound of his heartbeat thudded in his head, his ears ringing. Death was there with him, but he ignored its presence. He had to survive. For Aerina and his son, he had to.

"Rawn!" Lucenna shouted.

A troll wrenched him off the saddle toward its snapping teeth. A spear of electricity hit the creature, and he dropped. He rolled out of the way of its enormous feet and slashed through its throat. The forest filled with the sounds of blasts, screams, and the snarls as they fought for their lives. The stench of burning hide made his nose burn.

At the sound of a neighing cry, Rawn whipped his head around.

Fair ran from a troll chasing him until it cornered him on the edge of the waterfall. Rawn sprinted to him. He pulled out two long knives and slid on the muddy ground between a beast's legs. He sliced through its heels, leaping up to keep running for his horse.

Rawn leaped onto the troll cornering Fair and shoved his knives through its throat. He yanked out a bloody knife and impaled it into the back of the troll's skull. It went down and he went with it. It fell forward, forcing his horse to the edge of the falls.

Rawn lunged and caught the reins. He tried to pull him back to safety, but Fair was too heavy. His boots slid through the mud. They were falling. Fair neighed wildly at him, hooves kicking against the rock.

"No," Rawn grunted through his teeth as they slipped further. *"Reac erajed eton!"*

Fair neighed again, protesting.

"I will not let you fall!" He refused to let go of his friend.

Even if it meant falling with him.

He lost purchase of the ground, and they slid off into the open air. Purple light snatched them both. Lucenna held out a trembling hand to them, and the other pointed at the trolls with a beam of blazing Essence. Her legs bent, and she cried out from the effort it took to defend herself while keeping them from falling. She looked at him with glowing eyes full of fear and apology.

He nodded to let her know it was all right. It wasn't her fault. A troll knocked into Lucenna, and her magic winked out, her scream following his descent.

Rawn had only a moment to suck in a mouthful of air before he plunged into the ice.

CHAPTER 69

Dynalya

The trolls had them surrounded. Dyna let all of her power free, but it wasn't enough. She was running and throwing spell after spell. Cassiel and Zev were on her heels, his Seraph fire raging all around them.

"Look out!" Cassiel shoved her out of the way.

Dyna hit the ground as a troll's massive fist swung past her head and crashed into him. She felt the blow all the way through her bones. It hurled him across the forest, and he crashed into a tree. He didn't get up. She threw out a ball of Essence with a shriek and blew off the troll's head.

Pushing on her trembling hands and knees, Dyna ran for him. He was out cold.

"Cassiel?" Dyna shook him and patted his face. "Cassiel!"

Zev keened sharply. A beast had him by the leg. Dyna hit it with another Essence blast, freeing her cousin.

"Wake up!" She zapped Cassiel with a current of Essence and his eyes snapped open. He gasped for air, jerking upright. She threw her arms around him and squeezed him. "Oh, thank the God of Urn."

Cassiel hissed in pain. "My leg is broken."

She gasped and moved back to see it was bent at an odd angle. "Oh no, can you heal?"

"Yes, but—"

A swarm of trolls charged for them.

"Get out of here," Cassiel told her, trying to push off the ground. "Run!"

Didn't he know? She was done with all the running. Dyna rose to stand in front of him. Her vision filled with bright green light as she faced the trolls.

He shouted for her to leave him, but seeing she wouldn't, her mate flung his flaming sword in a last desperate attempt, sending it spinning in the air for the beasts. Zev took down another, but they couldn't stop the swarm.

Dyna knew what spell she had to use. It would take everything she had, and there was only one chance to get it right. Her body glowed as she opened all of her Essence channels. Every part of her body burned, and she slowly rose off the ground.

Dyna! Cassiel grabbed her arm with his flaming hand.

At his mental cry meeting her soul, heat flowed through the air. Power pulsed between them, and it surged in her veins, scorching her from within. It rushed out in a flood and she raised her other arm, palm held out against the charging beasts. Green tendrils spiraled over her hand and up her arm. With a scream of fear and rage, a blast of fire burst forth in a sea of raging green—and blue.

It tore through the wall of trolls in a massive wave, and continued through the forest, disintegrating everything it touched. All that was left behind were charred carcasses and the blackened earth. Ash and embers floated past her dimming vision.

Dyna stumbled back. Her Essence sputtered out, and she fell into Cassiel's waiting arms.

"Lev sheli." He tilted her chin, looking her over. "Are you all right?"

"Yes," she panted, her eyes fluttering closed. "That spell..."

Somehow, their magic had combined. Light sputtered weakly in her hands. Whatever that spell was, it drained nearly every drop of her power.

Whining, Zev limped over to them on a bad leg, blood leaking from his side. He nuzzled her cheek.

"I'm fine." She brushed his muzzle.

"We need to keep moving," Cassiel said. Leg, now healed, he stood while still carrying her. He searched the trees. "Wait. Where are the others?"

Zev spun around and snarled. It was their only warning before the bellow of trolls filled the forest. They lumbered out of the trees, more than they had ever encountered before.

Cassiel quickly kissed her, then pushed her in Zev's direction. "Take her and get her out of here."

"What? No!" She fought against the wolf, pulling at her dress with his teeth.

"Go." He walked out to meet the beasts, and his body flared to life with vivid flames, outlining his wings.

A troll came from the right, separate from the Horde—and it charged for him.

"Cassiel!"

Galloping hooves raced toward them, and it flooded her with relief. But instead of Rawn, someone else came galloping through the trees on a black horse.

A man layered in leather armor and armed to the teeth rose on the saddle and launched himself into the air. From the sleeves of his long, dark blue coat, he produced two gleaming knives and slammed them in the troll's throat. The blades burst out on the other side in a gruesome spray of blood. He jerked them out, and the head came off with a wet squelch. The troll's headless body teetered, then flopped down, the man landing gracefully at its side.

The icy wind tugged at his long frock coat, flaring behind him, and on his back was the white sigil of a bird's skull.

A symbol she had seen before.

The man glanced at them over his shoulder, dark blond hair falling to his jaw. A black mask covered the lower half of his face, only revealing his deep blue eyes.

Dyna recognized him anyway.

The ground rumbled as another thirty-armed men rode out of the woods on horses. The Captain of the Skelling Mercenaries mounted his horse and guided it front and center. He unsheathed the twin blades from his back, revealing their wicked serrated edges, each with a grinning skull for pommels.

"All right, men," Klyde called, looking at the massive Horde. "Go with God!"

"And may he receive me!" the mercenaries shouted in unison.

Dyna watched in amazement as they expertly killed the beasts with swift and precise attacks.

Their captain moved with a wild aggression, his blades taking down troll after troll. He barked commands, and his men moved into action. Grappling hooks shot from the harnesses the mercenaries wore, piercing the trees. The iron cables yanked them into the air toward the colossal creatures. Two men flew up, splitting limbs and heads with a swipe of their blades.

Cassiel pulled her away from the chaos to a safe distance. Clearly, they weren't needed.

A troll came roaring at the captain. He shot cabled hooks into a tree, and it catapulted him into the air. In a perfect arc, he flipped behind the troll as he came down, and his blades crossed at the creature's neck. Dark blood sprayed, leaving the severed head to fall into the bushes. He landed with perfect balance and straightened from his stance. His sharp blue eyes glanced around at the mass of dead trolls scattered around them. The men carefully walked among the enormous bodies and made sure each was dead by shoving their swords into every skull.

Sheathing his blades, the captain pulled down his mask, revealing a familiar face shadowed in thick stubble.

"That was a close one, lass," Klyde said in a mischievous brogue Azure accent.

Dyna managed a relieved smile. "Thank you, Captain. It seems I am indebted to you again."

When Lord Jophiel said sellswords lived on Troll Bridge, she hadn't expected to run into Klyde. But she was a little relieved not to find a complete stranger.

Another man approached. Beneath his brown curls was a black eye patch with a jagged scar going down his cheek. His brow set sternly over his visible gray-blue eye. He pulled down his facemask as well, and Dyna recognized him as the one who had accompanied Klyde in the Port of Azure.

"You..." Cassiel stared at them. "I remember you from the city. You're the ones my uncle spoke of?"

"Aye. I'm Klyde, Captain of the Skelling Mercenaries." He nodded to the man with the eyepatch on his right. "This is Eagon, my lieutenant."

"And you chose now to finally make an appearance?"

"You have no right to complain," Eagon said, his brogue voice thick and sharp. His coat hung open, giving her a glimpse of the two crossing belts on his chest containing a series of sharp throwing stars.

The rest of the mercenaries stood behind them. They were rugged, with scars on their face and hands. These men were not surprised to see them, nor did they react to Cassiel's wings.

Klyde's gaze leveled on him. "Per the arrangement between us and the lord of your mountain, Celestials are to stay out of our territory, and we agreed to stay out of yours."

"You are currently looking at the new Lord and Lady of Hermon Ridge," Cassiel said tersely.

"Pleasure to meet you." Klyde gave him a stiff smile and dipped his chin in a nod. "Well, *Lord*, you have entered here without our consent and disturbed the land with your noise and foreign scents. Because of it, the trolls are out hunting instead of hibernating at this time of year. The danger was something you chose to risk. Be grateful we came out here at all."

"We're immensely grateful, Captain," Dyna cut in, giving Cassiel a look to be nice.

"But there are only three of you." Klyde frowned. "I was told there would be five."

Dyna gasped and wildly searched the clearing. "Lucenna and Rawn, they're gone. And Fair? Where is Fair?"

They had gotten separated during the chaos.

Zev sniffed the ground, whining. They followed him to the bluff's edge and horror went through her to see the footprints and hoofprints on the muddied ground. The river below rushed out into the forest.

Cassiel cursed. "They must have fallen over."

"Then the river carried them away," Klyde said. "Pray to the God of Urn they survived the fall and haven't frozen to death. Better we find them before dark." He signaled, and the men mounted their horses.

"Wait," Dyna said at Zev's bark. He limped ahead for another set of smaller tracks. "They chased Lucenna off this way."

Klyde muttered something tightly under his breath, rubbing his face. "Eagon, take half to search for the elf. Olyver and the rest will escort these three back to town. I will go after the woman."

Cassiel crossed his arms. "We are not going anywhere with them."

"We're coming with you," Dyna said.

Klyde removed a pack from his horse's saddle and slung it over his arm before handing Cassiel the reins. "I mean no offense, but you will only get in the way. We know the land and how to move through it unseen. Bringing you along will either end with your death or mine. As for your friend, she's headed straight for a troll den, and the chances of finding her alive decreases by the minute. That part of the Bridge is so perilous, the only one to make it out of there alive is me."

Dyna felt torn, but for all their experience, they weren't equipped for this.

"Then take Zev. He can help track her."

Klyde frowned at the blood leaking from the deep gash on the wolf's hind leg. Dyna ripped off a strip from the hem of her dress and tied it around the wound.

"With that injury, he would only be bait." Klyde nodded at Eagon. The lieutenant ordered the men to move out, and they rode south. "Trust me when I say the best thing you can do for your friends is to wait in my town."

Dyna searched his eyes, trying to perceive anything behind his amiable face. "If I'm being honest, I don't know if I do trust you, Captain. At the moment, you seem to be our only option. But Lucenna may attack you first before giving you a chance to speak. If she allows you to get a word in, tell her I said *sage*. She will know what it means."

Klyde raised his eyebrows. "Very well. I give you my word I will bring her back. Leave us to do what we do best."

"And what's that?" Cassiel asked.

The captain shot a grin over his shoulder as he turned away. "Killing trolls." Then he vanished into the trees.

The remaining mercenaries eyed them stoically.

Only a stocky man with a crop of orange curls gave them a warm smile. "I'm Olyver. Don't worry about your companions. They will find them." He motioned north. "Skelling Rise is this way. Come along then, it's a fair jaunt to town."

Dyna looked up at the overcast sky, noticing the icy rain had changed to flurries.

"It's not sticking to the ground," Cassiel said, reading her thoughts. "We still have time."

She nodded and pushed aside the unsettling feeling. He helped her mount Klyde's horse. Once she was seated, he slipped on his enchanted coat and climbed up behind her. Dyna's body sank into his divine heat, not realizing how cold she'd been. His arms came around her as he took the reins.

Sage? Cassiel's voice slipped in her mind. *Does it have some hidden meaning?*

She smiled a secret smile. *Something like that.*

CHAPTER 70

Lucenna

Lucenna blinked through her bleary vision at the tree branches above her. They seemed to swim past, stretching toward the dark sky as it wept soft white tears. Her back dragged over the cold, hard ground, forest debris stabbing through her clothes. A sharp pang went through her skull, clearing her consciousness. She snapped her head up to see a troll dragging her by the leg in the direction of a large, dark hole within a rocky ridge.

Panic fired through her. She called on her magic, but it pulsed weakly, and light sputtered in her numb hands. Sharp pain throbbed in her head again. Half of her face was stiff with dried blood. Last thing she remembered was Rawn falling, then something hitting her before everything went black.

Her mind scrambled for a plan. Attacking the troll now would only make it finish the kill when she had no magic to defend herself. It snarled, and Lucenna quickly shut her eyes, playing dead. The fright of waking up alone and trapped bubbled up in her chest, but she tramped it down. *Think!* She forced herself to calm down and breathe.

The minimal evening light faded as the troll dragged her into the cave. Her stomach rolled with the horrid stench of feces and other rotten filth. She inhaled a shallow breath, trying not to taste it. The troll's heavy steps thudded, making the ground rattle. Something cold poked her. She peeked through her lashes and bit back a scream at the thousands of bones littering the ground.

Lucenna felt around at her waist and drew out a knife. If she could stick the beast in the eye, she could make a run for it. A mewling sound echoed in the cave. She snapped her head to the nest of dried leaves and mud where cub trolls perked up. She only knew they were cubs by their stunted teeth and were half the size of a full-sized one.

The troll lifted her in the air to feed her to them, and Lucenna lashed out with her knife, slicing one of its eyes. The troll bellowed and dropped her outside of the nest. The knife fell somewhere among the filth. Lucenna scrambled backward. Her fingers came over a long, sharp bone and she snatched it in her hands.

A flash of black flitted through the cave—some sort of furred creature. It ran at the troll, lumbering for her, and leaped onto its back. Lucenna caught the flash of long, sharp claws before they plunged through the troll's thick neck. Blood spurted from its gaping mouth and the claws ripped the troll's throat clean away. The beast teetered over the nest. Wild squeals of the cubs cut off abruptly as it crashed on top with a heavy thud.

Lucenna gasped and jerked back when the furred creature looked at her. It had a deer skull for a face, sharp antler horns, and thick, dirty black fur covering its hulking body and hunched back. Not as tall as the troll, but still big. She had only heard stories of the Wendigo, and none of them were good.

It moved a step, and she lifted the bone. "Come near me, and I will run you through."

It made an awful sound that reverberated eerily within its skull. Was it laughing?

"On your feet, lass." That brogue voice, smooth and deep like the flow of the sea's current, carried in the quiet cave.

The creature reached up with a clawed hand and removed its face...only to reveal another. Lucenna gawked dumbly, her mind taking a moment to make sense that she was looking at a man beneath the skull. One she had met before. His jaw was layered with a thicker beard than when they first met, but she recognized that cocky grin.

Lucenna blinked, not sure if she was indeed conscious. "Klyde?"

"I'm rather pleased you remember me."

Well, he had certainly made an impression. Not that she would ever admit it.

Klyde took her wrist in his gloved hand, careful not to scratch her with the long, sharp claws fastened at the tip of his fingers, and hauled her up. "The fates have allowed us to meet again, after all."

"Why are you here? How did you—"

A roar rang outside.

"Questions later." He pulled her deeper into the cave.

"What are you doing?" She yanked to free herself, failing to slip from his tight grasp.

Klyde shoved her into a slim, shallow crevice in the cave and forced his way in with her. He pinned her arms to the cave walls, his hips pressing into hers. Their faces were inches apart, and she could feel *everything*. Heat rose to her cheeks.

"Get off—"

He covered her mouth. Infuriated, she tried to kick, but there was no space. Klyde's blue eyes widened irately, warning her to keep quiet.

A Horde of trolls entered the cave. They noticed the dead one and fell on it with a ravaged aggression. Klyde shifted his head to block her view, but he couldn't block her ears. Wet sounds and crunch of bones filled the cave, making her stomach roll. Her heart thudded wildly as she squeezed her eyes shut. At the moment, she didn't care that his warm body was indecently pressed against hers—or that he smelled awful. He was a wall between her and those creatures.

And she wasn't alone.

After a few minutes of listening to the trolls gorge themselves, Klyde made hand motions that seemed to give some instruction.

"I don't know what that means," she hissed under her breath.

Frowning, he slipped his skull mask on and slinked out of the crevice with her. Lucenna reluctantly let him extend his furred cloak over her head. It reeked of musky beast. His arm slipped around her waist, pulling her tight against him as he had in the witch's den, and he led them away. Where was he taking her? She focused on their boots hurrying over the hard ground. It grew darker and colder, the sounds of the beasts falling distant.

"Klyde," she growled after a minute. "I can't breathe under this thing. It stinks!"

Lucenna shoved off the fur only for her foot to meet open air. She shrieked, and he yanked her back. They were on a very narrow rock ledge, no more than a foot wide. Beyond it stretched a drop into the pitch-black darkness. Lucenna threw herself backward, and her back slapped against the rock wall behind her. Her vision swam as she gasped for air.

"Oi, are you all right?"

"Too high." She hyperventilated. Her legs buckled, and Klyde pinned her to the wall with his body. Of all the fears to have, unfortunately, heights were hers.

"Don't look at that. Look at me." He grabbed her arms, and the clawed points lightly prodded her skin. The sensation made her shiver. "I'm right here. Look at me, Lucenna."

She was.

A glowing crystal with a *lux* symbol hung from a cord tied to the antlers. He lifted the mask, leaving the crystal to dangle by his ear. It cast shadows across the planes of his features. Her mind stilled as she studied that fine jawline and long lashes. He had a very nice face. Hard and angled in all the right places. They stared at each other in the echoing silence for a long minute until she realized what he said.

She narrowed her eyes. "I don't recall telling you my name, and you have yet to explain your presence here."

"Your companions told me," he said after a pause. "Dyna also instructed me to give you the word *sage*? I assume that means something to you."

Lucenna continued glowering at him. They had recently used that herb in a defense spell, so it could only mean one thing. Dyna had sent him, but she was warning her to be on guard.

"We arrived before they nearly fell to the Horde," Klyde said, drawing her out of her thoughts.

She gasped. "Rawn."

"My lieutenant has gone in search of him. The others are waiting for you in my town."

She absorbed what he said again, and her eyes widened. "*Your* town? You live on Troll Bridge?"

"Aye."

Then her first assumption of him was correct. His uniform beneath the fur, his weapons, the sigil on his baldric—he was a soldier, but not for any king.

His breath feathered down her neck, making Lucenna's pulse jump. Her chest heaved, increasingly aware of every inch of his warm, sculpted build pressed firm against hers, his strength obvious and overpowering.

"You can let go now," she snapped.

"Only if you promise not to panic again."

"If I do?"

"I have other ways of calming you down." Klyde's husky voice elicited a rush of heat through her cold cheeks, and she inexplicably glanced at his lips inches away from hers. One end of his mouth hitched, a hint of a dimple appearing. "You're making an interesting expression, lass. What are you thinking about?"

Lucenna scowled. "I'm thinking about pushing you into the pit."

But he had her pinned to the cave wall. She wouldn't be able to shove him off, at least not physically. A purple hue sparked in the dark with the crackle of her magic.

"You have exactly three seconds to remove your hands before I remove them *off* you."

Klyde laughed quietly, and the rough, deep tone sent a cascade of faint shivers down her spine. "I must admit, that isn't how I thought to be thanked for saving your life."

"I will gladly show you how thankful I am," she gritted out.

His lashes lowered, and his head dipped, his next words brushing against her ear. "Provided we survive tonight, I look forward to it." His breath coasted over her neck, sending a flutter through her stomach, before he backed off. "Keep moving. We have a ways to go."

She resisted the instinct to grab the end of his furred cloak like a frightened child. Keeping her eyes locked on his back, she pretended they weren't a foot away from death. Their echoing footsteps and the soft crackle of rock falling over the edge made her breath come in heavy again. She needed a distraction.

It occurred to her he hadn't been startled by her power.

"Why did they send you?" Lucenna asked. "Dyna and Zev, they would have come."

"Aye, they certainly tried," he said, his voice carrying in the vast space. "But no one knows these caves better than I, and no one else would know how to escape a troll den alive."

"Why is that?"

"You weren't the only one brought home for dinner." His antlers and hunched form cast long shadows over the immense walls. They bounced with each of his movements.

"And the disguise?" she asked next.

"The Wendigo is the only monster the trolls fear."

So looking like one and *smelling* like one was a survival tactic. Lucenna had to admit that was smart. She followed his purposeful stride, reading the confidence in every step. "How many times have you gone through this cave?"

"As long as it took to learn each tunnel. I made it a priority to memorize every inch of the Bridge." Klyde led her through a narrow opening, and they entered a smaller cave. Nodding, he removed the crystal from his antlers and hung it on a stalagmite, filling the space with soft light. "We will stay here for the night."

"What?" she exclaimed. "No. We need to keep going."

"You lot have woken the trolls. Right now, they are in a frenzy, hunting for a last meal. Once they see there is nothing left to feed on, they will lose interest and hibernate." He lifted a hand when she tried to protest. "We will make our way out in the morning."

Klyde dropped his furred cloak and mask at his feet, unveiling his blue coat and the many weapons strapped to his body. He also carried a pack, explaining the back hunch. He removed it and pulled out a rolled-up blanket, a waterskin, and a burlap sack. "Here, have a drink."

Taking the offered waterskin, she downed the icy water. "We don't need to stay the night to avoid them," she said. "I can get us out of here."

Lucenna cast an invisibility spell, and Klyde's eyebrows shot up. But it lasted only a few seconds before it left her gasping from the effort. Her Essence needed time to recover.

"It seems your candle has burned out," he said, making her flush. Klyde motioned at the blanket and burlap sack he set out for her. "Best we rest here and try to stay warm, aye?"

Without waiting for an answer, he laid back on the ground and rested on the lump of fur like a pillow. A clear sign he had no intention of moving on. Klyde was completely relaxed, hands linked behind his head as he watched her restlessly pace. Was the air thinner in here?

"I can't wait until morning," she said. "You stay if you want. I will find my own way out." Lucenna pivoted on her heel and headed the way they came in.

Klyde instantly appeared in front of her. "Woah, there. You need to be patient and wait until morning."

"Move."

"I can't do that. If you leave now, you won't make it out alive. I gave my word to your companions that I would bring you back, preferably breathing, and that's what I intend to do." He held out a hand. "So please. *Sit*."

The command sent an odd current through her chest. She tried to dodge him, but he stepped in her way.

"I have no qualms with throwing you over my shoulder, lass."

"You wouldn't—" The ground dropped out from under her, and she fell with an oomph on something firm, her silvery hair swishing in her face. His shoulder moved fluidly beneath her stomach, and his boots crunched over gravel as he marched back. "Put me down!"

Lucenna beat on his back, but it was like punching a rock.

Klyde dropped her on the blanket, and his large frame crouched in front of her. "Even if you found your way out of the cave without drawing the trolls, it's sundown. The temperature falls dangerously low at night here. With what you're wearing, you would freeze within the hour."

She glanced down at her black leggings and fitted wool sweater. A chill had settled in her bones even if she was out of the elements. It must be worse outside.

"You have magic, but clearly it's run out. Tell me, can you hold a flame?" he asked. "For how long? How many hours can you defend yourself before you're depleted again? You don't know which direction the town lies or where else to find shelter. Trolls are not the only thing that kills out here, lass. The cold is a cruel mistress, and she is kind to no one."

Lucenna didn't answer because she had no argument.

At her silent compliance, Klyde stood. "Now, can I trust you to stay, or do I need to lie next to you and keep you warm?"

Startled by the question, her face grew hot again. This man surely liked to try her patience.

"Don't come anywhere near me," she hissed. "I'll stay, but if you try anything, I will smother you in your sleep."

A grin spread across his face, and two dimples appeared on his cheeks. Klyde removed his bracers and greaves to slip off his coat, and draped it over Lucenna's shoulders, much to her surprise. He dragged the smelly pelt between her and the entrance and laid down again. Now that he'd removed a couple layers, she could see how well fitted his white shirt was, and the mass of his arms as he crossed them behind his head.

He nodded to the sack beside her. "There's food in there if you're hungry."

The mention of food made her mouth water. After a pause, she reached for it and pulled out a bundle of cloth. Inside were pieces of dried white meat.

She bit into one, finding it chewy and gamey. It tasted strange. "What is this?"

"Basilisk."

"Ugh." She spat it out and pitched the sack back to him. "That's disgusting."

"Really? I find it suitable."

"You clearly care little about what comes out of your mouth than what goes in it," Lucenna snapped.

Klyde's dark chuckle echoed softly in the cave. "Lass, I am very selective about what goes into my mouth."

CHAPTER 71

Dynalya

It was dark by the time they reached the town of Skelling Rise. Icy wind and flurries blew past Dyna's face, obscuring most of her vision. Spots of tiny orange lights in a perfectly straight line glowed high in the dark like fireflies. It took her a moment to realize they were torch fires. They rested on a towering stone wall that rose beyond the forest against the backdrop of the night sky.

"That has to be easily over sixty feet tall," Cassiel murmured behind her. He was a constant source of warmth with an arm wrapped around her waist, but it couldn't ward off the biting air. It was so cold it nipped at her fingers and toes. Their horse nickered as the mercenaries came to a stop before thick iron gates. Beyond it was a black void that made her heart rate increase.

An enormous shadow bounded past, iridescent yellow eyes reflecting in the dark. Zev had stayed in his wolf form, probably out of caution. They didn't know what they were heading into, but at the moment, it meant shelter out of the harsh weather.

Olyver let out a sharp whistle at the wall, and there was movement on the ramparts. He waved his torch three times in some signal. Voices called back, and a horn blew one long blare. A loud, creaking groan followed, and the iron gates slowly lifted.

Nodding, he led the way inside, with the mercenaries coming up behind them. Their torches revealed they'd entered a short tunnel. On the other end was a tall set of fortified wooden doors. Once the gates dropped again, the doors were hauled open. Hooves beat on cobblestone as they cantered into the town.

Dyna could hardly see much, but from the twinkle of torches spreading into the distance, the wall circling Skelling Rise spread far and wide for several miles. She could perceive rolling hills and the houses built on them by the lights in their windows. As they rode ahead, the mercenaries broke away one by one, riding for the houses with their families eagerly waiting at the door, until Olyver and two other mercenaries remained. He led them through the quiet square, and they passed by a fountain with the statue of a beautiful woman coated in frost.

From the little Dyna could see, they were well established. How long had they been living on Troll Bridge? The ruins of Azurite must be far from here.

"Where are you taking us?" Cassiel asked.

"To the Lieutenant's house," Olyver said. "You will await him and the captain there."

They moved onto a road up a hill. There stood a modest home of two stories and a barn nearby. Three silhouettes waited in the doorway, and the smallest one dashed down the steps.

"Evin!" a woman called after him.

The little boy's bare feet pattered on the ground as he ran up to them with a big, excited grin, blond curls bouncing around his face. He was about four years old and wore nothing but a long nightdress.

His smile dropped when he got close enough to see them. "Papa?"

"Hello there, lad," Olyver greeted.

"Evin, I told you to wait inside, dear." A woman rushed forward and pulled him against her hip. Her dress fluttered in the wind, outlining her round belly. She was heavily pregnant. Blond hair whipped past her face, her kind blue eyes quickly bouncing on all their faces.

"Good evening." She offered them a smile, but it couldn't hide her visible worry. Her questioning gaze shot to Olyver. "Where is Eagon? Klyde?"

The other one at the door crossed the porch, and Dyna saw it was an older boy. A lad of fourteen or fifteen, with light brown hair and light eyes.

"They'll be back soon. No worries," Olyver assured her. "Some of their party was separated during the attack and they've gone to search for them."

"Oh, thank the God of Urn." The woman sighed. The next smile she gave them was much brighter. "I'm Gale, Eagon's wife. This is my son, Evin, and my nephew, Tavin."

The lad nodded in greeting.

"A pleasure to meet you," Dyna said, smiling in return. "My name is Dyna, and this is my husband, Cassiel." She glanced at the shadows near the barn. "The shy one over there is Zev."

The introduction prompted her cousin to slip out of the darkness and Gale yelped, a hand flying to her stomach. "Good Gods, is that a wolf?"

"He's friendly," Dyna said.

For the most part, Cassiel's retort slipped through her mind.

"I give you my word he will be well behaved," she assured them.

Evin ran up to Zev, not at all frightened. He cooed and giggled as he petted him.

"Oh, Evin, leave him be," Gale said uneasily.

"Come here, tyke." Tavin grabbed the little boy's hand, tugging him up the stairs into the house.

"Well, come in from out of the cold," Gale said. "I imagine all of you must be hungry."

The men happily dismounted at the mention of food, and they tied their reins to the porch rail.

Cassiel slid down first before taking her waist and lifting her off. *Have I told you what it does to me when you call me husband?*

She hid a smile. *No.*

He settled her on her feet and his hand drifted to her hip, shooting fiery tingles across her stomach. *It gives me the inherent desire to taste those words as they leave your lips.*

Zev chuffed at them in annoyance, and she blushed at being caught. They weren't doing anything wrong, but it felt like he'd walked in on them, sharing sweet nothings in the dark.

Cassiel smirked. "Behave or we will leave you outside, wolf."

Growling, Zev leaped up the stairs onto the porch. They climbed up the steps after him. Dyna glanced at the sky and some of her worry eased to see the flurries were lifting. She whispered a prayer that Rawn and Lucenna were safe and would be reunited with them soon.

They entered the house, and a welcoming warmth came over them. A fire burned strongly in the corner hearth. Some couches were set over a furred rug beside it. Gale called them to the kitchen, where a round table was set with a small feast. The mercenaries had plates with heaping servings of potatoes, sausages, and peas.

"The unmarried men like coming here to eat," Gale told her. "I always make sure to have enough for a few extra mouths."

"We come because no one cooks like you," a mercenary garbled through a mouthful.

"Swallow your food before speaking, Cam." She playfully smacked his shoulder and nodded for them to sit. "Help yourselves to anything you like while I get the drinks."

Dyna served herself and Cassiel helpings of roasted vegetables, cheese, and bread. Zev laid by her seat, still refusing to shift, so Gale set a plate on the floor for him. As the hour wore on, Evin fell asleep on his mother's lap. Tavin listened with eager excitement as the mercenaries told him all the gory details of taking down the Horde.

Now that she could see him in better lighting, Dyna thought he had a striking resemblance to Klyde.

The blare of a horn sounded in the distance. The mercenaries rushed to the door. Gale moved to stand and hissed through a wince.

"Here, let me," Dyna rushed to take her sleeping son, but Tavin grabbed him first.

"I've got him, auntie," he told Gale, shooting Dyna a distrustful look. "I'll put him to bed."

"Thank you, sweetheart."

The lad left the kitchen and his heavy steps bounded up the stairs.

Dyna helped Gale stand. "How far along are you?"

She laughed tiredly and rubbed her belly. "I'm nearly eight moons. More than ready to have this wee one. I told Eagon I'm finished having bairns, what with me mothering half the men."

She meant it as a lighthearted jest, but Dyna frowned at her worriedly. There was a gauntness to the woman's pretty features and dark shadows beneath her eyes.

The neigh of horses drew them to the den where all the gathered warmth had been stolen out the open front door. As before, the group of mercenaries split off along the road, riding on to their homes. Only a few men followed Eagon up the hill.

"Fair." Dyna smiled in relief when she spotted the white horse among them, but it faded at seeing the bundled body lying on his back. She ran down the porch with Cassiel and Zev. "What happened? Is he all right?"

"He found him unconscious a mile down from the cascades," Eagon said. "That horse of his pulled him out of the water."

"Well done, Fair," Dyna said. The horse nickered tiredly in response. She brushed away the wet strands sticking to Rawn's pale face and pressed two fingers to his neck. "His pulse is weak, and he's frozen half to death. We need to get him inside."

"Give me a hand," Cassiel said to Eagon. Between them, they carried Rawn into the house and laid him on the blanket Gale laid in front of the fireplace.

"Help me undress him. We need to get him warm." She turned away to grab her satchel as Cassiel quickly removed Rawn's soaked clothing and shoes. Once they covered him with more blankets, Dyna kneeled next to him. "Can you hear me, Lord Norrlen?"

She checked each limb for breaks and pressed her ear to his chest. Rawn's heartbeat was too slow and his chest struggled to rise. He mumbled something in his delirium. A name she couldn't quite hear. He was feverish.

"Something is wrong." She studied his breathing and the way each wheezing breath pulled against his bruised ribs. "I need to see inside."

"Give her some room," Cassiel said and boots shuffled back.

Dyna conjured a mist of swirling Essence. Tendrils of light spilled from her hands as she cast it over Rawn's still form. She closed her eyes and let her magic weave through his body. His ribs were fractured, and one of his lungs had collapsed. Soft gasps and murmurs hovered in the corners of her awareness as she worked to repair the damage and slowly bring his temperature back to normal. When she finished, he took a deep breath before settling back into sleep.

"He will be all right," Dyna sighed. Her power was at its limit now, and she was exhausted. Cassiel helped her back to her feet. "Thank you for bringing him back…"

Eagon, his wife, and the mercenaries—everyone was staring at her.

"What of Lucenna?" Cassiel asked Eagon, breaking the silence.

"If they haven't arrived by now, the captain must have taken shelter for the night. It's too dangerous to be out in this weather," Eagon said, still looking at her. "Klyde knows what he's doing. I trust they will return by morning. You're welcome to stay tonight and have a meal if you haven't eaten yet."

Cassiel nodded stiffly.

"Thank you," Dyna added, since he forgot that part.

The lieutenant asked Olyver to take Fair to the barn on his way out while the new arrivals went into the kitchen to eat.

"I'm tired, love," Gale mumbled sleepily to her husband.

"I will have some blankets brought down to you," Eagon told them, then he lifted Gale in his arms and climbed up the steps with Tavin following.

"I don't like the way they were looking at you," Cassiel said under his breath.

Zev growled faintly in agreement.

"Perhaps my magic startled them," Dyna whispered back. "They might think I'm a witch."

"We will take turns keeping watch. As soon as Lucenna arrives, we go."

After a while, Eagon returned with more blankets and told the men to take their leave. They settled in for the night with only the fireplace for light. Dyna checked on Rawn again before laying down on the couch with her head on Cassiel's lap.

But she couldn't sleep.

Her mind wouldn't quiet when an urgent anxiety made her aching body restless. Lucenna was out there somewhere, and time was ticking by. Winter hovered over them like a storm waiting to pour.

Cassiel's voice curled through her mind. *Sleep.*

I can't. She sighed and looked up at him. *I'm worried.*

His eyes caught the firelight as he looked down at her. *I know. I am, too. But you need your rest for the long journey ahead. We all do.*

She glanced at where Zev lay next to Rawn. His eyes were shut, but she knew her cousin was alert and listening to the sounds in the house.

I'm afraid to say it.

Then don't.

What if...

Don't think about it, Dyna. We will make it out of here.

They would make it out. She chanted it to herself, turning it into a prayer. They would reach a western port before the Saxe Sea froze, because they couldn't lose three months of their journey. They couldn't.

Sleep. Cassiel's fingers slipped into her hair and lightly massaged her scalp in slow circles. As if by magic, his touch drew out a low exhale that had her stiff shoulders relaxing. *Forget the winter. Imagine you are laying in a glade of wildflowers fluttering in a warm breeze.*

Her lashes drifted closed, and she smiled as he tucked the blanket around her. *There is a field exactly like that behind my cottage, full of poppies, marigolds, and cosmos. The air smells the sweetest there in the spring.* Her nose burned as wetness gathered behind her eyelids. *The Zafiro Mountains stand high and proud against the clear blue sky. Cascades spill off the range and stream into the crystal blue lake at the bottom near the village. Our home is nestled within the rolling hills with a view of it all.*

She could picture it so clearly. Her heart ached with a longing to see her family and home again.

It sounds lovely. Cassiel wiped away the stray tear rolling down her temple. *I would like to see it when this is all over.*

You would come with me?

Lev sheli, I would follow you anywhere.

That made her smile. Dyna cupped his hand to her cheek and imagined him in North Star with her. That too was a very clear picture in her mind, as if the future itself promised he would one day.

Fatigue finally caught up to her, and sleep came swiftly, carrying her to summer fields.

Dyna woke with a shiver. A gray darkness filled the living room with the heavy drapes drawn over the windows. The light of morning leaked through the edges. Thin curls of smoke drifted from the fireplace, orange cinders fading from last night's fire. Cassiel slept beside her. He was warm and solid with his steady heartbeat in her ear. She flushed at finding her body pressed against him, her leg shamelessly between his.

So as not to wake him, she gently slipped his arm from her waist and rolled off the couch. The pile of blankets by the fireplace was empty. The others must be awake. She stretched through a yawn before walking to the window and lifting one end of the drapes. Her mind must have still been half-asleep because she struggled to comprehend what her eyes were seeing. She didn't understand the frost on the glass or the white landscape beyond it.

The sky was a veil of thick clouds, and from it streamed endless white fluff. She stared at it for a long minute, blinking repeatedly.

Until it made sense.

"No..." Dyna whispered in dismay. "No, no, no!"

She burst through the front door. The frigid air fell over her as her feet sunk into the deep white carpet of snow, reaching to her knees. A blanket of white covered the entire town of Skelling Rise.

A spot of color stood out on a short hill ahead of her.

Rawn.

He kneeled in the snow, absolutely still. She ran to him. He didn't react when Dyna reached him. Didn't move at all. His mangled blond hair blew limply around his lowered face. For a dreadful second, she feared he had died out here when no one noticed. In his hand was a crumpled up envelope. The letter to his wife he'd been carrying in his pocket for the last two months.

And now he couldn't send it at all, because there was no leaving Troll Bridge.

"Rawn?" she called to him anxiously. When he didn't answer, she touched his shoulder. He was ice cold. "Rawn?"

Their wise Guidelander, who always had the answer, broke down. His body shook with quiet sobs. Kneeling in the snow, Dyna hugged the warrior and cried with him.

CHAPTER 72

Zev

Zev sniffed the morning air, searching for that telltale scent of lightning. He couldn't smell much past the usual pine and earth. They said Lucenna had gone west toward troll territory. He heard Eagon send Olyver to search for them before first light. If she wasn't back by the end of the hour, Zev would go search for her himself.

His paws sank in the snow as he looked out at the main road through town. Several houses spread out far and wide. Fallow fields and orchards on the west end, and cliffs on south. On the east was a thick forest. Beyond it, a large roof peeked above the trees.

Another gust of wind blew against him, and it drew his attention to the wall. They were close.

He winced at the blare of a horn announcing arrivals at the gate. It creaked open and a small unit of mercenaries galloped in with Klyde at the front. Lucenna rode on his horse with him.

Zev tracked their journey across town on the trampled path to Eagon's house. When Lucenna saw him, she smiled with relief, but it was tired and bleak.

His tail wagged of its own accord, glad to have the last member of his family returned.

Klyde dismounted and tried to help her down, but Lucenna ignored his hand and slid off herself. She was dirty, her clothes torn, and her lilac eyes lacked their usual vibrance.

"I'm all right," Lucenna said at his worried whine, and she leaned against his shoulder. "I need a bed and three days of sleep."

"That is one massive wolf," Klyde said, studying him warily. "Is he tame?"

She smirked. "Only with those he likes. Shall we see if he approves of you? Why don't you give him a little pet?"

Zev growled. He didn't particularly dislike the man, but he didn't trust him either.

"I think I'd rather keep my hand, lass. Come. Let's get out of this cold."

Zev's paws clicked on the porch steps as they went into the house. He quickly picked up loud voices talking over each other.

"You will let us pass."

"I cannot."

"You can't hold us here!" Cassiel shouted at the mercenaries standing between him and the front door. Dyna was trying to calm him down.

Behind them sat a catatonic Rawn on the couch. He had been quiet since they woke to a land coated in snow. Zev sauntered in and went to lie at Rawn's feet. It was all he could do right now for his friend.

"What's all this, then?" Klyde said, announcing their arrival.

Dyna's face lit up, and she rushed to embrace Lucenna. "I was so worried about you."

"I'm fine. It seems we have bigger problems."

She sighed. "The lieutenant says we cannot leave."

"The blizzard is picking up." Eagon turned to Klyde. "I tried to explain to them it would be a death sentence if they attempted to cross now. It's too late for them."

Zev didn't like the sound of that. *Too late.*

The Madness stirred in his mind, but it made no commentary yet. It hadn't spoken in days.

Klyde crossed his arms and leaned against the wall. "Aye, he's right. Troll Bridge is two hundred miles long. It takes about six days to cross on foot. Five days without sleep, because if you did sleep in those freezing temperatures, I guarantee you would wake at Death's Gate. Our winters are merciless and nothing like you're used to. This blizzard will seal the gorge by tomorrow. I'm afraid you're stuck here until the end of the season."

Zev heard Rawn's sharp intake of breath, along with Cassiel and Lucenna's low curses.

Three months.

That was how much time they would lose, at the very least. How much longer would it take them to find Mount Ida and return? Once the snow melted and caught a ship, the voyage alone would take months. He met Dyna's watery eyes. They had exactly until next winter to stop the Shadow.

"Which one among you is the leader?" Klyde asked.

At the long pause that followed, they all glanced at their motionless Guidelander. Rawn looked so thin and exhausted under the blanket around his shoulders. His turquoise irises were stark against his bloodshot eyes. Zev nudged his knee.

"Oh. Pardon," Rawn answered with a soft rasp. He stood and limply nodded to Klyde. "I am Rawn Norrlen of Greenwood, and these are my companions. Thank you for your assistance."

"There is no need to thank us. This was a job."

At their blank stares, Eagon clarified. "We're mercenaries. We're owed payment for services rendered."

"Pardon?" Rawn repeated.

Klyde smirked. "You didn't think my men ventured out there for free, did you?"

They stared at him mutely, and Zev decided then he didn't like him after all.

Lucenna let out a scoff, looking at the captain with disgust. "I suppose there is no use in helping someone unless there's coin in it."

His gaze slid to her.

"No one called for your services," Cassiel told him.

"Lord Jophiel hired us to see to your safety, Prince. He has yet to send the fee."

"How did he contact you?"

Klyde's mouth pursed in a thoughtful frown. "Through a mirror?"

Zev canted his head, not sure what he meant by that.

"We had it under control."

"Aye, of course you did." Klyde arched an eyebrow pointedly at their shabby appearance. "Except you were about to become minced meat, your leader fell into the river, and Lucenna was dragged to a troll den. Without us, whatever was left of you lot would be buried beneath the snow right now."

Zev bared his fangs. Dyna ran her fingers through his fur, whispering at him to stay calm.

Rawn exhaled tiredly and rubbed his face. "Enough. Arguing will resolve nothing. He is right. They saved our lives. We have payment for you, Captain. It's in my pack with my horse." At the reminder, distress crossed his face, and he glanced at Dyna. "Fair?"

"He's all right, Lord Norrlen. He's in the barn."

Rawn exhaled, his shoulders sinking.

"There was no pack with your horse when we found him," Eagon said. "It must have been lost when you fell."

They all collectively groaned. That meant their gold was at the bottom of the cascades. So much for swindling it from the poacher.

"Then, should you find it acceptable, we could barter for something else," Rawn said. "We have other skills that could be put to use."

As soon as he said it, Eagon's one eye instantly fell on Dyna. "Her."

Zev snarled at the same time Cassiel's fists flared with blue flames. Lucenna and Rawn also braced. They were severely outnumbered, but he didn't give a damn.

"Wait, let's not make assumptions," Dyna said, holding onto Zev's scruff and her mate's arm.

"You have been staring at her since last night," Cassiel growled. "Whatever your interest in my wife, know we will not hesitate to cut you down."

The mercenaries only looked amused, none bothering to draw out any weapons.

Klyde chuckled. "My, that was an interesting reaction." He glanced at Eagon. "What do you want with the lass?"

"She is a healer of some sort, Captain. Last night we witnessed her use magic to treat the elf." Eagon's gaze fixed on him, and Klyde's relaxed composure tensed. They held a silent stare. "I merely meant we could use her services for trade. Sigrid isn't fully recovered. We have elderly here and some ill. It would do well to have a healer on hand. And Gale…"

"What about her?" Klyde asked, his voice hardening.

"Oh, don't you start." They all glanced up at Gale standing at the top of the stairs. She rested a hand on her round belly as she carefully came down. "Both of you calm yourselves and stop putting our guests on edge."

"Gale." Klyde rushed to help her walk down the remaining steps. "How are you feeling?"

"Fat, Klyde. I feel fat. I can't get comfortable enough to sleep well at night. When I do finally sleep, I'm woken up by bickering. Is that what you want to hear?"

He chuckled and kissed her temple. "If my sister feels well enough to yell at me, then yes."

Zev sniffed the air, confirming they were indeed siblings. More heavy steps rushed down the stairs as the lad from yesterday came bounding down with little Evin in his arms.

"Klyde!" they both shouted together and threw themselves at him.

He laughed and embraced the boys, and all the tension that had been in the room earlier eased itself away.

"The house is getting crowded now," Eagon said to Olyver. "Head home and monitor the town in case anyone needs help during this snowstorm."

The mercenaries ambled outside to their waiting horses, and the sound of galloping hooves faded away.

"What do you say we get breakfast going, lad?" Klyde asked the youngest. "Come help me in the kitchen, Tavin."

"Keep Evin away from the fire," Gale said as the boys followed him through the swinging doors. She held Eagon's hand, and they faced them. "I'm sorry if my husband startled you. He isn't the best at explaining himself. It took me some time to get used to that."

Eagon's grim face softened.

"I was a sickly child," she continued in a quieter voice. "My immunities have always been weak. When we had Evin, I nearly died in childbirth. It was hard for all of us, especially Klyde. We didn't expect to conceive again, yet the God of Urn had other plans. But…it's been difficult for me. I'm always in pain and I can hardly stand most days." Gale looked back at the kitchen, where they could hear her family laughing. "This cannot be the birth that kills me."

Zev could smell it on her. The weakness. It oozed from her pores like a faint musk—and he also scented the old metallic scent of blood. The kind that only females had, but it didn't smell right.

Gale's watery eyes met Dyna's. "After we saw what you did for your friend yesterday…" Her voice broke. "It was like a miracle. An answer to the prayer we have been waiting for. I'm sorry you're stuck here, but I…."

"Hush." Dyna went to her. "You don't need to explain yourselves to me. I'm a Herb Master. I took a vow to treat whoever is in need, and I will help you as much as I can. Shall we go upstairs, so I may examine you?"

Gale nodded, wiping the tears from her pale face. She didn't look well. The couple thanked her profusely before Eagon helped his wife back up to their bedroom and Dyna went with them.

Lucenna sighed, sitting beside Rawn. "What are we going to do?"

He rubbed his haggard face. "Our provisions are scarce, nor do we have the proper clothing for winter. If we survived the trip out of Troll Bridge, the next town is not for another two hundred miles more. We cannot survive that long in the snow without shelter."

Cassiel stood by the windows with his arms crossed, watching the snow blow past. "I cannot fly for long in this weather, either. Travel is no longer an option."

They weren't going anywhere.

What's the matter, beastie?

Zev closed his eyes at the soft hiss. It was like claws scraping against his skull.

Oh, did you think I was going to leave you alone? No, you're not rid of me yet.

The fire crackled faintly in the grim silence.

"Perhaps this is good," Rawn murmured after a while. "Everything occurs for a reason."

503

They all stared at him like he had grown an extra limb.

"From the moment I left Greenwood, I have been on the run. Each of us has carried that burden at one point or another. We have been moving constantly, facing enemies at every turn and fighting to endure every day. We are all more than eager to complete our missions and return home, but it cannot be at the cost of our lives. Perhaps this is fate's way of saying we earned the rest." Rawn tried to sound optimistic for them, but he couldn't fully hide the dejection from his sad, tired eyes. "This will be a time to heal and to train. For all our power and skill, we nearly lost our lives out there. If we cannot fight trolls, then we are certainly not prepared for our destination."

Those beasts had been the first opponents Zev couldn't easily take down. Mount Ida was halfway across the world, within a perilous sea rampant with unknown monsters and magic. Yesterday proved they weren't ready for it yet.

"We have other reasons not to be here," Cassiel said.

At the nuance behind the statement, they all glanced over at Zev, then at the scars visible through his fur.

The moon is coming for you, the Madness hissed. *Are you ready to accept her light?*

He never was.

His body ached from the memory of his bones breaking and reshaping him into the bloodthirsty beast he truly was. Lucenna hadn't witnessed him change yet, though he had told her about his Other.

Lucenna straightened. "Is that why you haven't shifted?" she whispered. "Because you don't want to frighten them?"

Zev made the choice when they were brought here.

"They probably would not react well to learning he is a Lycan," Cassiel said quietly.

He wasn't a pureblooded werewolf, and that made him more dangerous than all the rest. If the mercenaries didn't attack him, they would most likely toss them to the Bridge. He could survive in the wilderness, but his friends couldn't say the same. It was best the townsfolk think him a domesticated wolf for now.

They fell back into grim silence. Zev lay by the fireplace and rested his head on his paws as he watched the fire dance. He was better off this way. On two feet, he couldn't seem to step out of the dark mist that followed him. In it, there was no light. No Gods. Only the emptiness of no purpose.

The others glowed like bright lights of life. But he was flickering like the weak flame of a dying candle on its last stretch of wick. It could go out any day if he let it. At least, as a wolf, he could detach from reality.

Lucenna came to sit by him. "Are you all right?"

He wasn't, but he was trying to be.

Lucenna gently ran her fingers over his furred ears. "We won't tell them until we have to. When is the full moon?" she asked the others.

Cassiel answered, observing the storm outside. "On the winter's solstice, in a week's time. It's going to be a long night."

"I'll keep you company," she told him.

Zev shook his head.

"You cannot be anywhere near him when he changes," Cassiel said. "Zev is not himself anymore when...it takes over."

It was possible to control the Other.

He had to learn how to first, but the ones who could teach him had returned to Lángshān. The only tools he had were his chains. They barely kept him contained, and he nearly killed Dyna twice. It filled him with such wretched guilt every time he glimpsed the jagged scars on her shoulder.

"Dyna told me what happened..." Lucenna said faintly. "I'm sorry."

Zev closed his eyes. He was sorry, too. He was so tired of Death following his shadow.

All we know is death, beastie.

"We look out for each other," Cassiel said. "There are sturdy trees outside of town. We will see to your restraints."

Zev nodded his thanks, but he dreaded that kiss of silver. He could already feel its burn. For now, this was what it took to keep going.

Soon after, Dyna returned with a worried look on her face. "I will need to stay close by," was all she said, confirming what Zev had suspected.

He looked out the window. The falling snow continued to thicken on the ground with no sign of stopping. Its color reminded him of the snowy hill from his dreams and the white wolf looking back at him.

"You must have all wondered by now," Dyna said under her breath. A wary tension filled the quiet as they all looked at each other with the same thought. "About the people who live in this place."

It surfaced the question that had been on the back of Zev's mind since they arrived. What's a secret town doing hidden in this place, and how did it get here?

CHAPTER 73

Lucenna

After breakfast, there wasn't much they could do but continue watching the blizzard come down harder. Lucenna alternated between napping, sipping Azeran's tea, and speaking to her brother through the orb. In the evening, she noticed Rawn was gone. Movement from the corner of her eye drew her to glance at the window. Rawn stood outside in the snowfall with his face pointed at the gray sky.

Their Guidelander wasn't all right. She could see it in the line of his shoulders and silhouette. He had always been there to support them when they needed him. It was her turn now.

Brisk wind blew against Lucenna when she opened the backdoor. Her boots sank into the deep snow as she waded out to him. The snowstorm whipped through them mercilessly, blowing her hair across her face. Rawn didn't move. His eyes were closed, letting the wind beat against him as though wishing it would carry him away.

"From the moment I left Greenwood, I have sent Aerina a letter every month," Rawn said. "Mere words on a page. It was all I could give her in the place of my absence. Though I could never receive a reply, I sent them without fail. I gave my word. She must have asked it of me, for it would be the only proof I lived. Yet, for the first time in twenty years, I failed to send my letter. I will fail to do so for the next three months." Emotion crossed his face before he wiped it away with a hand. "Life is a path of endless hurdles, and this is merely another storm. Hardship is what gives us the greatest opportunity to grow stronger..."

Rawn was the wise one of their group. He always knew what to say, but now it sounded as if he was attempting to give himself a speech of encouragement.

"It's all right not to be strong all the time, Lord Norrlen," she said softly. "That must sound absurd coming from me when I struggle with the same. We have relied on ourselves for years. It's hard to accept setbacks or to allow others to see us having them, but I understand." Lucenna patted his arm. "Your wife will not think you're dead. I'll get your letter to her. I can open a courier portal."

Rawn's startled eyes turned to her. "You have the power to do that?"

"My brother taught me how."

"I thought a moonstone was needed to open portals."

She shrugged. "Yes, but I can open a small one without a moonstone. I'm not supposed to use those types of spells because they require a vast amount of Essence, but I already cloaked this area." She kept to herself that portals could also be finicky. "I spoke to Lucien earlier, and he said the Enforcers have returned to Magos for the winter. My father isn't looking for me at the moment either, so I'd be happy to be your courier."

After staring at her for a moment, Rawn covered his face and laughed wetly.

"I'm sorry I didn't mention it before."

He shook his head and offered her a feeble smile. "Thank you, my lady. You have eased my burden."

"Of course." She motioned for him to sit. "You have locked on her Essence before, right?"

He chuckled and sat with her. "Yes."

Lucenna blushed, realizing it was a silly question. To lock on someone's Essence was as simple as touching them. Rawn had obviously touched his wife.

"I will teach you how to open your own portal, so all you need is a crystal to keep in contact with her. First, search for her Essence in your mind," she instructed. "We will essentially do a location spell first. Have you done that before?"

"I must admit, I have not."

"It's simple. It's similar to a tracking spell. The difference being you would use your Essence as a net and cast it forth in your mind's spatial dimension to locate her. We need to be careful. Mage magic and elf magic cannot mix."

"I understand."

Rawn breathed in deeply and his body glowed blue as he drew magic from the natural energy around them. They closed their eyes and Lucenna exhaled a low breath, letting herself sink into the *Essentia Dimensio*. She could feel and see his Essence spark wildly with excitement in the black void of magic. It took shape as a dancing teal light. Her purple Essence appeared next to his.

"I want you to picture your wife in your mind. Where she is. What she is doing. Her face. Her voice. How she makes you feel."

Lucenna couldn't see, but she knew he formed the image of her in his memories when his Essence sparked brightly.

"Cast it forth like a net," she said.

They watched his Essence flow forward. It spread outward like a blue web in the darkness, searching all points in the distance. As it stretched, the color of his untrained Essence wavered.

"Hold on to her, Lord Norrlen. On how much you wish to see her."

His Essence brightened and surged forward. Lucenna's Essence followed behind at a distance.

They sat that way for a long while as they searched and stretched their light across the country of Urn. The snow chilled their bodies and soaked their clothes. Time passed slowly. They were growing tired until they saw a tiny spot of white on the horizon of the dimension in their minds.

Ron's breath caught. "Aerina."

"Her Essence is white?" Lucenna asked, her mouth slacking in surprise. "Yes."

"Lord Norrlen, that is extremely rare. Your wife has a pure soul."

He sighed happily. "That she does."

"Go get her."

Lucenna pulled back her Essence. The teal light shot forth and latched onto the white light. Aerina's Essence leaped with surprise at first, then they entangled together, swirling like two vines. Her white light sparkled and danced radiantly around him with joy and relief.

"She feels you," Lucenna said. "She can use magic?"

"Yes," he whispered faintly, distracted.

"Now we need to open a rift in the spatial dimension, and it will reflect a portal in ours. It's going to require a lot of power to open one big enough to send your letter through. We spent most of our Essence, so it will be taxing."

"I'm ready."

Lucenna's sent her purple Essence forward and pressed it against the fabric of the dimension in a rapid spin. The more her Essence spun, it slowly cut a small rift in the space. She alternated with Rawn, and the rift grew leisurely, letting through a strip of light. The color of their aura faded as they lost power. Rawn's Essence fell away, having used all he could muster. Lucenna continued pushing open the portal, forcing it with all her might until her Essence died away too. It left her body feeling weak and her bones hollow.

"Open your eyes," she said breathlessly. Rawn obeyed, and they saw a small black hole in the air in front of them. It swirled with a black mist, no bigger than her fist. "Quick, send it through!"

Rawn shoved his crumpled letter inside, and they fell backward in the snow, completely drained. Cold sank through Lucenna's body as she trembled uncontrollably. Her mind was left foggy and dull.

Rawn laughed blissfully. "Thank you, my lady."

"Think nothing of it," she said through chattering teeth. Her power hadn't fully recovered from yesterday, and now she had pushed herself to her limits. "I'm depleted. I can't move."

"Forgive me. I should have considered that first." Rawn's brow scrunched and his leg twitched. "The feeling is returning to my limbs. I may rise soon."

"That's good…"

Elves didn't live off of their Essence like mages do. Rawn would be fine as soon as his energy returned, but it would take Lucenna a lot longer to recover. She used too much power.

"Are you all right?"

"Yes…" she mumbled faintly. "I'm only tired. I could use some sleep."

"No, my lady, do not fall asleep," Rawn said, sounding anxious.

But Lucenna's eyelids grew heavy, and she fought to keep them open. Hazily, she listened to Rawn grunt with irritation as he struggled to get up. Her lethargic eyes gazed at the overcast sky, watching the gentle snowfall fall.

It's beautiful.

"Lady Lucenna…"

At Rawn's shocked tone, she glanced at the portal still in the air. It trembled and grew, ripping through the fabric of reality. She forgot to shut it.

Lucenna cursed and used all of her willpower to lift a shaking hand. She pushed the last tendrils of her power to sew the seams back together. But the portal shoved against her feeble power, growing bigger. Lucien's alarm pulsed in her temples.

"Not now," she gritted out. Her entire weak body shook with the effort, draining the last of her Essence rapidly. If she lost hold of the portal, it would spiral out of control and cause a catastrophic tear through space and time. Why did she try to do this when she wasn't at her full capacity?

"Close, please close." Her power was fading fast, and her heartbeat thudded in her ears. *Hold on a little longer. Only a little longer.* But one of her Essence channels collapsed, and her vision skewed.

"Lucenna!" Rawn grabbed her wrist. His Essence clashed with hers, and purple and blue light blasted through the portal—hitting the edge of the house.

No...

Lucenna slumped back into the snow. Her vision blurred, and she lost consciousness in spurts. She caught the brief sound of screams, the orange flare of fire, the stink of smoke, and her absolute helplessness to stop it. Somewhere in the distance, she heard the horn blare twice.

It was so cold.

Someone was shouting her name.

A bearded face leaned over her, dark blond hair tickling her cheek. Deep blue eyes that normally held mischief looked afraid. Was he afraid of her? Lucenna tried to say she was sorry but couldn't speak. Voices milled all around, shouting and running.

"The mercenaries are coming."

"Are you hurt?"

"Evin!"

"What happened?"

"We have to put out the fire."

"I think I can do it."

"Lucenna." Hands cupped her cold cheeks, calloused and warm. That voice grounded her as he spoke, deep and worried, and firm. "Don't close your eyes, lass. Open your eyes. Look at me."

Look at me.

He had said that to her before. Lucenna blinked up at Klyde, perplexed by his concern and annoyed at how gently he held her face. She weakly glared at him.

Don't touch me... she hoped it said, since her mouth didn't work.

"Good. Stay awake." He slipped his arms underneath her body, one around her shoulders and the other beneath her knees. Effortlessly, Klyde hoisted her up, cradling her protectively against his chest. She fit comfortably in his hold, and she was finally warm. "Shite, you're nearly frozen to death. What happened?"

What...her magic. Her mind sluggishly tried to put it together. She had tried to close the portal, but then her magic...

"Lucenna?" Dyna called anxiously. "Is she all right?"

"Where are you taking her?" Cassiel demanded.

"I need to get her out of the snow," Klyde said. "Your other companion there needs help. He's unconscious."

Lord Norrlen? What happened to him...

Lucenna could hardly think straight. Klyde's arms were like hot coal against her icy body. She welcomed the warmth and could feel that rippling strength beneath his coat. Strength he was using to shield her against the cold.

As he rocked her with his steady stride, a new scent reached her. Something that smelled like cedarwood, leather, and the salt of the sea. A fresh, crisp scent that reminded her of misty mornings. It was soothing, but only for a moment, because she shouldn't be anywhere near this man. His warm breath drifted over her scalp, and she tried to suppress a shiver but failed.

"Put...me...down..." Lucenna garbled.

It was barely perceptible, but Klyde must have understood her because he said, "No."

Was this another one of his services? She didn't want his help. When he come for her at the cave, she stupidly believed he had done it out of his own good will, but now his sudden presence made sense to her. He saved her because it was his job.

Her eyes drifted closed. "How...much...?"

"Oi, keep your eyes open, Lucenna." He jostled her gently. "No sleeping."

She glared up at those rough-hewn features that were irritatingly attractive. "How...much?"

"What?"

"How...many coins...is this worth?" she mumbled.

Klyde's mouth curved again in that vexing smile of his, dimples winking at her. "We can settle that later. Keep those gorgeous eyes on me."

His brogue lilt was pleasing to her ears. She could fall asleep to his thick Azure accent babbling his nonsense. Her eyes grew heavier.

"Lucenna, stay awake."

Her head lolled to see where he was taking her. Klyde headed toward a wagon where his sister and nephew sat inside, under a mound of blankets. Eagon and Tavin quickly loaded the wagon with their belongings. Lucenna tried to peer back at the house, but all she saw were running mercenaries and the flash of blue lights as black smoke spiraled into the sky.

She did that.

Klyde jerked to a stop. A large black wolf got in his way, growling viscously. Lucenna tried to say she was all right, but she couldn't do more than lie limply in his arms.

Zev's fur receded in a blur, and his broad, naked body stood steaming in the cold. "Give her to me," he snarled.

Instead of shock, Klyde only looked amused. "I was wondering when you were going to come out, mate. I knew what you were, by the looks of you."

A menacing growl rumbled in the night, and he snatched Klyde's coat in his claws. "Then I should warn you of one thing. Werewolves are known for their fierce loyalty and violent protectiveness. Would you like to know what I do to those who provoke that instinct?"

A flash of metal zipped past Zev's cheek, and he snarled.

Lieutenant Eagon pulled out another throwing star. "You recognize that burning sensation. These are made of silver. Release him now or the next one goes in your throat."

"*Stop,*" Lucenna tried to stay, but it came out as a whimper.

Silver would kill Zev.

"Stand down, Lieutenant." Klyde's command vibrated where she was pressed against his chest. "That's an order." To Zev, he said, "This was not my doing. I found her lying in the snow with the elf, and she's freezing. I need to get her warm."

"I will do that."

"While nude?"

She barely had the energy to blush. There was a rustle of fabric and the crunch of snow before she was yanked away from Klyde. The heat coming off Zev's bare chest was sweltering. He was so hot the snow melted when it landed on his tan skin. It was almost too uncomfortable after being held by Klyde.

"God of Urn, your lips are blue, and you're shaking." Zev looked her over worriedly, his voice growing distant. He held her closer, rubbing her back to heat her body.

Lucenna tried to tell him she was fine. But she could barely move. Her power...

"Rawn?" she garbled faintly. Her eyes couldn't stay open anymore.

"Dyna has him. I think Cassiel put out the fire."

"The portal..."

"What?"

"Do you see...anything...a black hole?"

"No, nothing," Zev said. "Only smoke."

Thank the God of Urn. She closed it.

Then the weight of exhaustion won, and it dragged Lucenna away.

CHAPTER 74

Von

Von lowered his head against the icy wind blowing against him. Coal's hooves clopped in the quiet as they rode through the snowy streets of Indigo Bay. The night was bright, with a nearly full moon in the sky. It fleetingly reminded him of Dyna and her werewolf cousin. He wondered where they were now.

The bitter cold nipped at Von's cheeks and chapped lips. He pulled the collar of his lapels tighter around his neck and ears. His wool coat struggled to keep him warm, his legs nearly numb. His thick beard helped to protect some of his face. He hadn't shaved since leaving for his mission a few weeks past.

The hour was late and not a soul was in sight. Von cantered onwards through the empty roads to the modern side of town. He reached the pier and stopped before the three-story building of the Corvus Tavern. It had an elaborate stone elevation and glass-stained windows. The frozen masts of Tarn's ship were slightly visible past the roof. He'd docked it in the tavern's private port. The Raiders would be there, and Von had seen a group stationed at the entrance to the town. They would be on watch, and most likely already reported his return.

Once Von dismounted, a bundled-up lad came out to take the reins. It reminded him of the first night in Beryl Coast, but he didn't allow the faces of his companions to enter his mind. He couldn't think of them now.

He entered the quiet lobby of the tavern. The lavish lounge was made of black marble floors, dark wood wainscoting walls, and the ceiling was coffered in an elegant design. Large chandeliers flickered overhead. It looked empty of patrons for the night. The tavern only provided lodging for people wishing to remain discreet and with the means to pay handsomely for it. It was the reason Tarn left his ship in their port while he had traveled through Azure.

Von spotted a well-dressed woman standing at a podium, writing in a thick guest book. He made his way to her and cleared his throat.

She smiled at him politely when she recognized him. Her dark eyes flickered to what he carried in his arms, but her expression remained well-schooled. "Sir Conaghan, welcome back."

He nodded.

She handed him a key. "Your master is in room 206. He has reserved room 207 across from him for you and your servant."

His throat bobbed at the mention of Yavi. It was unlike Tarn to put her in a room. She always stayed with the camp, or in this case, the ship. He must have wanted to keep her close to translate the Sacred Scroll upon its arrival.

"Thank you," Von said, accepting the key.

He trudged through the quiet lobby and up the staircase. His heart pounded as he neared the second floor. He didn't know what he would say to Tarn when he saw him. He was out of excuses. This was a failure he didn't expect to survive. He only wished to see his wife one last time.

He reached the doors and stood unmoving between the two of them. Von knew which one he wanted to choose and which one he had to. He closed his eyes, knocked, and entered. Olsson stood at attention by the door.

Tarn glanced at Von indifferently from his chair near the window. He'd dressed completely in black. His legs were crossed, on his lap rested a book he was reading as he rested his chin against a fist. His white-blond hair fell over part of his face, shadowing the scar crossing his features from brow to his chin.

"I was beginning to think you died somewhere," Tarn said. "You were gone longer than expected."

His pale eyes flickered down to what he held. Von carried all that remained of his team to the bed. Len's head lolled on the pillow as he laid her down. The left side of her temple was black and bruised, a gash marring her face.

Von got down on his knees before Tarn and bowed until his head was an inch from the floor. "Forgive me, Master..." He said it out of habit but had no hope he would be. He felt Tarn's stare boring into his skull. "Len lives, but she has not woken, and I have no hopes that she will."

It was a miracle the blow to her head didn't kill her...yet.

"I will call for a healer," Olsson said.

The door shut behind him, and the crackle of firewood filled the still silence.

"What *happened?*" Tarn's cold voice was unnervingly soft, and it sent a chill through the air.

"We were confronted by a Xián Jīng assassin. He came for the scroll." Von raised his head enough to see him straighten at the news. "We were the only ones to survive. The others...I buried them in the temple ruins."

Tarn was unresponsive for a long time. Von didn't dare move or say more. The room was quiet with the soft crackling of burning wood. The strong winds rattled the windows, howling and wailing, carrying the voices of the dead.

"Novo was the first to fall." Von straightened from his bow but remained on his knees, keeping his eyes low. "His death came unawares and swift. He didn't suffer. Len was struck and Bouvier died next. Elon..." Von swallowed. "...fell after. They fought bravely."

The leather of Tarn's chair creaked as he slowly leaned forward. "Are you telling me that one man defeated five of my best? Out of all of you, I would have counted on Elon's survival."

Von swallowed the dryness in his throat. "We nearly had him, Master. But he laced his weapons with Fengu and wounded Elon..."

Tarn stared at the fireplace, his pallid eyes gleaming with the flame. "If you feel guilt, it's pointless," he said after a pause. "You wouldn't have been able to save him without the antidote." He glanced up at the mirror above the fireplace. "What of the scroll?"

At Von's silence, a draft seemed to blow through the room.

"You don't have it." Tarn lifted his goblet. "And yet you bothered to return knowing what it meant."

He lowered his head. "I accept my punishment. No one is to blame for this but me."

"Why *did* you come back? I would have assumed your death along with the others. This was your perfect chance to flee."

Von never considered it. "I have nowhere I would rather be," he answered honestly.

Tarn looked at him then, but there was no anger in his cool gaze. He flicked his index finger slightly, dismissing him. "Go."

It was so unexpected, Von wasn't sure if he heard correctly.

"I won't kill you tonight," he said, picking up his book. "I'll leave that for tomorrow."

Von stood slowly and backed out of the room. He struggled to understand why Tarn was giving him another night of life, but he wouldn't question it now.

He left the room and came to stand in the hallway. The golden numbers of 207 on the door seemed to glow. The key shook in his fist. Would she want to see him?

Something moved from the corner of his sight. Someone disappeared around the corner before he could get a clear look, but he recognized the auburn hair and the shape of his wife. Von rushed after her and glimpsed the ends of Yavi's cloak before she drifted down the stairs.

"Yavi?"

She didn't pause. Didn't stop to look at him. She kept going, carrying a lantern out the front doors, and vanished outside. Von ran after her, calling her name. He followed her outside into the bitter cold as she flitted down the streets into the shadows. But he knew where she was going.

Von slinked out of the town to the woods, going off instinct now. He soon reached a small cave where the scent of sulfur was strong. He followed the sound of bubbling water and spotted her lantern and cloak on the ground.

She stood with her back to him.

"Yavi..."

"Don't come near me," she said. "I thought long about us, Von. Sometimes I feel like we knew each other better before. When you were the commander, and I was the slave. Things were clearer back then. Now everything is muddled. A dirty pool where I no longer see my reflection. I'm constantly confused and hurt by the decisions you make. I'm tired of waiting for you to do something. How can we have a marriage when I don't know you? I don't think I ever truly did, and perhaps you never truly knew me." Her voice caught with the tears he knew were welling in her eyes. "We should never have gotten married."

It crushed him to hear that, and the back of his eyes stung. He choked on pain and wretched desperation. He couldn't lose her like this.

"Yavi, please let me explain."

She turned around, her wet eyes shone in the faint light. He moved a step, but she shook her head.

"Letting you near me is what led to this mess," she said. "It will not get us out of it. Perhaps if we could go back in time, then we could have prevented destroying ourselves."

"I...destroyed myself a long time ago," he said, taking another step, then another. "I lead a different life before you, and I have done things from which I'm ashamed. My sins have chained me to a vile existence I earned. You're right. I shouldn't have let myself want you." He cupped her cheek and brushed her tears away with his thumb. "I never once deserved you, Yavi. Never. But I will sooner drop to my knees and grovel at your feet for a mere shred of your forgiveness than to bear your hatred."

His cheeks grew wet, and he pulled her close, breathing in her scent. This was why he came. He wouldn't have tomorrow with her. Tarn all but assured he would die by the next sunrise, and this was his last chance to do right by his wife. He had to hold her one last time—before he set her free.

"I spent the last month missing you, wishing to crawl back to you by any means. I'm finally here. Whatever you ask, I will do. Whatever you need, I'll provide it. But please..." His voice broke. "For one night, please don't turn me away. I don't know how else to tell you that you have my heart."

"Why do you have to say things like that?" Yavi hit his chest, more tears spilling down her cheeks. "I'm so angry with you!" She continued to beat his chest, and he let her. He would take it all. "I think I hate you. I do. I hate you. I hate you." Yavi fell against him, soaking his shirt. Her whole body shook with her sobs. "But even when it feels like hate, I cannot stop loving you."

Von held her, silently crying with her. She would hate him more come the morning when he left her alone in the world for good. He couldn't stand knowing he wouldn't be around to protect her, and worse, that she would carry this resentment for the rest of her life.

"What do you need from me?" Von begged. "Whatever you want, anything, I will give it to you."

If she wanted to run now, he was insane enough to do it. Even if it meant killing Raiders.

Her hazel eyes lifted to his. He beheld the depths of gold and green and her eyebrows curled with such sweet sadness he despised himself for ever making her cry. Von brushed the hair from her face and simply looked at her, memorizing every soft curve of her face, breathing her in. If only she knew how much of him was hers.

"We will speak of our problems tomorrow," she said. "You said you would give me anything I want. Tonight...I want you."

That was all he needed to hear.

Von picked up her stiff body in his arms and carried her to the spring. It was dark with only the moonlight outside. The lantern's small flame cast enough light to see the steam rising off the pool and her streaming tears. Each one was a stone piling inside of him.

Setting Yavi down by the edge, Von gently cupped her face and wiped them away. "I die inside every time I see you cry," he said, his throat catching. "All the more knowing I caused you pain."

Her wet lashes closed.

Von kissed away the last tear trailing down her cheek. "Let me take away, love."

Yavi's eyes opened and searched his. They were sad, beautiful, and somehow despite all his failings, still here looking at him.

He reached for her waist, trailing his hand up her back to the loose laces of her bodice. He pressed his mouth to her shoulder as he pulled each tie free and simultaneously kicked off his boots. Yavi lifted her arms, letting him pull the dress over her head. She removed his coat, then tugged off his shirt. He held her gaze as her fingers unbuckled his belt, leaving his trousers to drop to their feet.

The way she was looking at his body from beneath her lashes elevated his pulse and flooded him with warmth. Sliding hands to the back of Yavi's waist, Von pulled her bare body flush against his. He tracked the path of her fingers, tracing the scar at the center of his chest.

"Whenever I see this..." She looked up and her eyes were fractured. He had earned the scar during her first week at camp when another had attempted to take her for his own. By luck, the Raider's knife had missed his heart, but Von's didn't.

"To be clear, I'm still angry..." she murmured in the pocket of space between them.

"I know."

"Don't stop kissing me..."

"I won't."

He gently pressed a kiss to her nose, over the tears on her cheeks, her forehead, her hair, until finally her lips. Her mouth didn't open to him. She was unresponsive, except for her pulse fluttering at her neck and the hitch of her breathing.

If Von somehow lived past tomorrow, he wondered if earning her forgiveness was possible. He wondered if they could repair what they had, or if it was too late. The thought made his chest tighten painfully.

Not once was he ever worthy of her, but the first time Yavi had kissed him, he was done. Every rotten, battered, and scarred part of his being belonged to her. Von wanted her so much. He needed her like the earth needed the sun, even if it meant losing his head.

Because without her, he had nothing.

So, Von held her as he pressed gentle kisses to her face and lips until the stiffness melted from her body. Yavi leaned into him with a sigh, as though in defeat. Her hands climbed up his spine and roamed his back, leaving behind a trail of sensations that sank through his body. She brushed her lips over his bruises and cuts ever so gently. So faintly, like the brush of butterfly wings leaving wishes on his skin.

And suddenly he didn't wonder anymore.

Von picked her up again, carefully climbing the stone steps into the hot spring. The heated water felt perfect. It rose up his legs as he walked further in, deepening every kiss. His feet reached the bottom, and he shifted her weight to wrap her legs around his torso, and her arms circled his neck. Yavi's body felt fuller in his hands, her hips wider. He felt her heat pressed where he craved her, and it stirred a wild desire. Her tongue slid against his, making him groan. And when she rocked against him, he was a hairsbreadth from snapping out of control. It had been so long since he last had her, he might buckle sooner than he wanted.

Von forced himself to place her on the edge of the spring and took a breath. "Yavi," he said raggedly. She smiled, knowing what she did to him. That single most beautiful action squeezed all the air from his lungs. He dragged a thumb across her plush mouth. His favorite feature. "No matter the rise of the day or the fall of the night, I find my lips will always seek yours."

She gave him that same fractured look again. The one that knew the truth.

He was enthralled by her.

Von kissed her again, but it was hungry, devouring, and demolishing. It was a mess of tongue and teeth. Her legs wrapped around him, pulling him closer. Taking a fistful of her hair, he tugged gently to expose her neck. Yavi panted and her nails dug into his arms as his mouth traveled along her jaw to her throat.

"Only the Gods know how much I missed you," Von breathed, inhaling her delicious scent. She smelled *so* good, her skin incredibly soft. "I dreamed of this," he said as he gently nipped her shoulders. "The feel of you." He grazed his teeth on the curve of her ribs under her breast, then the crease of her thigh meeting her hips. He kissed that sweet mouth, nibbling on her bottom lip. "Of your taste—"

Von groaned out a curse when she rolled against him, desperate to reach that spot, to ease the ache, and he was halfway to madness.

"Von," she pleaded.

"You need me," he growled.

"Please..."

The water lapped on the edge loudly as he helped her rock against his abdomen. He consumed every twitch of her face and faint moans. He could feel her pulsating. Holding himself back was unbearable. But he couldn't get enough of this, of her coming undone before he even took her.

"Where, love?" He pinned her hips down in place to stop her from moving. Yavi whined in protest. He hovered there, right there. All of him tight and hot, but not in. Not yet. "I want to hear you say it. Shall I..." He brushed his mouth against the shell of her ear as he whispered everything he desired to do to her.

She whimpered his name in a breathless plea, and that finally snapped his control. But when Von grabbed her wet thighs, Yavi suddenly flinched away from him. It confused him at first until he looked down at her leg. Not much could be seen in the low lighting, but he could feel the textured skin. The scars left behind from the fire.

A knot of emotion constricted in his throat, and he wanted to kneel in front of her and say he was sorry. That he should have been there. That he should have run with her. That it would never happen again. But that's not what she needed.

"Love." He cupped her cheek and made her look at him. "There is not a single part of you I don't find beautiful." Lifting her leg, he planted a reverent kiss over the scar on her ankle. His mouth trailed up her calf to her knee and kept going. "To me, you will always be perfect."

He kissed along her inner thigh, inching to that spot that he knew called for him. Yavi panted in anticipation, one hand bracing her against the ground. Her breath hitched when he was an inch away, then he pulled back and started from the other knee.

She moaned his name in protest.

Chuckling, he closed his mouth exactly where she wanted him. She gasped, one hand weaving through his hair to the back of his head. He fed on every sound she made, on the very essence of her being. And Von mourned because he wanted all of it.

All of her.

The worshipful kisses, the filthy words, the joining of their bodies, and idle days. The bad ones. Good ones. The highs and the lows. Every inch, every hour, every moment with her. He wanted them all.

But he couldn't tell her there would be no more. He wouldn't take this from her, too.

Tonight would only be theirs.

Yavi's breaths sharpened, and Von felt her pleasure climb, felt her grow hotter, and her fingers near bruising on his shoulders, until the sounds of her splintering filled the cave. She collapsed on the edge of the pool, shuddering as bliss swept her away. Leaning over her, Von brushed the sweaty strands from her temples to see her better. It was mesmerizing—the look of ecstasy trembling on her face, the pink flush of her skin.

But he wasn't finished with her yet.

He possessively took Yavi's throat, lifting her mouth to his. "You own every part of me. I will prove it to you all night long, if that's what it takes. For as long as you will have me."

That lit a fervor in her eyes.

Yavi's arms clamped around his neck, her lips crashing against his, demanding he keep his word. Von hauled her back into the hot spring. Her legs wrapped around his waist, and he lined her hips with his. She gasped as they seamlessly joined.

He groaned, burying his face against her throat. "Gods, Yavi, you feel so…"

Perfect.

She kissed him, slow and deep as they moved. His hands roamed over Yavi's skin, needing to feel all of her. He would never have enough of this. Of making love to his wife, of holding her, and knowing her. Of every pleading sound he could draw. She needed more, so he yielded and gave her everything.

CHAPTER 75

Dynalya

For the second night in a row, Dyna found herself under someone else's roof. After yesterday's fire, Klyde brought them to another house where they met Edith, Tavin's mother. She was an older woman with brown hair streaked gray and a kind smile. She received them openly, but their house was smaller than Gale and Eagon's. After a night of all of them sleeping cramped together in the den, it was clear they would need more space.

"We don't have any other choice." Gale glowered at her brother across the table as they ate their morning meal. "It's the only place in town with enough bedrooms for all of us."

Klyde didn't have any smiles or cheerful jests today. He sat stiff in his chair, mouth pinched. "No, Gale."

"Do you think I want to go there? My house is gone." Her lip wobbled, and she covered her face.

Eagon sighed and pulled her to him. He rubbed her back, murmuring reassurances. "It's not gone, love."

"The cornerstones are still in place. Only the back wall needs repair," Klyde said. "The men volunteered to help me rebuild it. Now I can put in that extra bedroom you wanted and extend the den."

"And meanwhile?" Gale asked. "Where else will we stay? We can't take over Edith's house."

The woman smiled at them as she poured Tavin some milk. "It's no problem, dear. You're always welcome."

"I know, Edith." She squeezed her hand. "But there are too many of us. Every house in town is small and meant only for the family that lives in it." Gale nodded to Dyna from across the kitchen table. "Don't worry. We will sort this out."

She was more upset that the poor woman and her family were out of a home.

"We can see if anyone can take a couple of our guests in," Klyde said."

Gale shook her head. "That is asking a lot of them, Klyde. You know they're skittish folk."

"She has a point," Eagon said.

Dyna pretended not to notice them discreetly shooting glances at her cousin in the den. Most of the mercenaries had witnessed Zev shift yesterday. The town had to know by now there was a werewolf in Skelling Rise.

Gale glowered at her brother. "We're going to the manor."

Klyde exhaled a frustrated sound and rubbed his face. "They can go there. You will stay here with Edith."

"I'm near my term. It's best I stay close to Dyna in case anything happens."

"Why would something happen?"

"It's a precaution, Klyde."

His jaw flexed as he and Gale locked themselves in a glare.

The Captain of the Skelling Mercenaries met his match in his sister, though, because Gale didn't relent. Dyna wondered what was so dreadful about the manor that he didn't like the idea of them going there.

"She's right," Tavin said next to his mother. "The house is too crowded. I say Auntie, Uncle, and Evin can take my room, but them lot—" His light-blue eyes narrowed on her and her friends angrily. "They can't stay here. What if they burn down our house next?"

Edith shook her head at him. "That was very rude, dear. They explained it was an accident."

"Bullshit."

"Tavin," Klyde warned in a low growl. "Mind yourself."

"We were all in the kitchen when the wall in the den blew. You saw it. The damn witch nearly killed us—"

Klyde's chair screeched on the floor as he jerked the boy to his feet. "Outside. Now."

Tavin scowled. He marched out of the kitchen, and they bounded out of the house. Dyna heard only a muffle of Klyde's raised voice saying he taught him the meaning of respect before the door shut, leaving them in awkward silence.

"I'm sorry," Edith said to them. "Tavin is a spirited boy, but he speaks before he thinks sometimes."

"You have nothing to apologize for," Dyna said, and looked at Eagon and Gale. "We're very sorry. Lucenna never meant for that to happen and I know she will feel terrible when she wakes. We will do what we can to help you rebuild."

Dyna glanced at where Lucenna still slept on her bedding near the fireplace. Zev stayed next to her, monitoring her heartbeat. Lucenna had drained nearly all of her Essence, more than when she fought the Enforcers. They simply hadn't had time to rest. Rawn sat in the chair across from them, watching her worriedly. He explained what had happened and felt he was to blame. When he noticed Lucenna's magic going out from trying to close the portal, he tried to stop her, inadvertently mixing elf magic with mage magic. It caused the explosion that blew out part of the house.

And now she wasn't waking.

Lev sheli. Cassiel's voice drifted through her mind. Dyna met his gaze beside her. *She will wake up. She only needs time to recover.*

But Lucenna hadn't depleted herself this severely before. She barely had a kernel of power left when Dyna got to her. She'd spent the night slowly feeding her Essence to Lucenna, rebuilding the Essence channels that had collapsed inside.

You are the one who needs rest now.

Dyna patted his knee. *I'm fine.*

Cassiel glowered, and his concern hummed through the bond. *You are not. I can feel you. That strange spell in the woods drained most of your Essence and now this. Let Azeran's tea do its work for both of you now. Please, no more magic until you have recovered.*

That spell...she didn't know what that was or how it happened. Her veins still felt strangely hot. What was that? How did they do it? Whatever it was, it must have been an odd fluke fed by their desperation. But...could they do it again?

Dyna sipped her tea, inhaling the rosemary scent. She was feeling much better by the time they packed up their belongings in the wagon again. There was more snow on the ground, but the blizzard had ended.

The mercenaries were scattered all over town, shoveling the roads and cleaning roofs. Dyna heard Klyde and Tavin's muffled voices and the thud of their boots as they worked on clearing Edith's roof. Zev, Rawn, and Cassiel were helping to clear the snow around the barn and the path.

"Thank you," Eagon told her as he placed a crate of potatoes into the wagon. "I haven't seen her this well in a long time."

Dyna laughed as Evin threw a snowball at Gale. She squealed, chasing after the giggling boy. The color had returned to her face, and she moved easily without wincing.

"You're welcome," Dyna said. "I magically strengthened her immune system last night, but I will make treatment she will ingest every morning. There is the possibility the baby may come early."

Eagon's smile faded. "What do you mean?"

"Gale may not carry to term," Dyna told him gently. "The pregnancy is taxing on her body, but she is in her eighth moon. Your baby has a very good chance of survival."

He listened intently, watching her as she spoke. "You haven't mentioned my wife's chances of survival." He was reserved, but she read the anxiety in the shadows of his expression. "Tell me the truth."

"With our new arrangements, I will be there to monitor her every day," Dyna said carefully. "I will do everything in my power to help her through this."

Eagon sighed as he watched his family. "I know you and your companions were upset by your stay here, but I can't say I'm sorry for it. You came when the need was great." He glanced at the roof, and his brow creased. "Do me a favor, lass. Please don't mention this to Klyde. He has enough to worry about without us burdening him further."

Dyna nodded. Their business was their own, and she couldn't betray that confidence.

Once the path to the main road was clear, they loaded into the wagon with a couple of months' worth of supplies. Klyde was quiet as he rode alongside them on his ebony steed.

Eagon led the wagon further away from town into an unplowed road through a patch of dark woods. The still trees were like solemn sentries watching them roll past. The high sun cast shadows through the bare tree branches on the untouched snow.

They left the woods and rolled through two brick pillars with open, rusted gates. In the distance rose an immense five-story structure with round towers on both ends. The decorative elevation was composed of gray brick, but it was coated in mold and desiccated vines. Several tall, arched windows lined every floor. It had a sharply slanted roof and peaks covered with snow.

The manor looked like a small castle.

Eagon brought the wagon to a stop beside a broken-down barn that had long rotted with the roof caved in. They all sat in silence for a moment as they looked up at the old manor.

"Who used to live here?" Rawn asked.

"Some spoiled toff before he was eaten by trolls," Klyde replied. He dismounted to help Gale down as Eagon carried their son, then he busied himself unloading supplies from the wagon.

Eagon and Gale climbed the steps to the front door, and she removed a key from her dress pocket. Sighing, she stared at it a moment before unlocking the front door. It creaked as it slowly swung open on its rusted hinges.

They paused at the doorway.

Dyna peered past them at the grand foyer cloaked in shadow. The windows were draped closed by heavy blue curtains, keeping out the sun. The floors, made of polished squared stones, were covered in a layer of filth. An iron chandelier hung overhead, coated with cobwebs. To the right was a stone stairway with iron spindles wrapped in more webs. It curved upwards, leading to the next floor.

Eagon and Gale entered first. Their footsteps echoed inside the quiet dwelling. Eagon set the crate of food on a sideboard in the foyer and put Evin down. His son's wide, curious eyes bounced all over the place before he excitedly ran further into the manor.

"Evin, wait dear." Gale hurried after him.

Dyna went in and a stiffness entered her shoulders as some sort of unease cast goosebumps down her arms. It was dreadfully cold inside. She followed them hesitantly to the grand hall.

It was vast, with towering ceilings. From it hung more chandeliers. A long rug had been rolled up against the wall. The furniture was covered in white sheets. Several covered sofas and wing back chairs circled around a large unlit hearth. Dyna's breath clouded in the cold air as she continued further. The space smelled musty, and a layer of grime coated every surface. A ray of sunlight filtered in through the thin gap between a set of tall heavy drapes, highlighting the dust in the air.

Cassiel frowned. "No one has lived here in a while."

"How many bedrooms are there?" Zev asked Eagon.

"Fifty perhaps, not including the servant quarters."

Zev let out a long whistle.

"Let's check upstairs," Gale said to her husband. "We will stick to the second floor."

Their footsteps faded as they climbed the stairs.

"I'll take this to the larder," Zev said, lifting a crate of food. "Is it this way?"

"Aye, up ahead there on your right, in the kitchen," Klyde said, carrying in more supplies behind him.

Zev and Rawn followed him through a set of large double doors. Dyna glimpsed a large dining hall. The long dining table was covered with another white sheet and the curtains on the windows were closed as well. Torn blue banners hung from the ceiling.

Dyna canted her head as she admired the intricate wood moldings. "This doesn't look like the other houses in town."

"It's small compared to most I have seen, but this is a grand hall," Cassiel said. "A lord must have lived here long ago."

A lord?

Dyna wandered into the grand hall. A strange sensation came over her like she had been here before. A large tapestry hung on the wall. One torn corner draped over it, but she could barely make out the faded coat of arms.

She gasped.

"Thank you for allowing us to stay here," Rawn's distant voice echoed in the hallway behind her.

"A pleasure," Klyde said. "There are plenty of rooms upstairs. But please stay off the fifth floor. It's unstable..."

Dyna faced the covered portrait in the grand hall. She walked toward it, her heart pounding in her chest. It couldn't be...but she had to see. She reached for the sheet.

"Dyna."

She halted with her fingers an inch away at the sound of Klyde's sharp voice.

"Don't touch that, lass. It's bad luck to look upon the dead, and I will have none of that here."

The captain bounded over to her and yanked the heavy portrait from the wall. He threw it inside the fireplace with enough force that Dyna heard something crack. Klyde took out a piece of steel and flint rock to beat them together. Unable to get a spark to catch, and he muttered a curse.

"Need help, mate?" Eagon asked uneasily.

"No."

"Here, let me." Dyna reached for the broken frame. Klyde caught her wrist and Cassiel's growl rumbled in the bond. She warily glanced at the captain. "I won't look," she said softly.

Klyde gradually let her go. She concentrated on her Essence, feeling its heat weave through her once more. At her command, a flourish of flames caught the edge of the portrait and quickly engulfed it, the sheet turning black. The fire burned high, its light glowing against their faces.

"Ah, thank you." Klyde chuckled as he rose to his feet. "That should help bring some warmth to this tomb. I will see about gathering more wood and repairing the roof. Make yourselves at home."

He strode out of the living room for the door and mounted his black horse. With a snap of the reins, Klyde galloped away. As if he couldn't get away fast enough.

"This place is haunted," Cassiel said, coming up beside her. "I feel Death here."

Yes, Dyna felt it, too. She hurried outside. He joined her as she stared up at the manor.

"What is it?" he asked.

It looked different in person, aged by time and neglect, but the crumbling stone held the truth of it.

"Can you take me up? I need to see something."

Letting his enchanted coat drop at their feet, Cassiel swept her into his arms. They shot into the frigid air, the wind nipping at her cheeks as his wings carried them high into the afternoon sky. The sun shone brightly over the land of Skelling Rise. Wisps of smoke swirled out of the chimneys on every white rooftop. She studied the curve of the hills, the forest, and fallow fields.

This place truly was a tomb.

Dyna hadn't noticed it when they first arrived. Secrets had hidden in the dark of night and beneath the snow, but she knew where they were now. The manor...it once belonged to Lord Morken.

They were in Azurite.

CHAPTER 76

V on

The rays of the early sun peeked through the edges of the curtains, casting Von's room in low light. He held Yavi in his arms, silently observing her every feature. She slept beside him, warm under the several layers of blankets with her head resting on his chest. It didn't feel real to have her like this. Instinctively, his arms tightened around her.

He knew returning to Tarn meant his demise, but on his return journey, he had prayed for another day with Yavi, and it was granted. He thought of Elon and how he had prayed for the same with his mate. The thought tightened Von's chest. He couldn't let anything happen to Yavi. Even if it was the last thing he did before he died, he had to get her somewhere safe.

Yavi mumbled sleepily as she woke. She turned her head up to him and smiled lazily, but it faded when she saw his pained expression. "What is it?"

He held her to him and kissed her head. "I don't want to leave this room or this bed. I wish I could be here with you forever, but it's not possible. Today is the day you need to escape."

She sat up on the bed, alarmed. "What?"

Von sat up as well and gathered her soft hand in his. "I wasn't able to retrieve the scroll. We were confronted at the temple ruins, and we were not prepared. Our opponent was only one man, yet he killed them all—Novo, Bouvier, and…" He couldn't bring himself to say Elon's name. "I had to watch them die."

"Oh, love," Yavi hugged him. She knew how much it affected him when his Raiders died. Each death weighed on him like a boulder of guilt.

Von rested his forehead against hers. "Yavi, I'm out of pardons. Tarn is going to kill me for my failure." She shook her head, choking back a sob. "When I'm gone, I won't be able to protect you anymore. But I can die in peace knowing you escaped his grasp."

"What? No. Where am I to go?" she asked, her lip wobbling.

"I think Hallow's Nest would be a good place to hide for a while before you can take a ship to Dwarf Shoe and return home."

"Hallow's Nest?"

"It's a quiet little town in the north." Von smiled at her faintly. "I saw Dyna there."

"What?" Yavi gasped.

"She's alive. Her sorceress broke the spell Clayton put her under, and her cousin also survived. They are out there, love. The divination remains in play. Tarn can still be stopped."

Yavi closed her eyes briefly and tears rolled down her cheeks. "She's alive."

"Yes."

"Why did you come back?" Yavi cried. "You should have run while you had the chance."

Von held her face. "I had to see you one more time. I console myself with knowing there is hope for this world, after all. My only regret is not being able to have a family with you and build you a house in the country."

Yavi looked into his eyes with anguish. "Von...I have to tell you something."

He brushed her lips with his thumb. "What is it?"

"I have one last thing I must give you before you leave me."

He smiled. "Again? I would die a happy man." Von aimed for a kiss, but she dodged him.

"Von, you're not listening."

He finally caught her tone and straightened. "What is it?"

Yavi sighed. "Please try not to overreact."

"About what?" At her long silence and fear, he grew anxious. "Tell me."

She removed the blankets around her and got off the bed to stand before him. Von admired her naked body. Her wedding band hung on a chain between her full breasts. They were larger than normal, but he wouldn't complain about that. Then his eyes then fell on the small mound of her belly. A light brown line ran over it vertically from top to bottom.

Yavi placed his hand there, tears gathering on her lashes. "I'm with child."

A stark stillness fell over him.

Von's wide eyes burned as he stared at her belly. He was absolutely still, but the sound of his racing heart beat in his ears. Fear drowned out his joy before it could surface.

Scrambling to his feet, he stumbled with the sheets tangled around his legs. Von shook his head as he looked around the room wildly. He quickly pulled on his dirty pants and shirt left on the floor. Then he ran to the cabinet and started throwing her clothes in a bag.

"What are you doing?" Yavi asked him. "Von?"

"I need to get you out of here," he hissed. "How far along are you?"

Yavi lowered her head. "Four moons."

He gaped at her in angry shock. "What?"

She kept it from him for four months! But she had been showing signs—the lack of eating, feeling sick, enlarged breasts and hips—he had been so stupid to not notice it before. Yavi saw the resentment in his eyes and tried to take his arm. He freed himself and continued packing.

"Von, speak to me," she pleaded.

"Why did you keep this from me?" he snapped.

"Because I was afraid!"

"You should be afraid, Yavi. Tarn will have your head." He shoved more clothes in the bag.

"I wasn't afraid of him. I was afraid of you..."

Von stopped.

She backed away, breaking into a sob. This wasn't the reaction she had wanted. Expecting a child should have been good news.

"I'm sorry." Von dropped the bag and lifted Yavi in his arms, carrying her back to the bed. She continued to cry in the pillows. Von gathered her in his arms and covered them in the blanket again. "Shhhh..." he told her, rubbing her back. "I'm sorry. I've been a downright fool. If I had given you the proper care and attention, I would have noticed you were pregnant."

"Are you not happy?" she asked in a wobbly voice.

He sighed. "Oh, love, I am. But I wish this didn't happen now. It puts you in so much jeopardy. I'm terrified for you now more than ever because I won't be alive to protect you. As soon as I'm called to Tarn's room, you need to escape. Novo had saved fifty thousand gold pieces before he died. It's in my pack. Take it and go."

She scowled. "No."

"You have to." Von's hand came to rest over the softness of her belly. "You have someone else to live for now. For our child's sake, you need to escape."

"Verik." Yavi's lip wobbled, and she laid her hand over his. "I'm going to name him Verik."

"We're having a boy?" A twinge ripped in Von's chest to know he will never see his child grow. A knock came at the door, and they held their breaths.

"Commander Von, I'm sorry to disturb you," came Olsson's voice on the other side. "The Master will see you now."

Yavi cried softly and buried her face in Von's chest.

"Thank you, Lieutenant," he called. "I'll be right out."

Olsson's footsteps receded, and a nearby door closed.

Von wrapped Yavi tighter in his hold. "Don't cry. You need to be strong now."

"No." She tightened her arms around him when he tried to rise out of bed. "Please don't leave me."

His vision blurred at her plea. "Yavi." Von closed his wet eyes. "Our son needs you now. As soon as I'm gone, you need to run."

"I can't!"

"Yes, you can." He gently ran the back of his fingers down her cheek. "You have to."

Von kissed her passionately, memorizing her lips and body. She pressed herself against him, holding on to him tightly.

"I love you, Yavi," he said against her mouth, pain tightening his chest. "More than anything. You must run while Tarn is distracted dealing with me. Don't let me die in vain."

Von pulled her arms off him and quickly stepped back. His wife sobbed on the bed, covering her face with her hands. He left the room and gently closed the door behind him. He stood in the hallway, fighting back tears as he heard her soft cries.

Composing himself with a shaky breath, he entered Tarn's room and stood at attention with his arms behind his back.

His master sat in the same chair as last night, staring into the flames of the fireplace. Von would have thought he hadn't moved if not for the slight changes in his dark clothing. The morning sunlight shone in the room, catching on the irises of Tarn's pale eyes.

But his bed was empty. Where was Len now?

Olsson nodded to him respectfully, where he stood by Tarn. "Commander Von."

He nodded in return. "Lieutenant."

Tarn glanced at him and frowned in annoyance at his appearance. "This is how you present yourself to me? Go shave and change into your uniform. We have much to discuss. Meet me in the restaurant downstairs."

Tarn stood and walked out of the room.

Olsson followed him and gave Von a smile. "Welcome back, Commander. The men will be glad to know you have returned."

Von watched them go, wholly bewildered. He had mentally prepared himself to die and now that it hadn't come, he couldn't make sense of it. Dazed, he walked back into his room. Yavi yelped at his arrival. She was in the middle of quickly packing, now dressed in a mauve colored wool dress with a loose gray cloak on top. It hid any sign of her pregnancy well.

She stared at the odd expression on his face. "Von?"

"Tarn wants me to report back after being properly dressed." He shut the door behind him, blinking at the floor. "He won't kill me..."

"Oh, thank the God of Urn." Yavi threw her arms around him.

"Why?" He croaked. "Why does he keep sparing me?"

"Tarn doesn't trust anyone the way he trusts you. You have been with him from the beginning."

The beginning.

Von thought back to the moment on Azurite when he wanted to perish among the dead, but Tarn didn't let him.

There is only one penance for your sins. From this day forward, you will serve with your life in payment for what you have taken from me, as the holy law demands. Until that debt is paid.

Tarn never planned to kill him.

There would be no end to this life, because nothing would repay Aisling's death. There wasn't anything that could ever equal the loss of a wife.

Von went to the basin placed on the dresser. He didn't recognize the haggard face looking back at him in the mirror. His sea-colored eyes were bloodshot and sunken. His light brown hair fell in a tangled mess around his thick beard. The man in the reflection was drowning in an endless cycle with no end.

His guilt and religious beliefs argued slavery was what he deserved. Tarn saved his life, so it belonged to him.

Does it?

For fifteen years, he served. When would it be enough?

Yavi led him to the bath behind the screen divider. She turned the knob and hot water poured out of the spout. He barely registered the unusual commodity. Von let her strip him naked again and he climbed into the bath. She scrubbed him down and brushed his hair before snipping the ends. She took out a blade next and shaved him. Once done, he stepped out, dried off and dressed in clean black clothes.

He turned to the mirror again as he slipped on his leather coat. He still appeared tired, but some of his youth returned. Yavi swept the wet hair out of his eyes.

"I'm sick of this life," he admitted aloud.

"Von." She held up the golden ring hanging from a thin cord on his neck. "What does this mean to you?"

"It means I'm your husband."

Yavi lifted her ring, too. "Do you remember the vow you made when you put this on my finger?"

"Of course."

"Say it."

Von pulled her to him, whispering the words against her cheek. "'For as long as I live, I vow my heart is yours. I promise I will be true. I will love you and care for you in plenty and in want, in sickness and in health, in failure and in triumph. I will be your hearth, your solace, and your home, and I will walk beside you through all hardships that may come. From now and forever.'"

He remembered every word. That had been the best day of his miserable life.

Fresh tears welled in her eyes. "You promised me forever, and I mean to hold you to it." Yavi cupped his face. "I want to know what happened fifteen years ago. No more secrets. Only the truth."

Von closed his eyes, and he told her everything. She cried with him as she listened to what he had done. The lives lost because of him. How his pregnant sister had her stomach torn open and was left there for Tarn to find.

Not once did her eyes hold any judgment.

Then she fell still when he told her the Seer from Arthal had given him a divination about them.

"I want to hear it," Yavi whispered. "Exactly as she said it."

He swallowed, the words scorching in his throat. "'Only whence she burns will she be free. Her screams will carry in darkness and in ice to haunt thee. They'll cut through thy ears as the scars on thy back. Breaking and mending that which thee lacks...'"

A shudder went through her.

"I served him to pay my debt for the loss of life," he said softly. "And to prevent the loss of yours."

Yavi shook her head. "You have more than repaid him. With your years and your will, but you're a slave no more." Her voice broke. "I already burned, and you heard my screams. That divination has come and passed."

He stared at her gruesome scars. Could it truly be over?

She made him look at her. "Let go of your fear. You're free. You have always been free, Von. I won't let you say no to me anymore. *We* are leaving once and for all."

Yavi rummaged through the bags she had been packing and pulled out a small round thing in cloth, opening it for him to see a moldy roll of bread. She ripped it open and out fell a slaver's key. It clattered on the floor between their feet, matching the brass bangles around her ankles.

Von sucked in a breath. "Where did you get that?"

"A gift from Dyna."

He remembered then she had given Yavi the roll on the day the knights came.

"We're escaping the next chance we get," she said. "I cannot have a life where every day is a question if I will live. I want every tomorrow with you until we are both old and gray. *Together*, do you understand?"

Von's vision blurred as he looked at his lovely wife. Why did he think he could ever let her leave without him? He had a master...but suddenly the weight of those chains didn't hold him down anymore.

What else is there to strive for in life but wishes and dreams?

His wish was to be free and to spend the rest of his life with Yavi. He now dreamed of the freedom to love his family without fear. Even if Von had to fight the fates, it was time he lived for himself now.

"Yes."

She blinked. "What?"

"Yes," he repeated, his answer coming out like choked laughter. "To the Seven Hells with him. I'm coming with you. I can't leave you. Why did I ever think I could?"

Tears spilled down Yavi's face. "Do you swear it? Don't lie to me, Von. If you betray me again—"

Von silenced her with a kiss.

He loved Yavi like the night loved the moon. Never would he stop. Leaving her wasn't a possibility. It never was. Losing his family would carve out his soul. Running would bring Tarn's wrath, but it was worth it. Because he could no longer strangle himself with the shackles he wore for years.

"I swear." He pulled her close, forming the words on her lips. "We're leaving."

He hated to think about it, but the death of the spies gave them a real chance. None of the Raiders had the skills to track them, and with the slaver's key, nothing would keep her locked away.

The final obstacle was Tarn.

"Even if we might die?" she whispered.

"If our only two choices are to die fighting or die in slavery, then I will fight until my very last. No matter what happens, I'm telling you now that I love you. I will follow you anywhere, Yavi. If we fail and these are our last days together, then I will break open every Gate and take on the Gods if it means finding you again."

Yavi laughed wetly through her tears with such joy that for once he allowed himself to feel it, too. He would strive to reach a new life with his wife and their child.

"We will plan it properly." Von kissed her temple, then her stomach. "Hide that key and pack our belongings. We will play our roles until the time is right."

When he walked out of the room, he exhaled a long breath and straightened his shoulders. Von would strive for what he wanted now.

May the God of Urn forgive him.

CHAPTER 77

Cassiel

Once they had cleaned the manor and removed all the dust, they settled into their individual rooms. Cassiel chose a large one on the third floor, facing the north with a view of the ocean. His bedroom was spacious but plain. Not much furniture was in it save for a wardrobe, a desk...and a big bed. He tried not to think about that part.

Cassiel glanced up at the sound of soft footsteps. Dyna walked into the room, her eyes traveling over the windows.

She gave him a hesitant smile, and her fingers tangled together. "I like the view."

"I chose it for the space," he said, coming to her. "Where are your belongings?"

She bit her lip. "In Lucenna's room."

He tilted his head, confused, until he put it together. "I see."

"Would that be all right?"

"For a man and his wife to sleep in separate quarters? The outrage." He half smiled and stilled her fidgeting hands. The bond's energy hummed at the meeting of their skin. "What would the neighbors think?"

"They would think what a shameless wife."

"No, they would think there must be something terribly wrong with the husband."

"There is nothing wrong with you." Her brows curled up. "I simply...should stay with Lucenna until she wakes."

But they both knew it was because she wasn't ready to share his bed.

Which wasn't the problem. They would wait for however long she needed. Even so, Cassiel subtly lifted his shield, careful not to let her know his thoughts, because he couldn't deny two things. It would be impossible to sleep in the same bed and not want her, but it would be ten times more difficult to be separated from her.

Not having Dyna in his sight drew out a feeling like smoke from a growing fire. The overpowering fear of losing her again. The Druid had predicted it. Death and shadow were what awaited her at the end of this journey.

Tension crawled over his body at the mere thought of it, and his veins heated with his flame. It was an instinct that surfaced to protect what was his. Cassiel nearly suggested he sleep on the floor for that semblance of space while still keeping her close, but no. This was Dyna's decision.

Her choice.

He promised to always respect that even if it went against his need to keep her safe.

But when did protection become paranoia? His mate wasn't in any danger. She was in front of him, warm and alive. Dyna couldn't be happy if he was constantly afraid something would happen to her when he wasn't there.

"I understand, *lev sheli*. We have all the time in the world to get to know one another." Cassiel brought her fingers to his lips, trailing his mouth across her palm to the fluttering pulse in her wrist. "Starting from today..." He planted a kiss there and made his way up her arm to her shoulder. "And every waking hour after that..." He pressed his mouth to her throat and heard her breath catch. "From now and until forever."

Cassiel trailed his hands up the small of her waist. The bond hummed with many desires—from both ends. Dyna's lashes closed, and she leaned into him.

Cassiel stepped back, leaving the cold air to fall between them. "Meanwhile, I will behave as a perfect gentleman should."

Dyna's eyes popped open with a shocked laugh. She nudged him into the wall. "You're terrible."

He pulled her back to him and kissed her. *You torture me, lev sheli. I cannot help returning the favor a little.*

A knock came at the door, and they looked up to see Zev standing in the doorway. They both froze.

"I'm headed to town with Rawn," he said, ignoring their positions. "We're going to look around now that we know where we are."

"Do you think we should be concerned?" Cassiel asked as he let her go, pretending Zev hadn't caught them kissing.

They knew nothing about these mercenaries. When Dyna revealed this place used to be Azurite, they all thought it odd that they built a town over a grave.

"I'm not sure yet," Zev said. "Want to join us?"

Dyna shook her head. "I'll stay to monitor Lucenna's condition, and I need to brew medicine for Gale. I should go get that started."

"I'm staying as well," Cassiel said when she left. He motioned to the long rectangular package wrapped in soft leather and twine on his bed. "Might be a good time to present it to her."

"I wish you luck," Zev chuckled.

"I will certainly need it."

Zev stepped back into the hall. "She looks happy. I don't think I have seen her smile this much since before she lost her family."

Cassiel was glad to hear that. "I know it was difficult to accept our bond," he said, leaning against the doorway. "Thank you, and I'm sorry for any hurt we caused you."

"Well, I suppose you can make it up to me eventually." Zev shrugged, giving him a shrewd grin. "Starting from today and every waking hour after that. From now and until *forever*."

Cassiel smirked. "It may be best you stop listening to our conversations. One day, you may hear something you would rather not."

The grin dropped from Zev's face. Chuckling, Cassiel shut the door.

Dyna, when you are permitted, could you meet me in the courtyard? Cassiel asked as he slipped off his enchanted coat and changed out of his clothes. *I have something for you.*

Do you? Came her playful response down the bond. *Should I dress warm?*

He turned to the gritty mirror on the wall and sent her the image of his reflection. *You will be warm soon enough.*

Her delight vibrated through their connection, and Cassiel smiled as he felt her hurry to finish whatever she was doing.

After he tightened his greaves, Cassiel tucked the package under his arm. His wings stretched wide as he entered the balcony, his long black feathers fluttered behind him in the breeze. Since arriving, he hadn't gone out for a flight. He breathed in the frosted air and let the sun fall over his face. It was cold outside but bearable for a little while. The land the manor rested on was more secluded within the woods that surrounded it. The townsfolk may know about Celestials, but he didn't feel comfortable revealing himself, so he was glad they were here.

He leaped off the railing and let the wind take him. Cassiel flew for the woods to give Dyna some time. The trees were dense out here. Mostly pine and or barren branches. He passed by a frozen pond in the middle of the woods. But there was something a little past it that caught his attention. It looked like a rusted gate leading to some sort of underground storehouse or dungeon, long out of use.

Cassiel continued another couple of miles, and the woods eventually gave way to flat coastal plains that ended with sheer cliffs on the edge of the sea. They were high, water roaring as it crashed on the bluffs. It must be the edge of the Bridge. The cliffs continued for miles in either direction, the town's wall in the distance.

Dyna's voice fluttered in his mind. *Where are you?*

On my way to you. Cassiel circled back to the manor. Within a few more minutes, he landed in the courtyard, cleared of snow. He found Dyna there riding Fair, dressed in her fae armor. Her red hair flowed freely behind her like a streak of fire. He might have stood there to watch her all afternoon if she hadn't seen him.

She smiled brightly. "There you are. What did you have to show me?"

"Your final light gift." Cassiel presented the package to her with both hands.

Dyna dismounted and let Fair canter off. Surprise rose on her features when she noticed the hilt sticking out of the leather. Steel sang as she drew it free. Sunlight reflected off the sword's blade. It was light, honed to a slender size, and made precisely for her. Dyna was awed as she lifted the hilt to admire the crossguard fashioned into wings like his. Instead of a sapphire, her langet glinted with an emerald that matched her eyes.

Her brows curled as she looked at him in a way that made him hold his breath. "Cassiel..."

He shifted on his feet. "Is it too much?"

"No, of course not," she said teasingly. "It's not every day a husband gives his wife a deadly weapon she can skewer him with. Thank you."

He grinned. It's a good thing he has divine blood.

"It's perfect." Dyna admired the craftsmanship, but her smile wavered. "You have given me so much. I also have a light gift for you, but...it's nothing as extravagant as this."

His brow furrowed, not sure of her meaning.

She reached into her pocket and held out her hand. In her palm were two rings. They were simple, polished bands that gleamed like silver, but as he stared at them, he noticed the grains of wood.

"Before we left Hermon, I asked my lady's maid to bring me a branch from the *Hyalus* tree," she said. "We were wed with borrowed rings. It was the symbolism that counted, but I still wanted to commemorate our marriage with something that held meaning to us."

It was the *Hyalus* where they met and where they found each other again.

Dyna flushed. "I'm not as skilled as Rawn at carving, but he taught me enough." Then Cassiel noticed the scrapes and nicks on her fingers from the tools.

His throat thickened, and he struggled to speak. "Dyna...this..."

"Do you like it?" she asked timidly.

"Very much." Cassiel took the rings and slipped the smaller one on her finger and the other on his. They were a perfect fit. She had no idea how much this meant to him. How much more he treasured her for it.

"Even if they are only wood?"

Cradling her palm in his, he brushed his thumb over the smooth band on her finger. "When I was eight winters old, my father took me to the smith caves in Edym, where I chose my sword and watched it be honed in the blessed fires." He glanced at *Esh Shamayim* strapped to his hip. "I can still remember the heat of the forge and how elated I felt to receive such a gift that was made only for me. These rings hold that same value, if not more."

A smile lit Dyna's face. He supposed that was the reason he gave her a sword. A part of him wanted to replicate a piece of that moment.

"I didn't know you were born in winter," she said. "On what day does it fall? We should celebrate."

The reminder stole the warmth that had been thrumming in his chest. "It's not something I celebrate, Dyna."

Cassiel busied himself checking her armor and making sure it was secured. He felt her watching him, waiting for an explanation.

"It falls on the winter solstice," he finally said. "I didn't wish to tell you because I know what that day means for your past. It's an anniversary I hate, too." His fingers stalled on her belts. Speaking of it uncovered an old memory of him as a child, sitting in the dark dining room alone. Waiting for something that would never come. "I turned ten when it was decided those sorts of things were not meant for me." Cassiel sighed heavily. "So I went out into the snowstorm to search for my mother. Whatever happened that night, I ended up with broken wings. The next day, my father sent me away to Hermon, and year after damn year, I'm reminded of that."

Emotion crossed Dyna's face, and her hand covered his. "Because you miss him."

It wasn't a question.

"There are days when I do miss him," Cassiel admitted quietly. "And days when I hate that I miss him. Other days, I think nothing of him at all."

Her fingers brushed his cheek, prompting him to look at her. "When you have those dark days, come to me, so I may either embrace you—or attack you."

A streak of sensations pulsed down his arm in the same spot where she had written one of her vows.

He chuckled. "Those are my only options?"

"Yes, and I will choose which." Dyna walked backward with an inviting smile bright enough to spread an indulgent heat through the bond. "Seeing as I'm holding a sword, you know we have to spar now, right?"

"*Lev sheli,* I was hoping you would say that."

After they had the basics down, they spent the afternoon sparring. It didn't take long for Dyna to adjust to the feel of her sword. She seemed to have some instruction, and she learned rather quickly. It would take more than a day of training to hone her movements, but Cassiel could foresee how amazing she would be.

Her blade slashed through the air, and the clash of steel rang in the courtyard as their blades met.

"Well done." He parried hers away with the training sword he borrowed from the armory. "Again."

She lunged forward, and he swept his sword as he retreated. They moved in a practiced dance. Parry, lunge, advance. Retreat, stab, dodge. Round and round they went through the courtyard.

Dyna pivoted out of the way of his next move, and instead of following the expected step, she shoved her sword forward. Her cross guard caught his hilt and forced his arms up, her dagger appearing at his exposed throat. "You're dead."

He gaped at her. "I did not expect that."

She flashed him a grin. "Expect the unexpected."

Smirking, Cassiel moved into position. "Very well."

Her actions flowed faster, her enchanted armor giving her speed. Some attacks were new and aggressive. Attacks that he hadn't taught her. Dyna slashed for him, and he blocked, spinning away out of her next swing. With each thrust, she advanced. Clashing steel ricocheted around them.

She was holding her own, and he loved it.

Cassiel picked up the pace and pushed. Dyna retreated into the snow. Her boot caught, distracting her. He flicked his blade and knocked the sword out of Dyna's hold, sending it arcing to the other side of the courtyard. It landed in the plush snow.

Cassiel pointed his practice sword an inch away from her neck. "Surrender?"

Dyna's chest heaved with wild breaths, a sly smile on those pink lips that he desperately wanted to taste. She hit the flat end of the blade away and dropped. Her leg swept out, and the next thing he knew, he was on the ground, staring up at the sky.

"You let your guard down again, *kohav*," Dyna teased as she ran for her weapon.

She truly had that effect on him.

He growled and rolled to his feet. "I find it adorable that you think you can outrun me."

Cassiel leaped up into the air. His beating wings swirled flurries through the yard. He dove for his target. Under his incoming shadow, Dyna spun around and screeched when he tackled her into the thick blanket of snow. Cassiel landed on top of her, pinning her arms above her head.

He looked into the striking green of her eyes. "Do you concede?"

"Never," she replied softly. "Perhaps a truce?"

He leaned in closer, their noses touching. "I may require some convincing—"

Dyna wrapped her legs around his waist and flipped him onto his back.

He laughed. "I need to stop underestimating you."

"Yes." Dyna's cold hands trailed up his shoulder to his neck, leaving a cascade of tingles in their wake. "You really do."

Cassiel pulled her down, taking her mouth in his. He circled her back with his arms and held her close as he kissed her slowly. Green danced in the edges of his vision, and he knew tendrils of her magic were sparking at his touch. He smiled against her mouth and rolled her under him.

He could do this forever.

Her arms circled his neck, bringing her body closer. Dyna shivered when he dragged a hand up her thigh encased in leather. His tongue flicked against her pulse, and he swallowed the soft moan she made. He could feel her heartbeat with every stroke of his fingers.

I left a pot brewing in the kitchen... came Dyna's reluctant thought. *Medicine. I should...go...* But she clutched him with no sign of stopping.

Cassiel kissed her once more, then twice, and couldn't help a third before he got to his feet and helped her up. She was all pink cheeks and shy smiles. He laughed at the snow in her hair and wiped it off.

"Go ahead. I will gather everything."

She hurried back to the manor as he collected their weapons and gear. Once he had Fair back in the barn, Cassiel put away their things and headed for the dining hall.

The evening sun shone in through the tall windows. A long table parted the room. He followed the bond through another set of doors and found the kitchen. There was a large furnace and baking ovens. A smaller wooden butcher's table stood in the center with a steaming kettle. Two other doors led to a pantry and a larder containing old barrels. Cassiel curled his nose at the foul potent smell overpowering the scent of rosemary.

Dyna stirred a pot she had hanging over a fire in the hearth. "It's ready."

"What is that awful smell?"

"It's Esha root. It has many benefits. In Gale's case, it will strengthen her uterine muscle."

"What are her chances?"

Her brow pinched. "She will make it as long as I can keep her strong."

"You're worried."

"Her placenta is at risk of dislodging and causing an abruption. That could be fatal for her and the baby. This tonic will help to prevent that, but it may be best to have Gale bedridden until the birth."

"It's not something you can magically cure," he guessed.

She sighed and used a cloth to pull the kettle off the fire to cool on the stone ledge of the hearth. "Essence Healing encourages the body to heal, but if the body doesn't have the strength to heal, then..."

Cassiel waited for her to answer, but when she didn't, something cold stirred in his chest. "Then what?"

"Let's not worry about it now." Dyna turned away. "It's merely a possibility."

"Oh, I don't think so." Cassiel picked her up by the waist and placed her on the counter. She stared at him from the shock. The buttery sunlight streaming in through the windows fell over her, lighting the soft, red waves falling down her shoulders. "You will not mention that and tell me not to worry. I won't tolerate any *possibility* of risk coming to you. We have spoken of this before, of life force being the source of your magic. I have not forgotten. What will happen if her body does not have the strength?"

She dropped her gaze. "I'm not a full-blooded sorceress."

He lifted her chin, making her look at him. "What will happen, Dyna?"

"Gale...will draw her strength from me."

Cassiel narrowed his eyes because he knew it wasn't as simple as that. "What does that mean?"

"The source of magic is essentially life. It's a cycle that flows from one living thing into another. From the earth to the trees, to the sky to the sun, from person to person." She sighed at the look on his face. "I studied this, Cassiel. The same way you trained to master the sword. Medicine is my mastery. I know what I'm doing. Trust me."

But he tensed with dread and he didn't understand why, only that she was telling him healing stole from her. He stood there mutely, angry and concerned and not knowing what to say or do other than to ask her not to help Klyde's family. He couldn't do that. Dyna would always want to help others, but why did it have to be at her expense?

Dyna brushed his cheek. "Thank you for worrying about me."

Cassiel sighed, his eyes closing as she brought her mouth to his. He held onto her thighs, her fingers sinking into his hair as he lost himself in the soft kiss.

"Are you hungry?" she asked between kisses. "I made soup. There's bread, too. Will you join me? I'm starved."

Hearing that his mate needed food stirred the instinct to fulfill that necessity.

Cassiel frowned. "You are trying to distract me. I will let this drop for now only because I can deny you nothing."

He caught the hint of a smile as Dyna hopped off the countertop to gather some bowls. "I know."

CHAPTER 78

Rawn

While Rawn strolled through Skelling Rise, he found it had an impressive irrigation system, paved roads, well-structured homes, crop fields, cattle, and windmills. It seemed the gold the mercenaries earned fighting other men's wars went to their town. He stopped at a hill overlooking the land peppered with houses and farms. It had the semblance of peace, yet beyond the walls, Death awaited the chance to barge in.

"What are you thinking?" Zev said next to him.

"Why settle here, of all places?" Rawn replied thoughtfully, his breath swirling in the brisk air. "Any day, the town could experience another Horde attack. The Bridge was abandoned because of the high mortality risk...unless that is the point."

"You think they are hiding?"

"Lord Jophiel mentioned the captain values his anonymity. The Azure Kingdom is not aware of their presence here."

"Then who do they pay homage to?"

Rawn glanced at the west, where he heard a distant hum of gathered voices. "Perhaps to themselves."

He followed the sound curiously. They reached the edge of town and came upon what seemed to be a training yard. The area was flat and paved with thirty-foot-tall wooden pillars. It wasn't the mercenaries swinging across them that astonished Rawn, but the twenty or so younglings watching. They were all dressed in thick, dark blue tunics with the bird's skull emblem on the left side of their chests, standing at attention. Boys and girls, ages ranging from about fifteen to eighteen. Among them was Tavin.

"Family isn't determined by blood," Eagon said to the gathering, walking along the line with his arms behind his back. "It's determined by who you fight for and who fights for you."

They released a hoot in unison.

"What is the one law we live by?"

"Protect Skelling and those too weak to protect themselves!" they chanted.

"That is the only thing we bleed for." Eagon came to a stop as Klyde swung down from the pillars and landed in a graceful crouch behind him. The younglings watched with awe. "Now gear up. We're using the grappling hooks today. Tavin will go first."

The lad grinned. They rushed to the other senior mercenaries to be fitted with the gear.

"You train children?" Zev asked, his voice heavy with disapproval.

Eagon and Klyde glanced at them.

"They are all of age to swing a blade, mate," the captain said as they approached. "We learned from a young age Death doesn't care how old you are. Inexperience and hesitation are a quick passage through the Seven Gates out here. Even within our stone walls."

"Every winter, everyone from the age of twelve and up receives basic training for their survival," Eagon said. "Whether they choose to join our ranks is purely optional. The minimum age requirement for that is twenty, and they must train on the wall for two years before ever being allowed to cross Troll Bridge."

"Why not simply exterminate all the trolls?" Zev asked.

"We don't kill if we don't need to," Eagon said as they watched Tavin shoot a hook into a pillar and his body zipped into the air in a perfect arc. "At winter's end, only a handful of them per year decide to join us. To be a Skelling Mercenary means to live a short life. They are made to understand that very clearly."

"What do you mean?" Rawn asked.

"The last step of their training is to slay a troll," Klyde said. "We're present when it happens, but that is the requirement to pass recruitment."

"Knowing how perilous the conditions are, I have to admit, I'm surprised you would allow your son out there," Rawn said.

Klyde's attention shifted from Tavin to them. It had been a subjective guess since the boy was Gale's nephew.

Zev had confirmed earlier the boy's scent marked him as their kin, but not strong enough to be Edith's son. If Klyde was his father, then who was his real mother?

"He bears your resemblance," Rawn added as the lad leaped off a pillar and swung for another with skilled agility. "Including in his movements. Did you train him yourself?"

"I did," Klyde replied after a pause. "Though I would say it comes naturally to him. Tavin descends from soldiers, so he was born a fighter. But you assume wrong if you think I want him out there. We train children because when the day comes that they have to defend this town, I want them to have a chance."

As a soldier himself, Rawn could see the logic behind their ways. "We are trained young as well, for there is no telling when Greenwood would find itself at war with Red Highland again. I have lost good men because others either lacked the preparation to survive battle or their fear."

"What rank do you hold?"

"I am Greenwood's General of the Armies."

"Aye?" Klyde's eyes widened. "What are you doing so far away from your King? Shouldn't you be at his side?"

"I'm on a mission," Rawn replied carefully.

"What mission?"

"I am not at liberty to discuss it."

Klyde's expression became pensive. "It has to do with Dyna, doesn't it? Who is she?"

Zev's eyes flashed yellow. "My cousin."

Eagon moved closer to Klyde defensively, but the captain only smiled. He was baiting him.

"Dynalya is the Lady of Hermon Ridge," Rawn said before Zev could reveal more than what they already mentioned. "I should warn you. Prince Cassiel is very protective of his wife. He would not take kindly to strangers asking questions about her."

Klyde chuckled. "Aye, I noticed. Pardon me if I offend. I can't help being curious about your story."

"There is no story," Zev said.

"Everyone has a story, mate. And I sense there is a good one behind you lot."

"Then may we inquire about yours?" Rawn asked.

Klyde shrugged. "Ah, see, everyone in my story is dead."

"Was that before or after you settled in the ruins of Azurite?" Zev asked.

So much for subtlety.

The captain didn't seem staggered by the question. His coat billowed in a gust of flurries; his expression indifferent. Eagon couldn't quite disguise the tension entering his shoulders.

"Death dances in all our shadows," Klyde said. "No matter where we are."

An answer without an answer.

"How long have the townsfolk lived here, if I may ask?" Rawn said as he casually admired the town with false interest. "Skelling Rise is very well sustained. The taxes must be high."

Klyde chuckled. There was a coldness to the sound that reminded Rawn of Lord Jophiel's caution. "If you mean to discover who rules this land now, the answer is *us*. We bow to no king, and I intend to keep it that way."

Rawn exchanged a look with Zev at the clear warning. He dipped his head. "You value your privacy, Captain. As we value ours."

A silent acknowledgement passed between them, from leader to leader. They both had secrets to keep and would do well to maintain them.

The afternoon rays streamed through the clouds to shine on the training yard. It highlighted gold strands in Klyde's dark blond hair. The light caught on his irises, changing the color to nearly piercing white. There was something about the man that nagged Rawn since they arrived. He appeared affable for the most part, but there was something dark and vaguely familiar hidden behind his gaze.

It vanished behind another one of his grins. "Well, I'm off to my sister's house to see what I can do to repair the back wall."

"I will join you," Rawn said.

"No need, mate."

"I must insist. The spell went awry due to my oversight. Please allow me to recompense the damages. I have some building experience."

"Very well." Klyde clapped his shoulder and nodded for them to follow. "Come along. You're welcome, too...Zev, was it?"

"Yes," Zev answered gruffly.

"It's a neat trick, shifting forms freely as you do. I wasn't aware werewolves could do that."

"I suppose you could say I'm not a normal werewolf."

"Should I be concerned about that?" Klyde casually asked as they made their way down the hill. "I'm a reasonable man. I understand the necessity behind your stay and the nature we sometimes can't control, but my priority will always be this town. There are over two hundred lives here. We have survived on the Bridge because I don't allow any risks within my walls."

Their boots trudged through the snow in the brief pause. Was he telling them to leave?

"If you're referring to the full moon next week, I will be outside of your walls by then," Zev said. "And if you prefer I stay out there—"

"I assure you, we have the means to contain him," Rawn cut in. "He will be far from Skelling Rise when the moon rises."

"What means?"

Rawn hesitated to answer.

"Chains," Zev said. "I use silver chains."

"Hmm. Well, if you don't mind, I will accompany you when the time comes to see that reassurance in person."

They both reluctantly nodded. It wasn't as if they could deny him when they were at the mercy of his generosity.

"How is Lucenna?" Klyde asked as they continued. "Has she woken yet?"

"I'm afraid not."

He frowned. "But she's all right?"

"Yes. We expect she will wake soon." Rawn hoped she would. He owed her his thanks for helping him reach Aerina once more.

Rawn was out in the barn, humming to Fair in Elvish as he brushed him down for the night when a knock came at the entry.

Dyna stood against the moonlight, smiling at him. "Here you are, Lord Norrlen."

"Were you searching for me, my lady?"

"Yes, I merely wanted to thank you for helping me with the rings."

Rawn smiled at her soft blush. He had enjoyed spending the other night helping her carve the silver bands. She now wore hers. "It was my pleasure."

Dyna picked up a mane brush and moved to Fair's other side. "Were you able to learn anything about the captain?"

"Only that he is skilled at evading questions and asking his own."

Dyna looked thoughtful. "Naturally, he would be curious about us as well. We must tread carefully."

Rawn nodded. They had enough surprises and enemies appearing from the shadows. Nevertheless, he could see how much Lady Dyna had grown as she faced those obstacles. She was becoming a leader and a fine warrior.

It made him think of his son, and Rawn wondered what kind of man he had grown to be. Did Raiden take after him? Or after his mother? How he wished to have been there to see him grow.

"Lord Norrlen?"

He glanced up through his blurred vision.

Dyna looked at him worriedly. "Are you all right?"

"Yes, my lady, pardon." He cleared his throat and blinked away the wetness in his eyes. "I have been feeling nostalgic as of late."

"You miss your family," she said, smiling sadly. "Would you...tell me about her? Your wife?"

Rawn couldn't bring himself to answer at first. Images of her came to him, of their home, and her golden hair fluttering in the summer breeze, passing over the rolling hills of Dynalya flowers outside of his estate. If Rawn was still enough, he could imagine standing there with her, hearing her laughter and feeling her soft hand on his cheek.

In his youth, she had been only a wish.

One he never expected to receive.

"There is a moment where we reach a point in the path of life that deviates our entire existence. Fate brings another to join you on that path and suddenly they are as essential as the rise of tomorrow. Becoming the very air in which we live." He swallowed, fighting the thickness in his throat. "That is my Aerina."

The emotion that crossed Dyna's face told him she knew exactly how that felt.

"You will go back to her one day, Lord Norrlen," she said fervently. "I will see that you do."

And somehow, Rawn wholeheartedly believed her.

CHAPTER 79

Lucenna

"Are you feeling better?"

Lucenna rolled her eyes playfully at her brother's worried frown within the orb. He was keeping her company on the vanity as she brushed the tangles out of her hair. "Yes, I'm fine now. Are you sure father didn't sense me?"

Lucien's frown deepened into disapproval. "As luck would have it, your cloaking spell hid the blast." Which broke, and now she needed to replace it today. "How many times do I need to lecture you on the importance of not meddling with advanced magic?"

She gave him a sheepish smile. "Perhaps a few more."

"Lu," he said sternly. "You mixed your magic with elf magic. That could have killed you."

Lucenna winced. "Yes, I know, I know. It was an accident."

She had only wanted to help Rawn send his letter, but she should have waited to cast such a spell when she hadn't been weakened. Opening a portal had drained her terribly. Even with Azeran's tea, it had taken some time to revitalize her Essence.

"Well, fortunately, the Enforcers have retired to Magos for the winter," he said. "I received word that father is also on his way back. I'd say it's in our favor that you're trapped there for the time being."

Lucenna was relieved to hear their father had given up his search, but she made a face at her large bedroom windows coated in ice. A constant draft hovered in the air. "Easy for you to say when you're not the one in danger of frostbite."

Nearly a week in this dreary place and she still wasn't used to the cold.

"Other than the weather, is it safe there?"

Beyond the frosted windows, she could make out the sleepy town in the early morning and the sixty-foot stone wall surrounding it. "For now. We're enclosed from the rest of the Bridge and the trolls have gone into hibernation. The only downside is that their town is led by some absurd man."

"The Captain of the Skulls?"

Lucenna looked around her shared chambers with Dyna, searching for where she left her boots. It was a spacious room with two canopy beds made of dark wood and a fireplace in the corner. "Yes, well, they call themselves the Skelling Mercenaries. He even named the town Skelling, whatever that is."

Lucien chuckled. "A Skelling is a predatory bird that existed in the First Age."

Now their emblem of a bird's skull made some sense.

"What is this captain called?"

"Klyde." Lucenna glowered, still not seeing her boots. "No family name."

"Everyone has a family name."

"He hasn't given it."

"Hmm." Lucien stood from his desk and slid on his deep blue robes. "How is Lady Dynalya?"

"She's doing well. Her magic is growing, and she's adapting to it naturally." Lucenna glanced at her empty bed. "Dyna is up and about. I will have her greet you next time."

He nodded. "Sure. Well, I'm on my way to meet up with the Liberation to update them on the current situation regarding the search for the Moonstone."

Lucenna sighed.

"It's not your fault, Lu. There are many things we can't control in life, and the seasons are one of them." Her brother gently smiled, and she felt his affection through their link. Wishing for better weather reminded her of the old days when she was still in Castle Ophyr with him and Everest.

"How is he?" she asked hesitantly.

Lucien cleared his throat and gathered a stack of books. "I'm not sure. I've been preoccupied, and so has he. We haven't spoken in a while. The duties of a prince take most of his time."

Lucenna nodded, searching his face for whatever he wasn't telling her. Lucien and Everest used to be close friends, but that changed, and she couldn't help worrying it was because of her. "I see. Do you think now that the Enforcers are not searching for me, I could...speak with him?"

He shook his head. "You know he cannot risk it, Lu. Neither can you."

It had been that way since she left. Well, what else could she expect when her purpose was to dismantle the Mage Code? She was a traitor to the Empire and Everest couldn't be associated with her anymore, at least not publicly. But after four years, Lucenna was wondering if *he* was the one who didn't want to see her.

She never got the chance to explain herself.

"I understand," Lucenna said when she noticed her brother looking at her worriedly. "Take care of yourself, Lucien."

"Lu—"

Lucenna waved, and the orb cleared. He would only give her more apologies she didn't want to hear. The light caught on her ring, but it didn't seem to shine anymore. It looked duller somehow.

Sighing, Lucenna sat on the bed and yelped. The floor was so cold it felt like ice beneath her feet. Who would want to live in this place? Frowning at what would be her bedroom for the next three months, it occurred to her to look under the bed. She got down on her hands and knees and grinned in triumph.

"There you are." As Lucenna reached for her boots, she noticed a marking at the bottom of the bedpost.

The shadows from the bedside table hid most of it. Her fingers traced the small letters carved into the wood. They were uneven and sloppy, smoothed by age. Lucenna squinted, trying to read the caved name. It looked like a child had done it—while hiding under the bed.

For some reason, that unsettled her. The name, it looked like...

At the sound of her growling stomach, she sighed and put on her shoes before heading for the door. Lucenna stepped into the dawn's light streaming through the manor's arching windows. She yawned, ambling along the hallway for the kitchens.

She glanced outside at the courtyard and stumbled over her feet, doing a double take. Klyde was outside in nothing but his trousers. He hung from a tree branch as he lifted himself up and down in firm, rhythmic motions. The muscles along his shoulders, arms, and back shifted under the taut skin in the most fascinating ways. Many pale scars marked his strong body, some disappearing further down out of view. Lucenna drew her lip between her teeth, staring at the muscles bulging in his arms.

By the Gods, what does he eat to look like that?

Klyde dropped from the tree. He pulled something out of his pocket and used it to tie his hair from his sweaty face. Then he moved on to fighting an invisible opponent, throwing kicks and punches, sweat dripping off his chest. The heat coming off his body and heavy breaths swirled in the morning air. Lucenna's eyes drifted over his jawline, following the shape of his torso and the defined lines of his abdomen. His trousers hung indecently low, and it drew her eyes to the prominent V of his hips.

"Even his scars are handsome," Dyna said beside her, making her jump.

Lucenna scoffed and crossed her arms. Heat rushed to her cheeks at being caught staring. "I find him ugly and off-putting."

Dyna leaned in over her shoulder and whispered in her ear. "Liar."

Laughing, she continued to the stairs.

Lucenna's face flushed further, but she might have deserved the teasing. She followed after her. "Does he have to stay here? I thought he had his own house."

"Apparently not. Klyde lived with his sister until, well..."

"Until I blew a hole in their house." Lucenna felt awful about that. "I apologized to them, but I wish they would let me help."

"Do you know your way around building houses?"

"No..."

Dyna smiled. "I think they have enough help since most of the mercenaries are there, but you should stop by. Perhaps Gale could use help with something else."

"I suppose I will. When do you want to continue your magic lessons?"

"Tomorrow, if you're feeling better."

Lucenna conjured a dance of purple electricity in her palm. "Fully charged. I need to stop by the wall first to put up another cloaking spell. Have you been careful?"

Dyna nodded. "I used small amounts of Essence and only during Gale's treatments."

"Good. You should join me. This will be another magic lesson."

They went to the dining hall to eat breakfast with the others. Cassiel wasn't happy when Lucenna announced she'd take Dyna away from him for the day.

"You need to learn how to share, Prince."

"I don't share," Cassiel replied curtly, but he begrudgingly relented, saying Dyna was free to do what she wanted.

"He cannot leave you alone, can he?" Lucenna teased once they were outside.

Dyna looked back at the manor worriedly. "I think it upsets him when I'm out of his sight for too long."

She had noticed that, and it was a little concerning. Cassiel had always been protective of Dyna, but ever since they got her back, he seemed more territorial—and anxious. After everything they had gone through and all the near deaths, Lucenna understood why he felt that way. Then again, they were newlywed and clearly in love. It made sense to want her close.

But she couldn't help wondering why Dyna had not moved to his room now that she was back on her feet.

They took Fair with them and gingerly rode along the perimeter of the town's wall. If Lucenna were to guess, Skelling Rise was perhaps ten miles wide.

She came to a stop, measuring by sight that they were in the east. "Here should do."

"We're individually cloaked, right?" Dyna asked. Her cheeks and nose were tipped pink. She huddled in Cassiel's thick coat that he insisted she wear.

"Yes, to prevent us from being tracked by our Essence. But now we must cloak the area to prevent our magic from leaving behind a trace for others to sense. To cover an area of this scale, a more intricate cloaking spell is needed. The first one I placed had been tied to me, hence it fell when I did."

"So, we need another power source."

"Precisely." Lucenna reached in her satchel and pulled out four crystals. Each uniquely shaped and about the size of an egg. They were a vibrant ultramarine. "Fortunately, magic is found in…?"

"In the sun, the moon, and the earth."

Lucenna nodded. "Crystals are of the earth element and they are used to enhance spells. You've seen them in mage staffs."

Dyna made a face.

"Most crystals are enhancers, but a rare few can be used as a power source. Like the Moonstone and the Sunstone, for example. Azeran had infused the Moonstone with his Essence, so it's now perpetually charged by his magic. I will do the same with these. Their purpose will depend on the spell I infuse them with. In this case, a cloaking spell."

"Why four?"

"Well, I will place them in each corner of the town, essentially creating a diagram of the area that will be spelled. Once all four are in place, I will connect them to activate the spell. As long as they are never disturbed, not even the Archmage could sense us here."

"Azeran cast a similar spell over North Star," Dyna said. "But it visibly hid us as well."

That was a much more complicated spell.

They were interrupted by the neighing of horses before Lucenna could answer. A group of three mercenaries were cantering in their direction, faces half covered by black masks. Lucenna discreetly hid the crystals against her hip. As they got closer, she recognized the one leading them.

Klyde brought his black horse to a stop and lowered his mask. "Morning ladies. Everything all right?"

Having him in front of her made her tense. They hadn't spoken since the incident, but she hadn't forgotten the feel of his arms holding her close against him. The image of him that morning was clear in her mind.

She pushed the memory away with a scowl. "Did you follow us?"

He chuckled. "As much as I would enjoy following you around, lass, life is rather busy for me at the moment. We're inspecting the wall. I do so every week during winter to check for any fissures that could cause a potential breach in the summer."

Lucenna tried not to blush for jumping to conclusions. She failed.

"But I am curious why you're out here in this cold." Klyde raised his eyebrows as his gaze slowly dragged over her outfit of all black leather. It was fitted to her form, trousers and long sleeves, leaving only a peek of skin above her bust. "Dressed like that."

How she dressed was none of his business, even if it wasn't a practical choice. She wasn't prepared for this vile weather. It was rare to see snow in the Magos Empire. Normally, her magic was enough to keep her warm, but it was working hard against the constant tunnel of the freezing breeze.

"Perhaps we should ask his permission about the spell first," Dyna whispered to her.

Right. It was his town, after all. Yet the thought of asking a man for anything made her stomach churn.

Lucenna shifted on her feet and stifled a groan. She held out the crystals to him. "With your..." She gritted her teeth in a tight smile. "...consent...may I place a cloaking spell over Skelling Rise? It won't affect the wall or anything else other than hiding our magic. It's merely for security."

The captain's eyes dropped to the crystals a moment before rising back to her face. He nodded at his men to continue on without him and dismounted from his horse. His boots sank in the snow as he approached. When Klyde reached her, his tall, broad frame blocked the assault of the wind.

"Tanzanite." Klyde took a crystal, lifting it against the light. "Interesting that you should use these."

"How so?"

One end of his mouth hitched in that same amused smile, and she instantly glanced at the faint hint of a dimple on his cheek.

557

"Aye, you can place the spell," Klyde said, disregarding the question. He returned the crystal. "Under the condition I observe its placement. As you say, for security reasons."

Lucenna frowned. "Fair enough. Then I need to bury one at each corner of the town. North, south, east, and west. Equally spaced."

Klyde took out a scroll from his mercenary coat and unrolled it to reveal a map of Skelling. "That would be these areas."

He pointed out four spots along the wall for her. She had been off by several yards. Well, perhaps it was a good thing he came along.

For the next few hours, Klyde did well to stay out of her way, quietly observing, as they watched her spell each crystal and magically plant it into the frozen ground. Occasionally, he asked a question here and there if he was curious about something she was doing. When they reached the third spot, Dyna's gaze grew distant, and she smiled to herself. Her mate was calling.

"Go on ahead," Lucenna said. "Once I finish here, I'll head back."

"Only if you don't need me." Dyna looked at her hopefully. Cassiel may not be the only one with an attachment.

"I'll be fine. It's snowing, so take Fair."

"But we're on the other end of town. It would be a long walk back to the manor."

"I will escort her," Klyde called from further ahead. He crouched to mark a spot on the ground.

Dyna looked at her, and Lucenna read the note of caution. She gave a small nod that she understood.

"Be a good horse and escort her straight to the manor." Lucenna petted Fair's velvety muzzle. "No detours, all right? It's colder than the Everfrost out here."

Fair nuzzled her cheek and rode away, leaving her alone with Klyde.

CHAPTER 80

Lucenna

An arctic blast blew against Lucenna, and she shuddered, wrapping her arms around herself. Cold gnawed at her fingers and toes. The better option would have been for the prince to carry Dyna back instead of giving up her ride.

"Here." Klyde started to take off his coat, but she waved him off.

"I'm fine." It was a lie, but Lucenna didn't want to ask for more of his help when there could be a fee behind it. She cast another ball of fire and left it hovering in the air, but the wind stole its warmth away.

"Is it possible to hide a town?" Klyde asked as she used her magic to dig another hole in the ground. "To make it invisible as you made yourself in the cave, I mean."

Lucenna cupped the crystal in her trembling palms, and it glowed brightly with her magic. "That's called a warding spell."

She handed him the crystal, and he dropped it inside the hole. With a wave of her hand, the earth fell over it in place. "Aye? Such a thing sounds impossible."

"Oh, it's very possible. They placed one on Dyna's village." Lucenna briefly closed her eyes, internally cursing herself. She was supposed to be careful around Klyde. They didn't know much about him or if he was trustworthy, even if he gave them a place to stay.

Klyde continued strolling beside her as he studied the wall, not seeming to catch her slip. "Would it be possible for you to ward Skelling Rise from outsiders?"

"Yes, but it would cost you."

"How much?"

"More than you can afford, Captain."

Klyde only chuckled. He mounted his horse and held out a hand. "Come, we will ride to the next spot."

Lucenna tensed at the thought of sitting so close to him on the massive thoroughbred.

As if he sensed her worry, Klyde patted the horse's neck. "I promise Onyx will mind his manners."

It wasn't the horse she was worried about. Lucenna accepted his offered hand and let him haul her up in front of him. She sat stiffly in the saddle, putting as much distance between them as possible.

After listening to the clomp of hooves for an awkward moment, she said casually, "You have a nice home. It's peaceful."

"Peace is fleeting," he said so softly she barely heard it.

Lucenna turned a little to peer at him. "I imagine survival is a struggle on the Bridge, with the brutal winters and man-eating beasts."

"With any environment, you learn to adapt. Life is harsh out here, but we live by our own rules, and die by them, too." A fond expression crossed Klyde's face as he looked out at the view. "The peace you see, we worked hard for it, and it's worth freezing our bollocks to keep it."

The way he talked about it, Lucenna could tell he loved his town. "I'm told this place used to be Azurite."

"Aye, it was."

"Did you arrive long after it had fallen to the Horde?"

His blue eyes slid to hers. "I take it that is the question your companions want answered. Did the lass send you to find out?"

Lucenna stiffened at being caught and faced forward. "Will you charge me for the answer? It seems everything has a price with you."

"Nothing in the world is free," Klyde said into her ear. "You must first share your secrets if you expect me to tell you mine."

His breath sent a warm drift against her nape, making her shiver. She elbowed him back. "If I did, then I would have to kill you."

Klyde's rich laughter echoed across the land. Lucenna didn't know if it should offend her that he didn't find her a real threat, or consider it an advantage.

He led Onyx up a hill and motioned to a crop of woods in the distance. "The last location will be in those trees."

Tension settled in her stomach. She didn't like the idea of going somewhere alone with him in a secluded area, but she needed to finish the spell.

With the gap between them, a stream of icy wind constantly blew up her back. By the time they reached the fourth spot, Lucenna's teeth were chattering.

"I should take you back," he said.

"I'm nearly finished."

Klyde dismounted first and moved to help her down. She ignored his hand and awkwardly slid down the massive horse on her own.

He chuckled again. "Your stubbornness amuses me."

Lucenna ignored him. She quickly spelled and buried the final crystal. Closing her eyes, all purple glowing points appeared in the *Essencia Dimensio*. She cast out her Essence and connected them like a conduit. Electricity crackled along her skin as her power thrummed across the land. The crystals pulsed and settled as the cloaking spell finally fell into place.

When she opened her eyes, Lucenna found Klyde watching her with a soft smile. "You're extraordinary, you know that?"

The words flushed more heat to her face than her own fire.

"I do know," she clipped. "Thank you for noticing."

Two dimples appeared at his responding grin. "My compliment annoyed you."

"*You* annoy me."

Why was he so lighthearted and playful? What was there to laugh about in this gloomy weather?

Amusement danced in his expression, as if he found her irritation endearing. "Are you angry with me or is this how you treat those who help you?"

Lucenna scowled. Another bitter gust blew against and she inhaled sharply, rubbing her arms.

"You're freezing, lass. Take my jacket." He handed it to her.

"No."

Perhaps it was the way she snapped at him or he simply had enough of her refusals, but she saw when Klyde's eyes shifted from the gentle blue of the sea to a churning storm. He strode to her with a sudden purpose. Lucenna filled her hands with magic, but he swung his coat around her and let it drape on her shoulders. Instantly it thawed her frozen body in a warmth so comforting she nearly moaned. He pulled her closer to him as he adjusted it so all of her was covered.

"Are you always this stubborn?" Klyde asked. "It's not a bad thing to admit you need something." He brushed the messy tangles from her eyes, and the stroke of his warm fingers shot a rush of tingles across her numb cheek.

"I don't want help from you. It might carry a fee I rather not pay." Lucenna ripped off the coat, shoving it back at him.

His blue eyes searched hers as they fell quiet beneath the snowfall. "Ah. I see." Klyde stepped close enough to shield her from the wind. "Over the years, I gained a special skill set that pays me well. Whatever the price, only I decide what risks my men take. Aye, they hired us to see to the prince's safety, but that didn't include entering a troll den. I went after you because I chose to, even if it meant I might not walk out."

Lucenna didn't know what to say. Which was preposterous because why did it matter? He was only a handsome stranger she met in an alley who risked his life twice for her when he didn't have to.

She backed away, suddenly aware of how close he was. "I will find my own way back, Captain."

He sighed and put his coat back on. "It's best you stay with me."

She ignored him and trudged through the woods to find the road again, but everything looked the same.

Klyde grabbed her arm. "Oi, lass—"

"Let go!" She yanked on his hold. It was like trying to uproot a mountain. Her boots gave out first and slid out from under her. Klyde's arms came around her back, twisting his body as they fell. They landed in a heap. She was well aware of his chest underneath her, one of his hands protectively covering her head, the other low on her waist. She lay there for a moment, too stunned to move. The scent of cedar and the churning sea drifted to her.

"Lucenna?" The sound of her name formed by his teasing voice yanked her back to her senses. "Can you stand? Not that I'm complaining. I'm rather comfortable at the moment if you prefer to lie here."

She quickly shifted back on her heels between his legs as he sat up.

"Are you—"

Lucenna whipped out a blade, bringing it to his neck. "Let me make one thing exceedingly clear," she hissed. "Don't expect me to fawn over you like the other women you're used to. I'm not some starry-eyed wench blinded by your charms and chiseled shoulders. I'm a different breed. The kind that would fry your nethers and laugh while doing it. Do *not* test me."

Klyde stared at her for a long second, then a slow grin spread across his face. "You think I'm chiseled?"

Face flaming, Lucenna cursed her thoughtless mouth. His laugh cut off when she used the knife to tilt his chin up. She expected fear, but something else radiated in his dark gaze.

"Good Gods." Those rapt words rumbled in Klyde's throat. His hand landed on her thigh, seeping heat through her clothing. "Do you know how to use that, love?"

Lucenna gritted her teeth. "Would you like to find out? I'm tempted to put a few holes in you."

One second she had the knife, then it was in his hand. He flipped her on her back and pinned her beneath his hard body in the snow, their faces inches apart. Lucenna's heart shot to her throat. Why was she always finding herself pressed against him?

He leaned in close, his voice nearly purring in her ear. "I much prefer being the one who impales."

"Oh, you disgusting—Get off!"

Chuckling to himself, Klyde helped her up. "Only because you asked nicely. I don't wish to frighten you."

"You don't. Giving you the chance to move was a courtesy. Do it again, and you will find yourself in so much pain you will regret ever crossing me."

"Did you forget I lead a band of mercenaries others have taken to calling the Skulls?"

Lucenna smirked. "Would you like to see whether I can best you, Captain?"

A sly curve lifted half of his mouth, drawing out one of those damn dimples. "Aye, I'll meet that challenge. Take the first blow."

"If you haven't realized it, I'm very powerful," she warned. "I could easily defeat you."

"There is more than one way to defeat someone."

Without warning, she struck her hand flat against his chest. Purple lightning should have thrown him clear across the forest, but it merely crackled against his coat, fizzling to smoke. Klyde caught her wrist, flashing that aggravating grin. She tossed spell after spell, and he disintegrated all of them with a sweep of his arm. The ground vanished under her feet as he wrenched her around, pinning her to a tree. They stared at each other, both panting heavily.

"You didn't say your coat was enchanted," she hissed.

"You didn't ask." He shrugged. "Magic is a powerful weapon, but it shouldn't be the only one you have. Without it, you're at a disadvantage."

She had seen that proven with her father.

Lucenna smiled sweetly, and the action seemed to stun him, his body falling still. "Do you know what your disadvantage is?" She leaned in and his eyes dropped to her mouth. "You underestimate me."

Her knee smashed into his groin, and he dropped with a grunt. She strode away with her chin held up high, but stopped when Klyde didn't make a sound. He laid curled in the snow, unmoving.

"Captain?" Lucenna rushed back and rolled him onto his back. He was unconscious. "God of Urn, I must have hit you too hard."

But her worry vanished when his fingers curled around her waist and a small smile played on his lips. "You missed."

Lucenna released a groan that bordered on a scream. "I have never met a more ridiculous man. Every breath you draw infuriates me!"

She kicked his leg before stomping off.

Klyde's husky laugh rolled through the woods. "Where are you going? The town is that way."

Ignoring her flush, she pivoted to where he pointed. They came out where his black horse waited.

Klyde mounted the saddle with graceful ease and motioned for her. "Come, let me escort you to the manor. The temperature drops mercilessly once the sun sets. If you try to make it back alone, you would certainly perish from exposure and only for the sake of pride."

Lucenna scoffed but that one breath invited a burning chill in her lungs, and she remembered how easily the cold kills on the Bridge. She was trembling and her toes were numb. Klyde was right. She was being prideful—and stupid—even if he didn't mention that part.

Lucenna begrudgingly accepted his hand. He easily hauled her up onto the horse as if she weighed nothing. Klyde draped his coat around her again and this time Lucenna didn't protest. Taking the reins, he nudged Onyx into a canter. She sat stiffly, not wanting to get so close to him, but trying to stay upright while riding was difficult to maintain. Not before long, she was leaning against him. Klyde didn't tease her about it, thank the God of Urn. He was exasperating, but without him, her spell wouldn't have worked and she would have ended up with frostbite.

"Thank you," she grumbled.

"What was that, love?"

Lucenna glowered at his coy tone, trying not to clench her teeth as she repeated herself. "I said, *thank you*. For your assistance today...and the other occasions you offered it. I admit...it was kind of you."

"Are you referring to when I saved your life or when I improved your spell?"

"Don't push it." She could almost feel him grinning again.

"I think you might like me by the end of winter, Lucenna. Even if we have to pretend that you don't already."

CHAPTER 81

Von

Planning their escape took priority in Von's mind. He considered every possibility and setback as he walked down the hallway of the tavern. Their best chance to escape would be from the ship when they were on the water. That way, they left no tracks, and the west coast would be within reach. Immobilizing Tarn was the issue Von needed to plan carefully. Once they were free, he would take his family to another continent. Yavi spoke several languages, so they would manage.

Von reached the lobby. A few patrons were seated at the tables, eating their morning meals. The morning sun shone through the windows over the polished floors. He walked past them to the private room in the restaurant. Two Raiders were guarding the entrance of the sleek black doors.

They saluted to him. "Commander."

Each grabbed a golden handle and opened the doors for him. He entered to find Tarn seated at a table in the back of the reserved room. Lieutenant Olsson stood at his side while he read the report in front of him. Sunlight gleamed on the polished surfaces of the dark wooden tables all around. Deep red curtains hung open at the tall windows behind him.

Tarn continued reading the page in his hands as Von approached. He bowed, then stood with his arms crossed behind his back to wait. He watched Tarn's pale eyes quickly move back and forth as he read. Once done, a faint smile hovered on the edges of his mouth.

That was never a good sign.

Tarn leaned back in his chair. "You know, it nagged me that the death of the Maiden was too easy. Especially since she had only gathered four Guardians."

Because there were two more yet to come. *A familiar face and a creature with the strength of ten ...*

"The prophecy is still in play," Tarn said. "She survived the fall."

Von stiffened and held his breath. "How...do you know that?"

"Dynalya is still quite impetuous, it seems. She stopped by for a brief visit a fortnight ago."

Von stared at him, not understanding at all how that was possible.

Tarn tapped a corner of the folded page against the table, a cool gleam in his eyes as he studied him. "You didn't see her on your travels?"

As a life-servant, Von was obligated to answer honestly. But for the first time in years, a lie easily rolled off his tongue. "No."

"She is in the mountains," Tarn said, looking out the window to the north. He didn't elaborate on how he gained that information, and Von didn't ask. "I have confirmation that there is another Celestial territory in Hermon Ridge. They must have taken shelter there for the winter before embarking for Dwarf Shoe in the spring. To reach the west, they have no choice but to cross Troll Bridge. Once the ice on the coast melts, we will set sail. I'm sending you with a group to guard the western gorge of Troll Bridge. Should they make it out alive, ambush them and recover the Maiden."

Von lowered his head to hide his grimace. He hoped Dyna was still in Hermon. If she tried to cross Troll Bridge, she would surely meet her demise before she ever reached the other end. He had to warn her somehow.

"I also seemed to have misplaced the journal."

Von did well to appear surprised, although he knew exactly where it was. "She must have taken it."

"Perhaps." Tarn crossed one leg over the other, rather unconcerned. He probably didn't care about the map anymore now that he knew where to find Mount Ida. "What else do you know about the man from Xián Jīng?"

"Nothing more than what I have already shared. The man didn't speak. He found the Sacred Scroll first, yet he stayed to attack us. He could have left with the prize and we wouldn't have known."

Tarn processed his words. "Perhaps the scroll wasn't his true target."

Von glanced at the ugly scar that ran from Tarn's right brow across his nose and the left end of his cheek. Could the Emperor be sending someone to finish the job?

But why now, after six years?

The double doors to the restaurant opened, and a servant entered. He wore the gray Corvus uniform, and he held a silver tray with Tarn's morning meal. Von met his black eyes and an icy rage filled him.

Von swiftly grabbed a knife from within his coat and flung it at the assassin's face. He dodged with a slight movement of his head and the knife pierced the door behind him. Olsson drew his sword, standing in front of Tarn's table protectively. Von ran at the assassin. The man whisked the tray at him like a disk. Von slid on the floor to evade it and food fell everywhere. His knife swiped for the man, but he darted and flipped over him, aiming for Tarn. Olsson swung his sword. The assassin twisted and kicked the weapon out of his hand, catching it in the air. He beat the hilt against Olsson's skull and knocked him down.

Von ran at them, taking out more knives and flung them at the man. With one flick of the sword, the assassin knocked them out of the air. Tarn used the distraction to kick the legs out from under the assassin and quickly disarmed him. He grabbed the man's throat and his arctic eyes filled with malice. Von had only ever seen that look when he killed the man responsible for his scar.

Lieutenant Olsson and Von came to stand behind the assassin, closing him off from all sides. They were ready to kill him if he so much as moved.

"So the Emperor of Xián Jīng has come for me again," Tarn said, voice as wintry as the weather outside. "I will send him my regards, along with your head in a box."

The man faced him with a serene calm. "I'm not here to kill you," he finally said, his accent thick and tonal.

"I know an assassin when I see one." Tarn stepped back.

Von grabbed the man by his hair and held a knife to his throat. His hand itched to plunge it into the man's flesh.

"My name is Sai-chuen, and I'm no longer a contracted assassin. I was exiled from my clan some years ago."

Tarn nodded at Olsson, and he yanked open the man's servant tunic, revealing a burned scar on the right side of his chest where the clan seal should be.

"Why are you here?"

"I have brought you a gift," Sai-chuen said.

Tarn scoffed. "You mean you're returning what you stole from me."

Von searched the man's clothing and pulled out the old scroll, handing it to Tarn. He took it, then went to sit at the table again. It was yellow and old, crackling faintly as he unrolled it.

"Lieutenant," Tarn said without looking up from the scroll. "Bring the slave woman."

Von's heart sank. He didn't want Yavi in the same room as this man.

Olsson bowed and walked out.

"I first heard of your legend when I was a child," Sai-chuen continued. "Your name was whispered among my people with fear. It was said you were a demon who took what he wished, including treasures no one was meant to find."

Von stilled, glancing at Tarn. Was this man insinuating that he knew they'd stolen an artifact from the Emperor all those years ago? It had taken careful planning to infiltrate the palace and break into the hidden vault kept below ground. It had been full of gold and other riches, but Tarn had only taken one thing. He never told Von why they risked their lives for a small chest or what was inside of it.

Whatever it was, taking it had resulted in Tarn's permanent disfigurement.

"They sent the best assassin after you." Sai-chuen tipped back his head as he studied Tarn's long scar. "Yet he failed, as did so many others. I knew such a man would be an honor to serve, but you are very difficult to find. Once I learned you desired the Sacred Scrolls, I went in search of them for you, so that I may prove my worth."

Tarn's hard gaze slid over to him. "You're not worth the lives you cost me."

The statement was unexpected. Tarn didn't care about the Raiders living or dying, but there was one he did care about. Len was his protégé. His prized fighter. But she was trapped in her sleep and may never wake.

"If I had known they were from your company, I would not have killed them," Sai-chuen said indifferently.

"Lies," Von growled.

"Forgive my mistake. Because of me, you now lack warriors. I will repay the loss by taking their place."

Had that been his plan? To kill his way in Tarn's services?

Von's knife pressed into his neck, producing a trickle of blood. "You will die for what you did."

Sai-chuen's black eyes flicked up at him, his mouth slightly curving. Either the man didn't fear death, or he didn't fear him.

The doors opened and Lieutenant Olsson entered with Yavi at his side. Her eyes flickered around the room, clutching a stationary box to her chest. It always scared her to be called upon, though Tarn didn't harm her. She feared him since the day he burned his slave mark on her back.

Yavi bowed, keeping her head low. "You have called for me, Master?"

Tarn beckoned her with a slight motion of his finger. "Translate this." He slid the scroll across the table to her.

Yavi hesitated before lowering into the chair furthest away from him. She opened her case and pulled out a stack of paper and a quill pen with a jar of ink. Then she carefully held the scroll in her hands as she read the faded scriptures. Her eyes froze midway down, widening. Yavi's mouth parted in a shaky breath and her wide eyes met Von's.

"Is it the one?" Tarn asked.

Her throat bobbed, and she nodded. "Yes, Master. It's the Scroll of the Unending...but..."

"But what?" he said sharply.

Yavi unrolled the scroll further, revealing the bottom half missing. By the smooth frayed edges, it was torn off a long time ago.

"I will tell you where the other piece is," Sai-chuen said. "As my passage to join you."

A muscle in Tarn's jaw twitched, his eyes like sharpened glaciers. "If you're still breathing, then we'll talk."

Von thrust his fist into Sai-chuen's face, throwing him back.

There was no time to wonder why Tarn didn't order the man's immediate torture instead. Initiations were only reserved for Raiders he considered employing. They had sixty seconds to survive Von's knife without being killed.

Well, he didn't plan to let the man walk out of here alive.

Von's blade caught the sunlight as he slashed for his throat. Sai-chuen leaped back and kicked him in the face. Stunned by the strike, he dropped the knife, but kicked it across the restaurant before Sai-chuen could grab it. They darted back and forth, blocking each other's punches. Sai-chuen caught Von's wrist again and sharply hit his elbow upward, sending a searing pain up his arm. Then he delivered a blow to Von's chest with two palms, throwing him back onto a table.

Von slashed for his vital points. Sai-chuen chopped his hand away, jumping to avoid his sweeping kick. Von brought his other knife around for his chest, but it cut empty air as Sai-chuen dropped to his back on the floor, then flipped back on one leg with perfect balance. He shot up straight in the air and kicked Von backward. The blow hurled him against another table. He quickly straightened to face his opponent, fighting to catch his breath. The kick had knocked the air out of his lungs.

Sai-chuen spun a knife in his fingers with a goading smile. Patting his belt, Von glanced down, stupidly leaving himself open. Sai-chuen slashed for his chest, and Von thrust himself back with as much force as he could muster, but the tip of the knife caught, and cold ice sliced across his chest to the right end of his stomach.

Yavi's shriek echoed in the restaurant.

Von ignored the pain. He swiftly blocked Sai-chuen's arm and jabbed his waist, striking the wound Elon had given him. The man hissed through his teeth. He hit Von's hand away, and they swiftly met with a knife at each other's throats.

Tarn snapped his fingers, signaling the end of the fight. "Well." He idly drummed on the table in a contemplative rhythm. "That was interesting."

Sai-chuen stepped back, straightening out of his stance. He was cool and collected, as if he hadn't been fighting for his life. Von was painfully aware of his aching body and the sweat rolling down his face. Blood seeped through his tunic from the shallow cut. Face burning, he picked up his fallen knives and bowed. He had never been injured during an initiation.

Never.

Not even when he'd faced off with Elon.

"You're lacking, Von," Tarn said.

"Forgive me."

He waved a dismissive hand. "In truth, I thought you might not win against a Wu assassin."

Von straightened at the revelation.

"I recognize that fighting style," Tarn said, eyeing the man narrowly. "The Wu Clan dedicates their lives to become living weapons for the Emperor or whoever will pay handsomely. They never fail to kill their targets, or so they say. Am I not correct, Wu Sai-chuen?"

Von tensed and reached for another knife, but Tarn raised two fingers as a sign to stand down. He nodded at Yavi to finish her translation of the scroll. She had been staring at Von's blood dripping on the floor. The quill scratched against the page as she quickly worked.

Sai-chuen dipped his head in a nod. "I was trained well."

"Why were you exiled?"

"A rival clan murdered my clan head. The Imperial Lord called for peace, but I chose to avenge him. This disobedience brought dishonor to my kin."

Tarn silently regarded him and the idea of having such a lethal man in his pocket, but Von had an unsettling feeling about Sai-chuen.

"Where is the missing piece of the scroll?" Tarn asked.

"It's in the hands of an old fae. He was there when Jökull and Sunnëva ruled at the dawn of the First Age. And he was the one who stole the vital piece of that scroll."

Von stilled, his mind reeling from the new information. "What's his name?"

"He has no name," Sai-chuen said. "He is only known as the Druid."

The Druid...

As in the one they randomly met in the woods years ago, who gave Tarn the Dragon Ring? None of that could have been coincidence.

Tarn must have realized it, too. He leaned in closer, interest gleaming in his cold eyes. "Where is he now?"

A sly smile crossed Sai-chuen's face. "The Druid is another who is hard to find, but I'm *very* good at finding things."

Tarn studied him for a long minute until he finally said, "Lieutenant, provide this man with a Raider uniform."

CHAPTER 82

Zev

Zev shivered, his breath leaving frosted clouds in the air. He grunted with strain as Rawn and Cassiel supported his heavy body between them, nearly dragging him out of the woods. The snow shimmered under the morning sun, streaming through the bare branches. Zev's stiff legs struggled to move, every step leaving behind bloody prints. Fresh burns and leaking boils left behind from his silver chains marked his skin. The winter solstice was the longest full moon of the year, and it left him near death.

Klyde walked ahead of them with the thick heavy chains hanging over his shoulder, clinking softly in the soundless woods. The group entered the clearing and headed to the eastern gate of the wall surrounding Skelling Rise. Klyde whistled sharply between his fingers to notify the mercenaries operating the heavy iron gate, and the blow of the horn sounded before the gate opened for them.

Olyver waited on the other side with an empty wagon strapped to a horse. Mercenaries held back the angry townsfolk. They shouted for the beast to be put down, to be turned away, to not let him in because he would kill them all.

Bloody truths or filthy lies, the Madness whispered. *Which do they be?*

Truths, Zev thought. He could smell the blood in their veins and hear the beating of their hearts. If he'd been free last night, the Other would have ripped them apart one by one.

Breaking bones or begging screams, which brings us glee?

For all of his attempts at fighting for himself, turning had left his will weak. The sun was shining, but he didn't feel its warmth or see its light. The world was gray.

"Do not pay them any mind," Rawn murmured. He and Cassiel helped Zev into the wagon and lay him inside. They covered him with a blanket, then climbed in after him while Klyde sat in the diver's box with Olyver. The reins snapped, and the wheels jostled over the bumpy road as they made their way into town.

Zev caught glimpses through his blurry vision of the townsfolk peering at him warily through their windows and doors as they passed. He closed his eyes, hoping sleep would take him, but the pain was unbearable. They rolled through the woods leading to the manor and he drifted in and out, catching bits of quiet conversations.

"Thank you for your assistance," Rawn said.

"Think nothing of it. Will he be all right?" Klyde asked.

"Yes, Zev only requires rest. He recovers quickly. We apologize for the discomfort we caused, Captain. It's not something that could be helped. However, I admit I am concerned there may be repercussions."

"I will post a handful of my men at the manor for your protection."

"Do you believe that is necessary?"

"They are skittish folk," Klyde said. "We have protected our town with no casualties for so long they fear a repeat of the overrun or anything that presents danger."

"That is understandable."

The wagon rolled to a stop and Zev's eyes fluttered open at the sound of footsteps running to meet them.

"Oh, Zev," Dyna said forlornly at the sight of him. "Quick, bring him inside."

Lucenna waved her hand and cast her Essence over Zev's body, lifting him in the air.

Klyde hopped down from the wagon as she carried him inside. "Post four to guard the road to the manor, Sergeant."

"Aye, Captain." Olyver snapped the reins and the sound of wheels rattled away.

"We will lie low for a while and keep Zev out of sight," Rawn said. "Thank you, Captain. We are grateful for all that you have done."

"Aye, if you need me, I will be with Gale working on the house." Klyde's voice grew distant. "Find me should something occur…"

Zev drifted again, then found himself laying in his bedroom with everyone huddled inside. Dyna poured an ointment over his burns before she carefully

BECK MICHAELS

cleaned them. Lucenna and Cassiel stood at the foot of the bed, arguing with each other in hushed whispers.

"We have to show them he's not dangerous. They wouldn't fear him if they knew him," she hissed.

"These people made up their minds about him. It's difficult to convince a bigot of anything."

"We must tread carefully," Rawn told them. "We are guests here and Zev will shift two more times during our stay. Perhaps it's best to leave early in the morning on the day prior to the full moon to locate him as far away from the town as possible. That should placate the townsfolk. They have asked for him not to take wolf form as well."

Cassiel scowled with disgust. "You would ask him to do that, Lord Norrlen?"

"Why expect him to act civil when wolves are wild creatures?" Lucenna added.

Rawn sighed. "We have to do what we can to diminish their concern. It's for his sake, as well."

"It's fine," Zev rasped. "I don't mind." They were quick to gather around the bed. He tried his best to smile, but his face hurt.

"How are you feeling?" Dyna asked.

"I'm all right. Just a little tired." He tried to sit and grimaced at the sharp pain at his wrists.

"I'll take care of that." She reached for him.

"No. Leave it."

"Zev," she pleaded softly. "You may feel you should endure the pain, but that doesn't mean you deserve it."

With a sigh, Zev conceded. He was too exhausted to argue anymore. Cool hands landed on his chest and they glowed brightly as Dyna sent her Essence forth over his body. The others watched in silent awe. It didn't cease to amaze them, no matter how many times they had seen it.

Zev's eyes fluttered closed with reprieve as warmth thawed his aching muscles and the pain dwindled to a soft throb. She worked on him until the burns healed into scars. When finished, her shoulders sagged, leaving her pale.

"Thank you," Zev murmured, his eyes growing heavy again.

"Of course," Dyna said drowsily. "Rest. I will be here." She curled up in the chair next to him and promptly fell asleep.

Cassiel sighed and covered her with a blanket. "She exerted herself once again."

"She's all right," Lucenna whispered. "Dyna healed him rather quickly. Once she has mastered her magic, there is no telling how powerful she will become."

His expression slightly tightened as he watched her sleep.

"Come. We shall leave them to rest." Rawn headed for the door.

"I will remain here," Cassiel said.

Zev listened to Rawn and Lucenna's receding footsteps go down the stairs. He had almost fallen asleep until he heard angry voices outside of the manor.

He peered through his lashes at Cassiel standing by the window, looking outside. There was a distant expression on his face. A mixture of anger and...sadness.

With a low groan, Zev wobbled to his feet and went to stand beside him. "Are you all right?"

Cassiel frowned. "I should ask you that, and you should be resting."

They both looked down at the farmers bickering with the mercenaries guarding the gateway by the woods.

"I cannot rest when I can hear them. They want the beast gone."

The Madness prowled around him as though to search for where to strike. *Should we run, or should we hunt? Which side do you see?*

Zev sighed at his reflection in the glass. All he saw was his colorless complexion, haggard and morose, one half of his face in shadow. Life had always been that way for him.

Half dark, half wearing.

A derisive sound rolled in Cassiel's throat. "They are fools."

"Not too long ago, you wanted the same."

"I came to see how wrong I was," he said, turning to him. "You have a heart of gold, Zev. Don't let those blinded by fear tell you any different."

The rare kindness and sincerity behind that statement made Zev smile. "Is this your way of confessing your love for me?"

Cassiel narrowed his eyes. "Tell anyone I said that, and I will end you."

All jesting aside, Zev couldn't ignore the change had weakened his spirit. Or perhaps he was simply feeling out of place. Since he left Lykos Peak, it had been one thing after another.

Being here in a place where he wasn't wanted reminded him too much of home. As much as he hated Lykos Peak, he still missed the forest and the freedom of the wild. Of not having to think outside of simply existing.

He had a sudden urge to run in any direction and see where it led him.

"Zev?" Cassiel grabbed his shoulders.

From the way he was searching his eyes, Zev realized he was checking for signs of Madness. It was there, but that wasn't what made him despondent.

"I think...I should take some time for myself," Zev said. "Leastways, while we are here."

"What do you mean? Are you leaving?"

He nodded. "It's best for everyone if I do. I will be out on the Bridge where I won't bother anyone."

Cassiel searched his face. "If I let you walk out that door, will you come back? I cannot face her if the reason you are going is to cross the Gates."

Zev looked over at his belongings, not sure if he had an answer yet.

Cassiel seemed to read his thoughts and his expression grew grim.

"I suppose we will find out when the next full moon comes," Zev said.

Cassiel said nothing as he packed up the last of his belongings. After writing something down on some paper, he went to Dyna and tucked the note in her pocket.

"Take care of her," he murmured.

"Always," Cassiel said.

Inhaling a deep breath, he crossed the room to the balcony and leaped up on the stone banister.

"Zev."

He turned at the soft call, crouching on the edge.

Cassiel stepped outside and searched his eyes for a moment. "Your pain is no less real simply because others don't understand it."

Zev fought the tightening in his throat. As they stood there looking at each other, he saw Cassiel had faith in him. More than he had in himself.

"You can count on us to be there when the moon is full. *I* will be there."

Zev nodded his thanks, not able to say more. He leaped off the banister and landed in the courtyard below. He slipped into the forest, avoiding the townsfolk, as he made his way to the front gate. When he reached the wall, he asked Olyver to let him out. Whatever was on his face, the mercenary didn't argue.

Zev headed for the dense line of trees, feeling guilty for leaving Dyna's side. He knew she would undoubtedly worry about him, but he needed to be alone right now. She would be safe with the others.

He hiked his large pack over his back and continued south into the woods, leaving deep footprints in the thick, untouched snow. He stopped only when he could no longer smell or hear Skelling Rise.

At last, his mind could relax. It had been so long since he'd been truly alone. He used to hate the lonely days in the woods, but now he missed them. He needed the solace and tranquility wildlife brought.

There were echoes of his father all around him. In his shadows and memories, in the scent of nature itself. Filling his lungs with an icy gulp of air, Zev closed his tired eyes.

If you hold on to the past, you won't catch up to the present, son. And I never taught you to give up.

When he returned to the large oak tree, he let his pack slide off his shoulders and drop at his feet. He kept going. On he walked through the snow, thinking of everything he held onto.

Hatred of his existence.

Grief and guilt.

The chains.

His Madness.

Zev breathed in deeply, smelling ice, earth, and fresh air. He kicked off his boots and stripped off his shirt, letting the wind tug it from his hands. His steps quickened to a fast pace, then a jog, then he was running. He ran on two legs until the wolf took over, and he simply let go.

Zev spent his days on four paws roaming the forest. It was easier that way when everything always ached as a person. As a wolf, his thoughts were scents, sounds, smells. Mere instinct of the wild and survival. Tomorrow's horizon was all he had.

But then he started feeling the impulse of Pack life. He didn't have one, and when he had the opportunity to join another, he turned it down.

"I think crossing paths with you means something," Ronin had said. "For Lángshān."

Zev had wanted it. The possibility of belonging somewhere, but that was not meant for him. Not while he was in a limbo between his Other and his Madness.

"You're mad," Ronin guessed when he hesitated to answer. At Zev's surprise, he merely shrugged. "Broken knows broken. We have all dealt with the Madness in our lives. It isn't something to get rid of, but to acknowledge. It is a part of you as much as the wolf and the Other. It echoes only the vile thoughts we truly think of ourselves, but it does so with a purpose. It won't go away until you understand what it's trying to show you or until you succumb to your wolf because you refuse it."

Show him? Had the Madness tried to show him something?

It did. Once.

The memory of when his father died.

Zev keened, his wolf whining at the pain the thought brought.

He pushed the feeling away and bounded through the snow, sniffing the ground for something to hunt, but all the white was distracting.

Because in the back of his mind was the image of her.

Merely a moment of their meeting. A passing memory. And yet, in some desolate corner of his being, it kindled...something.

Lara had approached him the night before the Pack left when he had been alone looking up at the moon. The first and only time she had spoken to him. It began with a "Hello."

That one simple greeting had been enough to make everything in him fall still. "Hello," he had said back, too afraid to say anything more. Let alone move from his spot by the bank of the creek.

Lara studied him with those vivid blue eyes as he was left incapacitated by her scent once again. "Pardon...I uh..." she looked down at her feet. "I have been meaning to thank you for helping me on the plains."

He shook his head mutely, offering her a shy smile because he couldn't quite bring himself to speak words when he was so attentive to hers.

"I overheard your conversation with my brother, but he forgot to mention one thing. The Madness happens when you're living in a body that fights to survive with a mind that wants to die." There was something in Lara's gaze that drew him in more than her scent, where all of him was focused on her. "You may feel as if you're clinging to a thread, but the reason you haven't given in is that you don't truly want to fade away. You're dying to live. I hope one day you will...Zev."

He held that encounter with him like a small ember in his heart.

It carried the sound of her voice saying his name.

And the wish in her eyes.

Zev lay face up in the snow as he stared at the gray sky through the pine branches. Snowfall drifted down, melting on his face. How many days had it been? He lost count. He had no interest in keeping track. What else was he counting down to but the next full moon?

Since he was a pup, Zev hadn't strived for anything. There had been nothing else but the wolf and the change. Then came the Other and the pain. It created a vacant hole in his heart. It grew day in and day out as he fought to stay alive.

But there had to be more than nothing.

The thought made a wretched tangle of feeling build in his chest. He couldn't describe it. Only that it was heavy, and it made his eyes and lashes grow wet before they froze. His wolf howled inside of him. Offering to take over so he could banish it away, but Zev didn't shift.

Maybe he was tired of hiding from the sorrow.

Is that not what you wanted? To feel nothing? The Madness asked. Only curiosity laced the question.

Zev thought that was what he had wanted. He sat up and looked out at the frosted forest. Beyond it was the hint of the sea and the distant crash of waves.

Then what do you want?

It was a question he hadn't asked himself in a long time.

He stood and kept going, wandering through the woods aimlessly. The wind tugged at his thin clothes, though the cold didn't bother him. He searched for the answers in each step he took. Searched for it in the icicles hanging from the branches and in the rustle of the wind.

Zev reached a frozen pond and looked down at his blurred reflection in the ice. A black wolf looked back at him with bright yellow eyes.

Bloody truths or filthy lies, the Madness recited. *Which do they be? Should we run, or should we hunt? Which side do you see?*

Zev spoke aloud. "Me."

Two sides of him. The wolf and the man. This was who he was.

What do you want? It asked again.

"I'm tired of being broken," Zev said to himself. "Of fighting to wake. To sleep. To go on in this world. I'm tired of simply surviving. I want to live. And I want that to be enough." When the voice didn't press him, he went on, "I want to feel ... everything. I want to embrace it with my whole heart."

Even the things that hurt you?

He allowed himself to ponder it. Could he withstand more pain? Peace was temporary, joy passing, but hardship and loss, pain, and failure, those were also part of life.

His friends and his family—Zev could somehow feel them standing there with him on the ice. Their love held him together. Their faith gave him strength.

The answer to the Madness' question came to him in the stillness of winter that he had always found both ruthless and beautiful. He was ready to let go of the past. Not to forget, but to strip it as he had his clothes.

To leave it on the ground where it could no longer weigh him down.

"Sometimes we may need hardship in order to appreciate the good," Zev said. "There will be days more trying than others, but I want to experience all of it, live through all of it. With them."

Then live, Zev. There was an odd fondness there as if the Madness was patting his shoulder. *Live.*

It was a gradual departure.

The presence that had stalked him for years released its hold from the corners of his mind. One claw at a time. Then he heard the faint clink of phantom chains falling away from his neck. It left him stumbling without the feral strength, because that's what it had been. The wild drive to fight for his life, subconsciously born from his self-hatred and sorrow.

The guilt was still there and the ache, but the five-year weight of misery ... was gone. Oddly, a part of him missed the presence that had been a part of his consciousness since that night. It left behind an impression of the chains that had kept him shackled.

That first clean breath after suffocating for so long was like his world flushing with color again, washing out the gray.

Zev choked on the breath rushing into his lungs. He fell on his hands and knees as his entire body shook with his sobs. He cried until he could no more. Until the tears became tracks of frost on his cheeks.

There was more the Madness had tried to show him about his past, but Zev sensed whatever it was he would remember when he was meant to.

Now it was his turn to keep going.

The wolf came forward, and Zev's trousers slipped off as he rose on four paws. Everything was clearer and brighter. His sight, hearing, and smell sharpened, the scents of nature and the chatter of wildlife rising to his senses. He shook out its thick fur, feeling lighter than ever.

Howling at the sky, Zev sprinted into the wilderness. His muscles rippled under his fur as he picked up speed. His paws tore into the snow, and he raced over fallen logs and through shrubs, the forest passing him in a blur.

In due time, he would find a way to forgive himself for the past and someday fill the vacant hole in his soul. But he found the Madness had left one thing behind.

A gift.

Freedom.

CHAPTER 83

Lucenna

"**B**uild the pressure of your Essence in your hands and body," Lucenna instructed. "When you feel the intensity of its heat, throw it at the target."

The sky was orange and pink with the rising sun at their backs. Dyna inhaled deeply as she moved into position. Rawn stood thirty paces away from them with his sword out and ready, his breath swirling in the frosty air.

Lucenna nodded. "Ready?"

Dyna's hands glowed bright green with crackling power, and she nodded.

"Rawn is your target."

Dyna held out her hands and released her magic with an exhale. A powerful green surge shot at him with an incredible force. With a quick swing of his sword, Rawn sliced right through it, and the Essence Blast dissipated into a puff of smoke.

"Again."

Dyna cast spell after spell, running as she leaped and dove. Rawn deflected each attack until he missed one, and it hit the shield Lucenna had placed to protect him.

"Well done," she told her proudly. "You're improving."

A bright smile lit up Dyna's face, and Lucenna was glad. She had been down the last week since Zev's departure. And it seemed she was upset with Cassiel for letting him go. Their magic lessons were the only thing that cheered her up.

Lucenna glanced at where the prince sat on the banister of his balcony, always keeping watch over his little mate, even when she ignored him.

"Let's move on to quick attacks," Lucenna said. "Not all of your opponents will be stationary. Watch me now."

Rawn readied his sword, then Lucenna bombarded him with a series of spells. Fire, electricity, shards of ice. His sword gleamed in the sunlight as he cut through them all at an unbelievable speed. The smoke cleared, and he was left standing untouched. They heard clapping behind them and turned to see Eagon, Klyde, and Tavin watching them by the courtyard doors.

Klyde nodded at Lord Norrlen, visibly impressed, as they walked over to join them. "How did you do that, mate?"

"My sword is enchanted to disperse magic. It's an elf innovation not yet traded to the rest of Urn."

The mercenaries inspected it like children awed over a new toy.

Lucenna remembered the first time Rawn cut through one of her spells. She had also been shocked and awed. The Magos Empire was unaware such a thing existed.

"Elves are well acquainted with magic, but for those who are not, enchanted weapons serve as self-defense." Rawn handed his sword to Eagon for him to hold.

The lieutenant balanced the hilt in his hand, testing the weight. "It appears to be a regular sword, but it's not very heavy. What ore was used, if I may ask?"

"Lothian," Rawn said.

"Elvish steel." Klyde inspected the sword next and wielded it expertly, the blade whirling as it sliced through the air. "Difficult to acquire, I take it?"

"I'm afraid so. It's only found in Greenwood, and forged exclusively for King Leif's army. Perhaps you may hire a Magai Master to enchant your twin blades with a similar spell should you visit Greenwood one day."

"Magai Masters are the elf equivalent of a Grand Magus," Lucenna whispered to Dyna at her questioning expression.

"I will certainly consider it," Klyde replied to him as he winked at her. "I have a feeling I'll have use for it."

Lucenna glared at him dully. "Is there a reason you interrupted us, Captain?"

"Right, we came to speak to you, Lord Norrlen," he said. "The recruits expressed interest in Elvish combat strategies, and I came to inquire if you would mind giving a lesson. It's not every day an opportunity like this comes through town."

Klyde clapped Tavin's shoulder as he spoke. The lad was a foot shorter, but no doubt would grow to be the same height. Lucenna couldn't help noticing how much they resembled each other.

Rawn seemed flattered by the request. "It would be my pleasure. I could join you later this afternoon, as I am currently preoccupied with..."

"Oh, please go on, Lord Norrlen." Dyna waved him away. "I'm to join Gale and Edith for tea anyhow. I will go in and change out of my armor."

"Then I will need mine," Rawn said. He started toward the manor with Eagon and Dyna. Standing, Cassiel's wings stretched wide, and he flew off into the sky, most likely to follow.

Lucenna had no interest in watching the recruitment, so she turned back around and continued practicing creating ice from the moisture in the air. It was new magic to her and out of her guild element. But she couldn't concentrate with a certain someone lingering behind her.

Lucenna exhaled sharply and glared at him. "What?"

Klyde tipped his head. "Good day to you, lass. The sunlight's grace pales compared to your beauty."

"Sod off." She continued casting spells.

He laughed and sat on the stone banister surrounding the courtyard. "Come now, I merely thought to spare a moment to have another one of our enjoyable conversations. You know, the ones where you pretend to be angry only to cover up the fact that you're fond of me."

"Are you always this arrogant?"

"Only if you consider confidence to be arrogance."

She glowered. His head must be full of cotton.

"Well, I am not in the habit of holding conversations with strange men."

"Wise of you. If I see any about, I will let you know."

Lucenna groaned through her teeth. "I know what you're doing. And your idle flattery won't work on me, Captain. I suggest you stop before I mention it to your wife."

Klyde canted his head. "My wife?"

"Tavin, he's your son, isn't he? Edith is a wonderful mother, and she doesn't deserve—"

His burst of laughter interrupted her rant. "Ah, right. Your companions assumed. I'm not his father and Edith isn't his real mother, but we raised him together, I suppose."

Lucenna stood there dumbly, not understanding their family tree at all.

"Tavin is half my age. I would have thought it was obvious," he said.

"Your beard doesn't exactly make your age clear."

"I'm twenty-eight, if you were wondering."

"Splendid," Lucenna retorted. "And I wasn't."

She continued to blast her magic at the field, melting most of the snow. The sky filled with shards of enchanted ice and they glimmered like diamonds in the air. Then she brought them down with a swing of her arms, and they impaled the ground. Lucenna breathed deeply, feeling a little drained. She wiped the sweat off her brow and turned to meet the mercenary's thoughtful stare.

"Who are you?" he asked. "What are you doing here?"

She glared. "It's no business of yours."

"I was hoping to hear what tale you would fabricate."

"I'm not a bard." Lucenna strode for the courtyard doors, giving up on training for the day.

Klyde observed her from head to toe as she passed him by. The way he was looking at her sent a nervous tingle down her spine. "Well, I presume you're highborn. From the way you walk and talk, you certainly carry yourself with importance."

She stopped to scowl at him. "Are you calling me conceited?"

Klyde's smiling eyes fell on her ring. "Let me guess. You hail from a noble family and your father promised your hand to an old king or prince, perhaps. Alas, you ran away before the wedding and now the jilted groom is desperately searching for his bride."

Lucenna gaped at him in disbelief and hid her hand behind her back.

He grinned. "I guessed right, eh? But why wear the ring? Guilt?"

"You have a wild imagination."

Klyde shook his head and came to her. "Oh no, I'm not imagining things. I have put a lot of thought into this. What I haven't figured out is why your unusual group came together, how you ended up in the most remote place of Urn, and why all of you have bounties on your head placed by a famous outlaw."

Lucenna stilled. "You know who placed the bounties?"

"Love, everyone knows. Tarn is the most wanted man in Urn and you will have people come after you merely to get to him."

She glowered at the courtyard. They had narrowly escaped the Port of Azure because the Azure Guards wanted to use them as bait to capture Tarn. "I don't know anything about him. We've never met."

Klyde's eyebrows shot up. "You don't know what he looks like?"

Lucenna shook her head.

"Yet he placed a bounty on you. Why?"

She unintentionally glanced at the manor and he noticed.

"Because of Dyna? Or does it have to do with the jewel missing from your medallion?" Klyde glanced at it in question.

"I won't answer your questions," she snapped. "Stay out of it."

He shrugged. "I have guessed most of your stories already. Rawn has two bounties, one by Tarn and another by Red Highland—no doubt having to do with his covert mission. Cassiel is a prince of Hilos, so he is hiding in general, and Zev is a unique werewolf who is related to a unique human who can use magic."

Lucenna failed to hide her surprise. Klyde had been studying them since they arrived. The thought of him paying that close attention to her made her tense.

He frowned thoughtfully. "Dyna is the one I am most curious about."

She pointed her finger at him, and electricity crackled around it. "I remember warning you what would happen if you continued to pry into our matters. Why do you keep insisting?"

"Call it curiosity."

"Have you ever heard curiosity can get you killed?"

His eyes gleamed, now more intrigued. "I'll eventually figure it out, love."

"I'm not your love." She tapped the tip of his nose. A bright voltage flashed, and it threw Klyde back into a pile of snow. His enchanted coat protected him from the brunt of it, otherwise she might have burned off half his face. He blinked at her, literally shocked. "Serves you right. Don't stick your nose where it doesn't belong."

Klyde chuckled. "You wield magic magnificently. I would like to see what you could do with a sword in your hand."

"I have no interest in using such a crude weapon. It's too long and heavy."

His dimples deepened at his responding smile. "Aye, not the first time I've heard that."

"Ugh." Lucenna clenched her fists, itching to punch the mercenary. "One would think you were raised in a barn. Why do you continue to vex me?"

He threw his head back and laughed, his blue eyes dancing in the sunlight. "I can't help myself. You're prettiest when you're mean."

She stared at him, stunned silent as a familiar heat rose to her face. "This is how you do it, isn't it?"

"Do what?"

"You flirt a little, say the right thing, and with a face like yours, you must have women falling at your feet," she said dryly. "Well, I'm not interested and never will be, so it's best you leave me alone."

Turning on her heel, she headed for the manor. But Klyde was in front of her in an instant and he caught her wrist. "Wait, Lucenna—"

Purple Essence burst from her skin, shoving off his hold. "I told you not to touch me," she hissed. "All men are the same. They don't understand the meaning of the word no."

As soon as the statement left her lips, she saw the instant change in his demeanor. His jaw tightened and his mouth thinned. Fury burned in every line of his face, giving his blazing blue eyes a breathtaking intensity that was very intimidating.

"We don't do that here," he said with all icy seriousness. "And frankly, I'm quite offended you would assume that of me. I should clarify that I would never force myself on a woman. I don't tolerate that filth among my men or in my town." His soft voice was so frosty it swooped a chill down her spine. "*Ever*."

As annoying as she found him, Lucenna believed him. It was his eyes that told the truth, the coldness in them that said he had faced such things in some manner or other. And she wondered then what happened if someone decided they wanted the warmth of a woman who didn't freely give it? What happened to the men who defied Klyde?

She looked at his strong hands, calloused and scarred from his violent life, and she suspected the punishment would be grave.

Klyde released a heavy breath and rubbed his face. His anger melted away as quickly as it appeared. He looked at her again, and the amusement returned to his face. "Besides, I never met a woman who denied me."

"There's a first for everything."

He grinned now, both dimples surfacing. "Indeed."

She rolled her eyes and turned to leave, but he caught her elbow again.

"Endure it a moment," Klyde said at her hiss. He moved her aside and nodded to the spot where her foot would have landed. "There is a stone missing in the cobblestone there. I was merely trying to spare you a sprained ankle."

Except the spot where he'd pointed at was covered with snow. With a brandish of Lucenna's hand, magic blew it aside, uncovering the hole. She definitely would have hurt herself.

"How did you know that was there?"

He shrugged. "I tripped over it yesterday morning when I was shoveling the courtyard."

The delivery of that lie was so clean, Lucenna might have believed it if she hadn't been watching him clear away the snow.

She crossed her arms, studying him. "Perhaps the reason you're so interested in our secrets is because we're living among yours."

He stilled. A slight tension hovered in the corner of his mouth and in his shoulders.

She glanced at the manor. "Might they be up on the fifth floor? You told us to stay off of it because it was unstable, but that was a lie, wasn't it? You know this place more than you pretend. What happened to the people who used to live here, Klyde?"

He looked up at the structure looming behind her, and something unreadable crossed his face. "All you need to know is that everyone who lived in that manor is dead."

"Even the little boy?"

Klyde's eyes snapped to her.

"In my bedroom, a child had carved their name on the left bedpost. At first I thought it was your sister's name, but it wasn't. That room once belonged to a boy named Dale."

They stared at each other in the windy silence, flurries swirling around them. Eagon came out into the courtyard with the rest of her companions now dressed warmly for the weather.

"All right?" Eagon asked Klyde. "What happened to your nose?"

His gaze stayed on her. "Lucenna took exception to something I said."

"You probably deserved it, then."

"I did."

"Do you want to join us?" Dyna asked her.

"No, thank you. I prefer to stay out of the snow." She cast an invisibility spell over herself and stalked toward the manor.

"Stay away from that one if you know what's good for you," Eagon said as she reached the courtyard doors.

Klyde shot a grin in her direction, as if he could see right through her spell. "When have I ever chosen what's good for me?"

The group strode along the courtyard path leading around the manor for the road to town.

"Word of advice, Captain," Rawn said. "Seeing as you may be a man who enjoys taking risks, should you find yourself facing off with Lady Lucenna, it would be wise of you to run."

She stepped inside the hall, Klyde's voice drifting to her. "I will keep that in mind, Lord Norrlen."

Lucenna's heels clacked on the floor angrily as she made her way up the stairs to her bedroom. The man had a death wish. Why else would he continue to get under her skin?

Her steps slowed as she reached the second landing. The manor was eerily still and quiet now that it was empty. Her eyes drifted up the stairs that led to the other floors. The shadows were more prominent there. Dark and ominous. As though to warn her of what might wait beyond. But Lucenna had never feared the dark.

She continued climbing.

It was her turn to get answers.

Reaching the fifth floor, the air suddenly felt much colder. It stroked her nape like icy fingers, and she shuddered. Webs hung from the ceiling, dust coating every surface. A set of doors waited at the end of the dark, narrow hall.

The Lord's chambers.

Lucenna continued onward, her steps echoing in the silence. Reaching the doors, she hesitated to take the knob. A part of her felt it was rude to snoop, but the other half argued he had it coming. With a flick of her fingers, the heavy bolt clicked. She had to use force to turn the stiff knob. The old doors unnervingly creaked as they slowly opened.

The chambers were dark, the air stale and foul from having been trapped for so long. Thick blue drapes were drawn against the windows. A massive canopy bed made of dark mahogany rested against the right wall, the pillows and sheets moth eaten. In front of it was a dusty old fireplace. She waved her hand at the heavy drapes and they parted at her command. Dust swirled in the rays of sunlight illuminating the bedroom.

Lucenna stared at it, not sure what she was looking for. Strolling in, she circled the room, seeing nothing other than it once belonged to a noble family. Something to the left caught her eye. Some odd shaped mound on the floor. She approached it only to see that it was a decomposed corpse with a sword pierced through its back.

Something bubbled in Lucenna's throat and she thought she might vomit. She stared at it in horror, frozen in place. A rusted stain marked the rug beneath the dried out corpse. The shriveled skin was brown and shrunken around the bones, preserved in the room that had been closed off for over fifteen years. The lips were pulled back against the teeth, open in a soundless cry. The tattered livery hanging on what was left of the bones was only worn by someone of high nobility. The sword's pommel held the emblem of the family crest that matched the faded banners downstairs.

"You're not supposed to be in here," Klyde said behind her, his icy voice so quiet it raised goosebumps down her shoulders. He truly could see through her invisibility spell. *His jacket*, a faraway thought reminded her.

Lucenna's heart pounded behind her ribs, falling completely still while staring at the corpse. "Did you kill him?" She held her breath, partially dreading the answer.

"Yes," he replied frostily.

She spun around and backed away from him. "Why?"

"What does it matter? He is a dead man either way you look at it."

Lucenna clenched her fists. "You're a murderer."

Klyde's mouth curved in a cold smirk. "Aye, that I am, love. And I'm *very* good at it. I'll make no apologies for that."

"Why did you kill the Lord of the Manor?"

"Because he deserved it, and that is all you need to know." There was a finality to his tone that warned her not to push him further. "Please leave."

"I won't until you tell me why." She scoffed at his answering glower. "Oh, pardon me. Does it annoy you that someone had the audacity to pry into your past?"

A muscle shifted in his clenched jaw. He made for the door. She waved her hand, and it slammed shut in his face.

He halted there with his rigid back to her. "Don't force me to show you who I am. You might not like what you see."

The cold warning made her stiffen, but she had to know.

Klyde's coat defended him against attack spells and revealed glamor spells, but how well did it work against spells that were neither? Lucenna drew the rune for a truth in the air and it briefly pulsed purple before fading.

"What happened?" she asked.

The question triggered the truth spell, and a shudder went through Klyde. He faced her and the look in his eyes made her think he knew what she'd done.

"That man…wasn't the Lord of the Manor. He assumed the position after the Lord died," Klyde said through his teeth. "The first thing he did was come for my mother."

An awful feeling sank in her stomach. The wind beat against the windows, making her jump.

"She was beautiful, and it wasn't the first time someone wished to possess her because of it. I should have known what he planned once he sent me and Gale away to speak with her in private. We returned to find her beaten and her skirts were torn."

"Captain," Lucenna said faintly. "You can stop now."

"You demanded to hear this tale," he said harshly. "Now you will listen."

She lowered her head.

"My mother…" Klyde's jaw worked, the muscle straining in his throat. "She was sickly and anything that could cause an illness would be fatal. That man knew it, but he violated her anyway and she died. But it wasn't enough. That lecher came for my sister next."

Lucenna sucked in a shallow breath.

"When I heard Gale's screams, I found them in here. He was on top of her...tearing at her dress. Over there." Klyde looked at the corpse, his gaze going distant. "So, I grabbed a sword...and I drove it through his back. I stood where you are now as I watched him die. Then we barred this room, and the manor, and we never stepped foot in it again until now." He exhaled a heavy breath, his hard eyes rising to hers. "The end."

Lucenna looked away from him, too ashamed of herself. She waved her fingers, and the door creaked open. "I'm sorry..."

For all the loss of his mother, for the intrusion on his past, and for forcing him to speak of it.

The anger was still on Klyde's face as his warm hand wrapped around hers. Even so, his hold was gentle. She let him lead her out of the room. Taking a key from his coat pocket, Klyde locked the chambers again, and she continued letting him lead her down the stairs.

Klyde brought her to another door. After a second, she recognized her borrowed bedroom. She sighed, feeling foolish for her personal vendetta.

Lucenna took the doorknob, pausing with another thought.

The ghost of a tired smile hovered on his lips. "Yet another question, love?"

"How..." she hesitated. "How old were you when...?"

"Thirteen."

"God of Urn. You were only a boy."

"Aye." Klyde turned away for the stairs. "And he died in that room, too."

Lucenna stayed there in the hall, listening to his footsteps head for the front door. She went to the window at the end of the hallway and saw him mount Onyx in a smooth leap. Reins snapping, he galloped away, leaving behind hoof-prints on the path.

She looked to the town of Skelling Rise beyond the forest. They had wanted answers to the mystery of this place, but Klyde's story wasn't her place to share. So she decided to keep this revelation to herself.

But as Lucenna stood there, staring blankly in the direction he left, a glaring realization came to her. By his age, the timeline put him here fifteen years ago.

During the overrun.

The townsfolk hadn't arrived after Azurite fell—because they never left.

CHAPTER 84

Cassiel

C assiel landed on Dyna's balcony in the late evening, once again, to plead with her to forgive him. After days of silent treatment, he was going mad. He knocked on the door before striding in. She lay in her bed with her back to him.

Dyna was awake. He could sense her awareness through the bond, as well as her shield in place. Sighing, Cassiel came to sit beside her. On her nightstand was Zev's crumpled up note.

I cannot ask you not to worry. All I can ask for is time.

I need this. But whenever you need me, I will be there.

Her sadness hovered over him, and all Cassiel wanted to do was hold her, but he felt a wall between them right now. One that didn't permit him to come near her yet, and he hated it.

But he wouldn't stop trying.

"Dyna," he called softly. She pulled the blanket over her head. He brushed against the bond, tugging at the door she kept closed on him. "Please speak to me. You have punished me long enough."

Why did you let him go? Her muffled reply came through, as though she spoke merely through the crack.

That little split of an opening was enough for Cassiel to push his way in, because as much as she was upset, he knew she needed him, too. Dyna sniffled quietly, and he tugged back the blanket to see her tears.

Sighing, Cassiel lay on the bed on top of the blanket and wrapped an arm around her, pulling her close to his chest. "*Lev sheli*, Zev will be all right."

"What if he does it?" came Dyna's faint response, her voice breaking. "I mourned his death once. I cannot do it again."

"You won't lose him."

"Why did you let him go?" she repeated.

"Zev needs some time to figure out himself right now. We need to give him that. He left with his pack and his chains. He would not have bothered if he was going to give up." There was a pause, then Dyna rolled over. He lifted her face up to him and wiped her tears. "Zev is strong—like you. It runs in the Astron family, I hear. He will find his way."

That brought a faint smile to her lips. Thank *Elyōn*. Cassiel inwardly celebrated. *Am I forgiven?*

Dyna huffed and turned up her nose. *Do you think I will forgive you that easily?*

He smiled at her clear voice in his mind and kissed her nose. She squealed at that, trying to push him away, but he clamped his arms around her.

"If you need me to beg, I will. If only to be spared the torture of your indifference."

Dyna stilled and looked up at him with a sudden mix of shock and remorse. It took him a moment to understand. Then he felt it, her sorrow at what he had gone through, ignored by his family, and that she had done the same to him.

He shook his head. "It's not the same. You were cross with me for a choice I made, and you needed space."

She gasped and covered her mouth. "With everything that happened, I forgot to celebrate your birth-date." Her eyes welled again. "I'm sorry." *I'm an awful mate.*

Cassiel chuckled airily, ignoring the faint tightness building in his chest. "I am the one who is to seek pardon here. I told you I don't care about celebrating that day. It's not important to me."

It's important to me. She hugged him, laying her head over his heart. *If you don't like that day, then we can pick a different date that is yours. And every year from now on, that day will be celebrated because I will be grateful that you exist. I will be grateful for this heart that beats and these lungs that breathe. For these arms that hold me.*

How did she have the power to dismantle him with only a few words? To make everything in him collapse and come back together? She couldn't fathom the power those words had for a ruined person like him. He came to comfort her, yet she was the one who continued to fill the little fissures hidden within the rotten core of his being. Like mending broken pottery with gold, bringing light to those imperfections.

She was a wonder.

His beautiful bliss.

He would forever be grateful and amazed she existed here in this instance of a universe. Where somehow he had been given something priceless.

Cassiel was content to simply be here with her for however long she would allow it. He needed nothing else. Dyna eventually fell asleep in the blue hour of twilight. He admired her by the light of her glowing crystal necklace, creating little rainbow refractions on her face. He would stay here all night if he could, but Lucenna would return soon to toss him out.

Rising, Cassiel brushed the corner of Dyna's mouth with his, and quietly slipped out into the hall. He made his way down the stairs to the kitchen in search of dinner. After serving himself some cold stew, he sat at the dining table with the others. Rawn was reading while Lucenna quietly spoke to Lucien.

Cassiel absentmindedly heated his food with a petal of flame. If Dyna wanted to celebrate, he would let her, but really, the date didn't matter. It was the reminder of what happened after his birth-date that soured ever having one.

He looked to the head of the table, where he saw the wispy image of a boy with black wings sitting in a chair. Simply waiting for something that never came.

Cassiel snapped back to awareness when Rawn jumped up from his seat and ran out of the dining hall. He and Lucenna frowned at each other in confusion until they heard a faint cry in the distance. Then it got clearer.

"Dyna!" A voice desperately screamed outside.

They jumped up and ran out into the hall.

"HELP ME!" Klyde's scream rang through the manor. "HELP ME PLEASE!"

Cassiel rushed down the hallway with Lucenna right behind him. Rawn ran out the front door to meet Klyde running up the path, carrying his unconscious sister. The captain's face was distraught with panic. Edith came behind him carrying Evin. The little boy was scared and wailing loudly.

Rawn helped Klyde inside, and he stumbled in through the doorway. Gale's gray dress—it was soaked in blood.

A dread sank in Cassiel's chest.

"God of Urn!" Lucenna rushed to them. "What happened?"

Gale wasn't visibly injured. The blood was coming from beneath her dress. Her face was as white as snow, and she was hardly breathing.

"She was in the kitchen," Edith wept. "Standing on a stool to reach something. I told her to get down, but then she fell."

"We need to get her upstairs to Dyna," Lucenna said. "Let me take her." She cast purple Essence over Gale and lifted her.

Blood was dripping everywhere. Cassiel had seen it before, but this…this left him standing there in a stupor because he registered danger—for his mate.

"Please alert Lady Dyna," Rawn told him.

It was the last thing Cassiel wanted. His every instinct told him this was bad, but he flew up the stairs to Dyna's bedroom.

She was already awake, sitting up groggily, probably startled by all the shouting. "What's wrong?"

"It's happening," Cassiel said grimly. "Gale is losing the baby."

It was all that was needed to fully wake her. Dyna got off the bed so fast she stumbled to her feet and ran out into the hall. She gasped as Lucenna levitated Gale into the hall with everyone else running up the steps behind her.

"Bring her now!" Dyna ran across the hall to Gale and Eagon's room.

Lucenna quickly followed her inside and released her Essence once she had Gale in the bed. Klyde came in after them.

"Please take him. He shouldn't see this." Edith handed a screaming Evin to Rawn before going in, too. He quickly hurried the boy out into the hall and into another room, out of sight to distract him.

"Lucenna, bring my bag. Edith, boil some water," Dyna commanded. They ran out of the room to complete their tasks. "I need privacy!" she said to Klyde as she undressed Gale. "Please step out."

But Klyde didn't budge. He stared at his sister's ashen face in dismay.

"Captain." Cassiel took his arm. "Let's wait in the hall."

Klyde turned sharply out of the room, and sunk to the floor by the door, with his knees up, head hanging low. Cassiel followed and shut the door behind them.

It would be fine. It had to be. But he kept thinking about what Dyna had said to him about Essence Healing.

"Prince Cassiel," Rawn called to him from a room a few doors down. "Someone will need to report this to Lieutenant Eagon. He is training the recruits on the west end of town."

Cassiel shook his head. "Please do so, Lord Norrlen. I cannot leave Dyna."

Rawn nodded and brought Evin to Klyde. Then he hurried down the stairs, nearly slipping on the bloody steps. He made it down and out of the house before Cassiel heard him galloping away.

Lucenna ran past them with Dyna's satchel.

Soon after, followed Edith carrying a pot of steaming water. "Pray for her, Klyde," she told him as she passed. "All we can do is pray."

Cassiel held the door open for her before closing it again.

Klyde stared blankly at nothing, his body resting limply against the wall as he cradled Evin to his chest. "Pray?" he repeated scathingly. "It's in moments like these where I have the least amount of faith in the God of Urn…"

Cassiel didn't argue with him. He knew that feeling well. "Dyna is a skilled Herb Master. You may place your faith in that."

"Is that why you haven't stopped pacing?"

Cassiel halted mid-step, not realizing he had been doing it.

Klyde lifted his head, his blue eyes simmering. "How long has your lass known something was wrong with Gale? Don't deny it."

He hesitated to answer.

Eagon had asked them to keep her delicate pregnancy a secret so it wouldn't distress him, but there was no hiding it now.

"Upon our arrival."

"Why was this kept from me?"

Cassiel didn't answer.

"Eagon," Klyde concluded on his own and dropped his head. "I'm a bloody fool. I suspected her immunities were failing. I should have known this was why he wanted Dyna here."

They fell quiet and waited.

Cassiel listened to Dyna's faint voice giving Edith and Lucenna orders while she worked to save Gale. Then silence. Time seemed to drag on. After what seemed like hours, the door opened.

Edith stepped out, smiling tiredly with relief. "She's all right."

Klyde quickly got to his feet and rushed inside. Cassiel remained in the hall. Gale was still unconscious. Dyna held her glowing green hands above her stomach as Edith gathered the pile of bloody sheets from the floor into a basin. Lucenna laid a fresh white sheet over Gale and handed the torn dress to Edith.

Eagon sprinted into the house, his heavy boots beating up the stairs as he shouted for his wife. His flushed face shone with sweat from riding nonstop. He gaped at the red pool of blood in the hallway, his horrified expression switching to anguish.

Eagon ran past Cassiel into the bedroom as Rawn came up the stairs to join them. His chest tightened at the soft sobs coming from the lieutenant as he sank by the bed and held Gale's hand.

"I stopped the bleeding, but she needs to give birth now," Dyna told him gently. "Any longer and the pregnancy may take her life and that of your child's."

He rested his forehead on Gale's shoulder. "Do it."

Edith and Klyde stayed. Lucenna left the room at Rawn's nod to give them privacy and they headed for the stairs together.

Cassiel reluctantly followed. He tugged on the bond as they went downstairs. *How are you feeling?*

I'm fine. But the exhaustion couldn't be hidden from Dyna's voice.

You used a lot of magic. He could feel it.

I won't use it again unless absolutely necessary.

Then the bond fell silent.

The hours dragged as Cassiel paced back and forth in the grand hall, trying to keep his apprehension from bubbling over. Rawn sat in a wingback chair by the fireplace, gently rocking Evin while he slept on his lap. Lucenna played with a current of purple electricity weaving through her fingers.

Cassiel muttered a curse and stopped in place. "How much longer is this going to take?"

"Labors are quite enduring," Rawn said. "The day my wife gave birth to our son, it took twelve hours."

Cassiel groaned. He fought the urge to tug on the bond again. It would only distract her. But there was an inexplicable weight in his chest that didn't let him fully breathe.

Lucenna smirked. "Calm down. It's not your baby being born."

He scowled at her. "I'm worried about Dyna using Essence Healing again after saving Gale. You know it exerts her."

"From what I can hear, the labor is going well," Rawn said. "I do not believe she will have cause to. It won't be too long now."

Cassiel rubbed the stress from his face and dropped into a chaise. Time seemed to drag until the cry of a newborn broke the long wait. The muffle of their excited voices drifted to the main floor, and he exhaled a low breath of relief.

But then came a silence that sent cold trepidation down his back.

The smile faded from Rawn's face as voices shouted in alarm upstairs.

Cassiel leaped up. "What is it? What's wrong?"

"Gale is hemorrhaging," he said, his expression dismayed. "They can't stop it."

Cassiel sprinted up the stairs, with the others following behind. The baby's crying resonated loudly in the hallway. They all heard Eagon screaming Gale's name. Klyde and Edith's shouting overlapped in a rising panic.

"Take care of the baby!" Dyna snapped at someone. "Everyone, step back now!"

A powerful green light blazed from the door frame and the magical charge in the air pressed against his every nerve. It was hot and electric, pushing against them with a painful force.

Cassiel clutched his chest as he gasped for air. Her life force. He felt it draining. "Dyna!" he shouted desperately. "Stop it!"

Power pulsed out of the room, and a force hit them in a sharp wave. It hurled him against the walls of the hall. It faded away and all he felt was cold. The others groaned, struggling to get up from where they had been thrown beside him.

Cassiel scrambled to his feet and stumbled into the room. Eagon and Klyde gawked at Dyna. Edith too, from where she kneeled on the floor with the crying baby in her arms. His mate swayed where she stood by the bed. Gale lay there unconscious, the sheets soaked in blood around her legs. It dripped to the floor beneath it. Her blond hair stuck around her white face and neck with sweat. They watched as the color slowly returned to her cheeks.

Klyde checked his sister for a pulse. "She's alive," he whispered in awe.

Eagon buried his face in her neck and quietly wept.

Dyna turned, smiling at Cassiel, "I did it..." she said with a weak laugh. "I saved her."

Then her eyes rolled, and she hit the floor.

CHAPTER 85

Lucenna

The moment Lucenna saw the Essence fade from Dyna's eyes, she knew what would happen before her cousin collapsed. Cassiel dropped at the same time, as though someone had snipped their strings.

"No," Cassiel gasped in pain, clutching his chest as he tried to drag himself to her. Lucenna leaped over him and ran for Dyna. Klyde reached her at the same time.

"What happened?" Rawn yanked Cassiel up.

"He's reacting to their bond!" Lucenna said as Klyde helped her flip Dyna over.

"Her heart," Cassiel groaned, slumping on the floor.

Lucenna pressed an ear to Dyna's chest, listening for her heartbeat. Panic filled her when she didn't hear it.

"She's not breathing," Klyde said, his fingers hovering over her nose.

Lucenna shut her eyes and went into the other dimension, searching for Dyna's Essence. But...she couldn't see it. Dyna's life force—it was gone. Her Essence channels collapsed one by one because no power was holding them together.

But she had seen this before.

"Don't touch her!" Lucenna shoved them out of her way. She placed a hand over Dyna's chest and a bright volt of electricity shot out. Everyone in the room gaped at her in horror.

"What are you doing?" Cassiel snatched Lucenna's arm.

She ripped free. "I need to charge her life force." She hit Dyna with another shock of electricity. They flinched at the violent wrench on her small body. They watched her, waiting for something to happen.

"I felt the bond," Cassiel said. "Do it again!"

Lucenna zapped her. Dyna's body jerked and the pathways to her Essence lit up briefly, before going out again. "Come on, Dyna."

"No, come back," Cassiel begged her, his voice breaking. "Please stay with me."

Lucenna's entire body glowed purple. She sent out a stronger voltage to her chest. The Essence Channels blazed bright—and stayed.

"Lev sheli?" Cassiel's trembling hands cupped her face. "Dyna?"

She managed a small moan, and they all collectively sighed in relief.

Lucenna laughed wetly, wiping her eyes. "You scared us, silly girl."

Cassiel gathered Dyna in his arms and carried her out of the room, with Rawn following.

"What was that?" Klyde asked as he helped Lucenna stand. "What happened to her?"

She exhaled a sigh. "Dyna used all of her power to keep Gale alive. We knew the pregnancy was at risk, but we didn't expect—" Lucenna cut off in a wince, realizing her slip.

The fury was clear on his face as he regarded Eagon and Edith. "You *lied* to me," he said through his teeth.

The lieutenant sighed. "Mate, I—"

He moved so fast, Lucenna missed the exact moment Klyde's fist collided with Eagon's face. The blow sent him crashing into the wall. Lucenna didn't move as he strode out of the room past them and went down the stairs.

"Klyde!" Edith shrieked. "Come back here and apologize."

"It's fine," Eagon said as he wiped his bloodied lip. He returned to Gale's side and looked at his wife with a raw brokenness. "I deserved it."

The hour was late when Lucenna went outside into the courtyard for some air. Unfortunately, she found the Captain of the Skelling Mercenaries there. He was perched on the banister, drinking by himself. The moon was bright, casting the courtyard in a silvery haze.

"I thought you left," Lucenna said, lifting the hood of her new black cloak lined with fur. She'd bartered for it in town.

Klyde glanced at her over his shoulder, and the corner of his mouth quirked in a faint smile. "Sorry, love. I'm not going anywhere while my sister is here." When she didn't respond, he raised his eyebrows. "No threats or insults this evening?"

"I'm trying to be nice. Don't make me change my mind."

"I didn't know that was possible."

"Why are you out here drinking your sorrows away? Gale is fine. She is awake now if you'd like to see her."

"Is Eagon there?"

"Yes."

"Then I'll see her later." He lifted his tankard to her in salute. "Cheers."

Lucenna didn't like seeing the grim side of drunk Klyde, but she would take it over the man who ran into the manor screaming for help. He had looked so terrified, she'd felt his fear and helplessness.

She sighed and sat down next to him. "They only intended to spare you. Gale mentioned how hard you took her first difficult pregnancy. They didn't wish for you to worry."

"I'm her brother. It's my job to worry."

Lucenna couldn't argue with that. Lucien was the same with her. It annoyed her sometimes, but she knew he did it out of love.

"Eagon feels terrible for lying to you," she said. "Don't punish him for too long."

"We'll be fine. He's been my best mate since we were tykes, and even then we liked to resolve our disagreements with our fists. We will settle this in the same way." Klyde glowered at the snow. "If I had known Gale was ill, I would have taken her to the nearest city to see a Herb Master at first notice."

"Well, how fortunate that you have by far the best Herb Master handling her care. No one else would have risked that spell. It nearly killed her."

"Aye," he said softly. "And you brought the lass back."

There was genuine wonder on his face, like she was some sort of marvel. Lucenna looked away from him to the horses grazing in the courtyard.

"How is she doing?" he asked.

Seeing Dyna drop had been scary. Lucenna was glad Zev hadn't been present to see it. "She's resting now."

"Who would have predicted that our meeting would lead to Dyna saving my sister's life?" He leaned his head back, inhaling the brisk air. "Odd it be the way of fate."

Lucenna observed him as he looked up at the night sky. Moonlight shone against his face, turning his irises into white pools. He almost appeared younger, if not for the mangy beard.

Klyde caught her staring and winked. "Have you fallen for me yet?"

"No." Lucenna rolled her eyes. "I was only wondering why you hide behind this ugly thing." She tugged on the bristles of his chin and immediately let go when she caught herself touching him.

His mischievous grin returned. "If I shave, then you won't be able to resist me. You would be so helplessly in love it wouldn't be fair."

She smirked. "You're delusional."

He hummed behind the rim of his drink. "A few weeks ago, you couldn't stand the sight of me, yet now you're out here. Doting."

The blush worked its way up to Lucenna's cheeks. She only wanted to make sure he was all right. "Stop drinking." She snatched the tankard from his lips. "You're creating fantasies in your head."

"Is that so?" Klyde leaned in close enough to brush his nose against the rim of her ear.

The fluttering touch sent a tingle down Lucenna's back. She shoved him off the banister, and he fell snickering into the snow. He was always doing and saying things that caught her off guard. It aggravated her.

"Why do you do that?"

"Do what?" he asked.

"You turn even the direst moments into another joke."

Klyde rolled on his side and bent his arm to rest his head in his palm. A soft smile played on his lips. Lucenna squirmed, realizing she unintentionally let on again that she was paying attention to him as much as he had been doing to her.

"Humor eases the strain of life. You should try it sometime. I bet you would feel better if you let yourself laugh for once. Don't take yourself so seriously."

"I don't."

"Then laugh."

"I cannot simply laugh like some madwoman."

"Very well. Let me help you." Klyde got up to sit next to her again. He cleared his throat and looked at her with a sudden intensity. "Listen carefully now. What do you call a lost wolf?"

Lucenna frowned at the odd question, not sure where this was going. "What?"

He grinned. "A *where*-wolf."

She stared at him for a stunned moment, but her mouth twitched at the stupid jest, and it didn't go unnoticed by Klyde.

"Ha! You nearly laughed. Admit it, you find me amusing."

"I'll admit no such thing. I find you to be an annoying bore."

He chuckled again, and the sound carried the jovial amusement she hadn't heard in days. "I think you're trying to convince yourself of that, love."

She crossed her arms. "Oh, no, I assure you there is nothing pleasant about you in the slightest, Captain. I loathe you."

"I wonder if you truly hate me half as much as you pretend." The next look Klyde gave her stripped her bare, because he was looking at her in a way no one ever had before. "I find you enchanting, Lucenna."

His eyes briefly trapped her in the shades of blue and black, and her pulse leaped.

Lucenna forced herself to look away first. "You're supposed to be some fearsome mercenary the rest of Azure only whispers about, yet they don't know what an absurd man you are." She frowned at the sigil on his sleeve. "Is the bird's skull part of your persona, or does the Skelling have any meaning?"

He studied her a moment before standing. "If you want to know, then come with me."

"Come with you where?"

Klyde whistled and Onyx cantered over from where the horse had been grazing with Fair. He mounted the saddle with a smooth climb and held out an inviting hand to her. "I'll show you."

Lucenna considered going back inside, but as he gazed at her beneath the stars, she suddenly felt a little...curious.

She moved past his offered hand. "Fair." At her call, the Elvish stallion came to her. Slipping her foot in the stirrup, she sat in the saddle and patted his neck. "Shall we go for a ride?"

They rode off into the forest together. Frost coated every branch and stretch of land shimmered beneath the moonlight. He brought her past a frozen pool that gleamed like glass. They kept going and at one point she spotted a set of old rusted gates built into a hill, chained closed.

"What is that place?" Lucenna asked.

Klyde didn't bother turning. "It's a dungeon made when Azurite first settled here. It's not used anymore."

As she watched him ride beside her, she found herself saying, "You were here, weren't you? When the trolls came."

"I was wondering when you were going to ask."

"Why not simply tell Rawn when he asked about it? Does it need to be a secret?"

Klyde was silent for a moment as he led them out of the trees into a clearing of vast open plains. "That time of our lives was filled with blood and loss. We saw our families and friends torn apart and eaten in front of us. Everything we knew was gone. That sort of thing leaves a mark." He glanced at the disfigured scars on his arms, revealed by his rolled-up sleeves. "The Lord and all of his knights fell that day. We had to begin anew and learn how to survive. For some reason, those left looked to me for that. Some whelp who had nothing and knew nothing of the world, only that we had been abandoned to it. Everything I have done since then was to change the powerless existence we found ourselves in." His eyes met hers and they reminded her of the ocean again, the way the blues crashed into each other like devastating waves. "We fought for the peace we made, and I'm severely protective of that."

Lucenna asked no more questions. She couldn't imagine what it would be like as a child facing all of that alone, but she knew what it meant to fight so others could live. The town was his moonstone.

"Peace is a rare thing," she said. "Many cross the Gates without ever finding it. But you did, and I won't let anyone take that from you, Klyde."

His face softened, and the way he was gazing at her again made her stomach pitch.

She scowled. "But if I find this is some half-cocked story to gain my favor, I will break every single bone in your body and flay you alive."

He laughed, and she didn't know why it sounded nice to her. "So vicious. Your sweet words are like honey to my ears."

"I mean it. Lie to me and I will hurt you."

"Oh, I believe you."

They came to a stop on the edge of sheer cliffs that faced the open sea. Below came the roar of crashing waves beating against the bluffs. The moon shone above it in the clear night sky speckled with stars, reflecting on the surface of the sea. It was a majestic view.

The moment, this place, there was something soothing about it. Perhaps because she understood a little more of Klyde, and she oddly didn't seem to mind him anymore, or she was simply becoming accustomed to his eccentrics that secretly made her smile.

"Why are we here?" Lucenna asked.

"I like it out here," Klyde said, his expression pensive as he watched the waves. "It's quiet. It wasn't always like that. During the First Age, the Skelling ruled this sea. It was under constant storm because it created treacherous monsoons, and any ship that fell to their waves were destroyed. They say if you ever see one to hide and pray, because it means the Seven Gates have opened and death will surely follow."

"Ah, so it *is* part of the identity of the formidable Skelling Mercenaries."

He flashed a shrewd grin. "Perhaps."

With a click of his tongue, they gingerly rode their horses along the plains.

"That's a grand legend for a bird who only makes a little storm," she said.

"The Skelling wasn't feared because of the storms. They were massive birds, as large and powerful as dragons." There was a look on Klyde's face that she couldn't quite interpret. "And it was the only creature that could kill the Ice Phoenix."

CHAPTER 86

Dynalya

Dyna woke to the sun shining brightly through her bedroom window. She was in the middle of her bed, warm under the thick covers pulled around her shoulders, red hair flared around her head on the ruffled pillow.

Dyna moaned, feeling lightheaded and weak. The center of her chest ached as if someone had punched her there. She heard running in the hall before Cassiel burst into the bedroom. His wild eyes found hers, his apprehension switching to relief, and she was already reaching for him when he ran for her.

Cassiel pulled her to him, raising her to her knees on the edge of the bed. Every part of him wrapped around her, his whole body simply thawing into hers. He whispered broken words against her cheek. She understood none but *lev sheli.*

Dyna rubbed his back. "I'm all right. I'm sorry for frightening you." He brought his arms around her waist and rested his head over her chest. She flushed at the sensation. "Cassiel—"

"Don't move." He held her tighter. "Please."

He was trembling. She rested her head over his and wrapped her arms around his shoulders. His body slumped against her, feeling comforted by her embrace. They held each other for a long moment.

"I thought...you were...." His voice cracked. "I thought I lost you."

"I'm sorry," she told him softly.

Cassiel pulled back a little to look at her with anguish. "What were you thinking? You could have died. What if you did?"

Gale had been dying, so Dyna did the only thing she could to save her. But then she sank into a void, where Cassiel's voice had pleaded for her to come back.

"I was scared, too," she whispered. "I heard you calling me. I tried so hard to find you."

His anger faded, but his jaw didn't loosen. A muscle jumped in his cheek as he stared at her. Then he dropped to his knees, and his arms went around her waist, pulling her to him. "You cannot die on me, Dyna. Please, never do that to me again."

Dyna sighed. "That was the first time I dared to do that."

He searched her eyes questioningly. "Did you know what would happen if you used that much power?"

She didn't want to lie, but she knew he was going to be angry if she told him the truth.

"Answer me."

Dyna sat back on her ankles and looked down at her palms. "Essence Healing is draining because I'm essentially giving my life force when I heal. But it's safe in small increments," she added quickly when Cassiel's mouth fell agape. "My life force replenishes itself."

His eyes narrowed. "What you did was *not* a small increment."

"That was a higher level of Essence Healing. It's incredibly powerful, but it can sometimes completely drain you..."

"Which is fatal for mages," he said tightly.

She fidgeted with her fingers. "Yes, but I didn't think it would be for me because I'm mostly human. Before the barrier, I wouldn't have been able to do that. I didn't know what would happen."

"Yet you risked it, anyway!"

Dyna flinched at Cassiel's shout. Fury overtook his face, and his silver eyes pierced her like shards. She had never seen him so upset. She heard the rustle of Lucenna sitting up in the bed behind her.

"Don't yell at me," Dyna said in a small voice. She reached for him, but he stepped back. "Please don't be angry."

"I am angry!" Cassiel said. "And I have reason to be. You exhausted your powers knowing how dangerous it is and it nearly killed you. Your life is not expendable, Dyna. Not to me."

"I'm not the only one to jump into dangerous situations. You do the same for me all the time."

"I'm your Guardian. Your mate. Protecting you is what I'm meant to do." He clenched his shaking fists. "Have you any idea what it was like to see you fall? To watch Lucenna strike you with electricity to make your heart beat again?" His eyes filled. "I was on the ground, fighting to breathe, as I begged you to come back to me."

Dyna lowered her wet eyes, unable to see his visible resentment. He hadn't raised his voice like this since they first met. Back then, Cassiel had chastised her stupidity when she risked her life crossing Hilos. He was looking at her now with that same outraged anger.

"You were at Death's Gate." He dropped his head, his hands trembling on the edge of the bed.

"I'm right here," she told him gently, brushing his hair. "I'm alive because of you. It was your voice that guided me back. I will be careful next time."

Cassiel looked up wide-eyed and his jaw set. "There *won't* be a next time. You will never use Essence Healing again. Swear it."

Dyna stared at him, shocked by the demand. "Cassiel..."

He scowled when she shook her head. "Can you, for once in your life, not be reckless? Stop making me worry about you every damn day. Or is it that you enjoy being on the brink of death? Are you so cruel to have me witness it again? I won't stand for it, so you will end this now. No more healing."

She sucked in a breath, staring at his unwavering expression.

"You won't order her about," Lucenna hissed.

Cassiel's sharp eyes didn't look away from her. "Stay out of this."

Dyna clenched her fists, feeling his tension seep into her. "I took an oath to cure and heal. Essence Healing is a part of that."

"You are a skilled Herb Master without it. You don't need it."

"I have saved *countless* people with it," she replied tersely.

"At the expense of yourself!"

"No, it's not. I told you it's safe to perform in increments," Dyna shouted back.

"It's killing you, but you are too senseless to see it!"

Dyna's eyes stung. He may as well call her stupid again. She didn't understand why he was being this way.

Rawn was suddenly there, taking his arm. "Prince Cassiel, peace. Lower your voice."

He jerked free. "Are you in agreement with this, too?"

Rawn didn't answer.

Dyna angrily wiped away her tears. "You're being unreasonable, Cassiel. I explained to you how it works. I only used that amount of power this once. It won't happen again."

He shook his head. "I don't believe that. There will always be someone out there in need of saving."

It was true, and that's why she chose this trade. Becoming a Herb Master helped her self-heal after the Shadow killed her parents and little brother. She came out of her depression by becoming someone who cured the hurts of others. It was integrated into her life.

"You're asking me to give up a part of who I am."

"You have me now," he said. "I can heal whoever you want with my blood."

"You can't do that and I won't ask you to. This is *my* choice. I made it. Same as you made a choice to let Zev go at the risk he may end his life."

Cassiel closed his eyes. He breathed in deeply, then slowly released it. "Dyna, that is different and you know it. I'm trying to keep you alive. That is my purpose. I need that."

"I don't."

He flinched, and she felt the echo of a sharp pang tear through her chest, the same pain that he was feeling now. Dyna's glare faded when she realized what her words had done to him. He opened his eyes, and the anger was gone. They were filled with dismay.

She slipped off the bed quickly, reaching for him. "Wait, Cassiel—"

He stepped back, hurt and confusion on his face.

"Saving lives, to me, it's worth the risk of my own. I don't need you to protect me from that. It doesn't mean I don't need you."

But he wasn't listening to her anymore. Cassiel headed for the door.

Dyna grabbed the end of his shirt. "Where are you going?"

He didn't look at her as his shield fell into place. "I need some time with the sky."

She came around to look up at him, though he wouldn't meet her eyes. "Are you running away from me again?"

He was quiet for a moment. "This is your decision."

She reached for him but stopped. "And you don't support it."

He pressed his lips softly against her temple. The kiss was tender, but brief. *I'm sorry.* The words brushed softly against her mind, regretful and broken. *I cannot.*

CHAPTER 87

Dynalya

It was evening when Dyna made her way downstairs with Lucenna. They found Klyde standing in the grand hall by the fireplace. His broad back was to them as he rocked and crooned dotingly to what he held.

"The poor girl will never have a chance, will she?" Lucenna said. "You will chase away all the lads in town."

Klyde chuckled. "Perhaps some beatings and threats, too." He glanced up as they entered and smiled. "I take it you haven't properly met my niece yet. Come see the wee darling."

Dyna hesitated before walking over as Klyde turned, revealing the small bundle cradled in his arms. She inched closer for a better look at the sleeping baby wrapped in a white blanket. Her chubby cheeks were rosy and round. There were a few golden curls over her bald head. She had little lashes, a little nose and tiny puckered lips.

"She's a sweet little thing," Dyna said.

"And nothing like you at all," Lucenna added.

Klyde looked at her and they exchanged a glance, this one lingering. "I will take that as a compliment, love."

Love? Dyna peered at her.

Lucenna flushed. "Don't call me that. Your sister says it's time for her feeding, and if you don't relinquish her baby, I am to remove one of your limbs."

He chuckled, but his smile faded when he noticed Eagon coming down the stairs behind them. Wordlessly, Klyde handed Dyna the baby. He went into the hall and motioned at Eagon to follow him to the courtyard. Once they were outside, Eagon threw a punch. Klyde tackled him to the ground, and they traded blows.

Dyna gasped. "God of Urn, what is that about?"

Lucenna shook her head and snickered. "Apparently, this is how they resolve their disputes."

Well then.

Dyna carefully proceeded upstairs with the precious bundle in her arms. She stroked the baby's tiny fist, curled by her chubby cheek. The little one was so sweet. Completely at peace and untainted. Dyna made a silent wish for her to always remain that way.

When they reached Gale's room, she lightly knocked before going in. Gale sat up with a tired smile. Edith was sitting beside her on the bed.

Dyna laid the baby down and did a quick examination. "Is she feeding well?"

"Yes, she eats a lot."

"Wonderful." Dyna continued to check the baby's stomach, her heart, feet and hearing. She finished and quickly wrapped her up again in the blanket. "She's perfect. I'm grateful the God of Urn kept you here," Dyna said quietly and passed the baby to Edith. "I brought you something, Gale." She handed her a glass vial containing hallow lily seeds. "These are a special contraception that cause infertility. Take one every year starting from today and there will be no more pregnancies to worry about."

Gale's eyes watered, and she pulled her into a hug. "Thank you, Dyna, for all you have done for us. I'm so sorry you quarreled with your husband because of it."

Dyna flushed, embarrassed they knew about their fight. She had been so gripped by their argument she hadn't realized how loud they were shouting. "You have nothing to be sorry about."

"I understand why he's angry. You nearly lost your life to save mine."

"I will never be sorry for that," she said. "Even knowing the result. Well, I'll leave you to rest now. I will come back again tomorrow morning to check on you."

Gale patted her hand and let her go.

Sighing, Dyna left the room with Lucenna as Klyde and Eagon came up the stairs. They were both beaten bloody, but they were laughing and shoving each other, seeming to have repaired their friendship. Eagon nodded to them before going into his room.

Klyde lingered behind. His eyes went to Lucenna first, sweeping over her face a moment, before dropping to Dyna. "Thank you, lass. For everything. I'm forever in your debt."

"No debts." Dyna held a glowing hand to his face and healed the cuts and welts. He wasn't in dire need of it, and she had not fully recovered from yesterday, but she didn't want to feel like she couldn't use her magic when she wanted to.

"Aye." Klyde rubbed his jaw when she finished and grinned. "You are a walking miracle." His eyes drifted to Lucenna again, as if he couldn't help it. "Oh, I forgot to mention half the town is coming to the manor in an hour or so."

"They are coming here?" Dyna asked, surprised.

Lucenna frowned. "Why?"

Klyde rubbed a spot of leftover blood from his lip. "The townsfolk always gather on the first night of a birth. Life being so fleeting here, we like to celebrate when it's made. We drink all night until the sunrise and dance until we can't stand. Our festivities get unruly at times, so expect a few fist fights, if not an engagement."

Any other day, it might have sounded fun, but Dyna wasn't looking forward to it now. She wished it was held somewhere else.

"Does it have to be here?" Lucenna asked, mirroring her thoughts.

"Aye, the manor has enough space to hold a good crowd. Besides, I think we all need a night to unwind, lass." There was a heavy knock at the main door below, and he winked. "It's begun."

Klyde bounded back down the stairs to answer the door. From the second floor, they could hear the boisterous voices of the mercenaries.

Dyna continued to their shared bedroom. It was dark inside, with the sun nearly set. She lit the fireplace as Lucenna closed their door on the noise filling the manor. Voices drifted from outside, too. Dyna went to the windows. Townsfolk strolled up the path to the manor, finely dressed and smiling. They looked happy. Excited even.

"Maybe we should go," Lucenna said. "That ridiculous mercenary is right. I think we all deserve a night to unwind."

Sighing, Dyna shook her head and plopped on the edge of her bed. "I am not really in the mood for dancing, Lucenna."

"Lady Dyna of Mopey Mountain." Lucenna sat next to her. "Cheer up. This is your first quarrel with Cassiel, and that's a good thing."

It wasn't their first argument, but this one felt more serious than all the rest. "In what Realm is that a good thing?"

"It means you're acknowledging each other." Lucenna frowned, looking down at her ring. "I don't think I ever quarreled with Everest."

Well, that could be because he didn't know she was using magic, but Dyna kept that to herself.

"What is your opinion? Am I wrong, or is he?" Dyna asked, because she wasn't sure anymore.

"Oh, no. I will keep my opinion to myself. The only thing I will say is when we are angry, sometimes we say things we don't mean. While struggling to say what we truly want to."

Dyna thought of Cassiel and the look on his face when he was shouting. Of the emotions she had not paid attention to when she was busy feeling her own.

He called her reckless because it was the truth. She had a tendency to rush in head first during high-risk situations, relying on faith that everything would somehow work out in the end. Perhaps that was foolish, but her choices were based on what she felt was right.

If she hadn't taken that risk, Gale would have died. Yet if Lucenna had not been there, if she had not heard Cassiel's voice, she would have died instead.

Then he would have been left behind to mourn her death.

It finally hit Dyna why he had been so hurt by her decision. Because she hadn't thought of what consequences her actions would have on him.

Your life is not expendable, Dyna. Not to me.

Who knows how many mortal years she would have with him, and she almost gave them up.

Lucenna wiped the wetness from her lashes. "Sitting here moping won't make things any better, Dyna. So get up. You are going to reconcile with Cassiel, and we're going to celebrate a miracle with a drink, then perhaps a dance." She wore a mischievous smile. "And I have the perfect dress. Once the grumpy prince sees you in it, I can guarantee one of two things happening."

Dyna's eyes widened. "What?"

"He will either be furious, or he will forget about your tiff because all he will care about is tearing it off you."

Good Gods.

"But how are you feeling? You're still pale. Is your Essence not fully recovered yet?

Dyna shook her head. "It will take a few days or so."

She had used nearly all of her power to save Gale. Unfortunately, they ran out of the herbs used in the tea that helped them recover their magic.

"Well, you know the other thing that could help with that, right?" Lucenna said slyly.

Dyna swatted her away. "Do you always think about *that*?"

Lucenna laughed. "No, but I think it's time you move out of this room."

It *was* about time.

Dyna had waited to share a bed with Cassiel until she felt ready for that step, and he took it all in stride. Her understanding mate.

She wanted to see him. Needed to. Now she was the one left on the other side of a silent bond, and she couldn't stand it anymore.

So Dyna got up.

They were bathed and dressed within the hour, but the flimsy thing Lucenna made her wear could hardly be considered a dress. The black fabric seemed to flow and cling to her curves in all the right places, revealing more skin than she was used to. The thin straps led to a curved neckline, the bodice with gold accents emphasizing her cleavage.

Dyna tugged at the high slits that revealed her thighs. "I think this is too inappropriate."

Lucenna swatted her hand away. "Leave it."

"I feel cold in places I shouldn't."

Lucenna snickered as she dusted gold powder on Dyna's cheeks. "Good. Now stop biting your lip or you will eat away the rouge and ruin all of my work."

She sighed and let her finish. It was a losing battle, anyway. And she was curious to see how Cassiel would react to the dress. Would he look at her the same way he had when she wore the nightgown?

Music and cheering floated up from downstairs, reminding her of their guests invited by their gracious host. One who was equal parts mysterious.

"Have you learned anymore about Klyde?" Dyna asked.

The brush Lucenna had been running through her hair paused, and she glanced at her in the mirror's reflection, then away. "He's as careful with his secrets as we are."

There was something in her tone Dyna couldn't quite read.

"He's not careful with you." She canted her head, taking in the red dress Lucenna wore. It was a deep garnet, falling in waves of chiffon. It tied up at her neck, leaving her back exposed. The sorceress looked absolutely beautiful. She always did. And Dyna knew Klyde had noticed because his attention was always on her. "I think he fancies you."

Lucenna scoffed. "The only thing that man fancies is himself."

Yet she had noticed he wasn't the only one who stole glances. "Perhaps you might...too?"

Lucenna glowered, her cheeks flushing pink. "Don't be absurd. He's so...."

Dyna hid a smile at the struggle on her face. "Handsome? Rugged? Charming?"

"Maddening, overconfident, and..."

"*And?*"

Lucenna huffed. "He smells of troll."

Dyna could tell from her shifted expression that was a lie. "Hmm. Curious that you didn't list Everest as a reason."

Lucenna froze before staring down at her hand with such a horrified expression, Dyna felt bad for the comment. She didn't know why she mentioned that.

"I'm only teasing." Dyna slipped into her shoes and looked down at herself. "Well, I suppose...this is it?"

Lucenna nodded absentmindedly with her brow pinched. "Let's go."

They left their room, following the buzz of voices mingling and the sound of cheerful music coming from the main floor. When they reached the bottom of the stairs, they found the manor was packed with townsfolk. The massive crowd was mostly made up of men, and all the ones standing in the hall looked up at them.

"I think we might have overdressed," Dyna said under her breath. No one else was in an elaborate gown or brocade jacket. "Everyone is staring."

"With interest," Lucenna mused.

The men were certainly *very* interested. They smiled up at them, some coming to the stairs to ask for a dance. Women were looking at them, too, though their looks were unkind. Most likely due to how revealing their dresses were.

The bond hummed with roiling energy before Dyna met a pair of silver eyes staring back at her from the end of the hall. They burned like molten steel forged by cerulean flames. As Cassiel slowly observed her, Dyna decided Lucenna was only partially right about the dress.

He looked furious enough to slaughter every male speaking to her now and like he wanted to devour her alive.

"Have a good night," Lucenna sang in her ear before she slinked down the steps. Their new suitors made a path for her, half following on her heels.

Dyna stayed still, watching Cassiel prowl through the crowd in her direction. Heat blanketed over them as he stopped in front of her. She wasn't sure if it was coming off him or if it was her nerves or both.

The remaining men backed away at the look he fixed on them and hurried on.

His gaze returned to her, traveling over her exposed thighs, sweeping slowly up the plunging neckline to her bare shoulders and finally back to her face.

A feral sort of smile curved Cassiel's mouth. *"Lev sheli,"* he said, his quiet voice bordering on a growl. "As someone who wishes to save lives, you have put every male in this room in mortal danger." His fingers lightly curled around her wrist, and the electricity of his touch made her heartbeat spike. They continued up her arm, leaving behind a blazing trail. He leaned in as his other hand slid to the small of her back, drawing her closer. "You belong to me. I'm torn between proving it to them or taking you upstairs and proving it to you."

She shivered at the flutter of his breath falling on her skin. Dyna had to make herself breathe before she took his hand and climbed one step back up the stairs. After a pause, she climbed one more.

Then prove it.

CHAPTER 88

Lucenna

Lucenna secretly smiled to herself as she watched Dyna lead Cassiel upstairs. Well, she shouldn't expect her to return to their shared room tonight. Finally.

"Lucenna." Klyde leaned against the doorframe leading to the dining hall, his arms and ankles crossed. His eyes slowly roamed over her.

She was staring at him, too, soaking in his every visible feature.

The captain looked different out of his mercenary coat. He stood tall in black pants and a loose white shirt with the sleeves rolled over his bulky biceps. Her eyes lingered on the glimpse of his chest left visible, that gave all kinds of hints about the defined muscle hidden underneath. Though she already knew what was under his shirt.

He cleaned up nicely, but if she had to admit it, she preferred his rugged style.

"You look undeniably exquisite this evening." Heat radiated from Klyde's gaze as it drifted from her face to what she wore, his blue eyes penetrating as if he could see right through her. "No better way to entice a man than with a dress."

"Not that I care to entice anyone," Lucenna shot back. "Don't think you had any influence on what I wore tonight."

He flashed her a grin, putting those damn dimples on display. "Then what did I have an influence on?"

"Besides my growing revulsion, absolutely nothing."

"*Oh*, witty. Someone's in a mood."

Rolling her eyes, Lucenna pointedly turned her back and searched through the many faces in the crowd. She fidgeted with her ring, twisting it around her finger as she ignored the mercenary still standing behind her. Guilt twisted through her because until Dyna mentioned it, she hadn't thought of Everest in days. It wasn't right, and yet she couldn't help that her awareness heightened to Klyde's presence.

"If you're searching for Lord Norrlen, he left a little earlier," he said. "Mentioned something about the noise being too intolerable for his ears."

So much for that.

Lucenna would rather not be stuck in a crowd where she knew no one, but she also didn't want to tuck tail in front of Klyde.

"Captain, you were to wear your best for this evening's festivities," Eagon said as he passed by. "Where's your cravat?"

"Respectfully, up your arse, mate. I refuse to wear that frilly thing."

The men hooted with laughter.

A glance around showed they had all cleaned up tonight, and by the way they were flocking to the women, Lucenna guessed this was more than a simple celebration. The music picked up, and she followed the sound to the grand hall. Couples danced in twirling paces across the room. It was more jubilant than the balls held in Castle Ophyr, and more intimate in the way they held each other close. It seemed fun.

"There's a rare sight."

"What is?" Lucenna asked absentmindedly.

"Your smile." At the suppleness of Klyde's tone, she looked up at him. Really looked up. It reminded her how much taller he was. And big. The smile she hadn't known was there faded at the rapt way he was gazing at her. "Do you want to dance?"

Her gaze skittered over Klyde's arms to his hands, imagining them on her. The thought elicited a curl of heat in her stomach.

"I do." But instead of taking Klyde's hand, Lucenna accepted the offered hand of the mercenary who approached her. She let him pull her into the throng and they moved with the sway of the music.

The mercenary twirled her around, pulling her back flushed against his chest. "You dance very well. We met before, if you recall. My name is—"

Lucenna leaned her head back to whisper intimately close to his mouth. "I don't care. Spin me."

She knew Klyde was watching. She felt the touch of his stare as she moved. With every turn, she caught glimpses of him leaning against the wall, those dark eyes on her. The nameless man held her close enough to make her stiffen. She glanced past his shoulder, only to find Klyde had left his spot. Well, it wasn't as if he would watch her all night.

"Another one?" the mercenary asked when the song ended.

She plastered a polite expression on her face to answer him with some excuse. A large, warm hand grabbed hers, and she was twirled into another set of arms.

"She's with me, Olyver." Klyde's hard claim vibrated where her other hand had landed on his chest.

"Aye, Captain. Pardon." Olyver backed away with a dip of his head.

Lucenna glared up at him. "Since when am I with you?"

Klyde's cool eyes slid to hers, and one end of his mouth curved in a way that was both dark and intense. "We can pretend that little display wasn't for me, but if you kept dancing with him the way you were, I would've had to consider breaking his legs." He raised their linked hands, and his other slid to the small of her back. The warmth of his palm seeped through the thin fabric as the next song started. "But I would rather have my hands on you," he purred in her ear, and she felt the husky words lick up her spine.

Klyde drew her into a dance, and she let him lead. For once, Lucenna ignored her misgivings. The music picked up to a faster, romantic tempo.

She danced with the man she shouldn't, because at this moment, she didn't care. Klyde was in control of the rhythm. Her arms ended around his neck, his fingers gliding up her waist. The curve of her hips moved with each of his smooth movements in constant harmony. Their eyes stayed on each other through every turn. His thigh slid between her legs as they swayed intimately closer. The sensuality of it was so incredibly arousing she could hardly breathe. Klyde hitched her leg up his thigh as he dipped her with effortless strength. He hauled her up, bringing their faces close. The song ended, and a cheer broke out from everyone who'd been watching. They breathed heavily, their eyes trained on each other. He was so close she inhaled the scent of him coming off his pores, and it was all forest, sea, and masculinity. Her treacherous eyes fell to his lips, a mere breath away from hers.

And she wanted...simply wanted.

Lucenna peeled her eyes away from him and stepped back, breaking whatever madness had fallen over her. "It's-it's hot in here. I need some air."

She dashed away from him. Practically ran from the way her heart was beating in her chest, as if it wanted to break free. Pushing through the crowd, she rushed through the courtyard doors into the wintry night. She leaned against the wall and breathed in the icy air as the wind quickly cooled the sweat on her skin.

What was she doing? Moonlight glittered over the pink diamond on her finger and the tiny shackle tightened. Lucenna closed her eyes with a groan. She'd forgotten the one who needed to drop their walls was him, not her.

"Shite, it's colder than troll's scat out here."

Lucenna's eyes flew open as Klyde approached, holding two steaming mugs.

"Here." He handed her one. "This will warm you up."

She hesitated a second before taking it. A sniff and taste confirmed it was cider. A few other people were out there, chatting among themselves, some aweing at the blue and green firelights floating away into the night sky. Lucenna was glad to see Dyna and Cassiel had made up.

Klyde nodded for her to join him at one of the bonfires built in the courtyard. They sat, and he slipped his jacket on her, then he grabbed the blanket she hadn't noticed he carried and wrapped it around their shoulders.

"I don't know why you like this weather." Lucenna took a sip, pretending not to notice how close he was. He'd chosen to sit on the side that blocked most of the frigid air again. She drank more and felt the cider sink heavily in her stomach.

Klyde's head tipped back, lashes casting shadows on his cheeks as he breathed in the night. He appeared perfectly at ease. "I never said I did. Between you and me, I could do without ever living with snow. What's it like in the Magos Empire?"

"A lot warmer than here."

"I imagine so, with it being in the south. You're quite far from your homeland."

Lucenna drank more to avoid answering because she didn't know if Magos was her home anymore. It's where she belonged and where her brother waited, and where many women lived who had no choice. Home was supposed to be a place of refuge, and she had none of that there.

"Do you miss it?"

"No," Lucenna admitted quietly. "That place…"

These were her secrets, a personal darkness that she wanted to keep hidden. Klyde shifted his body to face hers, his expression open and waiting to accept whatever she had to say, because that's what he had always done. When she'd pushed back and hit with both words and magic, he took it all in. As if he knew she needed it.

"That place isn't for women like me," she said to the fire. "To be a sorceress is to be locked away in a dark room like treasure if you're fortunate, or traded and beaten like livestock if you're not. But we are seen as no more than vessels for them to take and take until we're hollow." Her hand drifted to the Lunar

Medallion, and she gripped it tight enough to feel the diamonds prick her fingers. "We're stripped of all power if we ever think of using it. Killed if we attempt to leave. I risked my life escaping that prison to change that. I want to break everything they stand for. I have to." Her vision blurred, and she fought the tremble in her voice. "Because if I don't, it means my mother died for nothing. But I'm stuck right here. I'm stuck."

Lucenna didn't quite know why she told him that.

It simply poured out and kept coming until she was crying. Klyde only looked at her with a gentleness she couldn't stand. His warm hand cupped her cheek, turning it to him. The moonlight reflected in his eyes. There was something splintered in them, like crushed crystal.

When he spoke, each word was soft, falling like a breeze over the sea. "It's natural to feel as though you're not in the right place. Life tends to make us feel like we should be somewhere else than where we find ourselves. This may not be the place you planned to be, but I believe those are the times we are exactly where we are meant to." His thumb wiped away her tears, leaving behind a tingle on her skin. "Even if we don't know it yet."

As Lucenna listened to his voice, she felt warmer for some reason. Snow began to gently fall like endless dandelion wishes.

He watched her with a soft smile. "Home is sometimes where you make it. Other times, it finds you. One day, however it comes to be, I have no doubt you will have that, moonlit lass."

The sound of the new name was a strike of lightning, sending her heart thundering behind her ribs. For a moment he simply gazed at her, his eyes spellbinding and brimming with unsaid things.

"How will I know when I find it?" she asked faintly.

"When you feel safe."

All her life, she never had that. Every day had been a constant strive to survive, and to fight for that survival. Lucenna couldn't think of the last time she felt safe—until now, in this courtyard, sitting with this man by the fire. The one who looked at her the way he always did. Not like a source of power or the means to fulfill some other need, but like he could truly see past her magic, past her anger, and saw something he found beautiful.

She liked it.

And it was wrong.

Lucenna ducked her head. The movement removed his hold and her hair slipped down her shoulder, creating a silvery curtain between them. "Safety doesn't exist for the sorceresses of Magos."

"Where there is oppression, there will always be those who stand against it," Klyde said. "I imagine you're not alone in your mission."

"I am…part of the Liberation," she admitted. "But until I return with what I need to overthrow the Archmage, there isn't much they can do than try to discreetly help as much as possible. They used to help women escape, but that ended when Enforcers began hunting us. Most are not brought back, those who are end up siphoned."

His body grew rigid, his jaw tight. "By siphoned, do you mean…?" At her expression, he became grim. "They cannot fight back?"

She smirked bitterly. "When there are laws preventing us from learning magic, it's difficult to defend yourself, let alone hide. The fact that I can use mine is a rare but fortunate exception. I must always be careful to never leave a trace of magic in the air because they can sense it and use it to track me."

Klyde fell quiet, a pensive frown on his face. "That's why you cloaked Skelling Rise."

She nodded. "No magic can be sensed outside of it and it will never fall as long as the spell isn't broken. I will remove it once we leave."

"Don't. Contact your Liberation and tell them to send your people here."

Lucenna gaped at him. "Here?"

"Aye, you cloaked an entire town on the other side of the country. One that has a sixty-foot stone wall, plenty of space, and it's guarded by a band of mercenaries. This is the perfect place to hide."

"But why would you do that?"

"Like I said, there are those who will always fight. It may not be much toward change, but offering shelter, this I can do."

Lucenna felt like she might weep again. This would make Skelling Rise the next sanctuary. A place where her people could be safe. He didn't understand how much that meant to her. She covered her mouth, exhaling a shocked laugh. She wasn't sure how Klyde would manage it, but—

She glanced up and found him watching her with a warm smile, and she smiled back because she couldn't help it anymore.

"When?" Lucenna found herself asking. She was shaking, holding her breath.

"Whenever they can come. The journey might have to wait until after winter, but give your Liberation the news, so they can prepare."

Lucenna stood before he finished speaking. "Come with me," she said excitedly. "We'll do it now."

Klyde didn't hesitate. He followed as she rushed back to the manor and ran up the stairs. Her heel caught on the hem of her dress.

Without missing a step, Klyde caught her elbow and hauled her onto his shoulder with ease. "Watch your step, my lady."

Lucenna laughed. She might be a little drunk. "Put me down."

"I don't want to."

Oddly, she had no complaint. Klyde carried her the rest of the way and set her down outside of her bedroom.

Lucenna grabbed the door handle but turned around. "Should I be concerned that you know where I sleep?"

His mouth hitched into a sly smirk.

It occurred to her the way she had told him to follow her could be taken differently. "I hope you didn't misunderstand this as some lewd invitation to my bed."

Klyde stepped closer, making her flatten against the door. His large body caged her against it, his palms flattening on either side of her head. He leaned down close enough that his breath blew across her collarbone. "Love, that is one thing I won't ever misunderstand. The day I'm invited to your bed is because you made it very clear you want me there."

Heat flamed from Lucenna's face to her stomach, falling somewhere she hadn't felt in a long time. If she wasn't already supported, her legs might have wobbled. "You can't say those things to me, Klyde." She should have shouted it at him, but her voice came out like a weak whisper.

"Why?" he murmured back.

"Because it's inappropriate. I'm promised to another."

His eyes darted to her ring. It suddenly felt like it was the size of a mountain between them. Klyde remained standing close as they stared at each other silently. The air was thick, the space between them thin enough to feel his body heat.

After another pause, he stepped back, and she could finally breathe. Blindly searching for the doorknob, Lucenna quickly opened the door. It swung open, and she backed inside. Better she focused on what they came to do.

"I brought you here so we could speak to Lucien. He will pass on your offer to the Liberation, and they will decide how to proceed." She went to her vanity, where her orb rested on its bronze stand. "Have you seen one of these before?"

"Aye, I know what an orb is, lass."

Her mind immediately locked on the change of moniker. It wasn't formal, yet he had created distance with only one word.

It's what she wanted, so why did she feel...upset by it?

She sat and Klyde lowered his large frame into the extra chair next to hers. He casually leaned back in a lounging position, but the line of his shoulders was stiff as though uncomfortable. Maybe bringing him here was too inappropriate.

Lucenna lifted her leg to unfasten her heels. The slit of her dress parted, and the fabric slipped away from her thigh. He followed the movement, his eyes trailing down the length of her leg and lingering on her feet. Ignoring the flush rising to her cheeks, she quickly adjusted her dress and sat straight.

Clearing her throat, Lucenna peered into the orb. "Hopefully, Lucien is still awake," she said, concentrating on connecting with his Essence.

"Is Lucien the one you're promised to?" Klyde asked, flipping open one of her magic books.

She balked. "What? No." The question interrupted her focus and the growing fog within the orb vanished. "He's my brother."

"I see." Klyde picked up a piece of embroidered fabric she had been sewing runes into. "Do you call each other often?"

"Nearly so." She snatched it away. "Don't touch that."

Klyde crossed his arms. "And how often do you speak to your betrothed?"

She narrowed her eyes at the turn of his interrogation. "I don't see how that is any of your concern."

He chuckled, but it didn't sound amused. "I was merely wondering."

"About what?"

"About why you left him. I assume he isn't like the other mages."

"He's not," Lucenna said coolly. "I didn't leave him because I wanted to. I told you why I'm here."

Klyde hummed and one dimple winked at the hitch of his mouth. "No need to get feisty, lass. Who am I to question a man for leaving his woman unprotected?"

"I can protect myself," she hissed. "You know nothing about Everest. He has other duties."

The dip in his mouth curled. "*Everest*—pretentious name, if I may say so."

"Because yours is exponentially better?"

Klyde opened his mouth to reply, then closed it. He dragged a hand over his face, as though to wipe away some emotion she didn't understand. "Since this Everest isn't here, I take it those aforementioned duties are more important than you? Does he at least call to see how you are?"

"He can't, if you *must* know." Lucenna could hear how defensive her tone sounded. She forced herself to speak more evenly. "Due to his station, we cannot communicate. I haven't spoken to him in four years. We will reunite when it's all over."

Klyde straightened, and something shifted in him. His eyes marked the change—shadows weaving through their depths. His mouth curled into a harsh sneer of disgust. "You have been on your own for *years*, risking your *life* for the betterment of *your* people, and he doesn't bother to see you out of concern for *his* station?"

Lucenna's reply stalled on her tongue, the question leaving her stunned. It made her mind turn in a way she didn't like. He didn't know anything about them to make such assumptions.

"Lucien said it was for my safety." It was her defense, but her words came out quiet, unsure. He was confusing her.

"It sounds to me like this Everest has forgotten you, lass," Klyde gritted out. "The only thing your brother is protecting is the delusional lie you tell yourself."

"How dare you!" She leaped to her feet. It was one thing to question her engagement, but to insinuate it was imaginary sent anger and humiliation rushing through her face. "I don't need to explain my relationship to you. Why do you care?"

His eyes hardened. They were deep and dark and threaded with frustration. Tension rose in the room as they glared at each other. Lucenna braced herself for a fight, but then the stiffness melted from his shoulders, and his face softened with something else that made her still.

"Do you truly not know the answer to that, Lucenna?" The sound of her name in his guttural voice stole all of her focus to his mouth, reading the shape of the letters on his lips.

He stood, forcing her to look up at him. He was serious and earnest like only Klyde could ever be, and something surged in her. He stepped forward, bringing himself so close there was no air in the space between them.

His voice fell like a soft thrum against her pulse. "If you had been mine, I know for certain I wouldn't waste time speaking to you through an orb, or searching all of Urn for you." Klyde cupped her cheek again and his thumb caressed the edge of her mouth. Her stomach dipped, fluttering, all of her aware of his warm touch. His eyes were on hers, so endlessly blue, roving over her face. His next words were a soft whisper on her cheek. "Because I never would have let you go in the first place."

Her heart...it seemed to swell in her chest. Then it crashed inside of her like thunder when his eyes fell to her lips. He was going to kiss her. She saw the intent in his lidded gaze. His hands fell to her waist, cascading shivers throughout her body. Lucenna didn't move.

He leaned in. Waited. Breathed.

His mouth was a hairsbreadth away from hers, its energy a promise of a waiting kiss.

And she wanted it.

Wanted it so much.

Because she knew—*sensed*—to be kissed by Klyde would change her. It would be something magnificent and enthralling, lush and terrifying. She could feel it there on the tip of her tongue. What it would taste like to have his mouth meet hers, like mint and sweetness and a flavor that was only him.

But Lucenna placed her hand on his chest, over his heart. It hardly had any pressure. He could have closed the distance if he wanted. Stolen that kiss, and she would have let him.

Yet Klyde held still. Obeying.

Because he would never take what wasn't given.

"I think you should go..." Lucenna whispered, closing her eyes.

Klyde held still for a minute. She couldn't see him, but she could feel his eyes on her. Then he stepped back, cool air falling in his place.

When the door shut quietly behind him, Lucenna lifted her trembling fingers to her lips where the presence of his mouth still lingered. She closed her eyes again, feeling guilty for wanting...and for wishing she didn't have to stop.

CHAPTER 89

Cassiel

Cassiel let Dyna walk him up the stairs, and she headed for his room. He said nothing as she opened it to the darkness inside. She tensed for a brief moment. Then she flicked a hand at the hearth, fire sparking to life before he could do it.

She stood still in the room, facing away from him. He got a full view of the dress now in the dancing shadows. It sat low on her waist, leaving her shoulders exposed. She looked so beautiful to him, so fragile. He brushed the silky red locks from her shoulders and planted a kiss on her neck.

"Are you still angry?" she asked.

The question cooled the coalescing fire in his body. He wrapped his arms around her waist and rested his forehead against the back of her head. "Furious."

Dyna released a sigh. She turned in his arms to face him, but he looked away. Looking at her only reminded him of what she said to him, and it still stung.

"Cassiel."

"I am sorry I spoke to you the way I did. I was taken aback. But can we agree to not speak about it tonight?" He let his hands fall. "I rather not quarrel again."

"Ignoring it won't fix us either. We should discuss it."

Heaving a breath, he stepped back.

She shook her head and turned his cheek. "Don't do that. Don't push me away."

"You did that when you chose death over me."

The light in Dyna's eyes dimmed as she lowered her hand. He deserved her disappointment and resentment. Even if it carved something vital from him.

Cassiel turned away. He didn't know what else to do with himself but escape the twisting in his chest. He stormed through the balcony doors with every intention of throwing himself into the sky.

A choked sob escaped Dyna's lips. "Please."

He stopped in place and closed his eyes. The sound cracked something inside of him. He clenched his fists so tight his nails cut into his palm. Every part of her pleaded with him and there wasn't anything to do but give in. Cassiel whipped around. She had seconds to gasp before he yanked her into his arms, curling his whole body over hers.

If anything happened to you, if you ever died, I fear the thought. I can't bear it.

I'm right here. She rubbed his back. *I will always be right here.*

Her use of Essence Healing merely stirred up what had been brewing inside of him since she'd been stolen away. He was so deathly afraid of losing her.

"Feeling you torn from my soul, I cannot go through that again," he said into her hair. "Your heart…I have seen how beautiful it is. I know helping others is who you are, and I'm amazed by you every day. You have given me a happiness I wouldn't ever have imagined, but I cannot withstand that being destroyed."

"It won't be." She leaned back to look at him. "I have been thinking about us a lot, Cassiel. About why two people who couldn't be more different were given a True Bond, and I think I know the answer." Dyna turned over his hand between them. "Can you make a flame?"

Furrowing his brow, he created a bouquet of blue fire in his palm. It lit Dyna's face. She wove her fingers through it, and he felt the sensation curl through his chest. Her green Essence wrapped around it and the flame rose into the night air. His breath hitched in surprise. Their flames encompassed each other flawlessly.

"Another." She whispered.

They repeated the process until the sky was floating with orbs of dancing blue and green lights. Distantly, they heard the awe and cheer of their guests outside. It reminded him of the Festival of Lights, when the *Hyalus* released its leaves into the night with *Elyōn's* blessings.

"Your flame never harms me. It molds perfectly with my magic as it did against the trolls. Why? You said it yourself beneath the willow tree." Dyna's wet eyes met his. "You were made for me and I for you. My mate. My star. You kept Death at bay each time it came. It was your voice that called me back from the Gates time and again." She brushed the wetness he hadn't realized gathered on his lashes. "You will forever be there to call me back."

A gentle smile rose on her face, tears like dews of moonlight gathered in her emerald eyes. She truly believed in him, and that everything would be all right. She wasn't scared about what fate would bring, and he didn't know if that was heedless or admirable, but she was correct about one thing. Nothing would ever stop him from going through any darkness to save her.

Cassiel lifted a hand to her cheek and brushed his thumb over her soft lips. "How did you become so brave? I may need you to teach me."

He felt her pulse quicken under his fingers and it excited his own. She shivered and his large black wings wrapped around her, blocking out the cold.

Dyna looked down shyly and shrugged. "I simply..." Drawing her close, he lifted her chin, bringing her face to his. Her voice dropped to a whisper, his lips close enough to brush hers as she spoke. "Decide what I want and..." Her lashes brushed her cheeks as her eyes closed, her fingers clinging to his jacket. "...leap."

Their mouths met in a soft kiss. He lifted his hands to her cold neck, his thumbs tracing the edge of her jawline. The bond throbbed in his chest as his entire being sank into her scent. She smelled of wild honeysuckle and wishes.

"When I saw you in the woods that day, you saved my life. I was barely living before you arrived." He whispered the words against her throat, and she leaned her head back with a soft sigh. "You are the air I breathe, *lev sheli.*"

Dyna rose on her toes, her arms coming around his neck. He pressed his mouth hard into hers, asking—demanding—more. Molten heat dove through him. He picked her up and her legs came around his waist as he carried her back inside, booting the balcony doors shut. Cassiel sat on the bed with her on his lap. The slits of her dress parted and his hands skated up her exposed thighs to her hips and lingered there, savoring the softness of her skin. She was the fuel to his fire. The heat of their bodies quickly seeped through their clothing with every kiss.

Her hands slipped under his tunic and he exhaled a groan that needed her so desperately it was the most severe shape of torment. His excitement was beyond his control now. When she rolled her hips against him, he was nearly undone.

Cassiel stopped, his chest rising and falling. He was forcing himself to stop because he had truly meant what he said. Going any further was her choice. Dyna looked at him questioningly, panting to catch her breath.

He stood and placed her back on her feet. "It's getting late. I should walk you to your room."

But she didn't move, and neither did he.

Heat stirred in Cassiel's blood as he observed the strips of black silk wrapped around her body. She looked absolutely sinful in it, and all he wanted to do was take it off.

Dyna held his gaze, something like a challenge burning in her eyes. She took one step away from him, and another, then another, until she reached his bedroom door that was cracked open with the key still in the lock.

"What if I said I wanted to stay?" Her soft voice fell over him in the quiet, hesitant, and so full of frail vulnerability.

Cassiel stared at her, slowly processing her words, not sure if she truly meant what they implied. The bond beat wildly.

"Dyna...even I have my limits," he said thickly. "If you close that door, I will peel that dress off your body and devour all of you."

He felt the bond jump with her surprise at his ardent response before it was flooded with the warmth of her. Dyna's hand curled over the brass handle. The door creaked as it fully shut behind her, and the sound the lock made when the key turned sped his pulse.

"Good," she whispered.

Her soft words floated between them like feathers on a breeze. For the span of a breath, Cassiel didn't move. Every muscle was still, except for the beat of his heart. The first night he had held her in his arms, planted a need to know what her bare skin felt like against his. To live in her scent, to discover the most intimate planes of her.

And here she was, calling him.

So he leaped.

Cassiel strode toward her with purpose, driven by an unknown power woven through them both. He cradled her face in his hands and their lips collided as he pressed her against the door. She stood on her toes, hands skimming up his chest. He slid his fingers into her hair and cupped the back of her head, holding her to him. His other arm wrapped tightly around her back. His body buzzed with her touch and he instinctively reacted. He gripped her waist, her body so delicate in his hands. He pressed closer, wanting to strengthen the fire of need within him. Wisps of her Essence entwined with his, the tendrils holding on to his every breath.

He led her backward as he continued to kiss her until the back of his knees bumped into the bed. They both stopped, their breaths hitching. He waited for her decision to continue. It had to be her choice.

Always hers.

Dyna's shaking hands reached for his coat, and he watched as she unfastened the first button. Then the next. Cassiel didn't rush her. He let her take her time as he admired the soft curves of her face in the firelight.

The coat slid down his shoulders, dropping to the floor. Cassiel tugged off his black tunic next. Dyna's chest rose sharply as she observed him, her eyes marking the trail she followed from his pecs, down the ridges of his stomach, lower still to the evidence of his want. He hesitated, not sure, or perhaps still waiting for her to change her mind.

"Tell me if you desire to stop," he said, cupping her cheek.

Dyna leaned into his touch. *I only have one desire, and it's not that.*

Her words made the center of him heat, shooting streaks of fire along his spine.

"Have you taken the..."

Dyna nodded. "I cannot fall pregnant."

That was good. They weren't ready for that yet, but the thought of one day, of the future, didn't frighten him anymore. Possibility. It thrummed inside of him like a scatter of currents.

She laid her hand over his chest, and he covered it with his.

"Your heart is beating fast," she said, her face as red as his must be.

Cassiel pulled her to him and traced his lips over her neck. She trembled when his tongue darted out to trace where her pulse fluttered. "So is yours."

He thought she might not be breathing, or perhaps that was him. His hand drifted to the lace ties going down her spine, hovering. Every fiber of his being strained with the craving to take her. He wanted to drink her in. He wanted to touch her. He wanted to taste. He wanted to explore every part of her that no other had seen. He wanted to be in...

Cassiel leaned another inch with her breath warm against his lips. *Dynalya...* The thought carried his full adoration and supplication. That was all. A soft pleading and surrendering call, begging to kneel before whatever she would give him.

She looked up at him, the green of her eyes gleaming.

His throat dried, and he swallowed.

After another breath, Cassiel dared to reach for the lace ties of her dress. They fell undone with barely a tug, willingly opening for him. He lowered one dress strap and kissed along the freckles on her shoulder to her neck. Then he did the same with the other, planting one kiss at a time. The dress slid down inch by torturous inch until her thin chemise was unveiled. Again, he lost the ability to move or speak, want seeping through him. Dyna glowed in the dim candlelight and the white fabric barely hid her body. He could see through to the soft arcs and the shadowed area at the apex of her thighs.

Cassiel memorized every detail. Every intimate curve eternally embedding it in his mind.

The sight of it sent a heat through his stomach, sinking low. He followed the rise and fall of her chest with every breath, and she looked at him with nothing but pure trust in those sweet, emerald eyes. Her breath caught as he curled his arm around her waist, drawing her flush against his chest, and he inhaled a shaky breath at the feel of her.

Nothing else existed outside of this room. If he gave up everything for one power, it would be to have time to stop and to live forever in this moment.

I'm consumed by you, he confessed. As if she didn't already know.

Her hands traveled up his back, firing tingles across it, and his blood rushed at the sensations. She leaned back as he continued kissing along the path of her neck to her other collarbone, attending to every shallow dip. The curve of her chest pressed against his, the smooth skin so silky, it drove him mad. He slid a hand up her thigh, and she softly gasped at the first stroke of his fingers. Her hands trailed higher on his spine, accompanied by the light scrape of her nails, triggering every nerve there. When she reached the shoulder blades, it shot shivers through his wings and every part of him roiled.

Cassiel took her hand and pressed a kiss to the inside of her wrist, then pulled her onto his lap as he sat on the bed. She straddled his waist, applying a startling warmth over the very center of him. He let out a soft groan as he dropped his forehead against hers, very aware of the thin fabric between them.

Dyna caressed his left wing and his whole body trembled as he panted her name. She caressed the right, tracing the arch, and the sensation sank through his wings, down to the depths of him.

"You would give me everything?" he asked. "All of you? Because after this, you will become a part of me completely, and I will never be able to let you go."

She looked up at him with tears welling in her eyes. He touched her quivering lips. The bond hummed with a boundless joy to be right here with him.

"Take it. Every part," she whispered. "I'm yours."

Yours.

He nearly buckled then. To hear such a thing, he never thought he would.

Cassiel kissed away the delicate tears from her cheeks, following the line of her jaw. "I was yours when I caught you from the sky. I have loved you since the first night I held you in my arms, and I love you more than the day before last. Every part of me has always belonged to you before I ever knew it," he said against her mouth. "Now and always."

CHAPTER 90

Dynalya

Dyna focused on Cassiel's breathing, on how profound and elevated it was. The ambrosial scent of his fell over her, and she thought she might dissolve beneath his warm hands sliding up her back. Her heart matched the rapid beat of his as he kissed her, his lips soft, slow, and sweet. It was a deep, aching sort of kiss that made Dyna sigh. Cassiel's fingers came around her trembling arm, and he pulled her to him until they were face to face. He was so close. She wrapped her legs around his waist, feeling all of him. Dyna's cheeks warmed under his gaze, her pulse throbbing wildly in her veins, and she nearly forgot to breathe. She remained still, afraid if she moved, she would break the spell.

They pulled inches away, their noses touching as they looked at each other. Desire burned from both ends of the bond. His arms slid around her, pressing them so tightly together she could hardly breathe.

Cassiel stroked his fingers along her spine—light as a brush of silk. He leaned in closer still, eyes impossibly bright. His hand slid up her nape and he gently took a fistful of her hair as his lips traveled up her neck to her mouth. His kiss turned fierce and deep, and she felt the throbbing build with the slide of his tongue.

When Cassiel's lips left hers, her breath came out in short pants. Heat stirred her blood with the look on his face as his eyes roved over her.

His voice was low and thick when he said, "I need to hear it once more."

He looked at her with an intensity, his dark pupils nearly drowning out the silver. It held craving, but reverence too. He was her husband. There was no one else she would ever want but him.

All of her desired for nothing more than to become irrevocably his.

She traced his smooth jaw with her lips and curled her hand around the back of his neck, running his silky hair between her fingers. With the gentlest pressure of her hand, he moved with her inviting tug, closing the gap between them until the barest whisper separated their faces.

"Yes." She breathed the word on his skin, her lips finding his. *I want this. I want you.*

Deep in her core, something quivered. His hand curled over the back of her head, pulling her harder into his mouth—and every secret yearning she had suppressed surged through Dyna as she tangled her fingers in his hair.

He kissed her as if she was life itself, and an integral part of his being fought to live. Cassiel held her tighter, pressing their bodies together. There was no space between them, yet it didn't seem to be enough. She shook, throbbing and frantic with desperation for his touch. His hands stroked her everywhere, caressing her like he never had before.

He shuddered as her fingers lightly scraped up his back to his wings. Fascinated by the soft but firm stretch of muscle and feather, her fingers traced it to the rising arch. It drew from him that unhinged sound she liked, the one that made her thighs want to squeeze together. His mouth was hot, electric tingles left behind by each press of his lips.

"Mine," he growled, his fingers digging possessively into her waist.

She sighed and arched her spine so his lips found her throat. "Yours."

His kisses and tongue spoke of devotion on her skin. Each one leaving an imprint of adoration. The smoke of desire. The bond throbbed, sending waves through her body.

Cassiel shifted back onto the bed, keeping her locked around his waist. When they reached the middle, he rolled her beneath him. The tips of his fingers glided up her thighs, and he moved on to pressing his mouth over her cleavage. He kissed that area as if he couldn't get enough of it. Rising on his arms, his mouth continued its descent within the valley of her chest, brushing his lips on the soft, sensitive flesh over the thin chemise. The sensation made her squirm and moan.

Her mind wasn't quite working. As if struck by lightning, her body was scorching, at the point of melting. She held back a whimper, lost to the raw sensation of Cassiel all around her. Every part of her felt tight.

He nuzzled the peaks of her breasts through the silky fabric, sending a bolt of pleasure threading through her body. The sounds he drew from her were mortifying, but she didn't want him to stop. Dyna reached for his wings, stroking the feathers. Her touch extracted a deep groan out of him, and his hips ground into hers, instinctively searching for the release they both wanted. But he still wore his trousers and the barrier of fabric kept her from him.

Dyna tugged on his waistband. Cassiel knew what she wanted. He was more than eager to shuck them off, and his bare legs came between hers. Skin against skin, firm muscle against the softness of her thighs, and the warmth of him made her temperature climb.

With trembling fingers, she placed his hand on the hem of her chemise. His breath caught and his chest heaved with a shaky breath. Cassiel took his time removing the fabric, his shaking fingers lingering, as he unveiled every inch of her curves until finally bearing all of her to him. He stilled as his lidded eyes flamed. He observed her so intently, taking in every part of her body. She was painfully aware of the jagged lines running from her shoulder to her chest, and the scar on her hip and another on her knee. She was deformed compared to the flawlessness of his kind.

Cassiel's eyes caught the firelight as he gazed at her, as though every wish he ever made, everything he ever searched for and needed, was found right here with her.

His fingers traced the tree geas on her ribs, shooting tingles through her stomach. The slow glide of his hand went down her leg to her ankle, and he folded up her knee to press a kiss on the scar there. He touched and caressed her everywhere she ached, as though to learn every inch of her body, murmuring little inscriptions on her skin.

"You are everything I never knew I needed." He leaned forward, his breath falling over the intimate parts of her unveiled for him, and Dyna's mouth trembled. "You have left me completely..." His lips coursed up her stomach, leaving a path of flames in the form of kisses to her prickled skin. "and utterly..." She stretched her arms above her, and gripped the sheets as liquid fire filled her with every press of his mouth and tender nip of his teeth. His lips traced the jagged scars on her chest, following them to the curve of her throat. "...undone."

Cassiel lifted himself above her, caging her in his warmth, and Dyna felt him there at her center. His fingers wove through hers as he entranced her with an unyielding kiss that left her breathless. She melted into him until he had her panting and vibrating beneath him.

"*Gam nezach lo maspik itach.*" His husky voice feathered down her cheek. "With you, even eternity will never be enough."

Every word, every kiss, was a vow. A promise of love and forever.

Dyna closed her wet eyes, and she inhaled as he held her during the brief ache of pain when they joined. Then she was stretched and full, so full. He groaned against her neck, and the guttural sound reverberated through her.

The fit, the closeness, his body enveloping her. It was too much.

Cassiel's arms quivered as he deeply breathed and waited for her to adjust to him, and to regain control of himself. She smiled at that and he did, too.

"You're the light of every star in my sky," she whispered in his language, her vision welling with more tears. *"Ani ohevet otcha."*

With all of her mind, heart, and soul.

His lidded eyes filled with unspoken emotion. He didn't need to speak when she could feel everything, every exhilarating and worshiping emotion as his heart responded, throbbing in time with their bond.

I love you, it sang with the gentle roll of his hips. *I love you. I love you. I love you.*

He planted more heated kisses on her jaw, to her lips. She was consumed by the sensations he left pulsating through her mind and body. She clutched the sheets to hold on to something solid, but it was impossible. Her being seemed to dance, elevating her into the atmosphere where everything glittered.

The markings they had painted on each other during their wedding night lit up across their skin, glowing with the promises they made. Every meeting of their bodies was slow, every kiss tender and devoting as they both learned how to move together and find their rhythm.

Flickers of pleasure swept across his beautiful face, so consumed by each wave. Her pulse spiked, and her hands slid up his back, sleek with sweat, fingers threading through his hair. His wings fluttered with every sway. Heat pooled, and she soared on the rise they created, higher and higher, until she teetered on the edge. Like their vows, the bond blazed and tendrils of light wrapped around them as their souls fully merged, at last becoming one.

Dyna knew, after this, she would be marked as his forever more, and she would never be the same.

Then she flew off the precipice with him, shattering amongst the stars.

And it was pure magic.

CHAPTER 91

Von

V on stood on the frozen shores behind the Corvus Tavern. He shielded his eyes against the sunrise coming up over the horizon. Raiders used pickaxes to break the ice free from around Tarn's ship. He had decided not to wait until spring to sail, now that the hunt for the Druid commenced.

The grand 200-ton vessel was made of the highest quality wood. The ship's name, *SOMNIO*, was painted in elegant gold letters on the side of the ship. It had black, unmarked sails. Gun ports on both sides were in a straight line above the hull. The noses of cannons peeked out of each one. More Raiders were climbing the shrouds to undo the tangled rope. Others rolled barrels of provisions and gunpowder up the plank.

It truly was a marvelous ship and the one thing they didn't steal.

Yavi left the back doors to the tavern with Geon helping to carry her luggage onto the deck, and they headed for Von's officer quarters.

A tingle of excitement stirred in his chest. Now that he had time to process that they would soon have a son, he looked forward to the day he would hold his child in his arms.

They were headed out to sea, and their escape was imminent.

"Commander," Lieutenant Olsson approached him. "The men have finished stocking the cargo hold. As soon as the ice has been cleared, we'll be ready to set sail."

"Good," Von nodded and walked with him to the dock. "Have you been able to gather any more information about that man?"

"No, Commander. He keeps to himself, and the men avoid him after he's broken the fingers of those who challenged him."

Von spotted Sai-chuen where he sat casually in the crow's nest. He avoided any labor, and for the most part, kept out of sight.

"Continue to watch him," Von said. "Oversee the rest of the preparations. Come find me when it's time to break water."

The Lieutenant nodded and walked away, barking orders at the Raiders. Von entered the captain's quarters. The back wall consisted of windows giving a view of the sea. Tarn was at his desk, the surface covered in scrolls, maps, and books. It rested in the center, on a large red and gold rug.

"How long?" Tarn asked, studying a map. He used a divider to take measurements of the Saxe Sea channel from Indigo Bay to Dwarf Shoe.

"Not long now." Von stayed by the door, looking through the round window to watch the activity on the deck.

"The trip will only take a week if the winds hold," Tarn said. "Dwarf Shoe is a free state. They forbid the collection of bounties, so no one will hunt for me there. Regardless, discretion, as always."

The door to the officers' quarters opened and Yavi walked over to the ship's railing, the wind weaving through her hair. Von smiled as he watched her discreetly rest a hand on her stomach.

But then Sai-chuen climbed down the crow's nest and landed next to her. Yavi recoiled as he closed in on her, saying something Von couldn't read. He gritted his teeth.

She had told him the man was often watching her, smiling his creepy, perceptive smile. He had ordered Sai-chuen to leave her alone, but the man clearly wanted to die.

Yavi backed further away from Sai-chuen. He closed in, pinning her against the ship's rail. She became outraged at something he said and attempted to strike him. He snatched her hand, leaning in closer. Yavi's anger switched to fear.

Von grabbed the door handle.

"Von," Tarn snapped, stopping him in place.

Yavi elbowed her way past the man and ran away to their quarters. Von heaved a breath and turned around.

"What occupies your thoughts that you don't hear me?" Tarn said, watching him narrowly. "Has your wound caught infection and affected your head?"

As far as anyone knew, Von was still recovering from the cut to his chest. But Yavi took out the vial of Cassiel's divine blood he'd stolen from the port market, and insisted they use it. One drop was all that was needed to heal him.

"No, pardon me." Von forced himself to leave the door and come to him. "I was thinking about why Sai-chuen was allowed to join your regiment? We cannot trust him."

"I don't trust anyone."

"Not even me?"

Tarn fixed his pale eyes on him. "I trust you to do as I command and not to question my judgment."

But he did question it. Something wasn't right about Sai-chuen and it put him on constant high alert.

A knock came at the door, and Lieutenant Olsson popped his head in. "We are set to sail, Master."

Tarn stood and they headed outside.

"To your stations," Lieutenant Olsson ordered, and the Raiders scurried to their posts.

They soon had the anchor up, and the ship groaned as the bow began to fall off port and move away from the dock. Tarn and Von reached the quarterdeck, and the helmsman stepped back. Tarn held the wheel, guiding the ship out to sea. Raiders pulled on the ropes and the sails inflated with the current of the icy wind. The ship gained headway as they sailed out to sea. Tarn held up a compass in one hand while he turned the wheel south.

Sai-chuen climbed the steps to the quarterdeck to join them.

"Location," Tarn said.

"The Druid is headed for Kelpway. It's a small town on the coast of Dwarf Shoe."

Von's stare pinned on the man. He tried to read him as anxiety churned in his chest.

What did he say to Yavi?

Sai-chuen's black eyes met his, and a clear knowingness was in them. He didn't attempt to hide his goading.

He knows.

Von's thoughts raced with a hundred solutions, all screaming at him at the same time. One ultimate decision drowned them all out.

Kill him. Do it now.

The man looked away at something Olsson said. Von reached in his coat for a knife, but Sai-chuen caught the movement. A challenging smile tugged at the ends of his mouth.

"Von," Tarn called sharply.

He spun around. "Yes?"

Tarn's cool eyes narrowed. "Where is your mind at? I told you to retrieve the sextant. I left it on my desk."

"Right away." Von reluctantly walked away. He felt Sai-chuen's eyes follow him as he headed to the captain's quarters. His nerves pulsed with unease.

He needed to get Yavi out of here.

Entering the quarters, Von went to the desk. On the piles of maps rested the sexton next to the divider. He absentmindedly picked it up, accidently nudging something with a soft clink. He moved a scroll to search for the cause and the glass vial of Witch's Brew appeared as if it was a gift from the Heavens. Tarn never left it off his person.

It was a miracle if Von ever knew one.

He glanced around first, then removed from his pocket a small pewter vial. His heart pounded loudly in his ears as he unstopped it and curled his nose at the bitter scent of Dreamshade oil. Who knew he would learn a thing or two about herbology from the Maiden?

Von had to wait for his hand to stop shaking before he poured in two drops, then put the vial of Witch's Brew back where it was found. God of Urn. This was it. The next time Tarn used the potion, he would fall asleep, and they would make their escape.

Von was in such a rush to leave, he nearly tripped over a small chest by the legs of the desk. It was stamped with the sigil of Xián Jīng, gilded with decorative corners and a golden clasp. The artifact they had stolen from the Emperor. He never got to see what was inside of it. Maybe it was curiosity, but he wanted to know what Tarn had nearly died for.

Swallowing, Von reached out and propped the chest open. He blinked at the contents, completely bewildered. It was nothing but an old copper tea pot carved with some elaborate design of a bird and feathers. He frowned and lifted the lid.

A pale gray powder rested inside.

Were those ashes?

Why would—?

The boat creaked, startling Von out of his thoughts. He lingered too long. Quickly shutting the chest, he hurried back to the helm. Tarn was the only one at the wheel.

"The sexton." Von held it out.

Tarn's gaze bore into him as he slowly took the sexton. It unnerved Von, and paranoia made him sweat.

He bowed so he could look away from those piercing eyes. "Shall I take my leave and see to your morning meal?"

After another beat of quiet, Tarn said, "Go."

Von tried not to run down the steps. He speedily walked across the deck to his quarters. He found Yavi there, crying into her hands.

She looked up at him and sobbed harder. "Sai-chuen knows."

It confirmed what Von already knew. He locked the door and rushed to her side. "What happened?"

"Why am I so daft?" Yavi asked through her tears. "He provoked me and I tried to strike him. I acted out of my station, and he accused me of being a privileged servant. I'm sure he knows!"

Von exhaled sharply. "What else did he say?"

She laid a shaking hand on her belly.

"Yavi?"

"Nothing. He said nothing more."

Von started pacing and wringing his hands. Sai-chuen must have put it together, and he would seek any opportunity to climb the ranks. "I'm not risking another day. We're leaving tonight. Tarn will sleep. I made sure of that."

Yavi hugged herself and bit her lip as she watched him.

"We're going to take one of the rowboats," he said lightly, like it would be easy. "The coast isn't far. We can make it back to Indigo Bay and disappear." His wife nodded tearfully and her throat bobbed. "Wait here. I'm going to see Sorren about our provisions." He wrapped his arms around her and hid his shaking hands behind her back. Yavi trembled with the fear Von fought to contain within himself. "I won't let anything happen to you or Verik," he vowed. "We will be free. Of him, of this place, of our past. Everything. We will start a new life with no more secrets or darkness. That is my promise to you."

Yavi's face crumbled.

"It will be all right." He kissed her temple and turned to go.

"Von." She grabbed his hand. "I..."

"What is it, love?"

Yavi looked away to the floor. "There is something I must tell you about the Scroll of the Unending. I should have known that man's evil ran further than I ever thought possible, but then I saw the scroll." She covered her mouth. "I didn't want to tell you because I feared what you would say, that you would change your mind about leaving."

He took her shoulders. "Why would I? It's you and me now and our son. Nothing will change that."

"Whatever your choice, I cannot hold on to this any longer because I know it will eat away at me. I have to tell you the truth."

Dread accumulated in his chest. "Know what?"

Yavi sat on the bed and dropped her head in her hands. "I...didn't tell you everything Sai-chuen said. He doesn't care about us. I don't even think he cares about becoming a Raider. He knew what he was bringing to Tarn."

Von crouched in front of her and lifted her chin. "I don't understand. What did he say, Yavi?"

She closed her eyes. "'I'm curious, sweet linguist,'" she whispered. "'If your eyes are as sharp as your tongue, then answer me this. If your master knows where the Tree of the Unending lies, why search for the missing piece of this mysterious scroll? You and I both know it doesn't contain its location, but secrets of never endings and renewed beginnings.'" Her lip wobbled, and she looked at him with fear and dread. "'Rotten little secrets…like how to perform a resurrection from the ashes of the Ice Phoenix.'"

All the air left Von's lungs as he slumped back on his heels.

He spoke not a word when the cabin started spinning. Not while his mind reeled with every piece of his past. He kept seeing flashes of his sister's smile and her bloody body torn apart at Tarn's feet. He saw every person they had killed to get to this point.

He saw the teapot.

Then he remembered the Relic Hunter's last plea. *You must destroy it…*

All the pieces came together like a sick puzzle, and the vile picture was a revelation that made his stomach heave. Now, years later, Von finally knew what was inside the chest, and what Tarn planned to do with it.

Jökull's ashes.

He was going to use them to…

Bile rushed up his throat.

Von ran out of the room to the side of the ship and vomited.

CHAPTER 92

Dynalya

Dyna woke warm and cradled against Cassiel's chest. He lay on his side with one of his wings draped over her like a blanket, soft feathers tickling her cheek. His breath ruffled her hair with each soft exhale. All of her attention focused on the firm smoothness of his bare skin against hers. She smiled lazily up at his sleeping face. Soft black locks spilled across his forehead like ink. He looked completely at peace and so ethereal in the early dawn trickling past the seam of the drawn curtains.

Closing her eyes, Dyna breathed the smell of gooseberries from his soap and the ambrosial scent that was only his. Every part of her ached in the most satisfying way. She could still feel where his touch had branded her, and where his mouth had kissed.

A few black feathers peppered the rumpled white sheets. They might have gotten a little carried away last night. Once he had her, Cassiel was relentless until they collapsed from sheer exhaustion. Dyna glanced up at the headboard where he'd left the scorched shape of his hands. She laughed softly, making the small feather on her pillow flutter.

With a flick of her fingers, all the feathers floated away to where Dyna tucked them in the nightstand drawer for him. She didn't need them anymore. Her magic was as strong as ever.

Quietly, Dyna snuck off the bed to the bathing room to use the chamber pot and clean herself. By the time she returned, her mate was awake. She flushed under his lidded stare, suddenly shy to be completely undressed, even if he had seen everything last night.

Cassiel unabashedly watched her approach, silver eyes heating. "Come here." When she reached the bed, he hooked his arms around her waist and pulled her back to him, wrapping his body and wings around her. "I need you closer."

She giggled. "This is as close as I can get."

"It's not enough," he breathed in her ear, sending a dance of hot shivers down her spine. "I have a need to constantly touch you. Everywhere."

Good Gods.

"Why do you look so radiant to me this morning? You are glowing, *lev sheli*."

"Well, you may have helped me recover my Essence last night," she said shyly.

"Oh?"

"You know how life force flows from one being into another through connection and magic..." She quivered as Cassiel's fingers trailed up her waist. He nuzzled her cheek, his mouth planting more soft kisses on her jaw. "And well, we..."

"Did plenty of that." He chuckled against her throat.

He said he would devour her, and he did—many times. His stamina was absurd. They hardly had any sleep, and he was more than ready to continue.

"Have you not had your fill?" she asked, her breathless voice betraying what the stroke of his fingers was doing to her body.

Faster than Dyna could blink, she was flipped onto her back. Cassiel caught her hands and pinned them above her head.

"Impossible." He kissed her throat, eliciting from her a soft sigh. "If you make that sound again..." His tongue flicked against her pulse and she cried out.

His mouth crash into hers. She freely fell into him and the fire he created. Dyna soared, and she was lost to the stars again. When they were finished, they laid there spent and grinning like fools. She couldn't do much more than tremble as her body seemed to float on an afterglow of pure bliss.

"I don't know if it will ever stop," Cassiel said.

"What?"

He tenderly brushed her cheek. "Wanting you. It's the sweetest addiction."

She bit her lip, fighting back a grin. The bond thrummed between them, shining brighter than it had ever been. Giving herself to Cassiel, there was something about it that made her feel so connected to him further than their bond. Like he'd become completely a part of her. Being in this bed with him felt as if nothing else existed and could easily be forgotten if she let it.

"We should get dressed," Dyna said as she traced the lines in his abdomen to the trail of dark hair past this naval. "The others will wake soon and wonder where we are."

"Let them wonder. It's not as though they should be shocked. If any of them were standing outside of the door, this time their assumptions would be correct."

Her face grew hot, and she swatted his arm. "Cassiel!"

Laughing, he drew her on top of his chest. Dyna rested her chin on her hand as she watched him with a soft look. She would never be tired of hearing him laugh. It occurred more often these days. The sun had risen further and filled the room with a rosy golden light. It fell over him and his wings in a dreamlike haze.

He brushed the messy curls from her temple, tucking them behind her ear. "What?"

"Nothing." She sighed happily. "Every day I wake up to you. I share my heart with you. I end my nights looking forward to spending the rest of my days with you. Yet after all this time, I still sometimes wonder if you're real. I keep thinking I'll wake up one morning and you'll only be a passing dream."

Because perhaps it was with time against them. Nothing would change the fact that her mortal lifespan was much shorter than his. A sad flutter went through her and she squeezed him tight. "If one day all of it fades, promise you won't forget me."

To know he would be alone after her passing made her emotional. He worried about her dying before her time, but she worried about the time they would have. By the end of it all, the only thing left behind would be their memories.

His confused smile wavered, and she knew he sensed where her thoughts had gone. "Stupid human, you are unforgettable."

Sitting up, Dyna pulled the blanket around her. Her hair fell in tangled waves around her face as she fidgeted with the sheets. "It would be a lonely thing, to be forgotten," she whispered. "But worse to remember when no one else does."

How can a thing be real if not remembered?

Cassiel sat up and he lifted her chin so she would meet his gaze. "During our journey, I found myself always observing you. The way the light of the sun seemed to grace you as much as the wind. I could never decide if the red of your hair was the color I favored, or if it was the green of your eyes. Your honeysuckle scent that followed you everywhere was the most pleasant torture. I despised every moment that kept us apart, and prized every stolen moment I had with you. Those memories are seared into my soul. For as long as I live, I will never forget the moment beneath the willow tree when you chose me. If this has only been a dream, then you are the best one I could have had."

The notes of his voice formed a warm melody in her heart, and she could listen to them forever. He kissed away the tears from her lashes. A still peace anchored them together in the morning as he simply held her to him.

"Who knew you were capable of saying such beautiful things?" she said, resting her head on his shoulder. "You're terrible to everyone else."

"I have a reputation to uphold. I'm known as the Black Hearted Prince, after all."

"I hear it's made of stone."

"Perhaps they are right."

If only they knew how wrong they were. Beneath the rough, cold exterior, her mate was a softy.

Softy? Cassiel growled. Her eyes snapped open when his arms clamped around her back and under her legs, getting up off the bed. He carried her to the bathing room with a purposeful stride. "There is nothing soft about me."

"What are you doing?" she squeaked.

"You know what else will be unforgettable?" A wicked smile curved his lips. "Bathing with my mate."

Cassiel laughed at her protests. For all her squirming, she had no hope of escaping. He pressed his mouth into hers with another sigh-inducing kiss, completely winning that argument.

The tub was big enough for two. It was soon filled with water and heated with a touch of his flame. Once he had her seated on his lap and massaging soap in her hair, Dyna decided there was nowhere she would rather be. Cassiel took his time washing her, being very *thorough*.

She leaned back as he kissed her throat. "If you're trying—"

He flipped her around so she straddled his waist, and he nipped her ear. "Not trying. Planning."

Her body instantly reacted with want, but the soreness between her legs increased. She ached all over. Any more, and she wouldn't be able to walk.

Cassiel stopped, and his expression softened with worry. "I hurt you."

A shy laugh bubbled out of her, and she circled her arms around his neck. "It's a good hurt. I don't know where you find the endurance."

"It's an insatiable need to please you."

"Then you can please me later." Dyna blushed furiously for saying that.

"Anytime you want me, *lev sheli*." His eyes sparked with renewed heat and his hands slid up her thighs, creating little shivers down her legs. "But you are sore, and I'm tempted to tend to it now."

She wasn't sure what he meant, but by the look on his face, she had a feeling whatever it was, he would enjoy it—and so would she.

A knock at the door made her jump. They both stilled and fell quiet. Though, what did she have to be embarrassed about? After a pause, the knock came again.

He groaned. "The day calls."

She hid a smile. Thank the Gods for that.

Cassiel stood, and the water streamed from his back and wings. She had a wonderful view of his many assets as he stepped out of the bath. He was the most beautiful thing she'd ever laid eyes on. Body sculpted like marble, strong and molded to perfection. And he was all hers.

I feel you looking, he said through the bond.

I remember you saying I was free to look to my heart's content.

He flashed her a grin over his shoulder before stepping into the room. *And?*

I am very content.

His low, answering laugh floated into her thoughts. *Stay there.*

As if she planned on greeting whoever it was. A more insistent knock beat on the door. Cassiel bumped into something and cursed. The rustle of fabric followed.

"Seven Hells, this better be important." The door creaked open and his shock fluttered through her chest. "Zev."

Dyna stifled a gasp. Surprise, relief, and mortification had her quickly sinking in the water. He was finally back, only for her to be naked in the next room.

"What took you so damn long?" At the sound of his gruff voice, she decided embarrassment was worth seeing him before he ran off again. Dyna quickly clambered out of the tub and threw on a robe.

"I was—"

"Never mind that," Zev huffed. "I need to talk to you."

"Wait, you should probably—"

Dyna rushed into the bedroom as her cousin stormed inside. He stopped short when he saw her. She did, too, because he looked different. Lighter. Like the world had been lifted off his shoulders.

But Zev's yellow eyes grew wide. They bounced from her to Cassiel, who wore only unbuttoned trousers, then to the disheveled bed, his nostrils flaring with a sharp inhale. His face, she had never seen him turn so many shades of red.

He quickly looked away, clearing his throat. "Uh, I'm sorry to disturb you. I had to warn you. The both of you."

"About what?" Dyna asked.

Zev's grim expression filled them both with a sudden bout of dread. "King Yoel has come."

CHAPTER 93

Cassiel

Cassiel's nails dug into his palms, flames winding through his fingers. His father was *here*. In Skelling Rise. Was it time for his sentencing? Or had he come for something much worse? He looked at Dyna, and her eyes grew wet as the same thought passed between them.

Had his father come to wipe their minds again?

"I spotted him flying overhead with a flock of armed Valkyrie," Zev said, his voice growing distant. "I thought there might be trouble, so I ran to town. But they arrived not shortly after. Rawn and Lucenna have gone to bide time. Klyde is greeting them now."

"Thank you for the warning," Dyna said softly. "Are you back?"

Zev's perceptible pause made Cassiel glance at him. By his unsure expression, he didn't have an answer. Other than leaving for himself, the townsfolk didn't want a Lycan around.

Dyna looked up at her cousin, her eyes welling as she smiled. "I'm happy for you, Zev."

Cassiel saw it then, too. The dark cloud that usually followed him was gone. He defeated his Madness.

"Whether you decide to stay or not, I am grateful you came," she said. "Please tell them we will be down soon. Don't leave until we have a moment to speak, all right?"

Zev's expression softened, and he patted her head. "All right."

The reminder of his father waiting for them was sliding the ground out from under Cassiel's feet.

As soon as the door closed, Dyna's cool hands cupped his face. "I'm with you."

Somehow, it was exactly what he needed to hear.

"Don't worry," Cassiel said, though the emotion overflowed from them both. He kissed her forehead and held her to him. "It will be all right. Whatever he has come to say, I will always put your life above my own, Dyna. Without a second thought."

"I won't let him break us apart." At her fevering promise, the vow she had marked on his spine pulsed. "We fight."

Cassiel tried and failed to smile. "My little warrior. Always so valiant."

He would fight whoever to protect his mate, including the High King. But Cassiel had little hope to defeat him, if it came down to that. Not even he knew the extent of his father's abilities.

"But how did he come?" she asked. "I thought Celestials couldn't fly in this weather."

"We can, but not for long. The colder it is, we risk our wings freezing and falling out of the sky." It had happened to him before. The temperature had been milder the last couple of days, which explained how they made it here from Hermon. "Well, we should get dressed."

They both glanced at the flimsy black fabric she wore last night, left forgotten by the bed.

"Except…I can't wear that to greet the High King, can I?"

Cassiel smirked. "I would rather you didn't."

A soft knock came at the door. They exchanged a look. Cassiel went to answer it and exhaled in relief at the sight of the two standing there.

"Noemi," Dyna exclaimed when she saw her lady's maid.

"I thought you might need her," Lucenna said with a sly wink. She handed him Dyna's pack. "I brought her things, but I think Noemi is more than prepared."

The dainty female rushed inside with her arms full of packages, orange wings fluttering behind her. "I brought everything you may need, my lady. For you as well, my lord."

Lucenna backed out. "I will wait downstairs with the others."

"I'm sorry I disappeared last night," Dyna said, following her to the door. "How was the celebration?"

"Uneventful." The sorceress smiled, but it seemed a little stiff. She gave a dismissive wave at the subject and went on her way. Cassiel noticed his mate's worried frown as she shut the door. It was probably nerves regarding their visitors.

Within minutes, Noemi had them both appropriately dressed in regal clothing. She was very efficient and knew exactly what Cassiel preferred to wear unless his valets had informed her. He caught Dyna's reflection in the mirror of the vanity where Noemi had her sitting to brush out her red hair in soft waves. The bond was shielded on her end, but the nerves were clear in the way she bit her lip.

"Oh, I also brought your crown! I shall get it."

Uncertainty crossed Dyna's face. The skirts of her silvery gown glimmered like streams of starlight as she stood. "Oh, um, no crown today. Save it for a grand occasion."

She looked like royalty, regardless.

Cassiel held out a hand to her. "Ready?"

"As I will ever be." Dyna's fingers linked with his. "Thank you, Noemi. You saved me."

She dipped in a curtsy. "It was my honor, Your Highness."

Cassiel took a step, but Dyna hurried to her pack. She pulled out a small, dark green bag made of velvet that was the size of her palm. He barely glimpsed the embroidery before she stuffed it in her pocket.

"What's that?"

"Only a sachet." A shaky smile surfaced on her lips. "The scent helps to calm my nerves."

Cassiel weakly smiled back. He would need more than sweet-smelling herbs to help calm the roiling in his chest.

They left the room and made their way down the hall, arm in arm. Zev, Rawn, and Lucenna waited for them at the bottom of the stairs, all dressed in black, standing at attention. It wasn't simply a role to play anymore. They were Dyna's Guardians. The statement of support straightened Cassiel's shoulders.

"They are in the hall," Rawn informed them under his breath when they reached the main floor.

Cassiel nodded. They followed a few paces behind as he led Dyna into the grand hall. The sofas had been pushed back out of the way. Valkyrie stood in two rows, forming a path leading to the wingback chair set before the fireplace where the High King of Hilos and the Four Celestial Realms sat. Klyde and

Eagon were speaking to him quietly, their broad shoulders blocking Cassiel's view.

On the right of the chair stood Lord Jophiel. On the left were two members of the King's Royal Guard. The hall had become an impromptu throne room. But any retorts Cassiel had died when the mercenaries excused themselves and moved aside.

Dyna's fingers tightened on his sleeve. *God of Urn.*

Cassiel nearly stopped at the sight of his father. He had changed drastically since they had seen each other last. Age had found him and rather unexpectedly quick. His blond hair had thinned, fading to a yellowed gray. His face was timeworn, with many more new wrinkles around his mouth and sapphire eyes. His body was thinner, shoulders hunched.

They stopped a few feet away from him and deeply bowed. Rising, they kept their heads lowered. The silence stretched, the only sound being Klyde and Eagon's retreating footfalls as they left the room.

His father's presence remained every bit as powerful as his voice. "Son." The stern tone stiffened his spine. "We have much to discuss, but if you don't mind, I wish to speak to Dynalya first. Alone."

Cassiel met his stare, and he worked to keep his tone leveled. "I do mind. And I'm not going anywhere, sire."

His eyes narrowed. "Very well. You may stay, but you will not interfere."

The command settled on him like the roots of a tree, weaving through his body and mind, holding him in place.

Dyna's hand on his arm faintly trembled. A soft pink colored her cheeks. For a fleeting moment, she looked scared, but it quickly disappeared under a determined expression. Shoulders straight, she stepped forward with elegance and poise. That bravery filled him with such pride.

But his father's next statement was a slap to Cassiel's face. "Dynalya Astron, I'm here to annul your marriage to my son."

King Yoel's words echoed through the manor, or it was the sharp disbelief reverberating inside his head. Cassiel attempted to shout that he would never allow that to happen, but his mouth wouldn't open, let alone speak.

His alarm climbed. Why couldn't he speak?

Dyna didn't appear shocked. She held the High King's gaze head-on. The sunlight streaming in through the windows softly haloed around her head. "With all due respect, Your Majesty—I refuse."

Everyone stared at her, astonished by the blatant response.

Yoel arched an eyebrow and canted his head. "You would refuse a King?"

"Only in regards to my bond. The one thing I know is that marriage is for life, at least for Celestials. If it's my heredity that you find intolerable or my lack of nobility, you will also find that I'm very determined to prove myself worthy to stand by his side."

"As I understand it, there was an attempt on your life for the position you now hold."

Cassiel's fire stirred in his veins at the reminder.

"Our people do not regard change well and think very little of humans," his father continued. "Any discordance you may have experienced will pale in comparison to what awaits you should you choose to remain his wife. Your union will be laden with backlash and burden."

"It would be a lie to say I didn't fear their hatred, sire. But for him, I would gladly face whatever the future may bring," Dyna said.

King Yoel studied her for a quiet moment. "I'm told this marriage came about through mishap, a bond forged by illegal endowment and neglecting all proper rites. Could you have truly cultivated this level of faithfulness in such a short time for a half-breed who took your hand by force? I have a mind to consider it infatuation or interest in your sudden station."

Whether he said it as a test or to provoke her, the statement still drove a spear through Cassiel's chest. To not only call him that, but to question her integrity was beyond reprehensible. Anger roiled through the bond, and after a second, he realized it wasn't his.

Dyna's expression remained perfectly neutral, even as her neatly folded hands flickered green. "Would you call the events in the Port of Azure, and the destruction of the throne room at Hermon Ridge, infatuation? To lay down our lives for each other, to fight by whatever means, that is not merely faithfulness but devotion."

"Are you saying you love him?"

"Yes," she answered without hesitation. That one simple, ardent reply diminished Cassiel's rising tension. "Regardless of how our marriage occurred, we are True Bonded. That means we are meant to be. Take my title, and whatever wealth comes with it, but you cannot have him. He's *mine*. By your sacred laws and that of the Heavens, nothing will change that." She inhaled a breath before adding, "And I would kindly ask His Majesty to please not refer to my mate by anything other than by name."

Her outward claim and possessiveness were flint to his fire. If Cassiel could move, he might have kissed her right there and damn whoever it offended.

A slow smile crossed the High King's face, and he rose. "Valkyrie." The females stood at attention, and the clanking of their golden armor rang in the room. "Here stands the Lord and Lady of Hermon Ridge. Will you serve?" They beat their fists over their hearts three times in perfect synchronization. Yoel's smile widened, and he held out a hand to her. "Welcome to the Soaraway family, my dear."

The rigidity that had tethered Cassiel in place released, and his lungs expanded with a full breath. From the moment he had bonded with Dyna, he carried a load of anxiety over how his father would react. He didn't know how heavy the weight had been until it was removed.

Dyna's shoulders slumped, her expression falling to a mix of relief and surprise. She took the King's offered hand. "Thank you, Your Majesty. Does this mean you approve?"

"I can imagine no other by his side. He will need you."

Cassiel frowned. "What is that supposed to mean?"

"One thing at a time." King Yoel motioned to the female warriors. "Now, Lady and Princess Consort of Hilos, you require a Royal Guard."

"Oh...but..." She glanced at their friends standing by the doors.

"I see that you have your Guardians. Nevertheless, it stands. Someone in your position can never be without too much protection." His father sounded calm, amused even, but something about the statement made Cassiel's heart rate spike. "Yelrakel is bound to protect her Lord. Otherwise, you may assign whoever you wish among the Valkyrie to guard you."

Dyna bit her lip as she regarded the female warriors. Cassiel sensed she didn't feel comfortable giving any type of orders, let alone assigning positions.

"My King." One of the male Royal Guards stepped forward and lowered to one knee. "If it would please you, it would be a great honor to serve Her Highness."

His father's eyebrows inched up, but he seemed pleased. "Well, Zekiel, if that is your objective, I would trust none other than the guard who has protected my family for many decades to now protect my daughter by law."

Except Cassiel didn't share the same sentiment. He studied the pureblooded male with long blond hair and an amiable demeanor. Zekiel had been part of the Royal Guard for as long as he could remember and had never shown him any contempt, but Cassiel wouldn't allow simply anyone around his mate.

"Sowmya." At his call, the female stepped forward. "You are hereby tasked with leading Dynalya's Royal Guard."

She bowed. "I'm honored, Your Highness."

"Glad that is settled." His father returned to the chair. "Please excuse us, my dear. It's time for my son and I to have a talk."

"Of course." Dyna gathered the sides of her gown and curtsied.

You could stay, Cassiel said through the bond.

But I shouldn't. The back of her fingers brushed his as she passed. *Try not to lose your temper.*

He would *try*.

Cassiel watched Dyna go. Zev and Rawn opened the doors for her, then they and Lucenna followed, her two new Royal Guards bringing up the rear.

"We will have the room," his father said to the others.

The Valkyrie marched out in a line, and Lord Jophiel patted Cassiel's back on his way out. Then the grand hall soon emptied until only the other male guard remained. He was a stoic Celestial with short hair and a stern manner. He took his duty seriously and was always guarding either the High King or the heir.

"You as well, Amriel. Leave us."

Amriel's mouth slightly thinned, the only sign of displeasure. He obeyed, and the echo of the heavy door closing settled in the quiet. Cassiel faced forward. Perhaps it was cowardice, but he couldn't look his father in the eyes as he waited for the consequences for his actions to at last befall him.

"Why do you suppose I have come?"

Cassiel paused. "Is this a formal inquisition, or may I speak freely, sire?"

Yoel waved a hand. "Why follow propriety now when you have done what you wished thus far? Speak and explain to me your reasoning. Jophiel has told me more than enough, and I have pieced together the rest."

"If you are not here to break our bond, then I assume you came to punish me."

"For which crime, exactly?" he asked sharply. "There were *several*. Violating my confidence and venturing across the country without permission, giving divine blood to a human, exposing your people, avoiding the Valkyrie, defying my summons, using Seraph fire without reservations, destroying rooms in the Hermon castle, threatening your council, nearly killing your brother, banishing him next, and abandoning your duties as Lord." His voice grew harsher as the list went on. "Your every action was a wanton show of disrespect against me and to the Realms."

Cassiel noticed the accidental bond wasn't on the list of crimes, nor any mention of the challenge won. "I had my reasons."

"Oh, of that I'm sure, and she walked out that door."

Dyna was the reason for everything, and the reason his blood heated now. "Whatever your verdict, it will fall on me alone. She will not be held accountable for any of it."

"That is for me to decide."

"No one will decide anything regarding my wife," he snarled.

The High King stilled in his chair as blue light bathed the walls.

Cassiel caught his reflection in the windows. His eyes were ablaze. His father glanced at his clenched fists encompassed in flame.

He quickly stepped back and put out the fire. "I'm—forgive me, sire. I didn't mean..."

King Yoel rubbed his face. "It's worse than I feared. You cannot help it, can you?"

Cassiel didn't understand what he meant.

"This power you have, it's not normal. The only purpose of Seraph fire is to protect and destroy. With that ability, in addition to the fierce instinct to guard a True Bonded mate, you are a danger to anyone who presents a perceived slight against her in any way. When I was speaking to Dynalya, your eyes were already lit aflame. Your attention did not leave her once. Break your bond?" His father scoffed airily. "I would not dare. For I think not even I would be spared your ire."

Cassiel swallowed, a new sort of fear cooling him. "I would never..."

"You did not spare Malakel."

He clenched his jaw. "He threatened her life. I had no other recourse than to stop him before he tried."

"Well, you certainly stopped him, Cassiel. But your performance in the throne room put many on edge. Some believe it's a sign the first king has returned."

He rolled his eyes. "Since when have you taken an interest in gossip?"

"When it presents a dire concern," his father said sternly. "One thing is for certain. If you were enraged enough, nothing would stop you from eliminating anyone or anything you deemed a threat to your mate. You would forget your principles, your family, and yourself. I know because we have lived through this once before. At the first hint of history repeating itself, you not only placed a target on your back but on hers."

The vision of fire raging through the council room and the echoes of frightened screams in the throne room rang through Cassiel's mind. His show of force only proved he was a living threat to his people. The scheming whispers in the halls, the attempt on Dyna's life, the kidnapping. He was responsible for all of it.

"You brought the Valkyrie here." Cassiel blinked at him. "Legion warriors. Welcoming her, granting her a Royal Guard, that wasn't merely for show..." His body burned inside as flames climbed up his arms like living serpents. "Leaving Hermon did not matter."

Dyna was the other half of his soul, and now the Realms knew it. No one would attempt to confront him directly. The only way to eliminate him was by eliminating her.

His anger evolved into feral animosity. The feeling consumed him with one thought that concluded the best way to protect her was to burn—

Cassiel? Dyna's frightened voice in his mind yanked him back from the brink of his madness.

He gasped, and the fire died away. His hands shook at the vehemence behind his thoughts. His plans.

"Their fear...it's valid," Cassiel said faintly. "Because when she is threatened..."

His only instinct was to attack.

King Yoel looked at him somberly. "I have not come to punish you, Cassiel. I came to give you a chance. Because if you do not place your Seraph fire under control, it will consume you, and then you would become the destruction of the Realms."

CHAPTER 94

Cassiel

C assiel's wings brushed the floor as he paced restlessly in the rooms Klyde had prepared for the High King within a tower suite on the fourth floor. They were much more spacious and grander, offering a view of the sea in the distance. And it gave them the privacy needed to continue their conversation. He needed to know more about his abilities—and other things.

"I fail to see how any of this makes sense," he said.

"What part?"

Cassiel glowered over his shoulder at Yoel where he stood by the windows, watching the flurries float by. As if revealing that he was a force of destruction wasn't frightful news.

But...his father looked thinner in his winter robes, paler. The sunlight streaming over him revealed the visible veins behind his skin and the spots on his hands. His white wings hung dull and limp.

"All of it," Cassiel said, studying him. "You, most of all. Are you going to explain your appearance? Don't tell me this is natural when uncle has hardly aged and he is only younger than you by five years."

Yoel's reflection in the glass was thoughtful. "We all grow old one day."

"Not like this. Not so soon."

Their kind used to live nearly as long as the Elves until the High King started aging rapidly. Because of it, Celestials worried *Elyōn* was slowly giving them mortal lifespans.

"It's the price I chose to pay," came his father's idle reply. "Everyone must answer for their actions in time."

Cassiel thought of the city his father helped burn to the ground out of revenge for the loss of his mother. It had been home to thousands of humans. Killing them had been a great transgression against their original purpose in the Mortal Realm.

"Do you mean this is your penance for Gamor? If so, why only you? Many joined in the slaughter. You are not the only one with human blood on your hands."

"As the ruler, I bear all responsibility, and one day you will find the crown's weight is heavy."

Cassiel halted in place as everything in him went cold. He read the sudden stiffness in his father's shoulders. "Now I understand your true purpose here."

Yoel sighed at his reflection in the glass. "Malakel challenged you for everything and those terms applied to him as well. When you defeated him, his inheritance lawfully became yours. That makes you the heir apparent, Cassiel."

"This is why you have come? To force this upon me?" Cassiel's mouth twisted with a sneer, even as his stomach pitched. "Gods. I admit, you nearly, very nearly, had me convinced. I should have known when you arrived only at a time that was most convenient for you."

His father didn't come when he was nearly exiled, assassinated, or when he wedded the love of his life. He came only to force him to take the throne.

Yoel's gaze cooled. "Aside from the weather, I could not come sooner. Duty bound me to make way for the Blue Capital first, and discuss with King Lenneus the events of the Port of Azure. He was furious, with due reason. As was I, seeing that questionable actions were made, but the rest does not bear repeating."

Cassiel glanced at the goblet Yoel held. His glowing hand clutched it tightly, the heat of his power causing the cider to bubble and steam.

"Nevertheless, they broke the Accords." He set the goblet down. "I made it very clear to the Azure King that should he desire retaliation, the Realms will respond. By the end of the war, I will have wiped the port and every major city in his kingdom off the face of the earth. There will be no ruins like Gamor. Nothing but ash to fill the records of history. I may aspire for peace with humans, but I will never allow any harm against my people—least of all my *son*."

Cassiel was struck silent by the quiet fury on his face. It confused him, this show of care.

After a breath, his father calmed. "Given what occurred, you had no choice, and there is not one now."

He scowled. "I don't want to be king."

"It's not a matter of what you want. As the crown prince, you are heir to the throne," Yoel said sternly. "I am trying to see to your future."

At that, Cassiel lounged on one of the sofas, crossing an ankle over his knee. "As I see it, there is no future to foresee when I no longer have the prerogative to take your place. I'm not who I was when I left Hilos." With a snap of his fingers, a curl of blue flame danced on his fingertip. "I have killed for her, and make no mistake, I would gladly do it again."

Yoel stared at him in bewilderment.

"Do you understand now? Scores of men have fallen at my hands. Any divinity I had is tainted." Cassiel leaned forward, holding his stare. "Have I made you proud, *Father*?"

Yoel canted his head, an edge sharpening his voice. "Yes, I certainly see you are not the same, yet you are still contemptuous and prone to forgetting yourself. It would be wise to mind your impertinent tongue."

The cool warning was enough to make Cassiel straighten in his seat.

His father sat on the sofa across from him. "My decision stands."

"Why? By my deeds alone I'm unworthy, nor should I be a wielder of Seraph fire. It came by some strange mistake that I assume *Elyōn* will correct in time. A half-breed murderer has no place taking the throne. Let Malakel wallow in Edym for the year, then he can be restored his birthright."

"The ascension can only be given by the High King or taken through challenge. You have both. It was never about the state of your divinity. Your brother assumed the position as heir apparent because the last five rulers had all been the elder, but I had never declared it so. I chose you, and the moment you defeated your brother, the crown legitimately passed to you. This is acknowledged throughout the Realms and by law. Not even Malakel can contest it."

"Then let him challenge me again and he can have it," Cassiel retorted.

"That is not where it will end. Right now, Malakel is in a deep sleep as his body slowly recovers from the wounds you dealt him. When he wakes, it will be to make you pay for his humiliation. If he takes the throne, he would not hesitate to shear you. Even if you run, his reach will extend to all four Realms and you will have no one to defend you from him."

A shudder sank through Cassiel's wings as he recalled what Malakel once told him. *Remember, one day I will be High King, and my first command will be to exile you.*

"Do not give him that power," Yoel said. "Take your rightful place in Hilos—with Dyna at your side."

"What?" He blinked, leaving the fog of his thoughts.

"As True Bonded and consummated, no one can dispute your union."

Cassiel was struck by the uncomfortable comment of his marriage bed. Then it was a question of how his father would know. It must have happened when he took Dyna's hand. He had Soul Searched.

"When you commanded me to be Lord of Hermon Ridge, I assumed this plan to make me High King was forgotten." Even as the words left his mouth, Cassiel saw the truth on his father's face. "None of this was a coincidence, was it? That is why you so readily agreed to let me leave Hilos. You intended this."

King Yoel didn't deny it. "What did you feel when you first met Dyna?"

Mine. The single word thrummed in his mind.

The moment he saw her in the forest, begging for help, it surfaced a need to keep her safe. To keep her close and put himself between her and danger. Cassiel had been drawn to her since that day. He'd been so confused by the strange protectiveness he held for the odd human when he had no reason to be. Saving her life had changed the trajectory of his.

"I knew it from the first that she was meant for you. Of course, I did not imagine you would bond in such a way, but it may have simply been instinct. You knew what to do even if you didn't understand."

It was the reason Cassiel granted her immunity and felt compelled to keep her safe. Because his soul had recognized her before he did.

"Except you knew who Dyna was before she ever trespassed into those woods." Cassiel narrowed his eyes. "I know you erased my memory of her nine years ago. You could have erased our meeting again, but you welcomed her into the castle and told her of our history. Then in the study, you didn't need to bring out those books after hiding them for so long. You wanted me to go with her."

With a heavy sigh, Yoel came to sit next to him. "You were becoming obsessed with Mount Ida as your mother had. You were following her path. Hiding the books was my way of stopping that, but when Dyna arrived, something sparked in you. You were not happy. I thought if you were with her, you finally would be."

Cassiel frowned, perplexed by all of this. "Then what about the engagement to Sarrai?"

"If you had yet to discover who Dyna was to you, I hoped the engagement might awaken the instinct to choose your mate, but you already had. You love each other. It burns strong through you both. I could not hope for more. It assures me you will not be alone in Hilos."

All Cassiel heard was that he'd been manipulated. "If you think I will subject Dyna to the same cruelty mother bore, you are sorely mistaken."

"You have my word. It will be different this time."

What an irresponsible thing to say. There was no way he could guarantee that when their abhorrence was a palpable thing Cassiel sustained since his infancy. "You cannot keep that promise."

"It will be different because Dyna will not be a consort but your High Queen."

High Queen.

The title slashed him like a whip, and all he felt was fear.

It would never work. They would never accept her. The thought of Dyna crushed under the hatred of his people would be another spear in his chest. He didn't want that life for her. And it would be a terribly short one. If they would attempt to remove her for simply being his mate, they would certainly come for her if she ruled over them.

"As for Mount Ida—"

"I'm going to that island, no matter what you say. You may have given up, but I will find my mother if only to prove she's dead."

Yoel flinched as if Cassiel had struck him.

Perhaps he was wasting his time going to that place to search for someone who left him behind. He was grasping at the hope that she was out there because he didn't want to consider the possibility that his mother never wanted him, either.

"I will not stop you from going. It will be good, I think, to find answers and to have time to adapt to the idea of your new life." Yoel stood. "I shall speak my command clearly from the onset. When this journey is over, you will both return home to be properly crowned as the new reigning power. You will be the High King of Hilos and the Four Celestial Realms, and Dynalya will rule by your side."

Cassiel stood, making his response also very clear. "No."

Yoel's expression hardened, and his wings loomed behind him. "You have forgotten your place. I am your King first before your father, and you shall obey."

The pressure of power lined the order, but Cassiel didn't bend into submission. "I am your subject, sire, but Dyna is *my* wife." His eyes must be glowing again by his father's wary expression. "I would march through the Seven Gates and grovel to the Gods before I ever allow her to suffer their hatred."

Pure shock crossed Yoel's face, his mouth parting. "By all that is sacred, Cassiel. You know not what you say."

"I'm doing what you should have done for my mother," he growled. "My mate is my only priority. She is the keeper of my loyalties. I care nothing for no one else."

Yoel's expression softened, and he sighed, laying a hand on Cassiel's shoulder. "I have followed your exploits and those of Dynalya. She has proven she can withstand adversity. I believe she will withstand the politics of palace life."

He shook him off. "Can we not do this? Where you pretend to care?"

"I do. Why be here if not for you?"

He scoffed at the pretty painted lie.

"Is it so hard to believe I want to be a part of your life?"

A bitterness churned in Cassiel's stomach with the wretched poison he carried all his life. "If that were true, then you would have been part of it when it mattered," he said tightly. "But it was made clear to me a long time ago that I'm nothing more than a bastard. A walking reminder of your shame." His voice grew harsher and strained behind his clenched teeth. "Not once was I part of the family, and nothing proved it to me more than when you cast me away to Hermon. I made my way without you and I don't need you now, so don't presume to find any kinship between us."

The hurt that crossed Yoel's face was almost believable. "You are angry. I understand that, but I have always cared for you."

Cassiel took a deep breath and exhaled it slowly to help control his temper. "I have reached a point in my life where I no longer believe you."

Yoel briefly closed his eyes. "In time, you will understand why I had to make these difficult choices. Regardless, I saw to your well-being. I made sure you had everything."

Cassiel's hands curled into fists at the ugliness brewing in him from that statement. "You are right. I did not want for anything but the warmth of your affection and acknowledgement. What explanation do you have for that?"

His wings drooped like wilted leaves, as if the question broke him. "When standing so close to a picture, it's difficult to see its entirety."

For some reason, that answer made Cassiel's nose burn and the back of his eyes sting. It surfaced an old memory of him sitting in the large dining room of Hilos as a child on the day of the Winter Solstice. "I waited for you," he muttered. "I still believed that you had not forgotten me. That despite you ignoring me for the rest of the year, that one day, you would be there. So I waited. Even when the candles were put out, and the dining room grew empty and cold, I waited." His throat constricted as he saw the memory so clearly, because that's when everything finally made sense. "I sat there, staring at the doors for hours, counting down the seconds you would walk through them...but you never did. I failed to understand what your absence meant until that day. Then I saw the picture for what it was. You did not want to remember my existence, and I questioned...I questioned why..."

Why had he been born when he was unwanted? He felt like that child again. Lost and purposeless. It made him feel sorry for breathing, because what had been the point to any of it?

"Son—"

"Don't call me that," Cassiel snapped. "Not once have you treated me as a son. I have only ever had one father, and it was not *you*."

It was his uncle who raised him and gave him a place to belong. Going to live in Hermon kept him alive.

Yoel's eyes saddened, and they lowered. The act only infuriated him more. "I'm—"

"Don't you dare say you are sorry." He was so sick of those words. They meant nothing to him now.

"I know I failed to care for you in the right way, Cassiel, but that does not mean that I do not love you."

Dry laughter and something thick built in his throat, lodging there like bile. "You have no place to say those words to me." Cassiel headed for the door with the urge to throw the man he once called father to the wind, but he spun around. "You know, for quite some time, I believed that feeling to be a fantasy. Something poets spoke of but never see. I doubted it was ever real until I found it with my true family." He swallowed back the emotion lacing each word. "And I was made better because of it. Being with them, I learned one thing for certain. You don't abandon the people you love."

They stared at each other in the strained silence.

When Yoel finally spoke, his voice was faint. "Trust me when I say you were placed with your uncle to keep you safe."

"Safe from what!" Cassiel demanded, throwing out his arms. "I'm beyond the lies now. We both know I was tossed in Hermon Ridge because I am the weight of your greatest disgrace. And thus, it stands, you have forsaken all rights to be part of my life. It's far too late for that." The accusations kept pouring out, painful and jagged, like shards of glass in his throat. "Where were you when I bore my wings? Where were you when I withstood their cruelty? When I was left alone to fend for myself? You left me when I needed you. You—" Cassiel's voice broke. "You *left*." He clenched his fists, forcing himself to breathe. He tried and failed to keep his voice steady. "You don't know what I like and what I hate. What I feared and what I endured. You know *nothing* about me!"

The shout tore out from the deepest pit inside of him. It seemed to resonate through them both, filling the air with the blemish of his despair.

Dyna's sadness swept through the bond. He had forgotten to maintain his shield, leaving everything he felt to reach her. Cassiel blocked her concern, and after another broken breath, he wiped every emotion and the wetness off his face.

This life had turned him into stone, and that's what he would be.

"The version of me that begged for your acknowledgement is gone," Cassiel said stoically. "You are only a memory I wish to forget. I don't give a damn about you, and I don't give a damn about the Realms. I will not be king."

He strode for the door.

"I am not finished speaking, Cassiel. Don't walk away from me."

"You have long taught me how."

"Stop," Yoel's command rang clear, halting him in place.

He saw the door handle, but his hand wouldn't take it. He couldn't move. "What is this? What have you done?"

"Come here."

His body rotated of its own accord. Cassiel fought against it, but no matter how much he resisted, his legs forced him to walk back and stand in front of his father.

"You used your compulsion on me," he growled. "As you did earlier in the grand hall."

"We are not finished," Yoel said firmly. "You also do not know what I endured. None of it compared to seeing the hate in your eyes and carrying the brunt of your resentment. For years, I let you walk away from me, but I cannot anymore."

He went to where his luggage had been placed and lifted his sheathed sword, drawing it free. Blue fire swiveled around the blade.

Cassiel inhaled sharply. Only blessed Celestials were supposed to receive it.

"Seraph fire is not a blessing made for those of pure souls without sin," his father said. "It's the badge of a Celestial who has fulfilled their original purpose and that is to *protect*. To lay down their lives unreservedly. You did that when you fought for your mate in Willow's Grove—and in North Star."

His heart was pounding against his ribs, his mind whirling. He could hardly breathe. Something was coming, and he wasn't ready.

"It's time, Cassiel."

"For what?"

The High King raised his hand as it began to glow white. "The truth."

CHAPTER 95

Dynalya

D yna sprinted up the stairs to the fourth floor. She'd felt Cassiel's anger and sadness, then his shock and panic. It beat against her senses, making her heart race. Since the moment High King arrived, she held the sheer fear it was to sever their bond. To erase their memories of each other again and take him away. Yoel welcomed her into the family, but it had all been a ruse to lower her defenses for one thing.

To get her mate alone.

Dyna clutched her heavy gown as she ran to where the bond led her. The guards shouted at her to halt. Dyna threw them back with a green blast of her magic. Zev, Rawn, and Lucenna were right behind her, fighting back the guards, creating an opening. She bolted ahead and ripped open the doors with another explosion of magic. Cassiel stood frozen; his eyes stretched wide as his father reached for him with a glowing hand.

"Stop!" Dyna screamed. She threw her arms protectively around Cassiel at the same time Yoel touched his cheek.

White light flared and stole her vision.

Then she sank.

A deafening roar split her ears. The terrible sound seemed to shake the earth and the *Hyalus* tree she hid in trembled.

The Shadow had come.

Dyna whimpered and burrowed into the warm body holding her. The tree kept out the dark but not her fear.

"It's all right," he said. She looked up into the boy's silver eyes, who was no more than ten. He looked so beautiful in the tree's light. He patted her head and his mouth curved with an encouraging smile. "I am here."

A warmth filled her chest. It banished the cold for a moment as she looked at the Seraph. For once, she felt safe. Home.

"Stay here," he said.

Then the boy grabbed his sheathed sword, crawled out of the burrow, and marched into the snowstorm. He was a small soldier in the dark. His black hair and wings shimmered with winter frost.

Cassiel, he called himself. *Cassiel.*

The name echoed through Dyna's mind, and her thoughts cleared.

This...this was a memory.

She gasped and tried to scream for him to come back, but no words came out. He walked across the white landscape as a large black mist appeared from the barren trees. Those molten red eyes burned in the dark, filling her with terror.

No. No!

The boy drew his divine sword and called to the Shadow demon. "I am Cassiel Soaraway and by the power of *Elyōn,* you will not touch my *mate.*"

The white flames of his sword blazed, and they turned a vivid blue. They burned so hot it warped the air.

Cassiel flew at the demon, and his sword slashed through its arm. What should have been smoke solidified beneath the Seraph flame. The Shadow screamed in pained fury. It regarded him now with a new intelligence and bared its fangs.

It whooshed in a gust of black smoke too fast for her eyes to track. It swiped at Cassiel. He dodged the first strike, but the second time those claws came, they ripped through his small body and Dyna screamed. He went flying and hit the *Hyalus* tree with a sickening crack.

He dropped into the snow.

She scrambled out of the burrow to him and rolled him over. His torso was slashed. Hot blood poured out of him, painting the snow red. Dyna wept as she pressed on his wounds. His wings were splayed at odd angles, feathers scattered around them like black petals.

He coughed up more blood. "Run..."

But she wouldn't. She couldn't leave him. As his heartbeat slowed, something inside of her cracked. The Shadow's cold stare brushed her back, and she knew she would die here, too. Cassiel reached up, and he brushed the tears freezing on her cheeks. His trembling fingers flickered blue.

"Do you cry for me?" he asked weakly. A hint of a smile tugged at his pale lips.

Don't go, Dyna's soul begged. Her child-self hadn't known who he was to her, only that she was losing him again.

Light faded from Cassiel's eyes like a star going out. Dyna felt the life leave his body and everything in her grew dark. A whimper shook out of her. Her fingers curled over one of his fallen feathers and it glittered gold faintly before the moonlight vanished. She looked up at the Shadow demon towering over her in the snowfall.

It killed her family. It destroyed her innocence. It stole half of her soul.

There was no more fear in her.

Power burned through Dyna's body in a rising wave. Her hands reached for the creature and a scream tore from her throat. Green light burst out of her and hit the demon. It crashed into the snow with a screech.

The magic stole her breath and Dyna swayed, her vision blackening. But it hadn't been enough. The Shadow rolled back to its feet as she dropped next to Cassiel, tears spilling down her nose. She hadn't been enough.

Her weak heart quivered with each of the Shadow's heavy footfalls.

It was coming.

A flash of white slammed into the demon. Pearlescent wings spread wide as a male Celestial whipped out his divine sword. Cerulean light bled through the white flames, turning them blue. "Stay away from my son," he snarled.

King Yoel.

He flew with an incredible speed as he slashed and cut the Shadow, fighting it back. It roared as it tried to cut Yoel out of the sky. He spoke the language of the Heavens in a rising chant.

The same glowing red line took shape in the snow. It grew as Yoel continued fighting the demon, developing into pickets made of black bone ending in sharp spindles. Its presence released something evil in the air.

The Netherworld Gate.

It creaked open and there was only darkness, frightening screams, and growls beyond.

"Return to the pit from whence you came!" Yoel thrust out his hand, throwing the demon backward through it. The Shadow's roar cut off as the Gate winked out of existence.

Dyna cried from relief, her vision dimming. She was so cold. Her heart beat slowly, as if it didn't want to beat anymore.

Yoel kneeled next to them and his face fell into distress. "Cassiel?" He reached out with shaking hands and pulled the boy into his arms. "Cassiel?" His eyes welled with tears as he brushed his pale face. "Son?"

But there was no waking him.

"He's gone," she said faintly. Her lashes frosted with her frozen tears. "I will follow him through the Gates."

Yoel started when he saw her, as if he didn't know she was there until now. He touched her cheek and a trickle of electricity sank into her. "You..." he said, his eyes widening.

A white light glowed around Cassiel's body like starlight from within. Pain crossed Yoel's features, his mouth tightening closed. He lay his son next to her and covered them with his coat. "Is this your justice?" he shouted at the night sky. "If so, I will lay upon your scales and pay for my sins. Not him."

Standing, Yoel turned away from her. His fists shook at his sides as Cassiel's body glowed brighter. Dyna reached for him, only for her hand to go through his fading form.

The God of Urn was taking him.

Yoel's voice called out in the language of the Heavens. The words reverberated through her soul and at that moment, she understood each one. "I call upon the Seven and the Seven Gates of old. Take from me my life and return that which was once whole."

A golden line appeared on the ground. It grew into massive luminous gates and they pulsed radiantly as they opened, revealing the light of stars and galaxies beyond. Yoel went inside. She didn't know how long he was gone. Her bleary eyes slowly blinked once, twice, then Cassiel inhaled a deep breath. The light from his body vanished as his father reappeared and gathered the boy in his arms.

But the King looked different. The gold of his hair was dull, the luster gone from his wings, complexion weary and aged.

After wrapping Dyna in his jacket, he tucked her into the burrow. "You must stay here."

She tried to take Cassiel's hand, but Yoel stood and her fingers only brushed his before falling to the snow. "Will I ever see him again?" she asked, her teeth chattering.

Yoel gave her a sad smile. "If the fates are kind, dear one, I hope not." His gentle hand came over her forehead and warmth seeped into her body. White light filled her vision as his power moved through her mind. He washed away her memories from the last hour and remade them with others.

Then the doorway to her magic was shut and locked away again.

"Don't move..." a fading voice whispered in the darkness. "Don't make a sound. The Shadow is coming..."

The Shadow is coming. It repeated in her mind, spoken through her lips over and over as a howl rang in the distance.

Dyna was yanked out of the memory when Cassiel shoved his father off of him. Yoel stumbled back a step. She slid her arms off her mate, her mind still dazed and slow. The King had been there on the night of the Shadow Winter. He made them forget...

Cassiel stared at him, his eyes wild. "I died."

"We cannot instantly heal wounds made by demons and black magic," Yoel said faintly. "Divine blood would have kept you alive, but with your wings broken, you were mortal."

Dyna's vision blurred as she understood what happened. "You retrieved his soul from the Gates," she whispered, looking at his aged face. "And the cost..."

"There is a balance to all things." Yoel sheathed his sword. He looked more tired and paler. "One cannot take without giving. Your time was lost when you died. The only way for you to live was to give you the time I had left."

"Why did you do that?" Cassiel asked, his voice strained. "Why did you give your life to me?"

"So that you could have one."

Cassiel sank to the sofa and dropped his head in his hands. Dyna sat next to him, resting a palm on his back. The bond trembled with all the emotions roiling through him. Her guards and friends stood at the doorway, grim looks on their faces.

"Mirah sent me there," Cassiel mumbled. "Did she know what would happen?"

"Someone sent you to North Star, but it was not her."

He muttered a curse and pressed on his forehead. "How much of my memory did you change?"

Yoel sighed. "As much as I needed to. I do not tell you this to burden you."

"How is this not a burden?" Cassiel snapped. "To learn that I—"

King Yoel swayed on his legs. Cassiel jumped up to catch him, but Lord Jophiel appeared and supported his elder brother against him.

"I think that is enough for today," Lord Jophiel said. He raised his hand when Cassiel's eyes widened and he tried to argue. "Yes, I knew the truth. It was difficult to keep this a secret from you, but we did what was necessary."

"I don't understand."

"There is much more I must tell you," King Yoel said, his voice becoming weaker.

"It can wait one more day. Right now, you need sleep." Lord Jophiel helped him to the large bed and made him lie down.

"Putting me to bed like a child."

"I did say using your power so soon after Azure would take a toll on you, Yoel," he chastised him gently. "You need your rest. We can reconvene tomorrow."

There was no more protest as his father's eyes drifted closed and his breaths evened out with heavy sleep. Lord Jophiel motioned for them to step out with him. Cassiel took her hand and led her back into the hallway, quietly shutting the door.

"Amriel," his uncle called to the male Celestial with short hair. The Royal Guard took his post outside of Yoel's door, then Lord Jophiel headed for the stairs.

"What did you mean?" Cassiel whispered sharply under his breath. "Why did he use his power in Azure? What is happening?"

"The Azure King was not content to accept your father's apologies or the affirmation of the Accords," Lord Jophiel said as they made their way down the second landing. "I think he merely wanted a reason to go to war, despite knowing they would clearly lose. Regardless, the losses on both sides would be great, and it would expose us further. That is not how your father wished you to start your reign. Therefore, he compelled the entire city of the Port of Azure to forget what happened."

Cassiel's shock clashed with her own. That was the power of the High King?

"Your father will discuss it with you later." His uncle sighed. "But you must sense he does not have long."

Cassiel's hand squeezed hers as they stared at Lord Jophiel.

"He may not ask you to give up your journey to Mount Ida, but I will. For the sake of your father and the Realms, you must take the throne."

CHAPTER 96

Dynalya

Upheaval fell over the manor with the presence of their guests. At her mate's command, the Valkyrie stood guard on every floor, in every corner, and wherever Dyna went, they weren't far behind. The day passed in silence as everyone held their breath for Cassiel's decision. Her mate didn't eat, didn't speak, or move from his spot by their bedroom window. He merely stared at the sky, perhaps waiting for the answer to come.

Whatever troubled his mind was kept from her. His shield had remained up since that morning. To learn they truly met each other that night only for him to die and be brought back—the payment for that would weigh on anyone. Whether or not Cassiel accepted the throne was something only he could decide for himself.

Dyna slipped away to check on Gale. Sowmya and Zekiel followed her a few paces behind like silent ghosts. That would take some getting used to. She tried not to let it bother her, though their presence felt like sap on her back. When she reached Gale and Eagon's door, she ordered them to stay in the hall. Sowmya's mouth pursed in silent protest.

Dyna entered and sighed in relief when the door shut behind her.

A soft laugh drifted from the bed. "Oh, dear." Gale smiled at her where she sat propped up against the pillows, nursing her baby. "I know that look."

"Mind if I hide in here for a bit?" Dyna asked as she came to sit beside her. "I'm sorry I haven't looked in on you. We had guests arrive early this morning."

"I heard. It's quite exciting to have the King of the Celestials here." Gale adjusted her clothing and burped her baby. "I wish I could meet him, but Eagon says it's best we stay in our room for now."

That probably was best.

Dyna leaned back into the velvet chair, simply enjoying the stillness. Soft afternoon light streamed in from the windows, giving the room a hazy sheen. Evin played quietly with blocks in the corner.

"How are you doing?" Gale patted her hand. "He is your father by marriage, after all."

Her thoughts were in a disarray when it came to King Yoel.

Why did he pretend not to recognize her? Why erase her memories and separate them only to allow them to reunite again? Yoel must have assumed Cassiel would follow her. If anything, she had a sneaking suspicion he planned it.

The placement of the barrier bothered her the most. Why had he done that to her? She was afraid of the answer. Her future seemed uncertain again and for different reasons. She wasn't prepared for any of it, yet when was she ever prepared for anything?

"He seems to approve of me."

"But?" Gale asked when she fell quiet.

"But I feel a little out of my depth. What do I know about being a princess?" Dyna waved a hand, laughing it off. "Enough about me. I came to see how you were feeling. Any concerns?"

"We're perfectly fine." Gale nuzzled her sleeping daughter's cheek. "Gwendolyn is growing strong. I named her after my mother."

"It's a lovely name." Dyna recalled a similar name on the plaque of the fountain in the town center. "The monument is dedicated to her, isn't it?"

Gale nodded, her smile becoming sad. "Klyde made it. His hands would better serve him building than killing. I didn't think it was possible to fix our house before winter's end, but he spent nearly every day there. It will be complete by next week." She looked around her room. "He must have hated coming here."

"Why does he dislike the manor?" Dyna asked.

Gale looked away. "Bad things happened here."

The way she said it made Dyna straighten. She held quiet, waiting for her to continue.

"When I was a little girl...a man...tried to force himself on me," Gale whispered. "Upstairs on the fifth floor. My brother stopped him."

Dyna felt awful to hear that. She held Gale's hand.

"We lost more than our innocence that day."

"I'm so sorry," Dyna said. "How long ago did it happen?"

She looked out the windows. "About fifteen years ago."

Fifteen.

Dyna pretended to let the information pass her, but that was the time Azurite fell to the Horde. These people didn't happen to come here and construct their town. They...they were survivors.

Gale seemed to catch herself and shrugged with a weak laugh. "I...suppose this place also reminds him of our previous life...in Old Tanzanite Keep. Stuffy castles and stuffy rules. We didn't have the best relationship with our father. My mother was the sweetest, kindest woman, but she was sickly...and it eventually claimed her life."

Dyna gently squeezed her hand. She knew very well what the loss of a mother felt like.

Gale reached under the blankets and pulled out a small portrait. She lovingly brushed her fingers over the painting, her lashes growing heavy with fresh tears. "I wish I'd been blessed with her eyes rather than her illness."

She held it up for Dyna to see. The cracked painting displayed a beautiful woman in a garden. Hair as gold as the sun, eyes a pale blue as a crystal stream. She had a gentle face and full pink lips, dressed in a lavender gown. She elegantly sat on a wooden chaise with a little girl on her lap. That must be Gale. Next to her sat a boy that was surely Klyde. His blond hair is worn short, his lip curled in his familiar smirk. A man in blue livery stood at her elbow. Their father, Dyna presumed. The scene was bright and colorful. So much that she nearly missed the shape standing beneath the shadows of a tree.

Everything inside of her frosted over at the sight of that pale face with wintry eyes.

"Wasn't she lovely?"

"Yes..." Dyna faintly whispered.

"I understand now how hard it was for them, but I miss the days when we were all together like this."

She couldn't look away from those eyes. Her heart rate climbed.

"I think my brother secretly wishes we could go back, too," Gale said. "He didn't always go by Klyde. That's what he chose for himself after we lost our family. I suppose he left his birth name in the past. He left much behind, I think, while I clung to it instead." A tear rolled down her cheek and splattered on the canvas. "I was so angry at him for easily laughing and smiling when I remained trapped in my grief. I see now he faced everything that way. Klyde chose to be a source of merriment when all I wanted was for him to be angry with me."

Gale's lips trembled as she fondly traced the faces of her family. "I thought he didn't care... but when he burned the portrait downstairs, I realized why the manor sat empty for fifteen years." She laughed weakly, a choked sound that was part sob. "Those smiles and exasperating jests were for me, while he buried everything inside. Now I wonder if I truly ever knew him at all."

Dyna returned to their bedroom with her mind spinning. Cassiel had moved from the window to the bed. It was early evening, but she silently changed out of her gown and slipped under the blankets. He curled his body around hers and tucked his chin over her head. She listened to his heart, counting the soft beats, infinitely grateful for each one.

They needed to talk about what she discovered, but it could wait.

Time passed them in silence as they held each other. Their bedroom grew dark with only the light of the hearth when Cassiel finally spoke.

"You jumped in to save me, although it went against the High King."

"Nothing would have stopped me," Dyna said. Protecting him was one of her vows, too. "I thought he planned to take you away from me."

He sighed, his breath tickling her cheek. *"Hasrat achrayut."*

She leaned back to glower at him. "Are you insulting me in your language again?"

"No, my reckless girl." The ends of his mouth tugged in a faint smile that never fully surfaced. The anxious way he looked at her made her worry. "What am I going to do with you?"

Before she could ask him what he was thinking, his warm lips kissed along her throat. He tugged on the lace ties of her nightgown, then his touch caressed her everywhere. Weaving through her hair, on her burning skin, in her pulse.

Dyna panted as his kisses left heated imprints down her stomach. She gasped and sat up when he continued further down. "Cassiel."

His dark lashes lifted, and those silver eyes met hers. A blue glow flickered in them. They burned with craving, but they also begged for a reprieve, for a moment where nothing else mattered.

"Lay back for me, *lev sheli.*" His voice was ragged, a near growl. Flames licked along his shoulders in winding trails as he took her ankles. "I said I would tend to you and I plan to."

Dyna's heart thrummed faster at the wildness on his face. Behind the inferno in his eyes rose a feral creature made of divine fire. The bond pulsated with his possessiveness and need, sparking her with frenzied desire. He stole her ability to speak at the first light touch of his mouth. She trembled as her body grew hot and hazy and too much. Her fingers dug into the sheets, needing something to hold on to, but it was all right because he had her.

And he always would.

She succumbed to Cassiel, and to the heat of every deliberate, worshiping caress, carrying her on a rising tide until she simply...ascended. Everything that weighed them down was forgotten beneath the wisps of blue flames licking along her skin, left to be burned away.

Perhaps because they fell asleep wrapped around each other, Dyna was pulled into Cassiel's nightmares. They were a jumbled web of images caught in the smoke of dream walking.

She saw him as a little three-year-old boy, screaming in bed as feathers slowly tore through his back. A woman with long black hair sobbed at the door on her knees, begging for someone to bring ointment for her son's pain. Dyna tried to get a closer look at her, but the scene spiraled to Yoel's study. His mother sat at a table with a pile of books in front of her. She wept over the pages with the illustration of a volcanic island. Cassiel, now an older child with black wings, reached for her. His fingers swept through her image that dissolved like fog, and they were thrust into a dark hallway. A cloaked figure hurried through it, her soft cries echoing around them.

Cassiel chased after her across the castle courtyard, but he couldn't keep up. She slipped past the castle gates and they clanged shut behind her as she walked away into the night. He cried out, his small hand reaching through the bars, begging her not to leave him.

The cloaked figure turned, and Dyna's heart jolted to see her own face.

She woke with a soft gasp. The fire in the hearth had died, but the crystal necklace she wore glowed softly in the dark room. Dyna brushed the hair sticking to the sweat on Cassiel's forehead and guided him into a dreamless sleep.

The nightmare...it was only his fears revealed. Not of her leaving, but that he would lose her against everything coming their way.

Having no love makes one so fiercely defensive once love is finally given. The need to protect that is soul consuming...Can you withstand everything that will come for being his wife?

The reminder of Sarrai's question left her unsettled. Dyna pressed a kiss over Cassiel's heart, then she slipped off the bed. After putting on a robe over her nightgown, she peeked out into the hall. No one stood guard outside their door.

Good. She needed some space.

The light from Dyna's necklace guided her down the hallway. A cup of tea would help her go back to sleep. She did her best to ignore the dark shadows in the quiet manor as she made her way down the stairs, but the hairs on the back of her neck stood on end when she reached the first floor. Dyna glanced over her shoulder into the pitch blackness of the foyer. It had been a while since she last felt the touch of darkness watching her.

Nothing is there, Dyna told herself.

So much had happened recently that the Shadow and her childhood fear of the dark were the furthest things from her mind. But facing it now made her pulse speed because she sensed something was indeed there...looking right at her.

A large shape dropped from above, and Dyna nearly screamed.

Sowmya's glower appeared in the light. "My lady, please don't wander without an escort," she said sternly under her breath. "My duty is to protect you."

Dyna pressed a hand to her chest, gasping to catch her breath. "God of Urn, Sowmya. You gave me a horrid fright."

Really, all the fanfare was unnecessary. There were better chances of her heart stopping from a scare than anything happening here.

"I'm headed to the kitchen for tea. Would you like a cup?" Dyna continued on. When they reached the dining hall, voices floated to her.

"His abilities come natural to him. In a way that is only seen with decades of training, yet he's had very little direction."

Dyna recognized Yelrakel's voice.

"Is that to say you believe the rumors?" King Yoel asked.

"I don't pretend to know any truths, Your Majesty. Whether your son is indeed the reincarnation of King *Kāhssiel* or not, with the force of Seraph fire at his hands, he will have no trouble finding supporters—as well as enemies."

A rush of gooseflesh prickled down Dyna's arms. She thought the gossip in Hermon Ridge had been merely that. Gossip.

Sowmya frowned at her disapprovingly for eavesdropping, but she ignored her.

"The Realms already fear him," he said. "They cannot help it when half of our people were lost to *Kāhssiel's* fire. It was a genocide of unprecedented scale."

"It's a history we cannot forget."

"As I do not forget those who rose against him. When the time comes, my son will choose you as his general. If one day he loses half of himself and his wrath burns through the Realms, what would you do?"

Dyna held her breath in the beat of silence. She dared to push slightly on the door to peer in the crack. She couldn't see much, only Yelrakel's bowed head past the long dining table where she knelt.

"I'm loyal to the royal family, Your Majesty," she said. "My will is my King's will. When he takes the crown, I will serve him as honor demands until my last day."

"I am trusting you with his life, Captain. He is the future, and for that, we must pray. Not only for the Realms, or the world, but that nothing should ever befall his mate. For if it does, *Elyōn* have mercy on us all."

A cold current that felt like a premonition crawled down Dyna's spine.

Someone yanked the door open, and they met the glare of the King's Royal Guard. Sowmya yanked her back, putting herself between them.

Past the guard's shoulder, Dyna met King Yoel's gaze where he sat in a chair a few feet from the Captain of the Valkyrie with Lord Jophiel on his right.

"Let her through, Amriel," he ordered. "You stand before a Princess of Hilos."

The guard stiffly backed away and his head barely lowered into a perceptible bow. The affront didn't bother her. It was something she would have to get used to, but as Dyna saw him in better lighting, she thought he looked familiar.

Sowmya hissed something at him as they entered the hall. His cold eyes followed her, and she finally recalled Amriel had been one of Malakel's guards in Hermon. It was his job to protect the High King and his heir, so he probably held a grudge against her for striking the prince.

Dyna dipped in a curtsy. "Pardon my intrusion, Your Majesty."

"Not at all. Come join me, Dynalya." He motioned for her to take a seat across from him at the table set up with a pot of tea and bread and cheese. She hesitated. "Oblige me."

He nodded to his brother. Lord Jophiel bowed and silently left the room with Yelrakel and Amriel. Sowmya murmured she would be waiting outside the door before leaving, too. Dyna sat as King Yoel poured her some tea. The scent of cinnamon and something floral filled the air before he passed it to her. She wrapped her fingers around the cup, waiting for whatever would come next.

"Are you shaken by what you overheard?" he finally asked.

Dyna let out a weak laugh. "Well, Your Majesty, I'm on my way to a magically hidden, treasure island in search of a relic that contains the power of the sun to slay a Shadow demon. Not much shakes me anymore."

He gave her that smile where she couldn't tell if he was amused by her answer. They were silent as they looked at each other. "It seems you want to ask me something."

She did, but another question arrived first. "The day of the wedding, I overheard you speaking to Lord Jophiel. You said, 'Nothing can interrupt what must happen tonight'. Were you referring to..." She flushed. "Our..."

His eyebrows shot up. "Oh, my dear, of course not. That is no business of mine. I merely meant nothing should interrupt the ceremony, so all may witness the light of your True Bond. I hoped it would silence the majority of all protests against your union, and it worked."

"Oh," Dyna said with relief. "I see now."

He canted his head and waited for the other question that she truly wanted answered.

"Why...?" She trailed off, lacking the nerve to ask. "I suppose you had your reasons for separating us, but as much as I try, I can't understand why you placed a barrier on my magic. No, you *reconstructed* the barrier...because it had already been placed." She didn't look away from him, swallowing back her emotions. "That means you knew me long before that night. I could have saved my family from the Shadow if I had my power. Why did you take it from me?"

Sympathy settled on his features. "I am very sorry for what befell you that night. If only I had known..." He sighed heavily. "When Azeran first came to me, it was to seek asylum on my land. I gave them the gorge that became North Star, and he placed a warding spell on the village to conceal it from the

Archmage. However, barriers were occasionally needed for children born with a vast amount of power. You were one of them, Dynalya. At your birth, everyone in North Star felt your abundance of magic, and your father feared it would attract the Archmage. Thus, Baden brought you to me."

Dyna's heart sank. Then it had been her father.

"The night the Shadow came, you somehow put a crack in the barrier and I had to fortify it again. Although as you grew, undoubtedly so would your power." Yoel gave her a soft smile. "It seems you have removed it. I knew there was something special about you." By his expression, he meant more than her magic. "You have bloomed into something far beyond my expectations. I see your strength, and I suspect you will need it for what is to come."

Dyna sipped her tea. "Do you mean because of the position I hold or my marriage with Cassiel?"

He glanced at her crystal necklace, and his brow creased. "Both, I suppose. The burden of power can be painful at times. Prepare for everything, my dear. Your destiny is in your hands and no one else's. We have to fight to survive. Sometimes, the cost is more than we thought to give."

The memory of killing Benton flashed in her mind.

"More than blood," Dyna whispered to herself.

"Pardon?"

She set down her teacup. "Someone once told me survival demanded more than blood. That it demanded your soul."

The King nodded with a sigh. "It very well could cost your soul, if not your life."

They shared a look again, and she knew they were thinking about his sacrifice.

"Do you…regret it?" she dared ask in a small voice.

"I have many regrets. Some regarding my wife and the one who should have been my wife." He rubbed his face. "But never will I regret giving up my life for his. I am relieved and so very glad that you accepted him. If either of you had rejected the bond, it would not have killed him, but it would hurt nearly as much as a broken bond, and broken you both." He looked away to the window, remorse crossing his face. "I did that to Mirah very slowly over the years, seeding her heart with hate. But I cannot change the past now. I can only hope for a better future."

Dyna sat in silence, reading the words he couldn't speak. "I know it isn't my place to say this, Your Majesty. Regarding those we wish to reach, sometimes it's hard to say what you mean, and easy to say what you don't. It's no easy feat to open one's heart, but I find that's what it takes for a chance to see theirs."

As the King looked at her, his eyes grew misted. "Thank you for being by his side, Dynalya Astron. Take care of him for me when I'm gone."

She discreetly blinked away her wet eyes. "I will."

He cleared his throat. "Well. As I remember, it was Cassiel's birth-date last week. I have brought him something, though he may not wish to accept it yet. Could I leave it with you to give to my son when the time is right?"

It would be the very last thing he would have of his father. The thought made her incredibly sad.

Dyna rose to her feet and inclined her head. "Of course, Your Majesty. You can entrust it to me."

CHAPTER 97

Von

V on's heartbeat was as loud as thunder in his skull. The ship creaked
quietly in the late hour as he stood frozen in the captain's quarters,
trying to make himself move. Tarn slept soundly in his chair with his
body slumped over the desk. Wine glistened in his cup, smelling of the tainted
Witch's Brew.

It was an odd sight. To see him like this. Sleeping. *Vulnerable...*

When he woke, his wrath would be a terror.

Kill him.

A thought urged Von. Kill him and get rid of Tarn's obliteration from the
world. Yet he couldn't bring himself to reach for a knife. Maybe because they
had once been friends. Family.

Out of love for his sister, Von couldn't.

His hand shook as he slipped the Scroll of the Unending out from under
Tarn and tucked it in his coat. Von picked up the Xián Jīng chest as he backed
away slowly, keeping his eyes on the deadliest man alive. Tarn didn't stir.

When Von reached the door, he peeked out the round window, straining
to listen. The ship was dark and still in the night. A light fog drifted over the
black sea and the deck, offering a veil. He spotted Geon where he waited
behind a cluster of barrels with Yavi.

The lad had traded his apron for a Raiders uniform to better blend in. He
insisted on serving as the lookout for their escape. The only Raider on duty
was unconscious at the helm, courtesy of the ale spiked with a few drops of
Dreamshade oil.

Once Geon made sure it was clear, he signaled. Von slipped out of the door and crouched by the steps to keep watch as they silently ran across the deck to the davit on the other side of the ship. It held a rowboat suspended next to the rail, ready to board.

Then Von rushed to meet up with them. "Are you all right?" he whispered to Yavi.

She nodded. Her wide eyes glistened in the faint moonlight streaming through the clouds. He gently squeezed her hand, willing her to feel reassured, but inside his pulse was racing.

"Did you get everything, lad?"

"Aye, Commander. Here are the rations for your journey. Good for a week." Geon shakily handed Von a sack. His face was pale and shining with sweat, reflecting the apprehension they all felt.

"You tell him it was me," Von said as he quietly placed their bags and the chest in the boat. "Blame me for all of it."

Geon nodded and swallowed. "What will you do with it?" he asked, glancing uneasily at the chest. The golden inscriptions looked unsettling in the night. They had told him what it contained.

Von pressed a hand over his heart where he'd tucked the scroll. "Burn it to the high Heavens."

Because he wouldn't allow Tarn to do such an abominable thing. They had done many awful things over the years, but resurrecting the dead? Not even the Gods would pardon that.

"Live long and happy, Geon," Yavi whispered to him and they embraced tightly.

"You do the same," he said, blinking back tears. "Safe travels. I pray one day we meet again."

Von helped Yavi climb into the rowboat. "Careful now. Sit and lie low."

She gave him a watery smile. "Not until you kiss me."

"It's a terrible thing to be married to such a stubborn woman." He sighed, leaning out to cup her face.

Yavi kissed him. "You married me of your own volition. Now you must bear the consequences all your days."

All of his days. He liked the sound of that.

"We're going to lower you first, then I will climb down the hull to you," he said.

Yavi nodded and crouched down between the seats. Her bangles caught the light before she hid them under her cloak. As soon as they were far away from the wards, they would use the slaver's key.

Geon smiled at him sadly. "I will miss you."

"Aye, me, too. I wish you would come with us, lad."

Geon shrugged with a small smile. "I can't leave that grumpy Minotaur behind. He needs me. Your place is with Yavi. My place is here. It won't be the same without you both."

"Geon..." Von swallowed. "I'm sorry for..."

Emotion crossed Geon's face. "I know. You did what you could for him, and I can't ask for more than that."

He exhaled a shaky breath, hoping and praying that Dalton found peace.

They each took a handle to the radial davit and slowly spun them to lower the rowboat. Von cringed as it creaked faintly, each sound causing his heart to beat faster. They carefully lowered the rowboat to the cold black mirror below. Frothing water tumbled away from the boat's stern. The night was quiet and still, as if it held its breath while it watched. He wasn't able to relax until the boat made it safely down in the water. Geon rapidly tied a rope around a metal cleat on the railing and handed it to him.

"It has been a pleasure, Commander." He saluted.

"Thank you, Geon." Von patted his arm. "I'm within your debt."

"Let's consider this even, then"

Von chuckled and climbed over the rail. "Farewell. Promise me you will leave one day and see everything you dreamed of. Find your way, Geon. Don't wait as long as I did."

He nodded. "I promise."

Von scaled the side of the ship while looking up at the lad's bright smile. He waved goodbye to them cheerfully, watching him go. Von wished he could have taken him, too. Geon had much more to live for than being a slave cook. He was going to miss him.

Geon flinched, his eyes going wide. A breath shot out of him, fogging in the night air, then his limp body fell over the railing. It was a slow descent in Von's sight. He fell past him and splashed into the dark sea. Yavi's scream pierced the silence. Von gaped down at the body floating face down in the water. Motionless.

"Geon!" Yavi cried.

She yanked on his clothes, trying to pull him onto the rowboat. Impaled on the back of Geon's neck was a glinting throwing star. Cold horror sunk in Von's chest. He looked up at the ship to find Tarn looking down at him. His mind went blank at the pure ice frosting in those pale blue orbs.

Von couldn't move.

He couldn't breathe.

His heart hammered in his tight chest.

Lieutenant Olsson and the rest of the Raiders appeared at the railing. Arms lunged for Von and yanked him back over, tossing him onto the deck. Sai-chuen leaped off the shroud he had been perched on and walked over to them. He tossed another throwing star and cut the rope tied to the cleat.

Von looked at Tarn and rose. "Wait, Tarn—"

A swift kick to his face hurled him back onto the deck. His ears rang sharply from the blow. The Raiders worked fast to reverse the radial davit and bring the rowboat back up. Yavi sobbed over Geon's body, her dress stained with his blood. She screamed when the men tore her away from his corpse and they forced her to kneel.

"You have taken me for a fool," Tarn said coolly. "If you thought I never knew about her."

Von tried to protest, but Tarn tossed something at him. It clattered on the deck, whirling gold in the moonlight before settling.

Yavi's wedding ring.

She gasped at the sight of it and touched her chest, realizing too late it was missing. Sai-chuen sneered at him. He grabbed her arm, and she fought him wildly.

"Release her!" Von shouted.

Yavi scratched Sai-chuen across his eye. Enraged, he smacked her, knocking her down. Von lunged for him, but Olsson tackled him to the deck.

Sai-chuen dragged her forward. He unsheathed his short sword and his black eyes gleamed like oil under the lanterns.

"No!" Von cried out. He fought against Olsson, but his hold was unbreakable. "Tarn, Please!"

Sai-chuen cut open Yavi's dress, revealing her bare back to them. Above her right shoulder blade was the slave seal that had been burned on her two years ago. A pale scar was slashed across it as the sign of a free slave. Yavi held her dress to her chest, crying softly.

Tarn's jaw clenched. "Not only did you have the nerve to attempt to poison me, you *stole* from me."

Olsson whispered an apology before reaching into Von's coat and pulling out the scroll. He handed it to Tarn.

He checked it briefly, then tucked it away. "Though I suspected you were not the same when you returned from Beryl Coast." His piercing, wintry eyes locked him place. "Primarily when you no longer called me Master."

Von's dread climbed as a Raider handed the Xián Jing chest to Tarn. He flipped the lid open and showed it to him. It was empty...

The teapot was gone.

Somehow, he'd known.

Why didn't the Dreamshade work? Von shook where he kneeled, his body having gone cold as his mind reeled with all his mistakes. Tarn was never asleep in the first place. Because he didn't consume anything, Von didn't taste first.

"You cannot hide anything from me, Von. Not your scheming. Not your weak heart. Not your secret marriage. And not your unborn child."

Ice.

That was all he felt forming inside of him as fear and horror crystalized over his soul.

A murmur passed through the gathered Raiders.

"You know the punishment for this is death."

Von crawled to Tarn on his hands and knees and bowed at his feet. "Master, I beg your forgiveness." His vision blurred with tears. "I was wrong to have defied you. I'll accept any punishment you see fit. But please, I beg you for her life."

"You misjudge me. I'm not quite the monster to kill a woman with child."

Von looked up at him, daring to hope.

Tarn reached into his coat and pulled out a long knife. "That is something only you do."

Von gaped at him. "W-what?"

"You want to be free? This is your debt repaid." Tarn held the knife out to him and the moonlight caught on the sharp edge.

He could only stare at him in shock. "But why? You have the Scroll of the Unending and Jökull's ashes. It was for her, right? All of this was for her. You want to bring my sister back to life and now you can, so you don't have to do this."

Tarn tilted his head and laughed airily. "Von...did you think even now it would be that simple? Or have you forgotten the legend of Jökull and Sunnëva? She stepped into the fire, because for life to be given, life must be taken."

A sacrifice.

"I had everything I needed until you let her go."

He stopped moving. Stopped shaking. Stopped breathing.

You let her go.

Dyna. She was meant to be the sacrifice?

"So Yavi will take the Maiden's place. I think this is much more fitting, don't you?" Tarn's eyes were orbs of frost, glowing eerily in the night. "A *wife* for a *wife*."

Von shuddered as, at last, his sins came to confront him. His mind filled with images of his pregnant sister's torn body in the hall of her home, Tarn's anguish at the loss, and the gore of every death he caused in Azurite. "Please. Don't ask me to do that. Please. I beg you."

"It's not a request. It's an order." He tossed the knife, and it stabbed the deck next to Von's hand.

"Then take my life for Aisling's as payment."

"Don't speak her name," Tarn snarled.

"You still need Yavi to translate the last half of the scroll," Von cried desperately, tears freely falling. "I'll die in her stead. Please, Master. I will do anything. Kill me instead. Kill me. *Kill me!*"

The scent of Witch's Brew was strong in the air as Von looked at the man who was once his friend, searching for some shred of mercy. Either spelled or buried, there was no trace of who he had been.

"You will end her life—or he will," Tarn said. Sai-chuen raised his sword above her head. "Now pick up the *knife*."

Von's quaking hand reached for it. He tugged the blade free of the wood and took Yavi's hand to help her stand.

She sadly smiled at him through her tears. "Don't be afraid."

He shook his head, biting back a sob. "Yavi...forgive me."

"It's all right, my love. There is nothing to forgive. I'll wait for you in our next life."

Her words ruined him.

Von lowered his head and streaks of tears rolled down to his chin. He held her in his arms, crying in her hair. "I love you."

She clutched him tightly, her body trembling. "How much?"

"This much."

Ignoring those around them, the swaying ship, and the impending threat to their lives, Von swept Yavi against his chest and kissed her. She entwined her arms around his neck. He crushed his mouth to hers urgently, every part of him shaking.

He didn't care that the others were watching. It was only them. From the moment he captured her, Yavi had captured his heart and gave him something beautiful in the misery that had consumed his life. She was his bane, and he would never stop fighting to give her what she deserved.

Von ended the kiss, gazing at his wife for the last time. "You are free."

He lifted Yavi and threw her onto the rowboat. She shrieked from the unexpected toss and landed on top of Geon's body. Von cut the davit rope suspending the rowboat, and she fell shrieking with it to the sea. The boat landed with a loud splash. Her head hit the frame of the boat, stunning her.

"Yavi!" Von shouted at her fearfully. She blinked up at him, struggling to sit up. "Go!"

She reached for the oars as the Raiders fell upon him. Von whipped out his knives. He cut them down as they came, leaving bodies sprawling over the deck. He buried the guilt of killing his men under the determination to save his family. Whoever stood in his way would fall until he did.

Large arms grabbed him from behind. "Commander, stop!" Olsson squeezed tight, causing Von to lose air and the hold of his knives.

Tarn walked to the rail and looked out at the rowboat floating away. Yavi hadn't recovered from the blow to her head. She swayed, struggling to row.

"You could have ended her life quickly, Von." Tarn met his gaze. "Remember that."

He walked away and climbed the steps to the captain's quarters without looking back. Von didn't understand until he saw Sai-chuen take an oil lantern hanging on a mast—and pitch it over the ship.

Von's cry echoed across the sea.

The lantern sailed clear through the night and shattered in the rowboat by Yavi's feet. Flames burst out and flared into the sky.

Then she began to scream.

Yavi's name tore from Von's throat. He fought madly against those holding him back, desperate to break free. The ship sailed away from the bright orange flames burning in the middle of the black sea as Yavi's agonizing screams slashed through his ears. Von screamed with her, his soul ripping to shreds. Olsson pinned him against the rail to keep him from throwing himself overboard.

A blow smashed against the back of Von's head. He fell onto the cold deck, all strength leaving his limbs. Then the world faded away, taking the last of Yavi's screams with it.

CHAPTER 98

Dynalya

The sound of distant screams woke Dyna from a deep sleep. She sat up and looked around in a sleepy daze, not sure if she was still dreaming. She touched her cheek, finding it wet. Had she been crying? Reaching out for Cassiel, her fingers landed on the cold, empty sheets. Where had he gone?

A knock came at the door, then Noemi came in to help her dress for the day. Sowmya and Zekiel followed her in to stand guard at the door. They had brought a cart to her with a pot of tea, porridge, and a covered plate that must have some sort of pastry because the air smelled like lemons, but she wasn't hungry. Her mind kept turning over Cassiel's dream.

"My husband?" Dyna asked them. She slipped on a robe over her nightgown and went to the wardrobe to search for clothes. It had been stuffed with dresses brought from Hermon.

"He stepped out at dawn," Zekiel said. He must have also been up early on duty because he looked tired.

"The captain is with him, Your Highness," Sowmya added, giving him a sharp look. "Refer to my lady with due respect."

He looked at her with sudden concern. "Oh, I apologize if I offend."

"No, of course not." Dyna waved it away with an awkward laugh. "Please, you need not be so formal, Zekiel, nor either of you," she said to Sowmya and Noemi. "I'm no one to bow to, truly."

They frowned at her, but the male guard smiled warmly.

"If it should please you," he said.

Sowmya shot him another glare.

"Sit, sit," Noemi ushered her to the vanity. "I will pick out a dress for you to wear."

"Something warm, please. I would like to go outside."

"I will prepare the Royal Guard, my lady," Sowmya said.

"Oh, um, must they come?" Dyna asked, twisting a red curl around her fingers.

"They are there for your safety."

Zekiel hummed, shrugging. "It should be fine this once. I think she would like to have a moment alone with Prince Cassiel."

"The Royal Guard must always accompany her," Sowmya said stiffly. "It's for her protection, a duty that is mine to see to."

"Of course. I merely meant she must be feeling overwhelmed and crowded with a constant armed parade of warriors in her shadow. All of this is very new to her, but the manor is well-guarded. We can allow her some space."

Dyna was warmed by his advocation and how easily he understood her, even though they had barely met.

"There is no need for both of us to crowd her." Zekiel chuckled lightheartedly. "I will gladly escort her outside."

"I won't leave my lady's side," Sowmya said, nearly growling. "If you are so eager, go and have the Royal Guard take their posts in preparation for Her Highness's arrival."

Zekiel's smile never dropped. "Right away."

He stepped out, leaving behind an awkward silence.

Dyna frowned at Sowmya's reflection in the mirror. "You looked ready to cleave him in half."

Sowmya flushed. "Forgive me, my lady. I don't like him."

"Because he is male?"

"Because he is terribly rude," Noemi interjected. They must have two different opinions on what she considered rude. He had seemed polite to her. "Not once did he refer to you with due deference, Your Highness."

"I asked him not to. It makes me uncomfortable to be regarded as royalty. I didn't grow up in a castle, so all of this is a bit much." Dyna started to stand. "If I'm going to trudge through the snow, I should wear trousers."

Noemi waved her back. "Oh no, no, no. You are a Princess now, and soon you may be Queen. You must be fit for your station and referred to with respect. If not even the guards follow decorum, the court will look unfavorably upon you."

They already looked down on her simply because she was human.

"It's all right, really. I don't care what they say about me."

Noemi huffed. "You must care, Your Highness. Your first days at court will reflect how your reign will be."

Dyna had come to terms with the fact they wouldn't fully accept her. But by some miracle, the King approved of their marriage, and she was fortunate in that.

Noemi held up a dress made of deep red velvet and trimmed with golden embroidery. "I made sure to bring dresses lined with wool to keep you warm. This one will complement your complexion beautifully."

It was lovely, but not very practical. Dyna decided to wear an extra layer beneath. Noemi made a disapproving face at her fae armor but said nothing as she helped her slip the velvet frock over it. It was certainly warmer than her other ones, if not a little heavy from how thick it was. The soft sleeves sat low on her arms, highlighting the curve of her shoulders and chest. Noemi herded her to the vanity table and worked on her hair.

"We cannot forget the most important touch," Noemi said as she cheerfully opened a polished box to reveal her sapphire crown. The stones glittered beautifully in the sunlight. Dyna wasn't sure how she felt about wearing such prominent jewelry, but it was a gift from her mate, and she wanted to please him.

The crown felt cold and heavy on her head. She didn't know if it really belonged there, but whatever answer Cassiel gave would change their lives.

Dyna rose and picked up her sheathed sword resting against the wardrobe. Noemi sighed, but knew it was a useless argument. It would go with her everywhere. Since arriving in Skelling Rise, they had trained nearly every day with weapons and magic. The journey would only get harder from here, and she needed to be ready now more than ever.

Once her sword was buckled in place, Dyna swished her skirts aside to strap her opal knife to her bare thigh and stepped into her boots. Noemi pulled out a long gray cloak with white fur lining and helped her slip it on. It hid her sword out of sight.

She left the bedroom with her guards marching behind her, their presence like a heavy blanket. Sowmya meant well, but having a flock of guards and holding a constant poise was exhausting.

Was this her life now?

As she came down the steps, she caught Klyde and Lucenna talking quietly in the foyer. Dyna paused, letting their voices float up to her.

"You have my word. I won't do that again," he said, searching her face. She wouldn't quite look at him. "Not until you ask me to."

"I won't." Lucenna turned on her heel and headed for the kitchens. Dyna made a note to ask her what happened the other night, because it seemed something did.

Klyde lingered in the hall as he watched her go, a strained look on his face, but then his eyes flickered up, and Dyna was caught. She came down the rest of the steps.

He swept an arm across his chest, inclining his head. "My lady."

"I thought the Skelling Mercenaries bowed to no one," she said with a surprised smile.

Klyde winked. "We make exceptions for our favorites." He was in full gear with his captain's coat and weapons.

"Headed out?"

"Aye, I'm on my way to the wall. The High King paid us generously to keep an eye out for any potential threats." Klyde shrugged. "No one will find us here, but if it makes him feel better, who am I to dispute it?"

"*They* found us."

"Aye, but Lord Jophiel knew where to look. I doubt anyone else would trudge through this Gods' forsaken place. Perhaps I should hire Lucenna to ward the town." He bowed again. "Well, I'm off, then."

"Klyde..." Dyna called hesitantly. She searched his kind face for answers to her questions, and she found the truth had always been in front of her, but she had been too distracted to see it. He canted his head questioningly. "I have wondered," she finally said. "Why did you decide to live here? Most of the year, you're either battling trolls or the winter."

He smiled.

To anyone else, it would look like all the other smiles Klyde gave. Playful, carefree... sincere. But Dyna was watching him closely, and because of it, she caught the flicker of an edge to his eyes. It was the wash of a storm wave. Violent and swift. It crashed on frozen shores before it was pulled out to the calm seas he hid beneath.

"The beasts we have learned to live with, and well, I've always despised the winter, but every season has its purpose," Klyde said as he turned away. "In the ice we mold our truth, even whence hidden by the snow."

Dyna watched him stride for the door with two voices echoing in her head. She left her thoughts there in the corridor to be picked up at a later time.

Right now, her mate needed her.

The bond led her to the courtyard where Cassiel was lying on a landscape of white, gazing up at the gray sky as the snowflakes fluttered down. He wore his enchanted navy coat that kept his wings out of sight. The snow half buried him there, and she thought he might not move until it did completely. It was a beautifully sad picture of a prince not ready for the next chapter in his life.

Yelrakel stood guard by the doors, her attention never leaving Cassiel. Sowmya took her spot on the other side of the entrance. Zekiel and the rest of her Royal Guard flew up to take posts on the roof and in the trees with the other Valkyrie. It wasn't privacy, but it allowed them some space.

Dyna brushed against the bond. Cassiel's silent warmth answered back. Taking that as permission to approach, she walked over and removed her crown before lying down in the snow with her feet pointed in the opposite direction of his, leaving their heads side by side. Her furred cloak protected her back from the frost.

It was peaceful, simply laying here and watching the snow fall.

"Living in Hilos, you cannot imagine what it's like," Cassiel said softly. "Its beauty is smothered with hatred. There is no light there. I don't want that life for you."

Dyna had been sheltered her whole life, from living in a small village, to being coddled by everyone who thought her too weak. She'd even been held back by herself. By her fear. Her fault. Her own insecurity of feeling like her abilities were never enough to protect the ones she loved. But these last few weeks, she left all of that behind. It was peeled off her by the world, by living, by training, and beatings. It hardened her, and she was not afraid.

Not of what may come.

And certainly not of court.

At feeling all of this from her, Cassiel closed his eyes, snowflakes catching on his lashes. "Dyna, if anything happened to you, I think I would lose my mind…" Blue fire crackled on his skin as it always did, she realized, when his need to protect her was triggered. It released a tremendous heat and the falling snow hissed as it landed on his face. "Perhaps it's because you are the other half of me. This need to protect you intensified by the thousands the moment I made you completely mine. The very thought of any threat against you, it ignites me with this indescribable craze." Cassiel's hands flattened on the ground, and his taut fingers dug in the snow, melting it. "I cannot lose you again. I won't survive it."

She curled her arm up around his head to cup his warm cheek, heated by the divine flame alive within him. "You won't lose me."

His silver eyes opened to meet hers. "Tarn, Malakel, Leoake, the Realms...I am haunted by the paranoia that you are not safe. That if I leave you unprotected for one second, they will tear you away."

Hearing that elicited the memory of Tarn's wife. Her death had ruined him. That could easily happen again.

"Cassiel, you cannot live your life afraid. Fear begets anger, and anger begets hate. I have seen what that does to a person. You cannot let it happen to you." He fell silent, and she searched through the bond to understand what he wasn't saying. "Am I truly the only reason you won't take the throne, or is it because your father requested it?"

His expression hardened.

"He's trying, Cassiel."

"Yes. Ten years later, because his time has run out, and he wants to cross the Gates with a clean conscience."

"He loves you. He may not have shown it well, but he is here now because he wants to be."

"How can I attempt a relationship with him, when all I feel is anger when I look at him? He abandoned me. Whatever his reason, I don't know if I can ever forgive him." Cassiel laid an arm over his eyes. "Now he wants to be a father by revealing I owe him my life? How am I to feel knowing every breath I take was stolen from him? He came here to guilt me into taking his place to rule over a kingdom of bigots. Why? I care nothing for them."

"I think that is what you tell yourself," she said gently. "It's easier to hold grudges than to acknowledge how we truly feel."

His low exhale clouded in the air above him. "What does the bond tell you? I'm too blinded to see, so tell me."

She turned her face toward him. "You are afraid."

Cassiel sighed. "Yes."

"Not because of what the Realms will think of you as their High King, but that you will fail to meet their expectations. That you won't be strong enough to protect your people. And...that you will repeat your father's mistakes...with me."

The bond jumped with his shock at the realization of what was buried under all of his resentment. She saw his apprehension, felt it grow when he dreamed of his mother. The thought that he would only bring her suffering and lose her in the end, either by his doing or by others, terrified him.

Anguish creased his features when he looked at her. "I could not live with myself if you bear the consequences."

"You can't protect me from everything, Cassiel."

"I will. I have to. Without you by my side, everything else is meaningless." He closed his eyes. "Why does it have to be me? Why, when I know nothing about ruling?"

"The burden of kings is dire," she said. "I cannot pretend to know the matters of court, but I know the weight of a crown is heavy. Yes, many will look upon you for leadership and question if you should have it. Regardless of what anyone would make you believe, being a half-human does not make you unworthy. It makes you the bridge between Celestials and humanity, and for that very reason, the throne couldn't be in better hands than yours."

Dyna saddened at the feeling that stirred in him to hear her say that. All of his life, they told him he was a mistake. A nothing.

"You are a *Guardian*," she said firmly. "Not only for me, but because that is who you are. There is no other clearer sign than your Seraph fire. That which only comes to those who answer the call to protect others at the expense of themselves. Because of it, the Realms will be safe in your hands. I believe this is your destiny. However, I'm not your mother." She stroked his jaw, and his solemn eyes met hers. "And you are not Yoel. He may not have been a good father, but he was a good King. You have the potential to be a great one."

He curled a lock of her hair in his fingers. His *Hyalus* ring glinted with the faint sunlight fighting to shine through the thick clouds. "Why do you think more highly of me than I do myself?"

Dyna smiled. "As I said before. I see you, Cassiel. I see you for who you are and not what you have lied to yourself about."

He looked at her as if she was his serenity. The sweep of his thumb left a heated trail behind as it stroked her cheek and hovered over her lips like the breath of a kiss. "I wonder when you gained the power to make everything inside of me either fall tranquil or surge into a frenzy."

"I could ask you the same," she said faintly, feeling her body heat beneath the path of his touch. If she could, she would melt into him forever.

"I searched the skies for the answer to what I must do, but I think I already know. I simply lack the courage to do it."

"I will support you in whatever you decide."

"If I do this..."

"I'm coming with you to Hilos," Dyna said definitively. "Once our journey ends, of course." Because nothing would impede her from going to Mount Ida. Not when her family was at stake, and she wouldn't let him give up on his mother, either. "Wherever you go, I will follow. You made that promise, and it's seared into my heart along with all the others. I know it won't be easy and many will oppose us, but I don't care what they say. Through the darkness and through the flame, I'm with you, *kohav.*"

Cassiel gazed at her fondly, though his unease didn't fully fade. The delay in his reply planted a little seed of worry.

"Promise me whatever comes, I will be by your side to face it with you." Keeping her safe was all that mattered to him, but she didn't need a shield. All she needed was him.

Cassiel's hand entwined in her hair and his fingertips brushed her neck, leaving little imprints of heat behind. "Whatever may come, I know one thing will always be true." He inched closer, his silver eyes on her mouth. *"At haor sheli."*

His soft lips enveloped hers, and fire wove through her being. The sheer affection behind the upside down kiss was a force like no other. One that left her dissolving beneath his touch as the snow, completely and irrevocably helpless at his hands.

And she was prepared to endure such a subduing sensation all of their days.

CHAPTER 99

Cassiel

Might we retire for the evening? Cassiel sent the thought through the bond as he helped Dyna up and brushed the snow off her skirts. *It's still morning. You wish to retire now?*

Cassiel picked up her crown, placing it back on her head where it belonged. He let his hand cup the back of her cold neck and drew her to him, grazing her cheek with his nose. *I wish to continue what we started last night.*

Dyna choked back a cough, her cheeks blooming pink. He sensed her remembering the feel of his lips traveling up her inner thigh, and it elicited a curl of heat sinking through her stomach. *Your Majesty, that was very direct.*

The formal address of his new status only stirred him further. He had the urge to have her under him, warm, close, and protected from any harm. She was so dear to him. Her heart, her mind, her body, her soul. He wanted all of it in every way possible. After having her, he couldn't imagine any other existence.

Cassiel trailed his fingers slowly from Dyna's wrist to her elbow. The bond was fully open because when she shuddered, he was aware of the electric currents running up her arms and down her spine. *That is the beauty of having a wife.* He brushed his lips on the edge of her ear and he was gratified by her soft sigh. *I can be direct because I feel how her body responds to mine, and she quite enjoys it when I touch her.*

Dyna covered her face. *Cassiel!*

He chuckled and tucked her head against his chest. "You are adorable."

He wanted to have her forever, to hold her like this every day. To kiss her, tease her, care for her, make her sigh at his touch, but also laugh unreservedly every day. He wanted to love her and be loved. He wanted to finally be happy. If this was what it felt like, then life couldn't be any more perfect.

At the clearing of a throat, they both looked up at Zev standing with his arms crossed a few steps away, Lucenna and Rawn behind him. Dyna's cheeks went from pink to bright red.

"Do I even want to know what you said to make her blush like that?"

Cassiel grinned. "No, you don't."

But the brief sunny moment passed into shade as they all looked at him with sudden seriousness.

"So, you will take the throne," Zev said.

Cassiel inhaled a deep breath as Dyna slipped her hand in his. Her support fortified his decision, and he nodded. The acknowledgment seemed to shift something among the Celestials.

Circumstances continued to back him into a corner, forcing his will. He didn't want to be king, but he felt obligated after learning what his father had sacrificed. More so, knowing what was at stake. The resolve to accept his fate was jarring. It left him adrift in a wind with no sense of direction.

Zev surprised him when he said, "I have decided to stay in town. I think you'll need me."

"The transition of power is a dire time." Rawn's sharp eyes scanned the trees. "And it appears your father thought well ahead to plan for every possibility."

The Valkyrie were all over the manor, their gold armor glinting in the daylight. Legion warriors, about two hundred in number. Some were out of sight, but Cassiel knew they were watching. Dyna tensed because she must sense what he did the moment his father had arrived. Heavy anticipation hovered in the air, like something was waiting to drop.

"The mercenaries are also on guard," she said. There was a peculiar tightness in her tone.

Lucenna crossed her arms. "Our one advantage is that no one else knows we're here. I don't believe there will be trouble, at least not yet. But we haven't forgotten about the voice in Hermon."

Those threats were very real, regardless of how eccentric they sounded.

Cassiel would leave nothing to chance.

The Valkyrie stood at attention and clanked a fist over their hearts. They bowed as the High King strolled through the courtyard doors with Lord Jophiel. His father's complexion looked much better than yesterday, and he moved without a hint of feebleness. Sleep had wiped away the frailty, but not his age.

His heavy crown and royal robes had been replaced by trousers and a winter coat. They shared a long look in the windy silence.

"Walk with me." His father continued on without waiting for a reply.

Dyna gave Cassiel's hand a gentle squeeze before he followed. They headed for the gravel path, away from the others. Only Amriel and Yelrakel shadowed them. The snow crunched under their boots as they walked the paths of the gardens. It couldn't truly be called a garden when it was mostly dried vegetation and mud coated in frost.

When they were at a suitable distance, his father said, "You have decided."

It wasn't a question. Of course, he must have had someone reporting to him.

Cassiel crossed his arms behind his back. "Though, I still question why you chose me to be your successor when you have two other pureblooded, true-born sons."

"There are reasons Malakel and Tzuriel are not suited to be my heir, which we can discuss later." They stopped on the further end of the gardens and his father turned to face the manor. "She means everything to you."

Cassiel looked at where Dyna stood among their friends, laughing at something Zev said. She looked so happy and beautiful, simply radiating. The clouds parted, bathing the courtyard in warm sunlight, as though to highlight the center of his world.

His life had always been unstable, with no solid course. The moment Dyna accepted him, there had been no other possibility that didn't include her. Perhaps there never had been. He had done everything to push her away, to be harsh and difficult, to the point of being despised. And yet she still offered her hand when he tried to run. Listened when it was so hard to speak. Cried for him when he couldn't.

That was the difference between being a burden and being wanted.

"She does," Cassiel said softly.

His father grew serious. "Now, imagine her vanishing when she is cut down."

The vivid image played horribly in his mind. Flames flared out of his body and melted the snow at his feet. The instinct to destroy surged like a feral animal. His head snapped toward movement on his right. Amriel halted, his expression dark, hand primed on his weapon.

Cassiel let out a snarl. He was filled with the sudden urge to kill the Celestial, instinct having marked him as a threat.

Yoel waved his guard back, looking at him curiously. "All it took was a suggestion to activate your flame. We are standing quite aways from Dynalya, and made no attempt to approach her, but we became your targets."

Cassiel exhaled sharply and his fire vanished. "What was the point of that? I could have harmed you."

"I am testing a theory." He nodded to where Sowmya stood by the manor doors. "The lieutenant is sworn to you and to your mate. She would never harm Dynalya, but imagine her doing so while suppressing the instinct to attack."

Flames instantly sprouted from his fists. Cassiel tried to hold back his power, but his veins burned from the strain. The fire slowly spread from his feet, inching toward the manor. It didn't matter who it was. His instinct to protect would prevail, and Cassiel doubted it could be controlled. If this was how he reacted with someone they trusted, how would he react when it was a diplomat or a noble who looked at Dyna the wrong way?

"Cease to resist," his father said. "Allow the force to flow through you. Balance can only be found when you move with the current of the fire and not against it. Accept it. To become one, there is only one way. Be the flame."

Cassiel glowered at him dully. "What does that even mean?"

Captain Yelrakel cleared her throat. "It means your fire must be allowed to move freely with you, Your Highness, while maintaining control. Don't subdue it. Let it flow and call it back."

She had already trained him to do that. Cassiel made the flames swivel around his body before extinguishing them into smoke. His veins settled.

"You are right. He has no problem wielding it," his father said thoughtfully.

The captain nodded. "Yes, Your Majesty, but summoning had never been the issue."

Containing it was.

"I prefer you not to speak about me while I'm standing right here," Cassiel said, crossing his arms. "Clearly, the issue is me. If I cannot resolve it, will you have Uncle put witch bangles on me again?"

His father's brow furrowed, and he glanced at the manor. "No...Nothing good would come from containing your power, and bangles would not stop you. Controlling your flame is the way."

He had easily burned through the bangles before. Other than Skath metal, nothing else could resist Seraph fire. "What if it's impossible?"

"Impossible is only an opinion." Yoel canted his head as he looked past him. "The one to control your flame is not you."

Cassiel followed his stare to Dyna as she and Lucenna began their morning magic lessons. She moved to the far end of the courtyard from the others, so they would be out of the blast area.

The day in the commons, when he had gone after his brother, he'd been so enraged nothing would have stopped him if she hadn't arrived. Her voice pulled him back from his feral madness, and she had walked through his flame to reach him.

Unscathed.

"Dyna...can touch my fire," he admitted. "I don't know why."

"Your fire will never burn her because Dynalya is your balance. Two parts of one soul. Only she can quell it."

Sensing his stare, Dyna smiled at him, and it held the light of a thousand stars.

You were made for me and I for you...

"How could you possibly know that?" Cassiel asked, turning to him with narrowed eyes. "There is no other pre-recorded mention of a Seraph fire wielder in our history, other than King *Kāhssiel*. When we were in Hermon, I visited the libraries to research on my new ability and to learn what caused him to harm his people. All that was mentioned was that fire consumed him, turning him into some sort of beast that could not be stopped. The armies banded together to fight him."

Yoel and Yelrakel exchanged a look.

"What are you not telling me?"

His father nodded to the captain and his Royal Guard. They bowed and left. He went to sit on a bench and motioned Cassiel to join him.

"You know, it was your mother who chose your name," Yoel said, looking out at the barren forest. "It means 'the speed of *Elyōn* and guardian of the Heavens'. She liked that for you. A great defender. I merely found it honorable to name you after our first king, but now I wonder if it was indeed the will of fate."

Gentle flurries blew past them, catching in his father's hair. "The reason you do not find the full story is the same reason any kingdom fabricates history. To hide their shame. King *Kāhssiel* was a benevolent leader, but very powerful. Nothing could oppose his Seraph fire. His compulsion took root with a mere thought. He was strong and fast, and he had other gifts that our people lost when they fell here. The reason he had Seraph fire was because he was never Forsaken. He chose to come to the Mortal Realm to help guide our people back to the right path. Because of it, he was favored by *Elyōn* and made High King. It created an envy among his generals, and they secretly turned on him." His father exhaled a long sigh. "*Kāhssiel* had no weakness until the day he met his True Bonded. Unfortunately, she was human. While our people were not wary of humans yet, they found the union abhorrent. When she became with child, they called it an abomination and used it as an attempt to overthrow him. During an attack, *Kāhssiel* sent her away with one of his trusted generals, not knowing he would be the one to throw her off a cliff."

Something cold sank in Cassiel's chest. His mind repeated all the moments Dyna had nearly fallen to her death over and over. He couldn't imagine failing to catch her in time.

"The loss should have crippled *Kāhssiel*, if not outright killed him," his father said. "They failed to understand how much vengeance can drive a being. Without her, Seraph fire consumed him and he draped the world in a sea of flame."

Cassiel's throat bobbed. "How long did...?"

"He lived for a year after her loss. The longest ever recorded."

One year with that excruciating pain?

"He only perished once everyone involved in her death was dead."

Something tugged at Cassiel's mind, but he couldn't quite grasp it. Something he struggled to remember.

"Her name?" he whispered, his throat clamping. "What was the name of his mate?"

Yoel looked at him in a way that made him hold his breath. "Sheli."

The air whooshed out of him, ice sinking through every corner of his body. *Lev sheli.* The affection he called Dyna by. His mind was spinning.

Cassiel had to swallow to make his voice work. "If you are attempting to tell me I am the reincarnation of some mad king, this conversation is finished. Whatever rumors you heard in Hermon were conjured by predisposed nobles desiring to slander my name. My abilities are a coincidence, nothing more."

His father didn't argue. He traced shapes in the snow that coated the stone bench. "I have come to find life is made up of coincidences. A monsoon blew through Hilos on the day I was to wed. It caused a shipwreck on our shores with only one survivor. Your mother. When I found her, I knew she was meant to be mine, but I was already bonded and it was too late." He lowered his head, dejection crossing his face. "I brought her to North Star, where she was taken in by a family descended from Lunar mages."

Everything in Cassiel was shaking. This was another story with an unhappy ending. The urge to flee had him leaping off that bench.

"The Astrons."

Cassiel halted. His shaky breath fogged in the air. He kept his back to his father, not wanting to look at him even if he couldn't stop himself from listening.

"Some time passed before we met again, fell in love, and had you. When you were a year old, Elia brought you to meet her adopted family. When your surrogate aunt embraced you, your eyes glowed blue with flame. Shortly after, she gave birth to a baby girl with bright red hair."

He had to lean on a tree to hold himself up.

"Elia knew what it meant and what tragedy would follow once the Realms realized who you were. So she went to Mount Ida in search of a cure for your Seraph fire. To spare you from the inevitable."

Cassiel sank against the tree's trunk. Anguish tore through his chest. He had always known she left because of him, because of what he was.

As a child, he remembered her rambling about wings and preserving life. He'd always assumed she meant for herself. Now he knew how unreliable memory could be.

"Why didn't you go after her?"

"I tried, but she had hidden herself from me. Elia did not want to be found. Perhaps because she was angry with me for not believing her. I did not want to believe it." Yoel closed his eyes. "I became consumed with trying to locate the island so I could bring her back. The night of the winter solstice, I realized I had not only forgotten about you, I had neglected to protect you. And once again, I was too late."

Cassiel's body spasmed with the phantom slash of claws ripping through his chest. He sank to his knees. "How much...how much time do you have?" he asked, staring blankly at the snow.

"Perhaps another year."

Only then was he able to take a full breath since yesterday.

They still had time.

"I admit, I was selfish," his father said. "When I gave you my lifetime, I held on to ten years because I wanted to see who you would become. I did, and yes, I am proud." Cassiel met his gaze, and a sad smile touched on his father's face. "Like you, I also conveyed to my father I did not want to be king. I considered shearing my wings to be free to live how I wished. In time, I found my path, and so will you. A true leader does not seek greatness. They are called to it. If you choose not to heed the call, you will still be who you have always been. My son."

They had lost so much time to secrets and misunderstandings. Wedged between resentment and affliction. His parents sacrificed everything for him, and he had resented them for it. The veil that had muddled his life lifted, and now all he felt was shame.

Cassiel fought the lump in his throat. "You...you let me hate you."

703

Yoel sighed. "It's what I deserved for what you sustained. My greatest sin was perhaps separating you from Dynalya. It was essentially a form of rejecting your mate. That pain left you both catatonic for days. Had there been a bond, it might have broken you. When you woke, your Seraph fire had fallen dormant, and you looked empty inside. I thought if I erased that night and sent you to Hermon while she remained in North Star, it would change your fates. Yet your paths crossed once again by a *Hyalus* tree. It was a sign from *Elyōn* that I could not stop your destiny. I could only prepare you for it."

Cassiel never understood the meaning of destiny, and he didn't understand it now, but some dastardly Druid once told him that was the thing about fate.

Nothing was ever certain.

"You asked me why it had to be you." His father placed a hand on his shoulder. "The answer is simple. The throne has always been yours."

The declaration sent an electrical charge through Cassiel's chest, and with it a sudden clarity. The feral animosity that surged at any threat against Dyna wasn't merely because of their bond. It was because he had lost her before in their past life. "All of this began because of who I am. Now that the Realms know I have the power to destroy them, someone is after my mate merely to take me down. I will obliterate whoever comes for her. I will do whatever it takes to keep her safe, even if that means disappearing, because I have someone precious to protect."

"Going into hiding won't stop him."

Cassiel stilled, recalling something his father had said yesterday. *Someone sent you to North Star, but it was not her.*

"You know who it is."

But Yoel was no longer looking at him. His wide eyes stared at something past his shoulder. Cassiel whipped around. At first, he didn't know what he was looking at. A refraction of light flashed on the roof of the manor as if reflecting on something. It flickered back and forth in a steady rhythm.

Like a signal calling to the sky.

"It's too late to run," his father said grimly.

The town's horn blared in the distance three times. It was the only warning they got before a host of armed Celestials blotted out the sun.

CHAPTER 100

Dynalya

Everything around Dyna faded to a dull hum, muffling the shout of her mate. She looked up at the mass of Skath Celestials diving for her like a flock of white crows. They had waited until she was out in the open and apart from the others. Her Guardians and Sowmya ran for her, but they were too far. Cassiel's cry reverberated through the bond. He raced for her with horror on his face.

His fear shook the bond to her very soul.

But for once, she wasn't afraid.

She was furious.

They had their happiness. Their peace. She would be damned if she let anyone take that from her. If bloodying her hands was the cost of protecting her future with Cassiel, then she would pay it—even if it meant dirtying her soul.

Dyna sprinted for him.

Her veins surged with magic, her vision flooding green. Cassiel instantly understood. His body flared with those beautiful cerulean flames, his expression switching to enraged determination. The host descended on them right as their hands met. A massive blast ripped out. Blue and green fire roared into the sky and blew through the first unit, disintegrating them to ash and embers. The detonation threw the remaining Celestials back through the sky with a scattering of feathers.

Cassiel crashed into her. His warm arms clamped around her body, looking her over wildly. "Are you hurt?"

"I'm all right," she assured him.

The Valkyrie surrounded them defensively, taking out their shields and weapons. Zev shifted in a snarling mass, Rawn and Lucenna arming themselves with sword and magic.

"Take her back inside now," Cassiel barked at Sowmya, but she stepped back.

"I'm not going anywhere," Dyna said. She let her cloak drop and her sword sang as she drew it free. "I will not cower and I will not bend. Let them come."

Cassiel stared at her for a stunned moment before his expression filled with admiration. This was her fight as much as his. His thumb brushed her chin. One light swipe of affection and approval. Because he understood her and what she would do.

For them.

Tossing off his enchanted coat, Cassiel unsheathed *Esh Shamayim*. Seraph fire licked along the blade, its heat warping the air. Rawn, Lucenna, and Zev came to her side. Her Guardians. Her friends. They would fight with her, too.

"We will cover the ground," Rawn said, and they all nodded.

King Yoel joined them, giving her a wink. "*Elyōn* has blessed me with one last fight before I go."

"Fates willing, this will not be your last," Dyna said.

At Yelrakel's command, the Valkyrie lined up in formation. They stood at attention, helmets on, sunlight glinting off their scaled armor and grieves.

Ready for war.

Sowmya, Zekiel, and the twenty members of her personal Royal Guard broke out of the lineup. They came to stand behind her. Their duty was to protect her first.

Dyna gripped her sword's hilt, and they all looked up at the small army that came for them. At least five hundred armored Celestials. Against two hundred Valkyries. The odds were unfavorable, but Dyna had seen how fierce the females fought. They were an unstoppable force.

And so are you. Cassiel's rich voice fluttered through her mind.

His hard silver eyes trained on someone among the mass of white wings. On the one leading the host of Celestials. He was a broad male with short hair and steel-plated armor, holding a fire shield. He flashed her mate a sneer before putting on his helmet.

"Lord Hallel," Cassiel growled. "He brought his Vanguard."

King Yoel frowned. "So it would seem."

Had he expected someone else?

But this wasn't another challenge. Lord Hallel was breaking the peace treaty among the Realms for only one reason. This was a coup.

706

He wants Hilos. She sent the thought to Cassiel.

His chin dipped in a nod. *I suspect the same.*

Lord Jophiel strode to them as one of the Valkyrie handed him a sword. "Feels like old times." He came to his brother's side. "I hope you can keep up, old bird."

"Old bird?" Yoel chuckled. "I will show you old. Try not to fall behind."

Cassiel turned to his father. They stood face to face, twin blades of Seraph fire in their hands. They shared a smirk. Albeit cold and determined, it was united. He walked to the front of the Legion with his father and uncle at his side.

Her mate stood tall. Shoulders back, wings like a cloak of black smoke. He radiated strength and command, an esteem they all felt.

He looked like a King.

"Valkyrie!" Cassiel called, and they beat their swords once against their shields in response. "Skath has betrayed the crown. Kindly escort them through the Gates."

They hooted a cry and shot into the sky with him.

They were a storm of gold, aiming for the cloud of silver speeding toward them. They clashed and their colors blended into each other like paint, feathers bursting out.

Dyna kept an eye on her mate.

Cassiel was a comet of vivid blue rounding through the air. He blasted into the right flank, and Celestials were thrown back in his wake. Whoever was caught by his flame or blade plummeted from the sky and vanished into a flare of white light before they hit the ground.

Jophiel was graceful in his movements. Fluid as he soared through the sky, taking down opponents two or three at a time. Yoel let them come to him. He swept them back with his sword or with a flick of his hand before they ever touched him. The Skath Celestials around him began fighting each other as he wove through their minds with his compulsion.

The Valkyrie also battled with a stunning, wild aggression. They were better and faster—but outnumbered. For every three males they felled, one of theirs went down.

Lord Hallel cleaved through them with the force of a scythe. He was steadfast and heartless, severing wings from their bodies, so they would drop to their deaths. Dyna and Lucenna tried to catch them with their magic, but some they missed. The sound their bodies made when they hit the ground collided against her being.

Feathers fluttered down as Celestials kept falling from the sky, each one vanishing into light. The viciousness, the slaughter of it all, made Dyna's vision blur and her trembling jaw set with ire. Her heart raced wildly with Death taking souls by the hundreds.

She hated simply standing in the courtyard. She wanted to be up there. Currents of Essence hummed in her body, glowing on her skin, eager to be used.

Jophiel and Yoel continued fighting their way through the Vanguard, and they split the front lines. They were making a path, she realized. For Cassiel.

He was coated in blood and ash, his black wings gleaming in the sunlight. It seemed like all paused to see him. To watch as a cerulean glow wrapped him in a plume of flame. His wings rode on a tide of blue embers as he soared up through the opening—straight for Lord Hallel.

Cassiel slammed into him, becoming a blue beam as they shot through the sky. But Lord Hallel took the brunt of it with his shield. They broke apart and came at each other in a clash of swords.

Out of all the suspects behind her attempted assassination, Lord Hallel had been low on Dyna's list. His Realm was small. No matter his skill as a warrior, his army couldn't withstand a full affront against Hilos. It didn't make sense.

The horn blared through the air again.

More Skath Celestials had come—and they were flying right for the courtyard.

"Finally," Lucenna sneered.

Vivid purple light blazed around her silhouette. Her long white hair whipped around her in the rising wind as electricity radiated over her hands, up her arms, and neck. The power crackling in the air prickled against Dyna's Essence and hers responded in kind.

She felt Cassiel's attention switch to her as green light coiled up her arms to her shoulders. Dyna whirled her sword and her power hummed inside of her.

Her Royal Guard ran ahead with her Guardians to meet them, Rawn leading the charge. Skath Celestials teemed the courtyard in white flame and were hit with an onslaught of purple and green.

Dyna swept her blade and cast out spells, meeting every attack that came. She was sure in her movements honed into her through weeks of training. It felt as though she was made for this. A Celestial swung his sword for her head and it clashed against her enchanted shield. Dyna thrust her blade through his stomach before Sowmya wrenched him away. Another male flew at her. She captured him in the air with her Essence and threw him to Zev, who caught the Celestial by the throat and tore it free.

Her Guardians kept to her flank, taking down enemies all around her. The clang of steel and cries of pain rang out. The scent of blood and smoke filled the courtyard, white light constantly flashing in her vision.

Her Royal Guard was falling.

For all their power, they didn't have the numbers.

Lord Hallel bellowed a command. Half the Vanguard swarmed Cassiel—and the other half flew for her. They were taking their chance to kill her now.

Dyna and Lucenna stood shoulder to shoulder as they threw a barrage of massive attacks to take them out of the sky. The world shook, and the air hissed with their coalescing spears of lightning and flame. Cassiel fought with everything he had to reach her, but the flock caged him.

Her arms trembled with the attacks never ending. She read the exhaustion on Lucenna's face. They strained under the force of their magic. Power spilled from them in droves, quickly draining their Essence. She choked on the smoke of burning trees and feathers—

Feathers!

Dyna searched for ones that weren't scorched. When she found two, she called them to her, handing one to Lucenna. The glow in the sorceress's eyes brightened as it recharged them. All of Dyna's Essence channels opened. Green flooded her vision and magic spiraled up her arms with a vengeance, building and burning as it invaded her being.

Lucenna faced the courtyard, thunder rolling overhead. Dyna aimed her hands at the sky and screamed as she released her sea of green flame. It roared into the air and ripped through half the Vanguard, annihilating them into cinders. She slumped back and dropped to the ground.

That was it. She couldn't risk using more spells like that without harming herself.

Heavy steps clanked on stone, steel screeching in their wake. She blinked up through her blurry vision. Lord Hallel strode through the courtyard as fighting continued all around them. He dragged his sword along the cobblestone, shooting out sparks. He grinned at her through his helmet, knowing she was out of magic. Dyna searched wildly for her weapon.

Cassiel landed in front of her with a *boom.*

Flames skittered out, taking out anything in its path. His fire cleaved through Skath Celestials, brimming into the crevices of their armor and disintegrating them where they stood. Lord Hallel dodged his attack and flew back.

Cassiel spun to her, his eyes dancing with blue flame. He pulled her up, but her legs gave out. His arm clamped around her waist. "Get Dyna out of here!" he shouted at someone past her shoulder.

No.

Sowmya grabbed her arm, but she shook her off. "No. I'm not—"

"Dyna, please listen to me," Cassiel said, taking her shoulders. "There are too many of them. You did so well, but now I need you to go. I need you safe. If you die, we all do."

Because then he would fall, and without him, the battle would be lost.

The desperation in his voice, his fear of losing her, subdued Dyna's protests all at once. He pressed a crushing kiss to her mouth.

"Take her," Cassiel told Sowmya, his shaking hand clutching hers. "Hide her until the skies are clear. If I don't return by nightfall, fly her to Hermon. Now go and protect the future High Queen of Hilos."

Dyna bit back a sob.

She was pulled away, and their hands broke free. Cassiel leaped into the air for the remaining Vanguard. He bellowed out a roar, fire wrapping around his body.

Zev, Rawn, and Lucenna moved to follow her, but Dyna shook her head. "Stay with him."

She needed to protect her mate, too.

CHAPTER 101

Dynalya

They towed Dyna away from the battlefield. Sowmya kept her covered, pressing her tightly against the cold sharpness of her armor. Janel and Zekiel followed on their heels. The Royal Guard fought their way through the courtyard as they headed for the forest. Blasts of fire and spells provided extra coverage, taking down anyone who tried to go after them.

Her sword. She forgot her sword somewhere, but it was too late to get it.

Sowmya got her past the tree line into the forest and told her to run. They made it several feet when the ground seemed to shake again. This time it was with the rumble of racing horses. Dyna spun, catching only a glimpse of Klyde leading the Skelling Mercenaries into the courtyard. A clash of swords rang out.

"Oh, thank the God of Urn," Dyna said. "He brought reinforcements. We can go back—"

Arrows rained from above, zipping past her face.

Janelle went down. She fell at Dyna's feet, staring blankly at the sky with an arrow through her eye.

Dyna cried out. Sowmya dove to cover her, red wings snapping out like a shield. Her body spasmed with each arrow that pierced her through.

"Sowmya!" Dyna screamed.

The Valkyrie stumbled, blood dripping from her mouth. She gave her a bloodied grin and readied her glaive, blue flames spiraling around the blade.

"Go, my lady," Sowmya said, turning to face the group of Skath Celestials coming. She stood tall, even with the many arrows protruding from her back and wings. "I will deal with this."

"What? No!"

Zekiel's arm yanked Dyna back by the waist, hauling her away from her loyal guard. She quickly fell out of view behind the trees.

"Sowmya!"

"Leave her. More will come!" Zekiel urged. "I am charged with protecting you. Please come this way."

Dyna reluctantly followed him as they ran into the forest. The sounds of clashing steel and the veil of smoke and ash faded beneath the chill of snow. They ran and ran, the sound of her heart beating in her skull. The hem of her dress grew heavy as it was soaked through with melted snow.

Cassiel had closed the bond. She would give anything to feel him right now. What if, by running, she had left him to die?

Dyna tripped on a tear in her dress. Her ankle buckled, and she tumbled, leaving her crown to plop into the snow.

"You wore a crown," Zekiel said, and she thought he might have sounded a little derisive.

"Well, I didn't have time to put it away, did I?" Dyna scoffed to herself, pushing back on her hands and knees. She felt silly putting it back on now. That morning, she'd contemplated what it would mean to wear a crown before an army came to make sure she didn't. "Perhaps it fits the occasion."

"I suppose it does." Zekiel turned to go and something slipped out of his pocket.

Dyna picked it up, frowning. "Why do you have a mirror?"

"For my vanity." Zekiel snatched it away, not bothering to help her stand.

Putting any weight on her ankle made her hiss. She gripped a tree for support.

"We have to keep moving." He rushed past her and the scent of lemons came to Dyna again. It was so startling after smelling only blood and smoke that it made her head hurt.

"I need a moment."

He kept going.

"Zekiel."

"Hurry," he tossed her way sharply. "There is no time for your needless complaints."

The way he spoke to her was like a slap to the face. It was a ridiculous thing to worry about now, but Noemi was right. She couldn't allow this to continue.

"When I speak to you, I expect you to stop," Dyna said in full authority.

He halted.

"Your lack of decorum isn't appropriate. You will regard me accordingly when you speak. Do you understand?"

After a pause, Zekiel turned and deeply bowed. "Of course, Your Majesty. Pardon me. I was concerned about your safety and I forgot myself. It will not happen again."

Dyna nodded. "Please lead the way."

She limped on her bad ankle as they hurried onward to the north. Where did he plan to hide her when there wasn't much in this direction but the bluffs and the pond? Lucenna had mentioned the old dungeons were near here. They could hide in there.

The wind blew through her dress, and she shivered, rubbing her bare arms. Again, she caught a citrus scent. Why was it familiar? She had smelled it before, now that she thought of it. Where...?

Memories came to her in fragments. Malakel's sneer in the hallway. Hilos guards in the shadows. The shallow cave on the side of the Hermon mountain.

The night she'd been taken, only one male spoke, but there had been two in the cave, along with that scent. And now she knew what it was.

They left the forest and came to the pond. Zekiel searched the sky.

"You must have trouble sleeping," Dyna said, opening the bond. She let her thoughts and voice project to Cassiel. "Verbena oil is used to treat insomnia, and it has a very distinct smell of lemons."

Zekiel stilled.

"You were there that night in the cave. It was Amriel who abducted me, but you were there."

In answer to the revelation, the dark flare of Cassiel's mind met hers. *Where are you?* His voice was a savage growl.

The pond.

The battle is won. We're coming. Keep him talking.

She gave herself a second to feel relief before steeling her resolve.

"Are you waiting for Amriel again?" Dyna backed away as Zekiel faced her. "He must be the one to do the dirty work. You're merely the coward who breaks the wings of tied up females, the one who lurks in dark hallways at night—and who hides on the roof to signal our enemies with a mirror."

Cassiel's curse blared in her mind.

"Then there is silent Amriel," she continued, backing away further. "The guard who never speaks because he spoke to me before and couldn't risk me recognizing him. But he wasn't the one who spoke the night of the festival. This plan came from above you."

Zekiel narrowed his eyes, confirming her suspicion. However, he wasn't a Skath Celestial.

I don't think he serves Lord Hallel. She told her mate. *Someone else sent him here. Get him to admit who.*

"Do you know it's rather easy to guess when you are communicating with that Nephilim? You always wear a stupid little smile." Zekiel's blue eyes became as brisk and lifeless as the ice at her feet. His once kind expression peeled off like a mask, and she saw clearly her mistake.

Amriel could have killed her in Cassiel's room back in the castle. Instead, she'd been taken to Zekiel because he was the one she should have feared. All the times she'd been hurt by Tarn and Malakel had been to get something they wanted.

Zekiel would hurt her because he wanted to.

Dyna swallowed. "You were sent to kill me."

"Yes." He smiled, and there was no kindness in it. Only sheer elation at the thought of ending her life.

"Why? By who?"

Zekiel tsked, wagging a finger that he wouldn't say. But Dyna had two guesses in mind. Two Lords close to the royal family who stood to gain from this coup and a throne for the taking.

"All you need to know is that your death will return peace to the Realms. Don't resist, and I promise it will be quick and painless." He gave her a mocking bow. "*Your Majesty.*"

The last of Dyna's Essence powered inside of her and came to life at her fingertips. She decided then and there only one of them was waking to see tomorrow, because Cassiel wouldn't reach her in time.

Losing what they had wasn't an option. Even she fell, she still wouldn't be beaten.

Dyna filled her trembling hands with green flame. "You think I fear Death? I have faced it several times. By now, I would like to think we're familiar acquaintances."

Zekiel laughed as he prowled forward. "That's the only thing about you I mildly liked. You face the direst of problems with courage, even if you don't feel brave."

Dyna tossed out a flare, but he was too fast. One second he was several feet away, the next, Zekiel flew at her. She ducked past his knife and punched him with a blast of magic. He crashed into a tall boulder but immediately stood as if he felt nothing at all. The burn in his chest healed in seconds.

Take his wings! Cassiel shouted.

She threw out spell after spell, aiming for his feathers, but Zekiel caught on. He sped past her next attack and slammed her face into a tree. Dyna's crown ripped into her temple, pain bursting in her skull. She dropped like a sack. Her vision swam and her ears rang. Warm liquid leaked down her cheek, splattering bright red in the snow.

Dyna!

She whimpered, desperately calling on her Essence. A boot rammed into her stomach. The air shot out of her and she gasped a weak cry. Cassiel's furious snarl thundered in her head.

Get up! She internally shouted at herself, but she couldn't move. The blow had stolen the strength from her body. She fought to recover the breath knocked out of her.

Zekiel grabbed her ankle, and her Essence vanished, leaving her cold and empty. He dragged her limp body away. The soft cushion of snow was replaced by hard ice.

"He wanted you tossed over the cliffs, but I prefer a more poetic death," Zekiel said casually. "They say drowning is peaceful once you stop fighting. Well, for your sake, I hope it's true."

Dyna threw out a kick and it connected. Zekiel grunted, but instead of letting her go, he twisted her leg and she felt the bone snap. She screamed at the white hot pain ripping through her. His fist slammed into her face and the blow left her stunned on the frozen lake. Her vision danced with sparks, ears ringing.

Tears sprang into her eyes. At the pain. At the loss of her quest. And the impending demise that would steal her away from Cassiel.

His unbridled rage echoed the roar in the distance.

Her loss would break him, and in turn, break the Realms.

"He's...going to kill you," Dyna laughed weakly, the taste of blood coating her tongue. Her trembling fingers reached for her thigh. "He's going to kill you all."

"Soon, he will no longer be a threat," Zekiel said.

She felt a sudden burst of heat by her face. He raised his divine sword and stabbed the ice. Cracks shot out as it fractured, the white flames cutting through it until she heard the slosh of water.

Zekiel lifted her battered body and held her above the dark hole in the middle of the frozen pond. "My Lord bids you well."

Dyna managed to turn her head to look at him. "I will be sure," she murmured. "To send Lord Raziel my regards."

Zekiel's eyes widened.

She had guessed right, and it bought her a mere second.

Dyna slashed at him with her knife. Red spilled from the slit in Zekiel's pale neck, trailing down to his collar. His legs swayed and arms slacked.

Then she fell.

Her body plunged into the frigid depths. Needles speared her skin as it stole her warmth and the little air she had left. She gasped, and the water forced itself into her throat. Dyna reached for the fading light, urging her sinking body to swim, but the weight of the dress dragged her under.

Her lungs burned to breathe and her muscles locked up. She flailed uselessly, the water rapidly claiming all the feeling in her limbs. The pain faded as she went numb.

There was no fear here, only a lonely sadness.

She continued to gently descend, mourning again everything she would lose. Her family. Her future with the one she loved.

She didn't want to die. Not like this. But the panic ebbed with the last burble of air leaving her lips. Every nerve lost feeling, leaving her to float away.

She heard a voice, so pure and ethereal. It encompassed her mind and moved deep in her soul. Commanding her attention. *Dynalya!*

Bright blue light flared out in the dark and from it came Cassiel's face, his flawless features contorted in desperation.

He dove for her. *Swim!*

It's all right, she tried to tell him, managing a faint smile. *I'm right here.*

His voice cried out her name. His hand extended out as he dove, but the water caved in on her, and swallowed her in darkness.

CHAPTER 102

Cassiel

The pond was a frozen void. Cassiel cast out his flames, and they illuminated the trail of blood leading to Dyna's sinking body. She wasn't kicking or flailing. Only sinking. Diving as fast as he could, Cassiel begged her to swim. To fight. Her incoherent thoughts barely reached him. She smiled, trying to comfort him as if she knew this was the end.

Don't stop fighting!

Cassiel caught Dyna and instantly felt her gown weigh them down. He ripped open the bodice, yanking it off her. Underneath was her fae armor. Kicking off the lakebed, he swam toward the light with her in his arms. He broke the surface with a coughing gasp. The ice had melted with the blast of his fire. It forced him to kick for the shore. Their friends ran to meet them as the Valkyrie swooped down to join. Sowmya came limping out of the trees with Yelrakel's help, ripping arrows out of her wings.

"Take her!" Cassiel said once he reached the bank.

Zev grabbed Dyna and laid her over the coat Cassiel had left in the snow. He dragged himself out next to her. She was beaten and bloody, her lips frozen blue. So deathly pale, she already looked dead. Her broken leg was bent at an odd angle.

"Gods, what happened?" Lucenna exclaimed.

"The guard," Cassiel growled, glaring at Zekiel's body left on the frozen pond. Crystalized blood pooled around him.

Lucenna removed the water from Dyna's lungs. She still didn't move. Cassiel grabbed her wrist, checking for a pulse, but their bond was weakening.

He pressed an ear to her chest, listening for her heartbeat. Terror filled him when he didn't hear it.

"She's not breathing!"

"She's frozen," Klyde said behind them. "You need to resuscitate her."

Zev reached for her, but Cassiel shoved his hands away. He leaned Dyna's head back, sealed her icy lips with his, and forced air into her lungs. He pumped her chest in counts of three as she had taught him, then continued giving her air.

"Don't you dare die," he told her angrily between breaths.

Despair sunk in Cassiel's bones as he frantically worked on his mate. Her body jerked with each pump against her chest. He stared at her ashen face for any sign of life, but she was motionless.

"The bond?" Zev asked him frantically.

Still there. Fractured and fading. Cassiel laid his head over her chest, searching for a heartbeat. He found none.

"The bond!" Zev shouted.

"It's—" Cassiel grunted in pain, slapping a hand over his chest at the puncture of agony. It was so painful he only stayed conscious out of sheer desperation. "Come back, *lev sheli*," he begged as he pumped her heart.

Zev stared at her. "She...she's..."

"Don't say it," Cassiel growled.

Dyna looked to be asleep, but she was as white as a ghost. He continued anxiously working on her. Air. Compress. Air. Compress. Her ribs cracked beneath his force.

Cassiel groaned a painful cry at the bond fracturing further. "You are not allowed to die, Dyna. You said you would hear me, so listen to my voice. Come back to me. Come on, damn it! *Please!*"

She heaved a gasping cough, and water gurgled out of her mouth. The sound nearly toppled him. Everyone exhaled audibility with relief.

Cassiel rolled her over and patted her back. *"Lev sheli,"* he breathed and caressed her cold cheeks. "Open your eyes for me, love."

Her lashes fluttered weakly. He took her face and pleaded for her to look at him.

"Cassiel..." she faintly rasped, too weak to open her eyes.

He squeezed her tight against him. "Stupid human, you nearly left me again," his voice cracked. He thought she was uncontrollably shivering, but it was his body shaking against hers.

"I heard you..." Was all Dyna said before falling unconscious again.

Cassiel wrapped her up in his coat and brushed the wet hair from her face. His silhouette flared with his fire and he placed a hand over her chest, willing her his heat and taking her pain.

Dyna's crown laid half buried in the snow some distance away, the glinting sapphires stained with her blood. It filled him with a vicious rage. He may as well have delivered her to them himself. The others backed away as the flames licked along the ground in a circle around them, its intense heat drying his clothes and hair.

"Your Highness," one of the Valkyrie called to him, where she and another inspected Zekiel's body. "My Lady slit his throat, but he's still alive."

He was immensely content to hear that. "Good. Take him to the dungeon."

The Valkyrie lifted the traitor and carried him off the lake.

Whether Dyna forgot the only way to kill them was through the head or the heart, or if it was intentional, he now had the chance to deal with Zekiel himself.

Cassiel looked at Yelrakel. "Where is my father?"

"As soon as Skath retreated, Amriel insisted the High King be taken to his chambers as a precaution."

His eyes widened.

Amriel.

"Keep her warm," he told Zev. "Valkyrie, with me!"

Cassiel leaped into the sky. He raced for the manor, flying as fast as he could over the crop of trees. Overwhelming fear warned he would be too late. Minutes seemed to drag until he left the forest. The courtyard was littered with ash, feathers, and blood. Only the mercenaries and remaining Valkyrie were left standing. He rounded the manor for the fourth floor tower to his father's chambers. He spotted him through the windows, appearing to be arguing with his uncle. They were perfectly fine. Amriel must have flown off as soon as he realized Zekiel was compromised.

Cassiel landed on the balcony and ran into the room. "Father."

Yoel turned to him, his mouth curving with the beginnings of a smile, before shock wiped it out.

Too late did he notice the form swooping out of the shadows. Cassiel turned, a flaming sword already coming for him.

"No!" his father's shout rang through the room.

A force tore Cassiel away, and he crashed into the bookcase. His head spun, vision skewed as he tried to sit up. Blood splattered on the ground at his feet. Lord Jophiel choked on a cry, and Cassiel looked up. He froze, his mind and heart stopping. Amriel's blade—the blow meant for him—was pierced through his father's chest.

The Valkyrie crashed through the windows, and Yelrakel tackled Amriel. Cassiel caught his father's falling body, and they sank to the floor together. Yoel heaved a wet cough, blood trickling from his mouth. "Dyna?"

"S-she's alive..." Cassiel said shakily.

He smiled and sighed. "I'm glad."

Cassiel's fingers trembled as he lifted his father's coat to see the wound on his chest. It wasn't healing. Blood continued to spill, painting his clothing red. His heart. It must have been...

Still, Cassiel cut his hand and poured blood over the wound. He willed it to heal. Prayed for it. His internal cry of torment reached into his chest and squeezed his lungs, desperate for a miracle, but like all the other times, *Elyōn* didn't hear him.

"The Gates..."

His father shook his head, already knowing what he would ask. "You cannot return a life that was given, son." Every breath was a struggle. A cruel pull against his ribs. "Most people live only once, but if you do it right, once is enough."

Cassiel shook, his vision blurring. "No, Father...you have to stay." He felt like a child again, saying what he had wanted to tell him all those years ago. "Please don't go. Don't leave me behind. I cannot do this without you."

"You can. I failed you, Cassiel, and I am so sorry for all of it. I am sorry that I have to leave you again, but I know you can do this. Whatever you face or whoever you become, your reign will bring our people a new future." Yoel's hand glowed bright against his face. "Some will resist. Some will bend. But in time, the Realms will fly with you. In time, you will help them...see..."

White light flared into Cassiel's vision, and the room faded from existence. His mind flashed with memories he didn't recognize. Memories of another lifetime he lived ages ago. Then he found himself in the castle gardens of Hilos.

The sound of distant, familiar laughter reached him, making his breath catch. Cassiel followed it down the gravel path through the flowering bushes, and he saw her. His mother. Her long black hair shone beneath the sun as she swayed beneath the fruit trees, her blue gown swishing around her bare feet. His mother smiled lovingly at the bundle in her arms, a baby with a head of dark hair. His father sat on a blanket in the grass, young and happy, watching them both with a soft look he had never seen before.

She nuzzled the baby's cheek and lifted him into the morning air. "My dear Cassiel, from the moment you arrived, you have been my joy and my blessing."

He inhaled a soft gasp and found himself back in the same room again. As the memory faded, the ascension passed to him. The power rushed through his veins, surging through every corner of his being. It returned the last missing piece of his soul and settled with a familiar weight. A crown of cerulean flames formed on Cassiel's head.

Yoel brushed the tears from his cheek as divine light shone around him. "Elia loved you so very much. If you find her...please tell her I kept my oath..."

Then his hand dropped. His chest fell still. Eyes emptying of life. Light blazed off his father's body, at last returning to Heaven's Gate. The light grew brighter until he was glowing as much as the sun. Then it faded.

And he was gone.

His father left him behind again, and in his absence, all Cassiel found was grief. His fists shook on the cold floor.

It wasn't supposed to be like this. They were supposed to try to understand each other, to recover that which they once lost. But now, that opportunity was lost, too.

It had been *taken* from him.

"Yoel was well loved by the Realms. We will mourn his loss," Jophiel said, his voice strained with emotion. "And by his grace, the divine reign has returned. *Elyōn*, bless the true High King of Hilos and the Four Celestial Realms."

As one, the Valkyrie and his uncle lowered to one knee, bowing their heads. "Long may he reign," they said.

Long may he reign...

It was an echo of what Cassiel had heard once before. It was said for every king, but the words disturbed him.

His ring was glowing.

"Every *Hyalus* tree is now lit in honor of you," his uncle said. "They are proclaiming the new sovereign to the Realms."

Exhaling a heavy breath, Cassiel rose to his feet and turned to his court. They waited for his first words. For the leadership that would pave the way of their future.

"This won't go unanswered," Cassiel said. "Whoever had a hand in this will learn that I am the new age." The promise blanketed over his sorrow, sealing the oath. "Valkyrie."

The warrior females stood at attention.

"Your King calls upon you. Not a command, but a request for your loyalty. Will you serve?"

The Valkyrie beat a fist over their hearts three times. The sound of metal against metal reverberated through the room.

"We have sworn fealty to the crown and now to you," Yelrakel said. "Our lives are yours, My King."

"Then I name you my Royal Legion, for I trust none other than you. Go, and spread word of the assassination of my father—and of my Queen."

Everyone stilled.

Cassiel straightened his shoulders. "As far as anyone knows, Dynalya Astron was killed today. You are all sworn to this secret upon the pain of death. That is my command. I deem it so at this hour. Thus my will be done."

They bowed. The Valkyrie soared off the balcony into the skies to do his bidding, except for Sowmya and Yelrakel.

Cassiel glanced at Amriel where they had him bound and gagged on the ground, Yelrakel's boot digging in his back. It cost him a great deal of restraint not to behead the male right there. Though his insides burned, his voice remained completely calm. "Make sure this traitor is comfortable in the dungeons until I'm ready to see him."

Yelrakel yanked Amriel to his feet.

"I want names. See that he gives them."

Her chin dipped in a dutiful nod, her severe expression promising to do what was needed. They dragged him away.

"I'm sorry you came into the throne this way," Lord Jophiel said, grief aging him as he looked at the spot where his brother vanished. All that was left were a few smears of red. "Yoel had imagined a different coronation for you."

Cassiel's ever-present flame cooled to ice with a coming decision. "As I'm sure those who sought to end me imagined a different outcome today."

"Cassiel, I know you are angry, but now is the time to mourn."

"I don't wish to mourn. All I want is blood." He left the room to find his friends waiting outside in the hall. From the looks on their faces, they knew what had happened.

"Lady Dyna is in your chambers," Rawn said softly, lowering his head. "We removed this from her ankle."

Cassiel briefly looked at what he was given. He put it in his pocket and entered the dark room with only the fireplace lit. Zev was there as his wolf, keeping guard at the foot of the bed. He offered a soft whine of condolence and silently slipped out of the room. Noemi stood from the chair next to the bed, bowing to him. The door shut quietly behind them.

He sat on the edge of the bed and held Dyna's small hand in his. He watched her chest rise and fall with steady breaths. Cuts and bruises riddled every part of her body. A bandage covered half of her face. Cassiel gently removed it to expose the torn flesh on the right side of her temple. Her eye was already blackening.

722

Taking the twin knife from his boot, he sliced his finger. Very carefully, he brushed his blood over the wound. He healed every hurt he could find one at a time, watching her skin weave itself until nothing was left but his dried blood.

Cassiel cradled Dyna's small hand in his. All of his life, he kept losing what mattered. It began with his mother, then his father, and his place in the world.

When she had stumbled into his life by some encounter of fate, he had finally gained something beautiful that was only his, but they nearly took her from him, too. It wouldn't end here. Like in their past life, Dyna's death was the cost of being with him.

For she was his treasure and his weakness.

The fear for her life surfaced again and uncovered a truth he had long known but didn't want to see.

She would never be safe with him.

Realizing what he had to do, a tear spilled down his cheek. Then another. And another. Until Cassiel folded over and wept.

CHAPTER 103

Cassiel

The snow crunched softly beneath Cassiel's boots as he passed by the frozen pond. Dyna's crown was still there, half buried in the snow. He picked it up and looked at the hole in the ice that had almost claimed her life. It was half frozen already. He squeezed the icy metal in his hand, and sapphires cut into his skin. Warm wetness seeped through his fingers, and it dripped off the crown onto the snow.

He kept walking through the bitter dusk. A torch in the distance marked his destination. Sowmya waited by the dungeon gates. He handed her the crown and went in. The stone corridor was dark and cold, home to cobwebs and skittering rats. He followed the dusty path to the torchlight spilling from the last cell at the end of the dungeon.

"The Royal Guards live to protect the royal family," Yelrakel's voice drifted to him, then the wet thud of a fist against flesh. "You both betrayed that."

"I protect the true bloodline, *Nephilim*," Amriel panted. "We renounce the half-breed and will do away with his witch whore. They will never sit on the throne—" He cut off in a scream, the sound carrying down the corridor.

Cassiel entered, and Yelrakel looked up from wiping her hands with a bloodied cloth. Amriel and Zekiel were tied to wooden chairs. Amriel moaned, his head hanging over his chest. Blood dripped from his wounds, and sweat glistened on his forehead. Knives jutted out of their wings to stop them from healing. It must have been the only way to get them to speak.

Yelrakel handed Cassiel a page smeared with ink and blood. The list was long and contained names from every Realm—Celestials placed in strategic positions—but none of them were high-ranking nobles. This had to be the work of a Lord. They won't give up that name easily.

Cassiel folded the page and tucked it into his coat. "Who sent you?" His voice echoed in the cell.

At their silence, Yelrakel thrust her fist into Amriel's jaw. "Your King speaks."

He grunted, raising his head. Even with his position, defiance simmered in his glare. "You are no king of mine. I will never bow to you."

Yelrakel viciously twisted the blades in his wings and yanked them out, tearing from him an agonizing cry. Cassiel gave her a look. She bowed and stepped out, her footsteps fading away.

"Who?" he asked again.

Zekiel laughed. "Is it not obvious? We were sent by those still loyal to the pure bloodline. It was an honor—"

Cassiel didn't look at him. With a single thought, he sealed Zekiel's mouth shut. With another, he hurled the guard across the cell, and his body crashed into the wall before crumbling to the ground.

"You must not value your life," Cassiel said, ignoring their shock at his power. "You know the sentence for regicide. No one will speak on your behalf. None will seek your pardon. You have been abandoned to this filthy cell. Left to my mercy."

Amriel's wings shuddered, his heavy breaths clouding in the air. He fought against his restraints, and the rope creaked from the force. "I knew the risks. I may die, but it will not end with me. That power your witch expelled in Hermon, we all felt it ripple through the Realms. Her magic is a beacon. You cannot hide her from us. We will not stop. We will come for her. The Queen will fall." He spat a clot of blood at Cassiel's feet, twisting harder in his seat. "Then we will come after you—*Kāhssiel*."

His old name elicited images of his previous lifetime. Days of fire and darkness, but there was also sunlight, and the sound of laughter, and warmth.

Snuffed out before he could fully bask in it.

"All of this began with your wretched breed," Amriel said, the venomous words dripping with hatred. "But your pestilence will not be tolerated. We will end you and keep doing so with every reincarnation. Your only purpose is to die!"

Amriel wrenched open his wings, and the rope snapped. He yanked out the hidden knife in his boot, but he never got the chance to attack. He stood still like stone, his arm frozen above him with the poised knife. Veins protruded from his reddening face, and his body shook with desperate resistance.

"Brave words for someone who reeks of fear," Cassiel said as he stepped backward into the shadows. "For someone who cannot move."

His compulsion had woven through every strand of the guard's mind like steel strands. When his father died, most of Cassiel's past memories had returned to him. He learned many things. Like the full extent of *Kāhssiel's* abilities. Of *his* abilities.

At his command, Amriel dropped to his knees.

"What was this about not bowing?" Cassiel mused. The torch fire vanished at a flick of his finger, and darkness enveloped them.

Their shallow breaths were loud in the cold quiet as they wildly searched for him. They were right to be afraid. These pureblood elitists had stolen his mate from him before, and this time, they stole his father. Their actions had uncovered a fury cleaved into his soul an era ago. It had split through him, opening into a vast abyss, and he found it was terrible and bottomless.

"I will tell you nothing, let alone scream," Amriel said. "I will gladly die before ever seeing the filth of human blood take the crown."

They both turned to him at the faint glow of his eyes

Cassiel's voice, devoid of any emotion, floated through the icy air. "Then die."

Flames flared from his feet and snaked for Amriel. It caught on his boots and crawled up his legs, bathing the walls in blue. He gritted his teeth against the pain, his chest heaving with rapid breaths. Pieces of blackened flesh flaked away like flurries in a breeze. Terror flashed in his eyes when he realized there would be no part of him left to return to Heaven's Gate. Flames consumed Amriel in a tall pyre, and he released a blood-curdling scream. The heat was so tremendous it warped the air. His screams cut off abruptly when he burst into a cloud of smoke and ash. Shimmering blue embers drifted down to land on the scorched black pile where he had once been.

Cassiel's attention fixed on Zekiel next.

The guard yelped when his body rose of its own accord. He jerked against the compulsion, but could do nothing as he marched forward. Sweat coated Zekiel's pale face. Though he tried his best to look unafraid, he couldn't disguise the rapid pulse in his neck.

"You hurt my wife," Cassiel said idly.

Bloody bone tore out of Zekiel's shin. He screamed through his clenched teeth. Then Cassiel broke his other leg, and he collapsed to his knees with another excruciating cry.

"This will not be quick. Nor will it be kind. Your death will be exactly what I consider *poetic*."

Cassiel laid a hand on Zekiel's chest and flames bloomed from his palm like the petals of a flower. He burned a hole through him—so...very...*slowly*. Slow enough for Zekiel's divine blood to keep him alive as Cassiel's fingers dug into his melting flesh. Every scream wrought was beautiful. The tones and pitches merging into a pleasing song created from his wrath. The fire eventually won and Zekiel's rib cage caved in like brittle paper.

Cassiel grabbed a hold of that scared, beating heart—and ripped it out.

The burning corpse dropped to his feet.

"Tell me," Cassiel asked the organ as it blackened, crumbling to ash in his hand. "Did you find the honor to your taste?"

There was no answer.

Not that one was expected.

The ash spilled through his fingers as he left the dungeon and passed through the rusted gates into the frozen landscape. His Valkyrie moved to their positions at his side and he strode back to the manor. Amriel's voice followed him into the dark.

We will not stop.

We will come for her.

The Queen will fall.

With each step, ice crept into Cassiel's veins, weaving through the flame. It demanded retribution. It swore to destroy. And he welcomed it.

Soon, the news of what happened here would spread throughout the Realms. He would make sure they knew one absolute thing. The High King now commanded a sea of divine flame, and beneath his ire, they would all burn.

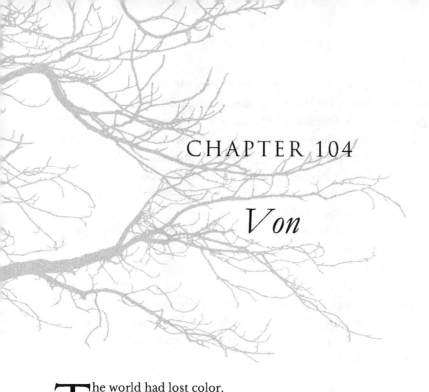

CHAPTER 104

Von

The world had lost color.

Everything was shrouded in shades of black and gray. One blending into the other in a depthless gradient. No end. No beginning. The bowels of the ship creaked as it swayed on the seas, though Von couldn't hear it. Not the drip of water leaking down the rusted cell bars. Not the scuttle of rats. Not the hazy hum of voices on the deck.

All he heard were the screams.

Over.

And over.

The blood that leaked from his ears had long dried into thin trails on the sides of his face. Von had beat them, tore at them with his nails to make the screams stop. They never did.

His stiff body had gone numb from the icy wet floor. He had no strength or will to move from the shadowed corner where he slumped against the wall, didn't bother reaching for the moldy bread left on a tray by his feet. He stared blankly at the rusted nail sticking out of a rotting plank.

On and on, she screamed.

And screamed.

Kill me. Please kill me. He sent the prayer to any god who would listen. His life had ended on those waves, consumed by flames. He didn't need it anymore. Why was he still alive?

Breaking and mending that which thee lacks.

What did he lack? What had killed his wife?

There was no sense of time, though it seemed to drag on endlessly as he listened to those horrid cries. Day and night were only marked by the cold in the air. Von's heart slowed further and his lungs struggled for breath. Then the coughs came and his vision grew hazy.

He was dying, and he was glad of it.

"You did this," a deep growl rumbled in the darkness. "This is where duty has brought you." A large shape moved in the cell across from him, and Sorren's snout appeared in the moonlight streaming in from the windows. "Do you feel fulfilled?"

Von blinked at the rats chewing on his pant leg. He felt nothing anymore. Every part of him was numb.

"Damn you, Von. Do you think becoming a mindless coof and wasting away will change anything? You don't think I want to forget? They killed the boy, too!" Sorren roared, and beat his fists against the bars. "Yavi—"

Von flinched. Her name struck him like a whip.

"*She* and Geon are two more names on that long ledger of lives Tarn has taken. Have you finally had enough?"

But the words were muffled beneath the screams he couldn't ignore. Sorren dropped back into the shadows in solemn disgust. Did he see the emptiness? The vast hole in his soul?

"Tarn has broken you," Sorren said. "Now we truly are forsaken."

The heavy door to the brig creaked open. The thud of boots neared and stopped outside of his cell. Keys jangled, then the cell door swung open.

Olsson crouched in front of him. "Commander."

Von's chest tightened. The title didn't belong to him anymore.

Olsson noticed his damaged ears and shook his head. "I'm greatly sorry for your loss and the part I played in it. I wish..." He sighed, looking away from his blank face. "Come, the Master calls."

Von was hauled to stand. Olsson half carried him, his bare feet dragging on the wet floor, step by slow step. The cries on the wind grew louder as they climbed the stairs to the deck lit by lanterns.

He closed his eyes so he wouldn't have to see the flames.

"This is yours," Olsson murmured under his breath and he quickly shoved something cold in Von's hand. Then his footsteps receded.

Realizing what he held, a shallow breath coated his throat with frost. Von squeezed the golden ring tight in his fist.

"Now that you have repaid your debt, your holy duty is finished." Tarn slinked forward from the shadows by the helm. "You are at last free."

The word shook something inside of him.

You have always been free, Von.

729

He looked out at the frozen seas at the call of her voice. Tears welled in his eyes. How unfortunate that he didn't realize that until it was too late. She died...because of him. Because he had been a weak coward.

"We have seen many things, you and I," Tarn continued behind him. "Spilled blood and lost blood, and it was all for a purpose only we can see through. We have come far and we have more yet to go."

We? Since when had it been we?

Von didn't understand, but he didn't care. Not anymore. He was free to choose what to do with his life now. The thing he lacked had been his *will*, as it had been twisted and bent to Tarn's whim. He had given up the rights to his freedom for the sins of the past and the person he loved most paid for it.

But that duty was over.

There was only one thing left for him to do, because for once, he had a choice.

And he chose the end.

Von walked away from Tarn. The bondage that held him down for years snapped with every step he took, one chain link at a time. His eyes stayed on the dark seas, knowing that was where he would find her.

His Yavi.

"Von?" Tarn called, confused. "What are you doing?"

He reached the stern of the ship and climbed up.

"What—Stop him!"

Raiders flooded the deck, shouting at him to come down. Balancing on the railing, Von turned. Tarn ran down the stairs to him, his wide eyes fixed with a look he hadn't seen in fifteen years.

Desperation.

Von finally realized why the man he once called Master had kept him alive all this time, despite causing his sister's death and constantly failing. As much as Tarn pretended to care for nothing, Von was the last piece of his past. The last shred of a connection to Aisling—and he couldn't help clutching on to it.

Taking that away filled him with sick satisfaction. They both should have died with her that day. It was the only answer that made sense to him anymore.

Von spread out his arms to the night sky as he felt the last of his chains break away.

"I command you to stop!" Tarn reached the stern, lunging for him.

"Piss off." Von let himself fall.

Tarn missed him by inches. Then he was claimed by the wind. It yanked him down and he crashed into the frozen sea. The churning waves swallowed him with a roar and he sank into its icy embrace. The water was so cold it knocked the air from his lips. The moonlight fell further and further as he floated away. The dark depths draped him in silence, and he found it calming.

No more pain.

No more nothing.

But an absolute peace.

A shadow dove toward him and he smiled, knowing who had come to escort him to his beloved. Death caught him, wrenching him through the darkness, and Von was grateful one god had finally answered his prayers. But it wasn't the Seven Gates that greeted him, only the burning gasp of air entering his lungs.

Von was hauled into a rowboat and dumped in a wet heap. He shivered violently as he vomited sea water before slumping over. Someone rolled him onto his back and he squinted up at the face above him. It was hidden beneath a black hood, except for a set of amber eyes.

"Elon?" Von rasped, not sure if he was dreaming. "What...why...why are you here?"

The elf sat back and picked up a set of oars. "You saved my life, Commander. Honor bound me to do the same."

Von's vision dimmed as they rowed away from the ship shrinking into the distance. He would live another day, and yet he felt cheated. Yavi fell out of his reach once more and tears froze on his lashes. The bitterness made him briefly regret giving Elon the antidote for Fengu venom, but as he clenched her wedding ring in his shaking fist, he thought perhaps the fates were giving him one more chance to do things right. A quick death was too easy when he could do so much more.

Tarn had stolen *everything* from him.

It was about time he paid for it.

CHAPTER 105

Dynalya

Dyna was aware of him before she opened her eyes. Cassiel slept in a wooden chair next to her, guarding her bedside. He leaned over the bed with his head resting over his crossed arms, one of his hands laying on hers. Fading sunlight gilded the room in an auburn hue. It graced the edges of his black hair and wings, bringing out the iridescent blues in the feathers.

Dyna's eyes welled at the sight of him. Her body ached, but she wasn't wounded, and her leg was healed. How long did she sleep? Perhaps a day. Maybe more. Her throat tightened as she remembered what happened in the woods, and the echo of Cassiel's voice screaming for her to come back.

As if her heart woke him, his lashes fluttered open, and his silver eyes found hers. They were splintered stars that flamed with nothing but pain.

Something happened.

His well of grief was so heavy, it fell over her and she could no longer stop herself from crying.

She knew before he spoke.

"My father is dead." The soft croak of his voice fell like dry leaves.

"Oh, Cassiel. I'm so sorry." Dyna tugged at his shirt gently.

He sat on the bed at her request. She wrapped her legs and arms around Cassiel, burying her face in his neck as she held him. He was stiff, and the bond silent. Instead of the usual warmth always hovering off of him, his body felt cold. The scent of ash and smoke lingered on his skin. They sat like that in the silence until the last rays of the sunset streaming through the windows fell beyond the trees, casting them in shadow.

"What happened...after. The battle, everyone else—" Dyna gasped and leaned back. "Zekiel."

He served Lord Raziel. She was sure of it.

"There's nothing left of him." The quiet wrath lacing each word sent a shiver down her back. The edges of Cassiel's face hardened into sharp stone. It told her whatever happened to the guard, he experienced the full force of her mate's retaliation.

"I need to tell you something," she said faintly.

But it was as though Cassiel hadn't heard her. He stood, effectively placing her on the edge of the bed. "Zekiel and Amriel have served the royal family since before I was born, and I now realize someone planted them there for a reason. The last day has proven to me what I have known from the beginning." His eyes rose to hers, and the air caught in her throat when she saw the starlight in them had vanished. As if they had been blown out and left behind nothing but emptiness. "I should never have entered your life, Dynalya."

"What do you mean?" She scrambled to her feet. "Do you say this because of the attempt on my life?"

He backed away at her approach, and she felt the wall he built between them.

Dyna shook her head, grabbing his arm at the sudden distress entering her. "I don't fear them! Whatever comes, whatever we face, we will endure it together. I told you, no matter the cost, I want to be with you."

"Your life is the cost and I cannot pay it." He removed her hold. "I'm sorry."

Dyna's chest heaved with gasping breaths when she understood what he meant. Her mouth trembled with the disbelief wrenching through her.

"No," she said. "You're not doing this."

Cassiel's face became an unrecognizable mask. It held no feeling. No warmth. As he looked at her, she found only endless desolation. "We don't belong together."

The light of their bond dimmed.

Tears rolled down her cheeks, and she shook her head. "I don't believe you."

"You deserve everything your heart desires. I cannot be the one to give it to you." He turned away.

Dyna threw her arms around him, weeping into his back. "Stop saying those things to me. You don't mean them."

"It was a dream," he whispered. "Now we have to wake up."

That response was a punch to her stomach. She felt something snap, like a thread splitting. The room skewed as pain followed, a swift, cutting line across her very being.

"If your fear outweighs any affections you have for me, then yes, all is lost. If you want to leave, then say you don't love me. I want you to say it plainly." She choked on a sob. "Speak the words that will completely break me, for that is the only way I will accept this."

Cassiel didn't answer. He couldn't.

Dyna circled to face him, clinging to his coat. "You said you would never leave me. You said it was the one thing you would never do. What happened to everything you ever promised me? It cannot mean nothing. It can't. You promised me always!"

But his gaze stayed on the wall behind her. His hands wrapped around her wrists, removing her with a gentleness that didn't match the indifference on his face. The threads of their future were unraveling at her feet.

"Cassiel," Dyna cried. "Please look at me." She leaned against him, needing something solid to keep herself from crumbling to pieces. Anguish pulsed around her in waves. Her pain was so potent it flooded the bond and his jaw clenched. "Let me in, *kohav.*"

His eyes met hers. They were dark and storming, and for a fleeting moment, his mask wavered. She felt him quiver, only enough to hint at indecision. All of her clung to that ounce of hope that she could still reach him.

Stay with me. Her soul cried through the brittle bond. *Stay. Stay. Stay.*

Cassiel looked away, and he slammed his shield between them, severing the link they both depended on. Dyna flinched against him. He stepped back several feet. When she tried to follow, he swept his hand sharply and a wall of Seraph fire cut between them.

Dyna scowled and stepped through it. She'd never been afraid of his flame. "We are bonded for life, Cassiel. I painted my every vow on your skin as yours is on mine. We are bound to each other and nothing you do will change that."

His eyes widened for a second as the flames died away, and his expression fell to cold resignation. "Then you leave me no choice."

She didn't understand—until a violent tremor shook the bond.

"You don't belong in my world," he said.

The blow landed, and she cried out at the first crack fracturing in her chest. Dyna recoiled away from him with a gasp.

"I don't want you in it."

She stumbled against the nightstand from the heartless attack of his words. His rejection frayed the edges of the bond, forming excruciating cracks through her heart. When she realized what he intended, an awful sob wrenched from her throat.

"Don't say it," she begged. "Please don't!"

Cassiel closed his eyes, as if he didn't have the gall to see her face. Her torn heart bled as he spoke the frosted words that tore her from him forever. "I don't accept the bond."

Dyna collapsed with a scream.

She had never heard a heart break until that moment, and it sounded like a rupture of glass. The rejection drowned her in agony as it split her very being into a thousand shards.

Cassiel let out a painful groan, and he doubled over. The bond drowned in a heartbreak so strong and painful, so intimate, it crashed over her.

It was his pain.

"I know..." Dyna sobbed. Her shaking hands curled into fists over her chest. "I know you're lying. The truth is, you don't have the courage to be with me, and that hurts far more than this."

Cassiel looked past her, his clenched jaw turning white. "This is where we say goodbye. You must forget this, and go on to live a long, glorious life."

Her eyes lifted to him, the first root of bitter betrayal weaving through her. "I won't forget. I will *never* forget. You have broken my heart, Cassiel. Why are you doing this?"

He swallowed and his quivering wings fell still as his expression wiped all emotion. "You are strong enough to withstand this pain."

"Please," She begged again, her voice a brittle sound. "Don't go. Please don't leave me."

Dyna cried as he walked away from her. She reached for him, but her fingers missed, forcing her to let go. That disintegrated the last of her hope.

The door closed behind him with a heavy sound echoing in the room, his decision slicing her heart open and leaving it there to bleed on the floor. The act held a finality she felt in the depths of her being. The brutal permanence of the end.

Pain lodged in her throat, full of disbelief and shock at what he had done.

"Cassiel!" Her scream rang through the manor. Dyna fell to the cold ground, shuttering from the torment of the rejected bond. It pulsed weakly inside of her like a dying worm.

The door burst open and Cassiel stumbled in. "I can't leave you like this," he gasped. "I can't. I can't."

Dyna sobbed with utter relief.

He came back.

Cassiel fell to his knees before her and pulled her limp body into his arms. Zev and the others paused at the doorway, their faces distraught and confused.

With her head against his chest, she listened to his erratic heartbeat and her vision blurred. "I know you, Cassiel Soaraway. From the moment we met, I felt your heart, and I knew I found my home. So please," she said faintly. "Please stay with me."

He brushed his hand along her cheek, the caress soft and warm as hearth smoke. "That is all I ever wanted." More tears spilled, and he wiped them away. He gently lifted her hand and slipped the *Hyalus* ring off her finger. "But I cannot let you relive the same fate."

She stared down at her empty hand and saw his ring was also missing. "Cassiel?"

Misery crept into his eyes as they met hers and the connection between them opened, his words a soft stroke across her mind. *I need you to know that my life was better because I met you. Thank you for being mine. For however brief it was.*

He cupped her face and pulled her into an aching kiss. Bright white light flared. The explosion of his power rushed through her body—and through her mind, invading every corner of her being.

This was wrong.

Something about this felt wrong.

The first thing he did was put her barrier back in place. The bricks were rapidly built one by one, locking away her Essence once more. The skin over her stomach pulsed and burned. Her internal scream burst through their connection.

I'm sorry.

She wrenched her mouth away from his. "No!" The strangled cry broke into a sob.

"What are you doing to her?" Zev shouted. He ran into the room with the others, but they halted mid-step, their bodies frozen in place. "Let us go, Cassiel!"

Dyna struggled as if her life depended on it, because it did. He was going to end it and leave nothing behind. If she lost him, she lost everything good she ever found. Her life would end with his.

"Cassiel, please stop." She tried to shove and kick against his hold, but he had her contained. His power wove through her, and she could hardly think. "If you do this, I will hate you! I will regret ever knowing you!"

He shuddered. *You will not remember me. It will be like none of this ever happened. It will be all right, lev sheli. I promise.*

She no longer had the ability to speak, or she would have told him his promises had lost all value.

He gently held her to him, and the bright light grew blinding. Dyna closed her eyes as darkness clouded her memories. He took from her, and it fractured an integral part of her soul.

And of his.

Her mind reeled as she clung onto anything to keep her tethered to him, but he was the one removing her grip, one finger at a time.

He erased the memory of when they first met by the *Hyalus* tree, then the time when he caught her out of the sky, the nights she slept in his arms, their kiss beneath the willow, the night he made love to her. He washed every single moment away. His face blurred next, and she started to forget the sound of his voice, the color of his eyes, the feel of his touch. However much Dyna pleaded, she couldn't hold on to them.

Each memory was a candle blown away, like wisps of smoke slipping through her grasp.

Cassiel's lips found hers for the last time. It tasted of tears and farewell. *I love you, Dynalya Astron. Forgive me for ever letting you think for one moment I didn't.*

And she felt it the moment her soul shattered from his cruelty.

Then everything they ever had faded, and he vanished with it.

CHAPTER 106

Cassiel

Cassiel took every memory of them. He tucked them away in a secret corner of her mind. Tears fell as he saw each moment they had, never knowing it would lead to this. He wiped away every part of her life he touched, and he filled them with others.

All he ever wanted was to stay by her side forever. To share her laughter and hold her close. To kiss her endlessly. He could be selfish and try to keep her, but that would result in the end of her life.

At first, he thought if he broke Dyna's heart and hurt her terribly, she would hate him and never think of him again. The words of rejection had burned on his tongue, yet it only unleashed an agonizing pain he couldn't withstand leaving her with.

He was a weed, and the only way to remove himself from her life was to remove all of him. Disappear so completely, the curse of his love would vanish with it. So that the one who was his heart would survive, he had to shatter their souls, and become nothing but flame.

When he finished, Cassiel carried her limp body to the bed and set her on the edge.

She blinked slowly. After taking in the room, she noticed him and her brows creased with confusion. Dyna looked at him in a daze, as though unsure if she was awake.

There was no recognition on her face, and it tore away another piece of him.

"Who are you?" she asked, her voice a weak rasp. "Am I dreaming?"

Cassiel worked his throat before he softly said, "Yes."

"Why do you cry?"

He looked into those blank eyes, feeling as if he would scream. "The dawn is gone."

The sun had set on his world and it wouldn't rise again.

Not for him.

Cassiel made himself walk away from his mate, from the one the fates gave him but wouldn't allow him to keep. Every step was more painful than the last. The band in his chest stretched and stretched until he thought it might snap and sever him in half.

He entered the next room, where his uncle and Yelrakel waited. Their faces were grim. Disapproving. She nodded at his prepared pack on the bed.

"Your father only wanted you to be happy," Lord Jophiel said. "That is all we ever wanted."

Cassiel stopped by the windows and looked at the twilight sky painted in deep blues and purples. "It must have been hard to be my father. One brought me into existence and the other raised me. You were my raft back then, Uncle, giving me a much needed place to belong. I never fit anywhere, but you I always counted on. I suppose you did what you felt was right."

"I have always done everything to guide you on the right path. I only ever had your best interest at heart."

"No. You had yours." From his pocket, Cassiel took out a piece of the bangle his uncle placed on him in Hermon. It was all that remained when he broke it apart in his fire. He held it out for him to see. "My father never ordered you to put this on me, did he?"

Lord Jophiel stilled.

"How about this one?" Cassiel held out the bangle they removed off of Dyna from his left pocket. The band had the same inscriptions that were on his and it matched the other bangle placed on her in Hermon. "I have been told time and again what it means to hold power, and shown the lengths many would take to keep it. Finally, I understand and I know what I must do."

His uncle's eyes widened, and he shook his head. "Cassiel, it's not what you think—"

"Don't feed me lies," Cassiel said softly, too tired of anger and treachery. He clenched his teeth as fire flickered around his fingers. "Or I'm afraid I may kill you where you stand. I did not want to believe you were like them. I did not want to believe the only one who cared for me never cared for me at all. You have damned me and I can no longer look at you."

Yelrakel and Sowmya seized Lord Jophiel's arms.

"Wait! Cassiel, please listen to me. I'm the only one who can help you!"

"The only thing I wish to hear from you is the name of the one who sent you."

"No one sent me. I didn't plan this. Those bangles were given to me by Zekiel. He said it was a command of the High King."

Cassiel searched through the apprehension in Jophiel's eyes for some truth, but he didn't have the strength to trust him anymore. "You should have left me to waste away in Hilos. I think it is only fitting that you take my place. When you receive word of my exploits, know you were part of it."

Jophiel's expression grew pained, realizing what he planned. "If you do this, you will hate yourself."

Cassiel laughed dryly. "I already do."

At the wave of his hand, Lord Jophiel slumped at their feet, falling unconscious. The Valkyrie dragged him away into the hall. He didn't know if his uncle had been merely used by the whole scheme, or if he was indeed part of it. Zev and Rawn would have recognized his voice if he had been the one behind the first attempt on Dyna's life. Someone else was after him and he knew it would only be those who stood to gain power.

Four Lords.

Four Realms.

He would go through them one by one.

Cassiel exhaled a breath. After another, he released his friends.

A few seconds later, a growl rumbled from the doorway. "What have you done?"

"What needed to be done."

Zev grabbed him and turned him around. "You used your compulsion on her. You took away her choice. How could you do that?"

A wretchedness speared into his being, and Cassiel inhaled sharply through his teeth. He loathed himself for doing it. For going back on his word and stealing something so vital from her.

"It may be tomorrow or years from now, but one day Dyna will remember what you did, and she will never forgive you for it."

His rotten heart deteriorated further in his chest, but it didn't change his mind. Cassiel removed his hold. "She is free of me, Zev. Safe. I can accept her despising me—so long as she lives."

He went to the bed and picked up his pack.

"Is that it, then? You're simply leaving her behind? Did you truly endure every trial together only to become strangers again? If so, then you don't deserve her."

He never did.

She deserved better. Oh Gods, she did. Much better than him.

"Now you've ascended to the throne and risen above those who spat in your face, but at what cost?" Zev snarled. "You fought for my blessing, Cassiel. You *begged* me!" He roared, his eyes shining wet. "I gave it to you because you swore to protect her and you—" His voice cracked. "If it wouldn't hurt her further, I would keep *my* word and rip that heart from your chest."

Cassiel felt miserable enough to let him do it, but he had things to do first. "I have not gone back on my word. Every assurance I made to you, every vow I made to her, this is my promise kept. I won't see her die for loving me. I must go so she can live, because nothing will ever be worth the loss of her life. Not even the preservation of mine."

No matter how much he wanted to crawl right back to her...he had to let go.

"What of our journey to Mount Ida?" Zev asked as Lucenna and Rawn entered the room behind him. "Are you abandoning the chance to find your mother, too?"

"The reason my mother was lost to me was because of *me*. Dyna will not suffer the same fate."

"But you are True Bonded," Rawn said. "A twin flame. Your souls were created from the same fabric in the ethers. Without her, your life will be incomplete."

A heavy bleakness fell over Cassiel's shoulders, but it merely fell back where it used to be. "I have lived all my life incomplete, Lord Norrlen. It's nothing new."

"Then go, if that is what you want," Lucenna hissed, her eyes glowing bright. "But you won't take Dyna's magic. Remove the barrier you placed on her. *Now.*"

"No." Cassiel held her glare. "She is powerful, and the trace of her magic can be used to track her. I cannot allow that. I have ordered the Valkyrie to announce her death and my time in mourning. As far as the Realms know, Dyna is dead. No one can know she survived, or more will come."

"What do you mean?" Zev demanded.

Cassiel reached into his coat pocket and handed him the crumpled page.

"What is this?"

"The names of everyone who wants her dead simply for being my weakness. For being a human with a crown. Do you understand now?"

Zev's eyes flared yellow as he read the long list, and the page crinkled under his shaking fist. "So what?" he growled. "When have we ever cowed before our enemies?"

"There comes a time for peace," Rawn said, his expression hardening. "And a time for war."

What monarchy isn't founded on blood and war?

As much as his father wanted to avoid that, Seraph fire was meant for battle.

Electricity crackled around Lucenna. "We will do away with whoever comes after her. We aren't cowards, Cassiel. We *don't* run."

"You misunderstand." He recovered the page, tucking it away in his coat. Then he grabbed *Esh Shamayim* off the bed and buckled the scabbard around his waist. "I made a promise to Dyna that I would always be her shield until my last breath. That page full of names is not the reason I run, but the reason I cannot stay."

Zev's eyes widened. "It's a kill list. You're going after them."

Starting with Lord Hallel.

"The day they decided to come after my mate—to kill my father—" Cassiel gritted his teeth. "Was the day they sealed their fate."

He'd been beaten down, spat at, despised, all for what he was, constantly living in the shade of resentment and hate. Whatever healing he'd gained blackened with the death of his father. He was the one who should have died. Both at the *Hyalus* tree and today. His father lost his life because of him, and that fact punctured a gaping hole in his chest, leaving him not knowing what life meant now.

They stole so much from him, but he would never allow them to take her.

When Dyna had come down the steps in her shimmering white gown on their wedding night, Cassiel knew one thing with absolute certainty. For her, he would set the world on fire merely to watch their enemies burn.

"Whoever shall contest it or not, I am now the High King of Hilos and the Four Celestial Realms. I will do what is necessary to protect my Queen, even at the cost of my soul." Blue fire burst from Cassiel's hands. It violently danced around his fingers and licked up his arms, swarming his body to flare behind him into massive wings of flame, filling the room with ominous shadows. "Those who oppose me, those who dare wish her harm—I will eradicate them all."

Zev, Lucenna, and Rawn looked upon his crown of fire, and they lowered to one knee, bowing their heads.

"Then we will fight with you," Zev said. "Dyna may be your Queen, but she's our Maiden. This is our battle, too."

They would fight. He knew they would. For her, it didn't matter the blood they would spill. But the price of his vengeance would cost more than he was willing to let them give. What he planned to do, there was no going back. For at the end of this path, he would find only death, and most likely his own.

"It's not," Cassiel said. "This battle is mine and mine alone. Your only duty is to protect Dyna—and to forget any of this ever happened."

Their faces went blank as his compulsion wove through their minds once more. Cassiel sent his power forth through the manor and Skelling Rise, so that whoever had seen him forgot. He erased their memories like cleaning away a stain with a cloth.

It was always him—the one who was left behind. This time, he would be the one to walk away.

So he did.

Cassiel walked out of that room and away from his family.

From every part of him breaking.

Away from her.

He leaped over the railing, letting his wings soften the fall. He strode past the foyer, the fading voice of his mate echoing in his skull. The glass doors to the courtyard were open. Sowmya waited outside in the dark. She knew her orders.

His lieutenant clanked a fist over her heart and inclined her head. "On my life, Your Majesty."

Cassiel kept walking.

His wings spread open, and the flames lifted him into the sky. The cold didn't reach him, only the fire of the destruction he had left behind. He headed north for the sea and flew as far away from Dyna as possible.

As he fell apart in the Heavens, a cruel realization came to him. He was never made of stone. For beneath it all, he was fragile glass, now broken so completely, the shards lodged in his chest, making every beat of his heart a torture.

He gained a throne he never wanted.

And lost the only thing he did.

Perhaps this was what it meant to love. Destroying himself so the one he cared for would live. Dyna had to live. He couldn't go on if she didn't. This would pass, and she would thrive as she followed a new path that didn't include him.

Cassiel shut his eyes against the torture, tearing him apart. Fire blazed through his veins, and he screamed with every part of his shattered soul as flames consumed him in a plume of blue light.

He forced his wings to carry him higher and higher into the atmosphere until the frosty air grew thin, and he could no longer breathe.

EPILOGUE

Dynalya

The air smelled of rot and rain. Dyna walked barefoot through the dark foyer to the front door of the manor as she followed the patter on the roof and the sound of crying in the night. Moonlight spilled across the sodden ground ahead. The cries grew louder, and the name it called rang clear. She stepped outside where a lad sobbed on his knees in the mud. He was young, still a boy. The rain beat down on him, his blond hair sticking to his face. Bloody bandages were wrapped around his arms.

"Come back," he wept. "Please don't leave me behind."

He's not coming back, Dyna said impassively. *That's what happens when people leave.*

Black smoke swirled around them as she left the dream. Dyna let her hand fall away from the one sleeping in the chaise, and went to sit by the fireplace. The logs crackled softly, sparking with embers.

It wasn't long before she heard the shift of weight and a soft groan. Klyde stretched, making his tendons pop, and he winced, rubbing his neck.

"Sleep well?" she asked.

The captain jumped and whipped around. "Dyna, you startled me." He chuckled uneasily as he drew up a blanket to cover his bare chest. "What are you doing up before dawn...in my room?"

Dyna continued watching the flames swivel and burn.

"It's rather early. Even the sun still slumbers." At her silence, Klyde slowly approached. "Lass?" He sounded worried, hesitant. Sitting with her by the fire, his blue eyes flickered to the small sachet in her hand. She absentmindedly traced the embroidered runes among the flowered patterns.

"I came to speak with you," Dyna said. "We have much to discuss, you and I."

"Aye? What about? Must be important if it couldn't wait until later when I'm better dressed."

"You were having a nightmare. What were you dreaming about?"

Klyde answered with another uncertain chuckle. "A man's dreams are too inappropriate to share with young ladies." After a pause, he asked, "Are you all right?"

"I'm fine."

"I...don't know if you are."

She looked at him then, the quiet carrying the spark of embers and crackle of wood.

His brow furrowed at her blank expression. "Are you unwell?"

"Should I be?"

To his credit, Klyde maintained his puzzled expression, but he failed to hide the tension in his shoulders.

"This scar." Dyna tracked a finger down the large, jagged curve running from his bicep to his forearm. "It must have hurt when the troll bit you and crushed through the bone, but it didn't compare to the pain you felt when he abandoned you in the rain."

He froze.

"How long did you kneel in the mud, screaming for him to come back?"

Klyde smiled, the edge of it a little tight, and he stood. "I'm not sure what you're talking about, lass. I think you may not be feeling well. Wait here. I will go find your prince—" He winced. "Pardon, I meant your cousin."

"No, you didn't." Rising to her feet, Dyna wandered about the bedroom.

The walls were blank, and the bed was unused. His boots were by the door, weapons left on the desk. Otherwise, the space held no character, or traces of the one who slept in it. She stopped by the chaise where his mercenary coat was draped on the armrest. She ran her fingers over the emblem of a bird's skull. Worn, folded pages peeked out from the pocket. Dyna plucked them out and glanced blandly at the wanted ads with their faces, letting each one float to the ground. When she got to the one with *his* face, a trickle of weak magic sparked at her fingertips. It caught the page on fire.

Klyde stood quietly behind her as it burned to nothing.

"A mage broke my mind once," Dyna told him. "I created a warding spell to protect it, so no such thing would ever happen to me again. I'm a slow learner, but I do learn." She tossed the sachet up and caught it, wafting the scent of sage through the air. Her fingers continued tracing the dissipation rune embroidered on it. The spell that broke spells. It pulsed with power, clarifying every memory of the one who betrayed her. "And yet, I regret to find my mind wasn't the only thing I should have been protecting."

The bond was still there, left weak and fragmented. It could only be completely broken by death, but other things had been broken. An unspoken feeling thrummed in her battered chest, filling the spot where her heart had been destroyed.

Dyna pulled the handfast sash from her pocket as she returned to Klyde's side. The wrinkled silk ribbons had lost their sheen. No longer white, but decaying brown. She tossed it to the fire, too. The edges curled, turning completely black as it was consumed.

She was so sick and tired of being taken advantage of. Sick of her naivety leaving her defeated. Of trusting the wrong people. Essence seared in her veins, but it beat against the thick barrier like waves on a dam. The little that slipped through crackled on her skin and the flames flared at her fury. Klyde flinched back.

"You knew who we were from the beginning," Dyna said. "I suspect you still do. I was once told your coat is enchanted against spells, if I recall. And I do recall a lot." Her hands sparked again at the emotions she couldn't quite hide yet.

But her shield on the bond, that was solid steel.

"Nonetheless, you didn't have all the details. You couldn't help but wonder who I am, and why my friends, who couldn't be more different, follow me. They are my Guardians. Prophesied to come to me by the fates, if you can believe that."

Klyde listened intently, completely still.

"One of...*divine blood*," she said tightly. "A Lycan, a sorceress, a warrior, a fairy, and finally someone with a familiar face searching for revenge." She turned to him, reading the tension gripping his body. "I found five, but the last one..."

When Gale showed her the portrait, Dyna had considered if Klyde could be her missing Guardian, but she felt no connection to him. There was only one other she felt that with, and he had been there since the beginning of her journey. Even though Von had saved her life several times, she hadn't let herself consider who he truly was because he served her enemy, and because she didn't want to think about what the divination could mean for him.

"Do you imply I am the sixth?" Klyde asked.

Dyna laughed. It sounded empty to her own ears. Cruel.

The flames dimmed, darkening the room.

"To be my Guardian, I would have to trust you. *Completely.*" Her voice sharpened. "Which I don't."

His eyes widened when three forms materialized from the shadows behind her.

"No, unfortunately it's not you," she said. "I know who the sixth one is, as I know who my husband was, Captain. And I know exactly who you are. Even though you were once known by another name, given to you long ago…by your *brother*."

Klyde bolted for his coat.

Purple mist whipped past Dyna and snatched him off his feet. Lucenna's magic constricted around him so tight, he jerked, gasping for air. Anger glowed in her lilac eyes. With a yank of her fist, she hauled him back to them.

"Lucenna—" His beg cut off at the snap of her fingers and a strip of purple mist covered his mouth.

Dyna had to admit, she'd briefly forgotten the reason she left North Star in the first place, while letting herself be distracted by sordid things like falling in love. But that was finished now. Completing her mission would be her only goal, and no one would stand in her way anymore.

Because she would be the beast.

The blade.

The one who drew blood first.

Dyna looked up at the helpless man with her Guardians coming to stand beside her. "I didn't see it at first, but you really do look like him." She brushed the captain's jaw layered in a thick beard that he had been using to hide that fact, and a cold smile rose to her lips. "It's a pleasure to meet you—Klydesdale Morken."

ACKNOWLEDGMENTS

With every book I write, I discover new things about myself, about the characters, and their world. *Shattered Souls* was an incredibly pivotal point in the story for everyone. It was definitely my biggest challenge. Not only because of the page length (I still can't believe all these words came out of my brain), but because I had to dig deep to really understand these characters and tell their story the right way with the care it deserves.

Which resulted in a HUGE book I didn't plan for, forcing me into unfamiliar territory as an author. It was difficult, if I am being honest, and I worried a lot if this was the right direction for the book, but I knew what the ending would be and what needed to happen to Dyna and Cassiel to get there. There was no other possibility.

Worry not, my dears! More is to come for our True Bonded soulmates. You can rest knowing I am a believer in happily ever after.

I received so much help from many amazing people that launched my third book flying out into the world. I hope you know I couldn't have accomplished this without you.

All my love and thanks to my husband, my mate, my bonded, Michael. Thank you for always being there for me, for being my sounding board when I was stuck, for answering my dude questions, for telling me I got this when I wanted to give up, and of course, for inspiring Klyde's witty personality. You're my always and forever. (PS-I adore your dimples).

Second, massive thank you to my incredible street team. I cannot thank you enough for continuing to shout about my books to the world and for cheering me on when I needed it. I can always count on you to be there when I want to gush about all the behind-the-scenes secrets I can't keep to myself. I absolutely love it when you DM me all of your reactions about my books (even when it's to yell at me). I'm so lucky to have you in my corner.

Special thanks to my beta readers: Katie Ryan, Cher Martindill, Mimi Corpus, and Devyani Saini. I put a lot on you with this messy monster of a book, yet you came through like Valkyrie warriors. Thank you for your insight and for taking the time to help *Shattered Souls* become what it is.

Thank you to Hadar Garson for sharing your beautiful Hebrew culture and language with me. I know in my heart *Elyōn* sent you my way.

Hina Babar, my magical editor. Thank you for telling me the hard stuff, even when I don't want to hear it, and for listening to my ramblings when I need to vent or cry about my setbacks, then telling me it will be ok.

Cher Martindill, my adorable sweet potato, I am so grateful to you. Thank you for continuing to help me run the reader group pages and all the extra stuff I couldn't keep up with. Between us, you're keeping me sane.

Of course, thank you to all the ARC readers, bloggers, booktokers, Instagramers, everyone who took the time to share about my books on social media. I appreciate every single post. It still feels so surreal and incredible when I see them.

And thanks to YOU, the reader. If you bought the book, read the ebook on KU, or borrowed it from a library or friend, I am so honored to have you join me on this journey with Dyna and Cassiel. It means so much that you have fallen in love with these characters as much as I have. Thank you for wanting to get lost in this world with me (and for sustaining me with all of your tears). You are the reason I get up in the morning to write.

This series has come far from that first letter on the page. It's grown and taken shape into something I never thought possible. I am living my dream come true and it would not be possible without everyone. I will never stop being so grateful to you, my Guardians.

Thank you!

I am forever within your debt.

Beck Michaels

CELESTIAL LANGUAGE
(HEBREW TRANSLATION):

At haor sheli: You are my light
Ata hakohav sheli: You are my star
Ani ohev otach: I love you (boy says to girl)
Ani ohevet otcha: I love you (girl says to boy or girl says to girl)
Lev sheli: My heart
Ata hakohav sheli: You are my star
Elyōn: Higher force (God)
Esh Shamayim: Fire of the skies
Elyōn azor li: God help me
Sheli: Mine, belonging to me
Kohav: Star
Hasrat achrayut: Reckless girl
Gam nezach lo maspik itach: With you, even eternity will never be enough
Eheye lach magen kol od nishmati beapi: I will be your shield as long as I live and breathe.
Harey at mekudeshet li be tabaat zot: You are blessed to me by this ring (altar vow)

FOR NAME PRONUNCIATIONS VISIT
WWW.BECKMICHAELS.COM/PRONUNCIATIONS

The adventure continues in...

RISING DAWN

GUARDIANS OF THE MAIDEN: BOOK 4

Printed in the USA
CPSIA information can be obtained
at www.ICGtesting.com
LVHW041940250823
755614LV00006B/25/J

9 781956 899030